THE GREATEST
SCIENCE FICTION
FROM
NEWFOUNDLAND

Published in Canada by Engen Books, Chapel Arm, NL.

Library and Archives Canada Cataloguing in Publication information is available upon request.

Print: 978-1-77478-151-7
eBook: 978-1-77478-152-4

Distributed by:
Engen Books
www.engenbooks.com
submissions@engenbooks.com

First mass market paperback printing: January 2024

Cover Design: Matthew LeDrew
Cover inspired by the esceptional work of Vaughn Marsh on 'Pulp Science Fiction from the Rock'

THE GREATEST
SCIENCE FICTION
FROM
NEWFOUNDLAND

ENGEN
BOOKS

'Always Greener'
dedicated to
'The Original Gig'
- JRH Lawless

'The Epic Quest for Terral B. Hylotz'
dedicated to
"My dad, Lloyd Pike
And the Engen community, especially readers like you.
Thank you for believing!"
- Andrew Pike

'Corporate Invasion'
dedicated to
"My incredible niece, Courtney Downey.
Your light, strength and courage will always inspire us. Your spirit
lives on in the people you touched.
You are missed."
- Teresita E. Dziadura

'Roxy Buckles and the Flight of the Sparrow'
dedicated to
'My grandmother, Susie Little
who encouraged my love of books.
And, as always, for Bridget and Suzie.'
- Nicole Little

CONTENTS

ALWAYS GREENER

JRH LAWLESS

1

RedCorp agent rank 57005
ARGYLE, Liam (age 41)
Status: Unattached
Summary: Weather presenter for 24-hour newsfeed on Stream 2. Ratings above par (marginal).
Highlights: Top "likeability" scores among current workforce from feeder synthetic personality testing. Second highest "mockery" scores.
Psych assessment: Repressed intellectual identity. WJ VI standard score 112 (High Average), Exner FABCOM1, PSV1. Mild depersonalisation disorder (DPD) under stress. Light anti-social tendencies. No medication required as per last medical inspection.
Employment history: Telemarketing ("summer job"). Unemployment postgrad. Directed to Stream 2 by unemployment algorithms (2053-present).
Education: Master's (Philosophy), University of London (see "known associates," Schedule A)
Personal notes: Former alcoholic (relapse perspectives: moderate), Mild Gaming addiction, Compliance level 4
Extracted - 08:23 13/01/2072

Ms. Heath stopped reviewing the AR[1] personnel file and moved it to the background of her heads-up display. The Chair, Ms. Preston, was about to open the board meeting.

"First point on the agenda. The ratings for *Reality Shock* are down for the fourth quarter in a row."

The stout and sharply dressed matriarch at the head of the conference table didn't have the usual AR profile floating in front of her. No title, no position in the corporate organigram, no family ties. None of the personal background and preferences that became the Corporation's property—and, in a large part, the Corporation's creation—the moment you signed on.

Everyone knew who Ms. Preston was. She didn't need any display.

---

1 Mere Augmented Reality, which is to say, "made bigger," as opposed to full Virtual Reality, which comes from the Latin for "manliness, manhood." Etymology proves once again that technology is size compensation by other means.

And ramming home the difference between "Management" and "management" was a side bonus.

"We had to make a tough decision, but we cannot wait any longer. It's time for a change. We're bumping *Reality Shock* back to daytime and launching a new feed for the Spring line-up. Mark?"

A squat boulder of a man squirmed in his chair. The words "Mark Underhill, Marketing Director" scrolled at the top of his display. He tried to draw himself up to a height he did not possess, making him look rather like a startled hippopotamus. He coughed and launched into his overly rehearsed spiel.

"Thank you, Ms. Chair, members of the Board. Our department has been hard at work over the past few months fabricating the next big thing. We decided the best way was to go back to the source and evaluate our past successes. Why did so many people tune in every night to watch *The Eliminator*?"

As he spoke, free-floating AR windows popped up to the left side of his ear. They showed a desperate, half-naked man running from unseen pursuers through a jagged metal jungle.

"How did a podfeed like *The Daily Diary* manage to topple local governments on three different continents?"

More windows appeared to his right. The newsfeed footage showed people, young and old, brandishing old-fashioned ink pens in the air. Confused and worried officials looked on from the windows of official-looking buildings.

"Why did viewers start watching the old, so-called 'reality television' programs in the first place?"

He paused, daring anyone to venture an answer to his rhetorical questions. Or even worse, to suggest he and his department only wanted an excuse to watch old vids of half-naked young men and women walking around flats. No one suggested any such thing. Satisfied, or close enough for management work, he continued.

"I'm not trying to give you a history lesson here. What we've been seeking is nothing less than the source of the terrible attraction of realpod. And we found it: voyeurism. The need to watch, observe, love, despise, scorn[2] and — above all else — judge.

"Today's society belongs to the individual, not the community. It no longer fulfils that basic human need to judge our peers. With realpod, we wrap all this up into convenient daily doses. Ready for consumption from the comfort of home, office, public toilet, or anywhere else you can catch the feed."

---

2 "to rip off someone's horns": graphic food for thought.

He paused, taking a sip of water and enjoying every second he made them wait. But the Chair, Ms. Preston, stared at him the way a dog stares at a fallen scrap, *i.e.*, not for long. He coughed and resumed in a rush of words.

"We already knew all this. And to be frank, as the Mirror's troubles show, we've run the concept dry." At his words, the previous two clips faded into the background. An animation appeared instead, showing the show's ratings over the past two years. It was like something out of a ski adventure sim.

"So, how can we make it fresh and powerful again? I'll tell you how." He started to pause for dramatic effect again, then glanced at the Chair and thought better of it. "The sources of realpod's historical popularity are more potent than ever today. Literacy reaching beyond a fast-food delivery menu has become a joke. People are more isolated from one another than ever before. Everyone is a victim.

"Not only is everyone a victim. Everyone's part of a world-spanning shouting match to get everyone else to recognise them as a victim. Children are suing mothers. Mothers are suing children. Psychoactive over-the-counter drugs are popped on an hourly basis by people of all ages, colours, classes, and creeds." He couldn't help but pause again, preparing his audience for the home stretch.

"So, what we asked ourselves was this. What if we gave every poor slob in the world the opportunity they've been begging for all their lives? A chance to have their unjust suffering recognised by all? What if we created an arena where these unfortunate souls would compete for our pity? What if we let the whole world watch them humiliate and reveal themselves, then vote on who has it worst?" He grinned, and his eyes gave a firm flick to the left.

"Ladies and gentlemen of the Board, I give you the Red's[3] greatest triumph to date. I give you ***The Grass is Greener***." You could hear the boldness.

The lights dimmed in response to the command. A tense hush fell over the assembly like a woolly comforter. A retro techno beat started up, with sound fed through bone conduction into each participant's inner ear. The walls disappeared from everyone's AR-enhanced view. Instead, there were

3 Cultural integration and the desire for generational distinction being unstoppable, it was only a matter of time before someone realised "red" was both a brandable colour in English and the word for *network* in Spanish, and it became the new fashionable term for the ever-growing interconnectedness of all things electronic, replacing the old *Internet*. At least, that was the official story. The millions put into advertising and product placement in popular media by the RedCorporation may have had something to do with it as well.

vast expanses of nothing, spotted with rare pinpoints of bright light.

A disembodied emerald-green hand appeared above the centre of the free-floating boardroom table. It snapped its fingers three times in rhythm with the beat, with unmistakable tactile cheer. Then it gave way to a slightly squished blue-grey ball, rotating with ponderous grace.

The planet—for such it was—fell through the void, spinning upon itself as its moon spun around it, and both spun around the distant sun.

As all this happened in dizzying precision, the table and viewers fell ever closer. Bits of brown, green, and black started popping up amongst the grey clouds and the blue sea. Soon, the screen broke through the cloud cover. It soared over a landscape of vein-like maglev tracks, huddled vegetation fighting a doomed rear-guard battle, and a triumphant conglomeration of urban sprawl.

"Earth," boomed a deep voice, perhaps out of charity for the slower viewers. "Our home. Since the dawn of humanity, we have lived in society, ever striving to shape our world to meet our needs. All this time, a single question has dominated human existence like no other: 'Why am I here? Today was supposed to be my day off!'"

The view merged with a random piece of sprawl. People milled about, as hard at work as the proverbial ant. The music's beat sped up with reckless abandon.

"We all have our load to bear, and the real question behind the human condition is this: Who has it worst? Is it you? Is it your neighbour?" Everything paused at this. Maglev trains stopped halfway around a bend. Ground vehicles paused in traffic. The rare pedestrians froze mid-stride, forever awaiting another leg to stand on. The camera swooped and soared, making a show of trying to take it all in.

"Let's find out, shall we? New on Red this season, the realpod feed that will become a legend. Together, let's see who has it bad, who has it worse, and find out where—" dramatic pause— "The Grass is Greener. Now taking applications."

The AR display faded to opaque silence. Both lights and walls returned to feed upon the gory aftermath. The only sound was a gulp as one executive, somewhere in sub-Saharan Africa if her display was correct, took a tentative sip of water. Everyone sat in what they no doubt hoped to be thoughtful poses.

A seasoned veteran, the Marketing Director allowed everyone their moment of posturing before he spoke.

"As I'm certain you have already realised, the title *The Grass is Greener*, which we ultimately retained at the end of extensive synthetic target-response testing, allows us to clearly describe the voyeuristic nature of the feed while avoiding any of the more... unfortunate connotations. With *'The GiG,'* as we've taken to calling it, we can give the main theme a positive spin, reducing guilt issues amongst feeders."

"Would we be looking at similar scheduling to *Reality Shock*?" asked a balding sprig of a man. An animated "Programming" logo played across his AR display in a misguided attempt at quirkiness.

"This would need a constant, twenty-four-hour broadcast as a base, but with a couple of novelties on top. Testing has shown moving the weekly feature broadcast from Friday to Sunday would reduce feeder turnover by up to fifteen percent. Our socioanalysts think this encourages 'religious' feeding behaviour. Our psychologists say it appeals to feeders trying to counter the imminent Monday dread and suicide rate peak. And the computer people running the simulations say, 'That's what the computer says.'"

As he continued, the Programming exec's bald pate shone like a small, hair-fringed moon. "Then there's the bit we're most excited about. Legal has figured out a risk-free way for us to force contestants to have our new eyeNet lenses implanted for the show. We're looking at full, first-person perspective coverage, all day, every day."

The matriarch butted in with one word: "Fred?" Nothing else needed saying.

Fred turned out to be a short woman sporting the kind of pink bow that's only appropriate on the head of a bear riding a small bicycle. She righted herself to attention. The sober word "Commercial" bobbed along with the display in front of her, the only one not animated or scrolling in any fashion.

She frowned in concentration as columns of data appeared before her eyes only. "First projections show annual advertising revenue of some eight-point-three billion fids[4]. A net growth contribution of one percent after advertising, supplies, maintenance, and personnel losses."

"Which brings us to the second item on the agenda," said Ms. Preston, not only hammering the point, but nailing it. "The success of this feed will hinge on finding the right kind of person to host it. Someone under our control; someone people can relate to, and maybe even 'like,' while still being able to condescend to him."

She stopped, considering what she had just said. "Yes, we need a male for this one. A woman could never fit that bill. Does anyone within your

---

4 Fids is the common abbreviation of Fides (pronounced "fee-dess"), which is itself a contraction of Financial Determinant of Sale, the international monetary unit born in the direct aftermath of Market War One. Nobody had ever used the thing to buy or trade anything, but it was still handy for comparing the obscenely large sums of money bandied around by the elite corporations, mostly just to show off.

units seem suitable?"

Some young thing sitting behind Fred—half a continent behind, in fact—let out an involuntary "Umm." It earned him the terror of Ms. Preston's undivided attention.

"Sorry, Ma'am. I was only thinking, sorry, wouldn't it be better to hire someone who is, you know, famous, to draw people in to watch the feed? Sorry," he punctuated again.

No hint of a smile broke the Chair's countenance. "Don't be a fool. A poorly trained lemur could host this feed and become a worldwide superstar overnight. We don't want some video-enhanced diva already loaded up with an ego the size of a planet. And even bigger pay expectations, no doubt. This isn't a celebrity gossip feed; this is about the nitty-gritty of life."

A sharp young lady halfway down the table let out a tactical cough. Her display read, "Ms. Alyson Heath, News and Weather," in prominent but sober font. "Stream 2 currently has in its employ a young man who seems suited. Liam Argyle, our evening news weatherman."

"Him?" scoffed the Marketing Director through the folds of his chin. "The tall guy with the stubble and the jug ears, to host our flagship primetime feed?"

The Human Resources manager drew up Argyle's psych profile and let out a loud "Hmm."

"His profile also says he is educated—in philosophy, of all things. Clearly, this was some time ago. Yet is he not a bit... mismatched for a host position such as this?"

"He does have a nice smile, though. Sort of authentic, you know?" This thought came from a Human Resources middle manager who might not be a resource himself much longer unless he guarded himself better.

"Yes," cut in the matriarch, addressing all comments at the same time. "And it is precisely because he gets such reactions that our Mister Argyle will be the perfect host for *The Grass is Greener.*"

She turned to the burly man with a red tie sitting on her right. "Les, get the full personality and background assessments started on him straight away. Make sure any of that high-horsed nonsense has been squashed out of him over the years. If he checks out, I want him on the job starting next week. Can you take care of the details, Alyson?"

"You can count on me, Ms. Preston," replied the younger woman, her face stonier than the cliffs of Moher.

"Well done. On to more pressing matters," said the Chair. As she scanned the faces around her, a scrolling list of items and prices appeared behind her head. "What are we having for lunch?"

2

Sunk deep within the embrace of the automated vehicle taking him home, Liam couldn't believe his luck.

The whole experience seemed alien. As removed from reality as letters to the North Pole, news of floods in eastern Kazakhstan, or the eternal feasts in the Halls of Valhalla.

The sheer impossibility of it all had been gnawing at him since the call on Thursday. Liam had braced himself for disappointment, fully expecting the ground car to fail to show up to take him to the Heath estate. Things like this didn't happen. Not in reality.

And yet, there the car had been—five minutes early, of all things. And off he had gone, stepping into the world of his betters. Hearing the offer again straight from the mouth of Ms. Heath, the goddess of his own personal pantheon.

His own show! And not just any show, the network's flagship feed! He hadn't dared to ask the question that seemed to loom over the whole affair like an elephant behind the settee. Why him? Liam didn't think of himself as ugly. Not in so many words. But the face in his mirror didn't belong to a Sanchez-Oda, or whoever the latest androgynous flavour-of-the-season was. Neither did the belly, added the deriding voice of integrity.

Liam almost slid into the abyss that was his despair over a four-year absence from the female front[5], but caught himself. He was fine as he was, he convinced himself once again, before wrangling his thoughts back to the day's events.

Why him? He wouldn't risk breaking the charm cast upon an otherwise sane and uncaring world by uttering the words out loud. And in any case, what was he supposed to do about it?

He'd tried to remain as composed as possible during the brief meeting. But it was clear he was no longer in control of anything. Refusing the offer was not only unthinkable. It was on par with one of those primordial Words of Power. The true name of some Great Old One, which if uttered would sunder the very fabric of reality beyond the skills of any passing cosmic Penelope to repair.

---

5 Among other fascinating sides of the female anatomy.

What's more, it was a silly notion. How could he refuse? It wasn't a once-in-a-lifetime opportunity. It was, from his experience of the universe, a never-in-a-lifetime opportunity. Or at the very least, never-in-Liam-Argyle's-lifetime. It was an astounding chance to finally take his rightful place with the movers and shakers of the world. To help the company make the world a better, richer place.

That was the problem with the covering the weather, of course. Weather affected everyone—it was far and away humankind's single greatest topic of conversation. But a weatherman didn't, contrary to popular belief, affect it. You put words to data other people, using expensive chunks of metal zipping through space, had worked out about what it might do next. You gestured at the maps and diagrams some other people displayed on AR lenses around the world. And yet, people reacted as if he were the weather's trainer in some great elemental circus. They blamed him when it broke loose, escaped, and took a member or two of the audience along with it. It must be true, after all—it was on TV.[6]

This show would be a chance to have an impact. To make a difference in the lives of so many people. His own, first and foremost. What did he have to show for his life up until now? A Philosophy diploma still stuffed down the side of one of the boxes from his last move. A second-rate job, a beer paunch, and a liver the size of a small bowling ball. They'd taken pleasure in showing him the MRI after the stomach pumping, on the night he'd decided to recognise his drinking problem.

And imagine everything he could do to help the poor slobs he'd be interviewing. To bring their problems out of the shadows and into hi-res nanoparticle light across the two hundred seven states covered by the Red. He could give them legitimacy. And along with RedCorp, he could bring them hope, he could help them better their conditions, while making a tidy profit for the company to boot.

Ms. Heath had been adamant about these possibilities, somewhere around the third glass of heady port. As a result, it all seemed a little hazy, but the heart of the matter was clear. Could he let nagging doubts about losing control over his own life get in the way of this sanity-rending opportunity?

A firm cough came from the front of the vehicle, where the human driver would have been, were such things not laughably obsolete.

"'Ere we are, mate," came the disembodied voice, oozing synthetic "personality."

---

6 An archaic expression that had somehow lasted long after the last "telly-vision" had been stripped for its rare earths. In terms of anachronism, it ranked right up there with "it's written in black and white."

There's nothing else for it, Liam realised with dread, marshalling[7] his thoughts.

He'd have to give her a ring.

"William," mothered his mother in her motherliest of tones, "you know you've always had issues with commitment. DPD isn't a personality flaw, you know. It's an illness, something you can cure."

Her picture, floating in the air before his eyes, was slightly distended. Liam's cheap AR lenses couldn't quite compensate for the alcohol messing up his iris reactions. But her frown of maternal concern came through loud and clear, nonetheless.

"Yes, Mother." She was the only one who ever called him William, now that his dad was gone. By the gods, he loathed that name with every quirk and quark of his being. And Willy, Billy, or anything of the sort.

"You've only just come to terms with that drinking problem of yours—"

"The rehab finished over a year ago, Mother. That's all over with."

"—and I know you think you're living comfortably now," resumed the monologue, thoroughly devoid of heed. "But you've always had so much potential, and we could use the extra income. My pension doesn't go far these days, and your father's benefits are running out in another year."

"I know, Mother," he said, surrendering to the inevitable, but doing his best to tune her out nonetheless.

"And you know I've never liked that hovel you're living in, William. You'll need a proper home soon if you ever plan on building a family of your own. Oh, speaking of which, I'm organising a get-together this Sunday with a friend from the horror movie club. Her lovely daughter is coming along too. About your age and with a promising career in interior design. She happens to be single and I'm sure would be most charmed to—"

"No, Mother, we've been through this before."

"I'm not getting any younger," she carried on, regardless. "And you do know how I'd love to see my grandchildren before I follow your poor father."

"Yes." Ye gods, how he hated being an only child. "Listen, Mother, what I called you to talk about was what you thought of this job," he finally managed to get in edgewise.

"Oh…" She paused, rallying with the ease of an accomplished nag[8] as

---

7 Or, more accurately, *mare*-shalling — yes, as in a female horse. Etymology is both weird and revealing.

8 Nothing to do with female horses this time. Through Scandinavian etymology, "to nag" originally meant "to gnaw." Food for thought.

he derailed the freight train of her rant. "Well, it sounds like the opportunity of a lifetime to me, and you'd be a fool to turn it down. But you know I'll be here to support you, whatever you decide is best."

"Yes, Mother. Love you, Mother."

This is the way the world ends. Not with a bang but a simper.

3

Liam peered at the card, turning it over between his fingers. He stared, mesmerised[9] by the gleam of sunlight on the plastic edges. He just wanted to avoid facing the full reality of what he now held in his hand. For another few seconds yet, at least.

He wasn't certain whether Corporate had sent the short, suited man next to him to give him a tour of his new workplace at the unfashionable end of the Thames or to act as his boss. But the man carried on with his speech, either unaware of, or uninterested in, Liam's fugue state.

"Now that we've got the card template on file, you can order them by the box from Corporate. Ask me for the form anytime you like. The tag inside is set to load the contact info into any local AR networks. Right then, let me get this open."

The bright AR-enhanced green of the show's "outstretched hand" logo shone brighter than anything else on the card. He stood staring at the words printed in bold and inescapable clarity underneath:

The Grass is Greener

The AR copy of the card in his hand popped up at the corner of his eye like an unwanted proposition, broadcasting his new lot in life to the whole world.

A good name for a show, all in all.

"Ah, here we are," said the little man, as if the matter were up for grabs and reality needed convincing on the subject. With a flick of a hand, he triggered some element in his AR overlay. The imposing warehouse doors clattered and raised at a nonchalant pace, bordering on spite. In a professional building like this, a lens somewhere would be capturing every detail of his face and anatomy, cross-checking them against his Corporate file. He'd stopped worrying about one of the machines getting it wrong and caus-

---

9 The term is the linguistic legacy of Franz Mesmer, 1734-1815, who conned the Paris elite into believing in an "animal magnetism fluid" that could be used to impose one's will on another. In hindsight, that's basically shooting fish in a barrel.

ing trouble for him ages ago. It never happened, despite what you heard sometimes.

That typical bizarre warehouse non-light bathed the space inside. The sort of light designed to make things harder to discern than actual honest darkness. In contrast, the address on his new card leapt out from his AR display. Was it some sort of typo? Surely nobody in their right mind would name a place...

"Mr. Argyle," boomed the man with the AR display identifying him only as 'The Editor,' "welcome to Tantamount Mews[10]."

Liam looked up. Doors loomed out of the non-light at him like suspects in the mythical police line-up. Embedded AR tags flashed their names, somehow resentfully: 'Networking,' 'Studio 1,' 'Studio 2,' 'Field team,' the improbable 'Lounge,' 'Agency Storage,' 'Editor/Producer,' and, last and most probably least, 'Host.'

Well, that's it then. Attributing emotions to doors. I've finally lost it.

Best to follow Emperor's-New-Clothes wisdom and avoid pointing out how ridiculous calling this place 'Tantamount Mews' was. The little boy at the end of that story can't have made many friends by laughing at the powers that be. Or by dispelling the collective illusion. The story doesn't say he lived happily ever after. Or lived at all for that matter.

"It's a bit rough still, I'll be the first to admit," said his new Editor. "We've had to get this old archive warehouse emptied out and geared up in a matter of weeks. But here we are, two weeks before filming starts and ready to go. I think the name also gives it a bit of a homey touch, don't you?"

"Oh, yes. A homey touch. Quite so."

On that note, the Editor ushered him over to 'Networking.'

The door opened, and the non-glare went from sickly yellow to actinic blue. A large man swivelled around inside, hauled himself to his feet, and lumbered over. He extended one greasy hand in greeting, the other nervously adjusting the professional-grade computer interface wrapped around the palm.

"These are the backbone of the whole operation," began the Editor, before pausing. He turned from the miscellaneous machinery banks lining the cramped room and stared at the room's occupant for a moment. He treated him to an expression both as fogged and as empty as a city sky by night. As Liam took the man's proffered paw, the Editor apparently succeeded in remembering what the man was doing in his studio.

---

10 Common throughout the UK, the term "Mews" designates a row of buildings converted from stables, named after cages designed to hold hawks while molting, and ultimately after the Latin *mutare*, "to change." Also, cat sounds and a bunch of legendary Pokémon.

"Ah, yes, Liam Argyle," he resumed, with a cough. "I'd like you to meet our, um, Infrastructure Technician, Mr..."

"Barry Fletcher, sir. You can call me Barry," said the man, going so far beyond beaming he must be forming his own closed rictus circuit. "Watch your feed every night, I do, and you've never led me wrong once. Well, except for that one time, what was it, three years ago now? But who could have seen that heat wave coming anyway? Pleasure to work with you, sir, a real honour."

"Likewise," replied Liam, acting out of get-rid-of-the-weird-weather-man-fan instinct. "So, err," he fumbled, sensing the uncomfortable silence stalking the conversation amongst the eaves. "What is it you do here exactly, Barry?" He didn't rank high enough in the corporate food chain to have any organigram info in his AR display yet.

The man couldn't have smiled further if he had been the victim of a particularly sadistic medieval torture involving cheeks, cables, and easily excitable horses.

"Well," he began, hooking his thumbs into the belt loops of his insulated overalls. "I take care of these here beauties." He followed this with the inevitable wink, jerking his head over toward the back of the room. Banks of eye-watering lights, humming metal, and jumbled cables sprawled along the walls like so many walruses enjoying a mid-afternoon bask upon the floe. "They're what makes all this possible now, aren't they?"

"Yes," added the Editor. Liam made a mental note. His new chaperone was the sort of man who couldn't stay quiet while people gave out information he wasn't controlling. Or at least taking credit for. "As I was about to say, these devices are the backbone of everything we do here. They're linked up to the Red central broadcast pod downtown, of course. They'll broadcast everything we produce here, after proper Editing,[11] of course. They'll also let us receive instructions from headquarters and keep contact with the field teams."

Barry grinned. "Yep, they may look old, but through these beauts, we'll be feeding onto every AR lens in the civilised world."

"Well, not quite directly," corrected the Editor, with a little sneer. "But the principle is there. In any case, Liam," he added, taking him by the arm and steering him toward the door. "You won't have much to do with this part of our set-up. It's important to know it's there. Comforting and so on, I'd imagine. But you needn't concern yourself with it *outre* mesure."

He opened the door and then turned to give a curt nod to Barry. The man nodded back, sliding back into his chair the way an avalanche might settle within a valley.

---

11 Audible capitalisation, naturally.

"We'll leave you to your own devices, then…" The Editor trailed off, realising his unintentional pun with an expression of horror.

Barry let out a deep belly laugh as the Editor retreated into the non-gloomy entrance hall/warehouse, pulling Liam along with him. Liam thought it was a good laugh though. Maybe this wouldn't be so bad after all.

His treacherous optimism was proven wrong the instant they breached the 'Field team' door, next along the line. A small metallic-sounding blur ricocheted off the doorframe and buzzed toward them before they had the chance to enter. Or even, as the case were, duck.

The blur and Liam's left ear entered one of those struggles typical of two objects convinced of their right to occupy the same space at the same time. Pain blurred his vision, and a fleeting smile of relief crossed his features.

There was the universe he was used to. He'd been starting to get worried.

4

"Zing!" came the complaint from his ear nerves. But his brain soon hushed it to a low grunt of discontent. It didn't have time to deal with such nonsense from mere extremities. Particularly such unbecoming ones as Liam Argyle's earlobes.

Inside the room, a clutter of faces not so much swam as bobbed before his charcoal grey eyes. He had either stumbled into a support group meeting for very flat acrobats or else someone had loaded AR mugshots into every open spot of air. The same someone had vandalised most of them with bright red virtual markers.[12]

There was a gasp, and two of the more substantial faces pierced through the AR curtains.

"You idiot!" snarled a plump-faced Asian woman in her early thirties. She stared at him for a moment, during which the only sound was the wet flap of something broken in the overhead air-conditioning. Then she jerked into motion and rushed toward him, her extended hand rending the air and clutter like the prow of an icebreaker vessel. But a tall, shaggy-looking apparition barged in from the far right to cut her off.

---

12 Though one would be hard pressed to earn any serious historic accreditation for the idea that Vandals may have acquired, and furthermore employed, such instruments as marker pens during the Sack of Rome.

"Very sorry!" gushed the hairy, hulking form of the newcomer. "Didn't see you coming, there. Lucky that didn't do too much damage, eh?" he added, pointing at the metal cup rolling across the floor.

Given the man's size and pilosity, Liam was surprised he was hearing words and not a sort of bear-walrus grunt. If movies were any guide, he should be making nonsense noises everyone else would respond to as if it made perfect sense, making Liam feel like a pillock.

Liam also reflected that people often had a different definition of 'lucky' than he did. Even a nice plain not-having-things-thrown-at-him would have been luckier than "only" getting his ear nicked.

Wait a second, was that an 'Eh?'

"Ah, let me guess. You're Canadian, yes?"

"Yup," said the shaggy man, for lack of a name. "Well, to be fair, I'm mostly Italian, what with my name being Carpentiere and all. But it's also true my gran, his wife, you see, was from a second-generation Iranian family, so that must count for something. And I'm also one eighth Algonquin, on my mother's side, so..." He paused. Everyone around him was mouthing the words out, trying to catch up. Or, in the case of the Editor, staring into the distance, probably waiting for the moment to insert the conversation back into his reality.

"Err, so yeah, Canadian. You betcha. It's all explained in my profile anyway," he added in a mumble Liam was sure was for his ears only. As if he could read anything in anyone's display through this augmented mess.

"Ah," said the Editor at long last. "Mr. Argyle, I see you've met our field team. Field team, this is Mr. Argyle. Our 'host[13],'" he added, chuckling to himself. "Feel free to mingle and so on, as you'll be spending a fair amount of time working together. Just remember that we want diversity and candidates within easy travel distance of the studio. You lot can sort that out together. I'll be back in a bit."

He seemed positively mirthful as he left and closed the door with an excited, "Hoho, oh yes, that's rich." His voice trailed away down the hall.

Action overcame the dam of awkwardness and seeped back into the room, roughly as fast as defrosting molasses and twice as stickily. "Coffee?" suggested the massive Carpentiere, by way of a peace offering. Liam took the proffered foam cup with a sigh of gratitude and relief. As the distinctive pitter-patter of caffeine crept down his spine, he was finally able to focus on the room, its contents, and its occupants.

"There's rather quite a lot of stuff in here, isn't there?" Liam said, with the mental equivalent of a wince, when he could no longer bear the si-

---

13 Amazing etymology there. Look it up, but consider this your spoiler warning!

lence.

"Yes," replied the short woman in an over-firm tone, having succeeded in negotiating her way around her massive co-worker. "We've received thousands of applications since we put the adverts out last week. We were just, err, discussing which tags to remove from the wall, to make way for some promising new ones that came in today."

"Discussing, were you?"

"Energetically," added Carpentiere.

"So," Liam said, bending down to scoop up the offending cup, "this was part of said discussion?"

"A mere contundant argument addressed to my esteemed colleague here," said the scruffy giant.

"One still awaiting a fair rebuttal, if I'm not mistaken," replied said colleague. Her tones were as calm and collected as the growing shadow of a freefalling anvil.

"Now then, Norma, there's no need to—"

"I told you not to call me that!" shrieked she-who-was-apparently-not-to-be-referred-to-as-Norma, her hand darting to grasp a handy silver letter opener. "That's Ms. Lee to you, buttmunch!"

"Ms. Lee, Ms. Lee, alright!" stuttered (Buttmunch?) Carpentiere.

"Yes, and I'm Liam Argyle, pleased to make your acquaintance, alrighty then. Well, that's done, and well done might I add."

He desperately tried to conclude the topic at that, fighting, in vain, against the question on his lips.

"So, if I followed that tantalising exchange correctly," he couldn't help but continue, turning to stare into the scythe-sharp eyes of the letter opener-clenching woman, "your full name would be—"

"Norma Andrea Lee, most pleased to meet you," she replied through gritted teeth.

The knuckles grasping the metal implement had already crested egg and were making their stolid way toward the purest angelic white. Where his personal resolve had failed, his sense of self-preservation kicked in. Liam somehow found the strength to cut back any attempts at a pun, at the last second.

A sudden wave of misplaced compassion seized him at that moment. So this is what life as an editor is like.

In any case, his new co-worker seemed satisfied for the time being.

"Maybe you can be the arbiter of our little dispute about these applications." Her tone didn't seem open to discussion, and Carpentiere nodded in agreement.

"Err, alright then," Liam said, in an utter failure of both prudence and eloquence.

In a bustle of activity as violent as it was sudden, the two set upon the room. They reached out to manipulate bits of the AR clutter here and there, gathering bits together. Then they stood facing Liam with the lot.

"What about this one?" asked Ms. Lee, thrusting forth an RFID displaying what looked like a CV to Liam. It even had a little picture of a droopy-looking middle-aged man in the upper right-hand corner. But it had the strangest entries:

Full Name: Richard Blaine Fields
Age: 42 (my God, already?)
Place/Area of Birth: Tool shed, Nr. Quarry Road, Cradwell (mother in transit to nearest hospital, after borrowing neighbour's car)
Work Experience (Previous): Plant Worker, Unemployed, Textile Worker, Unemployed, Telemarketer
Work Experience (Current): Senior Surface Technician (H-mart all-purpose Janitor)
Overall Work Experience: Dreadful - Duration: 12 years, 7 months, 16 days
Hours: potentially 24/7, never the same hours two weeks in a row
Conditions: Aggravated and dangerously rushed customers (on the store floor as well as in their vehicles in and around the building), draining and polluted setting, chronic depression and suicides among co-workers, falling items and appalling sanitary conditions in food storage and packing (part of duty being minimizing contagious disease risk from vermin and human wastes), harassment by robotic delivery drones
Health and Safety Issues: see above
Failed Ambitions: Ecologist, Veterinarian
Habits / Medical Conditions: Social drinking, Medium strength Valnex (psychiatrist prescription, no longer under therapy), regular use of painkillers at night for back troubles
Extraprofessional Activities: Had to give up bowling and then gardening because of back pains. Feed watching in chiropractic chair (game shows, Realpod, nature shows).
Last Meal: Fried Chicken

What insanity was this?

"Yeah, some of them had a bit too much fun with their applications," said Carpentiere, misreading Liam's reaction for amusement. "That's what we get for asking people to submit 'anti-CVs.' Still, as a marketing gimmick, it worked rather well, I suppose. They're good at that at Corporate."

"Too good, if you ask me," said Ms. Lee. "We need to trim this lot down to twenty-or-so applications by next week. And we already got rid of over half of them. We've got the rejection letters ready. We just need some help setting some guidelines for what needs chucking out."

She turned on Liam with enough force to make a sledgehammer rust with envy. "So, what did you think of that one?"

"It's, err, that is to say, I thought it was, umm, a bit… plain?" Liam finally replied. He watched their faces with all the painstaking attention of an obsessive-compulsive portrait artist at a discotheque.

"Plain." The giant swayed a little in the predominant breeze of uncertainty.

"Plain…" A frown crept up Ms. Lee's petite features like Saturn's ring rising over Titan. Something small yet fundamental deep within Liam quivered in abject terror.

"Sounds right to me," said Carpentiere, against all expectations.

There is much to be said for that overwhelming force behind human actions that is laziness. Humans need a damn good reason to do something. Especially when someone else has removed the need to do anything other than agree.

Passivity is the cement making society possible. Liam felt a sudden surge of gratitude and love for his fellow Man, so encompassing that he had to privately blame the air conditioning for making his grey eyes water.

But it is at one's own peril that one underestimates the drive to compete, even in matters of laziness.

"Right, too plain," added Ms. Lee. "Or not enough. Whatever. We need people so plain their platitude will make the commonplace seem extraordinary." She sent the application to the virtual bin. By this time, her colleague had already forced two more disembodied sheets full of intimate facts to the forefront. They danced before Liam's eyes like indiscreet ballerinas.

"Which of these two do you like?" he asked in a voice like a foghorn. "The dog stool texture and odour analyst for KibbleCo or the suicide hotline night shift lady?"

"Umm, I'd have to go with the dog poo guy…" said the erstwhile weatherman. "But they both have real pathetic potential," he added, eager to be helpful.

"Right, we'll keep her as backup then." Carpentiere added another layer to the vertical filer.

"What about these?" said Lee, pouncing into the opening. "I've got a disabled 50-year-old fast food branch assistant manager." She waved a poorly presented AR form in her right hand. "There's also this live support technician at SelectSat, who has a lisp." This, presumably, was the sad AR face she was waggling in her left.

"I'll take the support technician, any day," Liam was quick to say. Surprised to find himself enjoying the exercise, he sipped his coffee as he examined at the next pair proffered by the candid Canadian.

"The career shoe salesman, I should think." He took another sip.

"What? A desperately single monkey mating expert? Please, let's not turn this show into a farce. We'll go with the amusement park ride tester." He gesticulated in an excess of emphasis, pushing the coffee beyond the limits of the cup's tolerance and scalding his hand.

"Let me mop this up first," he grunted through gritted teeth, reaching for a few sheets of used stationary. He dabbed, then resumed. "Right then, let me have a look." And so he did, looking, then closing his eyes and looking again.

A pained look, not to be mistaken with a sudden attack of internal plumbing issues, squeezed his face. Suppressed memories pushed their way through the crowd to sock his consciousness a good one. And a well deserved one too, for that matter.

I've seen people like this before. Those guys in the construction jackets who ram people into commuter trains at peak hour. I've always wondered if they were actually paid to do that or whether foul people stepped up to do the work pro bono. Context sprang back to meet his conscience like a bungee jumper.

"Yes, he's a good candidate for the show. Who else do you have?"

Liam smiled to himself, thinking he could get used to this.

Then a muffled clamour started up at the other side of the cheap plaster walls. There were shouts there, growing more and more insistent.

Curiosity may be a known felicide, but its many other crimes are wholly unaccounted for. Liam decided to take his leave and put it to immediate investigatory use.

"Belay that, I need to get going," he said, making for the door.

"No problem, we have a good feel for the type of application we're looking for now," said Carpentiere. "Thank you for your time."

"And for taking an interest!" added Ms. Lee, not to be surpassed. "Looking forward to working with you!" With that, she shut the door behind him.

5

Outside, the voices reaching him from the next room, along with its dubitable "Lounge" name tag, couldn't have been louder if their owners had been holding a firearm to Liam's head.

"I'm sorry, sir," said a defeated feminine voice.

"Sorry isn't good enough! We don't pay you to be 'sorry,' do we? We pay you to do your job!" shouted a voice Liam recognized as the Editor's.

"Sorry, sir!" the first voice replied, tears audible, if perhaps not yet visible. "It's just that—"

"Just that what?" The Editor's voice wore an audible sneer.

"It's just," the female voice paused, swallowing, "just that in the out-sourcing contract it says that we're entitled to—"

"Entitled to loaf about in the staff lounge on work hours, hmm? Is that what you're entitled to?"

"It says we're entitled to ten minutes break per day, sir!"

What am I doing? Liam asked himself, somewhat hypocritically, yet without making the slightest attempt to move on or stop listening.

"Yes, ten minutes a day, to go to the bathroom or something, or to have a cup of coffee to keep you going, not to sprawl on Red property[14], having a bit of a ten o'clock snooze!"

"I'm sorry, sir—"

"And fancy[15] that, what a coincidence, me strolling in for a bun just as you were sitting down to 'rest your eyes'... Do you think I'm a fool? Do I look like a fool to you? Answer me!"

Liam pictured the Editor's brown-specked bug-eyes popping out of their sockets as if they were mounted on strings, and had to fight to suppress a guffaw.

"No, sir!"

"You've probably been asleep here for the past hour already, haven't you?"

"No, sir! I swear!"

"Oh, you swear, do you? Guide's honour? By the Gods, woman, what is this, preschool? I've a mind to cancel our contract with Mobile right now and let some other agency do our outsourcing from now on!"

"Please sir, no. I'll make sure it never happens again, sir."

The fear in her voice was, as they say, palpable.

"You can be certain of that." Liam could hear him gathering his smugness before delivering a dismissal all the more devastating since it had been introduced by that most desolate of clichés.

He couldn't let this happen. He barely had the time to register that the

---

14 Rousseau says civilisation, and with it, differences between Men, was born with the first delimitation of private property, the Latin "proprietas," which overlaps with the moral judgment of *propriety*.

15 *Fancy* is a contraction of *Fantasy*, and most often used sarcastically, when there isn't the least bit of fantasy involved.

hand opening the Lounge door was his own before he found himself being stared down by the combined glares of a wiry-looking woman of some forty years of age, her eyes puffed slightly red within their sunken sockets, and a petulant Editor, flustered at least as much by the interruption as by the realisation of the identity of its author.

"Err, Argyle, yes. Come in, and shut the door behind you." The Editor scanned Liam's face whilst composing himself. "As you may have heard, I was in the midst of disciplining this... agent of ours, after having caught her napping in the employee Lounge, here."

Liam sat down, with assurance that surprised no one as much as himself, beside the woman on the imitation leather sofa which must have been someone's gravely mistaken idea of a happy marriage between taste and budgetary reason. It was the centrepiece of the supposed Lounge, thought Liam, who was of only slighter-than-average build, would have been hard-pressed to actually succeed in doing anything even remotely resembling lounging in the squeaky little two-seater.

The thrum of the central air conditioning unit above his head did not add to the room's appeal, either.

"Liam Argyle, pleased to meet you, ma'am." He smiled, extending a hand which, after a reflex moment of wary inspection, was shaken.

"Mary, Mary Artworthy, sir."

The Editor turned a livid pale green, and Liam decided to press his advantage.

"I'm new here and just getting my bearings. So, what is it that you do here, Mary?" He could have drawn up her profile, but there was a lot to be said for the human touch, especially in a situation like this.

"Err... I'm an agency worker, sir," she said, looking as one who has just realised the reason something looked too good to be true was because it, in fact, was.

"I see. But what do you do?" he repeated, before the Editor could butt in without breaking the form of things.

"Well, I mostly do the cleaning up, and writing mail, and fetching parcels, and repairing a few things when they break down and so on, catering, odd jobs... You know, agency work." She gave him the sort of shrewd stare generally reserved for things found under shoes or stuck to the underside of tables.

Liam remembered meeting agency people before, or at least bumping into them in hallways. A furtive lot of people of all shapes, colours, and creeds, doing just about any menial job conceivable and only identifiable as a group because of their tendency to fade into the background, despite the bright yellow safety bands Health and Safety made sure they always wore on their arms.

But never before had he actually sat down and spoken with one, beyond wishing them a vapid "good day," motivated in equal parts by the overriding urge to distinguish himself with a bit of civility and the perverse desire to see whether this agency worker was the sort of person that would freeze in surprise at a demonstration of politeness, which often came across as an attack in this rigorously calloused world, or the sort that would rally and return the gesture with a profound dignity that would leave both parties elated.

Now, however, and in reaction to the Editor's obnoxious assault upon the poor woman, he somehow found himself going beyond mere genial toying with these people and considering one as, well, a person. It was evidently a new experience for them both, through which they floundered like dolphins brought aboard a tuna trawler: nobody had expected them to be there, nobody had the foggiest idea what to do now that they were, and it was all just a big public-relations nightmare as far as the head honchos were concerned.

"Erm, that's quite a lot, isn't it? How many of you are there working here?"

"Oh, just meself in the day, and Taylor who does night security and maintenance. It isn't really big enough a job to warrant the agency sending a second person in the day." She glanced up at the frowning face of the Editor as one might dare glimpse at a looming crimson moon before adding, "But we're all grateful for the opportunity to be part of such an important endeavour as this!" This, she spouted in the same tone as children spout poems that in other circumstances they might have quite enjoyed but that they were forced to learn by rote.

"Yeeees…" said the Editor, "and such an important part it is. I am certain that you will not be lax in the execution of such a fundamental contribution again." He seemed to take great pleasure in staring her down.

"Oh, certainly not, sir!" Her wide-eyed innocence and eagerness[16] were picture perfect.

The Editor studied her face for what seemed to Liam like just a moment too long, then gave a curt nod, turned, and made for the exit. "Argyle, if you would join me in my office." This was unquestionably a command, spoken with his back turned as he opened the door.

"Right behind you," Liam replied, rising off the sofa and making to leave, but not without turning to give… Mary, he forced himself to remem-

---

16 Interesting how both innocence and eagerness to comply with whatever someone else expects of one should command the same sort of facial expression and refer to the same child-like image. But then again, so does a deer caught in the headlights.

ber, a smiling wink. The exasperated eye-roll she addressed to the Editor's retreating back lifted Liam's heart and spirits in an entirely unexpected measure.

He made his way through the non-gloom past the "Agency Storage" cupboard and over to the final door, with its "Editor/Producer" AR sign, which played through the non-light in the warehouse entrance hall much better than any of the previous ones. The door stood[17] open.

Inside, Liam blinked. The light was so soft he was forced to pause at the doorstep to let himself adjust and focus.

Shelves of books lined the walls on either side, greeting anyone entering the room. Actual paper books! The collection might be worth a fortune, if the books weren't simply solid imitations, as he strongly suspected them to be. Such a collection would be enough to make a sizeable museum proud.

"Do close the door behind you and draw up a seat." Buried in the depths of his desk's padded chair, the Editor could have been sold off to the nearest aquarium as a rare new species of hermit crab. "It's a bit early for a tipple, but can I get you anything to drink at all?" he offered, listless and monotone, as Liam took in the rest of the room. The overall impression was that someone had put a great deal of effort and money into creating an inescapably imposing caricature of a classic gentleman's study. Even the obligatory desk podscreen blended into the polished imitation stone surface in order to be nigh on invisible, unless you knew what you were looking for.

"Yes, err..." said Liam at last, experiencing the mental equivalent of running to catch, or at least make desperate hand signals at, the retreating rear of a bus. "Water would be fine, please."

The Editor smirked. "Still or sparkling?"

"Sparkling."

"Glass or bottle?"

His defences finally depleted under this sustained assault of solicitude, Liam crossed the room, flopped into the padding of the offered seat, and answered with a resigned, "Glass, thank you."

A smile crossed the Editor's pudgy face like a freight train accident waiting to happen. "Chilled?"

"Please." The cocky bastard.

The Editor focused for half a second, and a deceptive panel in the imitation woodwork at Liam's side slid open to reveal a glass of gently frosted carbonated water. As he took it into hand, he couldn't help but boggle at the man across the desk, which visibly delighted said man to no end.

---

17 As opposed to laid down open, which would have suggested something else altogether. Not that "stood open" doesn't, necessarily.

Liam glared at him.

"It only does a small selection of drinks," came, at length, the Editor's concession, borne upon the back of a thunderous pause.[18] "The secret," he whispered, leaning in over the table toward Liam for no purpose other than effect, "is that every idiot says water."

"What?" started to protest his victim, before realisation hit. "Err..."

The man's smirk grew wilder. In revulsion at being made the butt, as it were, of yet another awful joke[19], Liam clutched onto the oddity that the man's public profile didn't contain his actual name, just his job. This was gross discourtesy, bordering on illegality in certain jurisdictions.

"Tell me... err, hmm, I don't even think you've told me your name yet."

"You don't want to know my name," said the Editor, looking more or less exactly as serious as a mime doesn't.

"Try me." Liam made a lacklustre attempt at a winning grin.

"I'd rather not," said the as-of-yet nameless one, his voice as dead as a pan.

"Oh, but I insist," said Liam with a voice like saccharine, which is to say, somehow managing to sound both sweet and horrible.

"Well, it's just that, err... my name is..." His eyes darted here and there, seeking an escape with equal parts of desperate determination and inevitable futility.

"... Ed," he grunted.

Ugh, complained both Liam's sense of good taste and his faith in humanity, joining forces in revolt to violently seize control of his jaws, tongue, and vocal cords, before collapsing back into the silence of a black hole.

"But wait," rallied his synapses and vocal chords. "You would have obviously known your name and what it would lead to as you were choosing jobs..."

"Fate!" said Ed the Editor, with a helpless lift of his hands.[20] "There just wasn't a thing to be done for it." He narrowed his eyes at Liam, waiting to pass judgment on his response.

As usual, whenever confronted with an awkward social situation, Liam fell back on literature and popular culture. "Sort of like Hook in *Peter Pan*, then? Or Scar, the lion in that old Disney movie."

---

18 Not to be confused with *paws*, though potentially just as sharp and hairy.

19 "A jest, sport or pastime" in the original Latin, from the Proto-Indo European word root for "word" or "to speak." Hence, "the whole word's a play." Shakespeare missed it by a letter.

20 An ancestral gesture meaning, "Bugger this, you take this load off me"; first use attributed to the mythological Atlas, if Ayn Rand is ever to be believed.

The Editor grunted with apparent satisfaction, and Liam counted himself lucky for choosing references so old that the man hadn't noticed both were villains.

"You look like a fate-bound man yourself," the Editor eventually said in solemn judgment. "And you're certainly an intelligent[21] man."

Liam eyed him in much the same fashion as a mariner eyes the oncoming storm. The Editor seemed to be sizing him up and could only, Liam assumed,[22] come up with the result "big," what with the man being a good three heads shorter than him and built like a hot dog.

"Tell me, Argyle... What do you know about etymology?" asked the Editor in unwitting horror house voice parody.

Liam sputtered like a proton frozen at absolute zero, or close enough for practical purposes. "What? You mean, words and such?"

"Indeed." The Editor's voice creaked like the first defrosting of a primeval glacier.

"Well, I suppose I know a bit... Words, they can be pretty interesting and all that. I've never really given it that much thought."

"As one only does at one's great peril." The man in black drew himself straight, ready to deliver his sermon from behind his desk. "Take the word 'editor,' for instance. Damn interesting word, editor. Where do you think it comes from?" The man's glare would have made a prison yard searchlight pale with envy.

"Well, the verb 'to edit,' I'd say." The only response Liam received was a scowl, which for some reason reminded him of his kindergarten teacher, Mister Saunders. "Err, that is where it comes from, isn't it? Person who edits?"

The scowl deepened like a valley. "Yes, yes, of course, but where does it actually come from? What does 'to edit' really mean?"

Liam's mind raced upon a circular track. All he could come up with was "to choose what stays and what goes," and he was convinced this would not be to the man's liking. Instead of risking sounding like a fool again, he remained silent, and shrugged.

The pontiff in the Editor came back to the surface. "To 'edit' is, literally, to 'say out.' Such is the essence of my function: I say what goes out and what remains."

Liam nodded in a gesture of understanding that was met with barely covered contempt.

---

21 *Intelligent* meaning, here, "marginally more civilized than a chimp and naturally far, far below my own level of intellect."

22 And, indeed, when you assume, you make an ass of you and me. Or Liam and the Editor, as the case were.

"Of course, it shares the same origin with the word 'edict,' which opens whole avenues of richness to the texture of the word." The Editor chuckled. "The point is, if you don't know what a word truly means, then how can you ever hope to know the essence of the object it describes?"

Liam's baffled silence was taken for assent.

"Well then, it is getting on, so it is my regret to have to make literal use of my named function and now say: Out."

Liam sat making sense of this. As he was making no visible attempt at moving, the Editor urged him on with a curt nod, and he eventually got the message, fitting form to function and turning the Editor's jumbled words into actual communication.

"Oh, err… alright then." Liam stumbled to his feet, knocked his chair out of place, righted it, reached the door, turned in complete bafflement, and managed to utter, "Well, err, g'bye then."

The Editor dismissed him without looking up from some display or another he had just opened upon his table top screen. "Farewell.[23] And I'll be seeing you bright and early on Monday for our first feed." The door drew shut with surrealistic silence.

6

Among the crinkled corn chip packets, demolished cheese board, and spilled remains of three of the most expensive bottles of wine they'd had at the H-mart, the heavy gaming-spec physical screens loomed like the half-excavated walls of some lost city of old, redolent with hidden threat and mystery.

Or maybe he was just in one of those moods, having been thoroughly thrashed by Kyla, his best friend since University, and the rest of the old gang in the opening sci-fi RTS game of their usual Friday "Wine and Warfare" gaming session. His mind just wasn't on the game—might as well rip the band-aid off and break the big news.

"What, you mean that new big feed they've been harping on about all day and night all over the Red?" Steve managed to cover both his beard and the table in cracker crumbs as he spoke.

"That's the one," Liam said. "The Grass is Greener".

---

23 Of course, as *Hobbit*-era Gandalf would have been prompt to highlight, had he been ambling past, the Editor's meaning here was the absolute opposite of "fare you well."

"How the hell did that happen?" he scoffed. Only good friends can expect to show this sort of callousness and still get invited back next week.

"Well... They just called me up and offered me the job." Liam didn't think he was convincing anybody, and least of all himself.

"Liam," Hank said in the calm, reason-filled tones of a well fed Hank, those self-same tones which would make the Archangel Gabriel hirself moult with envy, "the Reds must have armies of weathermen working for them... Legions! Not to mention the news anchors[24], hair stylists, office clerks and mail boys who'd make just about as natural a host for a feed like that as you would. Hmm..." He bent down to serve himself another hefty slice of cheese from the moribund board. "I'm happy for you, don't get me wrong," he said through the dairy mush with the confidence of someone who knows, through experience and much training of his audience, that they'll be understood anyway. "But why you?"

Following Kyla's cue, they sat there watching him like drying paint as he thought this over. He hadn't really had the time to stop and think about why they'd chosen him. It was hardly much of an assumption to think there must have been plenty of other candidates who had been interviewed as well. There must have been... but surely a board bigwig like Ms. Heath wouldn't have taken the trouble of seeing them all.

He tried to view himself from their perspective. Looking at himself through the mirror of his friends' minds, he had to admit that the perplexed-looking man before him seemed nice enough, in a non-assuming sort of way, but he certainly didn't cry out as being prime star material. If anything, he was the plainest, least assuming of the lot of them. Kyla, with her ever-changing hair currently coloured a rebellious orange, would have made a much more natural choice. Or a more interesting one, in any case. Even Hank or Steve were at least as good at speaking in public as Liam. So why him?

Had there been some sort of covert testing done long before that call from Corporate? There'd always been rumours about the darker sides of Red-based personality testing, but it only made sense to keep an eye on your people to make sure they were getting along alright, and to weed out the nutters. So he'd never really given the rumours much stock, despite the questionnaires that popped up on his display ever week, just like everyone else. Had something like that happened here?

"Well, it's awesome, whatever the reason is!" said Steve, rising to slap Liam on the back, much like a whale does the open sea. "Our Liam, a pod-star! The world won't know what hit it! I'd say this calls for that bottle of

---

24 Often submerged, sometimes beached, yet never truly at sea, if they're worth their salt.

champagne we've been saving in the cupboard, what say ye?" He was off before anyone had answered with anything more than a half-smile or, in Liam's case, a half-objection that he hadn't told Steve or anyone else about the bottle of champagne at the back of one of his cupboards.

Nonetheless, he was glad that he'd told them about the show, he indulged in telling himself as he studied the freshly formed bubbles on the side of his champagne flute. He'd been worried about how they'd take it, he now admitted to himself, worried that the news would cause some barrier to come between them. He had worked himself up so much that when he'd finally told them, it had seemed over almost before it had started, the memory being little more than a blur. Such was often the way the mind coped with moments of focused stress, or it was in Liam's experience of the world, at least.

They'd taken it very well, he had to concede to his essential optimism. They were all drinking and eating and chatting away, on that and any of a plethora[25] of other random topics; all was well with the world. Only Kyla seemed, to Liam's attuned eye, slightly subdued behind her good-natured grin—he had known her since they were teenagers, and he could tell.

"So, how do you feel about all this?" she asked him in private, as they cleared the debris off the table some hours later.

"Well, it's a lot to take in, you know, all at once, but it's an incredible opportunity. I feel very good about it." The fact that he welcomed the following intrusion of Hank with the thoroughly polished cheese board compounded his unease with a vague feeling of alienation and shame.

"We're still on for next week, aren't we?" Kyla asked as they made their way back into the waiting taxi shuttle.

"Definitely," said Liam, but not without a quiver in his voice. "Wouldn't miss it for the world."

7

Showing up at the show's outer London Tantamount Mews headquarters for the second time, Liam received his first taste of his new routine. It tasted a lot like grapefruit.

Before they left for their first interview, he eyed the copy of the first

---

25 Originally, an excess of bodily fluids. Thanks to the advances of medical science, our overflows are usually less physical these days, but they still need to come out *somewhere*.

potential contestant's AR anti-CV over crappy instant coffee in the Lounge: Finn Oldman, 34, single, and something called an "accounts facilitator" with Health Services.

A large vehicle was waiting outside to take him, Lee, Carpentiere, and most importantly, their expensive equipment down to the main Health Services offices in the northern suburbs of the city.

It was a long bumpy ride, and judging from the worn feel of the suspensions, the flashy Red logo nano-paint job with its constantly shifting patterns and colours had probably cost more than the vehicle itself. Liam gazed out at the criss-crossing maglev shuttle lines packed with an undying ebb and flow of commuters at all hours of day and night. Anything to avoid having to talk with the other occupants of the vehicle. The idea of having to open that social can of worms and, once conversation was started, having to find subjects to cover the entire drive thereafter seemed to be a terror shared by all present. None dared break that primeval ice, for fear of what might lie beneath.

It didn't even make sense that the suspensions would be bad. He hadn't been in a vehicle with suspension problems since he was a child. Everything was made from self-maintaining nano-materials these days. It either worked well or gave out altogether when the nanites reached minimum levels and shut down. You just couldn't get something that only worked half-assedly anymore, and yet these suspensions were unquestionably doing exactly that. If his AR encyclopaedia was to be trusted, for that to happen you'd need to somehow modify the basic nanite programming to drop all the safeguards and then keep running the parts down as they literally crumbled apart, burned out nanites dropping away like dead skin cells...

He shuddered, closing the AR search window. *Weren't we all supposed to have flying vehicles by the time I was an adult, anyway?* The idea was certainly good for a distraction, but it was also something he was truly passionate about. The promised future from his childhood stories was supposed to be the present now, surely. The technology seemed to be there, with superconductors you could fry eggs on. So why the hell wasn't this damn thing zooming across the skies to land gracefully on a roof-top platform? Why was it "too expensive for any practical use," as the media always said, when at the same time, the residential and commercial playgrounds of the corporate rich had private flight lanes into the urban centres, paved entirely with room-temperature superconductors? Was gross inequality the only way to realise the dream of flying cars that humankind had defined as "the Future" for so long?

The Health Services building, which eventually provided Liam with a welcome excuse to stop thinking about such things, was indescribable;

not merely indescript, which simply underlines a certain laziness on behalf of the describer, but quite literally indescribable, in the same way that the mind cannot truly describe things it cannot grasp, be they too vast, like the yawning chasm of the country sky above a city-bred child's head, or too horrible, such as the limitless potential of that self-same sky at night. One could say the building was grey, one could say it was bleak, one could say it was tall, but that would not be actual describing; those same words could apply to just about any building in a fifty-kilometre radius and, indeed, were in essence already contained in the word "building" in this setting. Those qualities[26] which made this specific building "Health Services" lay elsewhere. Somewhere elusive, beyond the merely physical and into a realm of quickly silenced despair and routine little bureaucratic evils that both beckoned and repulsed the mind of servant, subject, and onlooker alike. Nonetheless, inadvisably to Liam's mind, they entered.

Liam tried to ignore the obvious scene they were offering with their professional-grade pod-cameras[27] and sound recorders (sets of three eye-sized lenses to be positioned around the room for best feeding effect and, in a noteworthy demonstration of anachronistic conservation, referred to in the business as tripods) as they made their wary way across the desolate lobby, past the terminally unmanned reception desk and, after some debate and on the directions of a grimy and manifestly outdated AR directory, into the eventual elevator and up to the fifth floor, left wing, "User Relations."

A man whose AR ID introduced him as "Agent 1215084 – OLDMAN, Finn – Accounts" was waiting for them by the "employees-only" water outlet.

"I wasn't sure you'd really be coming," said the man, putting an end to a seemingly millennial state of relative inertness in order to gush forward to shake their hands, without taking the trouble to introduce himself any further than his ID already had. "It's not much, but here it is," he said, waving his arm in the general direction of the mess of meter-wide and long cubicles that honeycombed an office floor entirely devoid of proper walls, or even windows, for that matter. "Hey, is that thing on?" His gaze fixed upon the lit pod instruments in Lee's hands, his hunger evident and unabashed.

"Yes, but don't worry about it, just doing some preliminary light and sound tests and so on. Don't mind them," said Lee in the consecrated formula dear to seekers of "candid" footage[28] since the birth of the graven im-

---

26 For a given value of the word "quality."

27 The "chamber," a little space designed to capture a moment, lock it up, and keep it safe and deathly still forever more.

28 The imperial measurements will live on in etymology long after the metric system inevitably replaces them in all practical uses.

age reel.

"Shall we go have a look at your workstation?" asked Carpentiere, to general, if not particularly fussed, assent. They seemed to expect Liam to lead the way, so he did. Finn's cubicle was, quite precisely, three and a half walls, the patch of plastic floor they delimited, a chair, a small physical filing cabinet, a folding table that did not deserve the title its obvious function as a desk bestowed, plenty of bare wall for AR window display, and a mess of paper scraps. Writing implements were apparently at a premium, and the waste basket was out in the space between sets of, for lack of a better word, walls. One could only resist against dignifying this space with the title of "hallway."

Finn took his place at his chair, casting constant glances at the lens, while they stood next to him, outside the cubicle. He would occasionally burst out and say, "So is this going to be in the feed? Is it?" to which they'd calm him and tell him to just go about his business while they made certain all the settings were right.

Liam knew for a fact this was an outright lie because he'd half-listened to them discussing the matter toward the end of that interminable ride from the Mews to this wretched place. The feed had been live from the moment they'd left the van, and what they were doing now was trying to get the more-or-less candid work scenes that would be the filler for Finn's preview spot.

He wasn't all that comfortable with the idea of systematically lying to the applicants right from the get-go, but he couldn't deny that the only way to get people to look properly natural for the feed was to make them think it wasn't on. Since there was nothing to be done for it, he decided to let it go.

At length, Carpentiere broke the silence. "Alrighty then, I think we've got it. Mr. Oldham, could you please start by telling us what it is you do here." The man looked up from his podscreen, where, ostensibly at work, he had been frowning and sighing at an open file for a good five minutes now, and started.

"Oh, well, I work in accounts, see. When users sign up for HS coverage, they're filed, and we start up an account for them. Any treatment they undergo is billed to that account, where we validate any deductibles and bill the rest back to the users on a monthly basis..." Here he paused his rehearsed spiel, looking hesitant, maybe even fearful. When he spoke again, it was in the lowered tones of a conspirator,[29] or perhaps of a man who, faced with the choice, preferred to part with some of his throat rather than his cigarettes.

"The problem is, our 'users' are by definition the dirt-poor people who

---

29 "Breathing together." Ultimately, we are all conspirators.

can't even pay for perfectly affordable private health coverage, like Medi-calc™." Liam was reminded of an advert he remembered from some train ride or another. "So they can barely ever afford the seventy or eighty percent of the treatment cost that isn't covered. And then there are the incentives: Health Services gets a fixed envelope every year to cover all expenses, and that's not just to cover the basic treatment coverage for the users, but also everyone's salaries at HS. The budget is tighter than... well... it's very tight, so anything that doesn't get paid by the users ends up coming directly out of our pockets. That's why we need guys like me. Our job is to follow up on the users and make sure they pay every cent they can... even when, really, they can't."

Liam looked around him as he listened to the man. The cubicles around him were filled with women, men, and enbies who were ordinary enough, judging from the backs of their heads at least, and yet here they came, day after day, pushing society's most unfortunate to the brink of survival—he wouldn't allow himself to finish that thought to its logical conclusion.

"Take Fred Watson here," Oldman said, lifting his podscreen to face the lens. "I really shouldn't be showing you this, so don't go putting it on the feed now, but it really shows what I'm talking about. Fred here has two kids he only sees every other week but still needs to support, a second mortgage he can't really afford, and a budding thyroid cancer that should have been diagnosed years ago, and it's my job to make him pay up for the meds that will only postpone the inevitable at this stage anyway." Liam returned his full attention to the man. "Sometimes, that means using threats: repossession of the little flat he inherited from his mom, letting the Family Services in on his financial difficulties, that sort of thing... I suppose you could call us something of an uncivil service[30]." He chuckled, not so much balefully as like a literal long-forgotten bale of rotting hay. "But the thing is, Fred here is just so damn typical it's tragic. I deal with hundreds of Freds every day."

Liam examined Oldman's flabby lines, his receding hairline, and his nose hair in turn, and in mountingly horrifying detail. The man seemed to take the silence as a sign of expectant interest, for he continued.

"I have to study these files, take in all the details, and then go about my job making sure they pay up. Let me tell you, it's not an easy job, emotionally or psychologically." Always one for compassion, or so he liked to believe, even in the face of congenital antipathy, Liam had to cut in.

"Why don't you just get out of it then? Find some other job? Maybe we can help."

Finn raised an eyebrow. "Change jobs? What good would that do? I've

---

30 To be translated into French as "dysfonction publique," en français dans le texte.

been here a while now. I'm starting to get some decent benefits at last. I'm not about to give that up on a whim, and a man's got to eat, you know. No, what we really need is to have the psychological stress involved in the work taken into account by the Services and properly compensated. At the very least, we should get some coverage on our psychoactive medication. If you really want to help, you can put this in the feed to give us some media attention and force the Services to do something for us. That's why I sent in the application in the first place. So..."

"... this'll all be in the feed, right?" The large AR projection more-or-less tastefully thrown again the walls of the Editor's pseudo wood-panelled office froze on the man's eager expression of hope and greed.

"Perfect! This is precisely the kind of thing we're looking for. Despicable and pitiful at the same time." The Editor beamed like Pharos rebuilt. "We'll take out that last statement and cut straight to the scene at that hovel of his, with the indefinable mutt. People always root for the underdog[31]. It'll be pure synthetic pathos gold."

Liam knew the Corporation had to be right. That's why they were the Corporation, after all. But an odd thought trotted through his mind and past his lips. "Won't that make him seem... better than he really is? We spent about five hours filming with him, and it only took five minutes to see he was a pretty despicable guy. I don't know if I feel comfortable with the idea of making him seem almost sympathetic with a pitiful home life scene."

The Editor's first reaction was a quick glance at his desk's security-shaded podscreen. "Argyle, my dear boy," he said. His tone irked Liam to no end, as he knew very well that the man had all of five years on him, regardless of his obvious efforts to make himself look older. "What we are doing here is a service to the public. These kinds of situations need to be brought to the light if we're ever going to make a difference. You do want to make a difference, don't you?"

"Well, yes..." Liam said, in earnest. In a display of the sort of obliviousness that had earned him his job in the first place, he wondered when the callous Editor had become such a master of empathy, to be able to read into him so openly.

"Then what's a little doctoring here and there? The ends justify the means, and we could hardly honour the little git with an integral display of his lechery, could we?" Liam certainly agreed there. "Don't let it get to you. It's all for the greater good." He closed the conversation with what was undoubtedly meant to be a wise nod. Liam didn't know what to say, so he

---

31 The one who's getting it in the rear, that is.

stuck to what he knew.[32]

"That's that then," said the Editor. "You and the crew had best go grab a sandwich from the trolley in the Lounge. You've got a busy afternoon ahead of you. In the meantime, we'll start shaping this up for upfeeding back to Corporate." The subsequent silence made Liam think he was dismissed, but the Editor must merely have been pensive since, as Liam was making his way out to find the trolley, he added, almost as an afterthought, "Oh, and Argyle. Keep up the good work."

8

"That's your actual name?" If Liam hadn't taken such an instinctive liking to the next potential contestant, he would never have believed him.

"That's right," said the chipper young man, spreading good cheer like some sort of jovial plague carrier as he sat on his pub stool. "Usnavi. I know it's weird and supposed to be degrading, somehow, being named after the U.S. Navy because of a Cuban thrice-greatgrandmother who didn't have any other name for her child's father. But that was my grandfather's name, and his grandfather's before him. It's become a bit of a family tradition by now."

Smuggled into the country as a newborn by parents who were denied refugee status but came illegally anyway, there was hardly a thing in his voice or mannerisms to give away Usnavi Musibay's Cuban origins. Certainly, his accent was no worse than every other East Londoner's.

He seemed to laugh in the face of his ridiculous name, the withered right arm he made no effort whatsoever to conceal, and the world in general. It was difficult not to like the young man instantly, and Liam saw no reason to fight the impulse.

"Have you been, you know..." Liam gestured at Usnavi's arm. "Like that since birth?"

"Oh, aye. 'Upper Limb Reduction Defect,' the doctors call it, which is medical lingo for, 'You've got a withered arm for some reason and we can't do anything about it.'" He laughed. "Not that I want them to. This arm here is just like my other one, it's part of what makes me who I am. It's just one of them things, you take them as they come."

He shuffled a bit on his stool and took a swig from the pint glass gripped in his good hand.

---

32 *i.e.:* nothing.

"Of course, it's just as well that I look at things that way, since I certainly can't pay for any of the fancy prosthetics that might make it look like I have two good arms. Maybe someday, right? Especially if I make it into this big show of yours."

He drained his glass and set it back down on the gleaming engineered hardwood bar top.

"Until then, I'll just have to be like the Earth itself, in that Hitchhiker book. Not 'armless, but mostly 'armless."

Usnavi cracked up laughing at his own expense, and Liam didn't know whether it was appropriate to join in or not. He was very much in terra incognita as far as his political correctness charts were concerned. He decided to just go with it for a bit, then bring things back to business.

"So, Usnavi—if you don't mind me calling you that—what is it you do for a living?" Looking over at the young man, past his shrivelled arm, Liam realised how crass the expression "for a living" truly was.

"Well, for a long time, it was illegal to hire me, being here without paperwork and all, so I'd try my best to get a bit of manual labour now and then that pays under the table. But, of course, even that's hard to come by if you've got half the arms as everyone else begging for work. Then my family got rounded up and threatened with deportation back to post-war Cuba."

Usnavi paused as the server came back with a refill for his pint, ordered in perfect silence through his charity-bin AR lenses as he was talking. He rubbed the right side of his chest, beneath his worn Star Wars t-shirt, a reflexive action by all appearances. Liam encouraged him to carry on.

"We all thought there was nothing for it but to live on the street in what's left of Havana. Then, at the last minute, the immigrant app offered the only work visa it said I qualified for. I think the official title is 'Clinical Investigation Agent.' Sounds grand for a human guinea pig, doesn't it?"

Liam nodded. Obviously, new products and research needed to be tested on people before they could be opened to the public. It was one of those things you knew must be happening somewhere in the background noise of society. It certainly was strange to meet a human test subject face to face, though.

"What kind of research have you been involved with?"

"Oh, all sorts, but they've only started offering me the ones that really pay the bills this year, since I had my full medical and genetic details done up." He wiggled his withered arm for emphasis. "Other than this, it seems I came up pretty clear. Odd, really, since I usually feel like shite warmed up—excuse my French. But one of the doctors even said that I was a perfect test subject, whatever that means."

Usnavi put down his glass and lifted his good hand, ticking off the fingers. "New drugs, medical nanotech, cosmetics, all the classic stuff. You name it, I've done it. Right now, I've got a sweet deal trying out some new bacteria-fighting ninja virus strain. It's great, because I have go to lots of public places to expose myself to as much disease as possible, and they pick up the tab." He took another swig of lager, sighing in satisfaction. "Tastes all the sweeter when you know someone else is paying for it, but I suppose that can't last forever. There's another cool gig I've applied for, I'm just waiting for them to get back to me. All very hush hush, but it's definitely interesting. Maybe something the people watching your show might like, do you think?"

Liam couldn't stop himself from grinning at Usnavi's naked enthusiasm and resolved to make sure the young man made it onto the show, one way or another. This was the perfect example of a life that needed to be heard and seen. A chance to really change the world for the better.

They followed him around all the rest of that day as he gave them a first-hand tour of his life, from his favourite street Cuban *empanada* food truck down in Brockley, to the tiny little room he shared with three cousins in a lean-to extension around the back of the family's grey plastic labourer prefab, one of the thousands crammed onto the old parks in Redbridge.

When Carpentiere's drives started running out of room for footage, they realised they'd already stayed two hours longer than scheduled. *The Grass is Greener* team took their leave, with Liam promising to get back to Usnavi as soon as possible. Carpentiere loaded the podcameras and sound equipment back into the vehicle and, noting Liam's good spirits, matched the host's grin with his own.

"If you liked that one, Liam, wait until you see the plan for tomorrow morning. I hope your passport is in date, because we're flying to Hollywood."

9

At first glance, Liam thought they had taken a wrong turn and ended up in a clothing exposition room, the kind overweight people went to out of fear that their shopping app might get their sizes wrong again. Everywhere, manikins[33] in various states of dishabille loomed like fashionable

---

33 "Little man." Also used for robots in early sci-fi, before Čapek coined the truest possible term.

gargoyles.

Again, it was one thing to know that all pornography these days starred the robotic descendants of the humble vibrator. It was another to be confronted with a studio full of the things.

One of the super-humanly buff male figures in the centre of the room stepped forward and reached out to shake his hand. Liam rallied his runaway wits and smiled as best he could, finally recognising the figure from his profile pictures.

Spike Bighorn, the last flesh-and-blood porn star in Hollywood.

Towering over Liam, Spike—yes, that was his actual birth name; Liam had double checked the file before he could allow himself to believe it—wore a skimpy "Indian" brave costume that should have looked both racist and ridiculous. Spike somehow managed to make it look authentic.

Torn between curiosity and deep-grained moral dislike of the whole business, Liam stood there, hesitating to even take the proffered hand to shake it. He eventually decided to shake the hand anyway, before the situation got even more awkward[34] than it already was. Spike didn't seem to mind.

"Boy, am I glad to see you guys. They need me for another shoot, and I was starting to think you had gotten lost on your way here or something. Did the AR take you the scenic route?" His voice boomed, full of imagery of tomahawks and calumet pipes.

"Just a bit of hassle getting our luggage at the airport. They mixed up the tags on our case with the luggage of some South African tourist family, and the systems refused to release any of the luggage until we could get a supervisor to override it. I suppose that's what they call progress, right?"

Spike's laugh could have brought down a fighter drone at eighteen hundred meters. "It's the same here, friend, I can tell you. So, do you want to do the interview here, or would you like me to find an unused set for us?"

"No-no," Liam replied, a bit too fast for his own liking. "Here will be fine. I wanted to ask you about your relationship to your... coworkers, I suppose."

Spike let out a slightly less military-grade laugh.

"What, the Erobots?" He draped an arm around one of the nearest male manikins, reminding Liam that he had taken Spike for one of them just moments before.

"Beautiful craftsmanship, by all accounts. Skin like silk, and let me tell you, that's one hell of an improvement over the sandpaper they used to cover the first generation of these guys in." He let out a sigh, not intended to be dramatic, but coming from such heights and depths that it almost had

---

34 "Turned the wrong way."

to be.

"That's all just appearances though. Obviously, the adult entertainment industry is all about appearances, so that's only to be expected. Between the design improvements and the advances in AR enhancement, you can hardly tell the difference between a real person and an artificial performer anymore—and that's the whole problem, really. How are we supposed to compete with perfect tools who make a Turing test sound like a come-on, and will never mess up a take, miss a cue, or make a funny face?"

All around them, the mecha-pornstars stood in silence. Surely, it was only Liam's imagination which made it seem like they were listening? He had to break the silence. "It says in your application that you're the last human actor left in the Hollywood... adult entertainment industry. Was that just a figure of speech?"

"Nope, I am the very last real person working in front of the cameras. I hear they're not quite as mechanised yet in Krung Thep or Bollywood, but the last other guy around here was Harry Balzac, and he got his retraining orders over a year ago now. Last I heard, he was working as a sports presenter. Of course, the female co-workers were the first to go, what with power tool burn."

"Power tool burn?" Liam tried not to ask, he really did.

"Sorry. That's the term for muscle strain caused by piston-driven artificial members. It's been around for a while. Mostly affects the female performers for obvious reasons, through us males have not been spared from that ourselves. But at least I get to take turns."

Liam somehow felt that he should be taking some form of offense here, but Spike was just so damn natural and open about everything, as if android bisexuality were the most common conversation topic in the world. Liam liked the man.

They carried on with the tour of the set, but Liam knew it was a done deal. The Editor had been adamant about wanting Spike on the team, and Liam could see his point—so to speak. Who would resist the temptation of taking a peek through the eyes of the last human porn star in Hollywood? Imagine the ratings...

Following Bighorn through the set, between rows upon rows of frozen Erobots and boxes full of other tools of the trade, Liam began thinking about the viewers who would be watching all this, once the show finally started. What sort of person would they be, to be attracted to content like this?

10

One crammed and cost-effective transatlantic flight later, Liam and Carpentiere were back on the hunt for their elusive contestants. After a flop with an abattoir "surface technician" who had suffered from a terminal lack of charisma, they were more than a little antsy as they waited at the curb outside a residential unit in Chiswick for their next candidate.

"Where the hell is she?" asked Carpentiere, rubbing his hands to fight off the late fall chill. "We managed to get here on time, even though we only got the address at the last minute. Isn't this supposed to be an emergency service?"

A crash from inside shook the fronting of the building behind them. Both Liam and Carpentiere turned and looked up out of instinct, before shielding their faces with their arms as shattered glass fell down upon them both.

Liam brushed the bits off his jacket sleeve. Neither of them seemed to have been hurt. "Rough neighbourhood," said Liam, in a failed attempt at lightening the mood.

"I say we give her another five minutes and then we write her off," replied a nonplussed Carpentiere.

"Come on, man. This could be good."

"Ten minutes, then," said Carpentiere with a grunt, leaving them both waiting at the curb in silence, each lost in their own AR displays as their breath condensed to mist before them.

They shifted to one side as a heavyset lady stormed out of the residential complex's front door, bearing a case. She passed Liam, Carpentiere, and their equipment case before stopping and whirling around on them. The effect was terrifying and made them regret any sins they may have or may not have committed. The apparition was uglier than imagination cared to allow for.

"It's you, isn't it? From the Red reality show?"

Despite his sudden and profound desire that it not be them, Liam managed to stutter some form of confirmation. The lady, whom Liam could only induce[35] was their potential entrant, a Ms Juliette Binns, put a fist on her hip.

"Have you been waiting out here this whole time? You've only gone and missed it all, then, haven't you?" Liam presumed they had. "Just as well, though, I suppose," carried on Ms Binns. "It got a bit hairy in there today. You must have seen it when the guy broke the window, yeah?"

Liam confirmed that, sadly, this had indeed been an obligation, while scolding himself for getting into one of those distant moods again and trying his best to bring himself fully back into the moment.

"Well, the clients can get like that sometimes, in my line of work. There's a reason why all the AR service providers have to offer emergency on-site technical support teams, and that's because people freak the fuck out— can I say that?" she asked mid-sentence, addressing Carpentiere, who had already pulled out his podcam and begun recording. Liam found it highly interesting that the one holding the equipment was the one people turned to out of instinct, and noted that in an empty corner of his psyche for later.

"Feel free to say anything you want, ma'am," came Carpentiere's reply. "We want you to be as natural as possible."

"Well, I can do natural," said Juliette, with a smile. "So, yes, people freak out very fucking badly indeed when their AR systems fail. Whether it's due to a software crash in the operating system or some kind of hardware failure, the result is always the same. People are used to living with AR constantly editing the world around them, adapting how they see and experience it, and formatting their interactions with the rest of the world. When that protective layer disappears suddenly—well, naked, unaugmented reality can be a pretty scary place. They had us experience it ourselves as part of training, and it sure gave me the willies." Juliette shook, and not from the cold. "So I guess I can't really blame the poor bastards who lash out at us when the service interruption flag goes up and we arrive to sort things out. Some of them can get a bit nasty though, like that guy today, with his meat tenderiser."

She paused, a pensive look crossing her features like the shadow of a cloud passing over a particularly disturbing mountain range.

"Of course, it does seem to be a lot worse for me than for most AR emergency techs. I suppose that, well, this," she said, gesturing at just about everything from her collarbone up, "doesn't help things very much. The poor bastards are getting their first look at unfiltered reality in ages—probably in their lives—and they see this face coming through their door."

---

35 Yes, "induce," not "deduce." This is induction, a probabilistic hypothesis based on what facts are available, as opposed to deduction, a strictly logical and necessary consequence of those same facts. Sherlock Holmes never deduced anything!

At this, Juliette hefted her case and shrugged.

"Well, nothing to be done for it, I suppose, and it just means that I'm probably the most qualified tech around when it comes to handling panicking clients. Speaking of which, do you gents want to come back to the response centre with me and wait for another call? I could show you around the place."

Liam tried to hide his resigned sigh and failed miserably. "I suppose so, Ms. Binns."

The last thing Liam wanted to do was follow this lady any deeper into the world behind the comforting illusions that kept people entertained, informed, and sane. But orders were orders, and he needed at least another two hours of footage before he could run back to the Mews for a cup of tea and a sandwich.

Still, he mused as he followed the woman down the street to the Tube, a frontline soldier in the battle between reality and artificial paradise? The woman would certainly bring a unique perspective to a show like *The Grass is Greener*. He wondered what she'd make of their new lenses.

11

The next day was a Saturday, but that had little meaning for Liam and Carpentiere as the official-looking DMPC vehicle stopped in front of them. With a contented little pneumatic hiss, it opened its seating compartment door and they entered.

Liam smiled at the other passenger, a broad, muscle-bound man in a crisp uniform, and waited for Carpentiere to finish setting up the podcam surround system before speaking. The car was already heading at full tilt toward its own ends by the time he was done.

"Right then, Mr... Leigh, is it? Or is it Brad?" Their host acknowledged with a nod as stiff as a two-by-four, his hand resting on a case taking up the entire seat next to him, but remained silent.

"Excellent, " Liam lied. "Could you please tell us a bit about what you do, then?"

"Brad Leigh, Disease Monitoring and Prevention Corps number 2599401-51," reeled off their potential contestant, like a combatant resisting interrogation, "assigned to the fast-reaction target interception and vector pacification task force, sir."

Surprised, Liam double-checked the profile in his AR display. Looked like the right guy, and surely there couldn't be two people with a mug like that, even though his facial recognition app seemed to be having a tough time getting a lock on his face. "There must have been some mistake. I thought you were a Germ Bouncer?"

The man's stony facade broke into a rare smirk. "I have heard civilians refer to the task force that way before, sir."

"So, if you don't mind me asking, what's with the military get-up and all of the official symbols on the car? You'd think this were some sort of military police operation or something."

The smirk disappeared, to be replaced again by an utter, disdainful absence of features. Impressive control, and far more insulting than any anger might have been.

"As I am sure that you are aware, sir, the Disease Monitoring and Prevention Corps works under public tender in application of World Court jurisprudence and laws transposed in every State. We look like a military police operation because we act for the public good with the full weight of military status and police authority, sir."

"Oh, I meant no disrespect, of course," Liam was quick to backpedal. "I've always had the highest respect for the boys and girls in khaki. I was just surprised you needed to advertise it, though. Is that something you find helps in your day to day work?"

The atmosphere in the tight compartment relaxed a bit.

"Well, it never hurts to show our colours to the vectors, sir—the disease-bearing people, that would be in layman's terms, sir." Leigh seemed to relax a bit, and carried on. "You know, most of them still resent us and try to resist treatment. Some even act as if it were optional and they had any say in the matter! Between ourselves, that's why the brass decided we needed a contestant in this new reality show of yours, to make people fully aware of what we do, how we operate, and how important it is."

"I couldn't think of a more deserving cause," said Liam, wishing he were brave enough to make it sound as sarcastic as he felt it should. "But why would that be you, instead of any of the other agents, do you think?"

Leigh shifted a little on his seat. "Well, that would probably be because of my little... problem."

"Sorry, it doesn't say anything in the file. What problem is that?"

"Well, if you must know... it's my face, sir. It's common."

"Common?" asked Liam, with a blink. "I don't think any of us are winning any Mr. Universe pageants, you know."

"Not like that," growled Leigh, a red flush creeping up his neck. "Common, as in difficult to distinguish by the damn face recognition apps that seem to be everywhere these days." He sighed, and seemed a different man for a moment. "You know, when people say they have 'one of those faces'? Well, that's me. It's always been the same, ever since I was a teen and public buildings started using facial recognition security doors. If I had a cred for every time I've been pulled for interrogation because my AR ID tags don't match who a door says I am, I'd be rich enough to retire."

He paused a moment, pensive.

"It's a bit of a hindrance in our line of work, of course. Vectors tend to resist even more when their AR display tells them I'm not who my badge says. But then again, without all of those problems, I might never have felt the call to serve in the Corps. It showed me just how little the individual matters when it comes to public security."

A shiver ran down Liam's spine, and it wasn't one of the good ones. He was desperate to change the subject before he had to think about it too much. "So, do you think we'll get to see one of your.... interventions, today?"

"Of course, sir. I have an average of twenty interventions per day. Even more so on a weekend, when the public toilets are in full use and their sensors send all manner of viral and bacterial alerts our way. Public toilets count for a good half of my intervention workload on a day like today, sir—so I hope you don't mind getting your hands a bit dirty, so to speak."

Liam balked. "What do you mean, get my hands dirty?"

"Well, things can get a bit hectic with this sort of intervention, sir. Our response times are fast, because they have to be. We need to get to the vectors before they leave and start spreading their disease among the unsuspecting public. This means the vectors are usually still in the middle of their business, such as it is, when we arrive and commence treatment. Entitled pricks think they can keep us waiting, too. Selfish bastards."

"Wait, so you actually do barge in on people wherever they are and force medical treatment on them? I thought that was just an urban myth!"

"It is a necessity, sir. We do what we have to do, sir, however surprised the disease carriers may be to see us arrive."

"Well, why don't you let them know you're coming beforehand, give them some time to prepare?"

Clearly, this was the funniest thing, or perhaps just the most ridiculous, Leigh had ever heard. "What, and give them time to run off before we could possibly get there? Oh, that would certainly be one way of making my job easier, that's for sure! I didn't realise this was a comedy program!"

His laughter was interrupted by a flash from the car's interior lighting, clearly matched by an alert on Leigh's AR display.

"Buckle up, boys, we've got a live one. Influenza in the colon—looks like we'll have to bring 'em in to camp to apply enema treatment. Are you boys ready?"

Damn the Editor and his inescapably clear instructions. "As ready as we're ever going to be, Mr. Leigh," Liam replied, trying his best not to sound as horrified as he felt. "Unless you think we'd get in your way. As you say, Corporate has pretty much secured your place in the show anyway. You can just drop us off anywhere here, if we're going to hinder you in your very important work."

"Nonsense!" said Brad, dashing Liam's meagre hopes. "It's hard out there, fighting the good fight, day in and day out. We need all the publicity we can get! And I've yet to meet the sicko I couldn't handle on my own after a good lick of the taser."

"Oh, goodie," Liam sighed, turning to stare out of the car window at the blurred grey buildings speeding by. He would have been happy to walk all the way back to the Mews, through the slums, if it got him away from Mr. Brad Leigh any faster.

12

Their next interview was only a short ride away from the Mews, but it felt like an alien planet. Liam sat in the sad little academic office in the unfashionable end of his old alma mater, the University of London's Birkbeck College, and wondered what he was doing there. Perhaps the equally sad-looking man sitting across the desk from him had the answer.

"Professor Fourka, if you don't mind me asking, sir... Why did you send in an application for *The Grass is Greener*? You do realise the point of the show is to see who has the worst lot in life?"

The professor, Dr. Ali Fourka according to the profile in a corner of Liam's AR, smiled a little and shrugged his tweed-clad shoulders. "Of course. However, if I remember the advertisement correctly, it mentioned 'all walks of life,' yes? Surely, this means you aren't just looking for the destitute,[36] the sick, and the maimed. 'All walks of life' includes all of those who have suffered the most from the... let's say 'evolutions,' to remain polite, of modern society. Since they shut down LSE to replace it with in-house Corporate government and business directorship programs, I'm the only political science academic left with a position in all of the UK. Even that, I sometimes fear, is only an overlook. Once they get around to auditing the books and see that they still have a Professor of Political Science on the payroll, I'll be

---

36 Etymologically: Abandoned, put away.

queuing up for reassignment by the employment algorithm as well. Already, they're reducing my classes and giving me the worst time slots. The students are gently encouraged to mock me, when they show up at all."

Liam thought he remembered crossing paths with Prof. Fourka, as they both ambled about the corridors of Birkbeck. He certainly hadn't seemed dangerous or undesirable, and probably less offensive than some of the other faculty. Perhaps he was just being paranoid, which had been known to happen among academics after reaching a certain age without obtaining tenure.

"Why would the College want to get rid of you, specifically, Professor Fourka?"

"Isn't it obvious, Liam? If you don't mind me calling you Liam, that is. It's quite simple. These days, nobody wants a political scientist around providing critical thought about the abdication of the political sphere in favour of the world of private business. Not when we're all so busy living it."

Liam had thought as much in private himself, but the podcameras were rolling, and he felt it was part of his job to play devil's advocate.

"I'm not certain it is quite that simple, Professor. You speak as if we no longer had a political system and everything was decided in Corporate boardrooms, but we still elect our politicians. We still have Countries, Parliaments, Governments, Councils, Mayor—the whole lot. Certainly, the Corporations now have their own extraterritorial Courts and their own Law system, but that doesn't mean we've sold our political decision-making power to them."

Professor Fourka tilted his head somewhat, considering Liam before he responded. "What sort of people do you find in these elected positions, these days?"

"Yes, I see where you're going. Most of them are business people and have business ties, but that doesn't mean Corporations are running everything. That's just the people's choice, since the business world is where all of the most talented people work. People were fed up with the old crew, the professional politicians. They want elected officials who know how to make money, who will get rid of the bureaucrats and get the job done."

"Ah, yes, getting rid of the bureaucrats. They've certainly done that. Let's take a look at the core prerogatives of the State. Do you know who runs the Police service and the Tax system in our own country, these days?"

"Well, the Government and Parliament, obviously."

"Really? So, when you receive your income tax notice, or if you are taken in for police questioning, then you are dealing with State-employed civil servants, are you?"

"No, all of the actual hands-on management is outsourced nowadays to companies like RedCorp and the Revenue Corporation, obviously. But all of the actual policy decisions are still made by the elected politicians."

Across the table, the smile on Ali Fourka's face contained less actual cheer than a clown's wake. "Are they? I think you'll find that the first thing an elected official will be keen on 'outsourcing' to a third party is the responsibility for an unpopular police enforcement measure, or tax hike. Deniability is the main goal of the government outsourcing program, Liam, not efficiency or cost reduction. That can happen sometimes, certainly, but it is entirely coincidental, and the outsourced services are usually more expensive than the opposite. Private business exists to make profits, after all, and the taxpayer has to pay those at some level."

Liam glanced over at Carpentiere and the podcams, whirling away to provide a full, three-dimensional recording of the discussion. Damn it all, he didn't want to be arguing against this man, he wanted to buy him a drink! "These are all very interesting theories, Professor Fourka. So, if I understand correctly, you think your treatment here at Birkbeck justifies a spot on *The Grass is Greener*? Presumably, you would use this to expound upon these ideas of yours?"

"The way I see it, your show is a bit of an epiphenomenon, a frontier where control may not be quite so tight. With a bit of publicity, maybe I could make myself more trouble to get rid of than to keep. I'm not holding my breath, but I've got to try something. I'm sure you understand."

Poor bastard. They followed the Professor in silence as he gave them a tour through the worn-down University halls. Professor Fourka had a snowball's chance in a fusion reactor of actually making it onto the show, Liam told himself, so at least he'd be spared the public humiliation. The Editor would never let the show turn into a platform for these kinds of ideas.

13

Back at the Mews, the Editor beamed at Liam from across the empty, polished surface of his desk.

"Thank you for coming straight in to see me, Liam. I just wanted to congratulate you on the excellent job you've been doing. We are well ahead of schedule regarding the candidate interviews and selection. I've been reviewing the footage you uploaded, and there are so many good candidates there, we are embarrassed for choice. I'm confident the last few interviews already lined up for next week will provide us with the final two contestants, giving us a full complement of eight in time for the live weekly pre-mière next Sunday."

Liam's brain did a couple of mathematical gymnastics flips and did not like the scores he came up with. "Sorry, sir, but did you say two more contestants? I'm not certain we have six definite contestants after the in-terviews so far. You aren't counting the abattoir cleaning lady, surely? We could have congealing porridge as a contestant and it would be more inter-esting to watch."

The Editor made a show of looking pensive. "No, my count is correct. With Professor Fourka, that makes six."

"Professor Fourka? But... well, I had assumed that..."

"What? That RedCorp wouldn't want that sort of anti-Corporate opin-ion voiced through our show?" He actually laughed at this, taking the cari-cature beyond breaking point. "Liam, my dear boy, you have so much to learn. Would you like a drink?"

"No, I'm fine, thank you," Liam responded by rote. His alcohol rehab conditioning had been worth every penny, even though he suspected it might be put to the test over the next few weeks.

"Very well, then." The Editor steepled his fingers and leaned forward across the desk. "Tell me, Liam, did you know that Bedlam[37] Asylum was one of the biggest entertainment venues in Georgian London? Toffs would pay quite handsomely to go view and mock the inmates, the insane, and the political activists alike. Ninety-six thousand visitors in one year alone! It was quite the popular and commercial sensation."

Liam had no idea where the Editor was going with this, and wished things could remain that way.

"So, as you see, *The Grass is Greener* has a proud heritage and is only the latest iteration of an old tradition—probably as old as humanity itself. People have an instinctive need to see, and to mock, other people. Our con-testants are the inmates of our own little asylum, and will be treated and in-terpreted as such by the viewers. Professor Fourka will be a grand bit of fun when he airs those crazy ideas of persecution, especially when put along-side the life of someone like Usnavi Musibay. Nobody will take a word he says seriously—quite the contrary! We will make sure of that."

Liam felt sick and regretted not accepting that drink after all—at least he would have had an excuse for feeling sick, then. The Editor carried on.

"But, of course, it is our viewers who hold the power and will vote to decide the ultimate winner of our little bit of entertainment, so who knows? Maybe even Professor Fourka will have a chance. But none of that will mat-ter if we don't get the final two contestants lined up. So, once again, keep up

---

37 Originally, Bethlehem.

the excellent work, and I look forward to seeing your interviews."

Dismissed like a pop-up ad, Liam skulked out of the Editor's office. Standing in the non-gloom of the Tantamount Mews central warehouse area, he shuddered to think that, in a matter of days, he would be broadcasting from this same cavernous room to networked eyes and minds around the globe. He felt lost, dwarfed by the enormity of what lay before him.

Sucking it up, he grasped onto the only thing he could, the job in front of him. All he could do was deal with this task, and then the one after that. He would just have to see it though, come what may in the end.

Steeling himself, he set off to grab a bite to eat from the trolley. If he were quick, there would be just enough time to wolf down a sandwich before they had to leave for the next interview.

14

Liam hoped it was just a trick of the light and the podcams would see things more objectively than he could. To him, the dark-skinned woman leading them up the stairs looked and moved like she were at least twice the age of thirty-five, which was listed on her profile, under the name Azar Acquah.

"People always make fun of me when I say I'm a Dumb Squad freelancer, but it's not my fault the company decided to call itself that way," she said, panting slightly as she reached the landing at the top of the stairs. "It's not that bad a name, after all. Everything has been made 'smart this' and 'smart that' — we just make them dumb again."

After checking they were still following, she made her way down the corridor and over to the apartment door at the far end of the hallway.

"Don't worry," Azar continued, and Liam was unsure whether she was talking to them or to herself. "The clients always set up entry authorisations for me when they want me to come treat their house while they're out, which is most of the time."

She stood in front of the door and waited for the security system to pick up her AR network ID. A loud click confirmed the system had decided it liked her enough to disengage the bolt, and they entered the apartment.

After the dark corridor, the light streaming in from the tall windows blinded Liam a bit, and his AR glasses just made the glare worse. Still, he had to admit it was a very nice apartment, if you were into that centre city style of living. He stood, appreciating the retro-swing era decor that was so fashionable these days, and Azar must have noticed his interest.

"Yes, the clients have some pretty swank places. They're the ones who can afford to have their devices disconnected." She laughed a bit, and the creases at the corners of her eyes only served to draw attention to the glassy lifelessness of her left eye. "It's funny, really. You would think it would be easier not to put all of the connected chips into all of the products in the first place. Does your toaster really need to communicate with your wallpaper and your socks? But even with all of the medical proof now of how bad that constant EMF soup is for your health, no one is willing to buy a product that isn't so 'smart' it should know better than to sell itself in the first place. Hah!"

She pulled out an EMF scanner, as well as what looked like a long pair of tweezers, attached to a bulky battery at her hip. Leaving Liam and Carpentiere to their own devices, she walked over to the living room sofa and started slowly running the EMF meter across its surface.

"No, apparently it's easier to cram everything full of smart chips anyway, and then have those who can afford it hire the Dumb Squad to manually go over each and every consumer item in their house, to hunt down and deactivate every non-vital bit of electronics. Nice for some..." She sighed, but never paused in her painstaking work, even as she crawled along the base of the sofa. "Still, it's what keeps me in work, and at least I know I'm doing something useful. God knows I could have used something like this when I was a girl."

At this, Liam cleared a knot in his throat and spoke up. "Yes, your profile says something about an illness?"

"If I had only one illness, I'd be a much happier lady today. I've been sick for as long as I can remember, and they say it's all down to the early AR implants my parents gave me for my seventh birthday. Of course, we all know now that those things had less EMF-shielding than a box of cardboard and were basically see-through cancer coins. But my parents had no way of knowing that. They were sold on the idea of being cutting-edge and offering me a leg up in the Augmented world of the future. Since then, I've also come to realise that, for a relatively well-off couple of busy professionals, AR implants may have seemed a lot cheaper than employing a Nanny to keep their only daughter calm, entertained, and traceable at any time."

She prodded the sofa with her tweezers and sent a crackling discharge into the fabric, lighting her features up like a Cinco de Mayo mask. The podcam lenses twinkled and twirled as they recorded every glimmer.

"That was before I started getting seizures and they finally took me in for testing. Eye cancer, brain cancer, the whole shebang. Textbook case for these first generation AR lenses, and far too late to do anything about it by then."

Azar broke into a coughing fit at that point, leaving Liam to wonder how much of that was dust and exertion, and how much of it was psycho-somatic, given the topic of conversation. Either way, she soon pulled out of it and lifted herself from under the couch.

"Maybe it would have helped to get my lenses upgraded. Those new ones are supposed to have much better EMF shielding than back in the day. But what would be the use, even if they weren't so damn expensive?"

"Wait, you mean you still have the lenses?" asked Liam, baffled. "Even though they gave you cancer, and are probably still making it worse? Why didn't you just have them removed?"

Azar paused, halfway between the living room and her next targets in the kitchen area, and turned to face Liam. Her expression was one usually reserved for things found crawling under stones. "What, just remove my lenses altogether? Without replacing them? Frankly, I'd rather live with the cancer, so to speak. I don't know what I'd do if I didn't have my shows to distract me from the work and keep me going. I'm re-watching one of my favourite old comedies right now, if you must know."

She gratified Liam with a little smile, as if asking for forgiveness after her outburst, and resumed her walk over to the kitchen linen drawer. Pull-ing out one kitchen towel after another, she scanned each one and zapped them whenever necessary, talking all the while.

"Of course, it hasn't been all bad. If I hadn't gotten sick, I would never have heard about the Dumb Squad. After all the medical bills, my parents couldn't afford that sort of thing, but they took me right in when I applied for a job there. It's funny how it all works out in the end, isn't it? As if ev-erything has a purpose."

She paused, kitchen towel in hand, and turned her smile upon Liam once again.

"It's just like your show, really. I just happened to see the advertise-ment, and when I read the application paperwork, I learned you'll be of-fering free, latest-generation lens implants to all of the contestants! Now there's a sign I'm meant to be part of the show, if there ever was one."

For all of his scepticism regarding lazy, superstitious reasoning, Liam couldn't bring himself to disagree. As he followed busy Azar from one luxury apartment to the next, he realised there were lots of ways of do-ing good, big and small. Maybe helping someone like Azar Acquah get the lenses she could never afford otherwise was the realest kind of good he could hope to do through the show. And, at the end of the day, probably the one that meant the most.

15

What a week! he informed himself, nursing the remains of his second gin and tonic. *I know, I was there,* came his own surly answer, and this made him snort slightly in laughter. If he hadn't been safe in the comfort of his own seedy armchair, he might have felt embarrassed. But he deserved to let loose a little. They'd gone through three more applicants that afternoon, and out of those, only one had turned out to have any real potential for the feed.

Of course, it had to be the bitch of an inner-city Post-Top.[38] He tried to repress the shudder this thought provoked, and failed. The woman had been utterly terrifying, a raging monolith with a bone to pick with the entire world, preferably one supporting some vital organ. He poured himself a well deserved third as the memories rose unbidden, in a sort of mental acid reflux.

"Where do you come off, thinking you can barge in here, hide behind your little machines and pretend to judge me?" she began to rant as soon as the light on the recording lens turned on. There was no bullshitting that one. "People aren't some damn insects for you to study. Trying to profit off people's misery by making a spectacle of it. You make me sick." She physically spat, missing the nearest lens by a finger's width.

"And YOU!" she continued, pointing an index at the lens, as if warning it, just in case it thought the worst was over with the saliva's near-miss. "Watching all this in your underpants, on your settee, in bed, or possibly on the damn bog! Have you no shame? Have you no dignity? Have you truly nothing better to be doing? So, you think we're pathetic? Pah, what does it say about you that you don't have anything better to do but sit there like the

---

38 In a world where "topping oneself," the most common euphemism for suicide,* had become so routine it had a dedicated and specialised service industry, post-suicide cleanup companies, or "Post-Tops" in common speak, were in high demand.

*There also used to be "Human-Caused Delay," specifically used in PA announcements after a suicide on public transport rails. However, the term fell into disuse after new laws removed any obligation for the trains to clean up or gather any remains until after they arrived at destination.

idiots that you are, gawping at US?"

At that point, she grunted and pushed them out of what she had just decided to be her way, knocking the lens to a tilted angle as she clambered into the passenger cab of her service vehicle, with all of the cleaning equipment—and the mind hesitated to consider what else—stored in the rear cargo section. The heavy-duty engine gunned like hell's doorbell, and the door swung open. The post-tops' ugly mug leaned out to haunt them.

"I've got to get this load to the crematorium and then sluice the truck down by sundown. Are you maggots going to come along and have a chat or are you wimpin' out?" she asked them, with high expectorations.

The others had been struck dumb. "Err, no, that's okay. Our camera in the cab will give us plenty of footage. We'll just use that, and get back to you," Liam eventually said, mainly just to bridge the gap, since nature abhors a void.

"Har!" had been her only reply as the door shut and the engine left them wallowing in a cloud of fumes as thick and dense as the woman had made him feel. He took another swig of gin, but was shocked and desolated to discover the glass was dry. Can't be having with that, now, something located at the top of his spine told him in irrefutable terms, and the arm already pouring another healthy dose of gin seemed to be in agreement.

Well, it was all done and dusted, now. Eight contestants, all lined up to receive their implant lenses at the first live show on Sunday. He had asked why it was on Sunday, and the Editor had spouted some nonsense about religion and suicide and something or another. These managerial types really had far too much time on their hands. And the editing! He was happy enough to put it down to the stress of the approaching deadline, but surely it couldn't be right to distort all of the initial interview footage like that. The way the Editor was putting together the intro sequences for the first live feed, he would be turning the real-life people, and their honest stories, into either heroes or villains. It wasn't a proper show anymore. It was a Frankenfeed, and Liam shuddered into his gin at the thought of the monsters such a soulless construct would beget. *Ugh, watch out,* he caught himself. *You were slipping into one of those moods again.*

It was a shame he'd had to cancel the Wine and Warfare meet this Friday. The Editor had scheduled a major screening meeting that evening. He'd sent a com message to the gang during the subway ride back, and he hoped they weren't too disappointed about it.

Still, he had to admit, the GiG team had done a pretty good job, really, especially given the circumstances. Now that they were done with the selection process, he'd be able to keep a closer eye on the editing process, to make sure they didn't stray too far from the truth. They'd be ready for the première, no problem, and he'd be able to keep the show on track. He was going to make certain that the feed stayed focused on helping people, on making a difference. Yes, everything would work out just fine... And on these soothing notes, he lulled himself to sleep, fully dressed and marinated, among the debris of his living room.

16

He hated make-up.[39] He used to have to go through the ritual caking of orange muck every night back at Channel 2, and he'd been looking forward to only having to do it once a week from here on in. Once a week... how odd that seemed, minutes before the première. He needed to get through that first, preferably alive, before he allowed himself to indulge in the soothing waters of routine.

Mary was doing quite a professional job on the make-up, though. She was a lady full of hidden resources, and he made a point of telling her so.

"Oh, go on. You are too kind." The woman blushed and scolded him as she continued to apply the bright goop, a smile on her face.

"You deserve it, Mary. This place would fall apart in a matter of minutes if you weren't around." And it was true. She was always zipping about, tending to something or another, cleaning, doing maintenance, posting AR notices, sending memos to everyone, pushing her little trolley... Her sandwiches were satisfactory, nothing to write home about, even if there were anyone at home to receive such, but better fare than a lot of work food he had tasted in his life. Mary simply smiled and went on with her work.

Liam didn't have time to push the pleasantries any further, in a doomed attempt to avoid having to confront the looming trial by fire. It came back with a vengeance when a figure he only vaguely identified as Carpentiere came to tell him that it was "fifteen minutes to feed time" and that they needed him on set. Shock clouded his mind like water cast upon a campfire.

"Five minutes!" shouted Barry Fletcher, from the depths of his plasma-lit lair. At these words, what he tried to think of as a battle calm descended upon Liam, as would a well aimed ball of catapulted glue. He took in his surroundings with the eyes of a newborn.

The gaping warehouse entrance had undergone, since his first non-

---

39 Something that sounds like having to apologise after an argument simply can't be good.

glimpse of it all those days ago, the kind of plastic surgery that could open up wide avenues of future crime and profit for even the most actively sought-after menace to law, order, and morality.

Where darkness and shipping boxes had once reigned, there was now a caricature of a sterile, gleaming medical operating room. Doctors, nurses, orderlies, everyone was present—and some of them weren't even bit actors called in for the evening. The decor was only skin-deep and didn't go any further than the immediate area of the operating table, but that hardly mattered—the rest would be edited in for the full, AR experience.

Behind the scenes, Mary shepherded her little flock of contestants, and her presence helped calm Liam somewhat. She was certainly a lady of many resources.

The little blinks in the darkness were the tell-tale signs of so many active pod lenses, ready and undoubtedly raring to feed his every movement through Barry's fortress and the Editor's live scrutiny to Corporate, and from there all the way to the hearts and minds of nearly a billion screens, AR lenses, and glasses, around the globe. A fair amount of these would probably even be in use at the time by their owners, and that was the part Liam was still having issues with.

His lingering doubts about the final applicant roster chosen for the première did not help in the least. He was quite convinced they'd gotten the best of the applicants they had been to interview over the past two weeks, and he had no qualms whatsoever over the quality of the work he, Lee, and Carpentiere had put in, under the circumstances. However, he couldn't help but wonder about all the evident candidates who had lives far worse than the blue collar fools they'd spent most of their time interviewing, but who hadn't seemed to enter into account at all for the feed.

Where were all the down-and-out hobos he flicked AR charity coupons at every other day in the subway stations? Surely, they were the ones who really had it bad, who needed the help and attention the feed could provide, more than anybody else. Where were the terminally ill? Where were the Fourth World poor? Surely there were enough of them about to find at least one to include in the feed. He had broached these concerns with the Editor only the day before last, and the response left him perplexed.

"Argyle," he said, the rainbow reflects in his eyes betraying the fact that he didn't even take time to put his AR display into standby before answering, "you don't seem to grasp the fundamental resource we're tapping into here. To put it bluntly, people watch these feeds because they need someone to pity, and you can only pity someone you identify with. Feeders just wouldn't see enough of themselves in a hobo or in some damn Fourth World ghetto child for them to be of any practical use for the feed."

He raised a hand, anticipating a swelling tide of indignant protest. "I don't have time to explain it to you properly." The Editor tossed him something the size of a pebble. "Here. Why don't you take this and copy it onto your drive." Liam caught the tiny bookchip in wary silence. "It's Rousseau's *Inequality between Men*. It'll tell you everything you need to know. You'll find the important bits bookmarked. Just leave it in my box when you're finished copying it."

The shape weighing gently against his suit pocket lining reminded him that he had yet to indulge the Editor in his strange new fancy, but he had a feeling that he might do so once this première was over with; he could already feel the need for a good read wax bountiful within him, like the harvest moon.

Still, they were an interesting crowd, these candidates of his. He was glad they would all get their contractually guaranteed two weeks of fame and annihilation of privacy before the first elimination session was scheduled. Eight lives and only two preliminary launch feeds in which to expose their pathetic daily antics to the world. He diagnosed some bizarre paternalistic emotions stirring within him, and he wondered how he would deal with having to part with the losers.

He dismissed this as the resounding call "One minute to feed!" shook his mind like an Etch A Sketch, wiping away any stray grains of thought.

17

The contestants milled about in a vague sort of line, like poorly disciplined schoolchildren. Liam had no mental energy to spare for them as he stepped into the neon-lit, AR-enhanced studio simulacrum of an operating room.

Who were they trying to fool, anyway? Every child over the age of four knew AR implants were easier to install these days than having your ears pierced, and certainly didn't call for a full operating theatre. But perhaps that was the point, after all. It was all a theatre, all a show, and sometimes the props, the clichés, are more real than what they're meant to represent. So be it, then. Liam would do his part, however meaningless it may be.

Was that truly his own voice, trying to pontificate[40] about how simply and utterly *ecstatic* he was all these viewers had tuned in to join in what would undoubtedly be the "greatest live feed of the century," whatever

---

40 "To build bridges."

historians and marketing directors may have to say on the subject? He was no longer certain. Everything around him seemed to take on a strange new colour—something on the far side of the spectrum, a sort of blacker-than-black. With each passing heartbeat, his glands pumped more and more stress-induced cortisol into his system, completely upsetting his natural diurnal rhythm, effectively tricking his body into thinking he was actually in a dream-state, which was a comforting thought.

The contestants seemed just as stunned as him as they made first contact with the world at large, but at least they had the protection of the group. For that one brilliant moment, they were all equal before the invisible hundreds of millions of viewers. Soon enough, if the Editor had his way, which he naturally would, cocky Brad would be throttling the weaselly Finn, and a terrified-looking Juliette would no doubt clash against Azar, who looked as if she had found a winning lottery ticket inside a fast food fortune cookie at the idea of getting her shiny new top-of-the-line AR lenses. But, for now, they were all equal before the ophthalmic micro scalpel, and it pained Liam to be the one who would have to burst that bubble.

Something was beeping behind him. His body seemed to know something he didn't, and turned to face the blinky-whirly contraption on the far wall which he barely recognised as being called a camera. The camera lights were the only bright points in the ambient gloom of the stage. The blinky-whirly stopped blinking and simply sat there, watching his body gesticulate and talk in a frantic, whacked-out on life sort of voice he hoped to the Gods was not actually his.

It might just have been his depersonalisation disorder talking, but as he ushered Usnavi, his first little volunteer lamb, to the Augmented Reality slaughter, he kept telling himself that he must have misheard Barry. There was no way that there were actually one-point-five billion viewers for tonight's feed. One with nine zeroes, with an extra five and eight zeroes thrown in for good measure? They always made sure you spelled out the number in letters when signing documents, it made it more real that way... But these weren't zeroes, they were people.

An insistent cue appeared in his AR view and, mechanically, he waved an arm in a grand sweeping gesture. The nervous smile on the face of the Usnavi strapped into the operating chair was soon replaced by the genuine smile of the Usnavi in the new, free-floating AR video window. As the pretend doctors and nurses descended upon the real Usnavi, chromed instruments gleaming with all desired dramatic effect, the viewers were free to look away—if they so desired—and watch the sequences filmed the previous week, introducing Usnavi and exposing his life to the world.

Liam couldn't help but feel a tingle of pride at the idea that he was doing his part to bring injustices like Usnavi's to the light, to redress some of modern society's wrongs.

And yet, with flawless timing, the interview sequence faded to black at the very second when the operation was finished and the new AR implants came online. The AR video feed now twitched, and a blurred bar appeared down the middle. The bar widened and soon showed a first-person perspective chaos of blinding lights, blue surgical scrubs, and himself — Liam — half visible in a corner and looking off someplace else entirely.

Liam took no pleasure, despite his rehearsed[41] tones, in vaunting to the world this amazing technology which would now allow them to view the world through Usnavi's eyes, night and day, whenever they so desired, between now and the end of his participation in the show. Liam hoped Usnavi would be among the last, and maybe even the winner. He certainly had more to complain about than most of the rest of them.

Jill elbowed her way in next, seeming to dare the assembled actors and medical personnel to lay even a finger on her. They did, nonetheless. When Jill's own flatteringly edited intro sequence was replaced by her first-person live feed, she immediately returned into the ranks of her fellow contestants and put her new advantage to good use by capturing the most unflattering close-up footage of them possible. Liam would have laughed at how obvious these antics were, but he was still front and centre, escorting the next contestant, Azar, to the operating chair.

Azar wouldn't stop thanking him, which made him feel even more of a hypocrite than he already did, but at least she was thanking everyone else around her as well, as they sat her down and came at her eyes with sharp, gleaming instruments of ocular doom. When her own intro sequence had finished and her live feed came online, they thought there must be a problem and started to adjust the lenses, before realising that the blur was simply due to the tears of joy cascading down Azar's worn ebony cheeks.

Spike took his eye shot next, not seeming to mind big things looming in close to his face. Ali Fourka seemed to take it all with stoic resignation, as opposed to Finn Oldman, who sweated and threatened to sue the Network if they messed up so much as one of his eyelashes. He obviously hadn't bothered to read the extensive liability exclusions in his contract when he signed on, or even looked up the definition of corporate extraterritoriality, for that matter.

Brad scowled at Juliette as she urged him to go on before her, and stepped forward to do his duty for the Corps, as he took great pride in declaiming at every opportunity. This left Juliette as the last contestant to

---

41 Is that what the expression "death warmed up" means? When you are "rehearsed"?

submit to the surgery, and she proved the most difficult by far.

"Is this really necessary for the show?" she seemed to not so much ask as plead, as if oblivious to the fact that one-and-a-half billion people were listening to her every word and no doubt enjoying her discomfort immensely. "Can't there be one contestant without the new lenses? Just to shake things up a little?"

It pained Liam to have to be the one to remind her of the obvious, but at least he could try to sound caring and sympathetic about it. "Juliette, you knew what you were getting into when you applied for the show and when you signed the contract.

"Signed the contract?" Juliette lowered her voice, as if whispering would prevent the viewers from hearing her. "You know what AR contract systems are like. All I did was look a bit too long at the accept button and my interface thought I had clicked to accept. I was probably going to say yes anyway, but I didn't get to look at any of the fine print."

"Regardless, you have an obligation now, and I really don't understand what the problem is. You work with fixing AR implants all day, and I would have thought that, of all people, you would have no problems with our little broadcast setup."

"That's part of it. I know what an AR implant can and can't do, and these new twenty-four-hour broadcast implants have done away with so much EMF shielding, they're bound to—"

"Now, now," cut in Liam, in response to an urgent prompt from the Editor over his AR display, "I'm beginning to sound like a broken record here, but do I need to remind you of the non-disparaging clause in your contract regarding Corporate products and intellectual property?"

Juliette scowled at Liam. "There's no need to get vulgar. I get the message. And that's not even the real problem." She sighed, and went silent, as if deciding whether she should say whatever was on her mind live on the show. For her own sake, Liam wished she wouldn't, as he couldn't see a single scenario where this turned out well for her. But if wishes were fishes, there'd be no such thing as industrial devastation of fish stocks and, accordingly, she carried on. "It's just that, well, I don't like the idea of having strangers looking out through my eyes. And not just one stranger, but millions of them, man, woman or child, anywhere around the world, looking out of my skull and seeing everything I see. It makes me feel dirty."

"Juliette, that is a perfectly understandable response, but really, why overthink it? Surely you can see that it makes no real difference to you, not so long as you continue acting naturally and don't let it affect you." Liam thought this was utter shite, but it was what he had been trained to say and he could spout crap with the best of them. On the spot, Juliette seemed unable to point out the gaping flaws in the official logic, so Liam pressed the advantage. "And it's all for the good of the show, really. We want to make the best show possible, don't we, and I'm certain that you want to do well in it."

With a visible shudder, Juliette steeled herself. "Let's get it over then."

Five minutes' work later, Juliette reopened her eyes. The complete set of eight first person perspective feeds were live and available for browsing by anybody with an AR interface. It was entertainment history in the making. Why, then, did Liam feel like he needed a shower so hot it could scour his soul?

18

The Editor was in his office, with one of the live feeds displayed in high resolution on his new, ostentatious physical display screen. Liam was hardly surprised to see it was his friend, Suicide Jill. The Editor had been adamant they keep her on the show, and he was now fawning over her picture as she spat her contempt at the world and all its lodgers.

"She is so ultimately precious. Look at how her sneer reflects off the mirror... Listen to the beautiful harmonies underlying her snort..." The man had then stopped and simply stood upright, swaying slightly, and with a dazed look. "She's... she's perfect. Perfect, I tell you! There's nothing to edit! Nothing I could remove could make this any better!" He paused before the monumental[42] realisation. "By the Gods... I think I'm in love."

Jill tactfully, or perhaps out of some little-known quantum sense of self-preservation, chose that precise moment to expectorate violently and launch into a rant about "those booky wimpling types who wouldn't know a good lay if it came and hit them in the frontal lobe with a maglev carriage." The Editor allowed himself only the briefest moment of registered shock before editing this out as well and declaring, "Well, nobody can be *perfect*, of course."

He coughed, adjusted his tie, and carried on as if nothing had happened.

"That's precisely why we need to keep a tight rein on everything that happens in these so-called 'live feeds.' As you interact with our contestants during the weekly features, please keep in mind that any slips or unfortunate comments will need to be edited out, by myself or one of the team here

---

42 From the Latin *monere*, "to warn," specifically of the presence of a grave.

on those rare occasions when even I must sleep. I do not plan for there to be many of those, not with so much riding on this show being a complete success, but nature will out."

Liam had managed to remain quiet and just nod up until now, but his impish nature got the best of him. "Nature will out what, sir?" he asked, his grin conspicuous by its absence.

"What?" The Editor seemed astounded that part of the furniture of the room had just called him out on his phrasing. "Oh, Argyle. Shouldn't you be out there rounding up the staff to go have a drink or something? I'm sure I'll be along shortly."

If everything didn't still seem so distant and so unreal to him, he was sure he would have found that funny.

The gin did him a world of good. He could feel his senses returning, watch things sharpening and becoming whole again. It was odd, and slightly disturbing, how moments of stress seemed to put his consciousness into a sort of sleep mode while his instincts dealt with the situation. He gulped with relish.[43] Still, his little semi-fugue state had seen him safely through the first big show, and everyone seemed pretty pleased with the results.

After the première had finished, and the fully armed and operational contestants were sent back to their various conflicting realities, the GIG team had migrated, at the behest of their native guide, Barry Fletcher, to the nearest watering hole. For some reason, Liam was amused to see that it bore a superimposing AR sign identifying it as The Hive. He was now coming back out of the feed haze at last, amidst a dream of steel-topped bars, an orange dance floor, soft lighting, and ancient classic rock music. The stucco and mirrors at ceiling-level were a rather nice touch though, he felt.

He ordered a second gin without a thought and turned to find himself alone. Eh, good riddance. Everyone had been crowding around him, eager to clap him on the back, which he hated, and trying to bask in the reflected glow of his new host status like some media-minded lizard, which he hated even more, since he didn't feel any such glow himself. They didn't even have the decency to leave him enough time to have a proper drink and gather his wits. Other than this largely unwanted attention from his crew, he'd been receiving glances from random people in the bar, some of their eyes still shot with the reflected rainbow glow of their AR pods.

How odd. It must have been the first time in, well, ever, as far as he could recall, that he actually took notice of the podjockeys sitting around the place. People crouched over podscreens or reclined with eyes twitching had always been there in the background of his life. They were as much a

---

43 Not literally, thankfully.

part of the scenery as road signs in the city or the horizon in the rare open country areas which remained. Yet now, for some reason, they stuck out in his mind like the sore cortical homunculus of a thumb.

As he was entirely occupied by the task of securing a second refill for his gin, he did not notice the woman's reservedly grand entrance, nor the hushed silence that fell over those parts of the bar which were not already silently basking in an asocial flickering light. In fact, he did not register her presence at all until she strode over and tapped him on the shoulder.

"Argyle," she said in a voice as sharp as the crease of her suit, "I must congratulate you." Somehow, the "must" sounded less like emphasis and more like the statement of a necessary chore.

Liam turned. "Ms. Heath," he managed to get out between sputters. Gin and nasal passages do not make good barfriends.

"I followed the feed tonight, of course," she continued, having the good grace to pointedly ignore his floundering, even in the face of all evidence. "Well done, all in all. You held up your end of the affair quite well, although of course, we knew you could, and would."

Liam could have given an early "moving picture" a run for its celluloid in an Olympic speechlessness event.

"I won't keep you from your just revels. I simply wished to let you know that we at Corporate are all behind you, and are keeping a keen interest in how the feed evolves. Rest assured that you can count on our support every step of the way. We'll be watching," she added, without even an attempt at the smile that a lesser person would have allowed circumstance to dictate.

As he watched her leave the bar in the same wraith-like fashion in which she had entered, Liam was somehow far less assured than before the intervention. Resting was entirely out of the question. Nope, sullen drinking was all there was for it. Such desperate times called for desperate measures, and preferably generous ones too, of something single malted.

In the end, it was only the sheer horror of a well lubricated Editor in a *good mood* which brought him straight out of his own depths and into frenzied flight, in the general direction of where his shiny new car had parked itself.

19

Success.

He was a success.

The show was a success.

He had the attention of the entire world.

The attention of the woman in front of him, however, seemed far away. Kyla sat across from Liam in the new, deep plush chairs in his sitting room and frowned into her barely touched glass of gin. "Being host of a show like *The Grass is Greener* gives you a unique perspective. No doubt about that," she said, breaking the silence.

But deep in the combined comfort of his armchair and his own third glass of after-supper tipple, Liam merely smiled and nodded. "You're right. The show is so unique." He grinned, loving the thought of it.[44] "It's such a privilege, to be in a position to look into the lives of so many people."

"Yeah, lives all lined up for everyone around the world to see," muttered Liam's best friend in the world. Her hair, dyed an uncharacteristically subdued mauve for the occasion, dangled lankly, half-hiding her face. "Sounds like hell to me."

Anger flashed through Liam's merrily intoxicated mind. Kyla was the only one of the gang who'd answered Liam's invitation to come over, so they'd just watched a movie and ordered a curry in instead of playing. He was grateful she was there. After the première, he felt he needed some grounding. But if all she wanted to do was rain on his parade, she might as well not have come at all.

"Hey, I don't make the rules, okay," Liam said, bits of spittle flying from his lips. "People's lives are the way they are, and that's just the way the world is. All I do is make sure they get the recognition they deserve!"

Kyla raised her head, sadness filling her stark blue eyes as Liam took a deep, angry swig from his glass. "I wasn't accusing you of anything, Liam. I'm on your side here. But you must know what I mean. Seeing all those lives laid bare. The chains and dependencies set up to keep people firmly

---

44 Or, in other words, becoming philosophical.

in their place: education,[45] health, work, mortgages…" Kyla paused as a shiver ran through her, head to toe. That only made the anger roiling deep inside Liam flare higher.

"But that's just the natural order of things, Kyla. The right order of things. It's just like they taught us at back at school, like Hobbes said. People left to their own devices would destroy each other and themselves. That's why we need the Corporations, right? To bind everyone together and make us better than individuals, so everyone ends up better off."

Liam chuckled at the thoughts pouring from his own mouth, and stopped to crack open a fresh can of mixer. His glass was empty again, and this philosophising was thirsty work.

When he looked back up again, the sadness was gone from Kyla's eyes, replaced by sharp steel. "Is that what you really believe, Liam? That the Corps are doing those poor people in your show some kind of favour? That your show is actually helping them?"

"Hey, they volunteered, didn't they?"

"Do you think they had any actual choice? Next time, have a good look at your contestants. At all the innocent little factors which, stacked up, become a structure more secure and more unbreachable than any physical prison ever built. Do that, and then tell me that they had any other option, any other hope, than to sell their souls to that show of yours."

Liam chuckled again, swirling his fresh glass to get the mix just right. "So now we're talking about souls, are we? What is this, the Bible by Foucault?"

"Yes, exactly!" said Kyla, a fresh flush of hope rising in her voice. "It's Foucault all over again, Liam. *Discipline and Punish*. But now, the all-seeing prison warden is every single one of us, with our displays and our pod-cameras. Ten billion wardens paying for the privilege of watching over ten billion prisoners, all dancing to the tune of the Corporations, just because they're the ones who give us the chance to act as our own jailers."

"Never thought you'd turn out to be a modern-day post-structuralist, Kyla."

"There's no such thing as a modern-day Foucault, Liam. There can't be. Nothing of note ever comes out of the Universities nowadays. It's all been said and done as far as the world is concerned. And nobody would read a scholarly publication anyway, even if they bothered."

"You know, that reminds me of something my boss said." Liam lifted an arm to flick through his interface, then let out a choice swear as he knocked the glass over and emptied its contents onto his new Persian rug. With a

---

45 To educate is "to lead out of." It says nothing about "into what or where," "by whom," or "to what end."

cry, both he and Kyla sprang into action, all philosophical debate forgotten for the time being. Kyla pulled some tissues from her pocket while Liam ran to the kitchen for the paper towel roll, and by the time they were done soaking most of the junipery mess out of the beautiful scarlet rug, they were both giggling at the incident, best of friends once again.

It felt good. So much so, in fact, that Liam almost wished Kyla hadn't remembered he was about to show her something before he knocked the glass over.

"The Editor RedCorp has saddled me with at the show is an odd bird. The sort who'd read Foucault's panopticon like a Do-It-Yourself manual. *Domination for Dummies*," Liam added, with a chuckle. "So I'm not sure how I'm supposed to take this. But he transferred me this, before the show."

On the new wide podscreen mounted on the wall of Liam's sitting room, the Editor's book-file loaded up: "*Discourse on the Origin and Basis of Inequality Among Men* by Jean-Jacques Rousseau" read the title on the front page.

"Wow, that's old school," said Kyla, leaning in toward the screen. "And surprising. I read this one ages and ages ago, but from what I remember, Rousseau is all about man's natural pity for his fellow man. And that's not exactly what your show and your employer are known for, is it?"

Deep in the plush comfort of his chair, Liam bristled. "Isn't it? The show is all about pity for your fellow man."

"Liam, that's not pity," said Kyla, sadness flooding back into her voice. "That's exploitation. Social jockeying. Exactly what Rousseau hated about man in Society, taken to lengths the world has never seen before. It's dangerous."

Before he realised what he was doing, Liam was up on his feet, looking down at a cringing Kyla and nearly shouting. "Dangerous? I'll tell you what's dangerous. Hiding behind ideas and the so-called spark of 'nature' to justify selfishness and laziness. That's a dangerous spark, Kyla. In an instant, it could burn away everything humanity—organised, orderly humanity—has managed to build."

He paused to catch his breath. "You know, I think that's what the Editor was trying to tell me, and damn if I don't agree with him. It's no coincidence that the old nation-states have surrendered all the really important decisions to the Corporations. They're the only ones who have the skills and the leadership. Who aren't tied down to a bit of land and can see the big picture."

"Even if they aren't accountable to anyone?"

"Without having to pander to a million competing interests and to election cycles, you mean?" replied Liam, adding a scoff of punctuation. "The

Corporations are more accountable than any government ever was. And not just to their accountants," he added, leaving Kyla alone as he started pacing across the room. "But even more so to the women, men, and enbies in the commuter train. To their customers. If they stop seeking progress, the best new product that creates the maximum amount of happiness for the greatest amount of individuals, then the next Corporation in line will do it instead. They'll eat them up, without remorse or hesitation, because competition is fierce. And competition is right, since that's the only way to guarantee the most important thing always comes first: the best results, at the best price, for the greatest number of people."

It was Kyla's turn to stand up, but without any of Liam's anger. "People used to have a name for what you're describing, you know. Do the words 'corporate state' ring a bell at all?"

Liam stopped mid-pace and spun to face Kyla once again. "And what if they do? The Corporations aren't just pretending to serve some meaningless 'common good.' It's not just lip service. They actually do make things better for everyone. They don't have a choice."

"So that's it then. That's what you see around you, is it? One happy world, united under the almighty profit?"

"It beats the alternative," spat Liam. "Local politicians who say they stand for accountability and against corruption, but are just a bunch of clowns, surfing on the fact that people know the old system is broken. Even if they were serious about accountability, how could they possibly do anything about it using the tools of the past?"

Taking a deep breath, Liam turned away and retrieved his empty glass, to fix a fresh drink and replace his lost one. The system was right, he fumed. And he was right to be part of it.

Kyla stayed silent the whole time, gazing at him with an infuriating pity in her eyes, and waiting for him to speak.

"Look," Liam said at long last. "The main thing is that I'm in a unique position to be a force for good. And I'm going to use every opportunity[46] the GiG offers me to help my employers and make a difference in the world."

Kyla nodded, but not so much in agreement as confirmation. "Well, I'd better get going if I want to catch the last tube train. You just make sure you don't forget what's important, you hear?"

"Never," Liam promised, meaning it with every drink-sodden fibre of his being. He went over to give Kyla a big hug, holding her small, tense frame against his for an instant, before escorting her to the door.

"And don't forget, I'm always here if you need me," Kyla added, before closing the front door behind her.

---

46 Literally, "every prevailing wind coming toward the port."

A smile on his face, Liam headed back to the sitting room, picked up his glass, and flicked through the Rousseau on the wall screen. A minute later, with a profound sense of well-being, he slumped deeper into his comfy armchair and fell fully-clothed into the sleep of the self-assured just.

20

Why does everything have to start so damn early? He fought a losing battle against his brain as it tried to get back into working order. He so desperately wanted to preserve that delightful worriless slumberfuzz numbness which could so easily become all a man could ever want. His first rational thought of the day was that he'd probably stumbled onto the reason why chemical paradise-inducing drugs are known as narcotics. On that note, he eventually set about squirming out of bed and grabbed his bathrobe from off the floor.

He commiserated with his reflection as the bedroom mirror gave him the unadulterated damage report. It was a long-standing oral tradition amongst free-thinkers and celebrity interview podfeed hosts that a man or woman's thoughts in front of their mirror, first thing in the morning, were their most honest ones of the day, and revealed much about who they were and where they were going. Liam stared into the deep grey of his own eyes, searched deep, and thought how much he needed to use the bathroom.

This task took a mere few blissful seconds, but as it was trickling to an end, Liam realised that other organs were seizing the opportunity to demand their fair share of use of the facilities and, always one to recognise willingly that the king of the body is indeed an asshole, Liam sat down to business.

He had to make sure his resolve to act remained intact, rose the thought, above the supremely physical yet cathartic strain. The previous night's resolutions, everything he'd said to Kyla, were fundamentally right. He should be doing everything in his power to make life better for his contestants, and through them, for the world as a whole. But just saying it wasn't the same as getting it done. In practice, it could take some time before he was in a position to do any real good. In the meantime, he needed to play my cards well. He finished, then stripped and clambered under the steaming shower. His thoughts dissolved under the assault of heat and the touch of the water, before slowly recomposing.

The best he could do for now was to play the game and work his way up into a better position to make a difference, from the inside. And that started with earning a bit more respect, and a bit more power, around the Mews. He turned off the flow of water, groped for his towel on the toilet seat, and gave himself a summary drying, letting the air do the rest far better than his towel ever could, while he brushed his teeth and shaved.

It is notoriously hard to think anything much over the noise and the invasive taste of tooth brushing. But afterwards, as Liam ran the sharp metal of his razor across his face in carefully learnt movements, the resolve took a clear form in his mind. A plan of action.

First thing, when he got to the Mews today, he'd march straight in to see the Editor and tell him enough was enough. The man couldn't have his cake and eat it too. If he wanted Liam to be managing the production team, then he'd have to give him the official status to go along with it.

Executive Producer would do just fine, he added in silence, with a determined swipe of the razor. It had a nice ring to it, and it meant Liam would be in a much better position to protect his contestants, and make sure the truth of their lives didn't get manipulated and sacrificed for whatever reason, however noble the Editor could make it sound.

As he got dressed, he also mused there might even be a pay rise in it for him, if he played his cards right. That wasn't the point, of course, but it wouldn't take much for him to finally reach the sort of income where he could afford a proper house, farther away from all this urban mess. Something with some proper parking, more light, and a few trees or something. Maybe even something with access rights to the superconductor highway, straight into work!

He made his way out the door and off to find his car, twitched his fingers through the virtual commands that would have something hot and mostly edible waiting for him at the local drive-thru, and set off on his way through the suburban sprawl to the Mews.

A deep thrill[47] buzzed at the back of his brain as he prepared himself for the confrontation with the Editor. And damned if, despite his better judgment, he wasn't looking forward to it.

21

"Let me get this absolutely clear," said Ed the Editor, leaning forward across his imposing desk and steepling his hands. "The reason you just

---

47 From the Old English, "to pierce, penetrate." Presumably with emotion, but I'm sure Freud would have a thing or two to say on the subject.

barged in here is to demand a promotion to Executive Producer on the show. Does that sum it up?"

Liam felt a rush of blood redden his cheeks and fought to stay calm. There was so much riding on him making his point firmly and clearly. "Absolutely. And I'm going to have to be firm here, Ed. It's vital, and I won't take no for—"

"Fine. It's a great idea," interrupted the Editor, leaning back into his padded leather chair with the sort of smile usually reserved for particularly smug crocodiles.

"—an answer, and I... Wait, say that again?"

"I said fine. You've been doing great work so far, and you're right. It's high time we recognised that and gave you some more responsibilities around here." The Editor paused, flicking a hand through his AR interface and opening up a new tab. "Even though 'Executive' might be a step too far. Supervising Producer, that's the ticket, at least for starters. Shall I send the recommendation to Corporate straight away?"

Liam blinked, feeling lost at sea. He'd been prepared for a fight, and this complete capitulation made him feel like there was something he was missing. "Yes, that'd be fantastic. But you're definitely sure you agree with my promotion?"

"Absolutely," replied the Editor, treating Liam to that reptilian grin again. "Why wouldn't I agree?"

"Well, no reason really, I suppose." Liam had to stop himself before he started arguing in favour of the Editor fighting him on this, even though it seemed like the man had just given away a huge chunk of his power base at the show, without the slightest resistance.

"In fact," carried on the Editor, filling in Liam's silence, "this suits me to a 'T.' The show benefits from having stronger, direct management of the nitty-gritty of daily production woes, and I benefit because I get to leave that to you and focus more on the big picture decisions, and interfacing with Corporate. Everyone wins!"

Liam had enough experience with the Editor to be wary of his "everyone wins," which coming from his mouth usually meant "everyone who matters"—to wit, Ed, and Ed alone. It all felt too good to be true, but that alone wasn't a good enough reason to pass up the opportunity.

"'Everyone wins' sounds good to me," he said, trying to match the Editor's unnerving grin.

"That's my man," replied the Editor. "Let me sort it out with Corporate while you go announce the good news to your team. And don't forget, I'm always right here if you need any advice managing your new responsibilities. Make sure you close the door on your way out," he added, dismissing

Liam with a wave of the hand.

Liam's first new responsibility was less glamourous than he'd been picturing: there was a gap in the contestant monitoring schedule, and he was the only one available to fill in, so he ended up having to spend his first morning as Supervising Producer monitoring Spike Bighorn's feed.

At least he managed to get Barry to scrounge up an ancient physical screen for him so he wouldn't have to watch it direct in his AR display. He wasn't sure how he would have coped with direct visual immersion into the ins and outs—such as they were—of a professional android fornicator. This way, he could keep some form of distance and control, which was a good thing, because the man was unquestionably in full swing.

Liam was, at best, an amateur when it came to pornography, but it certainly seemed like the Erobots were putting Spike through his paces. From the first-person perspective, the orgy of limbs and erogenous masses took on a bizarre grace, like an acrobatic ballet routine. As Spike gave and received in kind from his various partners of either nominal sex, his own fleshy and well practiced moans meshed with the recorded voices around him, so that one was indistinguishable from the other, at least to Liam's inexpert ears.

It was such an alien experience, to view this intense pornographic orgy, scripted to within an inch of its non-life and executed with mechanical perfection, from within the eyes of the only human being in front of the podcams. From between a pair of spread android-gynous legs, there was a glimpse of what were presumably other human beings, as they milled about their various off-screen production activities. But instead of being reassuring, the presence of other people simply added to the bizarreness of this robotic orgy, experienced from the inside and performed in grunting silence. Liam felt like he should be getting aroused, almost on a moral level, but something just wasn't working for him—a blessing, undoubtedly, since he was, as he just remembered, still in the workplace.

The weirdness of the whole experience reached its summit when one of the electric jezebels took a shot of synthetic semen along an exposed joint, creating a short-circuit that sent her leg twitching like an epileptic tap dancer. The director called for a halt from her seat behind the main podcam console, and the mass of writhing plastic flesh crystallised into so many individual statues, each frozen position more ridiculous and more grotesque than the next.

The malfunctioning madam was removed, and Spike eventually disengaged enough limbs and orifices to pull himself out of the frozen orgy. With one last glance back, he headed over to his own little corner and towelled himself down—with a towel bearing a massive advertisement for the production company, Galatea Entertainment, Liam noted with a smirk.

In fact, having noticed one advertisement, he became aware of all of the other product placement logos located throughout the set, strategically placed on various bits of skimpy clothing doing absolutely nothing to cover the 'actors,' reflected in mirrors and on bed covers... Even Spike's own less-than-genuine Native American bead bracelets were embroidered in a pattern which, from his angle, was clearly a stylised rendition of the well known "chemical hazard" logo of the world's most popular and expensive sugar/caffeine/opioid power drink: RedCorp's very own Sinner-G.

Well, Spike's employers certainly hadn't taken very long to figure out that having one of their porn stars broadcasting live 24/7 was a great way to generate new advertisement revenue, with product placement touching— how many people exactly? Liam pulled up the viewership data for Spike's live feed. Yikes, over ten million concurrent viewers? At 10 o'clock in the morning. Of course, that was just in his time zone and meaningless for a large part of humanity. Nonetheless, there must be a lot of boys and girls in Europe and Africa whose idea of light, late-morning entertainment was a heavy helping of android sex, with a side dish of product placement.

Liam slid his hand off the editing panic button that would freeze the feed and reached over for his celluloid cup of sugar-free caffeine water. With viewership figures like that, Spike must be doing something right and wouldn't be needing editing any time soon.

22

After what passed in the modern corporate world for "lunch," and consisted in the cold objective light of noon of little more than a hunk of coarse bread—presented as "raw" but really just cheap—smeared with a nutrient paste it was best not to inquire into too closely, Liam was back behind his AR monitoring interface, with his finger on the big red editing freeze button as instructed by the Editor. He hoped that, whatever the Editor was doing with Corporate, he'd be able to respond within the thirty-second editing delay period they had built into the live feeds, because Liam certainly didn't want to have to be the one to call the shots and be responsible for doctoring the feed, should the need arise.

Luckily, his afternoon assignment was a breeze: good ol' broomstick-behind Brad Leigh, out on his Germ Bouncer rounds and taking his job far too seriously. The public seemed to love the man for some reason, though Liam was damned if he could figure out why.

It was hardly high entertainment, watching from inside Brad's eyes as he sat in the seating area of what he insisted on referring to as his "patrol car," checking and double-checking his gear, from the various syringes, nanotrackers and random pointy things in his medical kit to his operational gear, which included short and long-range tasers, straightjackets, and an actual combat-grade smartrifle. Liam had no idea how anyone could have thought it was a good idea to let a cowboy like Brad loose onto the streets with a weapon that was certified to pump out 20 individual headshots a second. That being said, he had to admit it gave him a peculiar thrill to see the smartrifle's targeting protocols load into Brad's AR display as he picked up the weapon and gave it an unneeded polish—more like a caress, really.

The live feed jostled as Brad's car arrived at the location of his latest unwitting target, which looked like a pleasant enough suburban residential unit, hardly a hotbed of disease and contagion. With crisp, practiced movements, Brad grabbed his gear, swung out of the car, and leapt into action. As soon as he started pounding on the door, his well oiled routine started running into trouble, in the form of an obstreperous door security AI.

"Greetings, Mr. Esposito. Please state the nature of your business with Ms. Perez, and refrain from knocking quite so violently on my door frame."

Even from within Brad's eyes, it was evident that he was getting agitated. Bits of spittle darted against the door as he spoke. "Goddamnit it, my name isn't Esposito, it's Brad Leigh, Disease Monitoring and Prevention Corps number 259—"

"Sorry, Bradley who?" interrupted the AI, somehow managing to sound smug at the fact.

"Not Bradley, you useless pile of zeroes and ones! First name Brad, last name Leigh, check my official ID tag already."

The AI actually made a point of letting out a pensive "hmm" as it pinged his ID and cross-referenced it.

"I'm sorry, but my facial recognition program lists your identity as Mr. Sam Esposito, Mr. Esposito. I can't corroborate this ID."

Liam let out a sigh of thanks that his editing instructions did not concern swear words or other expletives, which were given free rein and even encouraged in the show, because Brad, at the end of his wits, which were probably not very long to start with, let loose a torrent of vulgarity that may well have scorched the paint from the door.

Not that this would have mattered in the least.

"Fuck it, this qualifies as wilful obstruction." Reaching into his belt holster, Brad pulled out a pad of what looked like used chewing gum and stuck it to where the door hinges would be.

"Mr. Esposito, please refrain from vandalising private property or I will have t—"

Neither Brad, Liam, or the other viewers ever found out what extremes the door AI would possibly threaten, as the nanite paste rearranged the door hinges' constituent molecules into an explosive gas, which detonated—knocking the door flat into the corridor inside with a minimum of effort and a maximum of dramatic effect.

Brad strode over the fallen door, stopping to pick up the now inert nanite paste and pop it back into his pouch, with a little pat. The tasteful interior décor was difficult to appreciate, not just because it was covered in bits which were until recently part of the front door, but also because Brad didn't spare it a second glance as he followed the arrow in his AR display. Navigating him through a mini-map based on up-to-date planning records for the building, the arrow soon took him to the bedroom where the DNA tags in the bedding had flagged a woman with a potential outbreak of Andes hantavirus.

Brad drew his short range taser and swung the bedroom door open. He scanned the room, but the rumpled bed was empty and the single window was closed. A whimper came from beyond the closed en-suite bathroom door, and Brad made his way over to it, pulling Liam and hundreds of thousands of viewers along with him.

"Agent Brad Leigh, Disease Monitoring and Prevention Corps number 2599401-51, ma'am," he recited to the closed door. "Under articles 5 through 11 septies of the World Health Convention, and article 8 of the UK Disease Prevention Act, 2048, I am entitled to your obedience and cooperation in the prevention of a public health risk which has been diagnosed within your system."

"¿Uy, que quiere? ¿Que hace en mi habitación? ¡No me lastimes!"

"Damnit, it never rains but it pours, doesn't it?" muttered Brad to himself, as if forgetting that that included viewers all around the world. A flick of the eye switched a "Universal Translator" toggle at the bottom of his AR display to "on." and he spoke again.

"Can you speak English, ma'am, or do you have a translator app?"

Either she didn't understand him or chose to remain quiet. Brad's translator app helpfully provided a phonetic guide to saying the exact same thing in more or less understandable Spanish, at the same time his tactical analysis routine finished its structural report on the door, identifying the handle as belonging to a mechanism without a lock.

The choice must have been an easy one for Brad, since he simply shoved the door open, sending the short, terrified lady inside careening against a sink cabinet. Showing as little care for her feelings in the matter as he had for her property, Brad raised his taser and shot the home's owner with both prongs.

"I really don't have time for this shit," muttered Brad as he waited for the disease vector to stop convulsing, before walking over to stab her in the neck with a dose of viral antigen-administering nanites. "Assholes thinking they can travel all around the world and bring their filth with them. No respect for other people, that's what their problem is."

He printed out a paper copy of the bill for services rendered and left it by the sink. As he made his way back out through the breached door to his waiting vehicle, and the next vector on his triage list, he whistled with the satisfaction of a job well done.

23

Peoples' reactions to his new status as a major podfeed host were an interesting experience for Liam, and one which, if pressed, he would have to confess he rather enjoyed.

He was used to the odd, or sometimes even, stare of recognition from his years as the Channel 2 weatherman, but that had been little more than a passing annoyance that came along with the job. This was entirely different. It came with more perks, for starters, and sometimes even for entire meals, including the wine.

He got invited to parties, and not just the work ones you get sent an invitation to from some mailing list and where not a single one of the strangers there makes the least effort at pretending to be interested in your existence. No, these were proper parties, which he received proper invitations for. The secretaries knew who he was when he called up to confirm, the valets addressed him by name when he pulled up in his new sedan, and the waitresses remembered what he had ordered the first time for the well deserved subsequent rounds. Although, to be fair, it was true that all three were more often than not the same outsourced person.

These parties weren't all fun and feasting, mind you. As the various AR recreations of retro video games and pieces of abstract artwork attested, they were usually held by some corporate bigwig or another. A fellow swimmer of the entertainment shallows of the big commercial pond, or sometimes from a completely different area with some obscure tie-in which

Liam only realised upon watching the daily business news feed sometime later, after a major deal or merger had taken place.

It was always strongly intimated in private that attending these events was an integral part of his new function, and Liam soon realised that this was because he was a conversation piece. People flocked around "celebrities" in the same way various insects can't help having unfortunate encounters with the indiscriminate bug zapper. This aura he now seemed to radiate for some unfathomable reason was the ideal stimulant, it seemed, for the instant electronic knotting of indissoluble contractual bliss, as such things go.

For he soon came to admit to himself, despite his reservations, that this was indeed his new status: he was a celebrity. Host and Supervising Producer of his own show. Oh, he had no illusions as to how deep that celebrity went, and was all too aware of the fact that speaking of "celebrities" as a whole was like grouping sand and mountain ranges together under the "hard bits" category. It was nonetheless clear that he shared, even in the smallest degree, in that basking golden glow which tinges how the world at large perceives the famous. It was mediocre, but by the gods of entertainment, it was his, and he was enjoying it more than he cared to admit to anyone other than himself.

In fact, he soon learned from his nightly virtual and physical shoulder-rubbings with the affluent that it was the "done thing" to mock celebrity and deny, at every possible occasion and whatever the company, how much this phenomenon was a profoundly enjoyable one. After sticking to a strict policy of cautious listening, he had quickly caught on and, in order to avoid standing out and displaying openly how wrong this all seemed to him, he joined in, in carefully average measures. Having given it some thought, he decided this behaviour must be an attempt by the rich and the famous at curtailing jealousy and making themselves seem more in touch with the common Man, more "human." He mocked them in private, but as far as he was concerned, they could do whatever they felt like.

He could hardly complain, but the parties were definitely cutting into what meagre sleep time his demanding work schedule left him. He was sure that in the old days a feed like his wouldn't have been run with a production team of only five people, but such was the result of the constant push for maximum productivity and minimum costs. The live feed monitoring alone forced him to put in hours which defied all labour laws. It was wreaking hell on his health and, he had no fear of recognising it, on his frame of mind.

It was what he had signed on for, and in all fairness he had been prepared for it. If only the work had been living up to expectations, it wouldn't have been so bad ; but his resolve—to play the game while acting responsibly with regard to the effects of what they were doing—had been most sorely tried, right off the bat. It was the editing that did him in and forced him to take action.

"Sir," he eventually worked up the courage to say, barging into the Editor's office as politely as possible, "I would like to speak with you about the segments for this week's show."

The man didn't even bother to look away from his live feed screenings on the wall-vidscreen. He simply waved vaguely at a chair, presumably inviting Liam to sit down and continue, and not even registering Liam's refusal of the offer, which Liam found far more infuriating than anything the man could ever have said.

"Ed," he resumed after a calming breath. This most certainly caught the man's attention, and Liam had to repress a smirk before continuing. "This is important. I've been talking with the team, and we aren't comfortable with some of the editing choices in the segment rushes for the Sunday feature show." This was stretching the truth a little, since when he had briefly mentioned the issue to them, they had contented themselves with a vague nod while backing away, but it was for a good cause. The Editor turned to look at him, the silence hanging over them like a solid gold yet fully operational replica of Damocles's famous sword, displayed at the end of a very thin piece of string. Liam swallowed.

"I know we've talked about this before," he said, with a slight wheeze, "and last time was one thing, but in these segments it's almost as if we are intentionally playing the contestants one off each other."

The Editor rested his chin on his crossed hands and blinked, which Liam took to be a request for him to continue. "Well, that's a bit too close for comfort to actually manipulating the outcome, isn't it? I know that's what everyone expects, but it doesn't mean we actually have to do it."

"Argyle," broke in the Editor, like a brick through a display window, "we are here to entertain. What this means is that it is our function to 'hold things together.'" He clasped his hands in demonstration. In another circumstance, he might have been in fervent prayer. "This very literally implies a hands-on approach. The feeders demand that we intervene so that what we show them is what they want to see, something in which they will be able to take an interest. The contestants expect no less of us, that we make their lives interesting enough to create a bond between the feeders and themselves. This is what they signed on for. We would be lax in our essential function of mediation if we did not translate the raw material into a finished product, in a language all feeders will respond to. This requires us, and here is I think the central point behind your unease, to appeal to the base categories, the archetypes, which the viewers unwittingly identify with and expect. Oh, our contestants have their individual traits and their eccentricities, and therein lies their charm, but at the end of the day, they will inevitably fall into the feeders' preconceived categories of people and personalities. We are simply making this as easy as possible for everyone involved, because it is one of the keys to a successful feed."

He paused, as if watching Liam's thoughts race through the maze of this monologue, the kind which people tend to skip reading when they encounter them in a play script, or perhaps a novel, and rightfully so. Just as Liam was emerging and about to answer, Ed cut him off.

"Now, I fully understand your position, and it is justified. It is too late to modify the segments for this Sunday, but what I can offer you is that from here on in, you and your colleagues will be systematically included in their assembly, and will thus be able to contribute to keeping them as close to nature as possible. What do you say?"

Liam realised this was final, regardless of anything he might add. He nodded and made to leave of his own accord, before his dismissal compounded the pervading feeling that he was a schoolboy again, preached to and scolded by the teacher. Ed caught him in a verbal lasso before he could make good his tactical retreat.

"Ah yes. Argyle? One last thing. I have been discussing things with Corporate, and we think it is high time that you had a clearer leadership role in our little team here. From here on in, we'd like you to take a firmer hand in directing the collective efforts, and this matter is as good a starting point as any. I'll make certain they'll put out a memo to that effect tomorrow. Good day to you," he finished, addressing his live feed screen once again.

24

From there on in, it had only gotten worse. The hours, the little white lies, the big red ones... he had to not only take part in them himself, but he also had to enforce and justify them to Barry, Lee, and Carpentiere. He was their Supervising Producer after all, and the only one around to make any decisions—and take any blame when something went wrong—since the Editor hardly ever showed up at the Mews anymore, working nearly full-time from Corporate HQ downtown.

Sometimes, in his darkest hours, Liam saw himself as at least as monstrous a being as a Finn Oldman, if not worse. After all, he knew better. It was impossible not to take a personal interest, both in the contestants and how they'd be affected by their media-mongering machinations, as well as, more poignantly, in his co-workers.

Carpentiere's little girl had been sick on Tuesday night, and it was by all accounts rather bad. He was pretty choked up about it, but from what Liam had managed to gather, on Wednesday morning the child had been rushed to the hospital and was still there under intensive care. Carpentiere didn't seem to want to face going into the details, and Liam certainly had no intention of forcing them out of him. He tried to do what he could to let him off work early, but deadlines were deadlines, and every man, woman and, indeed, child had to be ready to make a few sacrifices.

Then there had been that business with Lee, later that same afternoon, obviously, as if the basic work wasn't more than enough to deal with as it was. He had the sneaking suspicion they were intentionally trying to make his life hell. Would they gain anything from breaking him? In any case, Lee had managed to mess things up for him with Corporate, already. He had received an irate-sounding ring from Corporate late that afternoon, just as he was about to call it a day.[48] They were after the expense slips from the previous week's contestant audition forays into the wild world at large[49] and didn't sound particularly happy about it. After a mental moment's jig and reel, Liam mustered enough sense to remember he had charged Lee with the task of managing the archaic yellow, cyan, and fuchsia stencil-copy slips they had to fill in for each and every expense. He assured the man that he'd sort it out post haste, and went to seek the answers. He did not overly enjoy them once they were found, and he had the sneaking suspicion that the people at Corporate would be even less partial.

"Hey, I sent them like you told me to," went her response, as she paused in her sequencing of the live feed coverage, "but it turns out that the ones you had given me were the wrong sheets. I had a word with them, and apparently they change the colour-coding every week, for security reasons. And you know that fuel we, and by 'we' I mean you, put into the van? They're saying we should have used Petronext, not Totaloil, since they belong to a rival corp. They didn't seem particularly fussed about the fact that Petronext doesn't have a station for miles in that part of the city, and are refusing the reimburse it. Sorry."

She had little else to tell him, so he decided to take it to the Editor.

"You can hardly expect Corporate to pay for fuel bought from a rival petrol chain, now can you?" Ed seemed profoundly amused, which irri-

---

48 The day itself is hardly ever bothered about what people choose to call it.

49 Not to mention wide, as a result of years of evolutive adaptation to the fat and energy-enriched fodder of global society.

tated Liam even further, after the half-an-hour rigamarole with secretaries at Corporate until someone could track the Editor down for him. "And as for this whole expenses business… well, it's unfortunate that you took the wrong week's slips, is all I can say." Ed conveniently forgot to mention that the forms had been in the Editor's own office, and Liam had only taken them following the man's not overly precise instructions. "Of course, it was technically Lee's mistake, but she was acting on your orders, and it was your role to supervise her. You are the Supervising Producer now, after all."

Liam clenched his jaw and held back an outburst. He hated the words "Supervising Producer" more and more each day.

"You don't just delegate things and forget about them, you know," carried on the Editor, patronising as ever. "There's a bit more to it than that. Why, any idiot could be in an executive position, otherwise." Ed chuckled, but Liam failed to see either humour or reason to humour the Editor, and so stayed respectfully, if reproachfully, silent.

"Well, the best I can do is put in a word for you at Corporate. I think you'll probably still end up having to foot the gas bill, but I'm certain I can convince them to be lenient regarding the slips, this one time." His picture in the comms window gratified Liam with a little smirking grin that was undoubtedly supposed to look comforting and understanding, but merely managed to make Liam feel like snails had suddenly started crawling all over his skin.

"In the future, do keep a closer eye on your subordinates, Argyle. Surveillance is the biggest part of a hierarchical position, after all. We can't have you going around shirking your responsibilities, now can we?" he concluded with the sort of paternalist smirk you'd love to smack.

"Responsibilities," Liam said to Mary, who was unlucky enough to have been dusting in Liam's little office when he entered, and thus became fair game for him to vent at in private, as he sat in the swivel chair behind his desk. "How dare the Editor, of all people, preach to us about shirking responsibilities? I mean, if a hierarchy just means having multiple people doing and re-doing the same work, how is anything ever supposed to get done?"

"Right you are, sir," replied Mary, leaning against her cleaning trolley with her sprayer and cloth still in hand. "Speaking of which, I suppose I should get back to—"

"But don't get me wrong," carried on Liam, cutting Mary off mid-escape attempt. "I'm a big believer in the Corporations. Always have been. I grew up idolising the men and woman who gave life to them."

Mary sighed, stowed her gear away in the trolley, and stood at attention. "Is that so, sir?"

"Please, no 'sir' here. It's Liam, remember?"

"Right you are, Liam," replied Mary, a corner of her mouth twitching with a little half-grin. "And why do you think you've always thought so highly of our employers, then?"

Liam opened his mouth to answer the question, then closed it again when the words failed to come. It was odd, come to think of it. He was over forty years old, and he'd never once stopped to wonder why he considered corporations to be naturally above individual people. Wiser. Stronger. More efficient. Less prone to irrational emotions. He hadn't questioned it when studying political philosophy or ethics in University, and he hadn't once blamed the corporate structure itself for any of his dissatisfaction with his career and work life. Not before *Grass is Greener* came along, that is.

But, so help him Adam Smith, he was questioning it now. Could his blind faith in the superiority of the organisation over the individual just be something programmed into him? Because what he'd just experienced today was the complete opposite of efficiency or moral strength. It was cowardice and irresponsibility rubber-stamped and enforced through corporate hierarchy.

Had there ever been any critical thought about modern corporate structure at school?

"Sir? I mean, Liam?" prompted Mary, a worried look on her face.

Liam gave himself a little shake. "Yes, sorry. I was just thinking about what our schools teach children about the Corporate Council, and all the good big organisations have done for the world. It's only the truth, at the end of the day. That's history in a nutshell. Social and technological progress goes hand in hand with the history of Corporations and organised labour."

Mary treated Liam to a tired, sceptical look. "Sounds nice and simple."

"It really is," replied Liam, drawing deep on his memories from school, and wondering why he was so eager to impress the cleaning staff. "The Maurya Empire and the Roman Empire were built on the backbones of legal Corporate entities. And the fabled Roman legions were run much more like businesses than the old national armies. The great early Corporations, like the venturing explorer-businessman, Venice, and the East India Company opened up the world."

"I guess I never thought about it that way," said Mary, nodding in resignation.

"The list goes on. The printing press. The Encyclopaedia and Enlightenment. The transition from the small, individual workshop to mass production chains. Consumer goods. Affordable comfort for all. The Space Race, followed by private Corporations carrying on in space where the old nation-states left off."

Mary nodded again, edging her trolley toward the door. "It all certainly sounds very good and proper when you put it like that. Like destiny, that sort of thing."

Liam's cheeks flushed with pleasure. "Well, I won't deny progress has been... bumpy, at times. But yes, stronger and stronger organisation has unquestionably made life better and better for the individual people being organised."

"Speaking of organisation," Mary tried once again, taking advantage of a lull in Liam's thoughts, "unless you need anything else here, I have a leaky sink to fix in the bathroom, before someone slips and I need to rush them to the hospital."

"What?" Liam blinked and looked up in surprise. "Oh, yes. By all means. Don't let me detain you."

Mary made good her escape before Liam could engage her in another rambling conversation. But Liam's thoughts were turned inward, and more troubled than he cared to admit.

So what if his nagging doubt were founded? Did it matter if his view of history and the world were just the product of a biased Corporate-funded education system? Did it make it any less true?

He didn't know the answers. The questions alone were enough to make his head hurt. Nothing a stiff drink or four wouldn't cure, but it had been a long day, and he figured that was probably enough introspection for now.

There was one thing he was certain about, though. He'd be taking care of those damn expense invoices himself from here on in.

25

Liam surveyed his open drinks cupboard. Maybe he should be watching the drink. He knew that was the rehab training talking, but the thought remained just as strong. He probably had been overdoing it a little of late, he admitted to his inner confessor. In fact, it had almost been like old times again.

If only they hadn't had to cancel the Wine and Warfare tonight. He wouldn't feel so damnably guilty about the idea of having a drink if they were all together, and he really needed to blow off some steam.

The IMs off of Hank and Kyla, saying they both had other things planned tonight, were still hanging just at the edge of his peripheral AR vision, where he'd shoved them with an angry flick. He had also received a Com call from Steve saying he was "real tired" from work this week and didn't think he could make it, so they'd decided to just cancel it for this week.

It's funny. Steve had seemed more preoccupied than anything else on screen, but then again, it was often hard to tell with such matters. Still, Liam really would have preferred to have them over: he thought he could use both the wine and the gaming release. Solo play just wasn't the same, so he decided to fall back on some more reading. He had forgotten just how many interesting books he had loaded onto his tablet back in his philosophy days at University. Like everyone else, he had only read a small fraction of them at the time, only excerpts really, and only as imposed by the coursework.

Resolutely shutting off his AR display for the first time in weeks, he scanned the tablet's impressive index. The first to leap out at him and tug at something deep within the onion-layers of his thoughts and self was Erasmus of Rotterdam's *Praise of Folly*. He thought he would placate this urge by simply skimming the medieval work, but found it to be a surprisingly engaging read. He only stopped when tectonic-class stomach rumblings made him realize it was now past 9:30 p.m. and he had been reading the thing, out of time, for hours. He put the tablet down as if it had short-circuited and scalded him, but only long enough to knock up a hot bowl of soup with barley and pre-cooked and chopped veg. He couldn't help but start to read it again, while trying not to splash soup everywhere—an evil he judged necessary.

Resolutely removing his AR reading glasses, as he knew he'd be tempted to flick the AR back on every five minutes to look up a definition or a name in the online encyclopaedia, he finished the tome some hours later. Sleep crept up his spine on hobnailed boots, yet only served as a sensory backdrop as he got caught by the web of cross-references in the footnotes and railroaded into flight about one hundred kilometres above the surface of Friedrich Nietzsche's *Twilight of the Idols*.

He went through something disturbingly close to what he imagined an out-of-body experience to feel like, and the tiredness certainly did not help in this respect. A strange cocktail of emotions, equal parts terror and elation, mixed with ample ice and put through the blender, ran through his consciousness as it sped over Nietzsche's marble-carven precepts and admonitions, taking in both individual features and panorama.

At geological lengths, he managed to pull himself free of the gravity well of Nietzsche's mind workings, and rose to glance at the clock. He could not remember ever being up quite this late and yet not having a single empty alcohol vessel strewn about his person. As this flashed through some isolated level of his consciousness, most of it merely clamoured that a visit to the loo was of the utmost urgency. Never one to repress such bodily diktat, he climbed the stairs and headed to the facilities—but not without a pause to grab his tablet beforehand.

Temporarily freeing the mind from the constant weight of having to control the centrifugal urges of the urinary tracts and the bowels is always a greatly pleasurable thing. Properly harnessed, it can also be very conducive to strength and clarity of thought. This was a large part of why Liam had always enjoyed reading on the can, as it were, and one at least as important as the objective fact that there had been very little else to do with that inescapable part of the day since the demise of handheld gaming.

He was one of those old school gamers who refused to recognise fuzzy AR timewasters as actual games, and only activated his AR during toilet time when it was absolutely necessary, or if he had forgotten to bring his reading tablet. In the present case, he used his moment of clarity to make a conscious choice as to what he was going to read on his way to bed, perchance to sleep: Thomas More's *Utopia*.

He rose, stumbled into his room and out of his clothes, then pulled the covers from the foot of the bed. Never having thought of himself as anything other than a bachelor, even during those brief stints of relative sexual abundance, he had never had to make the effort to understand the obsession with "making" beds. Unless someone was coming over for a visit and had some remote chance of entering the bedroom, for some strange reason, he really did not see the point. He certainly didn't mind an unmade bed, as you were only going to mess it up again that very night, in just about any case.

He only returned to the tablet once he was comfortably snuggled deep within the slightly ripe comfort of his bed covers. Utopia, he thought with a sneer; a banner for lost causes and idealists.

Liam basked in the silent glow of superiority, not unlike centuries of easy thinkers before him who hadn't bothered to read the book properly and made the same, basic mistake: assuming[50] that, since the book talks about an impossible ideal, it must be as sarcastic as they are. This is, of course, missing the point entirely: a utopia may be, by definition, unattainable; this does not reduce at all the very real merit, even the necessity, of pursuing it.

Silently mocking the generations of fools who fought and died for one utopia or another, Liam slid deeper into the mattress, and into sleep.

---

50 See supra, only very much more so.

Mind-flashes against the black screen of his eyelids. A mask, but then, it is a person. Same thing. Female. She looks vaguely familiar. She starts moving.

He still does not recognize her, but he knows she is Mary, the agency worker. Isn't that odd? They speak; the words register only as movement in that somehow blurred face. She moves past other persons. He follows.

The people change. The ground stretches and drops away, but somehow his feet are still on it, and he himself does not move. Blood pounds through his world at an alarming pace as he pulls and pushes, fighting to free himself from the mounting torture. His heart feels like it must explode—

—he gasped, not sure whether the scream had only been in the nightmare or if he also screamed out loud. His vocal cords made a mucus-covered "glug" sound deep in his throat, and he was suddenly aware of the chill of cooling sweat making the bed sheets cling to him. A pant. He would change them in the morning.

The people are milling about him. They seem interested. Perhaps merely curious.

The ground! It is still falling away! He arches into the tugging void as he struggles against the stretching. He will break! He cries out for help. Wakeupwakeupwak—

--rgh! Definitely out loud that time. He glanced over at the clock: 2:30 a.m. Not good.

He dragged himself up, stumbled to the bathroom, and turned on the lights. The searing blindness helped him focus. He poured himself a glass of water from the tap and sat to drink it on the toilet, feeling a little pang of guilt, as he often did, at betraying that supposedly quintessential trademark of manhood which is peeing standing up. He had to get some sleep in; there was still a lot of work to do to get Sunday's feed ready. Popping his AR glasses back on for a quick check of his inbox, he reminded himself there was no reason for him not to sleep, after all. He couldn't even remember what was bothering him anymore. As he eventually made his careful way, blinded once again, back through the darkness to his body-warmed bed, he reflected that it would be nice to have an actual weekend every now and then. Or even just a free Saturday.

He supposed it was part of the job description. "Nothing for it..." his fading consciousness was vaguely surprised to find himself actually mumbling.

The Moon. It waxes huge and full in the night. Fascinating.

It grows bigger. Fear me, it seems to say. It grows bigger still. Surely it must hit the Earth! The collision never happens, ever-imminent. Liam cowers under the oppressive moon-glare. He gives a mental shriek.

Again? He decided to force his eyes open and turned over to look at the clock. His eyes focused upon the time: an hour and a half until the alarm was supposed to go off. He slid over and fumbled with it a bit, giving himself an extra fifteen minutes, as much margin as he could allow himself. His mind felt like it had been stuck full of needles by an apprentice acupuncturist. He drifted.

The alarm screeched, and he silenced it without conscious thought. Had he slept? He had no idea. Too late for it now, in any case. There was half a bag of coffee left downstairs, he recalled, as he shambled over to his wardrobe. Should just about do it.

26

I must be allergic to this stuff, at least a little bit, he reckoned, as Mary set about him with the orange gunk. *It can't just be that I don't like it.* Couldn't the computers just edit the make-up in without him actually having to wear the stuff? They did that all the time, right? Surely it would look better than this mess.

This was the first real weekly feed, with the contestants all live on the set and jumping through the hoops they had set for them, he reminded himself with an internal sigh. He was looking forward to it like his first enema.[51]

Mary must have sensed his tension because she was quick to say, "That's enough for now. How about we give that some time to settle in while I go and fetch you a nice cup of tea from the trolley." Or at least something to that effect. He wasn't really paying attention but nodded anyway, and probably mumbled his thanks when she came back with the hot plastic cup. These outsourcing people did have their advantages, he reflected, as various adverts, alerts, and spam messages popped into his AR view, all demanding their usual share of his divided attention.

---

51 "Throwing in," though techniques may have evolved somewhat since Proto Indo-European times.

They finished make-up ahead of schedule for a change, so he went and stood to the side, watching the final preparations for the set and feed equipment. The contestants were standing by the water cooler, performing the delicate balancing act of avoiding his, each other's, and anyone else's eye, while still endeavouring not to look nervous. AR displays, even when not necessarily turned on, were a great excuse for the socially awkward or uncomfortable.

He was somewhat pleased to see that this included both Brad Leigh and Suicide Jill, but was put off to see Finn Oldman brazenly stop Mary as she pushed the trolley past their knot, managing to con a tiny bowl of snacks from her. Did he know what people thought about him? It's all fun and games until someone loses an eye. In his AR display, the numbers on the big clock shifted into the dreaded conjunction. Time to get his game face on.

He stepped forward onto the set Mary had installed in the Mews central warehouse area. Long gone were the surgery props and the fake medical team. This was to be their permanent Sunday feature set-up, and it was a spartan affair: a few uncomfortable-looking chairs, a podium for Liam to pose behind every now and then, and a great many stage lights, all set on a blue chroma key backdrop.

Nothing else was needed. Everything else about the show, from the scenery to the props to the free-floating AR windows showing the various pre-prepared footage sequences, would be rendered in real time by Barry's cave of machinery and displayed in all its AR glory in the product going out to the viewers. This was common practice, but their show had the added spice of allowing the viewers an easy and equally real-time glimpse behind the curtain, since they could still have each candidate's internal live feed going while watching the weekly feature broadcast in another window.

The set was bathed in a glare which seemed to have little other purpose than to block out the rest of the world. A funny thought really, since, in fact, its goal was the exact opposite. He smiled and nodded to the contestants as they filed past to their seats, like schoolchildren fresh off the playground at recess. Somehow, he felt much more in control this week, and his mind wasn't quite so torn this time around. Sure, he still had just as many misgivings about how they had spent the whole week doctoring the live feed footage to make it as interesting as possible, but he was much more grounded. It felt pretty good. Then, the red light lit above the podcams and all thoughts were crowded out by the rehearsed lines and stress-fuelled smiles of showmanship.

The initial sequences had always been easy, and things were even more so now that the cameras spent more time on the different candidates than on him during the middle bits where he had to introduce the next sequences. Everyone got their thirty seconds of fame as the show focused on the selected highlights from their week's activities, ranging from Brad's door-busting antics to Finn Oldman getting a commendation for his health claim rejection record. Liam flew through the sequences on gold-winged boots, every word, every stance oozing assurance and charisma. He was on a roll.[52]

Then came the new bit, the sequence they'd dubbed "Crossfire" despite Liam's vocal dislike of the name. The Editor had scolded him. "Don't change a recipe that works, and in the business, you'll be hard pressed to find anything more tried and true than the Crossfire. It's a classic." So they'd set up these chairs on little revolving plates, and sure enough, the contestants were soon swivelling from their well ordered initial lines to face each other in a crude and somehow angular circle. Set spotlights flared with rainbow edges in their eyes. Each contestant's implanted lenses had the feeders skipping from head to head, skin to skin, catching every glance and every nervous reaction to the new setting.

He took position at his little podium to the side. It was going to be a massacre. His mouth went on of its own accord, and he soon found himself having to run to catch up with it.

"Tonight, we will be opening up the voting for the first elimination round. To help you, our feeders, make your choice, we decided to ask our contestants to say a few words about what they think of each other. Here's what they had to say."

Ugh, why didn't I screen this before they showed it? Inner Liam groaned as he watched the first clip's victim, poor Azar, work her way through a venomous tirade against Juliette. She may only have met her in person for the first time last week, and even then only briefly, yet that seemed to have been enough to form a profound dislike.

"I just know about these things. I see someone and I know if they're up to no good," said a very confident Azar in the clip. Her current self was looking somewhat less sure of herself in her seat there, directly under the glare of the other contestants' combined first-person viewership, but she seemed resolute. "I mean, it's a privilege to get to participate in a show like this," continued the clip-Azar, "and we're lucky to be getting nice, new implants like these ones. Moaning about it is just plain rude, and very revealing about true character, in my books."

The display paused, just long enough for the contestants to start stirring and for tensions to escalate, before playing the next clip.

---

52 Less like butter, more like Branston pickle.

"I don't know about you, but I've had it up to here," growled the unmistakable tones of Suicide Jill, as she gestured to someplace above her ample frontage, "with suck-ups and phoneys like that Azar, let alone Spike Toaster-Porking Bighorn. People aren't stupid; they know that we're chosen by RedCorp and that the Corporation controls everything that happens here. They don't also want to have to watch us kiss their asses as well. Or just pretend that everything is hunky-dory, like Usnavi. I mean, personally, I like the kid, but he needs to wake up. I don't care how many people are looking out of your eyes—they can't open them for you."

The sound of Finn Oldman cackling brought Liam back out of his AR overlay and back into present focus. He was sitting back in his chair, laughing at the nastier quips in the sequences, goading the other contestants on, and clearly enjoying the whole proceedings as much as a cat in the aftermath of an industrial accident at a feather pillow factory. He was in such good spirits that he wasn't phased in the least when, in the next sequence, Professor Fourka called him "a conniving little twit with all of the humanity of a broken anvil," Liam noted.

The free-floating window kept on Augmenting reality with reckless abandon.

"Seriously," boomed the voice of Brad Leigh, "I don't see how anyone could possibly have it as bad as I do. My daily grind has me fighting on the front lines to defend the world against dangerous diseases, for crying out loud. The rest of them are just whiners. I think it's pretty clear that I should win the show." The set broke into[53] pandemonium, the contestants rising to their feet, spit flying as, enraged, every one of them defended their claim to shame.

A downward glance told Liam that the main feed had abandoned all pretences and was now focusing solely on the upcoming melee, switching between the various first-person perspectives and ceiling-mounted aerial views.

Finn Oldman was grasping the back of his chair all too innocently, he noted with alarm. While the chairs were designed to be riveted to the floor for safety, it struck Liam as curious that no one had seen it fit to actually do so. He snorted. *I'm even being sarcastic with myself now. Dangerous, that.* It looked like he was going to have to step in, since he could no longer see any excuses that would allow him to avoid doing so.

A discreet twitch of his left middle finger activated his pre-set alert function, which would turn on an equally modest red light somewhere in Barry and the Editor's displays, letting them know that he was about to improvise and they would need to adapt on the fly.

---

53 With a heavy crowbar.

"And now," he said, feeling like a ringmaster sent in to lead negotiations after a mutiny in the lion cages, "the time has come to see who *you*—" he was really getting into the swing of it now— "the feeders, think deserves to stay in the fight."

An eerie calm fell over the contestants, who suddenly understood what World War I soldiers must have experienced when the other side came out of their trenches and said the local equivalent of: "Hey, it's Christmas, so let's let the machine guns cool down for a while, have a drink, and kick a ball around, what?" Surprise, a new focus, and a common fear combined to make the drawn lines of battle nothing more than that, if only for a fleeting moment: drawings.

"It is now time to vote, and find out where," Liam paused for effect, feeling so on top of his game he must be able to spot his new house from up here, "the Grass is Greener. Voting is now open."

He risked a quick glance at his AR overlay to confirm that the control room had kept up with him and the voting interface had kicked in, replacing the live feed with blaring commercials. He knew the handy tactile voting box would sit in the corner of all of the show's feeds for the next week, giving plenty of time and incentive to boost the ratings as much as possible. So occupied, Liam did not see the diminutive figure approach him until it was too late.

"Hey!" protested Spike, squidging him in the ribs with a massive finger. Liam refused to consider where said finger might recently have been. "Where do you come off, calling to vote like that? My sequence didn't even get played. That's bias, that is!"

"Oh shut it," said Juliette, wading in. "You have nothing to complain about, unlike some of us who didn't get a chance to see if some others were ready to own up to their slander—to my face!" she spat, her tone rising toward the end as she glanced at Azar, who was putting on, albeit involuntarily, a rather good impression of a terrified coat stand.

Oldman brought up the rear, actually hopping in his attempts to get somebody's attention, to the tune of "Not yet! Not yet! I haven't had time to explain how bad our dental plan is yet."

At that, everyone seemed to break into cacophony, amidst which Oldman, as the resident expert in the cost, and therefore value, of a good knock upside the head, decided to give his chair a swing into the amassed lot of them, for good measure.

As luck dictated, he managed to miss connecting with any of the competition and sent the furniture-cum-bludgeon on its way, sure and true, straight into Liam's temple.[54] As the cheap engineered alloy of the chair struggled to

---

54 Leaving Liam, not for the first time, without a god to pray to.

occupy the same space as the carbon, water, calcium, and some-other-bits locally referred to as Liam's skull, all he registered was a blur like a sudden flight of startled birds, and a sharp percussion. Cool movies with intricate first-person perspectives of shell-shocked soldiers and car accident victims had set him up for a major let-down, as the last thing he thought before nothingness engulfed him like a blue screen was, inanely, *What was that?*

27

Beeping.

Sounds like a heart rate monitor. Am I in hospital? Oh, dogs, I'm in hospital, and I'm pretty messed up by the sounds of it, if I'm saying dogs instead of gods. Am I alright? What's wrong with me? Why can't I see? Am I blind? Am I paralyzed? Might I die? What happened? Wait, my sight is clearing up. Oh...

The statutory condom distributor was blinking its little red light at him to show, even without the AR notice, it was empty and in need of a refill. Somehow, he'd never noticed it made a sound before. Now that he could put it into context, it wasn't so much a beeping as a buzzing, and seemed strangely over amplified. Such a loud sound certainly couldn't come from a mere flashing light. In any case, even the shittiest hospital wouldn't have taken things quite this far. He was clearly in the bathroom.

"He's coming around," a voice bellowed, as his ears perceptibly tightened in adjustment to the everyday assaults of the realm of consciousness. Far beyond its routine spin, the world seemed to have a wholly new rotation to it. A few seconds of frenzied data selection and analysis tentatively led his brain to identify the voice as belonging to Barry.

The man's face loomed above him, as full and orange as a harvest supermoon, and a decidedly unwelcome "helping hand" forced his muscles out of their state of contented, if somewhat bewildered, paralysis and into grudging movement.

Liam groaned, not at any pain, but in protest at being forced to return to an upright position that he found about as desirable right now as open-chest surgery by an intern freshly out of anaesthetics and using a blunt spoon. His head throbbed violently at this convoluted thought and gave his second, deeper groan a much sounder basis.

"Glad you came around," said the moon face, "the Editor was afraid we would end up having to call in Health Services, and you know how much they charge you[55]..."

This fraternal call to union through shared lamentations, usually echoed unfalteringly by anyone who has ever needed a stitch or ten, went eerily unanswered, as Liam struggled with reality, the way an eighty year old obligingly tries to grope the prostitute a well intentioned but profoundly misguided friend has provided him for his birthday: while keeping a careful distance, and with the profound impression of having been cheated out of something that had always taken for granted and should by now be, by all rights, second nature, just like riding a bike.

Barry stuttered, and tried to fill the unexpected void. "So... err... just so you know, we had to wrap up the feed without you, after the accident."

Which bit was the accident precisely? pondered something within Liam. *That things got out of hand, or that he was the one who got hit?* He supposed that, in the literal sense of the term, being hit in the head with a chair is, in the long run, just as much of an accident as everything else.

"Luckily, it's mostly automatic after the voting's started. Everyone was very subdued after we carried you out. That Oldman guy was very apologetic, and then we cut straight to commercials. Now we're back on just the first-person live feeds. The clip from Oldman's point of view when he swings the chair already has more hits than anything else in the show so far, so congratulations are in order, I suppose."

Indeed, thought Liam, although the question remained as to what, or whose, order that was.

"So... erm..." Barry faltered, out of words and in decidedly uncharted territory. "Can I get you anything?"

The impulse to answer "a bottle of gin" rose to about chest-level before he could fight it back. "No," he said. He leaned over the sink to take a sip of water, then spat a bit out. Pink gunk swirled down into the drain. He must have bitten his cheek or tongue somewhere along the line. Nothing to be done for it now, so he postponed checking which it was and filed it for later examination. "Thanks, but I'm fine."

Barry needed no more excuse than that to escape. "Right then, if you're certain. I'll be off then. See you tomorrow, Liam," he added with a big grin about as credible as a missionary the day after the Judgment Day of your choice, and sidled out.

Liam stood staring at the stranger in the mirror and listened to the creaks, thuds, and muffled vocal sounds of the Mews winding down to its troubled automated sleep. His AR glasses lay, reverently placed, by the side of the sink bowl. Nanopixel filaments made a tiny, desperate bid for

---

55 They were famous for taking the expression "an arm and a leg" to greater lengths than ever before.

freedom from the jagged edge of the shattered right lens. The bathroom seemed to have been touched with a subtle yet nonetheless effective ward against intruders; a silent stigma, but no less real than that used in times of pestilence.

Urh. Liam surfaced, shaking himself both physically and mentally. *If I'm well enough to have that kind of thoughts, then I'm well enough to get on home.*

Leaving his broken glasses where they lay, he stumbled into movement and made for the door. If he could get past how strange everything looked without the AR trappings, then he'd probably be able to focus enough to remember where home was.

28

Liam convinced himself that he deserved this as he listened to the ice tinkle against his fresh whiskey glass, and grinned. The new job had its perks.[56] One of them was having enough funds available to be able, when putting his shopping order through, to go for the expensive stuff at the top end of the price list without any more qualms than were strictly necessary. He made his way over to his armchair with only the slightest stumble and melted into its nanomolecular-moulded padding. The bottle went on the usual table at his side, its height just right to make picking up and dropping the bottle effortless.

He took his first gulp. *It's a funny old world.* All this brain-power, all this effort, all these machines at work to make something like the GiG possible. All that attention and energy spent by people around the world following the stories, getting the latest info, preparing to place their vote. He took a slightly deeper drink than he had expected, and sloshed his lip and the tip of his nose. *It's not as if their vote matters,* he added, wiping himself dry with his sleeve.

And when you come to think of it, with all these people following and voting for rubbish like this stuff, what might actual politics have to learn?

The means are obviously there. Be it through AR glasses, lenses, and implants or even through old physical devices, people can access any info and participate in any debate, anywhere, with every bit of convenience and ease. Sure, the political process isn't like a reality TV show. But security shouldn't be an issue: the new generation models have much tighter se-

---

56 Diminutive of "perquisite" or, in Latin, that which is "thoroughly sought after." Perks aren't some sort of side benefit; they are the main event.

curity than any manual process in history ever had. Consumers wouldn't have it any other way, not with everything from banking details to porn internet histories at constant risk. He sipped, and refilled.

Our tech obsessions should be giving us actual info, on important things, and not be wasted on this trash! Liam was damn sure that if people could vote in an AR window, you'd get a fuckload more than the usual one-in-five people actually bothering to vote. *What's stopping it? Is it a lack of will?* It was so easy for society to believe that individuals just don't care and couldn't be bothered to take an interest even if it were handed to them on a silver plate.

I'd certainly take an interest, if I knew my vote would actually matter, and I really don't think I'm all that unique in that respect. I'm certainly no better than anyone else. How could anyone not take an interest when given a chance to have their say and help decide the matters that affect their lives directly?

Then again, would people be able to get as passionate about politics as they are about drivel like RealPod?

And then there's the fact that I would be out of a job if something like that ever happened. Hmm.

He pulled himself up and out of his slump, forcing his charcoal-smoke eyes to focus, through the pleasant ethanol blur, on the time display at the bottom of his new, state-of-the-art nanopixel retina implant display. The ones that came with the bone conducting sound implants. It was laughable that he had stuck to his old AR glasses for so long.

One a.m. already? No time to sit here remaking the world, I need to get to bed if I want to get any proper sleep in. Early start on next week's show in the morning, after all.

29

The Editor's oversized, wall-mounted physical screen displayed a face. A male face. The sort of face that is constantly wearing a pained expression, the same way a silver screen vampire wears its false teeth. The face belonged to Ali Fourka, and the Editor was currently staring it down with a look that would have made any passing small rodent or other animal of prey run for cover in a pawful of milliseconds.

The first synthetic voter polls had revealed that, after last week's feature show, Fourka was by far and large the favoured choice for elimination this week. Liam would have thought that maybe that bastard Oldman's over-eagerness with the chair would have counted for something, but knowing this business it had probably made people like him all the better, if anything.

The Editor had called a general meeting that very morning to present the fact of Fourka's elimination and to discuss how to make it as entertaining as possible for everyone involved.

"We should include the scenes where he was badmouthing Oldman, directly followed by those where he was cowering behind Jill during the melee," he said, visibly repressing a sigh, but with a look of longing he could not hide. "Any other ideas?" he quickly added, covering for himself.

"Err[57]..." said Barry, "I have a chum, err, colleague, who does the networking in the Publishing department. Maybe we could see with the bigwigs there about some sort of cross-promotion. You know, we put their magazines and such in the feed, they put some of our content in their magazines. If we hurry, we could get some stuff about Fourka out before Sunday. You know, coverage of the melee last week, some juicy rumours, that sort of thing. It could really build up some interest and excitement."

"Yes," said Lee, not one to be outdone. "And we could also start organising the post-elimination for him as well: the talk feeds, the live events, the merchandising, all of that business. With the popularity of the show, eliminated contestants are going to become household names for a while, and Fourka certainly needs to do his part to promote the feed in exchange."

"I like it. That's the kind of thinking I want to see. You two get right on that, and I want results before we leave tonight. Anything else?"

Silence. While this was indeed an excellent opportunity to show initiative, competence, and worthiness for promotion, that realization that it also entailed an unexpected amount of very real and immediate extra work left all tongues temporarily in the possession of proverbial cats. Tangible downsides did much to curb any potential enthusiasm at abstract advancement opportunities.

Regardless, Liam still ended up having to work late nights all week in order to prepare the best possible elimination for Professor Fourka. There was something particularly perverse about preparing the fallout of a vote that was supposed to be still underway, while at the same time keeping an eye on the various live feeds. At least the fancy new top-of-the-line AR implants the Corp bought him to replace his broken glasses made multitasking while keeping up with his share of the feed monitoring duties that much easier.

Professor Fourka seemed to be pretty much resigned to his fate as he

---

57 To "Err" is human, but to persevere in saying "Err" is worthy of the hottest damnations of hell, as the saying should go.

went about what academic duties Birkbeck hadn't taken away from him yet and preached to the sparse assembly of largely uninterested management students, as per his habit. Something about modern societies becoming "reality intolerant." Business as usual, there.

Suicide Jill's live feed was probably, to the Editor's delight, where things were moving and happening in the days following the weekly feature. True to Emile Durkheim's studies, Monday proved to be a particularly busy time for her, especially what with the days getting shorter.

Liam had been the one on monitoring duty, comfortably set in his new car on the way to work, when Jill had been called in for the most gruesome job they had captured on her live feed to date.

"Ugh, Hackney again," she said with a snort when the orders came through on her AR display. Her clean-up van made an automatic and undramatic left turn to take her there. "Why am I not surprised." Jill had quickly decided to provide running commentary of her own life for her viewers—she was the only contestant who seemed to be treating the show with proper competitive spirit, and the viewers loved her for it.

"I swear, if I have to see that pile of old rubbish they call the Hackney Road Conservation Area one more time, I'm going to take architectural justice into my own hands and knock the whole lot down, just see if I don't!"

She took a swig from her thermos, then paused as more data on the job scrolled into view.

"Hold the big white phone," she said in apparent surprise. "This one might be worth your while after all. I know that looks like a load of paper pusher gobbledeegook to you lot, but what it means is that we've got a double suicide on our hands. Probably a lover's pact, we get those every now and then. I blame Shakespeare, myself." Jill was on a roll, with the London urban clutter serving as backdrop for her latest rant.

"Bloody romantic idiots, what do they think they're trying to prove, anyway? They're lucky enough to find someone who doesn't just want to screw them, but actually likes them and wants to stay with them afterward. Do they even stop to think how many people out there would love to be in their shoes? No, they're too good for the rest of the world all of a sudden, best to end it there while the ending is good and leave it to the Post-Tops to clean up the mess."

The van pulled to a stop, and Jill clambered out with a sigh to unload her cleaning gear. "Bloody typical," was all she had to add on the subject. Lifting the machinery and coils of vacuum tubes and pulling a rubber cleaning jumpsuit over her street clothes stole her breath and rendered her silent, for a rare change.

She grunted her way into the depressingly average tenement building and up the filthy stairs. The yellow arrow guiding her was the only bit of colour she could see, and a blessing, as focusing on it allowed both her and the viewers to avoid having to look too closely at the surroundings and their evident multipurpose as urinal.

The door to the mess-makers' little single room lay half-open. By the looks of it, whoever had found the bodies hadn't bothered to close the door or secure the site behind them—there were bits of glistening tubing, which Liam refused to think of as intestines, hung neatly over the doorknob. The door had clearly lain undisturbed since the event. Anyone who might have been interested in robbing it knew damn well, from personal experience, that anyone living in a place like this would have nothing worth stealing.

Even after five years of experience and hardening, Suicide Jill couldn't suppress a little quiver of fear at what she was about to discover when she pushed the apartment door open. She resumed her running commentary, probably because anything was better than the silence.

"I've tried to ignore it, you know. To make each new corpse into a thing, just another impersonal job." She edged the door open with her toe and stood in the open doorway, steeling herself. "But, you know what? Try as I might, there's always some part of me that just can't forget the people that these messes were, not so long ago. Women, men, and enbies—like you and me."

Jill made a show of taking one last deep breath before stepping into the dark room, and Liam wondered how much of Jill's speech was honest introspection and how much was just a speech, for the sole purpose of the show. If nothing else, it was good showmanship, since it gave the viewers more time to tune in as fans got the word out via social media that something was about to happen on Jill's live feed. The viewing figures in the corner of Liam's display were probably the only thing around here that couldn't lie: it seemed to be working.

"Here we go, guys."

Jill's lenses auto-adjusted as soon as she entered the dark room, adding a surreal, night-vision tinge to the blood and guts that coated the room.

"I know you can see this, but you're really missing out on the smell, guys." Jill paused just long enough for effect, before delivering the punch line, with an apologetic shrug. "It's just offal."

Liam, just like viewers everywhere, was too engrossed in the scene they were seeing through Jill's eyes to care too much about the horrible pun. Primitive instincts yelled that the still-oozing, red masses littering the room belonged inside a person, not sprayed across the walls and cheap furniture like some sort of retro charnel house décor.

"Well," said Jill, once the silence had become unbearable, "I'm pretty sure the bits around here would add up to roughly two whole human beings, but it would be one hell of a puzzler to fit them back together…"

Responding to the combined horror and morbid fascination of millions of viewers, she took one tentative step forward into the room, then another. Navigating her way around the biggest chunks in her path, four steps were all it took to get her from the door to the rough centre of what was still, under all of the gore, a functional bedroom/kitchen/living room combination affair. With mounting horror for all involved, she bent down and took a closer look at a discoloured lump in the middle of the room.

"Is that—"

The bubbly mass twitched below her, and Jill leapt back, nearly slipping on a tube of some sort in her haste, and bolted back out of the open door.

"Oh, fuck this. Fuck everything about this. I'm calling it in."

Liam wondered if all the other viewers were feeling as grossed out and confused as he was, as Jill brought up her telephone interface and cycled through her contacts list with angry flicks of the eye. Eventually, she stopped the list and chose one of the names, a certain "Kader," with a virtual stab.

Whoever Kader was, he answered the call with the sort of grumble you get from someone who had been doing something infinitely more interesting in AR when disturbed, and was eager to get back to it.

"Kader, you fuck, this job is no goddamn suicide pact. I've got the residue from a nanopaint bomb still twitching in the middle of the room. Bring up the file and get the code on this one switched over to what it is, which is a fucking double murder. This is not our business, get the rent-a-cops in."

Vulgarity seemed to have done its work to get Kader's full attention.

"Now hold your horses there, Jill. Let me bring up the file. Right. Yeah, no can do, Jill. Secufax has already been on site. They were the first called, and their agent flagged it as suicide before we were even called in. They wouldn't like it if we try to send it back to them now."

"They can go fuck themselves, Kader. Their 'agent' never even opened the door. He probably just pocketed the bribe from the building's superintendent to keep everything hush-hush and walked off for an early lunch." Jill's audio seethed over the feed, and Liam could only imagine her expression. "In the meantime, the only people who have been here are myself and the killer, just before they lobbed in a plastic bottle full of shrapnel and wallpaper nanites set to populate without limits. There isn't enough left of them to be sure, but judging from the amount of gore and the names on the door here, I'd wager that 'Lucy' and 'Amanda' were two consenting adults who didn't ask to be blown to smithereens by some repressed bigot with a can of nanopaint. Now will you please change the flag on this one so I can get the fuck out of this stench and go take a long shower?"

Kader made one of those annoying teeth-sucking noises, which sounded all the worse for coming disembodied through an AR call connection.

"Yeeeeah. But seriously though. What makes you so sure it isn't a suicide pact after all? They could have just wanted to show how deep their love was with a grand gesture."

Jill was silent for a few terrifying seconds, and Liam could just make out her clenched fist at the bottom of the feed's view.

"Kader," she said, in tones as calm and patient as the grave. "I'll use my fist to show you how deep your asshole is if you fuck me over on this one. People don't usually stop to make souvenirs after committing agonising suicide all over the walls. Here, someone decided to leave a lovely selection of entrails draped over the doorknob for whoever would have to deal with this mess, and that isn't going to be me!"

"Jill, calm down, alright? Look, it's not our job to make a fuss about this. What's done is done. Just turn on your Funfilter and get to work with the machines, okay? It'll be done before you know it."

Jill sounded subdued, almost tired, as she answered. "Man, you know I hate using those filters. They make me feel weak."

"Jill, they're so popular for a reason. There are times when you have to deal with something you don't want to have to look at. When you've got an AR filter that will turn it all into flowers or ice cream or whatever else does it for you, then you'd be stupid not to use it, right? You buckle down and take care of it now, and I'll put you down for an hour's overtime due to stress. How does that sound?"

Jill sighed. "Sure, man, I suppose so. But you owe me one, you hear?"

"That's the spirit. Rock on, Jill." Kader's voice cut out without wasting a second, as he rushed back to whatever AR timewaster he kept himself entertained with between calls.

"Right," Jill said out loud to herself, as if remembering the millions of viewers who had followed that exchange. "Fuck me."

She flicked open her main app menu and loaded up a program called "Funfilter - Fun for all ages, from 2 to 102."

Liam remembered when Funfilter had just been a silly add-on to video messaging services, letting you look like an idiot with huge anime eyes or rainbows puking out of your mouth. It hadn't taken long before the geniuses behind Funfilter realised the real money lay in real-time filters which could remove and replace anything disagreeable from view. With disclaimers in place to cover the inevitable tripping-over-invisible-objects-and-down-stairs incidents, it was one of the biggest successes of the early AR boom. These days, Funfilter came loaded by default into all AR operating systems, and the owners were off living in some corporate paradise on Mars or something. Lucky bastards.

Jill busied herself getting her equipment ready while the filters kicked in. By the time she had the portable incinerator unit warmed up and strapped to her back, the bits of guts still swinging from the doorknob had been replaced by colourful festive garlands, bringing back many happy childhood memories for Liam. Even the door itself looked like a better, more trustworthy sort of door, and Liam was pretty sure the hallway had not been in such a good state of repair a minute earlier.

With her multi-purpose cleaning hose at ready, Jill walked back into the room. No hesitation marked her steps this time, and sure enough, everything in any way disagreeable within the room had disappeared. It now looked as if some unruly children had decided to have a food fight in their otherwise well appointed nursery.

In resigned silence, she set about cleaning up the smears of what appeared to be chocolate pudding, the trails of spilled spaghetti—no meatballs—and the chunky bits of cake and hard candy that the irresponsible children seemed to have scattered all over the place. A couple of particularly large pieces of fresh fruit were too big for the multi-purpose hose, even on its widest setting, so Jill had to pick them up and feed them by hand into the incinerator unit. She did her duty without any visible qualms, other than perhaps a little shudder, which may just have been a glitch in the broadcast.

Soon, the children's nursery was back to its gleaming, cheerful self. Even the stubborn toffee stain in the centre of the room had come up eventually. Jill exited, closing the door gently behind her, then peeled off her chocolate- and fruit juice-smeared jumpsuit and gloves, which she tossed into the incinerator as well.

With a twitch of her eye, she moved to turn off the Funfilter, which the program only accepted to do after multiple confirmations that this was what she really wanted to do and disclaimers regarding anything unpleasant she might see once the filters were off.

What passed locally for reality came back into focus, bit by bit, as the filtering dropped out. The corridor was just as dark as before, the paint just as peeling, and the closed door was once again a shabby, ramshackle affair. The only difference was that everything seemed a bit hazy, as if there were some moisture on the lenses in Jill's eyes—but surely, that was simply another glitch in the filtering program.

With the fun and games over, the viewer count started dropping, as feeders around the world moved on in search of greener, more entertaining pastures.

30

Usnavi Musibay's excitement was contagious. Liam was so proud of getting him onto the feed. If there were one saving grace about the whole sordid business of the show, it would be this one, that he had helped, at his level, to make the world aware of the plight of people like Usnavi, be they handicapped like him, displaced, or just plain down-and-out. The world would do something about it, would want to help, once they knew, once they had shared his reality. How couldn't they? The boy was just so damn likeable.

Today was a big day for Usnavi. He was due to start a new medical trial, and the Corporation behind it—a branch of SyneDeal, the freeloaders—were pulling out all the bells and whistles to turn it into a publicity event, given the show and its live viewers.

Usnavi was more than happy to abandon his usual routine, which from his explanation consisted mainly of unmarked commercial buildings and service doors, and took great pleasure in the VIP lab tour he was now getting, taking Liam and all of the other viewers along for the ride. They were even telling him a bit about what they were putting into his body, for once.

"We're all very excited about our new line of ninja viruses, Mr. Musibay," said the SyneDeal PR doctor with the white medical coat and the friendly AR nametag labelling him as "Doctor Flatt." He ushered Usnavi over to the middle of the room where an AR display had been set up, showing an entertaining but confusing combination of molecules and DNA helixes, rotating freely in the air. "Our proprietary ninja virus techniques are the way of the future, Mr. Musibay."

Liam guessed that Usnavi had been called 'Mr. Musibay' more times today than in the rest of his life put together.

"Bacteriophage viruses have been around forever, of course, and human beings have used them since before we were human. Our noses are full of them, for example, housing them and relying on them to feed upon harmful bacteria in the air we breathe." Liam decided he would take the doctor's word for it, and avoid visualising that too clearly.

"We've been using bacteriophages widely for decades now," carried on the presumably good doctor, "ever since bacteria strains resistant to the old antibiotics became prevalent. Of course, the medical body should have foreseen that this was only postponing the problem and that the worldwide use and abuse of bacteriophages would lead to the evolution of bacteriophage-resistant disease strains, in turn. It's basic natural selection."

Usnavi spoke up at this, possibly to show that he hadn't fallen asleep. "Does that mean we can never have a lasting treatment for germs? One they won't grow resistant to?"

"Excellent question, young man," answered the doctor, pleased as a dog with two tails, and just as surprised. "That's precisely where our ninja viruses step in. Through an alliance of bio- and nano-engineering, we've been able to create viruses that are armed and ready to deal with just about any kind of harmful bacterium."

The doctor paused, allowing the AR display to illustrate his point. As they watched, animated virus strings—equipped with humorous little virtual black masks and katanas—twisted, flexed, and penetrated crimson red bacteria globules with reckless abandon. When the cluster of bacteria had been entirely destroyed, the doctor carried on.

"Natural bacteriophages have evolved to destroy just one kind of bacterium, which is why you have to take so many different kinds of bacteriophages to be properly protected. Instead, our new ninja viruses will be able to feed off any bacteria they are programmed to, neutralising the development of any natural resistances by 'reacting' to them, if you'll excuse my use of the term, and adapting their methods of attack in real time."

"But what about the good germs. Bacteria, that is. Those are a thing, aren't they? Good bacteria, that your body needs to stay healthy?" Usnavi sounded pretty eager to show he was clever and attentive.

"Yes..." The doctor seemed less pleased with this question than the previous. "You are correct, of course. It is precisely because of this need to balance the power of our new ninja viruses that we are now moving into human user evaluations." The doctor smiled at this, his PR face coming back to the fore. "Imagine, young man. Thanks to your work with us today, billions of people around the world will soon be completely protected from all sorts of diseases. Aren't you a lucky one!"

"Oh, yes, sir!" replied Usnavi, his grin reflected in the polished chrome of the lab counters. "So, these will be cheaper than the current phage treatments, then, right? So that billions of people can get some? It's just that most of the people where I live can't afford to get the current phage treatments, the ones that don't hardly work anymore anyway. But I suppose it'll be cheaper with just one kind of ninja super-phage, right?"

The doctor coughed and adjusted his collar, which had suddenly grown tight somehow, before answering. "I'm sure they'll work something out, yes. Can't really say, that isn't my area, of course. However, if we're done here, perhaps you'd like to see what we've set up for your first dose of the new ninja virus?"

He ushered Usnavi out of the lab and on to the next stage of the scripted publicity tour, taking Liam and the live feed viewers along for the ride.

31

Liam couldn't get past the question: what was he doing here, still at the Mews, at this time of night, and on a Saturday of all things? He knew all too well that taking a long walk off a short pier would be a better use of his time than asking to actually be paid for all this extra time he was putting in. Everywhere else, the hour was nominatively happy, and he sure would have been happy to be able to partake.[58]

At least the late night on Friday hadn't made him miss out on Wine and Warfare. He hadn't heard from the gang, so he assumed they were still mostly laid up, tired, and so on. Or maybe everyone was stuck working to all hours like he was, he sighed, as a flick of the finger minimised the AR Solitaire game he'd been half-assedly messing with and he got back to the actual work.

Right, so he was supposed to open this sequence here, insert that here, and here, and here... He had had all of an hour's "training" in doing this, watching over Carpentiere's shoulder as the man caught up on some urgent sequencing one day during the lunch break, and now he'd been turned over to the uncaring arms of the tutorial software.

It really wasn't his cup of tea. He had been trained in the realm of thought, in the humanities. He had always thought of computers as a tool, something to be used as a medium in the professional field and as a means to his entertainment ends in the private. Instead, with his expensive new retinal implants wirelessly tethered to the sequencing unit before him, long after he should have been in the comfort of his home and liquor cabinet, the relationship had somehow reversed. The computer was using him, forcing him to jump through its procedural loops as it fed him inane and mind-numbing instructions (click, click... click).

The software was most definitely the master tonight, although perhaps the correct term would be mistress. Indeed, he shared a strange pang of

---

58 An example of what is known as a back-formation, from "to part-take," which is to say, to take part.

sympathy for the Frenchman who, given the task of officially naming these strange new computing machines so very long ago, had for some time hesitated between the masculine "Ordinateur" and the feminine "Ordinatrice."

And anyway, what good have these things ever done for us?

The involuntary Monty Python reference was not lost on Liam. He had, after all, received a classical education. And what's more, it was fitting. Was not the modern computer empire rivalled only by the Roman Imperium of old? The Red was everywhere. Not only in the economy and in growth figures, but also in the minds and hearts of billions. It was even in their very cells, every second of every day, energy pulses carrying all and any sort of information through the very matter of their being, any potential health consequences down the line be damned.

Still, there was no doubt that being able to perform just about any menial task with AR software guiding your every move, step by step, was progress, of a sort. The Red was the great equaliser, the great unifier. Without its cultural bonding, the true modern international community of values and references would have remained a pipedream. *A utopia,* Liam realised with a mental snort.

Having somehow finished the work while he pursued this runaway train of thoughts, he shut down the offending machine with a vengeful stab of a hardwired physical button. No gentle AR prompt to *please shut down whenever is convenient for you tonight!* It took its time and made him wait as it shut down several applications, but in the end, whirred off into uneasy rest. *That's one less mind for the Red, you bastards!* Liam quickly scolded himself for his silliness at the thought.

Well, that's done, came Liam's mantra as he blinked his retinal clock into focus. He couldn't stop from admiring how intuitive this new tech was, and how much crisper it all looked than he expected. Form was one thing, content was another.

Right. Factoring in an hour either way to get back home, and even if I forgot about eating and showering and somehow went straight to sleep, I'm looking at, what, two-and-a-half hours? Two-and-three-quarters, tops? Ugh.

Equal parts of resignation and disgust washing over him like secondhand bathwater, Liam hauled out the crappy emergency futon from the bottom drawer of the office supplies storage and spread it out on the ground. The room being what it was, this gave him the disturbing sensation of having to sleep at the foot of the computer terminal. However, his body would have none of this squeamishness, and so he crumbled to the feeble mattress, barely taking time to remove his clothes and summarily sling them over the back of the various office chairs. Before he remembered to set an alarm someplace, he was fast asleep.

A vague sense of confusion, of lack of control: what is this thumping? What is this rushing? What is this feeling of spreading, of spinning, of rolling so very thin?

"Ah!" said a choked voice. It echoed so perfectly with something inside him that he slipped directly from sleep to a certain degree of wakefulness, without an instant of that in-between part he had always taken such luxury in maintaining for as long as possible.

"Yes," he said in a surprisingly normal voice, as if caught mid-conversation, "I'll be right out. Thank you." He rose to shut the door in one viscous movement.

What a deep sleep. He couldn't even remember falling asleep, or anything else between then and now. Well, there was maybe something... a vague impression but nothing you could actually call a dream. A mostly peaceful night for a change, now there was something he hadn't had in a while.

It was only then that a slight draught shook him and helped him realise two things: first, that the voice he had just risen to answer was Mary's, and second, that he was naked.

32

It was some five minutes later that the door opened again to allow passage for Liam Argyle, whose resolutely composed, and even defiant, posture contrasted directly with his ragged hair, crumpled clothes, and bleary, sleep-encrusted eyes. He strode across the main hallway of the studio, trying to broadcast an unabashedness[59] that he desperately wished he could feel.

However, the empty warehouse slept uncaring, its AR tags still dim in their power-saving night mode, unaware that by nightfall it would again be transformed into a temple of voyeurism and decadence for feeders the world across and back again. In the meantime, Liam squinted into the gloom as he made his way to the bathroom, trying to avoid the embarrass-

---

59 Being "abashed" means being so embarrassed or upset that you lose control and simply leave your mouth hanging wide open. Give it a try yourself: "A-baaaaaah-shed." Yes, word origins are often that simple.

ment of running into Mary.

Luckily, she was, as always, the first one at the Mews, in order to get things cleaned up and do the computer maintenance. Unluckily, as Liam now discovered to his regret as he pushed open the door, the first function also included cleaning the men's bathroom.

"Ah," said Liam, echoing the woman's own exclamation in a similar situation a mere few minutes earlier. "Err, don't let me stop you, and, umm, sorry if I, err, scared you earlier." He coughed. "I'll just be taking a shower then." Hoping to leave it at that, he started sidling around the cleaning trolley.

"Oh, no, Mr. Argyle." As soon as Mary had gotten over the surprise of the Liam-shaped monster barging in on her usually peaceful morning routine, she had somehow managed to completely block his way to the little shower at the back of the bathroom. "It's me as should be apologizing, barging in on you like that."

"That's perfectly alright, I assure you. Umm, I'll just..." Surely ending the conversation would let him get past her and her trolley and into the shower—if you could call it that, without any extra jets or sonic or anything. A wooden bucket with a hole in it would have had the same qualifications.

"No, no, I wouldn't hear of it. You just stay right there and let me make it up to you." She rummaged about in some arcane[60] drawer of her over-laden trolley and pulled out a little pre-pasted toothbrush in a tube and a hotel-sized[61] bottle of something that was probably shampoo.

"Here, you take these and do what you need to do." She paused, considering[62] him a bit. "Oh yes, you'll be wanting these as well, I'm sure." She fished out a disposable razor and a mini-bottle of foam. "And here's a towel."

"Right, err, thank you. Always know where your towel is, right?"

She gratified him with a chuckle. "I'll leave you to it then. Come find me when you're done and I'll fix you up something hot from the trolley." She swung said offending object through the bathroom door and out into the pervading non-gloom of the main hall. With a thud, the closing door restored both Liam's privacy and a good part of his shattered dignity.

Well, a shower would do me a world of good. He looked down at the miscellaneous instruments in his hands with much the same degree of innocence and confusion which his first ancestor to have discovered fire must have

60 Hidden, and thus, etymologically, "well guarded."

61 As in, "of the size of those commonly found in hotels," not as in. "of the size of commonly found hotels." I can see where that might be confusing.

62 To observe the stars.

experienced while staring at the bright, inviting, yet surprisingly painful colours dancing on the stick.

By the time his self-awareness had recovered sufficiently to stop and analyse where his apprehension was coming from, he had already lurched over to the shower and entered the searing and mind-blanking heat of a decent wash. Vague recollections of classic myths of purification through water and of long-established religious ablution rituals started trickling through his thoughts.

Then, his new implants interfaced with the tags in the shower cubicle seamlessly, setting the water temperature to precisely match his preset preferences and automatically offering him a selection of shower-time AR games, local or multiplayer, and podfeeds to choose from. From that point on, there were no more thoughts, other than a pause every now and again to remind himself that there were definite benefits here, when everything was said and done.

33

It was a much cleaner, civilised, self-controlled, and therefore docile[63] man who emerged from the steam-filled washroom. He gave Mary a cordial greeting as he spotted her taking out the bins.

"Better?" She grunted the words as politely as she could manage from behind the stacked rubbish.

"Aye, very much better. Don't know what I would have done without you." He paused, the long-atrophied roots of chivalry, solidarity, and basic decency nagging at him as he watched her wrestle with the door. "Um, perhaps I could give you a hand there?"

The scene froze as abruptly as the nostrils of a scientist emerging from a heated plane into the depths of polar winter. It was a good handful of moments later that she replied, "Yes, that would be nice," in a curiously deadpan tone which nonetheless set the scene back into movement again, the dance of the planets resuming its regularly scheduled course.

Liam went over to help her get through the door (well, he held it for her), and then heave the bins into the dumpster out back (one, to her four), before heading back in to help himself to a nice warm bun and hash browns off the breakfast trolley Mary had knocked up, his just reward for a job well done. Panting slightly, she joined him a few minutes later, just as he was

---

63 Literally, "easily taught."

finishing off his first helping and pondering the merits of a second.

The hash dealt out, the bangers thoroughly banged, and the brown water supposed to pass for coffee poured and served, there was nothing else for it but to start up a conversation.[64]

She opened the hostilities with, "So, long night, I take it?" between a forkful of banger and a bite of a bun.

"Yes," he managed to say after tactfully wedging his food in cheeks and under his tongue. "I've been at it all week. So much work goes into the preparation of these live feeds, it's unbelievable."

Mary poured herself a cup of tea. "Aye, tell me about it. I'm the one who is going to have to cart out all the props from the store and get it all set up for tonight."

"Ah, yes." Liam's cheeks reddened with each heartbeat. "So, um, how is that going for you, anyway?"

"It should be ready for tonight," Mary said with an expression of utmost serenity, as she stabbed her banger. "That's if we don't get any major hardware failures, or any spills that need cleaning up. I'll already be plenty busy as it is."

"Well, I just hope it goes better than last week," Liam said with a wince, not particularly listening to what Mary had to say anymore.

"I'm sure it'll be fine, Mr. Argyle. After last week, they'll do everything to make sure things don't get out of hand, don't you worry. Just took us all by surprise last week, it did. Now we know what to look out for." Her hand came to rest on his shoulder and gave him a good firm pat. He looked up from his plate, into a face lit up with a smile like a scimitar catching the light of the midday desert sun.

"You know, we don't get to talk like this anywhere near enough," he said. Against all expectations, he was smiling as well. "It's always go, go, go. We never get to take the time for a good sit down and an honest chat. We really should do this more often."

"Right you are, Mr. Argyle," was her only response.

34

Where had the day gone? For one long, glorious, drawn-out moment it had seemed like he would be able to lean back and oversee the final preparations for tonight's live feed forever, that the time itself would never ar-

---

[64] "Conversation" literally means "the act of living with," just as "versus" originally means "to change with."

rive, like some temporal turtle that the arrow could never quite hit. The people had buzzed around like busy little drones all day long. Just looking at them had made him comfortably drowsy and numb.

And now, here he was, his face full of gunk, dressed up like the buffoon[65] that he, not to cut too fine a point, essentially was, and walking toward the set with a shambling pace that would have made even the most dejected of death row inmates, on their last legs, as it were, proud.

His step picked up a good deal more spring as he observed[66] his contestants[67] all sitting there, revealing different degrees of the same expression, both tame and wary. The fact that, by now, last week's chair-related antics had been entirely forgotten by the feeders had not been lost on any of them, nor had the immediate consequence: this week was very much up for grabs, and any of them could be getting the proverbial axe.

He slid with astonishing ease from being Liam Argyle to being approximately one-point-seven-five billion Liam Argyles on screens and overlays the world over. It was all so easy now; there was nothing out of the ordinary, other than a profound sense of inner balance and a slight floating feeling which for some reason reminded him of the bouncy castles of his childhood.

There was no stress, not like the other times. It was truly so very easy, it was child's play. There was nothing to do, other than say the right words at the right time. Everything else was designed to just follow its own course without any input or responsibility on his part… Not unlike the weather used to, come to think of it. It was all so very lovely. He could even come to enjoy it, in time, like one might grow to enjoy a scalding hot bath, or even the reportedly fiery lakes of Hell.

The AR set was perfect, his contestants all played their parts admirably, there were no technical problems whatsoever, and the sequences summarising the highlights from the weekly live feeds fired off with military precision.

Other than double-checking that the chairs had been securely bolted to the floor this time around, he didn't have a care in the world—in either of them, in fact, the real one or the Augmented one. The contestants were going through their usual posturing and in-fighting, but Liam didn't let it get to him or break his rhythm.

He was resolved that even the Crossfire segment wouldn't get to him this time. Jill was up to bat, again. Sprawling in the seat of her works van

---

65 "Someone who puffs out his cheeks" (Try saying it and pay attention to how your cheeks move on the "buff" part).

66 "Watched and kept safe."

67 "Those who call to witness."

as the urban smartgrid handled the actual driving, she ranted and cursed and swore and roared. She went on about politics, about how politicians were all such limp-dicks that they, the people, had to vote in clowns to do their work for them now. She went on about the economy, about how the real joke was that, for all their posturing about fighting corruption, the clowns didn't have any more of a clue about how things should work than the other bastards used to. She went on about the other vehicles on the road. She even went on about having to go on about everything. But first and foremost, she went on about the feed: its creators, its contestants, and, especially, its viewers.

People tended to enjoy that sort of abuse, especially when it came from a source so safely remote, and one whose existence could be turned on and off at will. In that respect, Suicide Jill had more than a smattering of the divine about her.

And, indeed, it seemed to be going down particularly well with the feeders. The first results from the composite feeder testing showed that, thanks in a large part to Jill, the show was maxing out attention levels from all socio-eco-demographics. The advertising brain time was ripe for the selling.

On cue, Jill's rant gently faded to deep blue—clinically proven to hold feeder's attention up to thirty-five percent better than the traditional black—to be violently replaced by a blaring announcement for Alimart, "Meals delivered piping hot to your door, three times a day, seven days a week. Please enquire about our special bachelor rates." Any poor, hungry soul who happened to touch the vidscreen at this point, or simply twitch their eye the wrong way if watching through AR relay, would be caught in the commercial web and would most probably not emerge before having contractually obliged themselves to a lifelong supply of reconstituted hash vaguely resembling traditional meals.

The advertisements then lapsed into a series of indistinguishable pushes for over-the-counter mood-altering drugs. Predictably, each promised more complete relief from reality than both the previous and the next, despite the well known fact that they were all owned, at the end of the myriad corporate labyrinths, by Khemtech Industries and were essentially the same synthetic oblivion in different coloured packaging. Liam's body seemed to be taking all of this in with its usual gaping idiocy, so much so that he nearly missed the next segment he needed to introduce during the break between advertisements.

"And now," boomed Liam's voice through implants, glasses, and pod-screens around the world, "we've come to the moment we've all been waiting for. I know I certainly have."

He turned to grin at the contestants, before returning to the main pod-cam.

"We're making history here tonight, folks. That's not an exaggeration. For the first time, people from all around the world have been called upon to vote, together, in a single event. And boy, have you answered the call. Over the past week, no less than two-point-two billion individual women, men, and enbies have signed up and cast their vote, and the last votes are still coming in, since voting doesn't close until I say so, in a minute or two. But really though: more than two billion people."

Liam paused, nodding in a caricature of thought as he let the figure sink in a bit, for emphasis.

"That's damn impressive, folks. Whatever the outcome of the votes, we've done something incredible here, all together. It's almost as if people were just waiting for the possibility to come together and vote at a world-wide level."

A little alert flashed on Liam's AR display, warning him to get back onto the prepared script, and he gave himself a little shake.

"Well, there you have it, folks. You've followed the lives of our contestants for two whole weeks now, you've cast your votes over the past week, and it all boils down to now, the moment of truth."

Liam took a step back to stand amidst the contestants, while still facing the main podcam. Once he had reached his mark on the floor, he opened his arms wide.

"I'm going to ask our technical friends in the back to close off voting now. Don't worry if you haven't had a chance to vote yet, because we'll be opening up the next week of voting the very second that the results are tallied and we announce who you, the people, have decided to eliminate this week."

Liam made a show of raising a finger for silence as he looked away, as if listening to somebody speaking to him, presumably a God of some variety.

"The results are just coming in now, ladies and gentlemen, and—oh, deary me, it's a doozy. Juliette," Liam said, pausing for effect, "you've dodged a bullet there today, since you came in second with thirty-two percent of the elimination vote, in front of Spike with twenty-one percent—sorry, big guy. But with thirty-eight percent, it's clear: Ali Fourka, the people have decided. You're out."

Professor Fourka's live feed appeared in a floating window for all to see, but only for a moment. Liam thought it was a bit over-dramatic, but the image of his live feed fading to black before shutting down altogether was certainly an effective one.

Liam went over to the man and put a consoling arm around his shoulders. "Hey, look at it this way. People have decided you have the best life out of all of our contestants. That's a compliment, really, isn't it?"

Professor Fourka nodded. He did not seem fazed by the news of his elimination in the least—most likely since it was not actually news for anyone in the know. He simply asked if he could say a few words before exiting, a wish Liam was more than happy to grant him.

"As I take my leave of this program, I would like to deliver a word of warning. To the viewers, first and foremost: be wary. What you are being presented with as 'reality' programming is anything but. It is a product of entertainment. You all know this, of course, since you participate in it and in the illusion of reality it creates, and this is not really a danger in itself. The danger is when you forget it is just entertainment, however grounded in reality it may be, because at that point the illusion becomes the new reality. It shapes your view and expectations of the world, and it reduces your possibilities of acting upon the real world even further.

"To the producers, corporate backers, and the host of this show, a word of warning as well: such deliberate shaping of society's worldview is a double-edged sword. Since it defines the perception of reality, 'reality' entertainment is inevitably political in nature, in that it affects and reflects the life of the City, especially in the modern global City, with its various regional neighbourhoods and national blocks. Be wary of this inevitable political effect. Neglected or mismanaged, it can do us all great harm, and yourselves the first. Need I remind anyone how the first generation of reality show 'celebrities' came to invade the political sphere, heralding the final victory of celebrity over policy, transforming political parties into cults of personality, and leading directly to the abdication of decision-making to the Corporations?"

On that chilling note, Professor Fourka took a little half-bow and exited the stage. The Editor decided this was a good time for an energy-pumping jingle and a commercial break, which Liam welcomed like the first cool evening breeze on a scorching summer's day. He popped off the AR set for a quick hit of caffeine water, and stopped as he passed the Editor on his way back to the set for the wrap-up and transfer back over to the live feeds.

"Hey, Ed. Listen. I was wondering... do you think we should cancel the talk feeds and promotion week for Pr—I mean, for Ali Fourka? After that little speech tonight, I don't know if it's in our interests to give him even more of an audience." Liam was both disappointed and proud that he had managed to say "our interests" without even a quiver in his voice.

"Liam, my boy. Well done out there tonight, first of all. As for Ali Fourka, I wouldn't dream of cancelling his scheduled promotion run. Trust me, the interviewers we've lined up won't give a hoot about his political science claptrap. They'll pepper him with questions about Spike's big horn and the size of Jill's cleavage, which is what their audience wants to hear about." Ed waved an arm, for emphasis, as he spoke. "He'll have his final lap around the racecourse, and after the next Sunday feature, your friend Finn Oldman will become the new eliminated flavour of the week, sending Fourka back into ridiculed silence in his closet office at Birkbeck, where he will be the University authorities' problem, and not mine."

The Editor inflicted another one of those hated smiles upon Liam and gave him a gentle yet definite shove back onto the set, leaving him little-to-no time to process what he had just been told about the result of a vote that hadn't even opened yet.

"The commercials are nearly done, believe it or not, so get back out there. When you're done, come see me in my office so we can talk this over some more, and prepare for Oldman's elimination next week. Ta!"

35

It is amazing, Liam mused, how human beings are geared toward routine, which always settles in, even in the most extraordinary of circumstances.

Three weeks in, and Liam already thought of himself as an old hand at this live feed monitoring business. It was easy, really. He had long since given up worrying about having to intervene in a feed. It was clear the Editor and the higher-ups were happy to let the contestants go about their lives and put on any antics they felt like. It seemed that, as far as the feed was concerned, everything goes, including potentially disturbing events, like Jill's clean-up session last week—or even Professor Fourka's subversive classes and speeches.

Not only was it easy, but Liam had to admit he was growing more and more fascinated with these live feeds. At first, he hadn't wanted to touch the things with a laser pointer, and yet now, he caught himself popping into the live feeds to check up on his contestants, even outside of work hours when he was back home—including in bed and on the toilet, which he didn't find as disturbing as it perhaps should have been.

So it was with pleasure that he logged in to the live feed server that Tuesday, only to have any possibility of pleasure dashed as he saw that he was assigned to monitoring Finn Oldman today.

Liam's instinctive hatred of the man had only gotten deeper over the course of the show—and would have even without the chair incident, he was prompt to reassure himself. Oldman was human scum. There was no other way of putting it. A product of modern corporate world-society, certainly, in the same way that scum is the product of the stagnant waters of its pond. But scum, nonetheless. The man didn't have a moral bone in his body. And yet, he seemed to be taking to the show like a fish in water—or perhaps that should be an eel or something, thought Liam, before reminding himself there was such a thing as taking a metaphor too far.

Today, Oldman seemed to be playing hooky from work at the Health Services, which was a blessing in itself, since Liam didn't think he could have taken another day of watching Oldman violate medical confidentiality on an industrial basis and receive commendations for how efficient he was at declining treatment coverage.

Instead, he was strutting through an upscale commercial district, probably one of those new corporate complexes in Runnymede. But instead of stopping to look at the products on display in the shop windows, his attention seemed to be focused exclusively on the ladies walking around or sitting at café tables. Liam wasn't certain what Oldman was doing, but he had the feeling he wouldn't like it and his hand slipped back into its old position next to the big red live feed interruption button.

As he watched, the man scanned an indoor café terrace and locked eyes upon an attractive, copper-haired executive type sitting by herself, sipping a coffee and messing with something or another in her AR display.

Bold as a brass monkey with polar fleece undies, Oldman marched over to her table and sat straight down. She jumped and sputtered, but he made sure to speak up before she had a chance to start protesting.

"Smile, my dear."

From the sound of his voice, he was clearly doing likewise. "You are being broadcast live to every *Grass is Greener* viewer around the world."

By the look on the poor lady's face, she knew what The Grass is Greener was, and those magic words raced through her brain to collide with her mounting indignation at the man's behaviour, leaving her shocked and speechless in the aftermath, which Oldman took as an invitation to carry on.

"That's right, I'm Finn Oldman, one of the contestants in The Grass is Greener. I'm sure you've heard of our little program, with our twenty-four-hour live feed implants." He raised a hand to tap his temple, looking his target up and down in the process. "It opens all sort of possibilities, taking part in a big show like this one, you know. It won't last forever, of course, but even afterward, there are plenty of opportunities for... self-improvement, once you've become so well known. And I'd really like someone to share those opportunities with."

A look of horror crossed the silent woman's face as Finn finally delivered his prepared pick-up line.

"So, what do you say? Do you have celebrity in you? And if not, would you like some?"

The woman blurted out something inarticulate, and ran away so fast she knocked over her chair. Rising, Oldman went to pick it up.

"Ah, well, I guess she didn't have it in her after all. No worries, there are plenty more where that came from." Oldman swaggered on to another part of the shopping complex, leaving Liam with mounting horror at the realisation that the man was right, there most certainly were women out there who would be attracted to him simply due to the meagre sort of celebrity he had achieved through the show. Heck, after today's stunt, he would probably be getting propositions before the end of the day.

At least they had avoided the full-out sexual aggression scenario Liam had dreaded for a moment there, he consoled himself, taking his hand off the big red button once again.

36

Thursday brought another difficult live feed, but for entirely different reasons.

Azar Acquah had called in sick at work—a first according to the records the show had obtained—and was now dragging herself on foot all the way across town to the no-premium emergency walk-in clinic. It was pitiful to watch the woman, who was clearly in even worse shape than usual, haul herself through the filthy sidewalks of "Greater London," an expression which was growing more and more oxymoronic by the day.

Safely ensconced in the efficient and uncaring self-driving transport system, private vehicle owners and public transport users alike zoomed past, just as uncaring as their computer-regulated vehicles. In an age where getting worker A to worksite B as fast as possible was the only metric by which the transport system was judged, the rare pedestrians who were too poor to purchase a public transport pass—or get a job where one is provided for them—were at best an embarrassment, and usually regarded as a nuisance, a throwback to the time all those decades ago when the city was defined as a throng of people in the streets, as opposed to the efficient, faceless mechanical hive the current generation had grown up with.

Being a pedestrian in 2072 was an extreme sport. The urban smartgrid left little to no provision for walkers. There was no such thing as a crosswalk. Every kilometre or so, each major road would have the mandatory underground walkway that allowed pedestrians to cross to the other side—if they could find a path through the refuse, homeless people, and piles of human effluvia which were a hallmark of these tunnels, which doubled as impromptu homeless shelters since all public support had been withdrawn and the subway system had been "cleaned up" and militarised with corporate security forces.

Trying to cross the street itself was a high-risk proposition. Since the rules stated pedestrians weren't supposed to ever be on the street itself, smart cars were not programmed to register them, or stop if detected, any more than they would stop, and hold up the entire system, for a stray cat or dog. This was the main reason why cars no longer had front or rear windows: so passengers had an excuse to ignore any bumps they may feel during the ride, since they had no way of checking anyway.

Aged beyond her years, Azar was in no shape for any sort of death-defying street dash. They all watched as she slalomed her way down streets and through noxious tunnels, looking worse and worse with every step. Liam was concerned at her video angle, bent over like a top-heavy willow. She must really be feeling like crap, he thought—while repressing the guilty thought that at least the viewers, and himself, were spared having to look too closely at the dismal city surroundings, which not even a mother could love.

Like an outboard motor boat running out of fuel, the woman sputtered, shuddered, coughed, and then, inevitably, keeled over. As Liam watched in horror, her angle tipped even further and, her legs turning to unwieldy jelly, she slumped sideways against the blistered dome of a broadcast Pod—identical around the world, State-implemented as per World Court rulings, and found anywhere there was electricity. Azar wasn't moving, and didn't seem to have much to say—hardly riveting entertainment.

The thought reminded Liam of why he was watching in the first place, and he reflexively mashed the big red button, freezing the live upstream and alerting the Editor for immediate action, since the thirty-second live feed delay immediately started ticking away into nothing, taking with it any possibility of managing the situation without interrupting the feed.

The Editor's voice instantly rose out of the air next to him, without Liam having even had to accept the call. The background sounds were muffled, but it sounded like he was at some sort of gathering. A meeting, perhaps?

"Argyle, what happened?" His voice snapped like a bullwhip, setting

Liam's every nerve on edge.

"Ah! Sir, it's Azar Acquah, sir."

"Yes, I can see that. What did she do?"

"She was having health issues, and now she's collapsed on her way to the medical clinic. Should we send a medical team, sir?"

The Editor let out an audible sigh, before resuming, all traces of tension gone from his voice. "I see. Just a moment, please, Liam."

Liam waited, and was surprised to see the live feed timer resume, without any input from him. The display in the corner of his admin feed told him there were only just over ten seconds left on the delay clock, but even as he watched, imperceptible micro-staggers of the feed started building it back up again, a few milliseconds at a time.

Azar still lay unmoving, eyes half shut and one gnarled black hand spread against the bottom of the Pod unit's gunmetal dome, when the Editor cleared his throat to announce his return to Liam.

"There we go, Liam. No harm done, "

Liam couldn't hold back the retort. "No harm done? Ed, she could be seriously hurt. She could be dying! We have a responsibility to do something."

"Now, now," scolded the Editor, his condescending voice feeding directly into Liam's skull through the small miracles of bone conduction and making a great impression of what he imagined the voice of a god might sound like. "There's no need to go around bandying words like 'responsibility.' Our sole responsibility is to do our jobs and make a great show, for the whole world to see."

"I'm not certain looking out through the eyes of an unconscious woman makes for a great show, Ed."

The Editor actually chuckled at this, making Liam feel sick. "I beg to differ. What you're looking at right now is precisely what we've been looking for all along on *The Grass is Greener*. Real life! Honest, chilling, riveting, and pure. Look at the viewer ratings, Liam. They don't lie. Word about this is spreading like wildfire. No show has ever let you look out live through a dying woman's eyes before."

"Dying? Ed, we can't just let her die!" Liam felt on the verge of tears, and was glad he didn't have live broadcast lenses fitted into his own eyes.

"Figure of speech, dear boy! Just a figure of speech. I'm certain Ms. Acquah will be perfectly all right."

Fate, ever a bastard, chose that very moment to prove the Editor right, as the view wobbled and Azar was turned over. She blinked and shook her head a little, then focused on the figure before her, a man in a cheap business suit, learning over her with an expression of concern.

"Ma'am, are you alright? Can I get you anything?" Some jaded part of Liam thought the question sounded a bit too mechanical, too rehearsed. Had the man actually been checking her to see if she were dead before lifting any valuables? Liam scolded himself, this time, as Azar came to her senses.

"No, thank you. No. I just had a bit of a dizzy spell, that's all. I was on my way to the walk-in clinic," she added, apologetic for some reason, as if she had offended the man somehow by falling unconscious on the sidewalk between his office and his bus stop.

"The one over in East Enfield? You were going to walk all that way?"

As she wobbled to her knees, Azar let out a choked cough, one she had clearly tried to hold back. "I couldn't seem to find my bus pass, so I didn't really have any choice."

The man didn't seem fooled and cut her off. "Let me help you, Ma'am." Azar must have looked as if, in what pride she still had, she were about to reject the offer, because he insisted. "Please."

Liam felt a wave a relief as Azar nodded and the man he helped her back to her feet.

"The bus stop isn't far," said the man, his tone reassuring. "That's where I was going anyway, and I'd be happy to buy you a pass to Enfield, and a return as well, if you'd accept it."

"That would be lovely. Really lovely," answered Azar, walking as best she could to keep up with him. "I can't thank you enough."

The fuzzy feeling percolating through Liam's mind was so unfamiliar that he almost didn't recognise it as renewed faith in humanity — at first, he thought it might be a stroke. Of course, the Editor soon broke the spell.

"Ha! A good Samaritan! What did I tell you, my boy? Real life, red in tooth and claw! That's how we make a good show, by Alan Sugar's ghost!" At this, the Editor actually cackled. "Let this serve as a lesson to you, Argyle. The red button is for real emergencies only! Like when a contestant is threatening to break the rules or attempt to sever the little window on life that we're offering the world. Not when someone falls over. Watch out for the feed itself, Liam, and let Nature sort out the rest. Are we clear?"

"As a dead man's agenda, sir."

The Editor was visibly thrown by the sudden morbid turn of Liam's thoughts, but seemed pleased enough. "Right. As long as we're clear. See you at the Mews tomorrow."

God, Liam needed a drink.

37

Back home, the tinkle of ice at the top of his second glass of gin whispered to Liam that he would probably enjoy a good, escapist fantasy read. Maybe something like Tolkien.

Liam didn't have the heart to start a re-read of *Lord of the Rings*, and he had never been able to read *The Hobbit*—the Dwarves' tasselled hats from the beginning of the book clashed too violently with the rough imagery forced upon him by the classic, action-packed films he had watched in his youth.

He just couldn't face fantasy anymore, not the kind of classic fantasy Tolkien, C. S. Lewis, or Ursula LeGuin would have been able to offer. Some mindless fantasy movie or game was another thing entirely. He could watch generic black and white characters smash swords into each other all day long, and if it had gratuitous sex and/or dragons, then all the better. But what he was still honest enough to call proper fantasy, the stuff that created a coherent other world and held it up as a mirror to our own, he hadn't been able to stomach for a while now. Real life was hard enough to deal with as it was, without trying to muster the energy to care about another reality entirely.

What he needed was an illusion world he could lose himself in, without having to think about it—and even more importantly, without having to feel or care about it.

How did everyone else manage it? Oh, right.

He poured himself a third drink and, for the first time in his adult life, did what he had always prided himself in not doing, what he had thought defined him as different from everybody else—he shut down his reading app and loaded up the mass-produced video entertainment network. Afraid he might second guess himself or lose his nerve, he stabbed at the series in the "Fantasy" category that had the highest viewer count and settled down into his moulded chair.

When, an hour later, he realised his bottle was empty and it was probably time to get to bed anyway, all he could remember of what he had watched was a blur of swords, the clank of armour, and splashes of blood.

Everything seemed to be accelerating around Liam, as if the Earth had gained rotational speed, in defiance of all natural law, and everything was somehow moving all the faster and more frenetically for it.

Another week down, another weekly elimination feature. The show seemed to pretty much run itself nowadays, like a hamster in its wheel. Liam refused to dwell too long on the comparison.

This was the best show yet, and not only because of the growing viewing figures. Though the voting wasn't finished yet, it was no secret that tonight would see the exit of Finn Oldman, which pleased Liam to no end. Oldman was quite the pain in the neck. Liam still had twinges from the chair incident, and he was itching for revenge. He didn't think the Editor would let him get actual revenge on the man—although perhaps he would have, had Liam asked, come to think of it. It would have made for an entertaining show. Shoot, too late to ask now, in any case.

Liam would have to settle for the satisfaction of seeing Oldman booted from the show and back into the Health Service office anonymity where he belonged.

Sure as broken New Year's resolutions, the votes came in resoundingly in favour of eliminating Oldman, with Juliette Binns and Spike Bighorn pulling up the rear—as it were—but with barely half the votes.

Liam considered whether he should be feeling guilty at taking so much pleasure in the man's elimination, but he told his conscience to stuff it, especially when he saw how Oldman was taking the news.

Far from being hurt or depressed, Oldman seemed to be treating his elimination like some reward, basking in being the centre of attention. Before Liam's astonished eyes, he even did a couple of victory laps around the set, before racing over to embrace what could only be his new partner—a bleached blonde woman with a chest so full of silicone it could have grouted an entire kitchen, with enough left over for a half bath. Who had let this woman into the Mews in the first place?

Oldman swung both her and her grouting—which seemed to have a mind of its own—around, and together they gave the cameras a cliché movie kiss. The weedy man grinned at the public at large.

"Sorry to leave you just when things are getting good," he said, "but a gentleman doesn't kiss and tell, or even broadcast. Argyle, be a pal and tell your people to shut off these lenses of mine now, there's a good fellow. Lynne and I have some catching up to do, if you know what I mean."

Liam sincerely wished he didn't, because then he wouldn't have to scrub away the mental image of that walking shit Finn Oldman and the stupidly grinning pile of chemicals next to him in the act, such as it may be. That a man like Oldman could have used his show, used Liam himself, to increase his social status and his reproductive desirability made Liam want to grab an axe and bust open the bottom of the gene pool, starting with Finn Oldman.

It was therefore with a sigh of relief that he finally saw the back of the man and announced that voting was once again reset and renewed, until next week's feature show.

After a hasty exit from the set, Liam sat in the bar-equipped comfort of his new car and tried to convince himself that, with a major pain in his backside gone, things could only get better from here on in. He very nearly succeeded, as well.

38

Surely there must be a law somewhere against shit hitting the fan before eight a.m. on a Monday, right?

He wasn't even supposed to be monitoring Juliette Binns today in the first place. His roster had him with Usnavi Musibay, a cakewalk and the perfect thing after a rough Sunday evening show and an even rougher Sunday-to-Monday morning trying to drink the memory of it into submission.

But then Usnavi, bless his soul, had to go and catch a fever or something, leaving him bedridden and dry heaving, his stomach contents long gone. Liam had tried to argue to Ed that there was plenty of merit in sticking with Usnavi, that there was important social commentary in the unwanted side effects of the so-called "ninja virus" and, especially, that there was no need to reassign Liam to another feed. Ed had replied in no uncertain terms that social commentary could go take a flying leap and would happen whether Liam was monitoring or not, and so now he was stuck watching Juliette Binns in her bathroom, trying to make herself look human again, after a long night shift.

Even in his foul mood, Liam had to sympathise. Being called out for a series of night-time emergency AR repair interventions, especially just after the stress of a big weekly elimination show, really sucked a big one.

And so Liam sat, watching Juliette look at herself in her bathroom mirror and go about her morning rituals. Riveting stuff.

Still in a huff, he walked over to the caffeine water distributor and concentrated on pouring himself a cup without spilling it everywhere. It took all of fifteen seconds, but it was long enough for Juliette to leave the mirror, make her way over to her affordable apartment's excuse for a toilet cubicle, and stop.

Liam sipped at his cup and watched as Juliette stared at the toilet, as if indecisive about something. *Come on, girl*, he thought. *You've either got to go, or you don't.*

But Liam was as misguided as he was uncharitable. Juliette seemed to steel herself up for something, and, just as she strode forward, the screen in Liam's AR display went black.

In a world with a more dramatic turn of mind, this would have been the perfect opportunity for Liam to perform the traditional "spit take." But this wasn't, and so he didn't, contenting himself with another befuddled sip of his energy drink while he waited for what he assumed was just some small technical glitch to sort itself out, as such things usually did in his experience.

And yet, even to Liam's untrained lenses, this seemed odd. Juliette's AR interface was clearly still working and broadcasting, since he could see her display, with its start menu, time, shop, and program tabs. Furthermore, he could still hear the watery sounds and muffled bangs from next door, which were the fitting soundtrack of any cheap apartment bathroom. Everything was still on and working. Whatever had happened, it was only affecting the visual feed. Almost as if—

The feed interruption alert flashed in his view, bathing his whole display in a lurid red. He looked over to the button, which remained resolutely un(im)pressed. A remote activation?

The Editor's voice pounced upon his consciousness again, as uninvited as a cougar at a stag party.

"Argyle!" boomed his voice, out of thin air. "Where are you? Why didn't you interrupt the Binns feed?"

"I—I was just looking into the malfunction, sir, and—"

"A malfunction, is it, Argyle? A human malfunction, then. Our Ms. Binns thinks she can break her contract and keep her eyes shut when she wants a bit of privacy. A bit of alone time. After signing on for *The Grass is Greener*! The cheek!"

Liam wondered, for a moment, whether he was referring to anatomy or attitude, but wisely decided not to raise the question at the present time. "I see," he lied instead. "The clock is ticking, Ed, and we'll soon be out of feed delay buffer. What can we do?"

Liam's question was meant to be rhetorical, but the Editor clearly took it as a challenge. "You're right, time is wasting. I'll show you what we do," he seemed to threaten.

As he finished the sentence, a bright red system error message flashed against the eyelid darkness of Juliette Binns's feed. However, as Juliette was qualified to tell, this was no classic registry error or nagging alert to restart the system. This message had teeth.

"User JBINNS: You are in breach of contract with THE GRASS IS GREENER, Section 5.4.9 entitled 'WILLFUL RESISTENCE.' You will cease breach of contract within TEN seconds or punitive action will be implemented as per Section 14.2.11 subclause 3 entitled 'ESCALATING ELEC-TRIC SHOCKS.' This is your only warning."

Scary stuff, thought Liam, but a pretty clever trick nonetheless. Hadn't he read about an early sociology experiment that went something like that? The seconds passed, and Juliette seemed to be calling the Editor's bluff. Her eyes seemed even more tightly shut than before, if anything.

"Well, Ed, it doesn't seem to have worked. Nice try though. What do we do next, go see her or something?"

"What you do next," intoned the Editor, with heavy emphasis on the *you*, "is march straight back to your post and flip open the pad with the feed interruption button."

Liam was there faster than you can say "Pavlovian," and sure enough, the dramatic big red button was actually a big red flap, covering a simple touch pad bearing the label "Electrics."

"Wait... You mean that we can actually do that?" asked Liam, with equal measures of revulsion and curiosity.

"Argyle, do you know how easy it is to administer pain when you've got high-powered equipment implants inside one of the most vulnerable parts of the human body? Well, you will do. We're nearly out of buffer, Argyle. Press the button."

Liam fought with a veritable menagerie of conflicting impulses inside him and tried to stall while he worked it all out.

"This button, right here?"

"Now, Argyle!" The Editor's voice ran out of his implants, through his bones, and straight down his nerves to his fingers, seeming to bypass his brain altogether. He pressed the button.

On Juliette's feed in a corner of his display, the effect was instantaneous. The feed seemed to twitch along with the electric convulsions of her eyes, and the little scream of literal shock Juliette let out confirmed that the button did indeed work. Her eyes flung open, and as they did so, the system message faded away—though for some reason, overexposure perhaps, the word "ESCALATING" stayed around a good couple of seconds after the rest had disappeared.

"Boom!" yelled the Editor into Liam's cartilage, yet again. "And the feed resumes, with a whole three seconds to spare on the buffer clock." He cackled. "At this rate, you'll be running this whole show soon, Argyle, and I'll be keeping in touch from Corporate Paradise Mars!"

Oh, gods, thought Liam. *An upwardly-mobile corporate beast.*

"The main thing," continued the Editor, oblivious to Liam's horror, "is to keep a constant watch on her and, especially, make sure the feeders don't find out about Ms. Binns's little act of rebellion."

The Editor paused, pensive.

"For now, at least," he added, and Liam shuddered as he imagined the kind of grin which was undoubtedly splayed across the Editor's features at that very second.

"In any case, don't worry about it, Liam," he carried on. "Juliette is the given favourite for elimination in this week's early polls anyway, so you won't have to keep up your solemn vigil for too long."

39

Misery loves company, and when company isn't readily available, it will often settle for the next best thing, which is, of course, either reality television or pornography. Spike Bighorn qualified as both—which wasn't as rare as it probably should have been.

As such, Liam probably shouldn't have been surprised to run into a new problem to handle on his first break from a week of solid Juliette-monitoring. The weekly elimination feature couldn't come fast enough.

To his augmented eye, it seemed like Spike was going through the regular motions—mainly different forms of thrusting and bucking as he penetrated and was penetrated in turn by his various mechanical Erobot co-stars. It was certainly more entertaining than watching Juliette's terrified toiletries, or Usnavi, who had spent most of the week bedridden, with his immune system going haywire. Still, super-realistic execution or not, the sexual act soon acquired a boredom all its own, especially when performed with such cold engineering, with the artificial stop and go of professional cinematic production, and without any of the musical and post-production trappings[68] that were such a large part of what made the final pornographic product so titillating.

There was very little risk of any *Grass is Greener* rule-breaking here, especially from Spike, who was as comfortable in the limelight as a bug in a whorehouse rug. Liam's attention was therefore partial at best when a

---

68 "Ornamental cloth for a horse." No, really.

scream, mingling human pain with mechanical distress, rang over the feed and through his head.

Spike's field of view was tilted at a strange angle, as if he were bent backwards, and to the side. Whatever was torturing the man, it seemed to involve his nether regions, and Liam was thankful, for once, that the feed's field of view was limited in scope.

"Cut!" came the bellow from the lady running the show, and who would probably have insisted on being called director. The screw-bots froze in positions each more ridiculous than the next, leaving Spike impaled and helpless on a mechanical schlong.

The bright advertisements covering Spike's android partners took on a macabre tone as Liam watched the man struggle and yell out in pain, trying to extricate himself from the—somewhat ironic—spike he was stuck upon, to no avail.[69] While this was unfortunate for Spike, there was clearly no rule-breaking going on here, and so Liam decided to pass the time in speculation about what had gone wrong. Surely this wasn't just another rip or tear, however unspeakable. A seasoned professional like Spike Bighorn could soon have gritted his teeth and pulled it off—or out, as the case were—as he had many's a time before.

This must be something altogether worse, which left two options. Either it wasn't just a rip or tear but an actual snag on something vitally important within Spike's own inner mechanics, which was terrifying and would probably be an issue for the feed, or else some sort of muscular problem was stopping Spike from making a rear-guard retreat.

The director seemed to have come to the same conclusions.

"Oh, alright then," Liam heard her mutter, before she bellowed "Cut!" again, this time gesturing at a set technician who eventually caught on and scampered off-camera and returned, after a few bangs, clangs, and choice swear words, with a hand-held rotary saw.

He moved into position behind Spike, making Liam nervous even though he was a continent and an ocean away.

"Don't worry, now," said the man, sounding nearly as nervous as Liam felt. "This won't hurt a bit," he added in tones suggesting he was mostly trying to reassure himself, and failing miserably.

"Just make it quick," Spike muttered through gritted teeth, and soon the whine of the power saw sent chills down the spines of everyone involved.

The whine changed to the shriek of tortured alloys and the feed's view started shaking and shuddering, presumably along with Spike. It was a strange experience. Hopefully, it was just the impact of the saw cutting through the offending mecha-member, but the saw could also just as well

---

69 "To have worth."

be slicing through the base of Spike's spine at that very moment, and neither Liam nor any of the other viewers would have any idea, unless some screaming started.

It served as a cold reminder that, however intimate, however immersed in the skull of the contestants he might feel, it remained just a gimmick. It was limited, nothing more than a glorified parlour trick. Would technology ever be able to fully immerse one person in another's experience of the world? Maybe these new synaptic interfaces the tradeshows kept harping on about, but even then—wouldn't that just be a better camera, letting you feel, smell, and taste, instead of just see and hear, but without giving the slightest real inkling of what it was to be the person in the recording, with their own experiences, outlook on life, and beliefs? He didn't know, and wasn't sure he ever would—but at least it made a good distraction from the terrifying saw-noise, which sounded like it was right behind him, and which, at long last, cut out.

The same agency worker was clearly on both technical support and medical duty, since he put away the smoking saw and reached for a first aid kit. Still wracked with pain, Spike managed to turn a bit and watched as the improvised medic withdrew a scary-looking set of clamps from the kit and took position by Spike's afflicted bottom.

"There's just this bit that stayed inside to get rid of," the techie said, apologetic. "One last blow for the team, right?"

Spike started to reply, probably to tell him just where he could stick his blow for the team, but was interrupted by further spasms of pain when the techie shoved in the clamps and found a good position, before ripping out the larger-than-life compu-cock end. Liam offered a silent wince of male sympathy, both for Spike and the mutilated manbot.

Spike fell into a writhing heap onto the floor, and the medic placed the excessively hard-ware into a secure toolkit before pulling out two nanite syringes, one labelled as painkillers and the other for medical diagnostics.

The first killed all of Spike's pain receptors, bringing a halt to the shudders of the feed and the motion sickness it undoubtedly induced in viewers all around the world. As the techie applied the diagnostic nanites to Spike's bottom and waited for the results to come in over his AR display, Spike was able to piece back together the understandably scattered threads of his mental cloth.

"You know," he said, with a croak in his voice entirely unlike anything Hollywood has taught the world a frog is supposed to sound like, "this is probably where, in one of the more story-driven classic pornos, I would be cracking a joke about how I usually like to be on first name basis before we start using the clamps."

He pulled himself up into a sitting position and turned to face the techie, who had a far-off look as he scanned the medical diagnostics coming in.

"Of course, these days, there's no such thing as first name basis anymore. Or rather, everyone's first name is public property, on display in the AR profile along with everything else. So, I suppose you could say everyone is on first name basis now, in a way. But I'm not certain it actually means anything anymore..." Spike shook himself. "Listen to me ramble. You must have given me some good stuff there, doc. So, tell me... Greg. What's the damage?"

While agency placement training covered basic first aid technician basics, along with cleaning, catering, electrical maintenance, software debugging, and all of the other myriad tasks expected of the modern outsourced wage slave on his or her zero-hour, zero-job security contract, bedside manner had, sadly, not been considered a necessary skill.

"Whoa," said the young man, who in another, kinder lifetime would have probably been known as Greg the Surfer Guy. "I've never seen reading like this before. Is Tetanus even still a thing? Man, I've got to look this one up."

Spike rose in careful steps, like a ziggurat, and stood waiting in palpable dread for the medical encyclopaedia's verdict. The studio warehouse was strangely silent all of a sudden, as everyone other than Spike, Greg, and the Erobots had long since found an excuse to disappear, proving once again that the risk of legal responsibility for a cock-up—literally, in this case—is far more effective at clearing any given area than a mere bomb threat or fire alarm. This psycho-sociological breakthrough had revolutionised the security industry over the past ten years, with all previous sirens and alarms, which only made people waste time standing around debating whether this was just a drill or something, now being replaced by stern voices demanding to know who had knocked a hole in the window. Even in windowless office spaces, evacuation response times were at an all-time low.

"Well," said Greg the Agency Dogsbody, finally making his way through the medical articles thrust at him by the diagnostics system. "The good news is that it's curable. That's about it for the good news. As for the rest, I've never seen an infection spread this far before it gets picked up by a DNA sensor. Come on, man, I'll help walk you to a medicar."

Greg moved over to offer Spike an arm on their way out of the building, which he shook off with a small wave of the hand.

"It's all over your muscles," carried on Greg, making conversation as they made their slow, aching way toward the door. "No wonder you were in such pain. It's a surprise you could move at all. For the infection to take root that deeply, it can't have been introduced at skin-level. You'd have to get it from something penetrating really dee—"

Spike was completely oblivious, shuffling along as best he could, with the memory of muscle cramps hiding behind the painkilling nanite haze like a teenage Facebook conversation—never quite erased. Liam, however, was very curious as to why the Agency guy had stopped mid-sentence, or, more accurately, he was very curious if his suspicions on the matter were right—which they were.

Greg let out a nervous chuckle as they reached the main doors. "So, it seems like we won't need to call a medicar in after all. Corporate tells me it's sent its own medical staffers to pick you up. I guess it's your lucky day."

The doors opened, letting in a trio of interchangeable men with smiles straight out of a dental nano-reconstruction advert and white coats labelling them as doctors, whatever their actual qualifications may have been— this was still Hollywood, after all.

"Mister Bighorn, and not a moment too soon. Look at how tired he looks, David," said the first in line, grabbing Spike by the arm.

"Right you are, Josh," replied the second in line, in tones so identical the men might as well have been joined at the larynx. "Casebook overexertion if I've ever seen it. Let's get him hooked up to some solution." He took Spike's other arm, and together they combined physical force and power of authority to usher him out of the building and into the bracing urban smog.

"Right then," Greg called out from somewhere behind Spike. "Hope you get better. I'm going for a caff."

The door shut behind them and cut off any other comments. Soon, plunked into a seat of moulded white nano-gel, with the best liquid oblivion medical science had to offer pumping through his impressive veins, Spike was so far beyond caring he could probably see it coming back around in front of him again.

Liam, however, had pointed questions, and he knew just who to point them at.

40

"Did I do something wrong?" demanded Liam, barging into the Editor's office with as much anger as he could muster.

The bastard never even bothered to look away from his desk display. "Argyle, just the chap, do take a seat. I'll be with you in a moment."

Liam resolved to make a point and remain standing, but his heart wasn't really in it anymore. Anyway, he couldn't even tell whether the Editor was aware of his small act of defiance and just pretending to ignore it, or if he was really so engrossed in whatever interface he was in that he really had no idea. Liam's resolve soon melted in the face of social awkwardness, and he decided to cut his losses and sit down as he'd been asked.

Coincidence or not, the Editor immediately surfaced out of whatever augmented system he had been obsessed with, and smile at Liam. "There we go, sorry for all of that. Now, you were saying?"

Liam tried to recover some of his anger, but suspected the best he could manage now was to blush, or perhaps look like he had a bad attack of wind. He ploughed on regardless. "I was asking whether I had done something wrong, not interrupting the Bighorn feed when he had his muscle spasm attack. That was your order to send in the medical team, right?"

Liam had been prepared for a shouting match, for accusations, for lies. The Editor's easy-going laughter disarmed him completely. "Liam, dear boy, you performed exactly as expected, and as needed. Have no fear. Have you seen last week's ratings? As far as I am concerned, you can do no wrong."

He smiled again, before adding, almost as an afterthought, "Of course, you are correct, as well. I called in the local office's medical response team to do a bit of damage control, but that was through no fault of yours. This called for something a bit subtler than the big red feed interruption button."

Ed the Editor waved his fingers in a passing imitation of Sir Alec Guinness's classic bout of Force-enhanced civil disobedience, and a medical display popped into Liam's AR display. Pulsing in real-time, it showed what Liam just about recognised as a spinal column and back muscles, lit up like a corporate Holiday Tree which wouldn't dream about excluding a single cash-bearing consumer over something as petty as religion. Reading the legend, Liam noted that the seething red blotches covering the display were sites of bacterial infection.

"Liam Argyle, this is Clostridium tetani. Clostridium, this is Liam Argyle." The Editor couldn't help but laugh at his own little joke. "I can't blame you if you don't recognise it, Liam. The poor thing has seen better days. You can't get within two meters of a rusty nail anymore without your safety interface blaring at you, and monitor nanos will detect and treat any Tetanus infection long before it actually has an effect."

The Editor went very serious and fixed Liam with a concrete gaze.

"Do you know where the name 'Clostridium' comes from, Argyle? Let me tell you. It comes directly from the ancient Greek term for the threads of fate, the spindle from which all of our lives are woven." He paused, presumably to let his big flourish sink in.

As he waited for the Editor to continue and get to the point, if there were one, Liam realised he really needed to go to the bathroom.

"That is what we are looking at here, Liam, and sadly, Clostridium has lived up to its name and sealed poor Spike Bighorn's fate, at least as far as the feed is concerned."

Liam perked up at this. More manipulation of the feed. At least he was on familiar ground again. "Spike? But he's so popular," he said, surprised at how tired his own voice sounded. "Anyway, I thought Juliette Binns was up for elimination this week."

"A mere reprieve, certainly," replied the Editor. "Intelligence is adaptation to changing circumstances, Argyle, and in this matter, our course is clear. A Tetanus infection like this one will take weeks, maybe months, to clear up, and we can't let the feeders realise Mr. Bighorn could only have gotten such a bad case from a poorly maintained Erobot phallus."

The Editor sighed and made another wave through the air, almost reluctantly. A shiny, animated, and surprisingly-graphic advert for what could only be an Erobot appeared beside the live medical display. Liam was surprised, then slightly embarrassed, at recognising the Erobot in question from some of Spike's pornos. It was an exact replica.

"This is classified material, Argyle, and you weren't to know, but a Red-Corp subsidiary owns these little beauties and has a major public launch campaign planned for next quarter. Now that Erobots are accepted as the norm in pornography, it is time to take it to the next level and give the discerning consumer the chance to make the most of that yearly bonus and purchase his or her own perfect copy of a favourite porn star, fresh and ready for use, straight out of the box. Plug and play, if you will.

"Of course, we cannot have rumours—however true they may be—spreading about catching Tetanus or a whole slew of new and exotic STDs from a penetrating robo-cock, now can we?"

Liam sat in silence, before realising that the Editor actually seemed to be waiting for an answer.

"Err—I should think not," he eventually stammered.

"Good man, I knew you would understand," said the Editor with a nod. "So I'll be counting on you to downplay the whole Juliette Binns 'thing' during the weekly show and highlight instead how Spike Bighorn has been living it up all week in privileged Corporate comfort. Almost as if he had already won his ticket to Paradise Mars!"

Liam wasn't certain, but was that a bit of froth he had seen at the corner of the Editor's mouth there, for a second? The man was quick to wipe his mouth with his fingers, disguising it as a pensive pose, before carrying on.

"Yes, we will make certain that you have plenty of material to use. Just a simple pulled muscle and general tiredness, and Mr. Spike Bighorn thinks he can lord it over everyone else. We'll have the public hating him in no time. They're all rather jealous of him in the first place, anyway, for some bizarre reason."

"I blame the parents, myself, sir," Liam replied. He felt like he needed to contribute something, and that usually worked in his experience with people who sounded like they had gone mad.

"Indeed," said Ed the Editor, eyeing Liam like an organ grinder who has just been handed a tax return by his monkey. "Well, see to it then, Argyle, and keep the Binns situation under control as well, will you? Increase the shock power a bit further, if you have to. Ms. Lee tells me that has been working well for her."

41

Over three billion viewers. A three with nine zeroes behind it. How could a single one of them be fooled by the skin-thin façade of happiness coated over the faces of his tortured and disturbed contestants, as they sat lined up in front of the Augmented global firing squad for yet another weekly feature? If all three billion viewers were fooled by this, they might as well all be zeroes.

At least Usnavi had made it out of his sickbed and over to the studio for the weekly feature. The Editor had told them all how vital it was—by contrast, it put the final nail in the virtual coffin of Spike Bighorn. There was poor Usnavi, everyone's little brother, soldiering on, while Mr. Bigshot Spike was, in all appearances and official soundbites, too tired out from screwing for a living and too whacked-out on designer drugs in a RedCorp medical haven to even bother showing up.

It was almost as if he thought he had already won the whole show or something. As if he were already living the corporate dream in the effortless bliss and chemical comforts that Paradise Mars held for the elite of the elite. And, of course, for the one least fortunate soul in all the rest of the world, courtesy of *The Grass is Greener*.

That was the Editor's favourite spin on Spike's colorectal misfortune, and Liam had to admit it seemed to be working. Envy and jealousy were powerful motivators.

Sitting next to ailing Usnavi, Juliette Binns somehow looked the worst off of the lot. Her eyes were Sarlacc pits, and her haunted gaze seemed to follow you around the room, like some cheesy Halloween rip-off of the Mona Lisa. Liam had to keep repeating to himself that it was all necessary, and for her own good really. She had agreed to let the show do whatever was necessary to protect itself when signing on to the show, after all, and it was only temporary—she would be eliminated soon enough. Liam was grateful she was at least keeping up appearances and chattering on, more so than usual, if anything. Her anxiety was obvious, however, and Liam winced a little every time she jumped in her seat, at the slightest noise or provocation.

Further down the line, Brad sat at smug attention, lord of all he surveyed—at least in his own mind. Jill lounged in her seat, which was impressive in itself, since these clinical, corporate chairs were designed specifically to be as uncomfortable and relaxation-proof as possible. The faint smile on her lips seemed to tell the world that she knew what was really going on here, and Liam wondered how much of that was still true, at this point, and how much was just posturing.

Sandwiched between the two of them, Azar Acquah managed to offer a brave face to the viewers, but she looked nearly as worse for wear as Juliette. She had recovered well after her day off, along with a few days of cheap and moderately effective antibiotics prescribed by the walk-in clinic on the off-chance her inflection wasn't entirely resistant. Luckily, she had won that particular evolutionary lottery and had been back at work the very next day, prodding away at the appliances, furnishings, and closet contents of the rich in order to make them "dumber" than their costs and aesthetics already made them.

Liam was worried about her, though. He had been monitoring her, on his own time over the past couple of days, and she had none of the energy she used to put into her work, her bearing, her life as a whole. In everyone's eyes, and in the show's endless marketing and spin-off commentary feeds, she was still the embodiment of bravery and positivity in adversity, especially since the previous week's "Good Samaritan" incident. But up close, Liam just didn't feel it anymore, or at least not as strongly. Her general happiness with her lot in life, which had always been so infectious, now felt faded, distant—like the signals from a deep space probe, speaking slower and slower until it loses the sun's energy altogether.

Liam was vaguely aware of going through the motions of his prepared speech regarding the unfortunate elimination of everyone's favourite porn star, and how sad it was that he couldn't make it to be with them all in person. Mostly, however, he couldn't stop looking over to the contestants.

The expected reactions played over their faces like notes from a well-tuned piano—neither Juliette's poorly-concealed horror at not having been eliminated this week nor Jill's blatant contempt for the whole process were any kind of surprise, and that wasn't what kept snagging Liam's attention.

No, it was the physical image of the five people before him that kept him glancing back again and again, almost as if he needed to keep checking that he had seen it right the previous time. Just five of them, lined up in front of the world. Was this really all that was left? Five lives, supposedly the worst the world had to offer. Five contestants remaining, and what had he done for them, for any of them, since the beginning of the show?

The show came to a close, and the voiceless crowd from around the world cheered Liam on, the roar deafening inside his brainpan. Liam was grateful Mary hadn't found the bottle of Sipsmith V.J.O.P. gin he had stashed behind the bathroom garbage bin—or, if she had, had left it there out of pity for Liam. Neat gin was basically just a martini without the fancy glass, right? *Right,* he reassured himself, as he took another swig from the already half-empty bottle.

42

"Good news, Liam," petite Norma Lee somehow managed to boom into his ear, waking him up from the little eye-rest he was having in front of his display at some ungodly hour the next morning.

She had the good tact to pretend not to notice, and carried on. "Looks like we won't need to keep increasing the shock power on poor Juliette Binns. Not that I minded it all that much, truth be told, but it's probably a good thing. I don't think I could have increased the settings that much more without risking some sort of visible damage."

Liam tried to shake the alcohol out of his thought processes, and just about managed to keep up with what his nominal co-worker was saying.

"I asked the Ed if we were going to need to bring Binns in for an 'upgrade' on her implant power cells, and he told me to stop the contractual discipline measures altogether." She let out a dramatic and entirely fake sigh. "All of a sudden, keeping her within the show's rules just isn't important anymore. I don't know. Makes me wonder why the hell I've been putting in so many overtime hours over the past week that the calluses on my shock-button finger have started growing their own calluses."

Liam's sodden brain was too busy considering what the hell "hungover"[70] was supposed to mean, anyway—hung over what, exactly?—to apply basic self-preservation filters, and, in a rare moment of honesty, Liam spoke the first thought that came to mind. "That's horrible."

Norma's self-preservation filters, on the contrary, were fully armed and operational, and she shrugged, dismissing the whole question as she stomped back out of Liam's personal space. "Eh, it's nothing a good mani-cure session won't sort out. Nice of you to say, though. I just wanted to let you know because I saw you're on duty with Juliette this afternoon. Toodles!"

Liam's rational mind knew his door was just a bit of cheap particle board—a.k.a. "engineered solids" because it sounds more expensive—but his senses told his rational mind to take a leap off any convenient salient point as the door slammed shut with portcullis force behind Norma Lee.

Understandably, Liam didn't feel quite up to another etymological punching bag session with the Editor, so he decided to employ the tried-and-true better part of professional valour, also known as email.

From: Argyle, Liam
[mailto: agent44269@entertainment.redmail.com]
Sent: 18-04-72 9:43 AM
To: agent2766@entertainment.redmail.com
Subject: J Binns measures
Hi Ed,
Norma has just been in to tell me we're ending the behaviour measures regarding Juliette Binns? Is this correct? What happened?
Best regards,
Liam

Liam was keen to keep things on a friendly tone, using the Editor's proper name to show how at ease he was with the whole thing. However, a savvier swimmer of bureaucratic waters would have known that putting anything in an email, with a written trace, can and often is interpreted as an attempt to build a case of some sort: a declaration of war.

From: agent2766@entertainment.redmail.com
Sent: 18-04-72 9:51 AM
To: Argyle, Liam
[mailto: agent44269@entertainment.redmail.com]

---

70 "A thing left over from before," first recorded usage in 1894. It only took eight years for it to become almost exclusively reserved for, well, hangovers.

Subject: Your enquiry

Dear Agent 44269,

There seems to be some confusion, as I have no idea what you are referring to. In my editorial capacity for 'The Grass is Greener,' I may not be privy to all choices made by the production team and yourself in the management of each individual contestant, which I am of course not involved with directly. I trust that you will inform me of any actions your team and yourself may have taken if these have any bearing on my editorial work.

Regarding Ms. Binns, I have received reports today, coming from various entertainment news feeds and 'fan' sites, that she seems to be unsatisfied with the privacy intrusions inherent in her participation in the show. In the absence of any possibility of withdrawing from the show, she seems to have used her professional skills to obtain raw internal footage of alleged instances of behavioural conditioning through electrical shocks, which she then sent on for public broadcast.

Are these the measures you are referring to? If so, you were perhaps in your legal rights with regards to Ms. Binns' contract to enforce her obligations toward the show. However, the moral side of things must also be carefully weighed in such situations. Of course, I know nothing of these matters, and it may all merely be hearsay.

In any case, I must insist, for the good of the show and its image, that any such measures, should they have ever existed, cease immediately. It is, perhaps, best to let the public judge the merits or flaws of any grievances Ms. Binns may have. That is, after all, the whole purpose of 'The Grass is Greener,' is it not?

Please do not hesitate to share any relevant information with me, I am more than happy to provide any assistance I can in this matter.

Kind regards,

Agent 2766

The Editor's response, put together with astounding speed, dinged as it arrived and hung in Augmented glory before Liam's eyes long after he had finished reading it. He sat stunned, as the lives he was supposed to be monitoring flitted by, uncontrolled, in his Augmented sight. It wasn't so much the stab in the back from the Editor—he had never trusted the little man half as far as he knew he could throw him, and often wished he could. His shock was more profound, like that of a man who hears the creak of thin ice beneath his feet, but who didn't even know he was on ice in the first place. Let alone what toothsome monsters lay waiting in the depths. His position was suddenly threatened, and up until then, he had had no idea it could be threatened.

He was still sitting stunned when the Editor opened his door, with the well-fed air he always had after a lunch time spent schmoozing up other corporate bigwigs in some Michelin-starred crab bucket downtown. God knows it wasn't what passed for food in those places that could satisfy a man; it must be something in the air, letting them feed off the social status which fell like marine snow, in a constant flow of filth.

Luckily, it was very hard to tell the difference between a Liam hard at work monitoring AR feeds and a Liam merely sitting in his chair, gazing off into nothingness and realising how tenuous his position in life truly was. Since the Editor clearly cared very little either way, he carried on regardless.

"Argyle, hard at work as ever, I see," he said, in the same tones one might use to comment upon how wet the rain is today, or how dismally the local sports team of choice was performing. "I just wanted to make certain there were no hard feelings about those messages earlier. I have to respect a man who tries to stand up for himself, but there have to be boundaries, you know."

The Editor was grinning at him, one toady to another from across the corporate lily pond, and yet all Liam could see was the fresh gravy stain on the man's lapel, still moist and shimmering as it soaked into the ostensibly expensive nano-engineered threads.

"Well, that's all behind us now, anyway," said the Editor, a bit unsettled at the lack of any response for him to edit into his own narrative. "There's no harm done, in any case. It's not like your team did anything wrong, of course. We just couldn't keep up the pretence, not after Binns managed to smuggle those raw videos out."

The Editor chuckled, startling Liam out of his stupor and making him chuckle as well, out of sheer nervousness. The Editor needed no further encouragement to label Liam as "one of us" and speak to him accordingly.

"And why would we bother with sanctions, when the public will do the work for us? Have you seen the latest feed from Entertainment Hourly?"

Liam tested out a noncommittal smile, which seemed to work well enough. "As you say, Ed, I've been hard at work."

"Oh, you have to see this, it's absolutely delicious." At a flick of the editor's fingers, the feed popped into Liam's Augmented view. The worrying, predatory look on the Editor's face was hidden behind a free-floating window showing the public's reaction to the Binns video leaks, with running commentary. Literal running commentary, that is, with an almost supernaturally fit entertainment "news" person of indeterminate gender sprinting through a crowded subway station with a giant Augmented sign over their head inviting one and all to share their opinions with the world regarding

The Grass is Greener. Just a sentence or two, before the reporter bolted off
to the next "person in the street" who flagged in their AR display that they
wanted their fifteen seconds of fame as well. There were many takers, and
there were no half-measures in their opinions—the show didn't give them
time to have any opinion more complex than black or white, anyway.

"What is Juliette complaining about, anyway? Privacy? Who can afford
privacy these days, anyway?" asked a salaryman in a run-down business
suit.

The camera-person bobbed away and ran over to the next opinion-
monger, a girl who didn't look old enough to vote, with a baby strapped to
her chest and a hazy look in her eyes.

"It's bad, of course, that she's suffering so much from being in the show.
But it's also, I don't know, a bit fun to watch. You know what I mean?"

This feed wasn't the sort that sat around answering rhetorical questions, and so zipped off to a group of stooped women, sitting around a tiny
café-style table, in full-body burqas. They laughed as the feed arrived, egg-
ing one another on to speak.

"You get what you ask for sometimes, you know," chittered the voice
under the snazzy violet-coloured number on the left. "She should not have
joined the show if she did not want to be there."

"It is very entertaining though. She has the most inventive ways of
showing how much she hates being on the show," added one of her friends,
from under a more drab, grey-brown coloured veil.

"Don't be so mean!" said one of their friends, her laughter turning the
reprimand into a joke. "It's not her fault! She needs something to make
herself look worse off than the others, after all! She was nearly eliminated
last week!"

The show's view left this cluster behind it, their laughter fading away as
it moved on in search of fresh victims. The Editor clearly felt that his point
had been made, since he shut the window in Liam's display with another
half-flick of his hand. Sure enough, the look on the man's face was still the
kind that would send a shark rushing back to its resting place, having just
remembered it left the cuttlefish boiling.

"Impressive," said Liam, using another of his noncommittal favourites,
which seemed to always be interpreted to mean whatever the other person
wanted to hear. He had yet to be proven wrong a single time.

"Isn't it just?" replied the Editor, confirming Liam's theory. "It couldn't
have been better if we had actually had the budget to hire actors again."

Liam wondered at the use of the term "again," but decided to keep his
mouth shut.

"Far from being negative for the show, the Binns leaks have turned into a decent publicity stunt! Amateurish, of course, but free publicity is free publicity. It might even carry us through to the season finale, without any of the traditional middle-of-the-season sag in the ratings."

"Even when Juliette—Binns, that is—is eliminated from the show?" Liam asked, before he could stop himself.

The Editor nailed Liam with a shrewd[71] look, along with an ostensibly pensive "hmmm" before answering him.

"Yes, you've hit the only potential issue, of course. With new popularity levels like this, we may have to review our elimination schedule. We simply can't give up an opportunity like this. We'll just have to keep our Ms. Binns around a little bit longer and find some reason to cut someone else this week. Azar Acquah, I suppose."

The Editor walked over to Liam's chair and clapped him on the back. The touch made Liam's skin crawl like one of those 3D-printed insectoid machines. He still managed to smile and nod, somehow.

"Oh, one other thing," added the Editor, as he made his way out of the glorified closet which served as Liam's office. "My friend at Corporate said they'd be sending some sort of personnel memo out today to all unit coordinators, which includes yourself for the team here, of course. I'm sure you can handle it, along with finding some dirt to use on Acquah, right? Great," he replied to himself, careful not to leave Liam any time to sort out the jumble of questions competing for attention in his cortex. "I'll get out of your hair and leave you to it then. Can't wait to hear what you've come up with at the editorial meeting tomorrow morning!"

The door shut, and Liam turned back to his interface. He toyed with the feed list, opened windows, then closed them all again. He closed his eyes, but still the AR interface from his fancy new lenses floated against the back of his eyelids.

It was funny, surfaced the thought. He had already grown so used to them that he had forgotten how strange it was to never be able to disconnect, not even with your eyes shut.

All such thoughts were soon chased away, however, by the flood of conflicting emotions and general bewilderment which broke through his poor attempts at ignoring them.

What the hell had just happened?

71 "Evil, malignant."

43

A large part of the answer came some thirty minutes later, just before the statutory mid-afternoon caffeine water and bathroom break, in the form of a pointed and disembodied "ding" from Liam's inbox.

He welcomed the excuse to stop digging through Azar Acquah's personality file and live feed analytics, looking for something he could say at the meeting the following morning to avoid looking like a total idiot. But there was nothing there. Other than her health issues, Azar was a model contestant; she loved the show, and loved the Corporation even more for giving her the opportunity to take part in it. And yet, he had to find some excuse for kicking her off the show and make it seem as if it were the viewers' decision.

Surely, any email that could give him a valid excuse to take his mind off Azar, and what they were about to do to her, was a good thing, he reasoned. He then read the email and realised the limits of such self-serving logic, which has nothing to do with reason.

From: noreply@corp.redmail.com
Sent: 18-04-72 2:47 PM
To: Unit Coordinator List
Subject: Budget Drive
Dear Unit Coordinator,
Please be advised that, in application of quarterly budget drive objectives, your unit's allocated downsize quota is:

1.1 FULL-TIME EQUIVALENTS
Report of reduction quotas being met must be received by:

25TH APRIL
Coordinators are reminded that, as per statutory contract conditions, failure to meet all or part of personnel reduction quotas will be compensated automatically, first onto the coordinator's position and, if necessary, across the rest of the unit.
Regards,
Corporate

Liam's mind reeled like an old celluloid war movie. They hadn't even bothered to pretend it was anything other than an automatically generated email, with the deadly little digits piped in directly from some algorithm's table.

They wanted him to downsize, or get fired himself, as the message made certain to remind him at the end. How the hell did you fire four-tenths of a person, anyway? The message neglected to specify how much each member or organ could be counted as. Maybe they had another table for that sort of thing? It sounded like the sort of thing the Editor would save in his browser window's favourites.

Liam shook himself, then grumbled in silence at the roughness of the shaking. There was no need to panic, he tried to convince himself. It was like this at the end of every budgetary year;[72] he had been through all of this many times before. Of course, that had been on the receiving end, the non-consenting victim side of things. He had never thought he would one day be on the side of the heartless bastards he used to mock and curse, a ritual he joined in along with everyone else.

Still—he could be a bastard, too, if he had to, he supposed. The important thing was that this was expected, normal. It would have happened regardless, whether he was unit coordinator or not, so it didn't really have anything to do with him, when you thought about. It wasn't actually him firing anybody, and he was in it just as much as Lee and Carpentiere. Even more so, since he was the designated goat for this particular sacrifice, unless they could agree something.

Surely the others would understand how much his genitals were in a vice grip on this one, and would help him find a solution. He'd just call them into a meeting, and they'd sort it out amongst themselves, like responsible adults. Yeah. There was nothing to worry about; he would have this all sorted out in no time.

After a nice still drink or two, he added, grabbing his coat. If they wanted him to take the responsibility for something like this, they would just have to accept him knocking off for once at three p.m.

Whoever "they" are, added a small voice, but Liam was already on the way to his car, on the way to hearth and cup, and was beyond caring.

---

72 The budgetary year is unequalled by any other measure of time ever established by humankind, in that it is not concerned so much with the passing moments of one's life as with passing movements in and out of one's wallet.

44

Was he right to feel guilty about Acquah? The show had done pretty damn well by her, when you got right down to it. Through the GiG, they had taken a penniless, tumour-addled recluse and turned her into, well... into a household name, for one thing. Even if the rest hadn't really changed for her, that still had to count for something, right? That was one change for the better, at least. Liam kept telling himself that as he finished editing the footage from Acquah's feed this week, to showcase just how fast her health was falling to pieces and justify her elimination on a sympathy basis.

The Editor had loved the idea, and now he had two hours left to get the sequences finished if they wanted to get them out in time for the big entertainment commentary feeds to do their job and spin his sorry excuse into a credible reason for Azar Acquah's elimination from the show on Sunday.

Was Acquah really that hard done-by, then? What about them: Liam, Lee, Carpentiere, and even poor Mary? They were the ones who had to take a massive pay cut, across the board, just to avoid anyone being fired and to keep the show running. It was him, Liam, who had had to spend all week listening to Carpentiere moan about his daughter's medical bills, let alone Lee going on and on about her other career prospects and threatening to leave the show if she had any share in the pay cuts.

He had convinced them, in the end, that the pay cut would be only temporary, that they could fight to get it re-established next year. He certainly hoped so, in any case. Even under threat of random sacking, Lee and Carpentiere only accepted the cuts after he agreed to take a thirty-five percent loss himself, versus only twenty-five percent for the other three. Still, traditional game theory had prevailed, and both of them had accepted to lose the twenty-five percent rather than risk a random chance of being fired altogether. Out of principle, Liam had made a point of including Mary in the discussions as well, even though she really didn't have any say in the matter as an outsourced Agency worker. They'd just replace her overnight if there were any problem — and anyway, it wasn't as if she were in danger of being fired. The show physically could not carry on without an Agency worker to do all the menial work.

Just in case Corporate decided to pull the same stunt next year, maybe he should look at getting an intern or something in, someone who could take the fall next time around.

Christ, was that how Corporate management thought? All the time?

For once, the regularly scheduled Sunday torture session came as a welcome distraction.

45

Seconds after Liam had made the announcement, Mary had already scuttled off with Azar's vacant seat, unnoticed by any of the billions of the Sunday elimination show viewers. The thought of the ever-shrinking row of contestant chairs depressed Liam so much that he pushed it back into his mind's vestigial secondary hard drive, focusing instead on the worn-down woman he was holding around the shoulders. It was a good thing he was focusing on her, too—she felt so light beneath his arm, he could have knocked her off the set with one involuntary twitch.[73]

Up until now, what with a busy week of fame and business opportunities to look forward to, the eliminated contestants had all taken it well, or at least with good grace—other than Spike Bighorn, obviously, who had only found out about it when brought out of his designer medical coma three days after his elimination. But even in the usual, stress-blackened state of consciousness that he relied on to get him through the weekly feature shows, he couldn't avoid noticing just how miserable Azar looked. It was so at odds with her usual steadfast happiness, even in the face of adversity.

Liam couldn't very well comment upon it to her, not at the key moment in show, with every single viewer watching their every move. Instead, he gave her an extra little squeeze to make sure he had her attention, then hit her with the full force of his fakest, most over-the-top show business grin. She got the message, and put up enough of an excuse for a smile for him to be able to carry on with the show.

"Now, Azar, I'm sure I speak for all of us here at *The Grass is Greener*, as well as all the viewers out there around the world, when I say how much we've enjoyed having you here on the show with us. Can I get a big round of applause for Azar Acquah, everybody?"

Liam paused, smiling and nodding, as if thanking the non-existent studio audience for their equally absent applause. And yet, he knew there was always that one person, in any given group, who would clap like a trained

---

73 "To pull apart with a quick jerk," *i.e.*, most Twitch streamers.

seal at the slightest hint from a show host. Raised to the scale of his world-spanning viewership, Liam was confident he had just caused enough clapping to counter-act at least two faerie-realm genocidal wars—perhaps three. He played it "by the tutorial," as the kids say, leaving the standard five seconds before resuming.

"Thank you, thank you. Everyone wishes you all the best, Azar, and with the stresses of the show gone, I'm sure you'll be feeling better and back to your old self in no time. I guess that just leaves one question everyone will want to know the answer to: what comes next for Azar Acquah?"

She cringed a little at his question, almost as if she wished he hadn't asked her to speak. Liam first thought she was having some sort of panic attack and only recognised her silence for what it was, the struggle to hold back something you've been trying not to say, at the same time as she lost that struggle and blurted out what she had been trying not to say.

"What about the lenses, Liam—Mr. Argyle, sorry?" Even under the liberal smear of orange goop on her cheeks, the beginnings of a blush were poking through, and her voice was a touch lower than usual. "Do you really have to turn them off, like you did to the others?" She latched onto Liam's shoulder like a mussel to a sea scum-covered rock.

He had never really thought about it before. Did they really have to decommission the lens implants when a contestant was eliminated? He didn't really see it as a big deal himself; lenses were cheaper than clean water these days—but he could see how someone like Azar could want to hang onto high-end lenses like these, since she couldn't afford the cost of a daydream about buying a set on her normal income. They had taken her old lenses out at the start of the show, and given her medical history, he could see how she could be touchy on the subject. He put on his most compassionate face to calm her down.

"Azar, I understand why you're upset, but there's no need to worry. Everything's going to be fine."

Azar carried on, clearly not listening to him—Liam hoped the viewers couldn't see that as well, it certainly wouldn't do his ratings any good.

"It's just that I wasn't expecting to be eliminated tonight. Not with being sick, you know. Why eliminate me and not Juliette, who isn't half as bad off and is begging for it?"

"Now, now, Azar," cut in Liam, speaking over the end of her sentence in an attempt to drown it out, "let's not go second guessing why the votes went the way they did, shall we? The people have spoken, after all." Liam chuckled, out of sheer nerves; but luckily, Azar didn't seem aware of having muttered a dangerous truth, and carried on speaking mostly to herself, as she tried to hold back tears of desperation.

"I don't understand. It can't be me tonight. I didn't bring any new lenses. I don't have any to bring. I—" she said, before stopping with a choke, as if the words were clogging her throat in their rush to escape from her inner turmoil. "I need the lenses, Liam. I've always had them. I can't just not have any. I'd rather go blind before going around without my lenses. Much rather go blind, in fact; you could just get one of those cameras fitted, the ones they wire directly into your optic nerves."

Liam smiled and nodded, terrified at this train wreck of a departure from the usual post-elimination preening he expected from the candidates. Behind him, he could sense Brad and Jill stirring in impatience at how long Azar was taking; Usnavi was too good-natured to comment, and Juliette was too vacant-stared to notice. At some point some, someone would probably start making faces at the virtual crowd, mocking her. Liam was slightly ashamed at himself as he realised that he really wished they would, if only to distract and entertain the viewers a bit while he sorted this mess out.

Azar, in the meantime, seemed emboldened by her own profession of faith in the advancement of technology. She mustered enough courage to try to barter with Liam.

"I don't suppose that, under the circumstances, they could just leave the implants on for me? Just this once? Of course, you can cut the live feed now that I'm out of the show, I don't need that, but can't you just leave the lenses online? At least for a bit?" Her tone was more full of wheedles than a starter Pokémon player's line-up.

Before she had even finished the first sentence, Barry's voice barged into his consciousness, in all its high-fidelity, bone-conducted glory. Liam felt like he should have resented Barry's voice barging in on him without warning, or giving him the chance to accept or refuse the call, but that was only a tattered remnant of his principles talking—and not very loud, at that.

"That's a great big negatory from a technical point of view, my friend," Barry's voice grated inside Liam's skull. "These new implants are designed exclusively to support our live feed. We can't leave them on after the broadcast has been shut down, and we certainly can't leave the broadcast on. We don't have the budget to give her anything else, and her old ones are in the biohazard landfill where they belong. You'll have to find some other solution here."

Liam blinked to show he understood, then turned to Azar, without missing a beat at the end of her final question.

"You know what, Azar?" he said, fake grin spreading from ear to unbecoming ear. "You've been such a good sport since the beginning of the show, I think we can do even better than that. Unfortunately, it's not technically possible to leave the show's lenses on, and we will need them back, but I will personally take you to buy a set of top-of-the-line, perfectly safe lenses as soon as we're done with the show. What do you say?"

A look of indecision was still plastered across Azar's face, but Liam basked in the worldwide cheer he imagined at his magnanimous announcement. It felt good. After all, he'd signed up for this to help people, hadn't he? It seemed like a lifetime ago, and a lot had happened in a few weeks, but that was still his purpose, right? To help make the world a better place, however small the gesture?

"I guess so," said Azar, making Liam jump back to focus. A brief rush of terror pulsed through his veins at the idea that Azar might have heard and answered his private questioning. "Yes, that would be lovely, Liam. Thank you!"

Azar gave him a nominal hug around the waist—he had been squeezed harder by rutting poodles. He checked to make sure his grin wasn't slipping, then returned Azar's hug with exaggerated care, before disengaging and leading her over to the lens retrieval booth so he could wrap up the show. Liam counted his blessings; after all of that, Azar was mostly unresisting.

46

Liam somehow managed to drag the words "See you next week" out into the full ten-minute outro sequence required by the advertisers, then spent half an hour being cleared of the hated orange nano-goop under Mary's tender care. He was finally feeling human again as he emerged and started hunting down Azar. He soon found her staring, rapt, at the clear plastic of the caffeine water dispenser as it bubbled and kept its contents fresh. She shifted out of her aquatic reverie as he approached and broke the silence.

"It's strange, Liam. Without lenses, without menus and advertisements overlaid over everything, you notice things that you would never have noticed otherwise. Simple things, but beautiful in their own way."

A look of fear crossed her face, and Liam felt a pang of sympathy.

"Don't get me wrong," she rushed to add, with a slight stammer. "I need those new lenses like anything. I can't tell you how grateful I am for your help, Liam."

He felt a bit uneasy at how comfortable she seemed to be with using his first name now, and not "Mr. Argyle," but decided not to hold it against her.

"Don't you worry, Azar. We'll have you sorted out in no time. Shall we?"

Feeling like a knight errant, he guided Azar out of the glorified warehouse doors of the Mews and tried not to gag as they were assailed by the unfiltered airborne stew of pollutants and human effluvia which passed for "air" as soon as you left the climate-controlled security of a proper building. His nose shivered visibly as it prepared for the onslaught, and they both soldiered on into the night.

In a society where everything you could want—and a large amount that you probably didn't—was available for delivery at the inadvertent flick of an eye, it came as a revelation to Liam that going to physically buy something could involve inconvenience, and even effort. Lenses needed to be tailored to the individual eye, as measured when ordered. It was a quick and easy process, but one which presented a problem when you didn't have an established vendor to order lenses online from, because you didn't have lenses in the first place and needed to buy some.

Hence, the single type of physical shop that had flourished in the largely virtual economy of the 2070s was the corner lens repair shop, where underpaid and possibly illegal workers would fire up the biometric booth and get you back into the Augmented world faster than it took you to browse through their selection of impulse-buy sugar-enriched snack foods and drinks.

That was the theory, of course, but after ten minutes of wandering out randomly, Azar trailing behind him like a very confused duckling as they both waited for his map app to locate a shop for them, he had to conclude there was no market for lens shops in the middle of corporate warehouses and parking lots. They would have to move further downtown, which, to Liam's great reluctance, meant he would have to give her a ride in his new car.

Liam was surprised at how strongly his instincts rebelled at the idea. Why did it matter if he gave her a ride? Wasn't he putting the time and effort in to help her, anyway? What difference did it make?

Both Azar and he were silent as they marched through the frigid night air toward the nearest parking lot and his waiting car. It was only as he signalled for the door to open, and watched as Azar slid into the seating compartment first, as gallantry commanded, that he figured it out. His car was his private space, a luxury provided to him by his newfound corporate status, and to some degree an extension of his self. Letting Azar into it meant a fundamental change in their relationship, one that he wasn't sure he wanted. After monitoring and managing—even in internal monologue, he stopped just short of saying "manipulating"—their lives for months now, he didn't know if he was ready to deal with any of his contestants other than as a host. With Azar eliminated, and now sitting there in his car across from him, they were just two people, almost equals.

Liam told the car to find the nearest lens shop for them, and it set off on its own merry way. Since Liam was still brooding, Azar was forced to make conversation.

"I wasn't expecting it to feel so odd, being dropped from the show and not having so many strangers staring out of my own eyes anymore. It feels... liberating, in a way, I suppose. I've often thought that all of these lenses and cameras everywhere forces everyone to be... I don't know. Well behaved? A bit false, maybe? Politically correct, that's what I mean, I guess." She chuckled at herself a little, clearly nervous in a situation as unnatural for her as it was for Liam. "I'm not boring you, am I, Liam? You need to tell me if I am. I have no way of knowing otherwise."

Liam forced himself to deliver a half-hearted "No, of course not. I've often wondered the same myself. Please, carry on." Apparently, half a heart was enough to keep the conservational haemoglobin flowing, as Azar launched into the rest of her musings and left Liam, much to his relief, to his own.

"Well, I suppose it all comes from how anyone you come across nowadays could be recording or even broadcasting your every move. And even more importantly, anyone could be watching—including people you know, and who know you. Work people, friends, family, whatever. You never know who could be watching at any time, so you have to always be on best behaviour, sort of by default. In public at least, that is.

"That should be a good thing, I suppose, but I don't know if it's possible to always be on best behaviour. Maybe that's why everyone is expected to be so miserable and selfish in private. Just to balance things out, that sort of thing."

Liam caught his brooding thoughts and focused on Azar for the first time since they'd entered the car. Was she having a go at him, with her reference to selfishness? No, he decided, she was legitimately pouring her thoughts out to him. With embarrassment creeping up his cheeks like a colony of red slime mould cells migrating to a richer food source, he spouted out the first reply which came to mind, just to show he was listening.

"You may be right, you know. That would explain a lot. With individualism repressed and pushed out of the public sphere, you would get all sorts of twisted versions of it in private. Unhealthy perversions of natural individual instincts."

Liam stopped as he realised that Azar was looking at him with tears in her eyes. Not the intended effect.

Without thinking, he reached across the cabin and put a reassuring hand on Azar's brittle-feeling arm, which again seemed to backfire, as his guest burst into full, gasping sobs. She had never done anything like this over her whole period on the show. Not once. Liam would have known.

"I'm sorry," she managed to say between splutters, eventually. "It's so silly of me."

"No, it isn't," replied Liam, mostly because he felt that was what you were supposed to say in this sort of situation. "It's good. It's natural to cry. Let it all out, then tell me all about it as soon as you're ready."

She sobbed a little more at this, before pulling herself together with a series of controlled breaths. She looked so frail. Liam wouldn't have thought she had that much water in her whole body.

She mopped at her eyes with a corner of her coat, making Liam feel ashamed again, this time at not having tissues at hand in his car for unplanned guests who might spontaneously burst into crying.

"I'm sorry, " she said again, as if it were some sort of punctuation mark you had to use at the start of every sentence. "It's just that... I don't know. All that talk about lenses and repressed individuality..." She looked at him, looking for something in his eyes which she clearly didn't find. "I've always had a bit of a blind faith in technology as a force for good, you know? Especially lenses, bringing new worlds to everyone, and bringing people together. I didn't have much of a choice in the matter, I suppose. Growing up with lenses since before I could remember." She chuckled at this, though Liam was hard-pressed to see anything funny in the situation. "Maybe it's just something I picked up at an early age from my parents, as they tried to justify leaving their infant daughter in the care of what essentially amounted to one of the old TV screens stuck onto her eyes."

Liam shifted in his seat. He wasn't used to this role, the silent confidant. But he figured he could shut up and listen with the best of them.

"So it comes as a bit of a shock to have to face the conclusion I've been hiding from for so long. Forget about the physical health concerns. The important cancer isn't the one in Azar Acquah's brain. The real cancer caused by our brave new Augmented world is everywhere, in everyone's brain. It's a corruption, twisting everything good and wholesome about people just being people into greed, consumerism, lies. Selfishness, and the belief that selfishness is all there is, all there ever could be. Everything these days certainly seems to prove them right."

Liam opened his mouth to say something, but was cut short by a sudden fierce look from Azar.

"Everything. Tell me, Liam. Honestly, just between the two of us. No lenses involved. Was I really voted off the show tonight?"

The lie rose to Liam's lips as naturally as the can of premium-grade bachelor sludge had the night before, toward the end of the bottle of gin. Also like last night, it somehow seemed to get stuck in his throat, and not want to come fully out.

Why was lying to Azar face to face somehow different, more difficult even, than lying to literally billions of people across the world? It made no rational sense—or, at least, none he was ready to admit to himself just yet.

He floundered, choking in silence on words he desperately did not want to utter—for some reason, it felt as if his life depended on it. It was silly, stupid even, but the seconds went on and still Liam could do nothing but sit there, flapping his lips more uselessly than a muted politician. Azar looked sick, watching him. After what seemed like at least 1.7 eternities, she looked away, lowered her head, and broke the tense silence.

"It's okay. It's okay," she repeated, as if convincing herself of the fact. "I shouldn't have asked. Forget all about it."

Liam cleared his throat, but his voice still sounded hoarse when he replied. "Azar, you know the rules of the show—"

"Please, Liam. Forget everything I said." She was messing with what was left of her hair, so Liam couldn't really tell, but she sounded like she might be about to start crying again.

"Well, on the bright side," said Liam, desperate to change the subject and lift the pall[74] which seemed to have fallen over the car, "it looks like we're coming up on a promising patch of lens shops." He stopped and chuckled to himself. "That's something I never thought I'd hear myself say."

Azar didn't seem amused.

"Well, then, my dear damsel in distress. Are you ready for this knight gallant to escort you to complete our epic quest?"

It took Liam's most ham-fisted routine—a strange expression, when you think about, since pigs have trotters and can't even form fists—to get a half-smile out of Azar and pull her out of her funk, but he was glad for it nonetheless. The car pulled to a stop in the designated area outside of what bright AR signs proclaimed to be a slightly more trendy and lively part of town, and Liam slid out, holding the door open for Azar.

"Onwards, my lady! Your scrying bowls await!"

Encouraged by the odd look he got from Azar, he took her arm to help her out of the vehicle—she was so damned light.

"Yes, it is a little known fact that modern AR lenses are just the latest in a long line of divination tools, going all the way back to the ancient augurs, who would tell the future by observing the movements of birds."

He hooked her arm in his to prevent her from blowing off into the flow

---

74 "Cloth spread over a coffin."

of automated traffic, and they set off down the walkway to the pedestrian commercial streets.

"Of course, that became a lot easier when they invented Twitter."

47

As they searched for lenses, Liam tried to keep his enthusiasm and his optimism intact. However, four closed shops later, both lay as tarnished and battered as an uneaten portion of fish and chips.

Liam shook his head and made to push on to the next shop on the AR map, even though it was obvious by now that they were all closed to business this late on a Sunday night and any poor unconnected slob wanting a physical shop to buy lenses from would have to wait until morning. Above them, the ring road overpass loomed like a cathedral, and the vehicles created a general buzz about them, mocking Liam and his pretentions.

Out of sheer pigheadedness, Liam refused to give in to the whims of so-called "reality," and it was Azar who had to grab him by the arm and pull him back, as best she could.

"Liam, there's no point. They're all closed." From her tone, she had probably been saying this for some time now—Liam must have blocked her out in his hubris to help.

"Well, if the shops around here don't want our business, then I'll take you to one of the big commercial areas outside of town! The Hyper-mart will have stacks and stacks of lenses. Sure, they'll be the disposable kind, but at least they're open 24/7. What do you say?"

Liam flashed her his best professional smile, but apparently, she had nothing to say, regardless. She just lowered her eyes.

"Come on, Azar," Liam said eventually, cheesy smile still plastered across his face. "Don't leave me hanging here."

Liam was mortified—his attempt to lighten up the situation backfired terribly, and Azar broke out into sobs again. He leaned forward, as if to console her once more, and this time she broke off, pushing him away.

"It's no good, Liam. Just... just leave it, all right?" She cut back her sobs and backed away from him. "Just leave it," she repeated one final time, before turning tail and running off down the pavement.

Liam stood, dumbstruck, as the feeble excuse for an urban London breeze failed to move any of the smog, or even Liam's trenchcoat, which draped like a damp flag in the mid-afternoon sunlight created by Liam's

AR lightning settings.

"Hey, wait up," Liam eventually shouted, taking a few half-hearted steps in the direction of Azar, who was already halfway up the little overpass arching over the ring road expressway, of all things. "Azar! Where do you think you're headed? Be reasonable about this!" Cursing himself for something he couldn't quite name but felt vaguely guilty about, he took up the chase, hoping to bring his former contestant to her senses.

Liam certainly wasn't in the best physical shape, but he didn't expect to take anywhere near as long as it did to catch up with malady-ridden Azar Acquah. The frail woman, aged beyond her years, now seemed possessed by some sort of desperate speed. Liam was panting and sweat-covered by the time he caught up with her at the apex of the overpass and grabbed her arm, bringing her to a spinning stop.

She turned to face him, and for an instant, her eyes burned with an intensity Liam had never seen outside of the worst kind of dramatic soap opera. If he didn't know better, he would have thought it was hatred—loathing, even. Whatever emotion was behind it, the strength of the gaze, especially coming from his meek damsel-in-distress, was enough to cut Liam short and leave him wordless, yet again.

The scene froze for a second or two, like a lagging video, while below them the pilotless vehicles sang the incessant, general buzz of modern life. The car lights sent the shadow of the scant overpass railings dancing across the two figures. Above them, not a single star pierced the urban gloom, not that this would have surprised any of the twelve million people huddled in Greater London, most of whom had never seen an actual star shine in their lives.

Liam looked down at his hand, which was still gripping Azar's ragged army surplus shirt sleeve. He let go, and shook his mind back into gear.

"What do you think you're doing, Azar?" he asked, pretending for propriety's sake that he had only been waiting to catch his breath.

Azar smiled, but instead of her usual, long-suffering grin, this was a rictus; it sent a chill down Liam's spine.

"Think? No, no more thinking, Liam. I've done enough of that. Finding reasons for everything—excuses more like. Putting up and shutting up."

Liam tried to interject, to tell Azar she was making no sense, but her gaze flared again in the passing headlights and stopped him in his tracks.

"I don't just 'think,' I know exactly what I'm doing, for once. I'm doing what I should have done a long time ago, instead of buying, mind and body, into the lie, the collective sham, the con behind our conformity, our confusion..." She trailed off and turned to lean over the handrail, her gaze locked on the lights coming toward her in steady, central computer-regulated waves.

"Listen," said Liam, with a nervous gulp, "it's been a long day for you, what with the lenses, and the elimination show, obviously—"

Azar cut him off with a cackle ripped straight out of the latest *Wizard of Oz* remake. "Elimination show? Yes, a show. Just like everything else. And what a show you put on. Isn't that right, Liam?"

Scared into honesty, Liam said, "Azar, I'm sorry about the voting, okay? You were right earlier, of course. It was completely rigged." It felt good just saying it, but Azar kept her back turned to him and just leaned a bit lower across the rail, waiting in silence for him to offer more. How dare she judge him?

"It wasn't my fault though, you know! It was all the Editor's doing, and some exec or another up at Corporate calling the shots, I suppose. I tried to stop him." He had, hadn't he? "There was nothing I could do." That, at least, was true enough. If only she would say something, or at least react, instead of just flopping over the edge of the rail like that. "Tonight was just your time to go."

This, at last, got a reaction from Azar. She flipped around like a snake on speed and, still leaning against the handrail, hit Liam with her full, teary-eyed glare.

"You know what, Liam Argyle?" She trembled as she said the words. "You're right. It was my time to go, and there was nothing you could do. It wasn't your fault, and there's no reason why you should beat yourself up about it."

"I'm glad you see it that way," said Liam, flummoxed.

"Yes, I'm glad I see things this way now, too," said Azar, with a ghost of her former, genial smile returning to her face. "I see a lot of things more clearly now. All it took was forty years of radiation to the eyeballs, and a brain tumour the size of a ripe damson." She paused, chuckling. Liam didn't dare interrupt. "You shouldn't feel bad about the show, Liam, and I hope you won't feel bad about this, either. It really has nothing to do with you, or with anybody, truth be told."

"What are you talking about?" asked Liam, in a near-perfect imitation of an Angus cow presented with a differential calculus problem. Azar, however, seemed beyond caring about him or anything he might have to say.

"I wonder if it'll look any different, without the lenses?" she said to herself.

And with that, she flopped in a boneless, graceless dive over the top of the overpass handrail. Her fall into the passing automated traffic took little more than a blink of an eye, far longer than it took for Liam's brain to register and process what had just happened before him.

There was a muffled thud, something like a pile of slightly damp laundry hitting the floor, followed by a series of shorter, sharper thumps and squelches. By the time Liam started moving and peered over the rail, it was all over, other than a few patches of unqualifiable gore which described a surprisingly neat semi-circle upon the asphalt, when seen from above.

The vehicles quickly identified a potential road hazard, at least for their flashy nano-paint jobs, and started avoiding the lane altogether, passing through the new chokepoint in a sedate, orderly fashion, not entirely unlike mourners at a funeral.

"Fuck," commented Liam, and he pushed himself away from the handrail before he sent his cheap, studio trolley excuse for a supper down to join Azar's earthly remains on the expressway below.

"Fuck me," he added, covering his mouth with a hand and pulling down, as if making his face resemble one of those masks from *Scream* would somehow make the situation any less real.

"Fucking shit," came the conclusion, and Liam started to move back toward the rail, as if to check to make sure this was really happening, before stopping himself. Of course it was real, and he had no desire to subject himself to that sight again.

It was real, and the consequences would be as well. So, what was he doing, still standing around at what could, under a certain light, be viewed as a murder scene by anyone—such as a police officer, to take a random example—who might not take Liam's word as gospel[75] under the circumstances?

Biting his lip, Liam flicked his thumb out, triggering the AR interface to send his car to pick him up. He walked as fast as he dared back down the overpass and onto the street below, and waited for his car, shivering in the suddenly chilly evening.

When the car finally did arrive, a little pop-up message appeared, apologising in copy-pasted terms for the delay, caused by adverse road conditions due to a "human accident." Fighting back another bout of vomit, Liam slid into the car's air-conditioned interior and set off for the liquid comforts of home.

---

75 Literally "good spell," in the sense of "story."

48

There were no corporate rent-a-cops banging at the door of his new house the following morning, no incoming calls for him to stress over and ignore, not a single message or report. It was as if not a single person cared that Azar Acquah had committed suicide the previous night. Looking at himself in the mirror, Liam wondered if that wasn't the truth of it.

Upon arriving at the Mews, the dreaded shitstorm also failed to materialise, and everything was business as usual, except, perhaps, for a look from the Editor that might have been a little too knowing—but who could judge, with a man like Ed?

Just as he was relaxing into his chair and had decided to allow himself to let his guard down a little, a terrible thought struck Liam, and he quickly pulled up the logs from Jill's live feed. Had she been called in to deal with Azar's little "human accident" the previous night? Thank Mars, no: right after the show, she had been called to a run-of-the-mill incident in a tube station on the complete opposite side of town.

Other than a few irate calls from publicists who were angry at having to find some other flavour-of-the-week to replace the scheduled interviews lined up for the latest eliminated *Grass is Greener* candidate, there was a shocking absence of consequence for Azar Acquah disappearing off the face of the Earth—other than a specific patch of the A406, of course.

A few hours earlier, her every movement was followed, live, by millions of people around the world. Now, nobody even cared the see if she were still alive or not. There was probably a lesson of some sort for Liam there, but he was distracted by work before he had a chance to reflect upon it.

Not that the following week brought any sort of drama. In fact, that was the problem.

Brad was busy combing the city, single-handedly fighting a decidedly unphotogenic gastrointestinal outbreak and saving England's economy from a sick day epidemic—if you listened to him, which nobody seemed to want to do.

Jill was sulking after Azar's elimination and refusing to provide any interesting social commentary whatsoever on her feed.

And as for Juliette, she had started ditching work and any other social activity, preferring to hide in her apartment bedroom, with all the lights off. Since she knew perfectly well about the night optics which were a core feature of the GiG lens, this behaviour mystified Liam and everyone else at the Mews; it hid nothing from the viewers. Liam figured anything that helped Juliette keep her sanity together while counting down the hours until the next elimination show was probably a good thing.

Usnavi was at least back on his feet, but being between medical trials, his daily exploits were no more interesting than any else's, and less than most.

At week's end, Juliette's entirely unsurprising elimination was the anticlimactic cherry on top a bland Sunday. To Liam, even the joy in Juliette's face when her name was called seemed subdued, if not downright perfunctory.

The problem, as ever, was ratings. The slump over the past two weeks was big enough for the RedCorp Marketing division to edge in and try to take over the feed, suggesting a new flashy host, home-sculpted by their own resident team of crack plastic surgeons.

Ms. Heath came down on Liam and the Editor hard and heavy. They needed to do something drastic to get the ratings back up, if only temporarily. By this, of course, she meant Liam had to do something drastic, and probably highly degrading on a personal level.

His suspicions were not disappointed. The News department execs were not long in planning a scandal for him, one tailored for maximum sensationalism while carefully minimising damage with the prude socio-demographic.

And so, that Tuesday morning, even in the wee pre-sunrise hours, Liam found himself under the trees in a secluded pond-side clearing in Hampstead Heath. As he watched the hired crew install the "candid" podcameras and wheel in all the hardware—including his partner for the upcoming performance. He wondered what he'd done in a previous life to deserve this.

Turning to Ms. Heath, he rubbed his arms to fight off the cold and said, "Is this absolutely necessary?"

"Do you want Marketing to take over the GiG and fire your weather-announcing ass?" replied Ms. Heath, tapping an expensive-shoed foot. "Didn't think so. So be a good boy and strip for me."

"But it's so cold." Despite his best efforts, Liam spoke in a whine as he buttoned down his suit jacket, wishing the whole time he could get his teeth to chatter the way his deep-frozen skin was telling him they should.

Ms. Heath was ostensibly above answering such a plea. She busied herself with checking that the crew weren't about damaging any of the equipment, until Liam was down to his checkerboard briefs. She then came over to inspect him one last time. With a curt nod his way, she turned and gave a signal to the burly temp staffers standing by the largest crate of equipment.

As one, they reached in and unceremoniously pulled out a rigid-limbed but anatomically perfect replica of Liam himself. Right down to the most intimate, and entirely exposed, details.

Under the fascinated gaze of all present, they manhandled—or rather, android-handled—the Liam Argyle-shaped Erobot model into position next to its shivering, flesh-and-blood counterpart, and started booting it up.

"This is ridiculous," Liam whispered to Ms. Heath, if only to get her eyes off his silicon-cast member's member. "How is it going to look for the show, having its Host sneak off to have early morning intercourse with his own damn Erobot in Hampstead Heath?"

"It'll look exactly the way we need it to look. Fresh and scandalous enough to give the ratings a boost for a week or two. And just murky enough from a moral point of view that we won't put off the small fraction of our viewers who still have principles about this sort of thing. Plus, it'll make great advertising for our new line of celebrity-model Erobots."

Liam opened his mouth to protest further, but Ms. Heath's stare chilled him more deeply than the freezing winter morning wind swirling about his nether regions.

"You are in no posture to complain, Argyle," she said loud enough for everyone to hear, further withering his already weather- and shame-withered manhood with her glare. "This is a favour we're doing you, you know. Now buck up and take one for the Company."

The Argyle model Erobot finished booting up right then, turned toward Ms. Heath, and asked for instructions. Soon, the sordid little scenario cooked up in the fevered and reality-starved minds of the News division execs played out before the podcams set up to mimic candid com-footage.

The pretence of candidness ensured the cameras stayed far enough away—and somewhat obscured by foliage—so that "below the belt" action could be simulated rather than performed, which seemed to greatly confuse the android's pre-programmed enthusiasm for its function. It was only when Liam was acting out his finale that it occurred to him that the use of two Liam Argyle Erobots would have negated the need for his participation at all.

"Don't be ridiculous," said Ms. Heath, when Liam offered his belated suggestion once the entire affair, as it were, was over. "You come much cheaper than these damn robots do."

Was… was that a pun?

"You know I didn't actually…"

The chill from Ms. Heath's glare once again shut Liam's mouth for him, a Pavlovian response that felt as degrading[76] as anything else that morning.

Of course, not a single soul in the pod-feeding world had let him forget these events ever since—not a single moment's respite, but plenty of spite, spite and more spite. Over and over again they had shown the footage, claiming he had been caught unawares after a night of binging and debauchery.[77] The blitz lasted even longer than Ms. Heath had hoped for, well over a month in fact, pushed on by a Corporate media machine that would not let up sales of the Liam Argyle Erobot finally tailed off, so to speak.

Still the painful contrivance had fulfilled its mission well enough— Marketing backed off, knowing a losing fight when they saw it. Sometimes, Liam wondered whether saving his job was really such a good thing after all. However, every time his thoughts turned to what he would or could be doing were he no longer "the *Grass is Greener* guy," he came up against an abyss.

The week's one saving grace was Usnavi.

A working synaptic interface had been in the works for decades, always announced as being "only five years away." So-called tech experts had founded entire media careers on explaining why full synaptic Virtual Reality was a lovely idea, but impossible in practice. And so, the Editor's excitement when he told the team about the idea he had cooked up with Usnavi's doctors was perfectly understandable, and highly contagious.

"This is the big one, guys," Ed said with a drawl, leaning over the conference table, which had been cleared of most of its usual pile of cardboard boxes. "Launching a show, that's easy with enough publicity. Seeing it through to a second season, that's the real trick." He gave them his trademark wink, cocking his finger at them like a very poorly maintained pistol. Liam, Lee, and Carpentiere all kept a wise, seasoned silence. "Well, let me tell you one thing. When the entertainment history fellers tell the story of *Always Greener's* rise to glory, they'll point to Usnavi's live operation on the Saturday before our season finale as the moment our show achieved greatness."

Ed closed his eyes, seeming to pause to physically savour said greatness, in some sort of strange, self-serving synaesthesia.[78] The pause went on

---

76 "To knock down a step," hence the Universal Declaration of Human Rights-based worldwide ban in 2046 of all Snakes and Ladders games.

77 "Enticing from work or duty" – idle hands and whatnot.

78 My deepest apologies to any eventual audiobook narrators.

and soon became uncomfortable. The others shifted in their seats and made thoughtful "hmm" sounds, but there was no sign the Editor was paying them the least bit of attention. As senior employee, it fell to Liam to break the silence, after an opening cough.

"That's great news, Ed. So, how are we going to go about it, exactly?"

As icebreakers went, it was about on par with the Titanic, but the Editor seemed content enough as he opened his eyes and a wide grin spread across his features.

"That's the best part. We don't have to do anything. The hospital's PR department has already planned it all out, including the advertisement campaign—targeted AR pop-ins, forum trolls, the works—and all kicking in this afternoon." He paused again, but only snickered a little this time. "Of course, it helps that DynaMed, who owns the new synaptic chip patents, is also a fellow RedCorp subsidiary. They'll be opening the VR chip pre-orders right there and then, during the show. All we had to do is provide them with a bit of stock footage for the ad campaign, and everybody wins!"

Ms. Lee nodded more enthusiastically than a pump above a dry well, while Carpentiere was a bit more reserved—as he always seemed to be of late. But after Azar, Liam was determined to keep a smile on his face and show everyone how good he felt about Life, the Show, and Everything; he couldn't afford to show any doubts.

"Incredible, Ed. And even Usnavi will come out of this a hero. The first human to be connected to full Virtual Reality. Thanks to us, he'll go down in history!"

"Like Neil Armstrong!" chimed in Ms. Lee, always proud to find appropriate uses for ancient trivia.

"Or Dolly the Sheep," added Carpentiere, in a half-mutter. Liam felt the man had somehow missed the point, here.

"It'll go down in ratings history, that's for certain," said the Editor. "It'll do us a world of good—although, if it turns out to be the commercial success DynaMed's PR people are hoping for, it might not be so great for the kid's chances of winning the show." The Editor made a big show of shrugging, as if he didn't care, really, but he seemed somewhat pleased at the idea. "Oh well, you know what they say. You can't make a reality show without breaking a few eggs."

The man knew damn well nobody in the history of showbusiness had ever said that, and also that none of them sitting around the conference table like so many network-connected potted plants would dare to point that out. Liam seethed in impotent silence.

Surely, somebody around here could bring him a drink.

49

Roughly three-and-a-half bottles of prime scotch later, Liam stood in the virtual limelight once again. His glassy-eyed stare was fixed on the free-floating AR window playing the highlight clips from the last week's feeds.

"These calls are always the hardest," narrated Brad Leigh for the benefit of the millions of viewers around the globe watching through his eyes as his patrol vehicle cruised down a quaint, tree-lined suburban street. His gaze lingered on the tidy lawns and immaculate doorsteps a bit longer than was comfortable.

"These people," he nearly spat. "Pensioners, self-employed workers, stay-at-home parents... Too good to be part of something bigger, like the rest of us. Oh, they're happy to know the poor disease control man in the street is keeping them safe. But only when he's far away, in the city. As if disease couldn't possibly spread to their gated slice of suburban paradise." He let out a long-suffering sigh. "My job is hard enough without having to explain to people that the Law isn't just for other people."

The disease control patrol vehicle coasted to a silent, electric halt outside a neat white-panelled cottage, indistinguishable from any of the hundreds it had passed along the way. Brad pulled his treatment kit together, hauled both it and himself out of the vehicle, and marched over to pound at the door, sending an orange-leafed autumn wreath swinging under the shock.

"Disease Monitoring and Prevention Corps! Open up!" he bellowed, loud enough for the whole street to hear. But only silence followed, other than a tense shuffling from behind the door.

"Typical," grunted Brad under his voice, for the benefit of the viewers, before raising his tone once more. "Under articles 5 through 11 septies of the World Health Convention and article 8 of the UK Disease Prevention Act, 2048, I am entitled to your obedience and—"

"There must be some mistake, officer!" interrupted a warbling male voice from the other side of the door. "There's no emergency here. There's only the two of us here, and we keep a close eye on all our health apps."

The feed gave a stomach-churning swing as Brad rolled his eyes.

"If you persist in refusing to comply, I am entitled to enter the premises and administer treatment by force. This is your only warning."

"But we don't—"

"Right then!" cut in Brad, anger and glee competing in his voice. It took him no more than a few seconds to whip out little pads of sticky putty from his belt, stick them to door above the hinges and lock mechanism, and step back.

"Here we go!" he shouted, breaking from script in his eagerness to trigger the flashing "Detonate" button in his AR overlay.

The explosion of the microcharges was an underwhelming muffled thump, completely drowned out by the geriatric screams from inside the house as the door fell inward. Brad marched in, opening his kit with expert ease at the same time while scanning the dust-filled hallway for his targets.

Back on the *Grass is Greener* main stage, Liam's own, horrified gaze was drawn to the russet-furred cat that dodged around Brad's legs to run out the now permanently open door. He hadn't seen one with those colours in a while, and any excuse was good enough to avoid looking at Brad's undoubtedly joyful face in the hallway mirror as he walked past.

The hallway opened onto an open, cosy living area, and that's where the human residents of the house stood huddled—two elderly gentlemen in matching green sweater vests, clinging to each other for support in the middle of a thick Persian-style rug.

"We've got a reported C. Diff. outbreak in this house, gentlemen. Got to nip buggers like that in the bud," Brad drawled, his invisible grin loud and clear in his voice. He lifted a nozzle-ended tube attached to a brimming tank of khaki-green sludge labelled "faecal bacteriotherapy."

"You know how this goes. C. Diff. is so contagious I need to treat everyone in the house. So don't make this any more difficult for us all than it needs to be," he added, advancing on the wide-eyed and blubbering owners of the home.

The taller of the pair managed to find his wits first. "You can't be serious. We're perfectly healthy! You can't use that on us," he protested, as they both backed away from Brad. Soon, they were up against the ornamental brickwork fireplace and could back away no further.

"Ho-ho, I think we've got ourselves a volunteer! Unless stool transplant therapy too good for you?" spat Brad. "I make this myself, you know. All in a day's work in the Disease Corps. And a damn sight more effective than antibiotics too! So don't be a baby about this. Whip 'em down, bend over, and let's get this done with, shall we?" He gave the nozzle's trigger a playful pump to illustrate his point, sending the brown slurry halfway up the tube, then back down again.

The shorter of the two men twisted to grab an iron poker from beside the fireplace and brandished it before him, less like a weapon and more like a talisman that could banish the demon from their home.

Brad laughed outright, this time around.

"That looks a lot like a weapon to me," he said, reaching around to a clip on the left of his belt. "Protocol Four it is, then!"

His hand, when he lifted it back up, was clutching an ugly yellow box with metal darts protruding from the end. It crackled with electric energy at his touch.

"Wha—What's Protocol F—" started to mumble the taller of the two men. But Brad clearly had no intention of letting him finish his thought and fired off the taser, with prongs hitting both men squarely in the chests. They fell to the ground in a jerking, sweater-clad mess, and the scent of scorched printshop wool wafted through the air.

Brad stepped toward them, flipped them over onto their stomachs, one after the other, and started fumbling with their trousers, complaining about entitled babies and irresponsible treatment dodgers the whole time.

The Grass is Greener studio went deathly quiet, all the usual background chatter during a pause in the live feed fading away. Everyone turned to watch through Brad's eyes, with uniformly haunted expressions, as he provided both pacified gentlemen with their complimentary stool transplant enemas.

Once again, Liam wished he'd found the nerve to demand the Editor not replay this whole scene again in this week's primetime show. Or the nerve to say anything about it whatsoever, for that matter. But what good would it have done?

He put his smile back on as the treatment reached its nauseating end and they gave him the five-second warning before the return to live feed. The clip ended—at long last—and the light on the cameras went red again.

"Quite the in-depth look into the work of our brave Disease Corps men and women," he said, cursing himself at the ridiculous attempt at making light of such a fundamental[79] violation of privacy and human rights. "Anything to add about what we've all just watched there, Brad?"

Sitting in his bright red, plush hotseat, Brad Leigh sulked like a toddler hit by a growth ray. "Listen, it ain't easy being on the frontlines, protecting all you lot from diseases you couldn't even imagine. And in my defence, it's not my fault the standard bathroom sensors aren't calibrated to tell the difference between a C. Diff. infection in humans or a damn pet. A spore's a spore; they would probably have gotten infected anyway. And what were those two fogeys doing taking in stray cats in the first place, that's what I'd

---

79 Yet again, quite literally.

like to know! Bloody bleeding hearts."

Liam wasn't sure their hearts were the bleeding bits they should be worried about here, but he bit back the retort and kept his silence.

Brad shuffled uneasily in his seat, before adding, "They got free treatment, and the Corps prevented contagion as usual, is all I'm trying to say."

Liam beamed at him for the cameras. If only smiles could kill. "And I'm sure the voters will take that into consideration as we move into the last minutes of —" He paused for effect, stepping into the centre of the stage and raising his voice to a carnival shout. "This week's final vote tally!"

From there on, all that was left were the camera smiles, the screams at the announcement of Brad's landslide elimination, and the fake tears and even faker sympathy as Usnavi and Jill said goodbye.

Brad was escorted off the stage in sullen silence, muttering something about ingrates to the security agents. Liam cast aside his sudden questions about when the show had acquired security agents and announced, with great piped-in fanfare, the two finalists of *The Grass is Greener*, Season One.

At the post-show wrap-up meeting, the Editor stood rubbing his brow while the team waited in uncomfortable silence.

"We managed to keep the last week entertaining enough," he said at last, in a low moan, "but I don't know how they expect us to keep the feed lively for a whole one-hundred-sixty-eight hours until the big finale with only two contestants left. We aren't miracle makers, damnit."

Norma Lee rose out of her slump to sit straight as an oversized schoolroom ruler. "Luckily, we already have the Usnavi Musibay live operation event set up with DynaMed. As long as Jill gets another juicy suicide or two to mop up, that should give us a solid base to mount up to the finale, right?"

"No, it is not 'right,' Ms. Lee," answered the Editor. "It's a start, but we will have to bend matters even further than usual in order to produce anything close to the build-up of viewer attention we need for a successful finale to our opening season."

He paused, and his grin reminded Liam of those two poor men, home invaded, tasered, and enema'ed with their assaulter's own faeces, due to an error in medical sensor diagnosis.

"Luckily, I have just the thing in mind," drawled the Editor.

50

The enclosed garden area inside the Elysian Fields private mental rehabilitation facility was highly photogenic. It made for a great backdrop for Liam's interview with patient Juliette Binns. Not to mention a welcome distraction from the woman's sunken eyes and dilated pupils.

"Thank you for agreeing to see us on such short notice, Juliette," said Liam, trying to put the woman at ease, both for her benefit and his own. He couldn't reconcile the twitchy, broken woman in the blue hospital gown sitting on the other side of the little plastic table with the defiant woman that he'd come to know over the first few weeks of the show. Perhaps more intimately than he was comfortable to admit.

At the sound of his voice, her eyes stopped flicking between the plants in the gently lit solarium, Carpentiere's recording equipment, and the white-suited orderlies always passing nearby. Her gaze fixed on Liam at last.

"I guess I should be the one thanking you, for coming to visit. After the stunts I pulled on the show, the last thing I expected was more cameras."

Liam smiled and shook his head, every inch the understanding host the viewers back home wanted to see. "Being part of a show like *The Grass is Greener* is an adventure, and a lot of stress. It's enough to make anyone act a little kooky[80] now and again."

Liam's grin became a little strained as the seconds went by. Juliette made no response, simply staring at him with those pitted eyes, as if debating something internally.

"You're a welcome break from routine here, that's for sure," she said at last. "Normally, at this time of day, they've got me wired into some VR therapy scenario or another. I'd almost forgotten what eleven o'clock sunlight looks like."

Here we were: the meat of what the Editor wanted from the interview. Showing off the state-of-the-art rehabilitation facilities eyeNet had generously—and compulsorily—provided for Ms. Binns after her little breakdown and her elimination from the show.

"Tell me a bit more about the facilities here, and your daily routine,"

---

80 Early 1900s U.S. slang abbreviation of "cuckoo," which itself comes from "cocu," which is both old and current French for a cuckold.

asked Liam, all smile and saccharin for the sake of the live podcameras.

Juliette blanched an even paler shade of white, which Liam hadn't thought was possible. "I'm not sure—I mean, I wouldn't want to bore[81] you, is all," she said, her eyes shooting toward something off behind Liam's shoulder.

"Please," insisted Liam, resisting the urge to turn to see what was so intriguing behind him. "We've had an outpouring of viewer comments since you left the show, all wanting to make sure you're okay. Just like us," he added, trying not to make it sound like the afterthought it was. "You said something about VR therapy? That sounds fancy."

"Oh, they've got all the best resources here, that's for sure." Juliette actually smiled as she spoke, and let out a relieved chuckle. Maybe this was a safer subject than whatever was worrying her a minute ago. "The doctors and the staff are nice and all, but treatment here is really all about retraining the brain with the VR scenarios they run you through."

"That's amazing," Liam said, nodding thoughtfully so they had something to cut to when editing the highlight clip. "If it's not too private, can you share some examples with us?"

Juliette chuckled at this—a slightly harsh, out-of-practice sound. "I think we're a bit beyond privacy considerations by now, Mr. Argyle. But there are so many different scenarios, I wouldn't know where to start. They're very proud of their in-house developed psychiatric software, but they do tend to all blur together after the first day or two." She paused, wrestling with her thoughts. "In this one program they—"

"Now now, Ms. Binns," boomed a voice so close to Liam's ear he thought he had forgotten to block his incoming calls for the interview. Juliette went instantly silent as the speaker, a tall, silver-haired orderly in a spotless white uniform, stepped out from behind Liam. "You know we don't talk about psychiatry here. What we do is brain training. Oh, sorry if I've interrupted," the man added, as if he had only just realised he'd barged in on a recording, "but I was just passing by and overheard Ms. Binns's little error in terminology."

He turned to smile at Liam, ignoring the recording equipment and the hulking Carpentiere as naturally as if he'd been born in front of the camera. "Ms. Binns is still very new here, of course, and it takes some time for our clients to really come to grips with the nuances of their individualised brain training program. Speaking of which, I think Ms. Binns is late for her next session today. VR room number five, if I'm not mistaken," he added, eyes

---

81 The verdict is out on whether or not being "boring" originally meant slow and painful discourse that "bores" into your mind. But it's funny to note that the original "bore" was a tool, not unlike many boring people.

glazing over as he read something from his personal AR display. "That's just down the hallway. I don't suppose you'd like to see the room before Ms. Binns begins, Mr. Argyle?"

Liam had to fight back a smile. He remembered a time not so long ago when he would have been surprised if a stranger knew his name.

"That would be lovely. And might it be possible to ask you a few questions as well before we wrap up the visit?" he asked.

The orderly smiled, and his identity tag, labelling him as "Felix Reiter, Client Facilitator" above the green rolling hills logo of Elysian Fields Rehabilitation Centre, finally loaded into Liam's display.

"It would be our pleasure. This way, please."

Liam stood, leaving Carpentiere to fumble with the recording equipment as he followed Reiter and a demure Juliette Binns through the pastel corridors, with their comfy chairs that seemed to have been dropped in random places by half-hearted movers and their AR-broadcast copies of inoffensive classical paintings and pop art works.

"Here's VR room five on the left," half-whispered Reiter, like a GPS navigation app with the volume turned too low, as they approached a closet-sized door.

Liam couldn't have told it apart from any of the other half-dozen identical, baby blue doors they'd passed.

Reiter pushed the door, and all three of them, including the panting and filming Carpentiere, followed him into a tiny, dim-lit room dominated by what looked like a high-end fridge set against the far wall. A single, padded chair in the near corner was the only other furnishing in the dark cubbyhole.

"This is where the self-improvement begins," declared Reiter, his white smock darkened to a mute grey without the bright sunlight from the solarium. "Inside this chamber, we can simulate any situation, probe any moral quandary, push any boundaries the client wishes to overcome with our help. And our guidance, of course."

Leaning forward, Liam stepped up to the glass-fronted unit and peered inside. It was even darker than the rest of the room in there, but he could make out a running mill-type floor and various nozzles set into the inner lining of the unit. It was just big enough in there for a person to stand, with enough room to swing arms and legs.

"The science is still rudimentary, of course, with a need for physical simulation of sensations of cold, heat, wet, and such, along with nebulised chemical stimulant delivery. But it serves our clients' purposes for the present," said Reiter, his thoughts trailing away into silence for a moment. "Regardless, our success rates are phenomenal. But privacy during brain training sessions is vital to success, so I unfortunately must ask you to follow me out after I load Ms. Binns's agoraphobia program."

He popped open the front of the unit, ushered an unresisting and stoop-shouldered Juliette inside, and shut it exactly like Liam did his fridge door back home after grabbing a drink. The orderly flicked his fingers through an AR menu, and the lights inside the unit flared to blinding life. Inside, Juliette stood in the glare like a museum specimen in her hospital gown.

"Perfect," said Reiter, turning away to open the door back out to the corridor. "That's all set for the next few hours. If you'll follow me, gentlemen, I'll be happy to answer any questions you'd like. There might even be coffee and biscuits in it for you," he added, conspiratorially, as he ushered them out of the tiny room.

As he emerged into the diffused sunlight, Liam turned to cast one last look past Carpentiere, at Juliette Binns. His former contestant stared straight back at him, mouth pursed shut and eyes like gaping skull-holes in the bottom-lit VR unit.

She didn't mouth a word, and neither did Liam.

There were biscuits and coffee, but neither did anything to wash the sour taste out of Liam's mouth. Reiter lounged in his seat in the bright, leaf-filled solarium area and smiled for the camera above his steaming mug.

"Our dream is that, someday, we'll be able to do away with all that clunky apparatus you saw back there," he said. "Direct sensory immersion is making leaps and bounds, and the therapeutic potential is enormous. In ten or twenty years' time, we'll be able to control every single sense within the simulations—we may even be able to make the client forget they're within a simulation entirely. Imagine the brain training possibilities!"

A shiver ran down Liam's spine. Something wrong with the temperature control in here, maybe? Whatever it was, the podcamera was recording, and he couldn't afford to take his mind off business. Liam made sure his smile was still in place before turning toward the orderly.

"And how would you describe Ms. Binns's progress and outlook, if it isn't a breach of confidentiality for me to ask? The viewers are dying to know."

The white-gowned man swept his hand through the air. "I'd be happy to. We're under instructions to provide you with any assistance we can for this interview, Mr. Argyle. And once again, we aren't, strictly speaking, a medical institution. We simply provide software and facilities to help our clients retrain their own brains. As for Ms. Binns, there was some initial resistance at first. Not that unusual really, and I'm sure you can relate to that after what she put you through on that show of yours. We're all big fans here, by the way," added Reiter, with an embarrassed chuckle.

Liam chuckled back, mostly to cover the sinking feeling deep in his internal plumbing. "The show wouldn't be anything without its fans. But as for Juliette, you'd say she's making progress toward a full recovery, then?"

"Oh, absolutely," replied Reiter, all smiles. "Our simulations are the best, allowing the clients to face their ethical dilemmas and personal trauma in a safe, controlled environment. Now that she's fully compliant, Ms. Binns's successful rehabilitation is only a matter of time."

The orderly paused, taking a pensive sip from a mug bearing the presumably humorous statement "Allow me to introduce my selves" before continuing.

"Of course, calling it a 'full recovery' might be a bit misleading. The brain is a wily beast, Mr. Argyle, and maintaining the desired personality traits takes more than a one-time fix. It's a constant work upon the self, and our clients never truly leave us. They always come back for more, if only for a few psyche touch-ups every now and again. And that's for people who've never had a breakdown like Ms. Binns."

Liam took an audible gulp and started speaking the question on his mind before his good sense caught up with him and killed the words before they left his lips.

"But don't you think this sort of immersive VR therapy, as powerful as it clearly is, could be dangerous for someone like Ms. Binns? Given the nature of her trauma, that is? I mean, she's here because she rejected her implants and the show's immersive technology. Isn't there a risk exposing her to more of the same could do more harm than good?"

Shocked silence descended on all three men—interviewer, interviewee, and cameraman alike. Liam swore at himself. When would he learn to keep his damn thoughts to himself?

Then Reiter chuckled again and broke the spell. "Your concern does you credit, Mr. Argyle, and your contestants are lucky to have such a caring host. But have no fear. Every therapy program here is tailored for and approved by the client. When she leaves our care here, Ms. Binns will be a new woman, free from her crippling and pathogenic anxieties."

After seeing the broken shell of what used to be Juliette Binns, Liam didn't know how the man could spout such blatant lies and keep a straight face. Then again, maybe it took a hypocrite to know one. The people here didn't care about Juliette. They were probably just happy for the paying subject, and the publicity.

"Well, our time here is up. Thank you so much for all your help today, Mr. Reiter, and we look forward to hearing great things from you in the future."

"Likewise, Mr. Argyle," said the orderly, his fake smile never wavering.

51

Suicide Jill's feed the next day promised to live up to the Editor's wild-est hopes for sensationalism and filler content to see the show through the last three days until Usnavi's big live operation and the finale the following day. And like every time the shit hit the fan, Liam was the one stuck on live feed monitoring duty.

"Dispatch, I can't go in there," she said in deadpan tones, standing stone-still at the low, rusted iron gate to a dilapidated terraced house in the eastern suburbs of the city. The hose of her multipurpose industrial clean-ing unit lay limp in her hand. "I know the lady who lives here. I can't take this clean-up job, chief. Personal conflict."

"Jill, it's already been over a day since the rent-a-cops flagged this one for us," replied the bored voice over her comms, relayed in real-time to the monitoring Liam and, thirty seconds later, viewers around world. "If we leave it any longer, we'll have Disease Control on our asses for endangering public health. And you know the tender's coming back up for grabs in six months. This is more than both of our jobs are worth, Jill."

She cursed into the cold evening air, and Liam flagged this segment as vulgar for the rare viewer out there who may not have turned off their profanity filters yet.

"Don't fuck around with me, man. This is my ex-girlfriend's house. I've been doing this job for three years now, and I know you can't force me to do a clean-up when there's personal conflict. Send somebody else."

"Damnit, Jill. You know we've already got everyone working double shifts, and we still haven't gotten over the Monday hump. There's nobody else to send. So get your shit together, load up your Funfilter, and get in there. Or resign right now and enjoy spending the next week in queue at the Job Placement centre. Your call. I'm covered either way."

"Man, could you at least try to give a shit? For appearance's sake?"

"I don't get paid to care, Jill. But you know, it might not even be your ex or whoever in there. All the Secufax report says is that's it's a single-sized clean-up, sex female. They didn't bother identifying. So sure, that could be your ex, but it could also be someone else. A visitor, a squatter, who knows? Are you even sure she still lives here? I mean, as far as registered addresses go," added the man on dispatch, in an embarrassed rush.

Jill was clearly beyond caring about poor word choice. "It's true, I haven't spoken with Jamila in ages. Almost a year now. I suppose she could have moved on by now."

"Well, one way or the other, I'd say she has," chimed in the dispatch man.

"You're not helping here, Rodrigo."

"My brilliant and underappreciated wit isn't the question here. So are you gonna stand there all night or are you going to do your job? I bet it isn't getting any warmer out there, either."

A cloud of condensed exhalation betrayed Jill's exasperated sigh to the millions viewing through her eyes. Then the AR filters fell over her eyes, and bright virtual sunlight replaced the grey, early evening gloom all around. The broken-windowed, crumbling-bricked terraced house before her was suddenly a charming, flower-decked cosy little home.

"That's my girl," said the dispatch man. "That's one hell of a Funfilter, by the way."

"Shit," swore Jill. "I guess I shouldn't be surprised you're watching this live as well."

Rodrigo chuckled. "Can you blame me? Oh, and hey everybody! Go listen to my DJ mixes at—"

Shaking his head, Liam edited the pathetic attempt at a plug out of the live feed. Trying to get free advertisement on the feed was a far worse offense than any profanity they could come up with.

"You silly shit," said Jill, half-chuckling as she steeled herself and stepped up to the front door. The security lock responded to her AR system's ping, and then both her and her bulky cleaning unit were inside the house.

In the rosy Funfilter glow, the house looked amazing, and about as unlikely a scene for a post-suicide clean-up as could be.

Jill rolled her equipment down the cheery corridor, lit by bright sunlight that made no objective sense, but was welcome regardless. Walking with the certainty of someone well-acquainted with the house, she cast a cursory glance through the wrapped parcel-filled kitchen at the end of the hall, filled with little buzzing fairy-bugs, but otherwise empty. Passing an equally empty sitting room, she marched up a bright green-painted staircase.

As she set foot on the landing, the thick, yellow carpet squelched slightly under Jill's boot—a sensation her Funfilter, after a few seconds' processing, translated by placing puddles of water along the left side of the landing, shimmering invitingly and begging to be splashed about in.

Heedless, Jill followed them down the landing, all the way to the house's only bathroom. The door had a giant yellow smiley face plastered over it and lay half open. Pausing only slightly, Jill stepped forward and swung it open with the touch of a rubber-gloved hand.

Inside, the ancient freestanding bathtub was filled to the brim with water. It shimmered with such impossible clarity and brilliance that the Funfilter must have been working overtime to hide something particularly unpleasant. Bobbing gently in the water, a fully-dressed female clown lay relaxed and stretched out, by all appearances fast asleep despite the large, goofy grin painted on her face, and untouched by the water all around. Little bonbon tubes were scattered within arm's reach at the base of the tub.

"Oh fuck, Jamila," whispered Jill, her swear at complete odds with the bright, cheerful scene. Dropping her cleaning hose, she rushed forward to plunge a hand into the water and grip at the clown's wrinkled, loose-fitting lapel. She gave it a shake, peering at the smiling, painted face for a reaction.

But the eyes stayed shut, the body unmoving, and the only reward for her efforts was when the lapel she was gripping ripped loose with a wet tearing sound. The body fell back into the bath, sending a wave of impossibly fresh water gushing over the rim and onto Jill's legs.

"Fuck!" she yelled this time, winning no points for originality, and jumped back, raising her hand to gaze in horror at the ripped "clown suit" still in her hand.

The edges of the fabric oozed with sluggish frayed strings, which flowed outward before dripping onto the gleaming tiles at Jill's feet.

Dropping the ripped bit out of suddenly limp fingers, Jill rushed past the recumbent form in the bathtub and bent down above the toilet in the far corner, heaving.

Liam and all the viewers around the world, in their homes or out and about, were treated to the live feed of Suicide Jill puking out a seemingly endless flow of colourful party streamers into the rapidly-filling toilet bowl.

"Oh shit," said Jill in a low, throaty moan, when the last bits of confetti were finally out of her innards. "Fuck this right off. I can't."

And without further ado, she pushed herself away from the party supply-filled toilet bowl and rushed out the door, across the squelching landing carpet, and down the cheerful stairs, hardly stumbling at all as she made it to the bottom step.

"You know I'm sympathetic and all," came the voice of Rodrigo from dispatch over her comms, as she laid her wet, gloved hand on the front door handle. "But it's my job to remind you that refusing to do your job there, whatever the reason, is the same thing as a resignation. No severance or benefits. Are you sure that's what you want?"

Jill stood uncharacteristically silent for a moment, staring at the bright Funfiltered paint of the house's front door.

"What I want?" she said at last, with a nervous chuckle. "What I want is for you to add 'Jamila Lewis' as the confirmed identity on that file. Then I want you to find your manager and tell them Jill Nowicki says they can go fuck themselves for thinking they can treat people this way. And their own bosses along with them."

Jill cut off her comms at that, swung the door open with filter-jarring violence, and stomped out of the house. Leaving the company vehicle behind her, she flicked off the Funfilter and marched on down the suddenly dark, smoke-filled road toward the nearest bus stop.

Leaning back in his swivel seat, Liam nibbled on a thumbnail, lost in thought, then reached a decision and called up the Editor with a flick through his heads-up display.

"Yes, Argyle?" replied a grumbling Editor, answering only at the sixth ring, and with the sound of other people speaking fading into the background. "I hope this is worth interrupting a meeting at Central."

Despite himself, Liam gulped. "It's Suicide Jill, sir. Have you been watching the feed?"

"Argyle," the Editor growled in Liam's ear, "assume I am always watching the feed. And assuming that you are calling about Jill's resignation from her job, I really wish you hadn't."

"But isn't having Jill badmouth her employer live a problem for the show?"

"People quit their jobs all the time. Do you know the number of applicants any company, even a suicide clean-up contractor, will have for any sort of menial labour position? They'll be beyond caring, trust me. And so should you."

"Yes sir," replied Liam, not knowing how else to answer that.

"As ever, Jill's timing is perfect," carried on the Editor. "We couldn't have hoped for a better show from her in the run-up to the Finale. And now we have a good explanation to give for her victory on Sunday, despite little Usnavi's big night with his live operation on Saturday. So chin up, Argyle, and back to the grindstone!"

The Editor cut off the call without waiting for a reply, which saved Liam the trouble of having to piece one together from the confused swirl that was his mind.

52

"Whoa, is all this for me?" asked Usnavi, his gaze swinging around the bright-lit operating theatre, from the blinking podcameras to the science and tabloid journalists rubbing shoulders against the far wall. His eyes finally rested on the operating table set under a bright spotlight in the exact centre of the circular room, with a hulking brain-imaging unit and a gleaming forest of specialised robotic arms at its head, and surgical tool trolleys on either side.

When he didn't get a reply, Usnavi turned to face the chisel-faced and smiling DynaMed doctor ushering him into the room. "It's just that, normally, it's all waiting around until the researchers are ready for me, then five minutes in a backroom, and I'm lucky if I get an Elastoplast afterward. This is swanky."

The DynaMed doctor carried on manoeuvring the boy in the freshly printed and ill-fitting grey suit into position, sitting him on the edge of the padded green operating table, moulded to human shape and segmented like a caterpillar. The overhead spotlights blinded Usnavi as he looked up at his assigned guide.

At last the doctor answered, "That's because what we're accomplishing here today, together, is something nobody has ever done before. You're going to be the first person to receive our patented new full-immersion brain interface implant, Usnavi. The first to enter the world of tomorrow, where everyone can access information and interact with the world of tech at the speed of thought, using all of our senses and not just a clumsy AR interface or unreliable external sensors."

The doctor smiled, an indistinguishable clean-shaven face half-hidden by the overhead glare, and put his hands on Usnavi's shoulders. "You're going to make history, young man! A modern-day Neil Armstrong!"

The view from Usnavi's eyes shivered, and back at the Mews, Liam wondered if it was excitement, fear, or both.

"That's amazing."

And a nice consolation prize for not winning tomorrow, added Liam in silence.

"But are you sure it's safe?"

Usnavi's eyes wandered from the doctor's face down to the tray already in place by the operating table, with its saw-like instruments, drills, clamps, forceps… "If you haven't ever done this on a person before, how can you know there isn't any danger?"

"There's nothing to worry about, Mr. Musibay," replied the doctor, all smiles as he used his grip on Usnavi's shoulders to guide the unresisting boy down into a horizontal position atop the operating table. "The interface has been tested extensively. AI simulations, live animals, cloned human tissue, you name it. And the success rates, with no impairment of vital functions whatsoever, were much higher than expected."

Usnavi nodded, reacting to the doctor's smooth, placating tone, then stopped suddenly. "Wait, what do you mean 'impairment of vital f—'"

"Oh look, here comes the operating team," cut in the doctor, finishing his adjustments of the seat to Usnavi's diminutive size and moving to strap his arms against the curved green armrests. "No need to worry about these, either," he added, pre-emptively. "Just like everything else, it's only for your comfort and security. Always a safe precaution when dealing with the ol' noggin wiring, you know."

Usnavi squinted into the glare of the overhead lights, trying to make out the emerald-green scrub-clad forms appearing all around the operating table. He started pulling himself back up.

"Doctor! I don't think—I don't think I want to do this anymore. I want to stop!" he cried.

"Shh," said the doctor, reappearing beside his head and giving him a gentle yet irresistible push back down onto the operating table. "That's just your nerves talking. And we'll soon have those sorted out," he added, with a bit of a chuckle he quickly cut short. "But seriously, you've already signed on for this, and everyone is here for you. There's no backing out now. You're going to make history, Usnavi!"

The camera gave a sharp jerk as Usnavi craned to look at his arm, where a no-nonsense nurse had just inserted an IV feed. It instantly started dripping with a clear liquid.

"There's nothing to worry about," cooed the doctor, easing Usnavi back down into a resting position once again. "That's just to make sure you don't feel any pain during the operation, so you can stay awake, see how the operation progresses, and share your impressions as the first human in history to enter the new, full-immersion digital world."

Let alone share the experience with a few hundred million non-squeamish viewers back home, added Liam. The Editor had been adamant that it would either be awake surgery, or nothing at all.

"Well, as long as I'm awake and can tell you if something feels like it's going wrong..." Usnavi said in a low, sleepy voice. The anaesthetic was already starting to take effect.

"That's the spirit," beamed the doctor. "And I'll be right here, standing next to you the whole time, if you need me for anything, Usnavi. You're an amazing young man, you know," he added, sounding genuine to Liam's ears for the first time.

Usnavi simply nodded in response, as much as the operating table's formed headrest allowed him to.

The doctors and nurses busied themselves in the glare surrounding Usnavi. They hooked up electrodes to various parts of his body, and it was strange to think that he probably couldn't even feel those bits anymore—no more than the millions of spectators watching through his eyes. Somewhere to his side, a monitor started bleeping; it rang like a stream of censored expletives in Liam's show-addled mind.

He winced in instinctive fear as the whirr of a drill started up in his ear and the head-clamps fastened into place. The view from behind Usnavi's eyes started vibrating as the robotic arms pulled in closer, but the boy himself didn't seem to mind in the least.

"You're doing great," cooed the boy's handler doctor, along with a dozen other sweet nothings, while the machines got to work opening his skull and exposing his living brain. "How do you feel?" he eventually asked, when the silence got too heavy.

"A bit foggy, if that makes any sense," replied Usnavi, the clamps keeping him frozen in place as he spoke. "But okay otherwise. No pain or anything."

"Perfect," the doctor said in absent tones as he peered around the busy robotic arms at whatever was going on at the top of the boy's head. At the edges of Usnavi's locked-down field of view, beyond the glare of the lights, the various spectators jostled for position, all craning for a view of what was going on at the top of his head a well. There was a slow pneumatic *whirr*, and then a small *whump* of pressurised air.

"Weyhey, there we go," said the doctor, his eyes sparkling in the spotlights. "The first relay implant is in! Congratulations, Usnavi, and well done!"

The boy giggled as best he could under the restraints. "I should be congratulating you guys. You're the ones who've done all the work. I'm just lying here."

"All our work is only to help you make history, my boy," replied the doctor, patting Usnavi on a strapped-down arm. Somewhere behind Usnavi's ears, the faintest of scratching sounds grew faster and faster.

"We're almost there now," the doctor said, carrying on his running commentary, both for Usnavi's sake and for the millions of viewers around the globe. "The nanoscopic manipulators are hooking up the artificial neurons to the key hubs in your visual cortex, so you might start receiving our test input any moment now." His voice trembled. "Make sure to tell us as soon as you see anyth—"

"Doctor, I think I see something!" interrupted Usnavi, a laugh escaping his lips. "There's a green shape. And it doesn't move when I move my eyes!"

Sure enough, the feed flicked from left to right as Usnavi tested his theory. However, all he was succeeding in doing, as far as the show was concerned, was make Liam and the viewers feel sick. They could only see what the ocular implants recorded and not this new signal coming directly from inside the boy's brain.

One of the scrub-clad people behind Usnavi's head started to cheer but was quickly shushed by their colleagues.

"That's great, Usnavi," said his handler, in guarded tones, "but we need to you to try to focus on the green shape. Can you describe it to us?"

The feed finally stopped moving as the boy focused on the green shape only he could see.

"It's long. And it looks like it's bigger at the end."

Someone sniggered in the crowd and was quickly shuffled off to the back row. Usnavi carried on, unphased.

"I think—I think it could be an arrow. A green arrow, with some other shapes in front of it. And inside it. They might be letters."

The doctor leaned in over Usnavi. "I need you to concentrate now. Can you read the letters and tell us what they say?"

"I don't think I can," Usnavi said, shaking his head gently. "It's too fuzzy."

"Please," urged the Doctor. "You can do this. Just concentrate on the picture."

Doctors and spectators alike, both in the room and around the world, all held their breath as the boy strained to decipher the signals from the implant.

"It's getting clearer now! I can almost read it. The bit inside the arrow says 'Med,' and the bit in front is... Oh, of course. DynaMed! That's you guys, right?"

"Right you are," answered the doctor, a finger dabbing at the corner of his eye. "And can you see anything else?"

"Yes! There's something written underneath the DynaMed arrow, in little letters. It says, 'A Red Company—Blazing Trails Since 2034.'"

Another cheer went up from the doctors and nurses at Usnavi's exposed head, and this time nobody cut it short.

"That's amazing, Usnavi. Well done!" said the doctor, squeezing the boy's arm in celebration.

Back in *The Grass is Greener* control room, Liam shook his head, marvelling at the simple beauty of the publicity stunt. Usnavi could see the company logo, but no one else could. It was the end of the world of physical AR. From here on in, it would all be about direct stimulation of the relevant brain centres. Talk about advertising: denying the viewers the same view as Usnavi was the best way to make them all desperate for their own implants.

"There's more here, too," said Usnavi, eagerness to please oozing from his tone.

The hand on his arm froze mid-grip. "More? What do you mean, more?"

"There's something else underneath it now. A big box, with lots of letters," answered Usnavi, squinting to read the invisible new signal from the implant.

The boy's handler turned his still chiselled but no longer smiling face to someone behind Usnavi. "What the hell is he talking about?"

Silence reigned for a few tense seconds as someone busied themselves conferring with the monitoring machinery.

"He's right," replied a young and trembling male voice. "There's something else coming in over the implant. Something we didn't put there."

"I think I can read some of it," said Usnavi, who was completely ignored by the assembly.

"Whatever it is, get rid of it," hissed the PR doctor. "It's messing up our event."

"I'm not certain that's wise, sir. Or even possible," replied the technician. "At this stage, with the implant connected, any interference could have serious repercussions, both for the equipment and the host."

"Oh," interrupted Usnavi, with a laugh that brought all attention back onto him. "It's just someone's public network profile. Millie Shardlow," he read. "Works at eyeNet Stream 4 Entertainment News, single, likes Thai food and science fiction comedies, dislikes 'haters,' whatever that means, and—"

"Where the hell is this coming from?" demanded Usnavi's handler, ignoring the boy completely.

Someone whacked a machine out of Usnavi's line of sight. "From somewhere outside of the system, sir. That's all I can tell for sure. There's a lot going on here."

"Ooh, there's something else now," said the boy strapped to the operating table, slurring his words ever so slightly. "It's moving this time—looks like an ad. There's no sound, but I think it's the MediCalc health insurance mascot, Timmy the Turtle. I've always loved that guy."

Looming above Usnavi, the doctor's face had turned a bright, apoplectic red, like an irate harvest moon. "There must be something we can do to stop it!" he spat, gripping one of the technicians by the sleeve.

"Powdered eggs!" Usnavi shouted, saving the tech lady from having to find a response. "Two cartons, twelve per. Satsumas, four large. Cultured yeast, five hundred gram jar," he spouted on, not even stopping for a breath. "Erectile stimulant—Doctor, why can't I stop reading this? Fourteen gels, generic by preference. Help me, doctor! Water filtration tablets, one kilogram box—"

"Do something, damn it!" shouted the PR doctor one last time, before leaning in to loom over Usnavi once again. A bead of sweat dripped down from his now frazzle-haired temple. "And you hang in there now, young man. Do you hear me? We're going to sort this out! Nothing can stop progress!"

"You—" whispered Usnavi. "Y—Y—You..."

He stuttered, then stopped, the words so eager to rush out of his throat they were jamming in his brain.

"Yes?" asked the doctor, leaning in even closer.

"You can finally make your neighbours green with envy," he shouted into the man's startled face, "as you ride to work in style and comfort in the brand new 2073 Lagrange Imperial! Available at employee prices with no money down and easy monthly payments of five hundred eighty-eight credits!"

His voice dropped at the end of this. Then he added, in little more than a whisper once again, "No credit check required."

Back in the control room, Liam sat transfixed, watching the screen. Was this good for their advertisers or not? Was it good for the show? Or, you know, morally decent, he added as an afterthought?

One of the monitors outside of the feed's field of view started bleeping a whole lot faster.

"Shit, we're losing him here!" shouted the female techie. The PR doctor's genial façade crumbled faster than Usnavi's brain cell count.

The sound of journalists dictating article snippets to their AR interfaces drowned out the frantic work of the medical team,and Usnavi's ever-weakening drivel—until the mad bleeping turned into a single, drawn-out, spine-chilling note.

"Shit," repeated the medical technician, no longer having to shout in the hush that fell on the operating theatre.

Usnavi's now redundant handler shook his head and backed away from the boy. "Brain-death recorded at 17:33 hours," he said, the same way a puppy-owner might say, "Oh, another mess on the kitchen floor." He spun on his heel and left Usnavi altogether, marching over toward the crowd of spectators at the back of the room.

That's when Liam realised that, while Usnavi was dead, the feed was still very much live. He, and the millions of viewers around the world, were looking out through the eyes of a dead boy.

Some vestigial shred of decency deep within him sent his hand shooting out toward the big red button in his interface that would kill the feed. But it didn't even make it halfway there before a priority call came in from the Editor.

"Argyle!" he shouted in all his bone-conducted glory straight into Liam's eardrums. "I hope you aren't even considering interrupting this feed!"

"But, sir," protested Liam, before he could stop himself, "Usnavi died! And the feed is still live! This is terrible!"

"This is no time to worry about the PR impact for our biotech sponsors," scolded the Editor, not unkindly, but completely missing the point of Liam's half-hearted protests. "You've got to see the bigger picture. Here, let me send it to you."

Sure enough, a picture file came through, and a speechless Liam displayed it on his AR desktop. It was a close-up screen save of *The Grass is Greener* live viewer count, and not unlike a radiation-belt construction worker's baby, it had at least one or two digits too many.

"You see those numbers?" asked the Editor. "They don't lie. The feed is now the number one trend on social media. People are sharing the link like crazy. They lap up this macabre nonsense."

At the edge of Usnavi's dead gaze, medical staff wearing disappointed frowns started cleaning up the equipment, while the PR doctor was shouting something along the lines of "All right, time to fess up! Who did this?" at the assembled scientific and entertainment journalists.

Liam couldn't find the words to express the conflicting ideas raging through his mind. "But it's just not... I don't know..." He cast about for a term to latch onto. "Decent."

The Editor paused for a full three seconds, before muttering something that sounded like, "I don't have time for this crap." In the background of his audio feed, someone laughed.

"Liam, my boy," returned the Editor's voice at last, cold and calculated. "I thought we were long past this. You need to stop thinking about things in terms of 'decency.'" The sneer on his lips was obvious in his voice as he spoke the word. "Think about what we do in terms of public service, yes?

We bring people a direct glimpse into the lives of those who, for whatever reason, can be seen as less fortunate than themselves. Someone they can look down at, so to speak, providing them with a vital boost to their self-esteem, their mental well-being. Just the thing to help someone who might otherwise feel unsatisfied accept their lot in modern society."

Liam mulled over this novel way of looking at the show, in silence.

Meanwhile, on the still-running feed, the implants behind Usnavi's still and rapidly cooling eyes caught the PR doctor's voice.

"Do you mean to say not a single one of you bothered to read the sign outside the door and turn off broadcasting on your devices before entering the operating theatre?" he yelled.

There was an indignant and in no way repentant collective outburst from the assembled journalists. One voice eventually emerged from the babble as a spokesman for the rest. "Well, yes, we all read it. But we didn't think you were serious," stated the man, as if this should be obvious to anyone with half a brain. "These are the '70s, man. And we're journalists. Why don't you just ask us to rip out our eyeballs and chop off our fingers before entering?"

The doctor grumbled, told the journalists to stay put so he could deliver an official statement from DynaMed, and stomped back over toward Usnavi's strapped-in corpse, where the medical and technical team was still packing away the equipment, whispering amongst themselves, and waiting.

As was the Editor, Liam realised with a shock that brought him out of his feed-induced reverie.

"Yes, I think I see what you mean," he replied, eyes still riveted on the view through young Usnavi's open lids. "If we're helping people around the world feel happier with their own daily lives, then that has to be a worthy endeavour, right, Ed?"

"That's the spirit!" boomed the voice in Liam's inner ear. "And it certainly beats the alternative, which is unemployment, eh, Argyle?" he added, with a half-convincing attempt at a laugh.

Liam gulped. On screen, one of the medical technicians jostled the operating table as they reached for a piece of equipment, and Usnavi's head tilted, his eyes sliding blissfully shut, at long last. "You've got that right," he said.

Though the feed's visual feed was almost completely covered by Usnavi's eyelids, the sound was still coming through loud and clear.

"So what's the official takeaway here?" said the PR doctor, in a tense whisper.

"Well, from a technical standpoint, the operation was still a complete success," answered the female technician from earlier, also whispering. "It's still the first operational human synaptic link in history. Just a little too operational, that's all."

"You know, I think that could work," mused the PR man. "Historic success, dramatic sacrifice, crucial data learned, all that jazz. And crucial changes will be implemented as DynaMed moves on toward full commercial release, of course."

"Yes. A touch less open connectivity, for one."

"Well then, I guess celebration is in order after all," said the PR doctor, no longer feeling the need to whisper. "Pass me that champagne bottle. Here's to success!"

The pop of the cork was deafening over Usnavi's forever blind-eyed feed.

"And scene," said the Editor into Liam's inner ear. He'd forgotten the call was still active. "You can stop the feed now, Liam," he added, and Liam pushed the button before he'd even consciously registered the instruction.

Usnavi's live feed went dark, for the last time.

"Now that's entertainment," the Editor purred. "And I don't think I'm giving too much away when I say we may have a new winner for tomorrow's big finale."

53

The full moon above the special outdoor finale set loomed large and bright, despite the set's bright lights. *Must be something about being up so high in the Andes,* mused Liam. *So much closer to the heavens.*

If only the altitude and Quito valley pollution didn't join forces to wreak havoc on his sinuses, he might actually be enjoying getting out of the Mews for the big finish to *The Grass is Greener's* first season. As it was, he just had to grin, take his place on the set built at the base of the squat Equator Monument tower, read the words in the AR teleprompter, and fake it. For just one more show.

"An overwhelming four-point-six billion have voted in this, the final round of *The Grass is Greener,* Season One." His own voice boomed through the speakers set all around Quito's *Ciudad Mitad del Mundo,* the commercial buildings and the sphere-topped Monument tower brightly lit in the show's floodlights, but dwarfed by the already soaring spire base of the future Quito Space Elevator.

"It's been a wild ride, and we couldn't have done it without you, folks. Thank you all so very much!"

On cue, the live audience of curious Quiteños and visiting GiGalos—as *The Grass is Greener's* ever-growing number of diehard fans called each other—broke into wild cheer. Liam let it play out the pre-defined five seconds, enjoying real, non-canned applause for a change, before signalling for silence with a casual wave of his hand.

"So many votes, and in just a few moments, we'll be ushering your two finalists in for the last, teary goodbyes—and the results we've all been waiting for. But first, I'd like to take the opportunity of this special show, broadcast live across the world from Quito's beautiful Equator Monument, to draw your attention to our magnificent surroundings."

Liam swept his arm upward, guiding the eye past the balled tip of the Equator Monument and all the way up the black, floodlit cathedral lines of the Space Elevator base. High above the upturned heads, little constructor drones were hard at work in the skeletal upper reaches of the spire, pumping out heat-absorbent polymers to build Elevator crawler rails and support beams for the cable itself—whenever it finally got down here from the hollowed-out asteroid that'd serve as ball at the end of the nanocarbon assembly chain.

"Take a moment to appreciate the sight, everyone. Really let it sink in. because what you're seeing here tonight is the Future. And I know that sounds cheesy," Liam added, wishing the bosses hadn't forced him to go through with the PR spiel—it was part of the deal with the other Corporations partnered in the Elevator Initiative so they could get permission to use the site for the finale, apparently. "But I really mean it. Once the Elevator is in place, it'll be cheaper and safer to get cargo and people up and down from space than it is to cross an ocean today. The next great step in humankind's expansion out into the Cosmos. Hell, maybe someday soon, everyone will be able to have their own private Paradise Mars, and we'll have to find another prize for the show!"

Once again on perfect, docile cue, the crowd laughed at his feeble attempt at humour. Liam didn't know if it were possible to loathe himself any more than he did at that instant—but he grit his teeth, smiled, and resigned himself to find out.

"What I know for sure is that, between the Elevator work and the tourism boom, business in Quito has never been better—isn't that right, Quiteños?"

This time, a weirdly tame roar of local pride met his scripted call, all according to plan.

"I'd like to thank you fine folk of Quito for welcoming us here tonight for this very special show. And for making it possible, too, by letting us use your fine Space Launch Tube to send your chosen winner on their way to their reward in Paradise Mars."

In perfect timing, a capsule finished its constant 1G acceleration through the maglev tube network woven around the Andes valleys and up to the launch point at the end of the half-built Space Elevator base tower, kilometres above. There was a dramatic flash of light as the air ignited under the capsule's escape velocity speed, quickly quashed as the smart materials absorbed and harnessed the energy to feed the onboard systems on their way to rendezvous with the interplanetary laser thrust railway.

Back down on Earth, Liam crossed the stage in pre-calculated steps and stopped before a swanky, gold-accented, advertisement-filled train terminal. A shiny green pill-shaped capsule bearing *The Grass is Greener* logo lay waiting, snug in the groove of the maglev track.

"A lot of viewers out there may never have even seen a picture of a Space Launch Tube station before, and that makes me sad. So, before we get started, I wanted to give you all a little glimpse at what humanity can achieve when we all band together and work as one united planet.

"Sure, a Launch Tube like this is expensive to run, and very few people can afford to use it today," he added, trading his manic host's smile for a solemn look. "But soon, with the Elevator, everyone will be able to get to Space if they want to. I call that real progress!"

Liam grinned his false grin again and walked forward toward the audience. "And until that happy day, *The Grass is Greener* is here to make Space dreams come true! So, without further ado, please give a warm round of applause for your 2072 *Grass is Greener* grand finalists!"

As the deep bass fanfare of the show's theme song blared from every speaker, and in the ears of viewers around the globe, the two final contestants were ushered onto the stage—so to speak. No-Longer-Suicide Jill entered on her own two legs, scowling like never before, while on the other side of the stage the show's ever-exploitable temp service worker Mary carried in a little urn, a tasteful black lacquered affair with gold highlights. Liam suspected the urn had cost the show more than the boy whose incinerated remains rested inside had earned in a year.

Above their heads, free-floating AR windows played each finalist's highlight reel—Jill's live suicide clean-up escapades, leading up to and including her last misadventure, on the left; Usnavi's smiling face and willing participation in his medical experiments, on the right. The latter finished off with pictures of spontaneous vigils organised by GiGalos around the world in the last twenty-four hours, since his death live on feed.

Liam tried to ignore it all and focus on what he was supposed to say next, once both contestants were, each in their own way, safely ensconced in their seats. Mary shrank into the background, ignored by all.

"It's been a long road, folks, and again, if we're here tonight, it's only thanks to you faithful viewers and voters back home. So let's hear a big round of applause for you guys!"

The audience broke into applause even more energetic than before, and Liam could only assume the cheers were echoed by viewers around the world. A planet united in obliviousness to how ridiculous it is to applaud yourself.

Next to him on stage, Usnavi's urn gleamed in the spotlight, and Jill hung her head.

"There's someone else I want to thank before we close the voting and check the final tally—so get those last-minute votes in, folks!" smarmed Liam, hating every second of it. "While you do, I'd like to take a moment to remember the contestants who weren't quite so bad off as our finalists, but who were brave enough to open their lives up to the world and help make the show the amazing phenomenon it has become. Let's hear it for the grateful eliminated!"

A spattering of applause greeted the new AR display that opened up at Liam's words, and all eyes watched the last highlight reel of the night, a hodgepodge of sepia-toned moments ranging from Professor Ali Fourka's brief tenure on the show to Spike Bighorn's robopornographic sexcapades, from Brad Leigh's heavy-handed public service to Juliette Binns's fearful submission to the live ocular implant operation.

Liam watched along with everyone else, not even turning away when Azar Acquah's haunting face smiled at him from the screen. Yet he seethed in silence. Why wouldn't the Editor even listen to his idea of getting live commentary, or at least fresh footage, from the eliminated contestants? Granted, when you started making a list, you soon realised how few contestants were physically able to make a recording for the finale. But even without intruding on Juliette's VR therapy again, they could have tracked down Professor Fourka, wherever he was now. And surely Spike Bighorn must have recovered enough to make a recording by now. The fans would have loved that.

But the Editor had been firm. A brief "best of" montage and then straight on to the final sequence. Who was Liam to argue? And what did it matter, anyway. The sooner he got on with this, the sooner it would be finished, and he could go hide in his trailer, where a non-judgmental and non-demanding one-litre bottle of aguardiente waited for him on chill.

"Wow, that sure takes me back," he resumed, as the reel finished and the teleprompter in his retina started scrolling again. "The votes are still coming in, so we'll leave them open just a few moments longer. Just long enough to hear from Jill."

Liam strode over to where the now-unemployed finalist formerly known as Suicide Jill sat glowering at him, daring him to ask her anything. But the teleprompter wouldn't have it any other way, so Liam gulped and soldiered on.

"So, my dear," he said, despite the evidence of his eyes, "how does it feel to have made it all the way to the grand finale?"

"Well, if you really need to know, it feels fucking ridiculous, Liam."

Liam laughed, a touch nervously to his own ears. "I suppose so, if you mean how ridiculously amazing the possibility of a lifetime of luxury on Paradise Mars is, and so close to hand, right, Jill?"

Jill's only response was to rise to her feet, barge past Liam with a sad shake of her head, and walk over to speak directly to the assembled spectators.

"How can you lot stand there and cheer on this nonsense?" she shouted, squinting into the floodlight glare, trying to make out the people in the crowd. "This show is a monster! It takes people, spreads their lives wide open, grinds them into nothing, and then spits out whatever is left. And you people, all you people watching, are what powers it. It's a consumer product, and your brains are the commodity it's selling!"

This wasn't quite on script, and Liam stood smiling and paralysed. Maybe the Editor had a point about avoiding live input you couldn't control.

As if summoned by the very thought, a priority text message from the Editor appeared in Liam's display. *Well played from Jill, but that's enough. Get her back in her seat.*

Easier said than done. She was in full tilt now, and even if Liam could somehow strongarm the woman back into her seat—which he doubted—he couldn't very well do it live in front of billions of viewers. He cast about for some solution to the problem and, seizing the first idea to come to mind, strode forward to stand beside Jill, cutting into her rant.

"That's the Jill we know and love. Strong and frank-spoken as ever. And the viewers can't get enough of it. The live comments keep pouring in. Let's have a look!"

Liam waved his hand, and a new AR window appeared in mid-air, with a streaming flow of live comments from viewers.

lul who does she think she is?
someone forgot their pill
salty

There was just enough time for Jill to get the gist of the viewers' reactions before the chat delay caught up with the live show and ruined the effect.

we're on the show!

hi Mom!

Best show evar!

Jill stared at the cascade of words, at a loss for any of her own.

"Is this really what you all think?" she finally said, in tones lower than her chances of winning the show, now that the Editor had decided otherwise. "Is this all just fun and games for you?"

The crowd responded with spattered applause, which turned into full-out cheering and hooting when Liam stepped forward and cocked an ear, urging them on. Jill's tense, confrontational stance melted as the seconds went on and the cheering showed no sign of dying down.

"Wow, you guys are amazing," said Liam, eventually, and it was only then the crowd stopped cheering. "And I've just had word that voting is now officially closed! We should have the results any second now, folks, so don't leave your seats!"

He ushered the unresisting and downcast Jill back into her own chair on stage and took his designated position in the very centre. A gleaming new window appeared above his head—the largest one yet—with both Jill and Usnavi's names appearing in sparkling green letters.

"The time is finally here!" he announced, voice echoing between the Andes peaks. "After months of hopes and fears, of smiles and tears, it's all come down to this one vote. Who has it the worst? Who deserves the ticket to Paradise Mars the most? It's time to find out—right after this brief word from our sponsors. Don't go anywhere!"

54

Standing, eyes shut, in the floodlights while the precious seconds of the commercial break wasted away, Liam didn't know which was more depressing: the votes coming in or the comments on the show's live chat from the voters.

Not that he was surprised at the final tally displayed against the canvas of his shut eyelids. After the... incident with Usnavi's operation, the Editor had all but decreed that the boy would be the winner. And Liam knew the man would always end up right, one way or the other.

No—what depressed him was his growing suspicion that Ed didn't even need to doctor the results this time around. Surely the man couldn't have faked the messages scrolling down the live chat window. Not all of them, at least.

Vote 2 to pay respects to Usnavi!

RIP little man! Now you can live forever among the stars!

Usnavi wins or riot!

One million votes after the next, the tally overwhelmingly declared Usnavi the winner, the worst off of all the victims of modern life and the most deserving of the one-way trip to Paradise Mars.

The prize was supposed to involve a lifetime of luxury at the end of the trip, but in Usnavi's case… Well, at least there wasn't any doubt about the Editor's motivation in pushing Usnavi to win.

"One minute to air," bellowed Ms. Lee's voice from somewhere beyond the comforting veil of Liam's shut eyelids.

He chuckled to himself. He'd spent the first forty-odd years of his life cursing how long advertisements lasted. Now that he was on the other side of the screen, they never lasted long enough.

Time to face the music. Announce that the collective wisdom of the human race has decided to send an urn full of ashes to Mars instead of a living person. The ashes of a poor neglected boy murdered in the name of science.

No, Liam told himself. This was no time for half-truths. Science had nothing to do with it.

Usnavi was murdered in the name of entertainment.

And here were the viewers, the ones his brain got fried for, acting like they were doing the boy some sort of favour by giving him the win. As if it'd make any difference to him now. Or to Azar. Or Juliette Binns, for that matter. After all, what was left of her in that chemical and virtual haze could hardly be called living.

"Thirty seconds!" Carpentiere shouted in a low rumble.

There was no escaping it. The second Liam declared Usnavi the winner, it would all be done and dusted. He would have added his rubber stamp to everything RedCorp had done to demolish the lives of these people. What he himself had done to these people. His people.

Eyes downcast, he stumbled out of the spotlight and off to the side of the stage. He made it right to the edge of the set before anybody took any notice of him.

"Liam, my boy," said the Editor, grabbing Liam by the arm. "Here, I think this is what you're looking for." Liam looked up, taking in the stiff drink in the shorter man's free hand, and the even stiffer smile on his hairless face.

A peace offering, unquestionably, but held in a hand of steel. The Editor saw right through Liam. There would be no smiles whatsoever if he gave into his doubts and didn't go back up there to do his job. The moment of truth.

There was the slightest of pauses. A lump caught in Liam's throat, stealing his voice. Then he swallowed it down and drew in a deep breath.

Fuck it all. What difference would it make, anyway? Would any grand gesture from him make Usnavi or Azar any less dead? Spike or Juliette any less messed up? It wasn't as if one man could make any sort of difference.

Filled with new resolve, Liam nodded in silent thanks to the Editor, took the offered glass, belted it down without even wasting time on figuring out what it was, and trotted back into position at the centre of the set. Without a second to spare.

"The people have spoken!" he shouted, with a glee that no longer felt difficult to fake. "We have a winner!"

Under Jill's sulking stare, he stepped over to Usnavi's chair, grabbed the little urn in both hands, and lifted it high above his head.

"I give you your grand prize winner, your choice by a landslide — Usnavi Musibay!"

Liam paused for applause. The clapping and hooting from the crowd cheered him up to no end. He marvelled at how beautiful the urn above his head looked, its gold accents glinting in the spotlights.

The show's upbeat theme song started playing, and Liam stuck to the game plan. He stepped over, smiling, to wrap an arm around a shrunken, disabused Jill. With the urn still under his other arm, he hugged both finalists for one last, photogenic, front-page-worthy shot. Then he rushed over to the waiting shuttle, trying not to stumble at the edge of the set and scatter grand winner ashes all over the rubbery launch station floor.

"Come on, everyone," he shouted, and waved in mock spontaneity, the second he reached the open door of the maglev shuttle. The barriers holding back the spectators flipped down, just like the script said they would, and the crowd surged forward, carrying Carpentiere, Lee, and the set's mobile podcameras along with them.

Hands, faces, and squashed bodies crowded against the shuttle's transparent shielding, with everyone desperate to get their own touch of the moment before the shuttle and Usnavi went on their way down the tube, up the launch plume, and off to Mars.

Ignoring the somewhat nightmarish sight and smiling for the cameras inside the shuttle itself, Liam carefully placed the no-longer-glimmering urn in the lone plush green seat and strapped it in snug, thanks to the convenient, urn-sized straps someone had thoughtfully planned for.

"Thank you, young man," he said, just low enough for the viewers to get a sense of privacy and intimacy. "And congratulations. Couldn't have happened to a better person."

His hostly duty dispensed with, he backed out of the shuttle and turned back toward the crowd. Behind him, there was a *whir* of alarm, and the door began to slide shut with carefully programmed and dramatic slowness.

Liam waved his arms, shooing the crowd away from the shuttle. "Back up, folks! Back up! It's preparing to launch!"

The door finally sealed shut with a hiss, and the deep bone throb of the maglev track powering up produced the effect Liam's warnings alone could not. The crowd backed away, and it was with mixed cheers and sobs that all assembled watched the little craft slide onto the maglev track and float into launch position. With a high-tension crackle, it set into motion and was soon speeding down the station track, before being swallowed by the tube, on its way to frictionless acceleration and launch into space.

That, of course, wouldn't be for another hour or so, after it had gained enough acceleration zipping through the warren of tubes dug through the local mountains and valleys. Some of the spectators might stick around to watch Usnavi's little departing flare, but Liam sure as hell wasn't going to. He had no time for that, and neither did the crew. There was work to do to tidy up the set. And as for Liam, he had a celebrity after-party to attend in downtown Quito.

He was surprisingly at peace with the outcome of the show. This was good. Everything about the finale and Usnavi's big send-off felt, somehow, pretty great. He really wished someone had told him sooner about how much simpler all your problems became when you just gave up, put your trials and tribulations into their proper perspective, and stopped taking everything so personally. If he'd known, he would have stopped giving a crap years ago.

"A huge thanks once again to all you folks back home for setting Usnavi on his journey to Paradise Mars," he shouted over the hoots and roars of a crowd eager to have their animal grunts heard around the world. "And thank you for accompanying us on our journey, the first of many, to find where—" he paused for effect one last time— "the grass is greener! See you soon for Season Two, everybody!"

EPILOGUE

The men and women in the designer casual suits lounged in their easy chairs and gazed through the low-G club's extravagantly large viewing port. Watching the local photonic thrust relay tease the latest shuttle into docking position at Paradise Mars always drew a few spectators. It was a reliable way to kill an idle afternoon cycle.

But this shuttle contained neither crates full of luxury goods from Old Smoggy nor queasy-looking fresh arrivals to size up before anyone else could get their hands on them.

"What's this about, then?" said one silicone-faced man to the grand dame sitting across the aisle from him. "Are we taking on genies now?"

The lady shook her head and smiled, quickly dismissing the search window she'd pulled up to find the answer to the question. "Don't be silly. It's just the shuttle from that show. You know, the one with the low-class people and the man with the ears. They found a way to give the grand prize to a dead person and avoid having to send anyone here at all, dontchaknow?"

"Well, it's a handsome enough urn, I suppose," grunted the first speaker, a man of keen aesthetic sensibilities.

The lady reached over to rest a hand on his arm as they watched the robot workers empty out the shuttle, urn and all. "Oh, isn't it just? I think it will look marvellous on the lounge mantelpiece. A real conversation piece."

Liam Argyle is back!

THE RUDE EYE OF REBELLION

Book Two of The General Buzz

NOW AVAILABLE
IN EBOOK & PHYSICAL MEDIA

CORPORATE INVASION

TERESITA E. DZIADURA

CHAPTER ONE

A stillness had enveloped Boston in these early hours as Jason made his way to the bus stop. Heavy, rain-filled clouds hung low, muting the sounds of the people just starting their day.

Once it had been a pleasant walk with a cool spring breeze, the city stirring to life, and the birds singing in the trees. Now, no birdsong greeted him while he ran beneath the green canopy. They were all hiding from the incessant rain. Everything felt heavy and oppressive as he darted into the protection of the shelter.

"Frigging soaked again," Jason thought as he huddled in the corner, shaking the water from his arms and trying to avoid the ever-growing puddle. It had been a full week of steady thundershowers and he hadn't seen the sun in weeks. It felt as if day had turned into night. Streetlights stayed on during the day, briefly dimming each time lightening arched across the sky.

In addition to the unceasing rain, it was hot like July in Louisiana than April in Massachusetts. The temperatures had started creeping up since the first of the month. The unseasonal weather was so humid that some of the runners had gotten sick and passed out during the already gruelling Boston Marathon. One guy had died of heat stroke.

On the news the night before, Jason had watched as meteorologists expressed their bafflement by the never-ending rain and heat that seemed to be focused solely on the Boston area. The clouds seemed to be hovering over the city in defiance of jet stream and other weather patterns.

It wasn't even 7 am and it was already in the nineties. Boston had become a sauna that was threatening to become a swamp. There were announcements for rivers that were inching towards overflowing their banks and sandbags were being offered for areas that were at risk for flooding.

Jason glared at the puddle as it made its approach. The puddle grew bigger with each raindrop that fell until it had him cornered in the dilapidated bus shelter which always smelled faintly of old pee. With the heat and dampness, it had begun to smell more like standing inside a urinal and the stench made him gag. His attention wavered as he heard the low drone of his bus speeding down the street. He watched it approach, late as usual, pass his stop and keep on going. He leapt the puddle and almost cleared it. Tepid water splashed up around his legs and soaked his Converse shoes as he ran through the downpour yelling and waving, hoping the driver saw him. With a screech of hydraulic brakes, the bus stopped and the doors opened, but not before Jason was dripping wet. He jumped on, swiped his bus pass and nodded to Ralph, the regular driver, as he headed to the back.

"Gonna be another great day," Jason grumbled to himself as he folded his lanky body into one of the seats. He poked his earbuds into his ears, cranked up his music, laid his backpack on his lap, and closed his eyes as pools of water formed at his feet. His dark auburn hair hung limp over his face. Jason's normal complexion was pale but today he was flushed with his short run in the heat, and it made the light freckles on his face stand out.

"What utter shit this is."

"You got that right, mac," a raspy voice said.

Jason opened his eyes to see an odd-looking man staring back at him. Greying black hair in a tangle of unkempt dreads, over a round weathered face. Cool grey eyes peered out from below a pair of bushy eyebrows. A long scraggly beard covered a tie-dyed shirt stained with who knows what, which was tucked into a pair of well-worn camo pants. A backpack sat on the seat next to the man.

"Beg your pardon?" Jason inquired, pulling the earbuds out.

"I concur with your assessment that this is utter shit."

"I'm sorry, I didn't realize I'd said that out loud."

"It *is* a Monday after all." The man smiled, showing off teeth that would give an orthodontist nightmares. "What's got a young fella like yourself in such a slump?"

Jason swallowed hard and tried not to stare. It was a well-known, unspoken rule of those who ride the bus: don't talk to strangers. You keep to yourself, hunker down and hope to go unnoticed. Jason had broken that rule, twice now, and he was trapped. "Ummm..."

The older man just sat there, looking at Jason. Waiting for a reply.

"I don't like to complain..." Jason continued. "But...do you catch this bus very often?"

"I'm on it with you nearly every morning."

"Oh. Sorry. I never noticed."

The man just laughed. "No offence taken. You fly onto the bus, listening to your music, and hop off in the warehouse district."

Jason felt a little creeped out by this but nodded. "Yeah, that's my morning routine. But doesn't it piss you off how it's always late?"

"I suppose it might if I had someplace to be to. I don't."

"Oh," Jason said.

The man shrugged. "It's better than sittin' out in the rain all day."

"Why'd you do tha—" Jason cut himself off as he looked from the back-pack to the man and back again.

"Yes sir, hobo extraordinaire," the man said with a nod and a smile. "Name's Frank, by the way."

"Jason. Pleased to meet you."

"Likewise, but you haven't told me why this Monday is so shitty. Ralph's always late. That's nothin' new."

"Keep it up, Frank, and you can go back to walkin'," Ralph called out.

"I'm sorry, Ralph. I'm the one complaining," Jason rushed to his new friend's defence.

"Don't worry, Ralph's not gonna kick me off. No one else will talk to him so he's stuck with me."

Ralph's reply was a simple disgruntled snort.

"So, other than Ralph's lack of punctuality, what's got you down?"

He looked at Frank, homeless but still upbeat and happy. Jason had been so upset over things like missing breakfast and sleeping in; when comparing his lot with that of Frank's, he felt silly.

He smiled and said, "You know what? Not as much as I thought."

"That's a good outlook to have, young fella."

Jason kept his fears of losing his job to himself. A frown slipped over his face as he thought of having to face his weasel of a boss. He'd already been warned twice. He'd been made well aware that management didn't give a damn about Jason's *excuses* regarding his transportation woes. Last time he was written up he'd been told, "That sounds like a you problem. If you need to, catch an earlier bus." Which would be perfect except this was the earliest bus.

How'd he ever gotten to this point? Frank stood and moved up to a seat near Ralph as Jason fell silent and adopted a far-away look.

It was heading towards midnight on a Friday. The bar where Jason worked was crowded with all the regulars; an interesting mix of leather-clad middle-aged bikers and leopard-print-wearing cougars. Tonight, there were a couple of new bodies that had shown up. They didn't seem to mind that the place smelled of stale beer and reeked of loneliness.

Jason looked around at his handiwork. He'd spent all afternoon preparing for tomorrow night's Fourth of July party and barbeque. Banners hung from the ceiling, a large flag decorated one wall, and the candles cast little star patterns onto the tables from the red, white, and blue holders.

"It's gonna have to do," he said with a shrug. He just hoped they lasted out the

night.

Jason began humming along to Willie Nelson's "Help Me Make It Through the Night" playing on the jukebox as he turned back to cleaning glasses and topping off the bowls of nuts.

"That's my theme song," Jason thought.

He was dead tired. He hadn't slept in over twenty-four hours after working the night before, classes all afternoon and then back to work tonight. He gave the bottles of whiskey that lined the shelves a quick wistful look. All he wanted to do was lay down in bed with a drink, some take-out, and Netflix for just one night. "After finals," he kept promising himself.

"Help Me Make It Through the Night" had finished and "Blue Eyes Crying in the Rain" came on.

"Jesus, Duke? Don't you listen to anyone but Willie?" Jason didn't hate country, but he was to the point that he probably knew more of the words to Willie's, Waylon's, and Johnny's songs than they did.

"Ain't nobody but Willie," Duke said as he racked up another set on the pool table for him and his husband, Bear. Duke and Bear were a couple of regulars and the unofficial bouncers for Wanderer's Roadhouse. They were big men with long shaggy beards, and they lived in leather and denim. They were the owner's best friends and Jason had standing orders that the couple could drink and eat for free, but they never did.

Jason started singing along with Willie, "In the twilight glow I see her, blue eyes cryin' in the rain. When we kissed goodbye and parted, I knew we'd never meet again."

As he sang, he moved to the far end near a small sink and counter to cut up limes. The pair he called the Tequila Sisters had arrived and they'd soon be looking for their line-up of shots. He had his back to the crowd but with Duke and Bear on guard he had no concerns.

He didn't even so much as look up when he heard the door open, not until all the normal sounds of clinking pool balls and chatter stopped. "What the fuck?" he thought as he looked in the cracked mirror that was behind the bar but gave a full view of the floor.

Jason's mouth went dry and everything went sideways. She was the most beautiful woman he'd ever seen. Every eye in the place turned to follow her as she made her way to near where Jason worked and slipped onto a stool. It wasn't just her looks; it was her presence. Jason figured she couldn't be more than five feet tall, but she carried herself like a six-foot queen. She owned the space she occupied.

More than one biker licked his lips as he stared at her. She was either a master at ignoring the unwanted attention or was oblivious to the leering she'd garnered from the patrons. A starving man wouldn't have looked at a steak as hungrily as these guys were looking at her. Even Duke and Bear were staring.

Jason dropped his paring knife into the sink and turned to serve her, hoping he wasn't gawping when she leaned against the bar. His mouth went dry when he tried to speak.

"Hey," Jason said.

She looked up at him inquiringly. Her bright blue eyes made his heart skip a beat, but he hid his interest behind his bartender persona. "What can I getcha?"

"Whiskey, neat. Please."

"Any particular one?"

"Whatever your top shelf is."

Jason laughed. "Here, that would be Jim Beam."

Her nose scrunched with distaste.

"Hmm. Bourbon." She hesitated. "Any Scotch?"

Jason shook his head. "No ma'am. Just straight American bourbon."

"That will be fine but add a little ice to it," she said with a sigh.

"You got it."

A small smile pulled at the corners of her mouth as she accepted the drink. "Thanks."

Jason stood there, feeling awkward, as she looked down in to the amber liquid, swirling it in her glass. Small waves of the bourbon splashed over the ice. She took a sip and closed her eyes, savouring it. "Not too bad," Jason heard her whisper to the glass.

He gave himself a shake and stepped to the side a little and picked up one of the glasses to give it a polish. He was still close enough for conversation if she wanted to talk but far enough to not be creepy. While he worked, he continued watching her from the corner of his eye. The soft lights cast her face in a gentle shadow. She was far out of the league of every guy and girl in this bar, himself included.

Jason desperately wanted to talk to her and hoped she would start a conversation. She looked like she was worried about something and his job was ten percent tending bar and ninety percent therapist, but she remained silent. It wasn't normal for him to feel this awkward around women, but the words didn't want to come. He just stood there, polishing that same glass over and over. He was so focused on her that he hadn't even noticed the background noise returning or the jukebox switching to ZZ Top's "Legs."

"Jase," a biker sporting a thick black beard yelled from the other end, making Jason almost drop the glass. "Stop staring at her tits and give me a god damned beer."

Everyone laughed and Jason flushed bright pink as the woman looked up at him, raising her perfectly sculpted eyebrow. Looking back and forth between the biker and the woman, he stammered, "I wasn't... I mean I'd never... I mean... Oh fuck it." Angrily he poured a beer and shoved the glass at the laughing biker. Beer slopped over the rim and the biker tossed a five-dollar bill at Jason.

"Fuck off, Jack," Jason said as he grabbed the rag and started scrubbing the bar top, focusing on anything except for her.

Jack laughed all the harder as he re-joined his friends.

His humiliation complete, Jason prayed she'd just leave. He didn't see the small smile crease the corners of her lips as she began to watch him.

***

"Another whiskey. Please?" said a soft melodic voice.

Jason had been scrubbing the same spot on the opposite end of the bar from her and hadn't noticed her moving. His heart stopped. It was her. His face flushed all over again.

"Sure."

He poured the drink and served it without once making eye contact. As he placed the fresh glass in front of her she said, "My name's Amanda."

"Jason." His voice cracked and it came out more of a croak.

She grinned and his face turned pink for the third time that night, but as their eyes met, time stood still.

"Hey baby," a rough voice broke the connection and the two of them looked away, embarrassed.

Amanda turned and found a middle-aged man sitting next to her. He was an unfortunate looking thing with mousy brown hair that was thinning on top and just a little grey at the temples. His gaunt face was sallow and sported two days worth of stubble. He was wearing a rumpled dress shirt with his beginner's beer gut hanging over the tops of his jeans. As he talked, he twisted his wedding ring around on his finger.

"Can I help you?" Amanda asked.

"My name is Colin. I'm one of Jase's regulars and I just wanted to ask you a question. Do you drink milk?"

Amanda looked at Jason, who was glaring at the man.

"Yeah, I know you. If it were up to me, you'd never set foot in this place again." Jason thought as he recognized the guy and had no use for him. Colin was married. He was a complete a leech who had trouble understanding the word no from the women he hit on every night.

"Does your wife know you're here?" Jason asked.

Colin glared at Jason. "Angie is staying with her mother. Now fuck off and leave me and this lovely lady to talk."

Colin looked Amanda up and down, stopping to stare down her blouse.

He didn't seem to understand personal space, but Amanda was not easily intimidated.

"To answer your question, no, I don't drink milk. Why would you ask a complete stranger such an odd question?"

Colin frowned. "You were supposed to say 'yes.'"

"Why? I don't like milk."

"Because then I'd say, 'Because it sure did your body good.'"

"Oh." Amanda paused with her head tipped to one side. She was looking at Colin with a perplexed expression. "What a bizarre thing to say."

Amanda spun her stool, turning her back to Colin and facing the bar top once again. She had just picked up her drink when a hand grabbed her wrist, making her drop her glass. It smashed on the floor beneath her feet. Scowling, she looked from the glass to the hand that was still holding her arm and up into the man's face.

"Let go of me."

"I just wanted to talk to you."

"I do not want to talk to you. You are weird and old." Amanda sniffed and wrinkled her nose in disgust. "And you smell like a dead skunk."

"You bitch," Colin snarled, his face screwing up in anger. Amanda's hands were in white-knuckled fists as she faced Colin, chin up and unafraid.

Colin stared at her in shock.

"I said, let go of my wrist," she said coldly.

Colin's bluster faded quickly, and his hand slipped from her wrist.

Jason moved to stand between Amanda and Colin, forcing the other man to step back. "Colin, I think it's time you went home."

"You can't tell me what to do."

"I can and I am. You're cut off. Now go home."

Duke and Bear had appeared beside.

Jason. Duke reached for Colin while Bear stood there with his arms crossed over his chest.

"Jason's right. You've had more than enough to drink tonight," Duke said, taking him by the back of the shirt, all but lifting him from the ground. His feet tapped the ground as he tried to stand on his own as Duke escorted him to the doors.

"We'll have a chat with the owner about your continued patronage," Bear said as they chucked the man out the door and tossed his jacket and briefcase behind him.

Duke snorted disgustedly.

"Accountants."

"Sorry about that," Jason said as he started cleaning up the broken glass.

"It's not your fault. I'm learning it comes with the territory of being female."

There was silence while he finished sweeping and mopping. He stepped behind the bar and said: "I'll get you a fresh bourbon. A double, on the house."

"Thanks." Amanda accepted the drink and took a sip. "What time are you off?"

"Huh?" Jason was caught completely off guard.

She smiled even wider. "What time do you finish work?"

"Umm, when we close. Two am."

"I think I'll hang around until then. If that's okay with you?"

"Sure?" he said.

"Thanks. We can grab a coffee and maybe a bite to eat once you're done."

Jason was flummoxed. "Kay," was all he said.

She didn't say another word to him until Jason announced last call and Jack yelled back, "Hurry up, boys, and drink 'em down. Jase wants to get laid tonight."

Jason flushed again while Amanda looked confused. Their reactions made the crowd laugh all the harder.

CHAPTER TWO

Dinner ended up being burgers and fries from Del's Diner, a twenty-four-hour greasy spoon not far from Jason's apartment. It was small, and while it wasn't in an old rail car, the diner looked like it had stepped straight out of a 1950's sitcom, long and narrow with booths along one window-lined wall, complete with black and white tiled floor. Worn dark blue vinyl bench seats paired with tables made of faded blue linoleum and trimmed with polished chrome sat across from a bar lined with stools. "Love Me Tender" played on the speakers. It always smelled of fresh coffee and pie and other baked goods that were proudly displayed in cases along the bar.

Jason held the door for Amanda and as he stepped inside, he took a deep breath and sighed. Coming here after work always made him relax.

It was one of his favourite places in Boston. It felt like home, cozy and warm.

"Hey, Jase," the waitress called when he appeared from behind Amanda. "Who's yer friend?"

"Oh hey, Marge. This is Amanda."

"Well, welcome to Del's. Finest pie in Boston."

Amanda smiled and inhaled deeply. "I believe that."

"You a friend of Jason?" Marge said with a grin and a wink.

Amanda smiled back, "A friend. Hopefully." Her eyes flicked briefly towards Jason as she spoke and while Jason was oblivious, Marge didn't miss the look.

"Ahhh," was all she said with a nod as she led them to Jason's regular corner booth by the big picture windows, where he could sit and watch the world outside while he ate, next to the ancient jukebox. With practised efficiency she set the faded blue linoleum table, placing paper placemats in front of them and giving each a set of cutlery. She finished off by placing a plastic covered menu before Amanda, stood up, smoothed her apron and said, "What can I get you folks?"

Amanda looked puzzled. "Doesn't Jason get a menu?"

Marge laughed, "Oh honey, he knows our menu better than I do." She turned to Jason and continued, "Your usual?"

"Sure thing," Jason smiled and looked at Marge.

"What's his usual?"

"That would be the house special. It's a classic bacon cheeseburger platter, a cola and a piece of cherry pie."

"That sounds great. I'll have one, too."

"Gotta warn yah, it's got chipotle mayo that the cook makes here. It's got some kick."

"I'm okay with kick."

"What do you want to drink?"

"Root beer, please."

"Perfect." Marge turned away and called out "Del? Burn two for the special and a couple of frog sticks."

Amanda gave Marge a concerned look as the waitress walked to the soda fountain and poured their drinks. "That isn't what we ordered."

Jason laughed. "It's diner lingo. It means burger and fries."

"Diner lingo?"

"Yeah. Diners have their own lingo.
You've had to have heard it before."

Amanda looked at him blankly and shook her head.

"How haven't you heard of it?" Jason laughed. "It's like verbal shorthand. So, if someone orders two poached eggs on toast, you'd hear the cook call it Adam and Eve on a raft."

"Strange. Why do they do that?"

"Dunno. Seems like it's always been that way."

Amanda looked at Del's burly figure as he bustled about the kitchen, putting everything together. "So, making up names for things with names already is a diner thing?"

"I think it's just a thing people do." Jason chuckled, "Where are you from that you've never heard it?"

"Ahhh. I'm…" she hesitated. "I'm from Canada."

"They have diners in Canada. I've been to Halifax, Toronto, and a few other places. They all had diners."

"I'm sure not all towns have diners." Amanda fidgeted. "I'm from a very small town. Not many places to eat out."

"That's too bad. I mean about the not eating out much, not the living in Canada." Jason laughed awkwardly. "Diners have some of the best food."

"Why thank you, darlin'," Marge interrupted as she placed their drinks before them, two iced tumblers covered in condensation.

Jason took a sip and shivered from the chill.

"Thanks, Marge."

"You're welcome. Food will be up soon." She turned and headed back behind the counter.

"Well, I guess I'll find out soon just how good your diner food is." Amanda inhaled deeply. "I don't usually eat meat but that smells really good."

"No meat? If you'd said, they could have gotten you a veggie burger. They have them."

"No. It's okay. I used to be a vegan, but some things in my life changed."

"Nothing bad I hope?" Jason looked concerned.

"No. Just some changes that caused me to re-evaluate my nutrition." Amanda shrugged.

"Cool. As long as you're happy."

She nodded and they lapsed into first date awkward silence. Jason stared out the window, watching the occasional car go by while Amanda swirled the straw around in her drink. After a few minutes of staring at the paper placemats in front of them, Jason broke the silence. "Soooo..." Jason began, "you're Canadian?"

Amanda was startled. She'd been lost in her own thoughts. "No. I'm American."

"You said you were from Canada." Jason looked confused.

"What?" Amanda looked perplexed before responding, "Oh, right. Yes, I'm sorry. I was born in Canada, but my family moved here when I was a teen. I'm an American citizen."

"Okay. Gotcha. Canada's cool. Like I said, I've been there a few times. You said you were from up north. Where up north?"

"You'll not have heard the name. We don't even have a dot on Google maps."

"Damn, that is remote. What had you guys living in such an isolated area?"

"My Dad's a researcher." Amanda didn't look at Jason as she spoke. She stared at the paper placement and spun her fork in circles.

"Your Mom?"

"She's an artist. She loved working with the local Indigenous artists."

"What did you do?" The conversation was interrupted when Marge showed up and placed the food in front of them. Amanda took this chance to change the topic.

"Thank you." She looked up at Marge and smiled, "This smell so good."

"You're welcome, sweetie."

"Thanks Marge. Thank Del for us, too."

"Will do," she said as she walked away.

Amanda took a bite of the burger and grinned, "So gwood."

Jason nodded and smiled back.

For a while they didn't talk much, just focused on their food. Jason was starved from working all night and wolfed his burger down.

Amanda matched him bite for bite.

"So, I've told you a little about me. Your turn."

"Not much to tell really. I'm from Boston. My folks live just outside of town. I live nearby in a crappy little apartment in Mission Hill. I go to MIT and I work where you met me."

"MIT huh?"

"Yeah."

"What are you studying?"

"I'm doing a computers program. You?"

"Biology. Genetics. I'm working on my masters."

"Wow. You've got your BSc already. That's impressive." Jason laughed self-deprecatingly. "I feel like a slacker."

Amanda smiled at him, her eyes sparkled, and Jason's heart skipped a beat. "Don't. I was lucky."

"More smarts than luck."

"That is luck. I did nothing exceptional to deserve intelligence. I was born like it; to me, that's luck."

"Okay, that's fair. You won the genetic lottery. But you made the most of it. Not everyone does that."

Amanda just shrugged.

"Anyway, I think it's impressive."

"Thanks."

At that moment, like magic, Marge rematerialized beside them holding a tray that bore coffee and pie. She removed their now empty plates and replaced them with dessert, then disappeared again.

"She's good," Amanda said.

"Yep. Love this place."

They chatted as they ate, discussing nothing of importance: funny cat videos, the weird weather and so on. When they'd finished eating Jason walked Amanda home. It was dawn by the time they got there.

"I had fun," Jason said. He was feeling awkward again.

"I did too," Amanda replied. "Give me your cell."

Jason handed it over. "What are you doing?"

Amanda handed it back to him, screen up. It was open on the contacts app and it read: "Amanda B. 617-555-4319."

"Thanks." Jason was grinning again.

"Can I have yours?" Amanda returned the smile.

"Sure." He took her phone and put his info in.

After a moment of awkward silence Amanda took a step up on the stairs leading to the brownstone where she lived. "Good night."

"Good morning, you mean." Jason stifled a yawn.

Amanda laughed; it echoed around the empty street. "Text me?"

"For sure."

With that she disappeared behind the heavy wooden door and Jason headed home.

It was full daylight by the time he got home and crawled into bed, but he could not sleep. Jason lay there tossing and turning for hours. Whenever he closed his eyes, he saw her face, those eyes a shade of blue like a tropical ocean.

He replayed the whole evening over and over. Criticized every stupid thing he'd said or done. He rewrote it with a much more suave version of himself, then he'd snort at his own ridiculousness and roll over only to play the scenario out a different way. He kept this up for hours until he finally dozed off, having convinced himself she'd given him a dummy number.

He awoke a few hours later to his phone buzzing. A low sun cast his room into a rainbow of reds, oranges, and purples. He'd slept the day away. Clumsily he scrabbled for his phone and flicked the screen as he rubbed the sleep from his eyes. He had three unread messages, all from Amanda B. He smiled sleepily. Maybe he would see her again.

CHAPTER THREE

"Heya, darlins," Marge drawled as Jason and Amanda stepped inside the warmth of Del's.

"Your usual table?"

"Yes please," Jason responded.

He and Amanda kicked the snow from their boots and followed Marge to their corner table by the windows as they pulled off their heavy winter jackets.

"The usual?" Marge asked.

"Ye—" Jason began.

"Actually Marge, can we see a menu please?" Amanda cut in.

Marge looked surprised but nodded and grabbed a pair from the counter. "I'll give you folks a couple of minutes to peruse and be right back." Marge headed off to tend to her other customers, leaving Jason and Amanda alone.

"Why aren't we getting the usual?"

Amanda looked at Jason and smiled, "Let's try something new."

Jason looked skeptical but picked up the menu. "How about the Double Decker?"

"Ugh, so much cheese and bacon."

"What's wrong with cheese and bacon?"

"Nothing, if you want a heart attack."

Amanda looked at Jason before she continued, "We've been saying we need to eat healthier."

"But this is Del's…"

"I know it's Del's, and they have some lovely salads on the menu."

"But–"

"At least take a look." Amanda flipped the laminated menu over and slid her finger down the list of soups and salads. "Here we go, look at this one, The Spinach Special. It has spinach, strawberries, almonds, and red onion with a raspberry vinaigrette. Or this one, The Killer Kale with fresh crisp kale, goat cheese, cherry tomatoes, mixed berries and toasted nuts with a balsamic reduction."

She looked up and Jason was making a rabbit face at her. "Seriously?"

"C'mon babe, it's Del's. Burgers and fries. Onion rings. Pie."

Amanda smiled. "Or…"

Jason looked at her skeptically.

"We have a nice healthy lunch and we can get ice cream to go for desert. We can take it for a walk through the park."

"I guess–"

"Great," Amanda chirped with a smile.

"So, you two decide yet?" Marge cut off any further debate.

"We'll have two of the Killer Kales and sparkling waters."

Marge looked from Amanda to a dejected looking Jason, who attempted a cheerful grin but instead looked a little sick, "You sure?"

Jason nodded. "Yes ma'am. We're trying to eat healthier."

"Alrighty then. It won't be long." Marge bustled away, bringing the order slip over to Del. Jason saw Del look at the order and then over at the pair. He caught Jason's eye, raised his eyebrows and mouthed, "What the fuck?" Jason smiled sheepishly, pointed to Amanda, and shrugged. Del rolled his eyes.

Amanda had been oblivious to the whole silent interaction. While they were waiting, she'd started flicking through the pages of a newspaper another customer had left behind.

"Did you see this?" Amanda handed the newspaper to Jason.

"What?"

"All of it."

Jason leaned over the table and looked at the headlines to see what had been so upsetting. Nothing jumped out. It was all the usual type of stuff: an article on some scammers taking advantage of the elderly, an Amber Alert for an abducted three-year-old, a convenience store shooting and so on.

"What kind of a society treats its people in such a fashion?"

Jason wasn't sure where this was going.

He hazarded a guess: "A crappy one?"

"Yes, a very crappy one." She looked both hurt and angry.

"I agree. Too many people see others as easy prey. There are sick people in this world."

"Something needs to be done about them."

"That's why we have police."

"They are inefficient at stopping crime."

"They can't stop everything before it happens. That's not realistic. They're only human. They can't see the future." Jason frowned as he looked at Amanda. This wasn't the date he'd been hoping for. "You seem pretty upset over this."

"I am. If I ever saw anything like this happen..." She trailed off and sat there, glowering at the paper as if willing a criminal to appear so she could deliver justice.

"Violence doesn't resolve anything," Jason said after a brief pause. He wasn't sure it was the wisest thing to say but he felt he had to say something.

"Do you think any of those criminals would listen to reason?"

Jason shook his head. "No. Probably not, but vigilantes are as much a bane as boon."

Amanda shifted her eyes from the paper to Jason. "So what would you do if you saw someone being attacked?"

"Jason's a lover, not a fighter," Marge cut in as she put their drinks on the table.

Jason blushed. "I try to live by the motto 'Violence is the last refuge of the incompetent.'"

"Who said that?" Marge asked.

"It's a quote from one of my favourite authors, Isaac Asimov."

She looked at him blankly.

"He wrote the Foundation series."

Another blank look.

"How about I, Robot?"

"Is that the movie with that handsome Will Smith in it?" Marge asked while Amanda looked at him bewildered.

"Yes. Sort of. Asimov wrote the book the movie was based on."

"Hrmm, I might have to read it," Marge said.

Jason didn't have the heart to tell her the book was completely different from the movie.

"I'll loan you my copy if you want."

"Thanks. Your meals will be right up." Pen and pad in hand, Marge stepped over to the next table to take their order.

Amanda had fallen silent during Marge's discussion and when Jason turned back to her she was staring out the window, watching the people passing by.

He took a sip of his drink before he spoke.

"You okay?"

"Yes." She turned to look at him. "You didn't answer my question. What would you do?"

"Honestly, I don't know. It would probably depend on the situation."

"Scenario: You are walking home from work and you see someone trying to rob an elderly woman."

Jason thought for a minute, "First I'd call 911. Then I'd try to scare the attacker off by running towards them and yelling that I'd called the cops."

"Would that work?"

"Hopefully," Jason said with a shrug.

"If it didn't?"

"I'd put myself between the old lady and the mugger. Tell her to run. Maybe try to reason with the guy."

"You'd allow the robber to hurt you?" Amanda's brows were furrowed.

"If it meant her getting away, yeah. I'd like to think I'd do this. I hope I never have to find out."

Amanda said nothing for a while. She sat there in silence, frowning at her glass as she sipped her drink. Jason didn't interrupt her. He knew this was what she did when she was mulling over something.

"Your solution is different than what most people would do."

"Probably."

"I think I like it."

She looked up and smiled at Jason. It lit up her whole face, turning his insides to pudding. He was saved from having to come up with something else to say by Marge, who had arrived with their food.

CHAPTER FOUR

The bus jostled as it hit a pothole, snapping Jason back to the present. He looked around blearily and rubbed his hands over his eyes. They were passing the barred-up gas station, which meant they were not even halfway to work, and the bus was filling with familiar commuters. He saw the goth girl who worked at the mall on his route, the pimpled kid who worked at the fast-food place and always smelled of French fries and then he saw the creepy, grey haired, animal print wearing, cougar who hit on every person between twenty and forty. She worked at the seedy adult movie store and the bus would give a collective sigh whenever she got off. Jason looked at his watch and sighed. As he looked back up, he saw the cougar turn her head his way. He dropped his head down and closed his eyes before she had a chance to see he was awake.

A smile came over his face as he slipped back into the comforting embrace of his memories.

Jason had gotten some time off for this year's Fourth of July. They spent the evening with his parents, eating barbeque and reminiscing about Jason's childhood. They never failed to embarrass him. As a matter of fact, Jason was certain they took pleasure in doing so. Their favourite, which they told with a particular glee, was the first story they'd told Amanda. They didn't even build up to it this time. It was their opening salvo.

Jason's Mother leaned forward over her empty plate and took a sip of wine. "Every summer, we'd vacation in Nova Scotia. That's in Canada." Amanda nodded and smiled, flicking a bemused look to Jason. "Every year we'd visit the Maritime Museum. It's Jace's favourite." His Mother gave him her most proud Mom look. "This summer there was a display on the history of deep-sea diving-"

"Speaking of deep-sea diving, did you see the news from the Sea or Cortez? Something about a new species of shark..." Jason cut off his mother's story, trying to redirect it to something nice and safe and neutral, like politics or religion. He failed.

"It was quite the exhibit. Vintage diving bells, DSV's and so on. Someone-"

"An asshole." Jason grumped.

*"**Someone**..." His Mother paused and shot her son a look, "...had animated an old bubble headed diving suit to activate when people walked by." Jason's mother laughed, "That person was Jason. The arms reached for him and he got such a fright that right there, in front of the tour group, he screamed and peed himself." She pulled out a photo of six-year-old Jason, wet pants and pink faced by the diver.*

"Mom! Did you prep for this?" Jason said, flushing red. His Mother smiled, "Of course not dear. I always keep this picture with me."

"She does." His Father said with a grin.

"Mom..." He rubbed his hands over his burning face.

Amanda laughed and grinning at Jason before adeptly changed the conversation to his high school years.

Now his dating life, or lack thereof was up on display but at least it wasn't baby pictures.

Once the sun had set and darkness covered the city, they set off fireworks. He loved the look on Amanda's face as she watched the colourful display of willows, palms and comets as they lit up the sky. It was almost childlike in wonder. If he didn't know better, he'd have thought she had never seen fireworks before.

Afterwards, he gave her a necklace for their one-year anniversary. A coal black pendent made of meteoric iron wrapped in titanium wire and hung on a simple silver chain. He'd had it made from a small meteor he found when he was a kid. She loved it.

They returned home to their apartment and were curled up on the sofa watching *Independence Day* when she threw her first curveball at him.

"Babe, your Mom and I were talking today."

"Uh oh," he said, grinning.

She shot him a look, so he continued,

"About what?"

"Wanderer's."

"What about it?"

"We think you should get a different job."

Jason was surprised. He knew his Mom didn't like the place and she'd often suggested he work somewhere else. She had this irrational fear the place was going to get him killed, but he hadn't expected his Mom and girlfriend to team up on him.

"We just want what's best for you," Amanda continued.

"But I like the bar."

Amanda's nose wrinkled in distaste. "It's gross. It smells. The people are nasty and you're always getting hit on."

"Danny is only horsing around. He's not interested in me, he's got a boyfriend," Jason said as he put his arms around her waist, pulling her close.

Irritated, she pushed away and moved to the other end of the sofa. "I don't care. What about those cougars that have their eyes on you?"

"The Tequila Sisters?" Jason chuckled at the absurdity, "Bev and Donna? Hon, they're in their seventies."

Amanda shook her head and scowled, "No. The one who always wears the skin-tight pleather pants and leopard print blouse."

"Dotty?"

She nodded.

"You seriously consider her a threat? She drinks like a fish, smokes two packs a day and smells like mothballs. I'd sooner sleep with Danny." Jason leaned back and looked at Amanda. "Jealousy isn't a good look."

Amanda shot him a glower that made him reconsider the wisdom of his last words.

Hastily he added, "I know you can't seriously be jealous of women old enough to be my mother."

With a sigh, Amanda said, "No. I'm not jealous. I just want better for you."

"I like the bar and some of those 'nasty people' are my friends."

"You need better friends." It was Amanda's turn to realize she'd stepped over a line. As Jason opened his mouth to respond, she cut him off, "I don't mean Duke and Bear. They're okay. I just mean friends that won't keep you away from me all night." She paused for a moment. "Or grab your ass."

Jason choked back what he'd planned on saying. Instead deciding to take a different approach, "I make good money off the tips."

"Only because you let the old women grope you."

"They do not grope me."

Amanda gave him a withering look.

"Okay, so not often and the ladies only get touchy if they've had too much. Even then they usually only grab my arm or touch my chest."

"Dotty. Two weeks ago."

"That was an exception. She'd forgotten she'd taken her pills before drinking. She was pretty wasted."

"Doesn't mean I have to like watching her grab at your ass."

"It's kind of flattering..." *Jason began, joking, but quickly retraced those steps when he saw Amanda's expression. She could have melted steel with that look.* "I mean to say, it's terribly objectifying."

Amanda huffed at his response. "You seem to enjoy it a little too much."

"I do not."

"You play up to them."

"Well, it's kind of part of my job. To make them feel... well, needed or special or wanted or something."

"It's a shitty job that expects you to allow someone to paw at you."

Jason sighed. "Amanda, I'm not going to argue this with you. I know it's a dive. It's not a high-end martini bar in the downtown area. The patrons expect a certain level of lewdness."

"Which is why you shouldn't work there. You're better than that."

"Well, if not Wanderer's, where do you recommend I get a job to?" *Jason said in exasperation.*

"CloneZone."

"With you?" *Jason was a little surprised.*

"Why not? It's a nice, respectable office."

"It's a call centre."

"It's a printing company."

"It's a call centre," *Jason repeated.*

"That's only a small portion of what we do. You know that. The biggest part of the operation is the printing for our corporate clients. We do tons of instructional materials, brochures, flyers, business cards, whatever needs printing. It's so much better than that bar." *She said "bar" like it was a dirty word.*

It was Jason's turn to scowl. "There are good people who go to that bar."

"They are beneath you."

"Do you know that Duke is an engineer and that Butch is a minister as well as a physicist?"

"So?" *Amanda stood and walked to the window, pulled back the curtain and looked out at the city skyline.*

"You're judging people because of how they look, not who they are. Get to really know them, Amanda. They could surprise you."

She gave a sigh before allowing the curtain to fall back into place. "Fine" She looked over her should at Jason, her lips drawn in a tight line. Stay working there. See if I care." With that she turned on her heel and went into the bedroom, shutting the door behind her.

Jason sighed and poured himself a whiskey, thinking this was the end of the discussion. It wasn't.

The next day Amanda tried a different tactic. She spent the day sighing and when evening rolled around, she ordered in Thai for them, cracked a bottle of wine and came out of the bedroom wearing a sexy dress she'd bought earlier that day.

"I wish we could do this every night," she said, sipping the chardonnay.

"Mmm." Jason murmured as he rubbed her legs. They were sitting on the sofa with the fireplace channel on the television. Amanda was leaning back with her legs laid out across Jason, who was slumped down with his head back and eyes closed. He was full and just a little heady from the wine. "It would be nice."

He felt Amanda pull her legs away and he opened his eyes to find her staring back, pinning him in place with her look. She leaned in and kissed him, long and passionately as she began to unbutton his shirt. "We could make that happen." She ran her fingers lightly over his chest and kissed his neck. He shuddered under her touch. "Mhmmm," he replied as he pulled her against him, and they tumbled to the floor.

Later that night they lay together on the floor, a couple of throw pillows propped under their heads and a throw blanket draped over them. Amanda had her head tucked into Jason's shoulder. She could feel him breathing and hear the steady thump of his heart against her cheek. He made her feel special when she was with him. Safe. Happy. Something she'd never felt before and she didn't know how to deal with these feelings. It was the truth when Amanda had said she'd love to spend more time with him.

"Babe? You awake?"

"Hmm?" Jason replied sleepily.

"I want this every night."

"Sounds exhausting, but I'm game to give it a try." He smiled with his eyes closed.

He could hear the disappointment in her voice when she replied, "But we can't. You're either at work or in school. When you aren't, I am. I wish we had similar schedules."

Sighing, Jason opened his eyes and looked down at Amanda. She was on her back now, looking up at the ceiling of their little apartment. The light from the television fireplace flickered over her face and reflected off the tears in her eyes.

"Aw fuck," Jason said under his breath.

He knew he'd been played—and well. "Fine."

Amanda's eyes turned towards Jason.

"Fine?" she asked far too innocently.

"Yeah, fine. I'll apply to CloneZone tomorrow."

Amanda squealed and threw her arms around his neck, pressing herself hard against him as she kissed him.

"You won't regret this," she said as she pulled him back down, and for that night Jason had zero regrets.

Those would come later.

CHAPTER FIVE

The squealing and popping from the old bus's brakes as it stopped startled Jason from his reverie. Joe always did Jason a solid by stopping across the street from the worn-out building that held the call centre. It saved Jason's ass since the nearest official stop was nearly a quarter mile in either direction. He shivered a little as he crawled out of his seat. His clothes had begun to dry a little, but they were still damp, badly wrinkled, and there was a wet spot on the front of his pants where water had soaked in from his backpack. He looked like he'd slept in his clothes and peed himself. Sighing, he thought, "Glad I'm not trying to impress anyone."

"Have a good one," he said as he passed by Joe and his new friend Frank. He hopped off the bus and ran across the deserted rain-flooded parking lot to the main doors. Water splashed him with every step. The building had been converted from a warehouse to a large open-concept office, but no extra money was spent on restoring the exterior. The years had not been kind to the red brick, and it was dingy and crumbling. The massive glass windows had been covered over with rusty, corrugated steel, leaving only two small filth-covered windows for natural light. Jason had always felt that the closer you came the building, the more depressed or perhaps oppressed you felt. It had a presence, one that weighed you down. "I need a different job," Jason thought as he ducked under the small overhang that sheltered the double glass doors.

He fumbled through his pockets and backpack looking for his ID badge that doubled as an electronic swipe key. With a sinking feeling he realized that he'd forgotten it, which meant he'd have to go through Walter, the security guard, to get in.

Jason pounded on the double glass doors, trying to catch Walter's attention. The cranky old security guard made a point of ignoring him, continuing to watch the show he had on his mini TV. Walter despised tardiness and seemed to take a perverse pleasure in delaying those that were already running late.

"When I was your age, I got to work an hour early. Busses didn't run then, so I had to walk ten miles each way in all kinds of weather," Walter lectured as he slowly picked out a temporary ID badge and keyed in Jason's name. Jason bit down hard on his tongue; anything he'd say would only make the old man go slower.

After what felt like an eternity, Walter finally declared the badge was ready and held it up, wagging it slowly back and forth. Jason grabbed the ID badge and bolted for the card swipe which would allow him access to the centre. Jason was now beet red in the face from containing his frustration and anger. He hoped that he might still sneak in unnoticed. As he swiped his card the machine made a loud buzzing noise. Startled, Jason jumped back from the obnoxious sounding machine. "What the hell?" he said as he turned back to the smug looking old man. "Walter?"

"There is a new policy. Your manager has to sign you in. What's your manager's name again? Larry? Garry?"

"It's Tony, Walter," said a defeated Jason through clenched teeth as he returned to the security counter and hung his head.

"Tony Walter? There is no manager named Tony Walter. Are you sure you haven't been terminated for repeated tardiness?" Walter asked with a sarcastic smirk on his face.

Jason closed his eyes and took a deep breath, trying to calm himself. He said through clenched teeth, "Walter, my manager's name is Tony Smythe, or Anthony Smythe if you want."

The smirk faded to a dead glare and Jason knew he was a dead man. Walter turned back to his computer and once again using the hunt and peck method, he searched for Tony's information. "Ah, yes, here he is. A most responsible young man." As he dialed Tony's extension, he looked at Jason and said, "You could learn a lot from him." Jason nearly choked on his own tongue trying not to respond as he slumped down into a worn chair as he heard Walter say, "Tony, I got me a smart mouth out here who forgot his badge. No rush."

"No hope of sneaking in now," Jason thought glumly. He sat with his legs splayed out before him. Jason realized that even though he managed to get soaked through again while running across the parking lot, the only spot that hadn't changed was the wet spot on the front of his pants. He still looked like he'd peed himself. Dejectedly, Jason let his head flop back to rest on the top of the chair and prayed for a quick death. He was trapped in the small lobby that reeked with the smell of the sardines that Walter loved to eat while Walter harangued his captive audience with stories of his time as a postal worker, which somehow managed to also be lectures on punctuality and reliability.

It felt like an eternity until Tony arrived to drag his sorry ass into the office. "A swift execution is better than a slow one," Jason thought as he sat up to see a very surly looking Tony standing in the open doorway.

"Come," was all that Tony said as he crooked his finger, indicating that Jason should follow him. Wearily Jason got to his feet and followed behind the scarecrow-like frame of Tony into the depths of a singularly unpleasant hell; also known as the call centre production floor.

Tony's "office" was a cubicle that was slightly bigger than the rest. The only thing different about it was a laminated sign thumbtacked to the top of the cubicle that said "FLOOR MANAGER: ANTHONY SMYTHE." Regardless of its banality, Tony felt that his office was a grey felted royal seat from which he ruled his subjects with an iron fist. A modern-day Sheriff of Nottingham for the corporate Prince John; executing their orders with glee. The employees considered it more like an evil villain's lair where he plotted ways to make their lives miserable.

Jason sat in the broken rickety chair that was permanently stuck at the lowest seat level. Tony had a bad case of Napoleon complex, which meant he had to make his staff feel smaller than he was. He did that with this broken chair that his staff had to sit in because it forced them to have to look up into Tony's bulbous pale blue eyes while Tony looked down at them over the tops of his thick-lensed glasses.

He folded his arms across his shallow chest, crinkling his pristinely white starched dress shirt, which he kept tucked into his sharply creased khaki trousers. Every pair the man owned were just a little too short for him, exposing his white sports socks over the tops of his black loafers. To Jason, Tony always looked like the quintessential used car salesman with his dark hair slicked back, making his narrow, pinched face seem bigger than it was, and he always held an expression that seemed to look mildly disgusted at everything around him. Tony was a middle-aged sycophant; a company man all the way who cared little about his employees' welfare.

Staring into those soulless eyes, Jason decided that the best defence was a good offence, so he took a deep breath and spewed, "I'm sorry I'm late but I was here on time. I forgot my ID and Walter took forever to get a temp card for me and then I had to be signed in."

Silently, Tony reached for some paperwork and sat there in the pregnant silence, occasionally looking over the tops of his glasses at Jason and shaking his head, his thin lips drawn down in a scowl. Finally, putting the papers down and shoving them towards Jason, he said in a clipped nasally voice, "It's a pathetic man who blames others for their own transgressions. Especially when they lay the blame on a dedicated employee like Walter. You've been late three times in one month. You, sir, are now on probation. Sign this notice of probationary status."

Briefly Jason wondered how long Tony had the attendance improvement forms ready to go, just waiting for this opportunity.

Desperate, Jason tried to plead his case, "But Tony, I really was here on time."

Jason kept to himself that he believed Tony had deliberately delayed the additional thirty minutes, probably while printing and filling out the probation form.

"Don't you think it's time you started taking responsibility for your own actions? I was manager at my first job by the time I was twenty-three. With a little determination and hard work, you could someday make something of yourself."

Jason's eyes flashed with anger, which almost always meant his mouth was going to start going without any engagement of the brain. "I am responsible."

"You'd never know that from your attendance."

His sense of self-preservation was sending off klaxon alarms of warning. Jason was in a battle between his brain and tongue whether he was going to tell this weasel where to go. Jason was sure he felt blood as he bit his tongue. It was a crap job but for now it paid the bills. For the second time this day he longed for his old job as a bartender.

He died a little inside, but his brain won the battle. "Tony, I try. Honestly. It's the damned bus. This one is the earliest but it's never on time."

"That is not my problem."

"Can't you give me a later shift or something?"

"No. There are no openings."

"For fuck's sake. C'mon, man. Please. Be reasonable."

"Are you implying that I am unreasonable?" He peered at Jason over the tops of his glasses. "Have I not given you multiple opportunities? I've been most magnanimous."

"That isn't what I meant. I was just sayin' that it's hard for me to get here in time for first shift with the bus the way it is." Jason held up his hands, pleading. "Tony. Please."

"Be thankful you have a job. Others aren't so lucky." He smiled, more malicious than happy. "I'll tell you what. If you promise to show up for some training today, I'll hold off on filing the performance plan."

"What training?"

Tony waved his hand, "Oh nothing drastic. Just something that might help with your situation."

Another small piece of Jason's soul shrivelled and died, but he nodded. If he lost his job Amanda would be disappointed in him and nothing was worth that, so he choked down his anger and said, "Thank you, Tony. I appreciate the chance."

"You see, I can be magnanimous. Now you'd best get to your desk. You're already quite tardy."

As Jason grabbed his gear and headed away, his step faltered as he heard Tony mutter under his breath, "I don't know what Amanda sees in that man."

His face burning and his damp cloth sticking to his body, he headed to his desk.

"'Goddamned troll fucker" Jason whispered to himself.

"What did you say?"

Jason started and flushed bright pink, looked over his should at Tony and said "Nothing, boss. Nothing at all."

Tony gave Jason a long scrutinizing stare before waiving his hand in dismissal. Jason turned back and headed towards his desk. As he walked across the call centre floor, his wet jeans chafed his legs. His body shivered, and goose flesh rose on his arms from the building's air conditioning, which chilled him to the bone.

CHAPTER SIX

Jason's desk was at the opposite end of the floor. It wouldn't take him long to get there, the room was not large. Most of the floor space in the building was set aside for the "Printing and Distribution Centre," which was separated from the call centre by a thick protective cinder block wall. Jason's feelings flicked from anger to relief to depression as he shuffled his way towards his desk. A parade of fantasies of all the different ways that Tony could meet his demise flitted through Jason's mind: Tony's tie getting caught in the shredder; a large stack of printing paper collapsing on him and squashing Tony flat like Wile E. Coyote; Tony being run over by a forklift; Tony being covered in one of the many corrosive chemicals in the printing room and screaming, "I'm melting," as he slowly dissolved; and many more. The thoughts brought a small smile to Jason's face as he passed row after row of grey walled cubicles while automatically dodging the buckets, half-filled with rain water. There were dozens of leaks in the roof and large wet circles ringed the buckets, making the industrial carpet always smell faintly of moldy corn chips.

A familiar deep voice brought Jason back to reality. "Mijo. Where are you going?"

With a small start, Jason stopped and looked over at Marc, the only real friend he had in this place, other than Amanda. Without a word he gave a small shrug as he backtracked to his station and shoved his backpack under his desk, dropped his sodden jacket over the back of his chair and plopped down into his seat.

Marc looked at his friend with concern. "Where the hell have you been man? You're almost an hour late. Tony's gonna have your head if he catches you."

Looking at his friend, Jason said, "Too late, I've been caught, and I've already served it to him on a silver platter."

"What are you talking about?"

"Dude, I was running late. Again. I forgot my badge. Again. Walter took his sweet time to get my ID badge. Then I had to wait on His Weaseliness to log me in. In short, he knew I was late. The fucker tossed around the idea of firing me or if he should put me on probation, but instead he is sending me to some stupid training thing this afternoon."

"What the fuck did you say to him?"

"I wanted to call him a soulless pencil pusher." Jason ran his hands through his hair. "Instead I begged for my job."

"Smart choice, Mijo, you are lucky to still have a job."

"I know. It just kills me to subjugate myself to him. He's a dick."

"No argument there, but unless you won the lottery last night, you need a job."

Jason nodded as he finished logging in.

"So, in more exciting news, I'm supposed to be going out with Amanda after work. She said she 'wanted to talk.'"

"Man, that phrase is the kiss of death. It's usually said right before 'It's not you, it's me.'"

"I know. When she finds out I'm in trouble with Tony again, she's probably gonna dump me for sure."

"Why would I want to do that?" said a melodic voice from behind Jason.

Jason jumped, his eyes going wide, and shot Marc a look of sheer panic. "Manda? What are you doing here? I thought you were at that hotel setting up for the job fair," Jason said, his voice shooting at least two octaves higher than normal.

"We finished setting up the booth early and I decided to come in to get some paperwork done." She frowned at him. "I've already been talking to Tony and he told me about your meeting with him this morning."

Jason swallowed a lump as beads of sweat appeared on his brow.

Amanda only smiled. "I had told him that with the right incentive you could become a very productive member of our team. I also promised him that you would be co-operative and do *any* extra training. That's why he gave you that option instead of terminating you, which is what he wanted to do." She glanced around before touching his cheek and looked deep into his eyes. "Most importantly, I promised him you'd curb your tongue." She wagged her index finger at Jason as if he were a naughty child. "You really shouldn't goad him."

Marc choked back a laugh but Amanda heard it and shot him a glare. As she turned her gaze back to Jason she smiled again, her deep blue eyes compelling him to agree. "You will? Won't you? For me?"

"Dude, you're a smart guy. So, for once, do the smart thing," whispered Marc.

Caught by the force of Amanda's will and Marc's urging, Jason quietly whispered, "Fine. Sure."

Amanda's smile broadened. "Perfect," she said, reaching down and giving Jason a quick hug. "You won't regret it."

She turned on her heel and took off back to wherever she had materialized from.

"Man, I can't believe that. You got a last-minute reprieve from the hottest governor ever. I told you she had your back," Marc exclaimed.

"Huh?" Jason asked.

"You were whining about Amanda being pissed, but she saved your ass."

"Yeah. She did. I should have said no. I wanted to say no. I hate this shit hole and I want out. The only thing that really scares me is what her reaction to me getting canned would be."

"Not wanting to disappoint your woman isn't a bad thing, my friend. It's why I still work here."

"Your wife is pretty chill though. She'd be cool with you changing jobs."

"True 'nuff, but I'd damn well better have a job lined up to go to if I ever quit or I'm a dead man. I'm sure Amanda feels the same way." Marc said taking a whiff of his sinus medication.

"You still on that crap?"

"Better than coke." Marc said with a dramatic sniff. He grinned and then shrugged. "Doc says I'm on it until the infection clears. Stuff sucks and feels weird, but at least I can smell stuff now." Marc sniffed the air and made a disgusted face, "A fact I sometimes regret. Anyway, as I was sayin', find a new job, one you emjoy and I'm sure Amanda'll be cool with it."

"Jason shook his head. "I'm not so sure about that. I think she's a lifer for this place."

He leaned back in his chair, recalling his first days at CloneZone. The warning signs were all there.

He should have made his escape then.

CHAPTER SEVEN

The call centre occupied a run-down brick building in Boston's waterfront district. The weathered red, white, and blue sign over the door read "CloneZone: Copy & Central Printing." It was a stretch of the imagination to see it as the nice respectable office Amanda had described. It wasn't the bar, but it was definitely a dive.

Jason's new manager, Tony, gave him and the other handful of newbies the grand tour of CloneZone's call centre. It should have taken five minutes, but Tony managed to drag it out to thirty. Jason had never seen someone so enthusiastic over outdated computers and grey felted cubicles before.

"Dude, if he extols the virtues of different types of printing paper one more time, I think I'm gonna scream," whispered one of Jason's new coworkers as Tony lead them to one of the classrooms. He was like a father duck with his four charges trailing behind him. This classroom would be their office for the next couple of weeks as they were trained.

Jason stifled a laugh but nodded.

The man extended his hand, "Marc Cortez." He was shorter than Jason with short black hair, olive complexion and built like a bulldozer. Solid and stocky.

"Jason Donoghue," he said, taking the other man's hand. It was a firm, confident grip.

"What did you do to end up here?" Marc asked.

"My girlfriend works here."

"Really? What's her name?"

"You might have met her. She works in HR, recruiting, Amanda Blue."

"Pretty blonde?"

Jason nodded.

"Ah, si. Yes. She hired me." Marc gave Jason an appreciative look. "Mijo, you are a lucky man."

Jason smiled and nodded.

Marc turned serious for a minute, "Is it gonna be weird working with your girlfriend?"

"No. She works in HR doing recruitment. She isn't in the office much."

"She's lucky."

"Yeah, she attends job fairs and stuff or works from home a lot." He looked over at his new co-worker. *"How'd you end up at CloneZone?"*

"My wife told me I'm gonna be a Papa, so I had to get a real job."

"Congrats, man. When?"

"Thanks. Next spring. I'm still in shock I think."

"I'd say. What did you do before CloneZone?"

"Maria, that's my wife, calls it being a professional student."

"Gotcha. I know a few of those from MIT. Guys who bounce from one degree to another."

"Si. That's me. You go to MIT? Nice. That's where I did my master's in anthropology. What are you studying?"

"Computer engineering. What were you back in school for if you had your master's? Doing your doctorate?"

"No. I was doing a bachelor's in history."

"Why?"

"It was interesting."

"And your wife was okay with this?"

"No. That's why I'm here," Marc laughed. *"She informed me it was time I grew up. With a kid on the way I guess she's right."*

With that the facilitator showed up and interrupted them.

"My name is Sue, I'm your trainer. Please introduce yourselves."

"I'm Jason," Jason said, raising his hand.

"Marc."

"George," said a larger man, a smile spreading over round face. He was in his middle years, his brown hair greying at his temples.

"Jamie," the woman squeaked, though you could hardly hear her. She looked around at the others nervously.

"Thank you. We'll start with a getting to know you exercise. I want you to each put something about yourselves on this piece of paper..."

"This is the fifth circle of hell," Jason thought as he scribbled something pointless on his piece of paper before Sue collected it for redistribution.

***

"Nice sweater," Amanda said, laughing.

Marc grinned. *"Maria bought if for me. And I quote: 'Honey, everyone needs a cute ugly Christmas sweater.' I didn't have a choice."*

"I think it's cute."

"I dunno," Jason mumbled around his slice of cold pizza. "I think that snowman is over compensating." He pointed to the large stuffed carrot nose that was protruding from the middle of Marc's chest.

"Haha," Marc muttered as he tried to squish the proboscis back in.

"What's wrong with its nose?" Amanda asked.

Jason looked at her. "It was a joke?"

"Yeah, chuckles was trying to intimate that I am not well endowed."

"Never said anything about you, just the snowman," Jason said, laughing.

"I don't see how that's funny?"

Marc laughed as Jason said, "It was a double entendre."

Amanda just looked at him and blinked.

"Never mind," he said.

The conversation lulled as they finished their meals.

"You guys are the only reason I'm still working here," Jason said out of the blue.

"Dude, I'm with you," Marc said as Amanda sighed heavily and rolled her eyes.

She'd heard this complaint too many times.

"You've only been here less than a year.

It's a start. Work hard and you can go places."

"Where? Where can I go?" Jason shook his head. "I want to finish my degree before I turn thirty, but you seem dead set on me staying here with you. Every time I mention working any other place, you get upset." The bar wasn't good enough, even when Marge at the diner offered him a job, it wasn't acceptable. Jason looked at Amanda; there was no way she could be jealous of Marge. "Once I graduate, I can get a job with NASA or SpaceX or something. Good hours. Good money. A better job. Anything. As long as it's not here. I can't even get back to school with the hours at CloneZone."

"I know it's not your dream job," Amanda reached over and placed her hand on Jason's, giving it a gentle squeeze. "Babe, you just need to stay positive. Good things will happen."

"I'm trying. I just don't fit here."

"Will you try to hold out a little longer? For me? There are new positions coming up that I'm sure you'd be perfect for."

"What are they?"

"Well, I'm not supposed to say yet." Amanda looked around. There was no one nearby. "There's a couple opening up in lower management and one in IT."

"What's the one in IT?"

"You'd have to be working closely with Tony. It has to do with some project he's been working on."

"That's a downside. Do you know anything more about it?"

"No. Not yet." Amanda frowned and stood to leave. "I need to get back to work."

Marc looked over at Jason. "You certainly know how to clear a table."

"It's a gift," he said.

Jason tried to keep his promise, to remain upbeat and optimistic, but the place slowly drained the life from him.

He'd grown to hate his job, his boss, the bus shelter that smelled of pee, the bus that was never warm and always late, his co-workers, the customers, the coffee machine that only worked sometimes, and the clunky old vending machines that ate your money but never gave you your nice salty pretzels. Every day he dragged himself to this soul-sucking abyss, and every day he realized he was stepping further and further away from his goals.

The call centre was where dreams went to die.

CHAPTER EIGHT

Most days, the three friends took lunch together in the dingy cafeteria. Jason sat stirring his Styrofoam cup of noodles, while Amanda nibbled on her garden salad and Marc started to wolf down his huge foot-long meatball sub, pizza sauce and cheese dripping out the sides. Jason always wondered how a guy who ate like Marc could manage to stay in such great shape.

"Just look over there," Marc pointed across the cafeteria with his elbow. One of their co-workers was sitting at a table. He had a lunch bag opened in front of him but wasn't moving. He was staring vacantly at the wall and a string of saliva dangled from his chin. "What the fuck's up with him?"

"He looks normal to me," Amanda replied, shrugging her shoulders.

"He is most definitely not normal," Marc said around a mouthful of his sub.

"Maybe he's coming down with that flu that's hitting everyone?" Amanda suggested. "Just yesterday someone reported that Lucas was sitting on the floor crying. But he wasn't." Jason and Marc both looked at her with a confused expression. "I mean crying. That is, he wasn't crying. He'd been coughing and sneezing like crazy all morning. When he went on break, he got really dizzy and just sat on the floor with his eyes all watery."

"It's a pretty brutal cold," Jason said as he started to wolf down his cooled pot noodles.

"Yeah. At least half the centre seems to have caught this bug. I had it just after I started. They found me asleep in my lunch and I ended up being off sick for almost a week," Amanda said.

"I didn't know that," Jason said, looking at Amanda.

"It was before we met," she said dismissively. "I don't think I've ever been so sick. I was so out of it my roommate had to look after me."

"Smee ris rah feehin wuggy," mumbled Marc, his mouth stuffed with sub. Both Amanda and Jason looked at him, raising their eyebrows in unison. Washing down his food with a gulp of soda, Marc burped and said, "Sorry. What I said was 'He is a freakin' druggy'."

The two continued to look at him, but Amanda started to frown.

"I mean Gary is a drug dealer who uses his own product. Everyone knows that." Marc shuddered dramatically and burped again. "They are always bad news. I don't trust those types." Marc gave Gary a hard look. The guy was an addict. Something most of his co-workers knew. Some even got their weekend weed from him. He was a failed chemist who'd had a good job with one of the pharmaceutical companies, but he'd taken too much of a liking to the narcotics he'd been developing.

Both Jason and Amanda shook their heads at Marc before Jason replied, "Well, I just know I don't want whatever bug he's got."

Amanda leaned over, touching her shoulder against his, and whispered huskily, "I'll take care of you."

Marc made gagging noises around his sub while Jason flushed.

Giggling, she sat back up. "Oh. Did you get an email from Tony?"

"Who? Me?" Jason and Marc asked in unison.

Amanda laughed. "Jason."

"Yeah, he wants me to go to the training session at three. Me, Jamie, and George. The annual meeting of the CloneZone losers club," Jason replied, sighing heavily. He realized he had been sighing an awful lot today.

"Must be," Marc said, swallowing down the last of his meal and wiping his hands on a paper napkin as Jason looked at his friend with a hurt look. He hadn't expected Marc to agree quite so readily. "I got an email, too. Tony must think you are having a negative influence on me." He smiled, taking the sting from his words.

"What?" both Amanda and Jason said in unison.

"Yeah. The email didn't say what exactly the training was, just that it's you, George, Jamie, and me at three PM, in classroom two."

Amanda sat with her brow furrowed, staring at the last piece of lettuce as she moved it slowly in circles with her fork.

"You okay?" Jason asked Amanda.

"What? Oh yeah, sorry. I was just thinking about what Marc said. It's just odd that Tony didn't notify me. I have to record what training you receive, and I thought there was only three of you scheduled for today."

"Probably just a miscommunication," Jason said. "It's probably just another stupid 'attendance is important' corporate brainwashing training. We'll be told how important we are and that being late or absent causes undue hardship to our coworkers and blah blah blah. You'd think that the world was going to end if we didn't show up."

"Yeah," Marc agreed. "I always feel like I've stepped into some sort of Orwellian indoctrination nightmare when I sit through those. Maybe that is what they're really doing to us. There are some sort of sci-fi subliminal messages embedded into the PowerPoint presentation repeating 'Obey your masters' over and over."

Jason chimed in, "We're really human versions of Pavlov's dogs. Someone rings a bell and we all answer, 'Hello, how can I assist you today?'" Both men laughed. They never noticed that Amanda's face had gone a sallow green colour or when she finally slipped away.

When they finally stopped laughing at their own joke, Marc said, "Where'd Amanda go?"

Jason looked around and shrugged as he tossed his empty noodle container into the trash and the two men headed back to their desks. "Probably to find out why she was left out of the loop about that training."

"Probably."

The two men returned to their desks and returned to work. It was busy so the hours flew by and before they knew it, it was almost three PM.

Marc stood and stretched before heading off to the training session. He passed Amanda as she headed towards where they sat. "Don't worry. He's coming. He's just stuck on a call, Amanda. It shouldn't be long."

Amanda didn't even acknowledge Marc as she brushed past him.

"Thanks for the heads-up, Marc," he said in a falsetto. "You are most welcome, Amanda," he said with a shrug as he headed off to class.

Amanda heard none of it. She arrived at Jason's desk, glad to see him still sitting there. After hesitating only slightly, she sat down in Marc's vacated chair, scooted over to sit closer to Jason, and waited impatiently for the call to end. She could see he was reviewing the finalized order and wasn't really paying attention to her.

"Jason, I need to talk to you," Amanda whispered, tugging at his sleeve.

"Okay. Almost done," he mouthed back and held up his finger indicating "one minute." Jason continued to finalize a priority order for 20,000 high gloss flyers to be printed depicting a chartreuse and lavender chicken, with country western fonts; once printed they were to be shipped via courier to Pretty Chickie's Country Emporium in Bird City, Kansas. Jason was struggling to keep a straight face during the call.

"Okay then. That wasn't weird at all," Jason said, laying down his headset.

"Sup?"

Amanda turned to face Jason and took his hands in hers, looking up into his eyes. She loved they way they sparkled with intelligence and gentleness. They made her heart skip a beat every time. She knew she should not feel this way, but she could not help herself. The emotions she felt were too strong to deny.

Shaking her head, she steeled herself and shut herself to the pain that surged in her heart and said urgently, "This wasn't how it was supposed to happen. I'm sorry, Jason. I'm so sorry. Marc is gone and you need to get out of here." She paused. "Right now. You can't delay."

"Go? Where? Training? I'm going no–"

Amanda cut him off harshly. "No. Away from here. Get as far as you can from CloneZone, from Boston."

Jason looked hurt and confused. "Why? Gone? What do you mean that Marc is gone? Are you dumping me?"

"No. Yes. Just GO. Please." Amanda was near tears.

"I'm not going anywhere without an explanation."

"Of course you aren't. You are truly a stubborn asshole, Jason Donoghue." Her switch to anger was like a slap in the face to Jason and he reeled back from her a little.

"Wow."

"You are. I'm trying to sav–" Amanda cut herself off before continuing, "I'm trying to help you and you simply will not listen. Just fucking GO already!" she screeched at him as she jumped to her feet and ran out of the building.

CHAPTER NINE

Marc really did love these training sessions. A couple of hours away from the phones and the pedantic clients was a gift from above. Two sheets missing out of 300,000 printed and their world comes to a screeching halt. "Who counts those things?" he thought as he walked into the tiny classroom with its dull beige walls and row after row of tables, each holding five semi-functional computers. There was no personal space here if the class was full. Just you and twenty-nine of your new best friends. Marc was glad there were only four of them today. These rooms were always close and stuffy. It was a crap shoot if the AC was going to work.

The trainer hadn't shown yet, so Marc flopped down into one of the chairs as far back in the classroom as he could go, shifted his sinus meds as the bottle dug into his hip and then leaned back as far as the chair would go. Meanwhile his two companions were chatting quietly. Marc had mastered the call centre survival skill of napping with your eyes open and took full advantage of it in the classroom. It would be a little harder today, with so few in the class, but he was willing to give it a shot. Until he had to feign alertness, he leaned back in the rickety chair and closed his eyes.

"Jesus," Marc thought. "Jason's going to miss another class." He was just wondering if he should start a pool on who's most likely to kill Jason: Amanda or Tony. The classroom door shut with a loud bang. "Ah, there he is," Marc mumbled under his breath, opening his eyes, expecting to see Jason. There was no one there. The three of them were still the only ones in the room. "Must have been the wind," Marc muttered as he closed his eyes once again.

George got up to open the door, but the handle wouldn't turn. He jiggled it up and down then leaned hard against the door. "It won't open," he said with finality.

"Wadda yah mean it won't open?" Marc grumbled.

The racket George was making was ruining his nap. He opened one eye a crack to see George violently yanking and shaking the door while trying futilely to twist the handle. With a resigned sigh, Marc got up to help. This training course wasn't working out like he'd planned. After a few attempts of his own, he realized the door was well and truly stuck. He could see people in the distance, so he pounded on the door and the glass, but no one came; they didn't even look.

"We're trapped," Jamie squealed, her hands raising to her throat.

"We're just gonna have to wait until the trainer shows up," Marc said, but continued quickly when Jamie gave him such a look of terror. "It shouldn't be long." He glanced at his watch. "They are already fifteen minutes late."

He looked at Jamie, who was pale and sweating. She kept making small squeaking noises and looking around frantically. She reminded him of a mouse stuck in one of those little mazes that he'd seen on science programs in school. The little white critters were trapped in narrow corridors and they weren't allowed freedom until they'd solved the maze or done their master's bidding. When they did well, the reward was a scrap of cheese and a bigger cage.

Marc shook his head. His thoughts were making him feel claustrophobic. As much to himself as to the others he said, "Chill. The door's just jammed. It's happened before. Let's see if we can get someone on the office chat to come and open the door from the outside." Marc turned to the class-room's computers and sat down at the computer next to Jamie and patted her shoulder.

"It'll be okay. Won't take long for someone to come." She looked at him gratefully and tried a smile. Marc thought it just made her look sick, but he smiled back in what he hoped was an encouraging way as he turned back to the computer and wiggled the mouse. Nothing happened. He hit the power button on the computer, but still nothing happened. He tried the next three computers in a row and none of them would start.

"They're all broken?" he said, looking over at George, who'd continued to pound at the door.

"I'll check this side," George said. After four separate attempts he looked over at Marc. "These won't start either."

"What the fuck?" Marc muttered under his breath. He took out his cell phone to call someone. "Of course. No fucking reception," he said, looking at the four empty little bars. "Goddamned concrete."

He looked at Jamie, who was pale and sweating. She was curled up tight but was making furtive little movements with her hands and feet, while her wide eyes flicked from Marc to George to the door. It was if she wanted to run but didn't know which way was safe.

"I guess that's it. Nothing else we can do. We might as well make the best of it." Marc said, resigned and opened his phone, "Either of you got the app for Cake Layers game? We can do a team round."

Marc heard a mouse being dropped back onto the desk and George's sigh. "Guess not." He muttered just as George said, "I don't get this. None of the computers will turn on." He'd moved on from trying to find one that worked to trying to find out why they wouldn't.

"Marc?" George said. Marc turned around to look at George, who was pulling on a computer in the last row, but the machine wasn't moving. "They're bolted to the fucking desk."

As he spoke the computer tore away from the desk with a loud crack, sending George tumbling. The computer flew from his hands, landed across the room, bounced off the back wall and smashed open on the floor. Jamie screamed at the sound of metal meeting concrete.

"Dude, you okay? " Marc said as he helped George up off the floor.

"Yeah. I think so," he said, rubbing his backside.

"That thing is obliterated," Marc said. "You know, they'll probably take the cost of it out of your pay."

"Of that I have no doubt. Won't matter why it happened."

"Nope and they'll probably charge you double what the piece of shit is worth too."

The two men stopped, looking down at a hollow box. There were no motherboard, hard drive, or memory cards in sight. Just the twisted metal frame of an empty box with a few colourful wires and empty tubing. George and Marc looked at each other.

Frowning, Marc whispered to George, "What the fuck is going on here?"

The room's lights flickered and dimmed. Jamie yelped and curled into a ball. Marc thought he heard a low hissing noise. It seemed to emanate from everywhere.

"You guys hear that?" Marc said to the others as he turned in a slow circle.

"Marc, some of the computers have lights on now," George said as he dropped into a chair in front of the nearest one and tried to get it to work. Marc looked down at the completely empty case and back at his companions.

He scrunched his nose. "Do you guys smell something? It's like lemon house cleaner or something?" He paused again, sniffed, and sneezed violently. Whatever it was it burned when he breathed. "It's like Mr. Clean but way stronger?" Marc's Spider-Sense was tingling like crazy.

Jamie gave the air a little sniff.

"Yeah," she said in a high voice. She hadn't moved from where she huddled in a chair by the door.

"Frig, my throat and eyes are burning," George said, rubbing them.

"Mine too," Jamie squeaked.

"It's giving me a headache," Marc added, rubbing his temples.

George was holding tight to the edge of the desk. "Guys, I'm not feelin' so good. Anyone else feeling dizzy?"

Both Marc and Jamie nodded.

"Carbon monoxide?" Marc suggested. The building was heated by a furnace, but it hadn't been on in weeks due to the heat. It was getting harder and harder to think.

"Guys, look at this." George's speech slurred as he lifted the end of a piece of flexible metal conduit piping that had been attached to the dummy computer. He was still rubbing his eyes with his free hand and coughed. What looked like a faint wisp of smoke wafted lazily from the open end and drifted towards the tile ceiling.

"It's empty..." was all he managed. George gagged and fumbled at the desk's edge as he started to slide from the seat. He stood and took a step, but his legs collapsed beneath him and he dropped to his knees. He looked plaintively at Marc and Jamie while his mouth moved but no words came out. His eyes rolled up into his head and he flopped the last few feet to lie on the floor, hitting his head on the desk's edge on the way down.

"What's wrong with him?" Jamie gasped. She was finding it hard to breathe.

The room was starting to spin. Marc's stomach rolled, and he fought the urge to throw up.

"Gas…" Marc said in a slurred voice as he looked at the humming computers. His vision dimmed as he dropped to his knees. Jamie never heard his answer. Never once moving from her chair, she now slid to the floor. Her head hit the carpet-covered concrete floor with a thunk.

Fighting against the gas, Marc tried to make it to the door. As his fingers brushed the handle his unconscious form fell, pinning Jamie beneath him.

CHAPTER TEN

Jason bolted after Amanda, brushing past a startled Walter who glowered at Jason's back as he disappeared through the doors. The old curmudgeon didn't hesitate to head to his computer to report what he'd seen to his favourite manager.

The rain was still coming down as Jason ran across the parking lot, scanning the horizon for Amanda. "Where could she have gone?" he thought. He stood in the middle of the parking lot looking as far up the street as he could, across the series of linked parking lots and along the waterfront's edge. Which route had she chosen? He was frozen with indecision while hundreds of scenarios tumbled through his mind. He looked at the water lapping against the piers. They often walked along those piers during lunch. She said she found the water soothing. He took a chance that was where she'd go, so he headed across the lot and began jogging along the water's edge.

As he jogged, the rain stopped, leaving a stifling humidity that gave a potency to the cornucopia of fragrances that proximity to the waterfront provided. The air smelled of damp, mixed with tang of salt from the ocean, the bitterness of diesel, the stink of rotting fish with just a touch of hops from a brewery up the road. The fetid air made it difficult to breathe and his chest was beginning to hurt from his exertion.

He was relieved to see Amanda standing on one of the small piers that jutted out into the water. She was standing on the wooden beams that edged the concrete wharf, with her back to him. She was staring down into the water's murky depths. Her shoulders were slumped, and he could just see her quivering as she choked back sobs.

"Manda?" he said quietly.

As he spoke Amanda made a small yelp of surprise and spun towards Jason. As she turned, the water-soaked wood beneath Amanda's feet betrayed her and she slipped backwards, her arms windmilling in a vain attempt to regain balance. It was not enough. Looking at Jason, eyes wide with fear, she let out a silent scream and fell backwards into the sea.

Time seemed to slow as Jason watched her fall. He dove for her, tried to grab her outstretched hand, but the distance was too great. Amanda slipped away from him. He heard the splash as she hit the water ten feet below the pier's edge. A new fear gripped Jason, freezing him where he stood.

He couldn't swim.

The impact drove what little breath Amanda had from her lungs, stunning her. Warm water enveloped her as she sank, wrapping her in a peace that drew her in, comforting her. She could see a watery sun above as it tried to break through the clouds. Bits of flotsam passed overhead, breaking the fractal beams that penetrated the water. Her lungs burned. They cried for air but found only the briny water that had filled them.

"This is for the best," she thought as she closed her eyes and succumbed to the sea. This was a far better fate than being forced to choose between her two worlds.

Then Jason was there, wrapping his arms around her as he held her tight and fought to drag them both to the surface.

"I'm gonna die," he thought, "but at least I tried."

Rough waves hit Amanda's face as they broke the surface. Air tried to force its way into her water-filled lungs. She choked and coughed hard.

"No," she tried to scream at Jason, but it came out as a garbled moan as gouts of sea water poured from her tortured lungs. She fought weakly against his grip, but he held tight and frantically pulled her to the wharf's edge. Jason grabbed hold of one of the barnacle-encrusted pilings, holding tight while the sharp shells made tiny painful cuts on his palm.

She fought vainly to pry his arm from around her waist, kicking against his legs. "Stop," he cried, choking as a wave washed over his head. "You'll kill us both." She looked over her shoulder. He was terrified as he struggled to get them out of the water. He was exhausted and struggled to hold onto the slimy beams as the strong current pulled at them. His hand slid along the wood, the barnacles cutting his hands. Each wave threatened to tear them away and pull them under. Reluctantly she stopped her struggles and took hold of the pier while treading water.

"Let me go," Amanda finally managed. Her voice was a raspy croak.

"Save yourself."

"No," was all he said. Frantically he searched for a way to get them out of the water. Wood and concrete surrounded them. He finally spotted a ladder on the pier opposite them.

"There's our way out," he said. "You need to help me get us there. I can't do it alone."

Amanda only nodded.

Jason pushed away from their precarious perch. The pier was forty feet away, but it might as well have been miles. Jason looked like a drowning moose; arms and legs flailing, gulping in the filthy harbour water, making him choke and gag. Amanda used what little strength she had left to assist. Together they fought against the waves and a current that tried to pull them out to sea. Jason was surprised when he felt his hand touch the rusty metal.

He swung Amanda around in front of him, helping her get a grip on the ladder's rungs. He watched as she climbed out ahead of him, collapsing facedown on the ground when she reached the top. Moments later Jason fell alongside of her, collapsing in exhaustion.

After they'd cleared themselves of all the sea water in their lungs they lay together on the wharf; Jason's arm was draped lifelessly across Amanda's shoulders. How long they lay there, Amanda didn't know. His arm was warm against her and she could feel his breathing returning to normal. She didn't want to move. She knew once the contact was broken, reality would return, time would start moving forward again, and she'd have to face him.

Suddenly Jason sat up, pulling his arm away. The separation was jarring. Amanda lay there, keeping her eyes closed.

"Manda?" he said quietly. "I know you're awake." He reached out and touched her shoulder. Amanda pulled away roughly and stood, walking a few steps away before stopping.

"Amanda," he said more insistently.

"Please. No."

Jason stood and walked around her, and she turned with him, keeping her back to him until she was facing the sea. The wind had picked up a little and waves crashed against the pier. It made her shiver. She was soaked and the wind was chilling her, but that didn't matter.

"Amanda, you have to talk to me," Jason pleaded.

"Why can't you just trust me? You need to leave. Go as far as you can as fast as you can."

Jason paused as he looked at her. She looked resigned or defeated; he wasn't sure anymore.

"Are you trying to dump me?"

"No," she said, shaking her head.

Her wet hair whipped her face, stinging.

"Yes. Oh, please Jason, just go."

"You want me to drop everything and leave. No, explanation, no reason." Jason paused. "That's crazy."

"You have no idea."

"I would, if you'd talk to me."

She said nothing, just stood there staring at a flock of gulls that bobbed up and down on the waves. She thought them fortunate. Free.

"Amanda?"

She shivered and took a deep breath, held it, and with a slight sigh let it out all in one breath.

"You'll never believe me."

"Let me be the judge of what I will and will not believe. I can be pretty open minded. 'There are more things in heaven and earth, Horatio, than are dreamt of in your philosophy.'"

"Hamlet?" Amanda said, looking up to the horizon. "I didn't know you knew Shakespeare."

"There are a lot of things you don't know. Now, give me a chance," said Jason.

"I can't."

"If you want me to leave, you have to trust me enough to tell me the truth."

CHAPTER ELEVEN

Marc's eyes fluttered as he fought his way back to consciousness. His head throbbed horribly, and his mouth felt like something large and fuzzy had died there about a week ago. With a groan he tried to sit up but brought up solid against the restraints that held him to the bed. "What the fuck?" he muttered as he tugged against the heavy bindings. There were three heavy leather straps: one across his lower legs, another across his hips, with the last across his chest. He felt sick to his stomach and tried to look around, but he could see almost nothing.

He fought back panic. Where was he?

What was happening? Why was he naked? Thoughts of all those stupid conspiracy theory and alien abduction shows he'd watched flitted through his befuddled brain. They were right? Had he been probed? He ran his thumb over his hand. "Nope, no implants," he thought. None that he could feel anyway. The strap across his chest was a little loose, so with effort he was able to wriggle his elbows under his body and prop himself up a little, giving him a little bit better view of where he was. His initial relief at the dim lighting was washed away in a need to see his surroundings. "The fuckers have taken out my contacts," he growled under his breath, squinting myopically as he peered into the shadows.

He could just make out two forms, one to his right and one to his left, both lying on tables of their own. Marc glared up at the few dim pot lights around the ceiling as if he could make them brighter. They cast a ghostly light down on the prone figures. The Force was not with him and the lights didn't get any brighter.

Marc squinted into the darkness on his right. He was pretty sure it was George; his unclothed rotund form lay unmoving on what looked like a hospital gurney. Leather restraints lay alongside George's immobile form and his arms hung limply over the sides. Marc thought he saw what looked like trickles of dark brown dried blood that had run from George's eyes and ears, forming a small pool just beneath his jaw.

"Fuck," Marc whispered. He lay back, closing his eyes against the horror. What the hell had happened? Where were they? He tried to sit, but heavy straps lay across his chest, hips and legs. Thinking hurt, his brain felt like it was on fire.

If that were George on his right, Marc was sure it would be Jamie lying cold and lifeless to his left. He didn't want to see her like that.

The silence was broken by a soft whimper from his left. His heart sped up and he slowly turned his head to look. "Jamie?" he said in as loud a whisper as he dared. He couldn't see much, but a pale halo of light from one of the pot lights right above her lit her face just enough that he could see her profile. She looked terrified. Her eyes were open but locked unblinking on an invisible spot on the ceiling above her. Unlike George, she was still retrained, and her hands were clenched tightly into fists and her whole body seemed to be quivering slightly. She looked like she was fighting an invisible battle; every now and then she'd let out another whimper. Marc didn't know if it was pain, fear, or both.

"Jamie," he said louder. Her only response was a whimper.

"Damn it. Fucking damn it," he yelled and started to fight violently against his bonds. Waves of dizziness and nausea swept over him. "Jesus help me," he prayed. He felt like he was trapped in a bizarre urban legend come to life. As his vision began to dim, he wondered that if he woke again would he wake up in a bathtub full of ice, his kidney gone, and a cell phone taped to his hand. That was his final thought as the darkness claimed him once more.

CHAPTER TWELVE

Amanda sighed as she fought back tears. She'd spent the last two years hiding in plain sight. She'd been trained in subterfuge, and now Jason wanted her to just tell everything. He had no idea what he was asking.

She turned and looked Jason in the eye. "I was going to tell you this tonight, but I guess it'll have to be now." She paused. "I love you."

"You what?" Jason asked, completely dumbfounded at this complete turnaround.

"I love you. I need you to know that before I say anything else."

"I love you too, Amanda," Jason said, smiling as he stepped forward to hug her, but she recoiled, just stopping herself from falling into the water once again. Jason stopped cold, his arms still held out before him.

"Okay," he said, lowering his arms. He sounded so hurt Amanda's heart nearly broke, but she steeled herself. She had to be strong.

"I love you, but you need to go. You need to go because I love you."

"That is about as ass-backwards a statement as I've ever heard." Frustration was seeping into his voice now. He sounded angry and Amanda was glad to hear it.

Anger she could deal with.

"Listen to me, it's a crazy story and I don't have an ounce of proof. If you want to know the truth, I'll tell you. Once I do, do you promise to go?"

"I'll make no promise until I know why."

Amanda turned from him again.

"That will have to do, I suppose." She took one final deep breath, held it and let it out all at once, steeling herself for what she was about to say.

"I know you were doing some astronomy in school."

"Yeah…"

"Well," Amanda paused and stared at the water glistening on the ground. Tiny prisms refracting in what little light there was. "You aren't going to believe it."

"Try me."

"I don't know how to start. It's incredulous to even me."

"Just say it."

Amanda turned and looked at him over her shoulder. "How many species do you think are on Earth?"

"I dunno, lots. Maybe millions?"

"Around 8.7 million."

"That's specific."

"It is. Species of all types from bacteria that can live by volcanoes to complex creatures like homo sapiens."

"Okay." Jason nodded but looked more confused than ever. "Where is she going with this?" he thought.

"With all that diversity, do you think humans are the only sentient species?"

"Of course not," Jason answered immediately. "We have dolphins and whales as well as other primates."

Amanda hesitated before continuing, "What about single-celled species?"

"No. "

"Are you certain?"

"I'm into computers not microbes, but no, there is nothing I know of on Earth that has any real intelligence."

"What about the ones they found from Mars?"

"They were fossils in rocks. I don't know anything else about them."

"So, you believe that there could be life elsewhere?"

"Of course. So many solar systems with so many planets. It's narcissistic of us to assume to be the only intelligent life in the universe. Why?"

Amanda continued, ignoring his question. "How much do you know about the Perseids meteor shower?"

"Random."

"How much do you know?"

"I know some. It happens in August. The meteors come from the asteroid belt for the most part."

"Okay. What if I told you that of all the thousands of meteors that shower Earth during the meteor shower not all of the meteors came from the asteroid?"

"I'd call bullshit and ask how you knew."

"Let's say I heard it somewhere."

"Then I'd ask when you started getting secrets from NASA."

"This isn't from NASA."

"SETI then, or do I want to know from where?"

"Probably not, but you asked. Do you remember back in 1993 NASA found fossilized bacteria from Mars in a meteor here on Earth?" Amanda shivered as a low ground fog crept its way forward like a predator stalking its prey. Its tendrils wrapped around them, shrouding them, giving them a sense of isolation. "How many of those meteors actually make it through the atmosphere and deposit debris or hit the Earth? And of those, how many are seen by people?

"Most likely hundreds, if not thousands, but I doubt many are seen by people. Ones like that big one that hit Russia a few years ago are rare. There's a reason meteor hunters have day jobs."

"So, do you think that it is plausible of the thousands of meteors hitting the Earth each year, some could hold life?"

"Like, alien life?"

"More or less."

"Statistically it's not likely."

"Why?"

"NASA tracks anything that doesn't come from our solar system, so they'd know if something like that came through, let alone had an impact course with Earth."

"NASA isn't infallible. They don't even have a full catalogue of all near-Earth asteroids, let alone small rocks." Amanda paused, wrapping her arms around herself, and shivered. "So, I ask again, is it possible?"

Jason stopped to think. He thought about all the things he'd read over the years. The writings of Sagan, Einstein, and Hawking. The universe was impossibly expansive. Sagan once said, "The universe is a pretty big place. If it's just us, it seems like an awful waste of space."

"Yeah, it is. Really anything is possible, but most things aren't plausible or even probable. If I apply Occam's Razor..."

"Occam's Razor?"

"You've had to have heard of it."

Amanda gave him a look of consternation.

"Occam's Razor states that the simplest explanation is usually the truth."

"Usually. Not always."

Jason nodded his acquiescence. "Fair enough. Continue please."

"The fact is some meteorites do contain active life. Most burn up in the atmosphere. No one ever knows. Others don't survive this planet."

"I'm still calling bullshit, but I do concede that Earth is a toxic place. Our nice corrosive atmosphere and water. It protects us quite well."

"Yes, it does." Amanda smiled weakly. "However, it's not perfect. A microscopic creature called a tardigrade can live quite well in multiple hostile environments right here on Earth. So why not other microbes?"

"You're saying some survive?"

"Yes. In 2008 a handful survived. They crashed into the Atlantic Ocean just off the coast of North Carolina."

"Right." Jason dragged the word out, so it sounded more like "Riiig-gghhhttttt."

"It's true. No one saw its spectacular fiery entry before it impacted the Atlantic Ocean, spraying water and steam a hundred feet in the air. It broke apart as its superheated exterior hit the cooler water, dumping its contents into the sea."

"How do you know all this?" Jason asked hesitantly. She hadn't answered this question yet and he had a feeling he didn't want to hear it.

Amanda continued, once again acting as if she'd not heard him. "This little meteor didn't come from Earth's nearby asteroid. Its journey was much longer. It came from the solar system called 70 Virginis."

"Okay, I'll play along. How frigging long did it take the space rock to get here?"

"If it had flown by itself? Billions of years. Six hundred and ten, to be exact."

Jason gave her an incredulous look.

"Fuck."

"Yes. Very much fuck. Some species are far more patient than others."

"How frigging far away is the Virgin system?"

"It's 70 Virginis, and it's around seventy-eight light-years from Earth."

"So, you are saying that bacteria survived for that long?"

"This species did. That little rock held an occupying force."

"A what? How?" Jason was skeptical.

"Thousands of the rocks were sent out from the Virginis system. The rocks didn't have propulsion systems as such. They were shot from a space station that orbited Acantha. Each given a destination planet that was thought to hold life. They could use outgassing for small manoeuvres. Newtonian physics was their best bet."

Jason nodded, getting caught up in the story. "An object in motion remains in motion unless acted upon by an outside force."

"Exactly. Like the gravity of a solar system. It slowed the rock, and the small gas jets allowed its occupants to align its trajectory with Earth."

"I'd love to study this rock." Jason was sure Amanda was having a go at him. No way was this true, and, if it were, there was no way for her to know.

Now that she'd started talking, she couldn't seem to stop. "It was a crap shoot that they would make it to a viable planet. Most probably never did."

Jason stood looking at Amanda's back, the fog twisting and rolling between them. She was shrouded in a cloak of mist; pale, with wisps of her drying fair hair fluttering in the wind, she looked like a wraith. The fog held her every word, letting it linger. Jason shuddered.

She took a breath before continuing. "Acanthans are similar to Earth's amoeba but their unique cellular structure allowed them to hibernate in the frigid temperatures of space, it protected against the hellish heat of re-entry and then the highly corrosive salt water. Remember tardigrades?" She gave him another deadpan stare.

"Alright. I get it. Who named them?"

"They named themselves."

"Amanda, I know I've said this before, so at the risk of sounding repetitive, I have to say again, bullshit."

"No bullshit, Jason. I promise."

"I asked for the truth and you give me some sci-fi bullshit answer. If you wanted to break up, you should have just said so." He was angry. "You didn't have to go to these lengths."

"I didn't want to break up with you."

"Didn't?" Jason looked angry and hurt.

"I don't."

"That's not how it looks to me."

"I promise. You wanted the truth. I'm telling you the truth," Amanda snapped, her own anger coming to the surface. "You promised me you'd keep an open mind."

Jason gave her a hard look. She stared back at him, defiant and yet so sad. He wasn't sure what to think anymore, but she was right, he'd promised. "Okay, Amanda. Assuming this is all truth, how do you know about it? You work for MIB?"

"Who?"

"The Men in Black. You know, the guys from Roswell. Area 51? Alien hunters?"

"No, I don't work for MIB. They aren't real," she said with a dismissive flick of her hand. It was as if MIB were the most ludicrous thing to believe in. Jason almost laughed. After the story she'd spun MIB sounded downright sane.

Amanda turned and looked out at the ocean. It was murky, and rain-swollen, but for so many species, both terrestrial and non, water was the birthplace of life and she'd always been drawn to it.

"Jason, let me finish, please."

She didn't see him nod but continued. "Unlike Earth's amoebas you can see Acanthans with the naked eye, but only barely and they are sentient. They have a mission."

"And what would that be?"

"To infect whatever species they found."

"Of course it is," Jason said derisively.

Amanda looked over her shoulder and glared. "What they found on the Carolina coast was a treasure trove of people who spent the hot summer months swimming in the warm water."

"Infect?"

"Yes, infect. Or perhaps finding a host body would be better."

"Host body does not sound better."

"Perhaps not, but it's more accurate." She thought briefly of all those thousands of Acanthan lost. At the mercy of the currents, some were torn apart by storms, eaten by phytoplankton; or swallowed by sea life. Less than one hundred of the nearly three thousand creatures that had survived millennia of space travel had made it to shore.

"How the hell do they find people? Chance?"

"They can track the electronic signal emitted by mammalian hearts. Any mammals that use the shallow coastal waters were targeted. They had no way of knowing so many species populate this planet."

"So not all of them found humans?"

"No. Some found their way into other animals like pets or wildlife. Only a handful made it into the bodies of humans and not all were adult humans."

"You mean kids were infected?"

"Of course. Microbes don't discriminate. They just want a viable host. Nothing more. Nothing less."

"Do I want to ask how they infect?"

"Probably not. When people are infected, they get disoriented and confused. Some might look or sound drunk."

"Like the people at work."

She turned, and Jason could see her playing with her necklace. She absently rolled the small black stone back and forth between her fingers. It was the one he'd give her, made from the meteorite. The irony wasn't lost on him.

"Yes, like them. Unlike normal terrestrial amoeboid brain infections, we don't usually kill the host. That would be counterproductive to our purpose."

Jason stared, open mouth, at his girlfriend. "Amanda, what do you mean, 'we?'"

Amanda paled as she realized her slip.

CHAPTER THIRTEEN

Amanda could feel Jason behind her. She could feel the anger and hurt radiating from him. She couldn't blame him; she'd betrayed him, manipulated him and, as he saw it, planned on killing him. She hated herself for it. Looking back, she knew she should have acted sooner, but how do you turn on your people? No matter what she did, she'd betray someone she loved.

Amanda thought back to the first human she'd processed. She had only been Amanda for a few weeks at that point. She was cold and analytical and had found a young girl, only thirteen years old, a prodigy. Without any thought to the girl or her welfare, Amanda had drugged her and brought her to Tony for processing. It was the first time they'd tried to process a teen. It did not go well.

Amanda looked down at the girl strapped to the table. She was so young. Amanda had reservations on how well this would work. As a biologist, she understood human physiology. Children were the easiest to process with their wonderful developing brains; next were young adults whose hormone levels had evened out. The elderly were also easy to process but it was risky as they were prone to brain degradation. Teens were a different beast, filled with a cocktail of hormones that sent their brains reeling. However, Tony was insistent. The girl was impressive: a chess master by the time she was eleven, able to solve complex mathematical problems in half the time of even the most advanced computer.

Right now, she was just a scared little girl who was begging for her life. She was stripped naked, strapped to a cold metal table, and surrounded by strangers. Humans were vile to each other and Amanda knew what the girl had to be thinking. She had no way of knowing that if this worked, she'd be elevated.

Sometimes when she closed her eyes at night Amanda could still see the news flashes: "MISSING GIRL IN BOSTON AREA: JESSICA LAKE" and above it a smiling picture of Jessica with her family, her pet Jack Russell snuggled up in her arms and looking up at her adoringly. The Amanda of now wanted to cry, the Amanda from then didn't care.

Tony handed Amanda a petri dish with four small amoebas swimming in the clear fluid.

"I've decided to give her to you," Tony cooed as he ran his hands over her arms and she smiled over her shoulder at him, while Jessica sobbed on the table below them. "These are your children. Pick one, give them life."

"Are you sure? At her age this could be problematic."

"I'm sure." He looked down at the girl hungrily and she began to cry. Amanda's only response was a nod.

Jessica looked up pleadingly at Amanda. "Please, lady. Let me go. I promise I won't tell anyone," she sobbed. Amanda looked down at her coldly, analytically. Tears streaked the girl's pale face and plastered her brown hair to her face. Gently Amanda brushed the hairs aside; they'd be in the way.

"Shush, child. Everything will be okay. We have no intentions of hurting you. We're here to help."

Maybe she'd be okay, maybe they'd let her go. That small spark of hope lit her face and she gave Amanda a small tentative smile. The innocence of youth made her want to trust someone. Anyone. She knew the man, who was now standing a few feet away behind the woman, was evil. The woman might had taken her, but she'd not abused her. The creepy skinny man was the one who had stripped her and tied her down. When she struggled, he'd hit her hard, splitting her lip and swelling one eye almost shut; but maybe the woman would help?

Her brief hope was crushed as Amanda took a squishy worm from the dish and placed it in the palm of her hand, where it squirmed and wriggled. Gently she stroked it and looked at it with affection.

"This is my gift to you," Amanda said.

"What... what is that?" Jessica asked between sobs.

"This is humanity's salvation," Amanda said as she slid her offspring off her hand and onto the girls' face.

Jessica whimpered and tried to shake it free. Her head was strapped down so her movements were small and futile. The slimy little thing held fast and worked its way into her nose. She could feel it slithering its way inside. She'd been crying hard and the mucous helped the Acanthan work its way in faster. It was only a few minutes before it reached her brain. The small creature latched onto the cerebellum and small fibrous tendrils dove into Jessica's brain, wrapping around it and fighting for control.

It felt like her skull was on fire. She screamed and thrashed as the Acanthan's tentacles burrowed deep. Screams tore her throat raw. Amanda looked at Tony, "We need to find a solution to this. They make too much noise and are going to harm the host."

"Yes. Anesthesia might be a good solution."

"We'll have to see how hard it is to get a hold of."

Amanda and Tony watched dispassionately while a war of survival raged inside the girl's body, Acanthan versus Earthling. In this particular battle, neither *would win. Jessica's eyes rolled up in her head as she began to convulse. Spasms wracked her body as her muscles involuntarily contracted and relaxed in rapid fire. There was a loud snap as a bone in her arm broke. Her jaw was clenched so tight she bit her tongue and bloody froth poured from her mouth. Slowly the spasms reduced to twitches which reduced to stillness.*

Amanda checked for a pulse and shook her head when there was no flutter of life beneath her fingertips.

"Damn it," Tony grumbled. "She was so promising."

"I feared something like this would happen, though I confess I was not expecting this violent a reaction."

"It was unexpected."

"Teens will be difficult, their bodies are in too much of a state of chemical and hormonal flux to adapt to the symbiote. They will carry a high risk of rejection."

"Pity," Tony said as he turned to leave.

"Dispose of her, will you?"

Amanda looked down at the lifeless form.

"Of course."

Jessica's body was found three days later by a fisherman who'd taken his kids out on the Neponset River. One of his children had spotted something pale bobbing in the water near the shoreline. The police retrieved her cold, bloated body from where it had caught on a tree. The police said it was murder, but they had no suspects. Amanda had made sure there was no link back to CloneZone or herself. She'd watched every news piece she could find on it. The girl's death bothered her. She couldn't figure out why but every time she thought about Jessica, she felt a little sick to her stomach and she wanted to cry.

It was very un-Acanthan.

Amanda felt weak and nauseated as the memory washed over her. She'd hurt so many people. Killed people. Children. At the time she'd convinced herself that she was trying to save them, to save humanity from it's violent and self-destructive tendencies. She shook her head, but it wasn't the truth. It was a lie she'd accepted to make what she did easier. An excuse to exterminate an entire species. The truth was exactly what she'd told Jason, they were an invasion force. Their goal was to spread, take over the sentient species of the planet, make them Acanthan.

She sometimes wondered if they'd come to humanity in peace, would some humans have volunteered? Likely not. Humans were a xenophobic species and clannish to a fault, and Acanthans were obsessed with spreading. From what she knew of people, most would prefer death to any type of control.

She couldn't do anything to bring Jessica or the others that had been sacrificed back, but she could honour them by saving those that she could.

Amanda looked out over the water. She took a deep breath and closed her eyes for a moment, forcing the tears for all those gone from the corner of her eyes. The ocean soothed her, and right now she needed soothing and to be able to focus more than she ever had before.

She loved Earth's oceans; they reminded her of Acantha, though it was the wrong colour. Oceans were the birthplace of so many species throughout the universe. Even here on Earth, all life came from the sea and the variety and number were staggering, an anomaly in the universe. Most of humanity, with their myopic view of day-to-day life, didn't stop to look at the beauty that surrounded them. A few looked up, but they were rare.

Amanda considered herself an Earthling. She'd been born here and by human measurement she was only a couple of years old, but by microbial standards she was born mature with a full set of memories from all her predecessors encoded on her mitochondrial DNA. She could access them as needed. She closed her eyes as flashes of memory flicked behind her eyes.

She was swimming in the warm pink ocean that teemed with microbial life. There were only a few multi-cell life forms on the planet and only one of them sentient. The two species developed on different parts of the planet, so they knew nothing of each other until the mammals began to explore. All it took was one of the mammals swimming, and it was sheer accident that the amoeba slipped in but when it did, it took the mammal as its recipient. Instead of being hosts, the mammalian Acanthan species developed a symbiotic relationship with their tiny invaders. The microbe and mammal shared a consciousness with each other. It was this hybridization that gave the microbes mobility and true self-awareness. Together they augmented each other. The Acanthan intelligence developed exponentially and it was only a few millennia before they'd achieved space flight. Interstellar flight and conquest came shortly after. Planets that the Acanthan body could withstand were rare so their invasion plan was simple: fill a rock with the microbes, shoot it at the planet from outside the solar system and wait. Simple and safe.

She remembered the feeling of the soft blue fur on her body, the colony ships, and generation upon generation travelling through space. Memories of being selected for colonization, being placed in the rock, years of travel in that little rock, the brutal entry through Earth's atmosphere and the shock of Earth's oceans flitted through her mind, bringing her back to the recent past.

How could she ever explain all of this to Jason? How could any human ever understand? Especially one who knew she'd been sent to get him.

"Amanda..." Tony cooed in her ear as he ran his hands over Amanda's shoulders. She fought hard to stop from pulling away as she sat in the briefing room with the two other members of the Earth-bound Acanthan leadership. Tony was

her superior officer and under Acanthan law, she and all other of his subordinates were at his mercy.

"Yes, sir?"

"We've a new assignment for you. A young human named Jason Donoghue."

"Yes, he's a very promising MIT student. I found him." Walter sat there smugly. Amanda refused to acknowledge Walter's comment and, as they held equal rank, she could.

His obsequious and sycophantic attitude irritated her. He did everything he could to ingratiate himself with Tony and it worked.

Tony smiled at Walter, allowing him his moment. "A computer engineering major. He's also got a biology background. He's perfect for the position we have available. We need to finish that project. Walter did well in finding this one," Tony said, giving Amanda a very pointed look.

"Even though he's not in charge of recruitment."

"Very good work, Walter," Amanda said with a brief nod. It irked her to give him any credit. If she didn't acknowledge Walter, they'd know how much this did irritate her and she'd never give them that pleasure. She turned to look at Tony, who'd gone to sit across from his protégé. "Standard procedure?" she asked.

Tony shook his head. "Not with this one. He really has some of the best potential we've seen in quite some time and he is easy to get to. As you know, the less afraid a subject is when processed the better the chance of success, so we want him to be as relaxed as possible."

"Very well, sir. What would you like me to do?"

"Seduce him."

"I beg your pardon?" Amanda raised her eyebrows so high it looked like they were trying to meet her hairline. "You want me to do what?"

"You heard me. Seduce him."

"That is not in my job description."

"It is now," Walter said as he looked her up and down with a look of disgust. "You've finally gotten an assignment that you should be good at."

Amanda rounded on the older man and growled. "Shut up, you old coot."

"Commanders," Tony snapped.

Amanda and Walter turned from each other sharply and faced their Captain.

"Yes, sir," they said in unison, though Amanda still managed to glare at Walter from the corner of her eye.

"Amanda, you can see that of the three of us, you are uniquely suited to this role. An attractive young woman, slightly younger than he is. You are both interested in the sciences and have much in common. You have a chance at striking up a conversation with him that is natural and would leave him unsuspecting of any ulterior motives."

Amanda nodded as Tony continued.

"*Neither I nor Walter have this in with him. He'd suspect something right from the start.*"

Amanda mulled it over for a while as she leafed through the small dossier they had on Jason. She held up a photo they had downloaded from MIT's database. Not bad looking at all, so this mission wouldn't be as dismal as she'd feared, and his dossier was impressive. A young software entrepreneur, he'd saved up all the money to attend school. He was only working to cover his day-to-day expenses. IQ of 155, foundation in engineering and human biology. Yes, he'd be a valuable asset if they could recruit him without any corruption. She put the photo down and looked at Tony. "Very well. When do I start?"

Tony smiled and said, "Go to the bar he works at, meet him there and work your magic."

CHAPTER FOURTEEN

Marc found himself fighting his way back to consciousness. It was like swimming to the surface after a deep dive; watery haloed lights flickered before his barely opened eyes. His arms, no, his whole body felt heavy. He lay still and listening to the sound of his breathing. There was a dull ache that thrummed through his body.

"I'm still alive."

Forcing his eyes fully open, Marc found that he was still in the same cold, dry, antiseptic room with the hospital smell, complete with the pervasive undertone of death that stuck in his throat, making him gag. Whatever they'd used to drug him must have been finally wearing off because the dizziness and disorientation were gone, thinking was easier, and his head didn't hurt so much.

Marc tried to sit but the effort was short-lived thanks to the thick leather straps that were still firmly in place. He gave a few futile angry jerks against the restraints.

"Fuck." His voice sounded hollow in the noiseless room and with a frustrated growl he let his head flop back down.

From his limited vantage point, Marc tried to look around. Someone had been in. The room was brighter, and a soft cotton sheet had been draped over him. Slowly he looked to the right again, hoping he'd been wrong about what he'd seen the last time he had been awake. No, he hadn't been mistaken, George was still dead. Whomever had killed him hadn't even bothered to cover the body. He was horrible to look at; his flesh was a pale grey and flaccid, with the purple bruising from lividity just beginning to show along the backs of his arms and legs.

Gulping the fetid air to try and keep from vomiting on himself, Marc looked back up at the ceiling and closed his eyes. Bile rose in his throat, burning. He suspected that puking in his current predicament wouldn't be pleasant.

He was afraid to look and see what had befallen Jamie while he'd slept. Would he see her cold and lifeless body, with creamy blue-white eyes staring into nothing? As soon as he was sure he had control of his stomach, he turned his head.

Jamie was alive and looking perfectly healthy. Her restraints had been removed, and she was sitting cross-legged on the gurney, dressed in a simple blue hospital gown with a blanket laid across her lap. She was holding her hands in front of her and was playing with her fingers. She was looking at them in awe, as if she'd never seen them before. She had a huge smile, and her red hair was hanging limply around her face.

He tried to speak but his voice was little more than a croak. He worked his mouth to summon a little moisture and managed a hoarse whisper. "Jamie, thank God you're alive."

She didn't respond. "What the hell?" His thoughts were quickly going from relief to surprise at seeing her free then to hurt and anger. "If she's free, why hasn't she bothered to try and help me?"

"Jamie? Jamie, you okay? Can you help me? Do you know where we are?"

Jamie didn't so much as turn her head but replied, "Why yes, Mother, I'd love some ice cream," and then began to pantomime eating a bowl of ice cream. Jamie should be freaking out about being in a locked room, but she sat there calmly eating her invisible ice cream.

"Shit," he said, letting his head flop down. He gave the room another look, as best he could from his awkward position. It wasn't overly large, only twenty feet square with blank white seamless walls and a ten-foot-high ceiling. The only lighting came from the pot lights spaced evenly about the ceiling. Only half of the lights worked and of the ones that did, most were flickering, giving the room a surreal strobing effect. Against the far wall he could just make out the outline of some cabinets and a sink, but his position prevented him from seeing the wall behind his head or the floor below. Lined up side by side in the middle of the room were four narrow wheeled gurneys with sides that could be raised. He, George, and Jamie occupied three; one was vacant. All the gurneys were adorned with the brown leather restraining straps and each gurney had its own instrument trays filled with bizarre looking tools and dishes.

"Fuck," Marc muttered again while giving another tug on his restraints. He didn't like feeling helpless. "We've gotta get the fuck outta here."

He was talking out loud to Jamie. He'd figured out she wasn't here mentally and probably wouldn't respond but talking out loud helped calm him. And he needed that right now: calm and focus. It was up to him to find a way out.

With deliberate actions he began to test his bonds. All three straps were still in place, but the hip strap was just a little looser. He didn't know if it was from all his wiggling or if it was someone's error. Either way, he wasn't going to waste this opportunity.

With some effort he managed to wriggle his right arm up until his elbow was bent at a very uncomfortable angle. His attempts were halted when his wrist brought up against the strap.

"No freaking way." Marc gritted his teeth and twisted his wrist, dragging it hard against the rough leather. Friction burned his skin and tore flesh. He bit down on his lip to stop himself from crying out. Blood smeared over his wrist, wetting the leather and lubricating the strap. With one final tug he pulled his lower arm free and then did the same with his other arm, but now he felt a little like a T-Rex. He could move and wave his arms from the elbows down but couldn't reach anything.

Blindly he felt around. He ran his hands over the leather chest strap but could not feel anything that might be a fastener. He moved on to the one on his hips. As he felt along, he touched cool metal. He lifted his head to try and see but the buckle was too low down on his left hip. It was a simple thick leather strap with a belt buckle fastener. He tried to pull it free, but it was too tight, and he was one-handed.

Taking a deep breath, Marc tried to relax his body as much as he could, hoping it would release the tension on the strap. His fingers barely reached, and he painstakingly worked the leather through the buckle. It felt like it took forever, but he finally heard a soft clink as the strap fell free.

This freedom gave him some wiggle room. Using the sides of the gurney as leverage, Marc grasped them and began wiggling and squirming. Slowly, he managed to work himself down the table until his shoulders and arms were completely free. The pressure from the leg strap bit into his bare flesh. Determined, Marc ignored it and pushed on.

The top strap was still high around his neck when he ran out of room to scrunch down, but by then his arms were free and he was able to quickly undo that strap. The moment he was unfettered, Marc sat up. A wave of dizziness washed over him, and he gripped the sides of the gurney for balance.

"Too fast," he said and shook his head while taking slow deep breaths.

He took a quick look at Jamie who was still sitting there examining the fine details of her fingers.

Once he was steadied, Marc quickly undid the final restraint. As it fell away, he stretched his muscles, feeling the cramping and stiffness. He must have been out for a couple of hours at least.

Finally, he stood. The floor was icy beneath his feet and with a start he realized that he was still naked. Shooting a bashful glance at Jamie, his normally olive complexion flushed a deep crimson. Someone, a stranger, had completely undressed him. There was a stack of gowns like the one Jamie was wearing on the counter behind where he'd been lying. He reached over and grabbed one, pulling it on quickly and tying the straps behind his back.

He felt violated. A shudder of revulsion ran down his spine as he thought about how completely helpless he'd been. He had no memory of anything after the classroom. What had they done to him? As he looked over at Jamie, who had gone back to eating her invisible ice cream, and George's lifeless form, Marc reached behind him to pull the gown closed over his rear end and wondered if he would even remember if anything had been done to him.

Or if he wanted to.

CHAPTER FIFTEEN

Amanda had done as she was instructed. Her job was to recruit; she was good at it and she knew that Jason wouldn't stand a chance. People trusted the perky young woman with the wide earnest smile. She'd recruited scientists, business people, politicians, grandparents. She'd tricked them all saying she was a student looking to do a work term or doing a report. No one suspected. Humans were gross and violent. They took pleasure in killing other species, even their own. What Amanda hadn't counted on was falling in love. Real, human emotional love. Acanthans fancied themselves logical. They did have feelings; however logic would dictate their course of action. Emotions were frowned upon as motivational forces.

Bonding with humans changed this factor. Their complex mix of hormones and neurochemicals associated with these emotions overwhelmed the Acanthans. It affected them all: in Tony it presented as becoming addicted to personal pleasures, mostly food and sex, while Walter was hooked on daytime and reality television, and Amanda, well, she'd fallen in love with her assignment.

A smile flicked at the corner of her lips as she remembered the first time she saw Jason. He was behind the bar in that dingy dive, wiping everything down as he went and laughing with the patrons. The place stank and it took all she had to not turn on her heel and leave. Especially after the bar's patrons started ogling her as she walked across the floor and climbed up onto a bar stool. Then Jason turned to her, smiled, and she'd looked into his bright green eyes as he said, "What can I getcha?" In that moment she had felt something. Something she'd never felt before: raw physical attraction. The part of her that was Amanda recognized it—she'd felt it before—but her Acanthan part flinched. This was not part of the plan. Gamely she tried to stay focused that night, but as they'd talked, she felt more at ease with him. It was almost as if they'd known each other for years as they'd talked about none-sense, a word she used when humans made small talk about nothing important, none-sense. It was foolish talk about school, the wacky weather, videogames, favourite moves, books, you name it and they probably touched on it that night. She'd had fun and she wasn't sure what to do about it.

Over the months she worked on building a rapport with Jason, convincing him to give up his night job and go to work at CloneZone. He didn't want to, but she'd told him how important it was that he have a regular job with regular hours. She'd convinced him that MIT would still be there waiting for him.

Tony and Walter were thrilled at her progress. They were going to get the computer engineer they so desperately needed. Tony was so anxious he wanted to process Jason on his first week at CloneZone, but Jason skipped work that day, calling in that he had a last-minute appointment. Next time he was stuck on a call. Then he'd been late. Every time they'd set up for a new class to process, Jason wasn't there. Amanda had helped by changing class time, but she'd been unable to do it all. Tony himself had set up some of the classes, but still Jason dodged the bullet. If she'd been religious, it was almost as if divine intervention were interceding on his behalf. Tony was getting impatient. He wanted Jason processed and working on the code they needed.

She shook her head and droplets of icy water spattered across her face. She'd grown to care for Jason and by extension humanity. Watching her co-workers, people she'd befriended, wander around bumping into walls, the blood curdling screams from those who had awakened during the process, and disposing of the bodies of men and women that didn't survive had eroded her Acanthan dispassion. Amanda's empathy grew with each person she helped process, and it became harder and harder for her to send someone to the grinder. She was trapped. Tony would kill her rather than see her defect or even if he suspected how *human* she'd become.

Even before Jason she had stopped being in the centre when a processing was happening. She'd found herself falsifying candidate information to make them less appealing or harder to find, she'd delayed adding people to training and she'd purposefully ordered scented nitrous oxide gas, hoping that the smell would alert the victims to their peril. The scented gas had worked, people had fled the room, and when it couldn't be explained by the manager, they left.

"Why the fuck did you order that shit? We lost three classes of hosts yesterday," Tony had yelled at her as he paced back and forth their staging room.

"You try finding a place that will deliver nitrous oxide gas to a printing company without asking any questions," she snapped back. "I had to get it from the black market. It wasn't easy or cheap and it was the only stuff available. If it's not satisfactory, you can do your own ordering."

She normally felt safe to speak to him this way when Walter wasn't around. Tony was her commanding officer but also her Acanthan parent. She'd misjudged his anger.

"Do you want to get written up for insubordination?" he hissed through clenched teeth.

Amanda looked at Tony in shock.

She'd never seen him this angry with her. Insubordination to an officer of Tony's rank was a capital offence. Punishment could mean removal from the host or worse. Did he suspect her?

"No, sir," she said meekly.

"Order more. Until then I'll get Walter to have the locks rigged to set automatically. That should solve our problem for now."

Still, she'd managed to slow things down and save a few people. It wasn't much, but it was a start. Then she'd met Jason. Initially she'd planned on finding a way to convince Tony that this kid wasn't worth the effort, that the dossier was wrong.

Today she realized just how much she really did love him. The reality had scared her.

Tony was printing off papers and grinning from ear to ear.

"Why are you so happy?"

"Your idiot boyfriend just gave me the chance I've been waiting for."

"What do you mean?"

"He was late. I put him on probation with required training. Training that you will schedule for today." Tony tapped his little stack off papers to the tune of shave and a haircut. "I am finally going to get him into that classroom."

"I hear a *but* in there."

"You certainly do. He called me a, what was it now?" Tony put his finger to his lips as he tried to recall precisely the name Jason called him. "Oh, that's right. He called me a 'Goddamned troll fucker.'"   "To   your face?"

"No. He didn't have the balls for that.
I heard him mumble it as he walked away."

Amanda tried to stifle her laugh. It came out as a snort.

"Do you find something amusing, Commander?" Tony said as he tried to puff himself up.

"He looks like an overstuffed chicken," Amanda thought to herself, fighting back more laughter.

"No, Captain. Please continue. What is your plan now?"

Tony smiled and it scared Amanda. "Oh Amanda, we are going to process him, but I'm using the next gens."

"Tony, you can't."

His head snapped up and a frown pulled his narrow lips down into a thin line. "You forget yourself. I can and I will." He gave her a long hard stare. "If I didn't know better, I'd say you were concerned."

Amanda drew herself up. "You misunderstand me. He's a valuable asset and they aren't ready. He'll go mad."

He nodded, "I've supplied Walter with a syringe filled with ketamine."

"Animal tranquilizer? Why?"

"If he goes mad during processing, we will deal with him. Permanently."

"Oh," Amanda said as she chewed on her bottom lip.

Tony was taken aback. "You do not approve?" he said sharply.

Amanda looked up quickly. "I was just thinking..." Amanda's thoughts trailed off as she tried to come up with some reason for her concerns.

"But?"

"As I already said, he's a valuable resource. I thought we were going to make the most of him. "

"That would be preferable but at this point I'll take what I can get."

"Let me look into it, see what I can come up with. Maybe we can increase the odds of his survival."

Tony waved her off with dismissive flick of his hand. "Do whatever you feel is necessary. Just ensure there is a nice, compliant and processed Jason waiting for me after work."

With a nod, she turned on her heel and left. She didn't want Jason processed, didn't want him to change, and certainly didn't want him dead.

She liked the Jason she had, but she had no idea what she was going to do between now and the afternoon to change things or get him out once and for all. Not without getting them both killed.

CHAPTER SIXTEEN

Amanda felt her world spin around her.

"Amanda. Answer me," Jason insisted.

Amanda couldn't look at Jason, couldn't speak. The words were stopped by the lump in her throat. She shook her head.

"Damn it, Amanda, don't dare you leave it there. Are you one of them?" Jason's voice was bitter and angry.

After what felt like an eternity, Amanda said weakly, "I meant they." For the first time in her existence Amanda was ashamed of what she was.

"Like hell you did." Jason wanted to throw up. "The truth. Now." Jason was desperate to know. "Or I'll go ask Tony."

With a sob she blurted out, "Yes, it's *we*." Once the words started, she couldn't stop them. "Me, Tony, Walter, all of upper management, the entire crew of the printing centre and by now most of the call centre."

"Fuck. Me." Jason felt weak. "So, you're saying I'm working for fucking brain-eating aliens?"

Amanda nodded as tears streamed down her face. She hated this human body sometimes and its weaknesses. Acanthans were creatures of logic, humans were nothing more than balls of emotion in a meat wrapping.

"I swear if I close my eyes, I'll hear Rod Serling." Jason paused to take a deep, steadying breath before continuing. "Where are Scully and Mulder when you need them?"

"Who?" Amanda asked.

Jason just looked at her and wondered how he'd ever fallen for her. It had to be some alien pheromone bullshittery. She/it/Amanda didn't know who Serling or Mulder were. "Assuming I believe this, is any of the real Amanda left?"

"Yes. I am Amanda."

"Bullshit. Pretty sure Amanda's real brain wasn't made up of cytoplasm."

"Her current brain isn't made up of cytoplasm. I guess it's really, *we* are Amanda. We don't erase the person. Not completely. We bond with them. Through the bond we get access to most of their memories and feelings. Once we're, well, attached, their thoughts become ours; ours, become theirs. We literally become them outside of some insignificant memory loss, . So really, no one has died."

"That is only a technicality." Anger flushed his face.

"An important one."

"So, you're a parasite and *my* Amanda is gone."

It was Amanda's turn to be angry. "We aren't a parasite. We're intelligent and she was never *your* Amanda. You didn't own her. Furthermore, you never met her. You've only ever known me."

Jason reeled backwards. "Wait. What?" he asked, dumbstruck.

"That's right. Me. You fell in love with a, as you put it, *brain-eating alien.*" She said the words with such venom and self-hatred Jason almost felt bad for her. Amanda saw her chance to finally drive Jason away. "The only reason we met was because Tony wanted to recruit you. I was *sent* to you. I was your recruitment officer."

"What the hell do you mean?" Jason looked as if he'd been slapped. All colour had drained from his face and he looked sick.

"I mean, the hierarchy wanted you. We've been recruiting highly intelligent people with specific skills. Any one of those jobs would have put you in a great position as one of our agents. They wanted you badly. A nice young, hormone-driven human male. Ripe for the picking."

She turned to look at him. She pulled the shield of Acanthan arrogance and superiority around herself. She stood tall, looking down her nose at him, even though he was taller than her. He was staring at her slack-jawed. Each word struck home like a knife. "So, we studied you and knew you'd respond to a pretty face. We groomed you. It was the long way of getting you in position, but it worked." She smiled evilly. "Processing is so much more effective when the host is receptive."

"So, I was nothing more than your assignment."

Amanda didn't answer his question. She couldn't. "You have a wonderful mind. We wanted it."

"You can't have it," Jason growled.

"I know that now. You'd have been processed by now if you hadn't missed every single training session. Tony was ready to cut you from the program. Take the loss. I thought you had too much potential, so I convinced him and scheduled you in one last time."

"The training session this afternoon." It was a statement, not a question.

"Yes."

"What would have happened if I'd gone?"

"You'd have been processed." Her voice was dead, void of any emotion.

Jason waited, letting her words sort themselves out in his reeling mind. He felt angry, confused, hurt, and scared all at the same time. Each emotion took centre stage for a brief, painful moment before being shoved out of the way by the next in a flickering emotional kaleidoscope. His head spun, and his stomach heaved as he sat down heavily on the wharf. He was shivering with a mix of cold and shock.

"Aliens?" he thought. "Fucking aliens."

He looked over at Amanda. She looked like a half-drowned rat. Her blonde hair was dirty and plastered to her head and face. Her wet clothes clung to her. He wanted to feel sorry for her, a small part already did, but he couldn't. She had this look about her. She looked like Amanda, but not the one he'd known. When she looked at him, he felt like a bug. As he looked at her, anger won out, pushing all the other emotions aside. She was a bug, but she considered him nothing more than a host to be taken. He was a meat suit. He shook his head and as he did some pieces of Amanda's story began to click together. He looked up sharply at her and demanded, "Where's Marc?"

Amanda was caught off guard and answered, "Training."

"You mean, processed." His words came out through teeth clenched in anger.

"Oh," she whispered, looking away again. "He'll be a host by now."

"Fuck," Jason yelled. "Fuck everything." He kicked a thick wooden pier piling, sending a shot of pain up his foot and ankle. He barely noticed it. He was angry. Angrier than he'd ever been. He was fighting back rage as he turned towards Amanda and she stepped back, her eyes wide. She'd never been afraid of Jason, but he seemed on the verge of completely losing it.

"Jason?" she said, a quaver in her voice.

He saw her look of fear and in this moment he didn't care. Something inside him had snapped when he'd realized he and his best friend had been betrayed by the woman he loved. "I'm going back."

"No."

"I'm not asking you for permission," he said flatly. He looked at her. He didn't even really know her, but he knew he couldn't save Marc by himself. Grinding his teeth as he spoke, Jason said, "As much as I don't want to, I'm asking for your help."

"Jason, I..." Amanda hesitated.

"No more, Amanda. You've told me repeatedly that you got me out today because you love me. "

"I do." Amanda stepped forward, hope in her eyes. Jason stepped back from her; the look of anger and disgust stopped her in her tracks.

"You have to choose. Now."

"Jason, please don't–"

He cut her off abruptly. "No. Enough. I'm not a fool. You've told me enough that I can guess some of what you've done. Now you can begin trying to make up for some of it. Help me save Marc."

Amanda hung her head. Jason had no idea that she'd been subverting Tony's plans for months. That she'd nearly been caught a dozen times or more, often only being saved by the fact that it was inconceivable than an Acanthan would turn against their own. Her chest felt tight. "Jason, I..." she again began to plead.

"Your next words better be 'I'll help.'" His face was hard, and his hands were clenched in white-knuckled fists by his sides.

Amanda sighed and dropped her shoulders in defeat. "I'll help."

A wave of relief washed over Jason and she could see him visibly relax.

"We need a plan," he said.

"If Walter sees you, he will alert Tony right away."

"I know. Is there a back entrance we can use?"

Amanda nodded as she turned to look back out over the water. "I can distract Walter, tell him I lost my ID, so he has to come let me in. You can use my ID to get in through the side door."

"Walter saw us run out. It was obvious I was chasing you. Even he's not stupid enough to let that go, especially when he sees your ID check pop up on his computer when I use it to get in." Frustrated, Jason scrubbed his hands through his damp hair.

"The only way you are going to get in unnoticed is to use the side exit."

"You go on in. You can tell him some stupid excuse about us having a fight. I'll go around to the side exit and once you get past Walter you can let me in through there."

Turning to look at Jason, Amanda nodded her assent. "Okay."

They walked in silence back to the building, Amanda running the past couple of hours over in her head, Jason thinking of nothing more than trying to save his friend.

"Shit," he said as he stopped abruptly, putting his hand on Amanda's arm.

"What's wrong?"

Jason pointed to a large boxy white security camera on the wall angled so that it was pointing down at the front door. "We forgot about the security cameras."

"Damn it."

CHAPTER SEVENTEEN

Marc was hungry, cold, and really pissed off. He scanned the walls looking for a doorway, but they looked seamless. There had to be a door. They weren't transported into a sealed room, that only existed in science fiction.

"Who or what would want to kidnap a bunch of call centre agents?" he said out loud. "And why?" His voice echoed back to him.

He couldn't think of anyone who would want to kidnap the three of them. He tried to think of any link. They didn't have any money and the company sure wouldn't pay to get them back. Call centre agents were eminently replaceable. Their families weren't wealthy. None of them were exceptional. Sure, they all had degrees, but in different fields; George had sociology, Jamie had done environmental science, and Marc had done meteorology.

So, they were all intelligent and well educated, which wasn't unusual in this business, but who kidnaps people just because they are smart? A memory from history class flitted through his mind: Nazis. Nazis kidnapped smart people and forced them to develop weapons. Marc shook his head at the ludicrousness of the thought; this was 21st century America, not Nazi Germany. Nothing like that could happen here.

A more likely culprit would be a psycho. But how would they target three random people or be able to boobytrap a classroom to capture them, let alone drag the bodies out of the building?

"Not helpful," he said to himself. His musings wouldn't get them out of there.

"Focus, you idiot. What do you think, Jamie?"

"Buttercups."

"Exactly. First order of business, I need pants." Pants, boxers, anything would do. He felt vulnerable with his freezing bits hanging out. A quick search of the cabinets resulted in some paper surgical pants, which he quickly pulled on under the gown. They crinkled and made swooshing noises when he walked, but at least his backside, and more importantly his front side, wasn't hanging out anymore.

He quickly went through the remaining cabinets, hoping to find something, anything, that would help get him out. They were filled with basic hospital supplies: boxes of gloves and masks, stacks of gowns, trays of forceps, something that reminded Marc of the speculums he'd seen when his wife was having their son, only much smaller.

"What the hell are those for?"

His imagination filled in that blank spot and sent a shudder down his spine. Quickly he moved on. There were syringes and a few scalpels. One cabinet was filled with vials of something called Ketamine HCL injection. There was something familiar about the name, but Marc couldn't recall it. He brushed the thought aside as he spotted a large brown box labelled "IV Needles," which still had the invoice attached.

"Hey, Jamie, this might have an address or give an idea of where we are."

Jamie only giggled. His heart racing, Marc reached for the box; the ink had faded on the form. He tore the sheet off the box and stepped under a light to read it. The needles had been ordered from a medical supplier in Chicago. An icy chill washed over him as he read the receiving address.

"What in the ever-loving fuck would CloneZone need IV needles for?" Marc asked of a non-responsive Jamie.

He looked at the signing name. "Amanda Blue?" Jason's Amanda? Marc's stomach twisted. What the hell was going on?

"Amanda. Amanda knew about this?" he said out loud.

Jamie replied, "Manda?"

Marc looked at her hopefully. She was still as vacant as earlier; she was just parroting him.

"What the hell is going on here?' he thought. Was CloneZone a human trafficking front? Working for the government doing secret experiments? Each idea was outlandish and even as he thought of them, he felt foolish.

As crazy as it seemed, there was something illicit going on. The classroom was rigged with knockout gas and he was standing in what was a moderately well-stocked medical facility. Looking from George's cold body to Jamie's crazed countenance he wondered again what had been done to them. He wondered what had been done to him. With a laugh that bordered mania, Marc cycled back to his earlier thought. Had aliens invaded? While he had missing time, he still felt normal, and he didn't have any weird memories of scientists, little grey men, or anal probing.

"Next I'll be buying tinfoil in bulk."

"Foil," Jamie agreed, giggling.

Panic and dread threatened to overwhelm him.

"Jamie, we've got to get the hell outta here. They got us in here, so there has to be an exit somewhere." Looking around the blank walls he couldn't easily see where a door might be.

"Chickens," Jamie said gleefully.

CHAPTER EIGHTEEN

They stayed well back, hiding behind the cars in the parking lot. The rain began to fall once more. Amanda's brow furrowed and she nibbled her bottom lip as she stared at the security camera. Jason saw her, it was something she often did when she was thinking, and he had always thought it cute. The unwelcome surge of affection for her angered him and he pushed the feelings aside. "She's an alien, you idiot," he thought.

Amanda turned and, for the first time since their argument, looked directly into Jason's eyes. She tried to ignore her stomach twisting at the look of revulsion on his face.

"Jason, you're determined to do this?"

"Yes, even if I have to go through Walter to get inside."

With a resigned sigh she continued.

"I've got an idea. But it's really risky."

"Shoot."

"See the smoke shack?"

The "smoke shack" was a semi-sheltered pergola where the office's resident smokers would go for their breaks and was currently occupied by five people, all huddled together like penguins in the middle. Puffs of grey and white smoke wafted up from the collective.

"Where are you going with this?" he asked.

"Tailgate them."

"What? They'll see me."

Amanda squinted to see who was under the pergola. Even with her augmented sight it was hard to see details between the wooden slats that surrounded the exterior.

"I'm pretty sure only one of them is processed." She glanced up at the sky, squinting as raindrops hit her face. "For once this rain will work to our advantage. Just keep your hoodie up and head down. When they head back in slip in behind them. Keep your card in your hand for show, but don't let it go near the sensor. You can follow them right in."

"Risky."

"I told you it was." She paused and looked at the doors, only a few hundred feet away. "I'll go in ahead and keep Walter busy. Once you are inside, go right, then down the hallway that leads to the emergency exit and wait for me there."

Jason looked at the group huddled in the small shelter. "We'll have to time this perfectly."

"We're probably going to get killed," Amanda said.

Jason nodded, his face set and determined. "Do you have any other suggestions?"

"Notify the authorities?"

Jason let out a quiet snort. "They'd have us committed. 'Officer, aliens have taken over CloneZone and they are about to stick a slug in my best friends' brain.'" He looked at Amanda. "It sounds insane. Without proof, all we'd do is give the cops a good hard laugh."

Amanda looked away but said nothing else.

"If we're going to do this, let's do it," Jason said and he went to step forward when Amanda stopped him with a gentle touch on his arm. He turned back to look at her. She was looking up at him with large doe eyes.

"Jason, promise me that if I don't show up in ten or fifteen minutes, you'll forget this plan and leave."

"Amanda, I can't…"

"Stop," she said in a commanding parade officer tone that brooked no argument from those on its receiving end. For the first time he could see the officer she said she was.

"You have to promise me. If I don't show up, it means Walter and Tony know, and I'm either dead or will be soon enough. You'll never find Marc without me."

Jason's heart lurched when she said "dead" with such finality. He did not want to feel anything for her.

"If you don't promise me, I'm not going in. You won't save Marc, but you can save everyone else. Leave and tell the world we exist." She paused and drew a deep breath. "There's a USB drive in our apartment. Taped to the bottom of the blue vase that I never use. It has video of processings and other proof of our tampering with the weather and communication systems."

Jason was taken aback by her confession. "Why?"

Amanda turned from him and shook her head. "There is not time for that explanation right now. Just promise me before I lose my nerve."

Reluctantly Jason said, "Fine."

"Say it."

"I promise."

Without another word, Jason headed towards the little shelter but his steps faltered when he heard her say, "Be careful. I do love you." He recovered quickly and continued without responding.

Amanda was hurt when Jason didn't respond with even a "You be careful too." She wasn't surprised and didn't blame him, but her heart still broke because he was so cold. There were times that these human emotions were so troublesome to navigate.

With a soul-weary sigh, she headed to the building, collecting herself on the way. By the time she reached the doors and shoved them open brusquely, she was a full Acanthan Commander, shoulders back and spine erect, a look of disdain fixed rigidly on her face. Walter was perched at his usual station, eyes glued to the TV screen until the door chime sounded and Amanda entered the foyer.

"Walter." She nodded as she went to walk past him. She knew he wouldn't let her go in without questioning her earlier behaviour. They were of equal rank, but he never seemed to acknowledge that fact. His age and being Tony's lackey gave him a false sense of seniority.

"You're wet," Walter said, stating the obvious. "Where have you been?"

"I've been outside and it's raining. Humans get wet when it rains."

Walter scowled at her. "Tony's been looking for you. It seems that your boyfriend disappeared from work and missed another training session."

"Not that it's any of your concern, but we had a fight."

"So, he left work?"

"Walter, let's cut the bullshit," Amanda said with a sigh as she walked up to the counter, positioning herself so she was facing the door, and leaned over the counter to peer down at the older man. He stood to face her, making her look up at him. She scowled in distaste, but his back was to the door and that's all Amanda wanted.

"I know you saw us both run out of here."

Feeling a little more confident in this position, he crossed his arms across his chest and nodded. "Yes, I did. Why?"

Amanda could see the small herd of humans, their break finished, making a run for the door to escape the heavy rain. All of them had their hoods up and were hunched over.

Amanda looked into Walter's watery pale eyes and smiled. Helping Jason had given her one small gift she hadn't considered; she no longer had to disguise who she was. She decided it would be the perfect distraction. "Quite honestly, Walter, it's none of your goddamned business."

His puffy face went florid.

The scanner beeped once as the first person swiped in and pushed open the door to get out of the pouring rain.

"How dare you speak to me that way," Walter growled under his breath. As angry as he was, he had to keep up the pretense of being a security guard.

Beep went the scanner as the second person came through the doors held open by the first.

Amanda thought the pompous old bastard might have a stroke and the thought gave her great pleasure. "I dare because it's about time you realized that we are the same damned rank."

The first two who had entered looked up at her comments. The first looked shocked. "Yep, Acanthan," Amanda thought. The second in line just looked confused as he held the door for person number three. Beep.

"I'm going to… I'll report… You'll be…" Walter sputtered.

Beep. Four.

"You will do exactly nothing,"

Amanda hissed at him. "Do you really want Tony to find out your particular human fetish?"

Now Walter paled to a pleasurable chalky white. "You can't know…"

Beep. Five. Amanda's heart beat faster.

"Oh, I know, and I have proof, you pompous, self serving old goat."

No beep but number six stepped through the door nodding thanks to number five as he let the door slide shut behind him. Just a few more seconds. That's all she had to buy as the smokers started to parade through the inner door.

Walter's mouth was working but no sound would come out.

"I've got all I need to bring to Tony, unless you choose to be accommodating."

After a few seconds he managed, "What do you want?"

"Any new recruits you find, you will tell me about them instead of Tony. Let one get through, and some papers will mysteriously be delivered to Tony. You will defer to me from now on."

"You bitch," Walter grumbled under his breath.

Her smile widened at the attempted insult as she watched the inner door shut behind Jason's back.

"You have no idea," she said. "Do we have an agreement?"

"Do I have a choice?"

"Of course, you do. You can choose to do as I ask or not and throw yourself on Tony's well-known mercy."

He looked apoplectic. "Yes."

"Yes what?" she said smugly.

Walter spoke through gritted teeth. "Yes, Ma'am."

Amanda nodded as she walked away from Walter, who was purple with rage.

"Now, that's better."

She pushed open the doors that led to the service hallway and with a sigh of relief collapsed against them as they closed. She looked down and saw wet footprints fading off into the distance.

"Jason," she whispered to herself and pushed off from the closed doors and headed down the hallway to the emergency exit.

Her heart skipped a beat when she saw him. He was standing just down from the security doors in a shallow alcove. He had his back turned to her and was looking down the other end of the hall. She wanted nothing more than to run to him and put her arms around him. Instead, she walked over quietly and touched his arm.

"Jason?" she said.

"Jesus Christ," Jason whisper-yelped as he jumped and spun to face her, his arms flapping. "Christ, Amanda. Don't do that. You nearly killed me."

Amanda wanted to laugh and tried to stifle it as she replied, "I'm sorry. I didn't mean to scare you."

Jason grabbed her arm and pulled her into the alcove, looking back down the hallway where he'd been staring. "Quiet. I saw someone down there a few minutes ago. I thought it was Tony."

Amanda frowned. "Tony shouldn't be here. He should be in the processing lab with…" Amanda let her words trail off as Jason turned, looking at her with a mix of sadness and revulsion.

"I'm sorry–"

"Marc. We focus on Marc," Jason said brusquely.

She only nodded and looked at his dripping clothes. Jason was starting to shiver, as was she.

"We need to find some dry clothes. We'll stand out too much walking around sopping wet."

He looked at her quizzically. "How do you propose we do that?"

"That's easy. I'll check the lost and found," she replied with a smile.

The lost and found was a rubber tub just outside the cafeteria, located just down the hallway from Tony's cubicle office. There was a year's worth of unclaimed items sitting there waiting to be pillaged.

"You stay here. I'll just be a few minutes." Jason saw her turn to go.

"Amanda?"

"Yeah?"

"Be careful…"

Amanda smiled when he said this, but Jason didn't see, he'd turned back to watch down the other end of the hall.

"I need you to save Marc."

The smile slid from her face. She turned without another word and headed to the lunch room, past the double doors and out onto the production floor again. Technically the office was closed now, so there should not be many people around. Most would be gone home except for stragglers who had been stuck on calls or working overtime. Everyone who usually stayed after normal work hours would be in the warehouse and already processed. "Better safe than sorry," Amanda thought as she pulled off her stilettos and, barefoot, slipped past the empty cubicles until she reached the corner. She peeked around to make sure neither Tony nor Walter was hanging around Tony's desk. An empty corridor greeted her. She heaved a sigh of relief and headed the final few feet to the lunch room door.

She spotted the big green bin filled with odds and ends just inside the open archway to the open room. One wall held a counter with a couple of microwaves in cubbies. There was a fridge and a coffee machine. A grimy window was flanked by vending machines and there were tables and chairs scattered throughout in no particular pattern. It was also vacant. Amanda slipped inside and began rummaging.

It didn't take her long to find suitable dry clothes: some jeans, a worn grey t-shirt with a zombie on it that said "Beauty and Braaaaaaiiinns," and a worn looking flannel shirt that looked like they'd fit Jason. Next a pair of mismatched sneakers that were luckily in Jason's size. "Dammit," she muttered. None of the pants were women's. She grabbed a pair of grey track pants that had an elastic waist that she thought would fit her, a t-shirt with the Rolling Stones logo on the front and a pair of ugly rainbow canvas pull-on sneakers that looked to be her size. She rolled everything into a ball and stood to bring the items back to Jason.

"Amanda, my dear. Why on earth are you digging through that nasty box of leavings?"

Amanda jumped and squealed, dropping her findings back into the bin.

"Tony." She gasped. "You nearly gave me a heart attack." She had her hand over her heart and could feel it pounding against her ribs.

Tony's face creased into something that on anyone else could be taken for concern. No one who knew Tony would assume that; it was just his front. "You look pale. Are you feeling well?"

"I'm fine, sir," Amanda said, straightening herself and standing tall. She could not appear weak in front of him. "I'm just a little cold. I got caught in the downpour."

"Why were you outside?"

"Jason."

"What about him?"

"You'll have noticed by now that he wasn't in the classroom."

"Yes. His absence was disappointing." He casually took a step closer. "Especially after you promised me he'd be there."

"We got into a fight."

"Hmmm. Walter told me he saw you both running out. That was just about the time Jason should have been coming to class."

"Walter is a senile old goat."

"Amanda..." Tony said in warning.

Amanda tensed. "Fine. Jason and I got into a fight. I left and he followed me. I didn't think he'd do something like that."

Amanda paused until Tony waggled his fingers, indicating she should continue. "We fought some more, then he left. I'm heading home now. I'll take a syringe of the ketamine and sedate him there. Once he's out I'll bring him in. I'm afraid that will be the best I can do."

"Oh, Amanda, that is disappointing." Tony pouted and took another step closer and sighed dramatically. "I suppose it will have to do." His eyes flicked down to the pile of clothes she'd been holding then back up to her face. "You never did answer my question. What are you doing digging through that pile of disgusting human cast-offs?" His nose wrinkled in revulsion as he spoke.

Amanda drew herself up to her full height. Even as petite as she was, she had a presence. Her eyes flashed in irritation, and, unwittingly, Tony took a half step back from her. "Obviously I was looking for something."

"Did you find it?"

"No. You interrupted me."

"Whatever could be so interesting in there?" he said, poking the bin with his toe.

Amanda thought frantically. What could she be digging in the lost and found for? As she thought her arm brushed against her pocket.

"I've misplaced my cell. I was hoping someone dropped it in there."

"How dreadful. Nothing important on there I hope?"

"No. I don't think so anyway. It was just my personal cell." She shrugged, "Still, I wouldn't want it to be found by just anyone. Just in case."

He glanced back down at the bin, wrinkling his nose once more, and then back up to her. "Agreed. Now is not the time I want our secret to be discovered. You'd better find it." He thought for a moment, "Check with Walter, he may have found it or had it handed in."

"I'll do that," Amanda said, with a smile. She began to relax a little as Tony turned to leave. Abruptly he stopped, turned back, and stepped in close and whispered in her ear before turning on his heel and leaving without another look back.

Amanda paled and her eyes widened but said nothing her breath was caught in her throat. She just gave a curt nod. Tony smiled and left her by the bin, walking down the aisle with a cocky step.

Amanda swallowed hard. "Fuck."

CHAPTER NINETEEN

"Jamie, what do you think would work as a weapon?"

"Ice cream."

"That won't work very well," Marc thought as he searched the cupboards for something that he could use to defend himself if whomever had kidnapped them came back. He had no intentions of ending up like George. He'd seen a box labelled scalpels in one of the cupboards. He grabbed it and pulled it open; it was empty. There was nothing else of any real use in the cabinets. Looking around the room his eyes came to rest on the trays. On Jamie's tray he discovered what looked like huge six-inch tweezers, something that he could only describe as a probe, and a petri dish that held a clear liquid with slightly gelatinous blobs floating in it.

"Well, goopy jelly isn't going to help," he said as his stomach growled.

He realized it had been a long time since lunch.

"Jelly," Jamie cried.

Looking back at the petri dish he muttered as his stomach growled once again, "Mmmm, jelly."

He shook his head and walked over to the tray that had been near his gurney. "Nope, not worth it." He thought. This tray held a more promising array of tools. It had the tweezers and probe and one of those small weirdly shaped speculums (he unconsciously clenched his buttocks when he saw this duo).

"Ah. Here we go," he said as he grabbed a small scalpel.

Feeling a little more confident with his paper pants and a mini scalpel, he began walking slowly around the room, sliding his hands over the smooth wall. He was looking for any imperfection, anything that might indicate a door. A crack would do. On the last wall, the one that he couldn't see clearly from the gurney, he found a faint seam right behind Jamie's gurney. Up close he could see the line, but from even a few feet away it was invisible.

"There you are," he whispered. "I knew there had to be a door."

Marc was not unfamiliar with the way locks worked. He had learned many skills while growing up in the ghettos of Argentina. Maybe now those skills would serve a purpose. Picking a spot on what he thought was the edge of the door, about where a latch would be, Marc pushed the scalpel into the seam. He pushed and wiggled the small knife, but it couldn't seem to work itself in far enough to catch any mechanism. The blade was thin enough, but the handle was too wide to fit in the tight space. Marc slammed his fist into the door causing the material of the door to vibrate with a high-pitched hum. There were no scratches on the door where he'd shoved in the blade.

"What the hell is this thing made of?" Marc said out loud, stepping backwards and bumping Jamie's gurney.

"Oopsie," Jamie giggled.

Marc turned to look at her.

"Jamie?"

Jamie was grinning. "You go bump."

Marc was stunned. This was the first time Jamie seemed to acknowledge him. "Yes, Jamie. I did." He swallowed hard. "I did go bump." He took a step close. "Jamie, do you recognize me?"

Jamie didn't reply. She sat there smiling and staring off into the distance.

Marc sighed. He'd hoped she was coming back; he could use the help.

The door was a dud. There was no way he was getting through there. He scanned the walls, looking for a weakness. The wall was seamless but worn, with spots of pale grey cinder block showing through where paint had been chipped away.

"Damn it," thought Marc, "I'm in a fucking sealed box. I don't want to end up like George or, worse, like you, Jamie. Nothing personal."

Marc scrubbed his hands through his hair; his wife's face popped up before his eyes. "Aww babe, I need to get back home to you and time is running out."

Whoever had kidnapped them would be back and every minute wasted was a minute closer to their return.

"Maybe I can cut through the wall?" Moving to a dark corner and squatting close to the floor, he proceeded to run the scalpel down the wall. His plan was rough: score the wall with the scalpel, marking out a rough rectangular shape big enough for him to crawl through, then kick out the drywall and get himself and Jamie out. It would be noisy, but it was the only option he had.

Holding the scalpel tight, he slid it down the wall. The blade made a horrible screeching noise, like nails on a chalkboard, as he slid it down. "What the...?"

Leaning in closer he could see it was made of the same strange material as the door.

"Fuck. Fuck, fuck, fuck, fuck, fuck."

Angry and frustrated, Marc stabbed the scalpel into the cheap laminate countertop and ran his hands through his shaggy black hair. He'd hoped to make his escape quietly and quickly, but he felt that he was running out of time and energy.

"I guess the door is my best bet," he muttered, pulling the blade from the surface.

Marc returned to the door and kept working at the area where he thought the lock would be located. Suddenly, there was an audible click and Marc jumped back in surprise as the door slid open. Bright light blinded him, and he raised his arm to shield his eyes.

"Tut tut, Marc. It isn't nice to destroy other people's property."

Marc knew that voice. Lowering his arm and squinting into the light he could just make out a familiar face peering back at him. With an eerie smile the figure raised its hand and sprayed something into Marc's face. He staggered back, coughing; it smelled like lemon cleaner. A wave of dizziness washed over him, and he stumbled back against a gurney.

Tony entered the room with that same evil grin fixed on his face and nonchalantly approached Marc.

"What the fuck are you doing?" Marc said, scrubbing at his eyes.

Tony gave Marc a pitying look. "That, I'm afraid, would involve a lengthy explanation and I simply do not have the time."

"Why?"

"There is no escape," was Tony's only reply.

Marc raised his arm holding the scalpel and took a futile swipe at Tony. Tony stopped just outside Marc's reach and the swing went wide.

"Now, be a good boy and get back on your bed. Things will go much smoother if you'd just co-operate."

"Jamie? Help?" Marc pleaded, making Tony laugh.

"She'll be of no help to you."

Jamie slid off the gurney behind Tony. She looked confused. After a brief glance at Marc, Jamie's eyes locked on Tony's back and she began to walk stiff-legged towards him. Marc was surprised to see her respond but it gave him hope.

"Fuck you," Marc snarled. He tried to balance himself better against the gurney. Stars floated before his eyes and his legs felt like jelly, but he was determined to keep Tony's focus on him.

"Now, now," Tony scolded. "I do believe Jason is having a negative effect on you, but he won't for much longer."

Jamie was right behind Tony and Marc had to fight the urge to smile. "Where Jason?" Marc slurred. Whatever Tony had sprayed him with was making it hard to speak.

"Jason isn't your problem," Tony said. He was patient. He could wait for the sedative to drop Marc to the ground. Marc was athletic, a body builder. Even with his enhanced strength, Tony would be hard pressed in a fair fight against the larger man, and Tony hated him for it; but no one could withstand the aerosolized version of this sedative. Tony just had to stay out of reach.

Jamie was moving better now, and Marc could no longer stifle his grin. Tony looked surprised at this. "What are you smirking at?"

"You," Marc said simply. Jamie wasn't a big woman, but he'd lay even odds on her against Tony any day.

The grin slipped from his face as Jamie walked past Tony and quickly closed the distance between them. She wrapped her arms around him and pulled him upright. "Jamie?" he wheezed as she squeezed the air from his lungs.

"Put him back on the table, my dear," Tony said as Jamie lifted Marc's one hundred and eighty pounds as if he was a bag of potatoes and plopped him down on the gurney. He struggled weakly as she held him down while Tony put the straps back on so tightly that they cut into Marc's skin. Once he was secure, she stepped back robotically.

Marc managed to focus enough to look into Tony's eyes. There was nothing behind them. They were dead. Soulless. Fear gripped Marc, adrenaline surged, helping to negate the sedatives effects. He shook his head. "Whadda you want?"

"You, Marc, just you," he said as he patted Marc on the arm.

Tony stepped from Marc's field of vision. "Now be a good boy and stop struggling."

He returned holding a petri dish filled with the same jelly-like blobs Marc had seen by Jamie's gurney. As Tony held it over Marc's face, he could see that the blobs were semi-translucent worms swimming in the clear fluid. Each worm was about half the size of a dime. Tony placed the dish on the tray and removed the cover. He picked up one of the speculum-shaped tools and turned towards Marc.

"Now, Marc, stay still. This won't hurt at all," Tony said with a smile that promised exactly the opposite. Marc tried to turn his head away but with a flick of Tony's hand, Jamie stepped forward and held his head in a vice-like grip. Tony slipped the speculum up one of Marc's nostrils, making Marc gag and his eyes water. Marc heard a click as Tony pulled the trigger expanding the blades. Marc yelped, and Tony laughed.

Marc blinked the tears from his eyes as he tried to see what Tony was doing. Tony turned around from the tray and was gently holding one of the worm-like creatures in the tweezers and carefully laid the cold, wet creature on the warm sensitive flesh just above Marc's lip.

Tony caressed the thing with a finger. Marc felt it wriggle at the touch and he shuddered.

Tony leaned in close and for one brief, irrational moment, Marc feared that Tony was going to kiss him, and he pulled his lips tight. Instead, Marc felt Tony's breath brush his mouth as he said, "Go, little one."

Marc felt the worm wriggle its way up his face and into his nostril. His eyes went wide with horror and tears streamed down his face. "Jamie, please, help?" he whimpered.

"The Jamie you knew is gone," Tony said. "You could say she received an upgrade."

Marc looked at Tony, his eyes wide in terror.

"You'll understand soon enough. Or not." Tony patted Marc's arm once again and peered down at the terrified man with hungry eyes. "We'll see which it is in a few minutes."

Marc could feel the creature sliding its way through his sinus cavity. He wanted to throw up. After a few minutes he lost where it was. He hoped it had died. It hadn't. It had worked its way further up his sinus. It kept going until it reached the sphenoid sinus cavity, just in front of the midbrain.

That is when the pain began, and Marc started to scream.

CHAPTER TWENTY

Amanda was wide-eyed and breathing hard when she returned to find Jason huddled in a corner vigorously rubbing his arms to stay warm.

"Did you find anything?"

"Yeah, a few things," Amanda said as she looked nervously up and down the corridor.

"Everything okay?" he said, taking the clothing from her as she handed the pieces to him.

"Yes," she said before shaking her head. "No."

"Which is it?"

"I ran into Tony."

"Shit."

"Yeah. He knows what I'm doing."

Jason's face blanched. "What makes you say that?"

Amanda recounted her inopportune meeting with Tony.

"Do you think he suspects enough to change your access key?"

Amanda paused and frowned. "I don't think so. His last words were that I had to bring you here tonight or that Walter would take my place."

"You don't sound certain."

"I'm not," she said.

"We'll find out soon enough."

Amanda nodded and took another glance up and down the corridor. "Hurry. We'll have to change here where it's darker. It's too risky in the open."

"In front of each other?" Jason sounded horrified.

She turned to look up at him. "Jason, it's not like we haven't seen each other naked before."

"Yeah, but that was before..."

Amanda flushed red. "Before you knew what I am," she finished for him.

They were suddenly both very awkward.

"How about we turn our backs to each other?" Jason suggested.

Amanda nodded, her eyes downcast.

They turned their backs to each other as they began to strip off their wet clothes.

They could hear each other shuffling and a pile of damp clothes grew by their feet. Jason paused when Amanda's pink lacy bra fell against his ankle, still warm from her body. He swallowed hard and looked at the wall in front of him as he dressed. The alcove was small and occasionally they would brush an arm or shoulder against the other. Muffled apologies quickly followed as they'd try to retreat closer to their corner. Finally, they were both dressed and turned back towards each other.

"I don't think we'll win any fashion shows," Amanda said, eyeing Jason.

His wet auburn hair looked almost black, and the grey zombie t-shirt was a fit perfectly showing off his muscles. Blushing, she quickly moved her eyes from his chest. The red plaid fleece shirt hung loosely. It was meant for a much larger man. The jeans were both too short and hung from his hips, bulging under his belt. One blue sneaker and one white one finished his ensemble. She grinned. "You look like a hipster lumberjack."

Jason snorted a laugh and despite himself said, "I think you look pretty good." Amanda beamed. Her clothes reminded Jason of the first time she'd stayed over and borrowed some of his clothes to sleep in. Her blond hair had begun to curl into ringlets as it dried, and the t-shirt was too small and emphasized that she wasn't wearing a bra. The track pants were too long so she had pulled the cuffs up, exposing her calves. Jason swallowed hard.

"Liar," she said, a small shy smile on her face as she turned away from him and picked up the pile of wet clothes.

Jason watched her as she shoved their wet clothes into a corner. She was risking everything to help. He knew that and part of him wanted to hug her for it, but another part wanted to scream at her here for all the things she'd done. Instead, he did neither.

She stood holding both their cell phones. Water drained from the corners. "I don't think these are going to help us much."

"No. Just toss 'em with the wet stuff." Jason sighed and continued, "Where do we go?"

"This way," she said, pointing further down the service hallway as she stepped from the alcove. "Walter said that Tony was going to the labs and he was headed that way when he left me."

They talked in hushed tones as they crept down the corridor. "Labs?" Jason asked.

"Yeah," Amanda replied. "There are research and experimentation labs."

"What would you be researching?"

"Research on adapting a planet to Acanthans. Improving the Acanthan integration process. Things like that."

"Adapting a planet? You mean terraforming?"

"Yes. Except I guess it would be Acanthaforming? We like it warm and wet."

"All that rain…"

Amanda nodded as she led them down the hall. "Yeah."

"Humans don't."

"We've realized that. Only some parts of the planet will be altered to accommodate the true Acanthan form. Mostly around the equator."

"Oh." He paused "Do I want to know what you mean by integration process improvement?"

"Probably not," shed said, shaking her head. "The, um, examining rooms are just past the labs," she said as they reached a door holding a swipe card and fingerprint reader.

"Pretty heavy security for a call centre backroom," Jason observed. "I'm surprised no one has ever noticed."

"They did."

"Do I want to…"

"No," she said flatly. "This leads to a short hallway with the two labs on the left and two examining rooms on the right. There is also a door to the printing and distribution floor further down the hallway." Amanda dug her pass card out of the track pants pocket.

"The examining rooms are where we implant our offspring into the new hosts. Some people handle it okay enough and leave only hours after the process. They may be a little confused or disoriented. Others take longer. Those are left in the rooms to recover. Marc will be in one of the examining rooms." Turning to look up into Jason's eyes she said, "Jason, if he's been processed, he may not want to come with us, or he might try to turn on us."

Smiling sadly at Amanda, he shrugged. "I know, but what else can I do?"

Turning away from the pained expression on Jason's face, Amanda swiped her card and held the thumb of her left hand to the scanner.

With a soft click the door unlocked. Amanda grasped the handle and turned it easily, opening the door to reveal a brightly lit corridor.

"Remember, labs are on the left, processing is on the right," she whispered over her shoulder.

"What about security?" Jason whispered back.

"None. We never even considered that a human could figure out what was happening here."

Reaching behind her, she pressed her hand to his chest. She felt the warmth of his body and his heart beating against her palm. Taking a deep breath to steady herself she said, "Let me go in first. If Tony is there, he'd be expecting me. I'll leave the door open and try to distract him. Then you can... well... do whatever it is you are planning on doing." She paled a little.

Jason's face was hard as he nodded to her.

CHAPTER TWENTY-ONE

Amanda stepped up to the first door on the right and swiped her card to open it, glancing quickly around. The poorly lit hospital ward style room was completely vacant. Amanda sighed and shut the door as quietly as possible. She moved on to the next door. "Voices," she mouthed back at Jason and tipped her head to listen.

Motioning Jason back against the wall, she stepped up to the door, closed her eyes to centre herself, squared her shoulders, lifted her chin, and put an expression on her face of arrogance. Jason was speechless at the transformation. She swiped her card and the door opened with a click. She pushed it open and walked inside.

Tony stood with Jamie by his side.

He had his hand on her shoulder as he smiled down at the thrashing form of Marc, who was crying out in agony. Amanda recognized Jamie's blank stare. She'd had difficulty with the transition and was lost, but she'd make a perfect drone. Open to suggestion and good for mundane tasks.

Glancing around the room she saw George's limp body. He was undoubtedly dead.

Tony didn't immediately notice Amanda's entry into the room.

"There you are, I've been looking everywhere for you," Amanda said. She glanced down at Marc and continued, "I thought he'd have been done by now."

Tony slowly pulled his eyes away from Marc, who was writing in agony before him. Glowering at Amanda over the tops of his glasses he said, "There were delays. Why were you looking for me?"

"I can't seem to find any ketamine. I told you I was going to bring you Jason. I need the drug for that."

"It should be in Lab 2."

"It's not. I was just there."

"Damn it. I do not want any further delays."

"Well, as soon as I can sedate him, I'll bring him. Unless you propose I knock him over the head with something and hope for the best."

"Harumph," Tony grumbled, turning to look at Marc, whose cries had reduced to whimpers and his writhing to twitching with an occasional spasm.

"Everyone else is still here. We're trying to get the last few shipments out. I *need* Jason to finish the damned program. That idiot that Walter found can't program his way out of an Xbox, let alone write a program that can be sent via telecommunications devices." He took a break from watching Marc's suffering and looked up at Amanda, who had walked further into the room. "I had wanted it to be a surprise for you." Tony seemed excited. "We are so close to completion. We're just days away. All we need is Jason to be one of us so he can finish off the program."

Amanda was shocked. "Days? I thought we were years from readiness?"

Tony waved his hand dismissively.

"Oh, the signal may not get to every human. That was somewhat inevitable as there are swaths of the planet without any cellular or radio service, but we will get many. Once they are under our control, they will be easy to process." Tony licked his lips in excitement. "However, that also means

some will need to be harvested the old-fashioned way, by going in on foot."
He looked at Amanda. "It's been too long since we had a good hunt."

"I've never been on one."

"That's right, you were born here. It's very exhilarating. I think you will enjoy it."

"It sounds... interesting. You will have to teach me." She smiled at Tony.

"Our estimate is that once the program is complete, we can go-live within twenty-four hours."

"You *have* been industrious," Amanda purred. She walked up to Marc's bed and ran her hand over his arm. She could feel his muscles twitching beneath her fingers and his head rolled back and forth. His face was screwed up in pain and he made small whimpering noises.

Tony smiled proudly. "It will give us immediate control over approximately 85% of the population, including their leaders."

Amanda had worked her way to the head of Marc's bed. Tony suddenly stepped close to her and took her into his arms. She looked up at his sudden movement and gasped. Tony's eyes were ablaze with a fanatical light. "Amanda, then I am going to rule this world."

"Really?"

"Yes, and I want you to rule alongside me." His hands were clammy against her arms and his breath reeked.

Repulsed, Amanda broke free from Tony's grasp, swatting his hands away. She managed to look down on him while looking up at him.

"No," she said coldly. "I would never be your concubine. You disgust me."

Tony's jaw went slack with shock, which quickly turned to rage. He was quivering with it. Amanda saw a vein throbbing in his temple as she pressed home.

"You say The Council will make you king? Will they still feel that way when they see how much difficulty you've had containing one simple human?" Contempt dripped from her voice.

She turned to look down at Marc, her face softening, and gently stroked his face. Marc's thrashing quieted to mild twitches and shudders as Amanda touched him.

She'd managed to turn Tony to fully face her, his back to the door. He was impotent with rage and for a moment she feared she'd pushed him too far, that he'd kill her before Jason could act.

Her dismissal of his offer and the way she was touching Marc was too much for the egomaniac to cope with.

"Your love of these creatures is disgusting. They are nothing more than beasts."

"You seem to enjoy some of the perks of humanity," Amanda sneered.

Tony's eyes bulged and his whole body quivered with fury. No one had ever had the audacity to speak to him like that.

"You bitch. You'd choose the likes of him over me?" Tony waved at Marc's prone form.

"Oh, I haven't chosen Marc at all." Amanda smiled at Tony, her eyes flicking to just above his left shoulder.

Tony didn't miss that look and spun around just as Jamie squealed, "Jason," and clapped her hands. Tony stopped Jason's fist with his face. Almost twice the size of the scrawny Tony, Jason sent the man flying into a tray, sending utensils flying in all directions. A petri dish shattered on the floor. Dozens of small worm creatures wriggled in the shallow liquid as it ran down the floor drain into the sewer below. Tony fell to the floor, blood running from a broken nose, his lip already swelling where it was split.

"Help me get him up on the empty gurney," Amanda said, grabbing Tony's legs while Jason went around to grab his arms. Tony was Acanthan and wasn't so easily subdued. He grabbed a handful of tools that had fallen from the spilled tray, and as they bent over him, his eyes opened, and he drove a set of forceps deep into Jason's arm.

Jason recoiled, grabbing at his wounded arm, and stumbled backwards. With a cry he gripped the forceps and pulled them free.

"You traitorous bitch," Tony snarled at Amanda through his swelling lips which gave his words a slurring lisp. He held a scalpel that he'd found on the floor before him. Amanda scrambled backwards, her hands held up in front of her to fend off any attack.

"Jamie," Tony said and the woman's blank face turned towards Tony. "Restrain Jason."

"Jason." She said and took a step towards him.

"Jamie, no. Stop." Amanda ordered.

Jamie hesitated.

"Jamie, I'm your Master. Obey me." She moved towards Jason again.

"Jamie, this is you commander." She summoned all her authority and ignored the fact that she was scrabbling across the ground. "It's Amanda. You will cease action and stand ready by the wall."

Jamie spun on her foot and walked to the wall where she stopped, turned and sat, with her back to the wall."

"Fuck it. I'll deal with Jason myself. Right now, I will enjoy killing you."

"Tony…" Amanda started, glancing over at Jason, who was holding the hole in his arm, blood seeping from between his fingers.

"Shut up," Tony snapped, waving the blade at Amanda. He'd managed to get to his knees and was crouching like a trapped animal, ready to spring.

"That trick won't work again." He stood and went over to Marc, placing the blade at his throat. "First you will watch your friend die."

Jason had also managed to stand and was holding the forceps in his good hand.

Amanda spoke quickly. "Tony, you're right. I am a traitorous bitch. I've betrayed the entire Acanthan population here on Earth. I deserve to die."

She pointed to Marc's recumbent form. "'"He's just survived processing. Marc's smart and strong. Don't waste a valuable resource just to get even with me." She swallowed hard before continuing, "Take me instead. I'll go peacefully. Just let Jason go."

"Amanda, no," Jason said, horrified.

Tony hesitated. He glanced at Jason, who was staring at Amanda slack-jawed.

"Please, Amanda, you can't."

"Jason, I can. I will." She looked Tony in the eye. "Well?"

Tony looked at Amanda and a horrible smile parted his ruined lips, his bloodied teeth making him look like a vampire.

"Very well," he said as he lowered the blade from Marc's neck and beckoned Amanda to come to him.

Jason looked from Tony to Amanda. He was a long way from forgiving her, but he could clearly imagine Tony sliding the scalpel across her throat and he was not about to let that happen.

As Amanda took her first steps towards Tony, Jason threw the forceps at Tony's head with all his strength. Tony's head turned reflexively as the forceps' tip hit, biting deep into his face, tearing a long gouge. His hand flew to his head as blood began to run.

"Fuck!" Tony screamed. Blood sprayed over Marc's face and gown.

"Fuck." Jamie parroted and then let out a chilling laugh, making Tony hesitate as he looked at her.

Jason saw his moment and dove, taking Tony at the hips in a football tackle, driving him to the floor. The force of the blow drove all the wind from Tony's lungs. As they skidded to a stop against the cabinets, Jason had rolled away, but Amanda stepped in with a heavy utensil tray in her hands. Raising it above her head, she brought it down on Tony with enough force to leave a Tony-shaped dent in the metal.

"I choose Jason."

Tony slumped to the floor as Amanda dropped the tray and ran to Jason.

His arm was bleeding badly.

"Are you okay?" she asked.

Jason was secretly pleased at the worry in her voice.

"I'll live." Jason nodded towards Tony. "Is he dead?"

Amanda glanced back at him and said, "No, but he's out cold."

"Good. What about Marc?" Jason said as he batted Amanda's hands away and tried to wrap the edge of his plaid shirt around the injury.

Amanda looked over her shoulder at Marc. He was mostly still now, but he looked pale in the washed-out lighting.

"He was processed."

"I got that. Is he going to live?"

"I think so."

"Can it be reversed?" Jason looked from his friend to Amanda. It killed her to tell him the truth.

"No. Any separation will kill the human host."

"What about the Acanthan?"

"Yes and no. If another host is ready, we can be transplanted but we won't survive long without a host." Amanda looked at the blood soaking through Jason's improvised bandage.

"We've got to get you patched up. We can deal with Marc after. He's not going anywhere."

As much as he hated to agree, Amanda was right. He was bleeding a lot. He was a little concerned that Tony had nicked an artery. "Are there any bandages in this place?"

Amanda nodded and jumped up, heading to the cabinets on the wall. When she returned Jason was sitting on the empty gurney with his plaid shirt pulled off and was carefully examining the hole in his arm. It wasn't large but it was deep. Any other time he'd have gone for stitches, but they would have to wait.

Amanda laid out her supplies: a bottle of antiseptic, gauze squares, and some tape. She took Jason's arm in her hand. He resisted.

"Please, Jason, you can't possibly do this one-handed. Let me help."

He hesitated before relaxing, allowing her to pull his arm out straight. She examined his wound.

"You need stitches."

"I know."

"I can do them."

"No. There's no time. Patch me up."

With a sigh she took the bottle of antiseptic in her hand.

"This is going to hurt."

As she spoke, she poured the liquid into the hole. Jason hissed through clenched teeth as the peroxide fizzed and burned. Once it stopped, Amanda wiped the wound clean, closed it as best she could with some Steri-Strips, wrapped it in fresh gauze, and taped it up. The whole process was done in minutes.

As she finished, her hands slid down until she was holding his hand in both of hers. "Amanda–" Jason began.

She dropped his hand and shook her head. "Not now. We've got to deal with Tony."

It was Jason's turn to feel hurt, but she was right. Tony wouldn't stay unconscious forever. Between them, they hoisted Tony onto the gurney and tied him down with the restraints that he normally used to hold his victims. They used torn strips of one of the hospital gowns to make a gag and then covered his whole body in a blanket.

Once he was secured, they tidied the room as much as possible, taking a few moments to cover George with a sheet, and moved him and Tony over to the side. They hoped if anyone looked in, they'd think it was two corpses ready for disposal.

Jamie had watched the end of the fight without much as flinching. She'd remained sitting while the trio fought.

Jason finally had a moment for Marc. He walked over the prone figure of his friend, who was now murmuring and muttering in his sleep, eyes moving rapidly behind closed lids.

"They really got to him, didn't they?" he asked without looking at Amanda. He'd hoped she had been wrong.

"Yes," she replied, stepping up next to him.

Patting his friend on the shoulder he said, "I'll be back for you."

Amanda looked up at Jason in surprise. "What do you mean back? I thought we came here for Marc."

"We did. But I heard what Tony said to you about being nearly ready." Jason turned to look at Amanda. "I can't just run."

Amanda couldn't answer that; she knew what the plans were and what would happen.

"I'm not the only programmer. They will find someone to replace me and finish the code. It may take longer but they will. Then what? I hide while my entire planet is taken over?"

Jason was getting angry again. She could feel it starting to radiate from him in waves.

"What kind of life is that? This is my planet. It's my people. I have to try."

"What can you do?" Amanda asked, her voice shaking.

"You mean what chance does a pathetic human have against the Acantha?"

"That's not what I–"

Jason cut her off with a wave of his hand. "It doesn't matter. I have a plan."

As Jason talked, Amanda could see a change coming over him. He was always quiet, somewhat shy, not outspoken, and certainly not aggressive. Now he was angry, and that rage fuelled his determination. He wouldn't go down without a fight.

Jason smiled grimly. "Well, I've got some skills. I'm going to use all that shit I learned in school. First of all, I need to get into that douchebag's office," he said, nodding towards Tony's prone form.

"Then I need to raid a janitor's closet. I'm also going to need containers, preferably glass or something that will break easily." He had a far away look as he thought and planned; his eyes had a shine of anticipation. Amanda was a little disturbed by the enthusiastic glint in his eye as he spoke.

"Last, where is the electrical room?"

"Jason, that's a lot of sneaking around."

"Yes, it is."

"Is there anything I can say that will change your mind?"

"No."

"I didn't think so." Amanda had a sense of déjà vu wash over her as she recalled their conversation out on the pier. "Okay. Fine. I'll help then." She smiled at him. It was a lopsided, resigned smile and, for the first time, Jason smiled back.

"Thank you," he said quietly.

"Okay then, Tony's real office is in the hallway, closest to the call centre floor. With almost everyone out in printing or distribution, it shouldn't be too hard to get there unseen."

Amanda nibbled her bottom lip as she thought, and Jason caught himself smiling down at her. He quickly reminded himself that this thing wasn't Amanda.

"There's also a janitorial closet on the way, so that makes things a little easier. I'm pretty sure there's a bunch of mason jars in the lunch room..." She paused, thinking. "The electrical room is slightly more problematic. It's on the other side of the printing centre, which is now filled with my fellow Acantha. What are you planning?" Amanda asked.

Jason looked up at Amanda. "I'm going to out-human these fuckers."

CHAPTER TWENTY-TWO

They made their way unobstructed to the janitor's closet. Switching on the light, Jason smiled at the cornucopia of chemicals before him. Immediately he grabbed a bottle of ammonia, bleach, drain cleaner, and, after a quick reading of the label, three large bottles of floor wax.

"Slide the mop and bucket over," Jason said. "We're gonna need some glass jars too. And a roll of tinfoil if there is one, or anything with aluminum."

She raised her eyebrows in question but did as he asked, pushing the large yellow bucket over to him. Jason poured two full bottles of the floor polish into the tub of the scrubbing bucket and piled the bottles of cleaner onto the ringer.

"We're taking it with us," Jason said, and Amanda wheeled the bucket and mop combo into the hallway. As Jason was shutting the door, he spied a beat-up old ball cap hanging on a peg. On a whim he grabbed it and stuffed it into his back pocket. Pushing the bucket before them, they made their way to Tony's office.

The lights were off, and the door was ajar. Their luck was holding; there was no one around. Slipping inside, Jason sat at Tony's computer. He felt a momentary pang of regret: it was a beautiful laptop, easily worth at least four grand, and it broke Jason's heart a little when he though about what he was planning to do to it.

Jason brought up the login screen. "Damn it. It's password protected. Do you know it?" he asked Amanda.

"No. He never trusted anyone," she replied as she looked around the desk for anything that Tony may have written the password on.

"Okay, you have some of his memories, right?"

"Yeah. A few older ones…" Amanda replied pensively.

"What are some things he may have used as a password?"

Amanda frowned as she thought.

"He's a creature of habit, narcissistic, and a megalomaniac. One of his past ones was Epic1."

Jason keyed in the password. "Nope. Try again."

"Dominator123," Amanda suggested.

"Strike number two," Jason replied. "We've only got one shot left before the system locks us out."

"He must be using a new one," Amanda frowned. "Try Independence-Day1."

Jason raised his eyebrow.

"He said it's his favourite movie."

"You sure?"

"No, but it's the best guess I can make."

He started to key in the password when Amanda grabbed his arm. "No, wait. Try SlaveMaster70Vir."

Jason looked at her with raised brows. "That's random."

"Not if you know Tony." Amanda frowned. "He's bragged about Acanthan superiority and that he's going to be humanity's slave master. 70Vir is the Earth name given to the star that Acantha orbits. Tony would think this is funny."

Jason shook his head; Tony was way more fucked up than he'd thought. With a flick of his fingers, he entered in the password and they both held their breath. They sighed audibly when the screen flickered for a moment before it finally cleared to show a black background with a glowing red electronic eye peering out and the caption "HAL: It can only be attributable to human error" in white font below it.

"Seriously?" Jason said to Amanda, pointing to the computer screen. "HAL9000?"

Amanda looked at him blankly.

"It's from *2001: A Space Odyssey*. Can an invading alien actually be geekier than a human?"

Amanda shrugged. She only had the vaguest idea of what he was talking about.

"Great job," Jason said as he started clicking on files and doing a quick perusal before moving on to the next.

"Not really," she said.

He stopped his searching and looked up at her. Grinning sheepishly, she held up a post it note with the password printed on it.

"You had it the whole time?"

"No. I just found it. It was stuck inside his planner."

Shaking his head, he went back to work. While he worked on locating the files he wanted, Amanda slipped out to the cafeteria to find his requested containers, shutting the door behind her. She found dozens of them kept in the fridge and cupboards, which she emptied and quickly wiped out before stuffing them into a backpack she'd pilfered from the lost and found.

Nearly a half an hour passed before Amanda slipped back in to Tony's office.

"Jackpot," Jason said.

Amanda was surprised to see him pulling a USB drive from the laptop.

"Where'd you get that?" she asked.

"I'm a computer geek," he replied with a grin, as he started to close down all the files he'd opened.

Amanda looked at him in disbelief.

"How... where... We were soaked."

"Okay, I found it in the pants pocket."

"The ones got from the lost and found?" Amanda looked at Jason, surprised.

"Yep, the same. And outside of some porn, which I deleted, it was blank."

She shook her head.

"Almost ready," Jason said.

Grinning like a Cheshire cat Jason put the cover back on the USB stick and stuffed it into his pocket. "I copied as many of Tony's files regarding the invasion to the drive as I could. It has a lot of information on Acanthans, how you got here, images of your species, info on how processing works. There are also files on every person that was processed. From Tony's CloneZone account, I emailed the information and what amounts to a recorded confession from Tony to every major newspaper worldwide, the FBI, CIA, Homeland Security, and ICE."

"Tony had recorded a confession?"

"No. It looked like he recorded every meeting. I picked a couple and got lucky on the third try. It was one between him and Walter where he did a full evil villain monologue. It was perfect."

"I wasn't there?" Amanda looked into Jason's eyes questioningly, holding his gaze.

Jason turned away. "Not on the one I sent."

"Is Jason trying to protect me?" Amanda thought to herself. "If so, why? He's made his dislike of the real me clear."

She wanted to ask him, but he continued before she had a chance.

"I also got into Tony's social media accounts and posted it there." Jason paused and looked at Amanda. "He had freaking social media accounts. Who'd have guessed?"

"We all had some, we had to keep up appearances."

"It worked."

Amanda didn't know how to respond to that, so she simply laid the bags of jars on the desk.

"Perfect," Jason said.

"What if no one believes it?"

"What?"

"The stuff you sent out."

"Well, that would suck, but it won't matter in the end. I've got a coup de grace."

"What are you?"

He was grinning from ear to ear. "Tony said I was good and he's about to find out just how good I am." Jason paused and looked up at Amanda. "With the info sent out, we probably don't have a lot of time left before the shit hits the fan."

Amanda suddenly put her finger to her lips, silencing Jason. She stuck her head out the hallway and looked up and down. There was nobody there. "I thought I heard something. We need to hurry before someone shows up."

"Just gimmie another minute. I'm going to need a couple more things."

Jason began digging through Tony's desk, grabbing a pair of scissors and stuffing them into his pocket. Once he'd grabbed what he thought he might need he took the polish-soaked mop from the bucket and spread the polish liberally around Tony's desk. Amanda paled. "What are you doing?"

"You'll see."

"Jason-"

"No time to explain, we have to hurry. Remember?"

Amanda nodded.

"What do you need?"

"Those labs we passed..."

"What about them?"

"You said they did genetic research."

"Yes."

"There's gotta be test tubes, sample vials, or something similar. Right?

"Yes. Why?"

"I need them."

Amanda thought briefly about trying to dissuade Jason, but when she saw his look of grim determination, she knew there was no point.

"C'mon," Amanda said, leading the way into the corridor. Jason followed, slopping polish from the bucket as he went. He shut the door behind them and headed the short distance to the labs, dragging the sopping mop behind him. The first lab they came to had a sign on the door that read "Genetics." She swiped her card and the door unlocked. Amanda turned the knob and opened the door, letting bright light spill into the hallway. Jason and Amanda squinted against the harsh light.

"Commander?" a baritone voice greeted her. "I wasn't expecting you."

"Jerome? Why are you still here?"

"Oh, you know the Captain." There was a chuckle. "He wants the latest numbers on the next gen, and if I don't get them to him, and I quote, 'by yesterday,' there will be hell to pay. He's put a major rush on the research."

"Yes, I certainly do."

Amanda nodded her agreement as she stepped into the room, motioning Jason to remain in the hallway. The room was lit with bright halogens and she wrinkled her nose at the smell of sanitizer and formaldehyde. It always made her think of mothballs. The walls were flanked with scientific equipment: a centrifuge, a DNA sequencer, microscopes and more; there were two metal desks facing each other at opposite ends of the room. Jerome was seated at the desk that was against the far wall.

"Have you seen the Captain?" Jerome asked. "I was expecting him earlier."

"I believe he's a little tied up with one of the processings." Amanda put on a disappointed expression. "It didn't go as planned, I'm afraid."

"Oh, that is unfortunate. Was it a valuable asset?"

Amanda nodded. "Yes. The Captain is displeased."

Jerome nodded back with an expression of mutual understanding.

"Who's that with you?" Jerome said, pointing vaguely in Jason's direction.

"A drone."

Jerome raised an eyebrow.

"Actually, the Captain sent us," Amanda interjected before Jerome could ask any further questions.

"Really?"

"Yes. He sent us to retrieve some specimen vials."

Jerome stood and went to a nearby cupboard. He took out a tray of small glass vials, sealed with plastic stoppers. "Will this do?"

"Perfect," Amanda said, smiling as she reached for the tray.

Jerome pulled them back and held them close as he looked back and forth between Amanda and Jason suspiciously. "It is my job to collect any specimens. What does he need them for and why did he send a Commander for such a menial job? And with a drone to help?"

"They are for specimens. I do not answer to you, therefore the why is none of your business."

"Specimens of…?"

She was beginning to sweat. Why was Jerome suddenly so suspicious? He was usually a rule follower, not one to question a superior's requests.

Amanda sighed melodramatically and replied brusquely, "If you insist. It's for a dead Acanthan's brain tissue. From the failed processing I told you about."

Jerome frowned. "The Captain would have normally just used the intercom to request me to come and take the samples. I am the one who normally does any necropsies. The Captain dislikes getting his hands dirty."

"There is an issue with the intercom."

"Then why send you and not a drone?" Jerome had stepped back to his desk and was reaching for the intercom button, regardless of the fact that she'd said it was not working.

She glanced out in the hallway and could see Jason crouching slightly, ready to do what had to be done. She made her second gamble for the night. She stepped closer to the desk and frowned.

"Jerome, I'd hoped to spare you this until we knew for sure. You are a damned good geneticist and an asset worth retaining."

Jerome's hand stopped a centimetre away from the button. "What?"

"Tony was going to page you, but..." Amanda shook her head. "You wouldn't have enjoyed it if he had." Amanda looked sad and disappointed. "I told him it wasn't your fault. That the host had been faulty, not the symbiote."

Jerome blanched. "What do you mean?"

"The specimen he needs to sample is from the failed processing tonight and he blames you."

"Me? How?" Jerome's hand fell away from the intercom and he paled.

"Well, it is *your* next gen that killed the host."

"Oh." Jerome looked a little green as he sat down heavily in his chair.

"Tony wanted to punish you right away, but I convinced him to let me do the necropsy. You are our best geneticist."

"I told him they weren't ready. That the recoding was not stable. There was a high risk of death instead of generating a drone that is nothing but a husk with augmented physical capabilities."

"Oh, sweet Jesus," Amanda thought, fighting back a rising dread. Tony had used a next gen on her friends. As she thought of Marc her eyes flicked briefly to Jason before turning her focus back to Jerome. He was so distraught she could have likely started tap dancing right in front of him and he'd not have noticed.

She pressed on. "Have you ever known Tony to be patient?"

Jerome shook his head.

"The Gen2 samples were ready and he had a host. That's all he needed to know."

"Why did he choose such a high value host?" He was visibly sweating now.

"He likely felt the benefits of having this asset as a Gen2 were worth it. We did have assurances that they were viable, if a little unstable." Amanda shrugged. "Other than that, why does Tony do a lot of the things he does? If you want, you can ask him that the next time you see him."

Jerome looked up at her in shock and shook his head vigorously. "No. I don't think I will."

"While I am a more patient person than Tony, my patience does have a limit and I'm beginning to regret my decision to help you." She extended her hand for the tray. "Now, if you want, you can go ahead and page him or you can give me the vials and we can pretend you weren't here when I showed up."

As Jerome held the tray out, the vials rattled a little as his hands trembled.

As Amanda left, she said over her shoulder, "If I were you, I'd lock myself in here and get that report ready." She paused briefly. "And it had better have very good news."

She closed the door behind her and nearly collapsed when she heard it snick shut.

"Fuck." She gaped as Jason grabbed the vials and held her by the elbow, steadying her.

"You were amazing," he said, looking down at her. She looked up into his sparkling green eyes and smiled weakly.

"I want to puke."

Jason smiled in sympathy. "Welcome to humanity."

CHAPTER TWENTY-THREE

Amanda parked the bucket and mop by the door as they re-entered the room. She sighed as she saw that Jamie was standing exactly where they had left her, still playing with her gown. What were they going to do with her? She next checked on Marc. He was still out cold, but he was no longer twitching or crying out. His breathing was slow, steady, and peaceful.

"He's sleeping," Amanda said as she joined Jason where he sat on the floor, laying his spoil before him.

Jason set the bottle of bleach and ammonia next to each other then paired up the drain cleaner and the roll of tinfoil. As he worked, he glanced at Amanda checking on their friends and he thought, "She played that geneticist. She controlled whole thing right from the minute she opened the door. How many times has she done that to me?" He thought back to all the times she'd asked something of him, and he'd complied, almost without protest. Their first date, moving in together and getting him to work at CloneZone. He shook his head to clear it. He had to focus on what he was doing. A mistake now could be fatal.

He sat cross-legged on the floor and grinned like a kid with his first chemistry set. He started by lining up all twenty-one mason jars and split them between the bleach and drain cleaner sides.

"Chlorine first," he said under his breath.

"What are you making?"

"Grenades."

"What?" Amanda sounded horrified.

"I hope I don't have to use these, but I need something in case I'm caught." He looked up at Amanda and said, "I won't be turned."

Jason carefully began to half fill the first ten of the jars laid out before him. Once that was done, he took the smaller specimen vials and filled them with ammonia, capping each one carefully with their rubber stopper.

He carefully wiped them clean and lowered each one into a bleach-filled jar and sealed it. With that task completed he turned to the other set of jars.

He handed the roll of tinfoil to Amanda. "Can you tear this into tiny pieces and fill the specimen tubes with it?"

"Ummm, sure."

"Don't pack it tight."

While Amanda did as he'd asked, Jason filled the remaining jars with drain cleaner.

Once again, he carefully lowered the vials into the murky liquid.

Before sealing these, he looked at Amanda and asked, "Anything not made of aluminum that we can put in?"

"What for?" Amanda looked confused.

"Shrapnel."

"Oh," she said, her voice subdued.

"The ones with the drain cleaner will be, more or less, frag grenades. Once the cleaner mixes with the aluminum, it will explode. Anything inside becomes shrapnel. They aren't powerful enough to kill, but I want them to make an impression."

Jason looked at her as she stared at the bottles arrayed out before him. "Second thoughts?"

Amanda's eyes rose from the jars to Jason, slipped around the room taking in Marc, Jamie, and George, and finally rested on the form of Tony for a moment before she looked back to Jason. She tried to smile; it was small and wavered.

"No." Her voice cracked. She cleared her throat and said firmly, "No."

"Good." Jason returned her smile.

Amanda stood and found a box labelled "sharps," which turned out to be about two hundred lancets. Small and wickedly sharp. Jason shared them liberally amongst his drain cleaner jars. Using latex gloves as barriers, he screwed the caps onto the jars.

"What are the other ones?" Amanda asked, pointing to the bleach-filled bottles Jason was stowing back into a backpack.

"Ammonia chloride," he replied.

Amanda just looked at him blankly.

"They are chlorine gas grenades. It's nasty stuff. When the ammonia and chlorine bleach mix, it releases chlorine gas. It will burn the eyes, nose, and throat."

"But it won't kill, will it?"

"Oh yeah, it can kill." He looked down at the bulging backpack. "Once this is done, I hope there isn't any evidence that this is what I used."

"What do you mean?"

"It's banned by the Geneva Protocol. I'd go to jail for life."

"Jason." Amanda was horrified. "You can't."

"I can." He held one of the gas grenades before him, slowly turning it around. The pale-yellow bleach swirled a little and the tiny vial of ammonia made a muffled clink against the glass. "I have to."

He put the jar in and stood, hefting the pack onto his back.

Jason looked down at his watch. "I need to hurry. We've been in here too long. They are soon going to start wondering where Tony is."

Amanda nodded then opened the door and checked the hallway. It was clear. She stepped out and tugged the bucket away from the wall and stood there holding the mop handle in her left hand. In her right hand she held her ring key along with her key card.

Jason stepped up close to her and held out his hand for her keys. "This is it, I guess. Do or die time?"

"Don't say that." She looked up at Jason longingly. "Please."

"It's just a figure of speech. Trust me, I have no plans on actually dying."

Jason's heart lurched as he looked into her eyes, as if seeing her for the first time. He didn't know if he was suffering from some bizarre form of Stockholm Syndrome, or maybe he was finally seeing the real Amanda.

Hesitantly, he touched her cheek.

She pressed her face against his hand. Reluctantly he took his hand back, and reached into his pocket, withdrawing the USB drive. Taking her hand in his, he laid it in her palm and closed her fingers around it.

Holding her hand Jason said, "Take this. I want you to get Marc and

Jamie, then get out of the building."

"Jason, no."

"Please. I can't do this unless I know you and Marc are safe."

Amanda's heart was breaking; he couldn't do this to her. Give her hope that there could be something more, then throw his life away. If he were caught, she had no doubts about how this would end. It was selfish, but if he died, she'd have no one, nothing.

"Let me help you," she pleaded, her eyes filling with tears. "You stand a better chance with me."

He smiled down at her sadly. "No. A couple of hours ago you told me you loved me."

"I do," Amanda said. Jason could feel her hands trembling inside his own.

"Then save my friend. Get him back to his wife and kid."

"Jason…"

"Please, Amanda."

Tears threatened to slip from her eyes and her voice failed, but she nodded.

Jason turned to leave, but at the last moment he paused. He didn't want to leave things like this. Just in case. Impulsively, he leaned in and kissed her. He stood and pulled on the ratty ball cap he'd found in the closet and began to "mop" the floor. He headed straight for the printing floor, smearing liberal amounts of floor polish around as he went.

CHAPTER TWENTY-FOUR

Amanda re-entered the lab to find Tony awake, wiggling and mumbling through his gag, and Marc semi-conscious. She pulled down the sheet from Tony's head revealing the large purplish bruise that had developed where Jason had punched him. Tony's eyes went wide when he saw her looking at him. She stood there, staring down at him, seeing the pure hatred in his eyes.

"I'm sorry," she whispered, "but I can't leave you here."

Relief flooded Tony's face as Amanda reached for the gag.

"Thank you," Tony croaked, his mouth was dry from the cotton gag.

Tony glowered at her. It might have had more effect if his face hadn't been so swollen. As it was, it only made him look demented.

"I knew you'd come to your senses." He still had a lisp from his swollen lips. "No one needs to know what happened here. Of course, you will be punished, but not severely, and your lapse will stay between us." Tony's voice, while still a little horse had grown increasingly commanding as he spoke. "Now, untie me and help me up."

Amanda looked from Tony and back to Marc, whose eyelids were fluttering. "He's coming around," Amanda thought. She glanced at Jamie and wondered if there'd be any of the old Marc left. She could still feel Jason's kiss and the warmth of his breath on her neck as he said good-bye to her.

She looked back down at Tony and said icily, "I think you misunderstand me."

Tony's eyes went wide with incredulity. "What did you say to me?"

"I said 'I believe you misunderstand.' I do not want to help you and I will not leave you here," Amanda replied, squaring her shoulders. She looked Tony defiantly in the eye. "I've tolerated you for years. Your groping hands and your creepy leering looks. I've done all you've asked but it stops here. I hate you. You're a narcissistic power-hungry bastard."

As she spoke Amanda reached behind her to the instrument table and grabbed something that felt like an ice pick.

"Today I am human," Amanda growled as she swung her arm around, plunging it into Tony's neck. Warm blood spurted out over her hand and she quickly yanked it away. Tony tried to scream, but it came out as nothing more than a gurgle. He started to choke as blood poured down his throat and filled his lungs. His wide eyes looked accusingly at Amanda as she pulled the sheet back over his head. He twitched and thrashed as blood soaked the white sheet.

Jamie yelled out, "Cantaloupe," and giggled.

Amanda looked at Jamie sadly and sighed. She looked down at her trembling, blood-covered hands and wanted to throw up. Grabbing a corner of the sheet, Amanda scrubbed the blood off. She wanted to curl into a ball and cry. She felt weak. These feelings weren't what she'd expected. Guilt, sadness, remorse. She hated Tony. She thought it would have been easy, but Amanda had never taken an Acanthan life before, and it was taking a far greater toll than she'd ever anticipated.

Marc moaned, drawing Amanda away from her thoughts.

"Marc, can you hear me?" she asked, turning her back on the blood-soaked sheet.

"Wha... what happened?" he asked, trying to sit up.

As much as she knew Jason cared about Marc, Amanda had no intentions of releasing him until she determined whose side he was on.

"Marc, you, Jamie, and George were taken by Tony. He may have done things to you. Do you remember?" she said.

"Amanda? Is that you?" Marc said, squinting to try and bring the amorphous blob that was his friend into focus. "It's not safe. You have to get out of here."

Marc tried to lift his hand to rub his face and found that he was still restrained. Suddenly everything came rushing back to him: Jamie, George, and Tony.

Marc's eyes were wide with panic.

"Oh my god, Amanda, it's Tony. He gassed us. He killed George and fucked Jamie up. Please help me?"

"Shhh. Marc. It's all right. Calm down. Jason sent me to help you, but I need you to tell me, what do you remember."

"Jason? He's alive? Where is he?" Marc looked around frantically for his friend.

"Yes, Jason's alive." She didn't add the little thought of "for now" that had popped unbidden into her head. "He's doing something. You need to answer me."

"Amanda, please unstrap me before he comes back," Marc begged as he jerked against the restraints. He was just barely holding his panic at bay. Flashes of Tony's gloating face, the feel of the thing on his face, and the pain flitted through his mind.

"Marc, I promise I'll help you, but you need to answer me. It's very important." Amanda steadied herself. She was scared and precious time was passing. "Listen to me, I don't have time to explain everything right now, but Tony used an anesthetic gas. Did it smell like lemons?"

Marc nodded.

"That's Sevoflurane. It works fast, but once you wake you are fine."

"I don't feel fine."

"I don't suppose you do. He was experimenting on people. Before I can untie you, I need to make sure that you're... you." Amanda held onto Marc's face, forcing him to look into her eyes. "Tell me everything you can remember."

Marc looked into Amanda's eyes, searching for anything that indicated she was involved. He hadn't forgotten the box that held her signature. Amanda saw his fear and suspicion. She couldn't blame him after everything he'd been through.

"Marc, you can trust me."

"Really? Where's Jason?"

"He's gone for help."

"Jason would never leave you."

"Marc, please–"

"No, Amanda. Now. Something isn't right here. Let me up."

"I have to confirm something first. Please. It's important. Tell me what happened, and I promise I'll undo the restraints."

Marc knew he was trapped. Amanda had the upper hand. What was she trying to find out? He was afraid to answer. If she was part of this, he was screwed. If she was really trying to help him...

"Fuck it," he finally muttered, defeated. He turned his head to look at her.

"The truth?"

She nodded.

He shuddered recalling the feeling of the creature on his face.

Taking a deep breath, Marc said, "I know it's going to sound crazy, but Tony put a weird slug on my face, and it crawled up my nose."

"And then?" Amanda prompted.

"You believed that?"

"Let's say I do. What happened next?"

"Then it felt like someone had poured acid into my brain. I think I passed out. Next thing I know I hear voices and you are standing next to me." Marc looked at Amanda. "Who were you talking to?"

"Jamie," she replied absently, puzzled by Marc's lucidness. If he'd been processed, he should be having problems remembering and talking.

"Marc, are you taking any drugs?"

Marc looked at Amanda as if she'd lost her mind. "No."

"Prescriptions, anything at all? It doesn't matter what or how insignificant."

"Well, my doc has me on a nasal spray for sinusitis. It wasn't really working though."

"Fluconazole?"

"Yeah, I think that's it. It's in my jacket pocket, wherever that is."

"Marc, fluconazole is an antifungal. It may not have cured your infection, but it saved your life," Amanda said. Grabbing Marc by the cheeks she kissed him right on the mouth.

Marc's eyes popped open wide.

"Whaph?" he mumbled around her kiss.

"It's is also used to treat N. fowleri." Smiling with relief, Amanda began to undo the restraints holding Marc in place.

"N flowers?"

"No, N. fowleri. A brain-eating amoeba."

"A what? Tony tried to kill me with an amoeba?"

"Not really, but something similar to it. I'm sorry I didn't untie you right away. I had to be sure it was really you and you hadn't been changed."

"Oh, I'm changed all right. I'll never be the same again," he said as he sat up.

Jamie clapped her hands and squealed, "Watermelon."

Marc attempted to stand, putting his arm around Amanda for support.

As he made it to his feet Amanda said, "I don't feel right leaving Jamie behind."

"I'm okay with leaving her. She helped Tony recapture me. We can't trust her."

Amanda sighed but she knew Marc was right. If Jamie was following Tony's orders it was only a matter of time before she became a liability. She opened the door and stepped out into the hallway. Behind them they heard the distinctive sound of a gun being cocked. The pair turned slowly. The barrel of a '45 was only inches away from them and it was shaking.

"I think Tony may want a word with you two."

CHAPTER TWENTY-FIVE

Quietly, Jason closed the heavy door behind him. It shut with a quiet snick that felt very final to Jason. Thoughts of Amanda and Marc almost made him turn back. They were his friends, and he was abandoning them. He paused with his hand on the knob and looked back over his shoulder at the grey metal. Maybe he should escape with them and let the authorities deal with Tony. He'd sent them everything they'd need, and he'd given Amanda the USB with everything he'd had time to transfer. It was enough. Why did he have to do anything else?

Jason thought of George's corpse, Jamie's loss of sanity, and Marc's whimpers of pain after whatever Tony had done to him. So much was at stake. If the authorities didn't believe the email or saw it too late, then Tony would succeed.

Taking a deep breath, he turned his back on the door and stepped forward. He couldn't turn back now.

He paused to look around. He'd never been in this part of the building before. Nothing was familiar to him and while Amanda had given him the layout, he really wasn't sure where anything was. Time was precious, but he couldn't just go blundering around.

The room was expansive, a wide open warehouse. He couldn't see much thanks to the stacks of paper and printing materials that turned the open space into a maze. The place reeked of oil, toner, and ink.

Off to his right, he could see the huge loading doors; they were closed.

They were also his goal. Next to them was a door he planned on using for his escape.

He'd have to circle the perimeter without being seen. His plan was to box the creatures in, to get as many as he could.

That thought turned his stomach to ice. He'd never killed anything in his life and now…

He sighed and took a quick furtive look around. Jason allowed his shoulders to slump, pulled the hat he'd found down further to mask his red hair, and kept his face down while he slowly worked his way between the printers and packaging machines, slopping floor polish in his wake, hoping no one would notice he wasn't the usual night maintenance man.

Adrenaline pumped through his veins, his heart raced, but Jason felt more alive than he'd ever felt in his life. Even if he was only mopping a floor. He'd always played it safe, never taking a chance, never really lived. He vowed that if he survived this, things were going to change.

Carefully he worked his way through the floor leaving a slug trail of the polish. Polish was the perfect incendiary. Even if it dried, the fumes were flammable. The over-stuffed backpack filled with hastily prepared drain cleaner and bleach grenades he'd made dug painfully against his back. He sent a silent prayer to whatever deity would listen that the grenades stayed stable until he needed them. Otherwise, he'd take himself out in a most unpleasant way.

"At least these bastards will come with me," he thought morbidly.

Jason worked his way through the warren of stacks, leaving puddles of polish as he went. At intervals he'd hold the sopping mop up against the flammable materials, soaking them in the hopes they'd go up like Roman candles. He grinned when he came across a pallet filled with canisters of printing toner with their small warning labels with a flame. Here he poured some of the polish, saturating the floor and wooden pallet.

"That'll get their attention." He moved slowly, avoiding Acanthans, as he worked his way around. It felt like an eternity but in reality it didn't take him long to reach the electrical room. It was right where Amanda had said, located against the far-left wall of the huge room.

Bringing the mop and bucket with him, Jason used Amanda's key to open the electrical room door and slipped inside and shut it behind him. It was pitch black. He fumbled around the wall until he found the switch and flicked on the light. The single bare bulb flickered to life.

The room was fourteen feet long and twelve wide and had been used as a maintenance and storage area. Piles of boxes, wiring, and supplies lined the walls, casting shadows. It was like something from a horror film. The room where the serial killer always caught the pretty girl.

"Friggin' creepy," he said with a shudder as he stripped to the waist and tore his cotton t-shirt into ribbons, throwing the pieces into the bucket of polish to soak. Pulling the black button-down shirt back on he turned his attention to the series of panel boards on the far wall. He quickly read through the menus that ran down next each of the circuit breakers, a variety of lights, outlets, and security doors. With each passing tab, he began to worry that the one he was looking for wasn't there. He moved to the final panel in the row. It was a much smaller panel that connected to the others by a grey conduit pipe. It had a faded label that read "Loading Doors."

"Never fails. It's always in the last place you look," Jason said with a wash of relief.

He'd been afraid they wouldn't be together, and he'd have had to search the whole floor. He'd never have been able to do what he needed to in time if this switch had been out in the open.

Jason grinned and pulled the lever down until it clicked, cutting power to the panel. His goal was to cook alien brain-eating slugs, not to electrocute himself. The panel was locked, but that was okay; he didn't need to access the panel directly. All he needed to do was get into the set of wires leading from the panel to the door.

Another, smaller plastic conduit tube ran from the bottom of the sub-panel. About a foot below the panel there was a join where it turned and ran parallel to the bigger conduit tube above. This was the weak point he needed. Jason gave it a tug, but it didn't budge; it was fixed solidly to the panel and the cinder block wall.

"I've got to find something to break it or pry it off," he said to himself as he looked around the room. He quickly found a toolbox poked behind a few stacked boxed of maintenance supplies. Pulling it into the light he discovered it was locked with a small padlock.

"Seriously?" he muttered. Hoping no one would hear, he picked up the toolbox and slammed it against the wall until the small lock fell to the floor, still attached to the double loop. He put the battered box down and foraged inside it.

"This should do the trick," he said as he stepped back to the panel with a claw hammer in hand.

He needed to break the pipe but not mash the wires inside. He raised his arm and gave the plastic a whack. It cracked and splintered but not enough. He jammed the hammer in behind the pipe and gave a hard tug. It loosened and more plastic tinkled to the ground.

The final blow shattered the plastic, exposing the black-coated wiring inside.

There was a knock on the door.

"Shit." Jason jumped at the sound. His heart raced as he looked around frantically for a place to hide while the doorknob wiggled back and forth.

"Hey, who's in there?"

The boxes would never conceal him.

He heard the soft snick as the door unlocked.

Jason jumped behind the door as it opened and hid it its shelter, holding the hammer tightly in his hand.

"Hello?"

The figure stepped in front of the door. It looked down at the bucket filled with rags.

"Who the fuck left this here?" He began to close the door. Jason knew once the door closed, he would been seen.

"Me," Jason said, stepping forward, hoping to bluff his way out. Just in case he couldn't, he kept his right arm tucked behind his leg, hiding the hammer from view.

"Jason?"

It was Gary, the pimply drug dealing dude. Even as an Acanthan he smelled faintly of cheap weed. The look of surprise was quickly replaced with a look of smugness Jason recognized; it was the same look Walter and Tony would get just before they turned your life to shit.

"What are you doing in here?" Gary said, looking at Jason suspiciously.

Jason started down at the shorter man, his mouth suddenly dry, while his heart beat frantically and beads of sweat stippled his brow like tiny pearls.

"I didn't know you had joined us?" Gary asked.

"Ah, yeah. Last night."

"Humph. They don't tell us shit."

"Not much different than working in the call centre," Jason said, laughing nervously.

Gary nodded. "Ain't that the truth. Looks like you had it easy if you're on your feet already."

"Yeah, everything went smoothly. Bit of a headache and a nosebleed but that's it."

"You're damn lucky. I was out for days. Felt like I was dying." Gary shrugged indifferently. "But I didn't end up a veg or a slab of meat, so it all worked out."

Jason blanched. "Yeah. Lucky."

"Guess we should get going," Jason said as he moved to step around Gary, thinking he'd have to double back for his supplies. He felt a hand on his arm.

"What are you doing in the electrical room?"

"Umm," Jason stuttered. "Amanda asked me to check on something. I'm an engineer. So, she thought I could help."

"Right," Gary said, the doubt clear in his voice.

"I'm serious. See?" Jason held up Amanda's badge and keys. "She loaned me her stuff since Walter hasn't bothered to get mine ready yet."

Gary looked back and forth from the badge to Jason's face. He was close enough that Jason could smell the marijuana on his breath.

"Yeah, that makes sense. Walter is so busy crawling up Tony's ass it's a surprise he gets anything done," he said with a shrug, his hand dropping from Jason's arm. "If I see Tony, I'll let him know I was talkin' to yah."

"Sure thing," Jason said as the two stepped outside the room, Jason starting to close the door behind them.

"Don't forget the big meeting tonight," Gary said over his shoulder as he walked away.

"Meeting?"

"Lemme guess? They didn't tell you."

Jason laughed quietly. "Of course not."

"Tony has some big announcement. Wants us all to meet at ten."

"Great. Yeah, thanks. I'll be there," Jason said as he watched Gary's back fade into the shadows.

Jason took a deep breath and turned back into the electrical room, shutting the door behind him.

He looked at his watch, it was almost nine. "I'll have to work quickly now," he thought as he returned to the toolbox and took out a heavy screwdriver, which he used to pry the thick wire a little way out of the conduit. With still trembling hands he tried to carefully peel back the outer coating to expose the bundle of wires inside.

Jason teased out a single red wire and, using the scissors he had taken from Tony's office, pared back the cover to get the copper beneath. With a little effort he tugged the wire further out of the tube, allowing it to dangle close to the bucket. He used the screwdriver to get the sodden strips of cloth from the bucket and piled them on the wringer. He then positioned the bucket right under the panel.

"Shit," he muttered, the wire wasn't low enough.

He looked in the toolbox and saw a wrench. He pulled it out and wrapped the copper around the wrench, letting it dangle just above the soggy mess. He stepped back to appraise his handiwork and nodded his approval.

"MacGyver would be proud."

When the switch by the doors was turned on to open the bay doors, it would complete the circuit and cause the wire to arc, sending 20,000 volts into whatever happened to be handy. Right now, what was handy was the pile of rags soaked in highly flammable floor polish over a bucket filled with the same polish.

"Boom," he whispered as he grinned and made the universal sign for explosion.

Jason then turned the breaker back on, carefully picked up the back-pack, took the mop, and dragged it behind as he went, leaving a trail of polish that looked like a giant slug had passed by. He turned off the lights and left the door slightly ajar.

A good fire needs air.

CHAPTER TWENTY-SIX

Walter forced Amanda and Marc into Tony's office and tied each of them to chairs. He called Tony's cell and tried to reach him using the intercom, but there was no response. With each failed attempt, Walter grew more and more agitated.

"C'mon, Tony, where are you?" he muttered as he turned back towards his prisoners.

When he saw the smug look on Amanda's face he snarled, "What have you done?"

She refused to answer. Instead, she shot Walter a look of pure conde-scension. Without warning he slapped her, rocking her head to the side. A trickle of blood ran from her lip. With a smirk of defiance, she spit the bloody mess into his face. Walter went florid with rage. He raised the gun to her face. She could see down the barrel as it sat millimetres from her nose.

"You will tell me what I want to know."

"Leave her alone," Marc roared, struggling at his restraints. Walter turned to look at him and grinned before turning his attention back to Amanda.

"I know you will not succumb to torture, *Commander*, but your friend here has had no such training."

"Commander?" Marc's struggles ceased as he looked from Walter to Amanda and back again.

"Marc, I'm sorry. It's complicated." Looking past the barrel of the gun, she stared directly into Walter's eyes before continuing, "We can't tell Walter anything."

"Aw fuck." Marc's shoulders slumped. He knew what was coming and mentally braced himself for the blow which rocked him back in the chair. Blood ran from a gash over his eye. More blows followed. One after another rained down on him, each one eliciting a cry or pained grunt. He felt a rib crack, the wind was knocked from his lungs, his lips began to swell. His attachment to consciousness became a thin thread.

After what felt like an eternity, he heard Amanda screaming and the hits stopped. His head lolled back and forth and bloody spittle dripped from his open mouth. He heard Amanda saying words, but they held no meaning for him.

From a distance he heard a door open and close. He thought he heard crying, but he wasn't sure what was real or if it wasn't his own tears. His eyes closed as he allowed himself to slip into the abyss and all sound ceased.

Jason worked his way around the building, working hard to avoid anyone, occasionally passing by pairs or groups close enough hear them talking. He never lingered to listen. He'd just tuck his head down and mop, betting on the fact that no one ever paid attention to a cleaner.

Their voices followed him. Haunted him. He looked down at his hands where they clutched the mop handle. He saw a little grime around his nails where he'd rigged the wires, but otherwise they were clean. After tonight he wouldn't be able to say that.

He stopped walking to pool some polish around a case of toner. He didn't know how combustible the toner would be, but it would burn dirty making a cloud of toxic smoke.

A laugh echoed through the air. Jason hesitated. A lump formed in his chest. He knew the consequences of what he was doing. Did he really have to? He turned to look at the slug's trail of polish in his wake. He could go back. It would only take him a minute to change the wiring back. Then leave. Never look back. Make sure the cops got the USB drive, knew about what was going on here, but he'd have no part of whatever happened to everyone.

He recalled what was on that drive, what he'd seen on Tony's computer. He'd only had time to transfer the highlights, hopefully enough to interest the authorities, but he'd seen more. Pictures of the unsuccessful, images of the creatures stuck to a human brain. Once you'd been processed, there was no going back. You weren't human anymore. You were a hybrid.

A monster.

With a heavy sigh Jason began to mop again. He had no choice. The police were a hope but no guarantee. He was here.

Now. He had to act.

Jason moved on, slopping the polish wherever he went. He soaked piles of paper and pooled the polish around more jars of toner, working his way around the building. Meter by meter he drew closer to his goal, the loading bay doors.

"I'm gonna make it," he thought. For the first time since he developed the plan, he felt real hope that he'd make it out alive.

A roar of cheering stopped him in his tracks. He stood there, frozen, listening as a familiar nasally voice rose above the din, punctuated by a scream of pain.

"It can't be."

CHAPTER TWENTY-SEVEN

Amanda struggled futilely against her bonds. Whatever could be said about Walter, he made sure his prisoners were secure. A quick glance at the clock on the wall confirmed her worst fear, their time was running out.

"Marc." He was unresponsive and his head hung against his chest.

"Marc?" she called, a little louder. He'd been through a lot and had taken one hell of a beating. Walter hadn't pulled any punches, and when he'd started pistol- whipping Marc, she'd caved.

Walter knew where Tony was, and he was gone to get him. It didn't really matter, Tony was dead.

Amanda looked at Marc closely. His chest rose and fell with even, steady breaths.

They still had a chance. She just had to get free. They didn't have much time before Walter would get back and when he did both their lives would be forfeit.

She worked her wrists against the zip tie bonds, feeling them cutting into the tender skin around her hands.

Her hopes faded as she heard the door open. Amanda turned to look, her stomach sinking as she saw Walter helping Tony into the room. Tony was deathly pale and had a heavy bandage wrapped around his neck, making him look like he was wearing a turtleneck.

"It's good–to see–you–again, Amanda," Tony wheezed, a tight smile spreading across his thin lips.

"How?" Amanda felt ill.

"I am not–so easy–to–kill." His words came in short panting gasps.

"I found him and gave him this," Walter said proudly, holding up a heavy syringe. His obsequiousness was sickening.

"I saved him."

"Yes–you–did." Tony patted Walter on the shoulder. He looked like a proud pet owner praising his faithful dog. She wouldn't have been surprised if he'd taken out a biscuit and fed it to Walter.

"What is that?"

"Oh, a little–something–from–R&D."

Tony gasped as he collapsed into his chair.

"It boosts our ability to heal," Walter finished for his boss.

Tony looked from Amanda to Marc, who appeared to be regaining consciousness.

"Now…" he wheezed. "Now you get–to be Earth's–first example of what happens–to traitors."

His speech was getting stronger by the moment. Amanda paled. "What are you going to do?"

Tony just smiled and said, "Walter, escort our guests–to the gathering."

Walter smiled. "My pleasure."

CHAPTER TWENTY-EIGHT

Jason couldn't make out a word the voice was saying. He caught snippets that sounded like "traitor" and "betrayal." He had to get closer. Carefully, he worked his way around from behind the bench, walking along the fringe of the crowd slowly. They were shuffling and moving about in their growing excitement.

As Jason drew nearer, he had to fight the fear that was threatening to overwhelm him. The blob on the end was certainly Walter, the other was Tony; he had to know if what he suspected was true. Using the stacks of boxes as cover, he finally found a position where he could clearly see the improvised stage.

The world lurched beneath Jason's feet as his worst fears were confirmed. He could see both Marc and Amanda on the bench with Tony. Marc was the shadow standing next to Walter who was holding a gun to Marc's head. Marc's face was a mass of bruises. One eye was swollen nearly shut; his expression was blank.

"What have they done to you?" Jason thought as he looked at his help-less friend.

Anger replaced fear when he saw Tony holding Amanda by the hair, her body pressed against his and a scalpel hovering perilously over her carotid artery. A trickle of blood ran down Amanda's pale throat where the sharp blade had bit into her soft skin. Her hands were bound tightly before her with a black zip tie. Jason could see where the plastic had cut her.

As he moved, he heard more and more of Tony's words, that whiny, nasally voice sending a shudder down Jason's spine.

"She killed the innocent. The helpless. Jamie and George were like new-borns. They could do nothing to help themselves," Tony cried as he moved Amanda forward.

All eyes turned to her as the crowd hissed and roared.

"Listen to me," Amanda called out, beseeching to her fellow Acan-than's. "He's lying."

Tony glowered and prepared to strike when a voice called out, "Why would the Captain lie?"

"He wants power. All of it," Amanda responded. "You don't matter to him. We're disposable. Look what he's doing to me?"

"Yes, look at what I'm doing," Tony cried. "I'm bringing a human-lov-ing traitor to justice."

"You were caught trying to help him escape," Walter said, using the gun to point to Marc. "But it was too late, so in a fit of rage you attacked us. Killed Jamie and George."

"I did no such thing," Amanda screamed.

Leaning, Tony whispered in her ear, "They'll never believe you. They're mine."

He then lifted his head and called to his followers, "She lies."

"Liar. Liar. Liar." The mindless mob echoed their master.

Her eyes flicked from face to face, hoping to see a glimmer of doubt. But there was nothing. What little hope she'd had fled.

Jason gritted his teeth when he saw Tony lean in close and whisper in Amanda's ear. She looked like she may vomit but remained still. It wouldn't take much for the scalpel to end her life.

Putting on an expression of false concern, Tony nodded towards Marc. "This poor soul has just been processed. He may be misguided or con-fused." He shook his head sadly. "So, I will withhold judgment on him. For now."

Jason's heart sank, his worst fear realized. He'd held out hope, but he'd been too late.

Tony gave Amanda a hard jerk, making her yelp as he pulled her hair, the scalpel cutting another fine line.

"This bitch I know for a fact is a traitor to our cause."

Angry fists waved in the air. Cries of "Kill her!" echoed across the floor.

"Oh, we will, my friends. But first you need to know all her crimes." Tony paused for effect. "She has been conspiring against us."

An angry rumble began to rise. More voices joining the chorus of hate. Punctuating Tony's words every time he gave pause.

"She, Marc, and Jason have been working against us for some time and tonight they attempted a coup."

Tony's face remained grim as he waited for the din to die down.

"As bad as those crimes were, our Amanda, your Commander, my Second, my own daughter forsook me," Tony lowered the scalpel from Amanda's throat as he ripped the bandage from his own to display an ugly puckered scar on either side of his neck.

"She tried to kill me," he screamed.

Jason looked from Amanda's face to Tony's. He had to be lying. He'd been unconscious but alive when Jason had last seen him. Bound and gagged, but very much alive. Amanda wouldn't have done that, would she? Jason didn't want to believe it, but there was Tony looking like a mockery of Frankenstein's monster with its bolts pulled off.

Amanda turned her head slightly to look at Tony then spoke loud and clear, "My only regret is that I failed."

The crowd was enraged. Jason was sure if Amanda fell from the bench, they'd have torn her apart.

Tony smiled; she was helping him.

"Fear not, my friends. The ever-devoted Walter has saved us."

Walter puffed up twice his normal size and grinned. Jason had never wanted to punch someone so badly in his entire life.

"Thanks to his dedication and diligence, the conspiracy is ended, and I have named him my Second."

The crowd cheered and applauded.

"Walter. Walter. Walter."

Amanda tried to pull free, but Tony pulled her back and put the scalpel to her throat once again. He waited, allowing Walter to soak in the glory. When he judged the time right, he raised his hand, quieting them.

"Now, friends. We have a difficult decision to make." He put an expression of sorrow on his face. "What are we to do with our Amanda?"

The simple chant of "Kill her" began again.

"Yes, of course," Tony said. "But I ask you friends, how?"

An unintelligible cacophony of answers ensued.

Tony smiled out over his followers. He could see the anticipation, the hunger, in their eyes.

"It must be a message to any who might consider following in her path." Tony paused briefly as he looked out over the sea of faces before him. Each one looking at him expectantly. Only he could guide them.

"Friends, human history is rife with ways to kill each other. They've furnished us with so many options to choose, it's hard to decide. We could hang her or burn her at the stake."

Tony smiled down at the fevered faces that looked up at him. "We could draw and quarter her or I think…"

He held out his decision for a moment, the crowd grew quiet in anticipation. Leaned in. Waiting.

"We will flay her."

The crowd erupted in one voice, "Flay her. Flay her. Flay her."

Tony beamed down at them. A proud father.

"She will remain alive until our conquest is complete. She will watch. She will know her failure to protect this pitiful species and despair."

Tony shuddered with anticipation as he finished, "This will be glorious."

A cheer arose. The sound was filled with a primal need that made Jason's stomach turn, and he slipped the backpack from his shoulder. He looked around at the gathering. He saw Sue from accounts receivable who rescued kittens, Jerry who sat behind him and was the biggest comic book fan. Nearest to the stage he saw Gary the druggie. Faces he'd known, who'd been his friends. Now they were twisted with hunger and rage. A desire for blood. For the first time Jason truly saw them as the alien beings they had become.

His eyes blazed with anger as he pulled his ball cap down tight and stepped from behind the boxes. The crowd's inhuman screeching drowned out Jason's howl of defiance as he reached into the bag and pulled out the first grenade.

Amanda saw Jason. His face grim. Despite the proximity of the blade, Amanda tried to shake her head, but Tony's grip fixed her head almost in place.

Marc's head bobbed loosely but a smile slowly spread across his face.

Jason hung the bag on his left arm, keeping the top open, and withdrew the first gas grenade. He gave it a quick shake, breaking the small glass vial, allowing the drain cleaner and aluminum to mix. The glass became hot against his hand. He threw it with all the strength he could muster. It landed a few feet from the makeshift stage and exploded. Fragments of glass and burning chemical pelted those nearby.

They fell screaming. The second grenade Jason tossed flew towards the right of the gathering, shattering against a table and landing amidst the crowd. This one was a gas grenade. The bleach and ammonia mixed, releasing the green noxious chlorine gas that burned the eyes and throats of all those within its cloud. They too fell screaming, tearing at their faces as the corrosive chemicals blistered the eyes of those it hit. Clouds of the gas began to spread, choking and blinding the Acanthans wherever it went, while another drain cleaner bomb exploded nearby.

Tony looked on in horror as his people succumbed to the chemical attack. The floor below was nearly covered in the low hanging gas that moved and swirled beneath the stage. Like a hunting predator, its tendrils reached out, brushing its victims, weakening them, before enveloping and claiming them.

A man stumbled to the edge of the bench, his hands reaching up to Tony, his eyes beseeching.

"Help me?" Gary pleaded. His blistered and bleeding hands clawed at Tony's legs as he stumbled back, repulsed. Angrily he looked up to see where the grenades were coming from.

"Where is he?" Tony growled. As he searched the sea of faces, he yelled again, "Where is he?"

Amanda's bound hands grabbed at Tony's. "I don't know."

A scream of rage and frustration tore from Tony's throat.

CHAPTER TWENTY-NINE

Walter couldn't take his eyes from the cloud of gas that stalked him. The putrid yellow fog crept forward as he took several clumsy steps back from the rising fumes, distracted, his gun arm lowered. Without hesitation Marc spun, shoving the older man. Walter stumbled backwards, off the bench and onto all fours. The cloud of gas wrapped him in its embrace.

Screaming and writhing in pain, Walter tore at his face as the gas burned his eyes and seared his throat. Marc waited for a moment longer, watching as Walter began to twitch and cough up blood as the chlorine ate away his lungs.

"Pendejo," Marc snarled as he turned away from the dying man.

Jason saw the sudden movement from the bench and froze as he watched, slack-jawed with a bleach grenade held forgotten in his hand, while his friend took Walter down. "Marc?"

Jason couldn't believe what he was seeing; Marc had looked almost catatonic standing next to Walter. His blank face had been reminiscent of Jamie's vacant stare.

Jason's eyes flicked to Tony. A quick glance confirmed that Tony had seen everything.

"Marc!" Jason yelled, waving his arms and pointing to Amanda.

Marc scanned the crowd. A stationary bright red ball cap stood out amongst the panicking people and he followed Jason's frantic waves.

Jason cried, "Run!" and threw another grenade, managing to land it right in front of the platform holding Tony and Amanda.

Tony stepped back from the fumes, his eyes wide in horror.

"No," he gasped, backing away.

He looked wildly from the approaching Marc to Amanda before giving her a shove towards the edge.

She cried as she realized his intent and tried to dodge. She made double fists and swung at Tony, but she lost her footing. As she fell, her shoulder hit his hand and the scalpel scored a deep gouge along her back. Amanda screamed as she fell from the bench onto to the concrete floor, hitting it with a sickening thunk. Tony leaped over Walter's still form & disappeared behind the cloud of gas.

Jason started to run towards Amanda, heedless of the gas that separated them.

"Jason, stop!" Marc yelled as he ran, stumbling for Amanda, smoky green tendrils of gas on his heels. "I've got her."

A cloud of gas passed between them and Jason had to turn back or be burned.

CHAPTER THIRTY

Tony was blind with rage. He stumbled through the maze of the warehouse with his shirt pulled up over his mouth and eyes squeezed tightly shut. As quickly as he could, he made his way through the burning gas.

"Jason," he screamed as he stepped from the cloud.

The only response was the screams of panic and pain from his acolytes and the crash of breaking glass as Jason continued to lob his grenades. The warehouse was filling with more and more toxic gas, burning chemicals, and shrapnel. Chaos ruled.

Tony tore strips from the bottom of his shirt and tied it across his mouth while stuffing more around the edges of his glasses. Protected as best as he could, he began his search for Jason.

"The bastard can't be far." Tony was quivering with the desire to strangle Jason with his bare hands. Once Tony got a hold of him, he would pay dearly for this attack.

How many had he killed or wounded? Tony could see bodies littering the floor. Some still whimpered and twitched feebly, others were crawling away.

"I'm gonna kill you Jason. You'll pray for death before I'm through with you." Tony paused as a fit of coughing wracked him. Blood speckled his lips.

Jason heard the threats. He peaked from behind some boxes and scanned the area, looking for the source. He sighed, letting his head fall back against the boxes; he just wanted this over with.

A low keening wail drew Jason's attention. A blistered figure crawled from a cloud of low-lying gas. He shuddered a little in revulsion at the sight. He'd called Tony a monster for his acts of violence and cruelty, but now here he was doing the exact same thing to the Acanthans.

Jason swallowed bile and turned away.

He could just make out the doors and he slipped from his hiding place to make a run for it, but a new noise drew his attention. Tony had staggered out. For the first time since Jason had met him, he felt Tony's appearance matched the personality. He didn't seem to notice the swelling or blisters that covered a face that was screwed up in a rictus of rage.

"Jason," Tony called. "Where are you?"

Jason's only response was to toss his last frag grenade towards Tony. As he did, he broke cover and ran towards the delivery doors. He had to reach that switch. Jason coughed and staggered as he ran through a tendril of the greenish gas, nearly bringing him to his knees, but his eyes were on his prize. The ramp that led to a pair of buttons labelled "Open" and "Close." Jason kept his focus on the green "Open" button. The grating of the ramp echoed hollowly under his feet.

"I'm going to make it," he thought as he reached out his hand to hit the button.

His fingertips brushed the button as he was slammed to the floor, the impact knocking the air from his lungs. A hand clutched his ankle and he was dragged down the ramp, the rough grating tearing skin from his ribs, arms and legs. Jason kicked at the hand. He had to get up. He had to get to the switch. He was so close.

He kicked. His foot made contact with something and he heard a yelp of pain and the hand released. Jason climbed onto his hands and knees.

"I didn't say you could leave." A whistle had joined the nasally whine.

"Tony." Jason stood, his hand gripping the railing. He turned to look at his adversary.

There was a trickle of blood from Tony's nose where Jason's sneaker had made contact.

"You know this was all pointless." Tony waved his hand in a sweeping gesture.

"How so?" Slowly Jason shuffled his feet backwards, working his way up the ramp.

"You've not stopped us," he laughed. "You haven't even really slowed us down. A few days, maybe a few weeks, at most."

"Slower is better," Jason shuffled a few more steps.

"You think you are the first creature to oppose us?"

Jason paused. He'd never even thought about that. With a shrug he replied, "I don't know."

"You aren't. Eventually all their races fell to us. Earth will fall too."

"You have no idea about humans, do you?"

"I do."

Jason laughed mirthlessly. "No, you really don't. You'll never *process* us all in time and we don't give up. Ever." Jason stumbled a few more steps, drawing ever closer to the switch.

"Amanda and Marc are both dead," Tony said suddenly. Jason staggered, his face blanching.

"I don't believe you."

"Your little bombs were quite effective. Perhaps a little too effective for your liking. I watched them die."

Jason's eyes filled, but he kept inching his way back up the ramp, Tony slowly following him.

"I watched them die." He shrugged. "It wasn't the execution I'd imagined, but their screams were music to my ears." Jason felt sick and his lips were white with the effort to say nothing. He was so close.

"Once you've joined them, I'll finish what I started. Your pathetic little planet will be ours."

Jason felt weak. Drained. Exhausted. He looked out over the warehouse floor; gas still churned and twisted, pushed by the air conditioning system. He felt the ramp edge under his foot. The platform itself was under his heel. He was only a couple of feet away.

Bile rose in his throat. His friends were dead. He was cornered. A desperate plan formed in his mind. If they were truly gone, well, he'd make their deaths count.

He looked at Tony. "You're wrong."

Jason turned, pushing off and diving for the button.

Pain. Jason's world was pain. An intense burning pain that seemed to radiate from his lower back. He flopped face forward onto the floor, his feet drumming a dull tattoo on the metal ramp. Jason could hear laughing. Confused, he reached his right hand behind him, and it came away wet.

"Blood? I'm bleeding?"

A pair of black loafers topped by white socks appeared before his eyes.

"I told you that you wouldn't win. You're only a human after all."

The pants rose above the end of the socks as their wearer crouched down and gently cupped Jason's chin in his hand, tilting his head upwards. Up close Jason could make out how much damage had been done to Tony's face. He could have been a grotesque from a travelling carnival's sideshow. He was bruised and there was blood matting his thin hair. Bits of glass peppered his face amongst the blisters that covered it like pimples. One eye was purple and swollen. Yet he loomed over Jason, triumphant and gloating.

"I win," he whispered.

Blood dripped slowly from a scalpel that he held in his swollen fingers. Weakness overwhelmed Jason and as Tony let go, he allowed his face to fall to the concrete. His vision went hazy and stars swam before his eyes. He could feel his life bleeding out with each beat of his heart.

CHAPTER THIRTY-ONE

Tony knew he had gotten lucky stabbing Jason in the back. It looked like he'd nicked one of Jason's arteries and it wouldn't be long before Jason took his last breath. He shrugged as he stood, letting Jason's face drop to the ground. He'd wanted to savour killing him, but this would have to do.

With a sigh Tony turned away to hunt for the other two banes to his existence, Marc and Amanda. He had no idea if they were alive or dead, but he planned on ensuring the latter sooner rather than later. He had a score to settle with Amanda, and he desperately wanted to exact his revenge.

A rictus grin of excitement distorted Tony's already disfigured face as he stepped off the ramp. He would take his time with her.

Jason knew he didn't have long. Staying conscious was getting harder with each breath. He watched Tony's feet disappear from view. Spots began to float before his eyes.

"And this is how everything ends? Not with a bang, but a whimper."
With a sigh he laid his head down. "Didn't someone famous say that?" he
wondered.

"At least I tried."

As he lay in a spreading pool of his own blood, Jason thought he saw
Marc and Amanda, each leaning heavily on the other. He smiled. They were
dead, but it was a nice thought, that they'd get away. Free for whatever time
was left.

His imagination showed them creeping between towers of boxes hiding from Tony and the Acanthans who were trying to rally their forces.
His oxygen-deprived brain was giving him a final gift before its final shut
down. He watched them as they slipped from cover to cover. Jason closed
his eyes. He'd soon be joining his friends.

"There they are."

Jason's eye opened wide and he struggled to focus.

"What?"

Now that they were closer, he saw the blisters on Marc's hands and the
blood staining Amanda's shirt. He watched the surviving Acanthans closing on them.

"They're alive," Jason gasped.

But not for long if they were caught. Tony would use Marc and Amanda as examples. He'd make it as long and slow as possible.

Darkness was forming at the edge of his vision when Jason saw Tony
appear and started creeping between the boxes his friends were hiding behind. He was hunting. Jason could see that he'd intercept them long before
they made it to the door.

They would never make it out.

Tony stopped. He was a predator waiting for his prey, a razor-sharp
metal claw clutched tightly in his hand.

Jason shot Tony a hateful look. Summoning what little strength remained to him, he pulled himself around and using only his arms crawled
the last few feet, dragging his legs up the metal ramp. He felt nothing as
they slid along the cheese grater metal.

"That's good at least," he thought.

Tony had finally done him a favour.

He looked over his shoulder and saw Marc and Amanda nearing Tony's
position.

"Damn it," he muttered. He had to go faster. He pulled himself the last
few feet to the wall and collapsed as stars swam before his eyes.

A scream brought him back and his eyes flew open. He looked around,
confused. He realized he must have fainted. He didn't have much time.

Frantically he searched for his friends.

His vision was blurry, but he spotted them. Amanda was on the floor. She had a new blossom of blood on the side of her shirt, but she was awake and crawling on hands and knees towards the small exit that was next to the loading doors. Marc was wrestling with Tony. He was a big man, but he'd been through hell today and Tony was Acanthan. He was buying Amanda time to escape.

Jason had to help. He closed his eyes to gather what strength he had left, then pushed himself up to sit, fighting back a wave of dizziness. He tried to reach the button from where he was but couldn't. His fingers could just brush the close button.

"Not fucking helpful," he growled.

He looked back to his friends. Amanda had made it to the door and opened it. She was holding the frame like a lifeline. He thought she was calling to Marc, who was still struggling against Tony. Jason could see he was weaker.

It was now or never. With a final heave he grabbed the railing and pulled himself up. He cried out as pain flared anew in his back. A wave of dizziness threatened to take him under, and black spots danced before his eyes. Gritting his teeth against the pain and dizziness, Jason threw himself forward, hitting the green button as he fell.

He collapsed hard against the wall and turned his head to watch.

There was a whooshing noise that came from the electrical room. The Acanthans all stopped and looked over their shoulders, Tony included. It gave Marc the break he needed. With all the strength he could muster he gave Tony a shove, sending him flailing to the ground.

Marc stumbled for the door, grabbing Amanda on the way.

The polish ignited, sending flames screaming throughout the centre. Volatile printing supplies transformed into accelerants. As the flames swept throughout the building, all the chemicals ignited, adding fuel to the inferno.

Small explosions could be heard above the flames as canisters under pressure burst, feeding the growing inferno. A secondary whoosh and a ball of flame soared, sending out clouds of black, choking smoke.

"The toner," Jason said with a weak smile.

All those who were standing on the newly polished floors caught fire as clothing ignited. Jason couldn't help but grin as he watched Tony stumble backwards from Marc's push. He'd landed in a pool of the polish. He stood angrily, his wet clothes clinging to his body. Jason watched as the wall of flame reached Tony and he went up like a Roman candle, screaming as his flesh burned.

"Acanthan superiority my ass, you arrogant mother fucker."

Jason began to laugh as he slid to the floor, his vision fading. The loading door had opened a few feet before the flames melted the wiring. It was letting in cool air that fanned the flames into a tempest.

The last thing Jason saw before the darkness took him was Tony's blackened body falling twitching to the floor.

CHAPTER THIRTY-TWO

"He's awake," someone yelled.

Jason moved and moaned loudly as pain flared throughout his body. He heard movement and felt something wiggle in his arm and the pain started to recede.

Other sensations slowly made their way into his consciousness. A smell of antiseptic, a slow steady beeping near his ear, a soft whooshing noise, people talking, and someone weeping off in the distance.

He tried to open his eyes. It was hard; they felt swollen. Slowly, painfully, he managed to open them a crack. A face swam before his vision. A man with dark hair and skin. "Do I know him?" he thought. Yes. Jason tried to smile but his face wouldn't work right.

"Marc?" His voice was rough and dry sounding. Like crumpled paper blowing in the wind.

The effort made him cough, wracking his beaten body with starbursts of pain all over.

"Yeah, mijo. I'm here." Jason felt a hand gently squeeze his arm.

"Where?"

"You're in Mass General."

"Why?" Jason wheezed.

"Dude, you got hurt pretty bad. Do you remember anything? The fire at work?"

Everything came flooding back: Amanda, the Acanthans, the fire. He heard the beeping getting faster and faster. Jason started to struggle. His vision went hazy, and Marc's face swam before his eyes. Marc's concerned face receded and was replaced by the face of an older woman. Deep brown skin stood out against her brightly coloured scrubs. Dark curly hair going grey at the temples and soft brown eyes that were filled with compassion.

"Shush. You're okay now. We'll take care of you," she said as she tugged at something in his arm. It stung a little when she did, but a few moments later peace washed over him, and he closed his eyes.

Jason was surrounded by columns of flame. Tony's grinning charred skull laughed at him from amidst them.

He had to get away, but he could not move. He looked down at his legs. Fire enveloped them, and Jason began to choke on the acrid smell of charring bacon.

He awoke, soaked in sweat. He was crying out and flailing in the hospital bed. Alarms screamed as monitor leads pulled away. The IV tore from his arm. Warm blood spattered his face and he screamed.

The scrubs-wearing woman was back and she'd brought friends. They held him down. He felt a jab in his arm. Slowly the panic receded, and he relaxed.

Darkness swallowed him.

This time when Jason opened his eyes it was easier. There was less pain. Breathing wasn't easy, but it didn't hurt as much. He lay still for a moment. He moved his face. It felt less swollen. He reached up his hand to feel. His fingertips brushed cool bandages.

A warm dry hand took hold of his.

"Dude, don't. Not yet."

Jason opened his eyes. Marc was there, a stack of dog-eared books and magazines next to him on the table.

"Why?"

"You got hurt. Doc's got you bandaged up. You shouldn't poke at it."

Jason relaxed his arm and Marc laid it back down by his side, patting it gently.

"The centre?"

"CloneZone is ash, and the cops are crawling all over it." Marc grinned. "Dude, you should see it. It's all over the news. All the shit you sent out. The little bastards can't hide now."

Jason smiled back. His face felt tight.

"Amanda?"

Marc frowned and shook his head. "I'm sorry man, she's gone. She got you out, then disappeared. I haven't seen her since that night. Cops have been looking for her."

Jason sighed. "What do you mean she got me out?"

Marc smiled. "You should have seen her. She went all Batgirl on me. We got out just as the fire started. When you didn't come out, she took off back in."

Marc caught the look in Jason's eye and held up his hands. "Honest, I tried to stop her. But you didn't see her that night. She took off back into the warehouse. I thought for sure she was dead. No one could survive in there."

Marc ran his hand over his chest. "Walter managed to break two of my ribs. I was done in. We both were. I don't know how the hell she could keep going. I could barely walk."

Jason just looked at his friend and tried to shrug, flinching with the pain moving caused. Silence fell between them as they each recalled that last day at work.

Jason awoke. The scrubs woman was with him. "Morning, sunshine," she said, smiling as she helped him sit up a little. "We've met before, but you may not remember. I'm Mildred, and I'm going to be your nurse. Your surgeon, Dr. Stanford, will be in later to see you. You feeling up to it?"

Jason nodded. "Water?" he rasped.

Mildred disappeared for a minute and returned with a small plastic cup and a bendy straw.

"Easy now." She held the straw to his lips and Jason drank. The cold liquid made him choke and he coughed.

"Don't rush things. It's gonna take some time."

"How bad is it?" Jason asked after he finished coughing.

Mildred looked at him, her face serious. "I've seen worse."

"Truth."

He looked at her. She was measuring him.

"Please?"

Mildred's evaluating look changed to one of pity. It didn't make Jason feel better. "I think we should let your doctor review your injuries. You want me to stay with you?"

Jason nodded and tried to pull himself up. He couldn't feel his legs.

"Mildred..." he said, panic entering his voice.

"Oh no. Honey. Hush," she said to him, reaching down and taking his unburned hand in hers. "It's okay. It's okay." He looked up at her, terrified of what this meant.

"It's not as bad as you think. I promise. It can happen after a bad trauma."

"How? How could she think this wasn't bad?" Jason thought.

"The doctor can give you the details, but I promise you it's only temporary."

"I need to know." The nurse looked at Jason. His eyes were pleading with her. "Please?"

With a heavy sigh she sat on the edge of Jason's bed and looked him dead in the eyes.

"I'm not the one to tell you. That will be your doctor. I will promise you that we will take care of you and I'll be with you every step of the way." She stood and tucked the sheets in around Jason.

"Now rest." Mildred turned and left the room, leaving Jason with his thoughts.

As he closed his eyes, he could see Tony's laughing face before him. He wished he'd gone up with CloneZone.

EPILOGUE

Jason leaned heavily on his cane as he stared at the red brick building before him. The double glass entrance of the Maritime Museum in Halifax opened and closed as patrons entered and left, yet Jason made no move.

What awaited him there? He looked at the doors and then down at his watch; it was almost 2:30 pm. His heart began to race, but he took a deep breath, moved forward, and pushed open the doors.

Cool dry air that smelled faintly like the pages of an old book hit him and sent a shiver down his spine. He wasn't sure if it was the change in temperature or foreboding. That nagging voice of doubt crept in again, whispering, as he lined behind some tourists to wait for his turn to pay the entrance fee.

"This is crazy." He thought, "What am I doing here?"

During Jason's months in rehab, Marc had convinced him to try. Now that he was here, he was filled with anxiety and almost turned back when the young man behind the counter called out "Next."

Jason was on autopilot as he paid for his admission and held his wrist out while the clerk paused putting the paper wristband with the words "Admit 1 - Day Pass" printed on it onto Jason's arm and stared at him. He was starting to get used to the looks people would give him.

The clerk was having trouble getting the wristband on. He was trying so hard to not touch Jason's scars.

I'm sorry, sir. I don't want to hurt you." The clerk flushed with embarrassment.

Jason just smiled and finished pressing the ends of the wristband together. "Don't worry about it."

The clerk watched Jason as he walked away, wondering what he'd been through to look like that.

Without another thought, Jason headed down a carpeted corridor leading to the exhibits. His feet made soft shushing noises on the industrial carpeting while a recorded female voice provided information on the exhibits that he passed.

He followed the arrows, freezing in place before a sign that read "Titanic Exhibit – This Way." In the distance he could hear Celine Dion singing "Every night in my dreams, I see you, I feel you. That is how I know you go on." A shiver ran down his spine.

"Let me help you," she pleaded, her eyes filling with tears. "You stand a better chance with me."

He smiled down at her sadly. "No. A couple of hours ago you told me you loved me."

"I do," Amanda said. Jason could feel her hands trembling inside his own.

"Then save my friend. Get him back to his wife and kid."

"Jason…"

"Please, Amanda."

Tears threatened to slip from her eyes and her voice failed, but she nodded.

Jason snapped back to reality. That was a year ago, almost to the day. He looked at his watch again. 2:47 pm.

"I'll wait an hour," he told himself.

He knew that was a lie. He'd stay until they kicked him out. Today, tomorrow, and every day after.

A deep breath and he entered the exhibit.

A flash of blonde hair made him turn his head, his heart racing. "Amanda?" He whispered.

The person turned and Jason's face fell. It was a teenage boy.

Wishful thinking. He walked past the heartbreaking pieces of the ship that had been salvaged, children's shoes, and ladies' gloves. Items that had torn at his heart when he was a child, but today he didn't even see them.

Every flash of blue or feminine laugh, each blonde head he saw froze him in his tracks.

He looked at his watch. 4:49 PM.

He'd been wandering for almost two hours. He felt drained. He didn't have the strength he used to, but the emotional rollercoaster of hope and failure was far worse.

Jason stopped next to a scale replica of the Titanic. He tried to lose himself in the details. It was perfect. He stared at the tiny wooden people on the deck. The tiny LED lights in the portholes. He felt the other patrons moving around him.

Someone brushed against him.

He ignored it.

A hand touched his arm, "Excuse me."

Irritated at the intrusion, Jason turned. He stopped cold when two bright blue eyes looked up at him.

"Amanda?"

THE
EPIC QUEST
FOR
TERRAL B. HYLOTZ

ANDREW PIKE

PART ONE | EARTH | WITH: FATHOM

I

Light blasted through the windshield with all the terror of a nuclear explosion, and waves of razor-sharp shards of glass rained over me like acid searing my skin. The smell of my blood mixed with the bitter cold of the storm. My arms strained against the ambulance's efforts to veer off its path, swerving left and right like I was dodging moose in some twisted game of frogger. *Had I hit one?*

The ambulance shook violently, its tires leaving the asphalt and rumbling over the rocks at the side of the road. I tried to swerve back, but it was too late. Shrubbery scratched the driver's side window like a monster trying to break in to berate me on my poor choices up to this point. *Had I driven too fast? Was I paying enough attention to the road? Should I have opted for a different career choice? Certainly.*

Trees vaguely appeared through the white of the storm. Hitting one would spell instant death, but I had now become resigned with a self-depreciating calm. It was really no surprise I'd land myself in a position like this. A perfectly reasonable ending to a life spent satiating the never-ending demands of the hospital.

A tree slammed against the side of the ambulance nearly toppling the whole thing over. Before I had a chance to regain control, the vehicle gained speed. This was it. The worst-case scenario. Nothing in the wilderness first aid books could prepare me for what was about to happen.

The ambulance halted abruptly on some obstruction causing the whole thing to jolt and I became airborne, floating as if gravity had no further interest in holding on to me.

In a surreal clarity of mind, I made peace with the probable reality that this was the end. *You really messed up this time, bud.*

◢

I stirred to the presence of another. No pain. But shock. I opened my eyes to see a whirling snow lifting and dropping around me with a chaotic unrest. There was a surreal quiet to it. If it weren't symptomatic of the looming apocalypse, it would be almost charming.

Two barren trees appeared through the storm, withered and pale, struggling to stay alive in our endless winter. A closer look revealed they were connected to a brown snout and two weary eyes. In my paralysis I panicked as if some unseemly tree-headed monster had come to collect my broken body—lunchtime. When the creature let loose a surprisingly haughty snort, I realized I was staring at a moose. Like me, it looked apprehensive and curious; two creatures face to face with the decimation of our planet, with not a clue what to do about it.

"What a state."

The words seemed to come from nowhere. I attempted to move but could not. After a moment of struggling, I passed out.

◢

"Fathom…this is…EMS…come in…over…"

The voice was distant, scratching through a barrier of white noise, barely intelligible. I exerted the muscles in my arm to lift it, but a cold, dull pain spread through me.

"Fathom…come in…over…"

I pushed through the pain and clutched at my radio. I pulled it to my ear. "Roger EMS, this is Fathom."

"Where are you?"

"Ten minutes from the Last Bastion base, near the Ridgeline Forest."

"…numerous reports of moose…keep an eye out…it's like they've got a mind of their own…"

"EMS, there was an accident…"

The radio sputtered with static, then gave out completely. I cursed, tucking it in my camo winter coat.

How did I get to this point? Years of studying the sciences, a residency of pasty hospital walls, belligerent doctors and apathetic nurses, first response, and now doomed to die in a snowbank. Hell, I shouldn't complain, the way the planet was going with this storm, we were all going to perish soon enough anyway.

I tried to sit up but was reminded once again of the crippling pain; my head was pounding. I surveyed the scene. I was waist deep in snow. My forehead hurt. There was blood in the snow. I unzipped my pocket and removed my last resort first aid kit, undoing a bandage and wrapping it around my head.

The ambulance was nowhere to be seen but its droning was barely audible beneath the roar of the storm, dying like the flatline of an ECG. *Had I fallen off a cliff?* I approached the trees of the Ridgeline Forest. Last Bastion must be close. The northern storms had begun to destroy smaller rural communities and remote locations like the base, leading to a full lockdown within cities. A small unfortunate few, including myself, were tasked with the dangerous job of retrieving those without food and bringing them back to the city.

My trek through the forest provided little shelter from the conditions. With whistling winds burning my eyelids, I walked from tree to tree working outward from the cliff towards—what I expected would be— the coast. I can tell you that the journey is not one I'd wish on anyone. The cold chill pained to the bone. It was enough to make you wish for a quick death.

Leaving the forest, the whistling ocean winds hit me like a heart attack. Though my reserves were bolstered at the sight of the base's spotlight that appeared in the distance like a beacon of hope in the storm. I made my way along the shore until coming upon a cliff below the base.

After a short climb I reached a sheltered summit which offered temporary relief from the storm. The moon cast a peaceful glow over the ocean but it was interrupted by spiraling snowy columns stretching up into space. It looked like a giant nebula had engulfed the planet.

The Last Bastion base had been converted from a lighthouse to a research facility to study the storm, but it had been a fruitless endeavor. Scientists had studied the strange cosmic powder on every possible level, but were no closer to unlocking its secrets. The storm just showed up one day, consuming all in its path, and showed no signs of relenting.

I found a path to the base and ascended a stairway to reach a side door. The lights were off. I banged on the door as hard as I could for at least ten minutes, then I slipped into a defeated squat against the side of the building. My mind raced. Without shelter, safe exposure to a Level 3 storm was estimated at two hours, and I had no idea how long I was passed out. I could die right here like this.

Then, the base door abruptly flew open, blasting me with a puff of warm air and sending clusters of snow swirling up into the night. I recalled a childhood memory of returning home to gingerbread cookies in a hot oven. Pleasant, until I was hit by a cloud of noxious cigarette smoke that burnt my lungs and sent me into a coughing fit.

II

"Right. You're the medical response, eh?" The booming male voice struck me as the porch light flicked on. I rubbed my sleeve against my glasses to clear the condensation. "Not in the best shape, are you?"

The man became visible through a hallway of dirty smoke. The place could have been burning down for all I knew. He had glossy slicked-back hair, a trimmed beard and tattoos covering every inch of his skin. He looked mid-twenties, like me, but his eyes bestowed a fiery wisdom beyond his age.

The man squinted at me. "How exactly do you plan on getting us out of here? You look like you just fell off a cliff." He pulled a cigarette from his mouth and laid a mop against the wall.

"Uhm, yes. I did. My ambulance fell over a cliff. There was a crash. I don't know what hit me." I stepped inside and closed the door taking a moment to orient myself.

"You sure weren't hit with good looks," he said, bursting into a throaty laughter. "I'm Aaron Myles. Janitorial Apprentice, level fifty-two. You?"

"Jacob Fathom."

"Fathom. Can't imagine a name like that."

"Uhm, well..."

"Come to think of it, knew a guy with that name back at West End Cleaners. Absolute wreck he was, couldn't keep a job, multiple divorces, had some wild out-there stories about the universe though. Musta been the drugs. Never could figure out what he was on about. But the man *could* fix a dishwasher."

I suffered another coughing fit.

"Right, sorry about all the smoke. Government recently reversed no-smoking laws in public facilities, result of the death storm of course. Guess they figured everyone's gonna die anyway, might as well smoke 'em if you got 'em." He took a long draw on his cigarette and exhaled in my general direction, as if he hadn't just then apologized for exactly that. "Between you an' me, they're just in the pocket of smoke companies, right?"

"Sure. Well, we should probably speak to security if we're going to get out of here."

"Right. Let's go for a little walk."

I followed him down a hall of portraits of political figures partially obscured by the smoke. These strong leaders supposedly had a plan for pioneering humanity's expansion into space, saving us all from the death storm. At least those were the talking points during elections. In actuality, storm research had been an ignored priority, until now, when it was too late. I coughed again, nauseous from the nasty substance.

Myles brought me to a lobby with a desk endowed with enough laminated glass to justify a tax increase for next year. He knocked on the glass with a rat-a-tat-tat that startled a woman with a long auburn hair and a navy-blue uniform who had been absorbed by some reruns of an old show I didn't recognize.

Myles pressed a button and spoke through a speaker in the glass. "Bailey, our hero is here to save us," he said, laughing.

She turned her head slowly, almost resentfully, as if we were a minor annoyance she had been hoping she wouldn't have to deal with. Her frown confirmed this sentiment. She pressed a button on her side of the glass.

"I'm guessing the hospital isn't sending its patients," she said, nodding at my bandage.

"I was in an accident." I recalled my head injury and checked it in the reflection of the glass. It was holding up better than I thought. Bailey cupped her hand up to her ear and shrugged her shoulders.

"You have to push the button," Myles said. I nodded, and pushed the button, repeating myself.

"I see," Bailey said. "Mister…" she paused to glance at a piece of paper lying on her desk, "Fathom, is it? Wilderness First Aid Responder? Is crashing your ambulance part of some advanced emergency strategy we're not aware of?" She gave me a sideway look as if she was gauging my competency. It was a look I'd encountered a good few times over the years, and I had no redeeming retort other than to shrug my shoulders.

I shrugged my shoulders.

She let out a deflated sigh and opened a drawer producing a set of keys. "The storm's going to be full force in two hours," she said, "and it's too late to call another responder. Looks like we're trapped here for a few days."

Myles took another drag on his cigarette. "Well then, we should be head'n up to Cabell to let him know."

Bailey pulled a bulletproof glass cover over the security cameras and spent a good five minutes locking various drawers and a safe. She unlocked the door to her security station, stepped out, and locked it up again in a swift reflexive motion. She led the way across the unfurnished lobby to an elevator and unlocked a glass box containing the elevator's call button, pressing it. The elevator arrived with a loud "ding" and we stepped inside. She unlocked access to elevator controls, pressed the third-floor button, and punched in a code to allow permission of the requested action.

After an unnecessarily slow ascent, the elevator came to an abrupt halt announcing its arrival with another obnoxious "ding" and the doors opened to reveal a long hallway with high windows on either side. The windows rattled slightly as the dusty snow of the storm came up against them. Bailey walked ahead of us dangling her keys with a refined boredom. When we reached the door at the end of the hall, she unlocked it with her security card, and we stepped into a dark room emitting a dull hum of computer fans.

A man sat in front of several computer screens with his back to us. On each side of him there was a coffeemaker apparently in perpetual mid-brew—oddly excessive. Beyond his desk was a broad window with snow piled up along the edges outside.

"Ahem," Bailey announced. The man did not flinch, fixated on his work. She flicked the lights on, and he swivelled his head around with a break-neck speed.

"What the hell?" Cabell said, his face reddening as if someone had just thrown him out in the snow. He was middle-aged, perhaps mid-50s, with a buzzcut and small rectangular glasses, and he was wearing a black blazer and white shirt.

"Time for a break. You've got company."

"Eighty-five percent of the planet is consumed with an imposing cosmic matter depleting oxygen levels to eighty percent of what they used to be, and you want me to take five-minute break?"

Bailey sighed. "Would it kill you to get up and walk around once in a while?"

"Alright Bailey. Five minutes. Good advice. I'll take a break as the state of the planet slowly drops to a ten percent habitability factor, and we'll be no closer to solving the problem of this vicious storm."

"She has a point, Cabell," said Myles.

"Brief exercise will help with mental fatigue," I added.

"Who the hell is this?" Cabell asked, as he pinched the bridge of his nose.

"This our first responder. You know that type of job, right? The one that involves walking, sometimes even running and—dare I say—saving lives."

"The lives saved by officials such as myself far outweigh any in the first response or security fields. Just because you can't see the numbers in front of you doesn't make the truth of it any less real. If we don't find a solution to this imposing cosmic matter situation, we'll be heading straight into an apocalyptic scenario, and you won't be around to complain about it!"

Bailey rolled her eyes. "Well, I hate to drag you from your *exceptional work* that clearly isn't having any impact at all on the storm, but we thought you might be happy to hear that you'll be spending another few days here despite our waning food supply."

The tension of the room was interrupted by a jarring ring. Bailey pulled out her phone and looked at the screen. "I have to take this" she said, walking out of the room and leaving us wading in an awkward silence. The winds outside continued to howl, almost mocking us.

After a good minute, Cabell spoke. "So, how's that toilet coming?"

"Right. Should be unclogged in a bit. Just had a distraction, that's all," Myles said.

Bailey opened the door and gestured for us to follow her. "Roy wants us all downstairs for a videocall. You too, desk prune."

Cabell sighed, locked his computer, and made his way to the door.

We rode down the elevator and headed for the lobby, passing the familiar short hallway to the door outside. With an unexpended blast, the heavy steel door flew open blowing in wind and snow from the blizzard, offering a plump, bearded late middle-aged man dressed in a heavy fur coat, Santa cap and a backpack big enough to sustain life for months in the wilderness. We stood agape.

III

"Hi hi hi!" The man greeted us, shaking our hands, icicles dripping from his bushy, graying beard.

"Christmas's come early this year," quipped Myles, the ashes from his cigarette falling on his mop. "I didn't realize Santa Clause visited government facilities."

"Just hold it there, buddy," Bailey cautioned with her right hand, "how did you get in past the gates? Myles, did you lock the door?" Her hand dropped to her waist-high taser.

"*Ho ho ho and bottle of gin!* That's how they say it on the Bartholomew Seas, just don't be grin'n your teeth at 'em! Or, *your mother is fine company and she speaks highly of you.* No?" The man looked around the hall as if he expected some recognition for his nonsense. "Right, then, Terral B. Hylotz!"

Again, he outstretched his arm to shake hands, but we stood idle, wary of his strange behavior. He looked like he'd been homeless for years and presently his odor supported that hypothesis.

"Right. Mister...Hylotz? Interesting name. Never heard it before." Cabell paused, as if mentally perusing the many faces he'd seen in his government career. "This is a highly secured secret base, how the hell did you get in here?"

"Ah! Clever face on you. Quite square, maybe a little too pointy for my liking. Known many suits like you. No need to worry I am not here to cause trouble. You see, friends, I am from the *great outside*, in the far, far above." He spoke with the awe of a magician revealing a trick that he himself was surprised actually worked. He raised his hand in the air towards the door as if it explained everything. His tone suddenly turned reverent, his head twisted back and upwards looking at the ceiling. "It's my home, and I'll make it back there someday but for now, we will drink, we will drink!"

The cadence of his ending phrase bestowed a finality that he appeared to think would immediately bring rise to alcohol, of which there would be none. I felt bad for him. He'd ventured a bit too far into the woods. Somehow, he'd stumbled through the storms of our world's declining environmental stability to breach security at a top-secret government base. His presence created quite an enigma.

"Now just wait" Bailey scolded, waving her index finger at him, "it looks like you've a good few too many beers already. This is government property, and unless you have enough stacks in that pack of goodies to put me in early retirement, I can't let you roam around and burglarize the place.

"You can't be serious," I said. "We can't just send him off into that deadly storm, it's a miracle he survived in it at all!"

"He's trespassing on government property," Cabell insisted. "He's already broken the law. To let him go would be considerate."

"Oh, come on," I rebuked, "He's obviously confused, his pupils are dilated and he's shivering under that coat. To turn him away would be negligence!"

"Fathom's right," Myles said, "it'd be pretty damn inhumane. Wouldn't want my name pop'n up in a headline 'Janitorial Apprentice Leaves Vagrant to Die, Loses Job, But Who Will Clean Up His Career?'"

"Enough of this," Bailey ordered, pulling out her phone. "We're obviously not going to turn him back into the storm. He can stay...for now. But we're going to need a photo for the record. Now Mr. Hylotz, please say cheese." Bailey pulled out her phone took a picture, the flash lighting up the room. Hylotz formed a wide toothy smile revealing two missing teeth and a level of carefree complacency I never thought possible. The flash reminded me of the crash. A shiver ran through my body.

"Cabell, bring everyone to the lounge. Fathom, treat him for any injuries. I'm going to print off the photo and speak with Roy. I'll be back shortly. Oh, and Myles, for God's sake, lock the damn door."

After reaching the lounge, we sat Hylotz down on a red couch next to a plant. We pulled up chairs, eager to learn more of his travels. A brown wool sweater was visible just under his winter coat.

"Now, Mr. Hylotz," Cabell asked, "exactly how have you weathered the storm out there? Studies have shown people can last no more than three hours, and that timeframe is dropping exponentially as we grow ever closer to atmospheric annihilation."

"Annihilation," Hylotz said, his arms gesturing up and down, back and forth. "Funny word. You know, if you change the sounds a bit, you can add a much better arrangement: And High Elation! That's much more friendly, wouldn't you say?" Hylotz had no grounding in reality. It was ridiculous.

"You see? Nothing but a raving lunatic," Cabell concluded.

"Lunatics? Oh yes, I've known a few of them! Wouldn't wish anyone caught in Duncan's cave. But the Ondas, now that's an ocean I'd gladly dive into."

Myles was standing idle at the door, his eyes glazed over, his cigarette nearly burned to his finger. "This guy is smoking some serious drugs," he said. "I'm completely serious—and I'm rarely serious—this guy is into some out of this world shit. And I *know* my shit. I've never seen anyone so completely and utterly fried. Maybe we should get security back here, this is completely new territory of insane."

"He's delirious," I checked his eyes with my headlight. While he'd been talking, I'd pulled out my Wilderness First Aid kit and begun the spot exam. "He is definitely suffering from hypothermia. Get him a blanket, Myles. He is acclimating to the temperature shift. He may be suffering from a head wound. Terral, can you remove your hat?"

The man removed his hat to reveal a gaping head wound. Immediately the blood made me queasy, I tried to ward off a loss of consciousness, but my head filled with stars...

...The same moose from before appeared. How did he get into my mind?

"Look man, sorry to interrupt your human meeting, but have you found a way to save us from this shit weather? It's a disaster out here, I mean, animal rights, and all that."

"You're an actual moose, an animal, I have no idea how you're talking to me. I don't mean to be crass but if I have a moose talking to me, I think I have more serious problems."

"Right, yet again it's so easy for humans to overlook the suffering of animals. Look man, all I'm saying is, we could help you out someday. We have connections, and—"

I felt the moose's voice fade into the sound of my ambulance's siren. Again, the vehicle collided into a silver, metallic object that caused an explosion of colour and stars...

"Fathom, Jesus Christ man, you OK?"

"I, uh...yeah, I'm fine." I woke up to Myles shaking me. I felt the bandage around my head to see if I'd started bleeding again. Thankfully I had not.

"What kind of first responder passes out at the sight of blood?" Cabell snapped.

"Give him a break," Myles defended. "Dude's been through a lot already. Still reeling from the accident."

"I'll be fine" I said, standing up then grabbing the bandage to treat Hylotz.

"Alright, Mr. Hylotz. You've given us quite enough of this run-around.

How about a little honesty here?" Cabell walked up close to Hylotz and kneeled eye-to-eye with him. "You're in trouble for even being here, at least with some honesty you can redeem yourself and gain some sympathy. Tell us, how did you manage to survive what clearly has to have been at least a two month walk in the wilderness from the city, in conditions that would see you dead after a couple of hours?"

"Time, yes, indeed, and space; interesting concepts. Without them, life would be meaningless. Introducing them separates us into so many different classes, places, 'liefs—the colour of life, they say. Like the 'liefs of the Breaus, what festive meals they have, my Breaus, I would die to be back with my Breaus once again." Hylotz's face grew overcast with a distinct sorrow. His type of mental disorder was hard to pinpoint. Schizophrenia, maybe, but one with a hypersensitivity to shifts between delusions.

"My friends, I think you have your answer on this fellow," Cabell sighed. Myles and I looked at each other and we knew that this man must be a crazy, rambling fool.

"Show's over," Bailey announced from the doorway, placing a photo of Hylotz she'd printed out on a side table. "I'm just off the phone with Roy, and we're going to have to lock down Hylotz in the basement. They're sending another first responder down, but it'll be a few days before they get here. Until then we are all just going to have to hamper down."

"Right. It's decided then," Cabell announced, with a satisfied resolve. There was a consensus throughout the room.

"Come on now Mr. Hylotz, we'll be taking you to a room in the basement," Bailey said. "Don't worry, it's quite homey, you'll be taken good care of. When we get back to the city, you'll get a better treatment, and maybe we'll find out where you came from."

I stood up with Hylotz and Myles and all five of us began the trek to the basement, passing the hall with the door from which Hylotz had entered. We approached the elevator to the basement.

"How's your head?" Myles asked me, grabbing the photo of Hylotz from the table

"It's fine. Only just a little woozy."

"Any more thoughts on what you hit in the accident?"

I paused. "You know, come to think of it, there was a silver metallic object..."

"The marsh," Terral cried, and before anyone could react, he ran to the outside door and blasted back out into the storm leaving us just as bamboozled as we were when he entered.

"Well don't just stand there," Bailey ordered, "We can't have him running around the base. We've got to stop him!"

IV

"Terral B. Hylotz." Bailey's words echoed through the lobby as she tucked her auburn hair into the fluffy hood of her blue winter coat. "What an unusual name."

"Not from the east, that's for sure," I said. "Homeless, maybe, from the south side?"

"He smelled like marijuana and regret," Cabell said, wrapping a blue scarf around his neck, while grabbing a walnut brown winter coat from the closet in the hall.

"Don't judge a book by it's cover. He could be a genius for all you know." Myles pulled on a white winter jacket.

Bailey opened the door to a security closet and removed a couple of two-way radios from an old emergency kit that had ceased production over a decade ago. "Hylotz may need on-the-spot medical attention, are you OK to come along Fathom?"

"I'm fine," I said, pulling a white cap over my head.

"I just don't get how he could have got past the security walls of the perimeter," Cabell said. "They're over sixty feet high and they completely block off the area. He'd have to have come by water or air and both are near completely impossible with the storm."

"All the more reason for us to stop him," Bailey said. "Who knows who else he's with, or what he's capable of. His confused appearance could be a front or a distraction for some other effort. Now listen, the radio's set on channel one. Fathom and I will take one each. Stick together and don't spend more than an hour max out in the storm. No matter what, come back after an hour." Bailey took a box of face shields from the closet and passed us each one. We pulled them on. "Ready?"

"Don't forget this," Myles said, tossing something that careened through the air before gliding to a landing on the floor in front of Bailey. She picked up the photo of Hylotz that Myles had folded into a paper airplane. She sighed, tucking the photo in her coat pocket.

We looked around the room at each other. With mismatched winter coats, face shields, snow-boots, furry mittens and caps, we looked more like Christmas carollers than a search team. And we certainly had nothing to sing about.

"Let's go!" Bailey said, pushing open the heavy iron door to the storm outside.

We trudged down the wheelchair ramp with boots squishing the snow.

For the most part, we were like clunky, unarmed soldiers. Bailey locked the base twirling the key around her finger. The storm had settled somewhat. Gentle cyclones lifted snowflakes into the air, dropping them off wherever they might disappear in a gust of wind.

A treeline became visible through the blurry white, with a dip where the bridge to the road was. Behind us, the base stretched high up into the night air, its searchlight strobing through the cold mess of snow. Once it would have guided ships to shore, now it remained a last-resort cosmic beacon begging for divine intervention to come save us from the storm.

"Got him!" Myles yelled, slightly left of path.

"What?" Bailey asked.

"Got his footprints!"

We walked over find him staring at a path of bulky footprints. They trailed off towards the bridge.

"Good job," Bailey said.

We followed the footprints to the bridge. A glimpse of the sea below reminded me that a small misstep could be fatal. At the end of the bridge, we stood idle, scanning the snow for the footprint trail.

We continued, heading in the direction the footprints had been going. We passed a vacant parking lot, then made it to the road. It was dark. Bailey pulled out flashlights for us each from her backpack, when a gust of wind roared through the air. The photo airplane she had placed in her pocket became airborne, and she fell back into the snow. She pulled herself back up and shook snow off her coat. We continued, heading towards the woods.

"I've got something," Cabell shouted. There was another trail of footprints, but it was drifting into the woods. We peered through the snowclad trees, hesitant, but we knew Bailey had no intention of stopping.

As we headed into the woods, the ankle-length snow was hindering, but manageable. The wind was freezing though. Disorienting. The light from our flashlights led us through the shadows with Hylotz meandering footprints becoming harder and harder to spot. We passed a small pond frozen over with ice.

"Oh no," Cabell said, looking off to the side.

"What is it?" Myles asked.

Cabell held up a boot which was, to our dismay, quite likely the property of Hylotz. "There is a small hole in the ice."

I shook my head. "It doesn't bode well for him if he is walking around without a boot. He'll need medical attention. We need to find him fast."

"That could be a problem," Cabell said. "Look." He pointed at the footprints we'd been following, which were now accompanied by two or three more smaller ones, hoofprints? Hylotz's footprints became indistinguishable. They forked into two different paths: one up, one down.

"We're going to have to split up," said Bailey. "Cabell, you join me. Myles and Fathom, you can take the left path."

"Right. Fair enough, lets go Fathom," Myles said.

We branched off from the other two and walked up the path. As it became darker, the cliff jutted out impeding our progress, and eventually we had no choice but to scale the cliff. Myles stopped, refusing to proceed. "I... can't," he said.

"You can't climb?"

"No I mean, I can but..." Myles paused, as if searching for the right words to use. "Look, I did a lot of wilderness expeditions as a kid. "There's something about being out here that just...brings back some bad feelings. I really need a smoke, maybe I should head back..."

"We can't head back! We've got to find Hylotz. Look, I made it to the base on foot and I can tell you, it's not the kind of situation you want to be alone in. It's very disorienting, and you can lose your way. If we split up that leaves one of us without a radio. It's not a good scenario. It's really not that steep and there's no other way forward. If it gets much steeper, we'll turn back, OK?"

Myles paused, deep in thought. "Alright," he said. "Let's go."

It didn't take too long before we reached the top of the cliff. The storm had eased off, allowing us a limited view of the snowy forest below. The now-faintly-visible footprints led us to the subtle moonlit glow of a clearing. I paused. Something felt off.

"What are you waiting for?" Myles asked.

Then I saw it. Nearly perfectly camouflaged against a cliff wall, there was an outline of something...some, creature. I felt an immediate spike of adrenaline, a heightening of my senses and tingling my skin with goosebumps.

"...There..." I said, nodding my head in the direction of the figure. Myles turned and pointed his flashlight directly at a moose looming with intimidating antlers staring straight at us. The moose did not move. Suddenly, I recalled the crash in my mind. *Did I hit a moose?* Something felt wrong about it all.

"Relax," Myles said. "It won't hurt us. It's not angry."

"Damn right I'm not angry."

I shivered as the realization hit me. Somehow, I could understand what the moose was thinking.

"Fathom man, you ok?"

"Look man, no qualms with you," the moose said. *"You can help us."*

"Myles, I think...I...need to sit down."

"Relax, the moose won't hurt us. We can just back up and leave..."

"He's right. Not going to hurt you. But you need to help us. All of us. Otherwise, things are gonna get messy."

My mind blanked. I knew, somehow, this moose could understand my thoughts.

"What do you want from me?" I thought, towards the moose.

"Man, we don't have the answers right now. But there are others, far away, there are many of us, and there is suffering. We need your help to stop it. We know you can hear us and we know the humans have tricks against the storm they are only now coming to learn. But with your help we can all benefit together, instead of fighting against each other to survive."

"Fathom man, come on, lets go!"

"What do you want from us?" I asked.

"We don't know everything right now. But we do know that you have been looking for the bearded old man, and we know of his travels. Many of us have spent time with him as well, and he holds the key to all of our struggles. And we know which way he went."

The moose moved aside to reveal a dark hole in the cliffside. It walked back into the woods. Myles shone his light towards the cliff. "A cave?"

He shone his light inside to reveal the outline of a person huddled over to conserve heat.

"Fathom, hand over the two-way!" I passed it to him. "Come in! Bailey, Cabell, Come in!"

"We have you. What is it?" Cabell's voice beamed through the radio.

"We got him."

V

The cave was eerily quiet compared to the storm outside. Myles approached with slow footsteps, but as he neared, it became evident that this was not a person, but instead a backpack.

"Well now," Myles said, picking up the backpack and looking inside. "What gifts did he leave for us? We've got some bags of leaves, a pipe and a lighter. Definitely smoker materials, but I've never seen these types of plants before." Myles shone the light further into the cave. Hylotz was nowhere to be seen. Another snowy entrance was vaguely visible at the end. I began heading towards the exit, only to turn to find Myles fiddling with the lighter.

"Myles!" I said. "This is no time to smoke, we've got to rendezvous with the others."

Myles put the lighter back in the backpack and lifted it over his shoulders, and we left through the second exit. There was a thick patch of bushes and a short decline down a hill, and we were back on the asphalt of the road to the base, not too far from the locked gate leading back to the city.

It was clear and quiet, like we were in the eye of the storm. Over the cliff, the ocean stretched on, clouded with splotches of the white storm like voluminous plumes of smoke flowing from an inextinguishable fire up into space. Flashlights flickered in the distance. It was Bailey and Cabell.

While we waited for them to catch up, I realized we were standing exactly where my ambulance had gone off the road. I could see the tire marks heading into the woods. Another path veered off to our left, into a small clearing.

"What is it?" Bailey asked.

"Wait," I said and walked towards the path of the object that had hit me. I motioned for her and the others to follow.

We entered the clearing. A big shiny triangular object sparkled through the trees. Rays of moonlight hit the metallic silver, creating a surreal sparkling. I'd seen nothing like it before.

"Not sure you should go near that" Cabell said. I ignored him, reaching out to feel the surface. It was oddly warm.

"Wow," Myles said, piecing it together. "*This* hit you?"

"Yes," I said. It was all making sense now. I replayed the crash in my mind.

"Well, you should probably step away—" the object flashed forcing me to jump back. The smooth metallic outer surface had disappeared in four spaces on either side of the structure, offering a clear view right through its dark interior. With padded seating, it certainly looked like a vehicle, but there was no apparent apparatus other than a black steering wheel.

"Careful," Bailey said.

I took another step back. "What's that down by the door?" I said, pointing at a colorful item lodged between the object and snow. Bailey picked it up out of the snow to reveal the photo airplane.

"What are the chances of that?" Bailey said, laughing. She walked around the object touching it gently, just like I had done. Then she sat inside.

Myles unloaded the backpack into the object and jumped in as well. "Come on Cabell," he said.

"Not my cup of tea at all," Cabell said. "I really need to get back to the washroom, can we please just head back to the base?"

"It's much warmer in here," I said, holding my hand in against the soft material of the seat. And it was. You could feel the heat emanating from inside, yet there was no heating device visible. There was enough space for about four people.

"Come on, Cabell. This is *some* device." Bailey began running her hands along what was apparently a dashboard, and the slippery surface seemed to bend, receptive to her hand.

Cabell, shivering, stepped inside.

"What could it be?" Myles said. "Very strange."

"It's not government technology" Cabell said. "Being an authority, I can say that—unless it's classified, but we stopped experimenting with classified vehicles after the arrival of the death storm."

"Well come on Fathom," Bailey said. "Jump in."

Who will take the pilot's seat?

Fathom
Continue Reading

Bailey
Go to Page 347

FATHOM PILOTS

I jumped through door. My seat was calmingly smooth and lukewarm. There was a flash of light from the dashboard, and the panel came to life with bizarre neon green symbols as wiry tentacles lashed out grasping my arms. The interior glowed bright green from the dashboard. The others shouted, banging against the closed doors.

The thing jolted to life. Unburdened by any apparent propulsion system, it simply rose with the cyclones of the storm. It accelerated at a suicidal pace, and through the windows, we could see the clouds of the storm over the water becoming more frequent, until our view was obfuscated by a white blur of snow.

We began to spin. The ship turned faster and faster, and it was getting colder, colder, freezing! The screaming, the spinning, it all coalesced into a piercing high pitch tone in my mind, and I felt as if I was falling apart stretching into a bitter... cold... *space...*

I trembled. My anxiety peaked. The stormy whiteness prevailed. I felt tiny, like I'd been compacted into a snowflake. Doorways appeared on my left and right, scrolling past me. I was flying through a long, drab hospital hall. Patients were belligerent, yelling at hospital staff. It felt like the worst encounters of my entire career all infused together. A window appeared at the end of the hall. Before I could consider the fact that I would really prefer not to crash through the damn thing, I crashed through the damn thing.

Still white, but now, control. The snow was mushy in my fingers. I pushed my-self upward. Snowclad trees were all around. They were like the ones near the Last Bastion base, but the snowfall was lighter here. It was a pleasant departure from harsher conditions I was used to facing. The flashing red and blue lights of emergency vehicles appeared through the trees.

I approached a highway just like the one near Last Bastion. The ambulances and police cars were lit, but empty. A single gurney stood alone in the middle of the vehicles. I had no desire to be here, even though this was my entire occupation. I approached the gurney. A sheet was pulled over a body. There was no movement. Were they dead?

Through the corner of my eye, I caught an outline along the treeline of figures, no, creatures. Gigantic antlers. Moose. Many, many moose. They were moving just slightly, their dark silhouettes only vaguely discernable against the darkness of the receding forest.

I suppressed the desire to run, but my heart was racing wild. Where could I go, anyway? I had no idea where the hell I was. With great trepidation, I reached my hand to the sheet covering the body and pulled it back slowly.

The figure sat up immediately, his bloody old face shocked me, his toothless grin shot me staggering back several steps. Blood soaked through his graying beard. I felt the urge to pass out, to run away, to leave this horrible job forever. But some-how, I couldn't.

The old man winked at me and pulled out a big brown pipe, lighting it. A few of the moose from the trees walked out. As the man smoked then exhaled, a feeling of ease washed over me. The apprehension and tension of the situation abated into a serene acceptance.

The man shuffled off the gurney and joined the moose as they walked back into the woods. I stared as they disappeared, at a complete loss as to what to say or think.

The winds quickly snowballed into a roar as the brutality of the blizzard re-turned. Again, I became immersed in white, and my vision began to quake as if shaking out of existence.

Was that Hylotz?

COMA CLUSTER | WITH: FATHOM

I woke to radiant sunlight glowing through the glass of the ship. The rays heated the air inside that surrounded my hunched body as if I were wrapped in the womb. The others were asleep.

Through the front window, I absorbed the breathtaking view. A vibrant valley with a lush evergreen forest extending off into mountains with snow-capped peaks. A bustling river wove into a lake near the horizon. The sunlight cast an iridescent brilliance speckling the sky with a rainbow of sorts: the entire spectrum of visible light was stretched on display like the palette of some epistemological artist. It seemed too beautiful to be real.

I opened the pilot door and a greater warmth immediately struck me, a stark contrast to our former predicament. Moreover, I was moved by the sounds outside. The chirps, the tweets, and the new sounds that I'd never heard before. There was a sense of an overwhelming presence of abundance; new, curious, evolving life.

I walked out into the rushing water and knelt down to feel it. It was tepid and smooth, unlike the freezing cold water near the Last Bastion base. It was perfect. Where the hell were we?

Rising to my feet again, I walked to the edge of the river, sending grasshoppers dashing left and right in reaction to me. Squirrels paused along the treeline, as if in contemplation of my arrival. As I began walking again, some of them dashed up into their trees, that were reminiscent of the Grand Firs of the island I grew up on.

I made my way down the river with a fascinated curiosity. I came upon a couple of deer enjoying a drink of water along the river. As I approached, they looked up, and I was immediately filled with a thought of *who the hell is that guy?*

That was weird.

Nevertheless, I continued on making my way into the forest. The soundscape was filled with insects whizzing past, water rustling, grasshoppers chirping and birds singing. The gentle wind brushed against my skin.

I entered a small clearing with two rabbits in the distance. I stood to watch them for a moment, absorbing my surroundings and I realized I could hear their thoughts.

"Jack from Paradama lost another two bunnies. Hunters ramping up 'cuz of the storm."

"Shocking."

"Waste, really. Holds no candle to the wrath of the Bies, though. Thousands of humans killed as a result of them."

"I'd like to say it's their own fault."

"Oh, definitely is, they don't deserve it though."

"No, no."

"Shame we can't reach either of them. I heard that…"

A stick cracked under my foot. When I looked back up, the rabbits were scampering away. Christ. What the hell was this? It all seemed so surreal, yet, at the same time, it was very clearly happening.

Making my way further through the forest, I heard a crying in the distance. I worked towards the sound to find a placid clearing with a waterfall. The source of the sound was a deer calf caught in a foothold trap, crying and unable to escape. I cautiously made my way to it. The poor creature sprung away from me as I approached, tearing its ankle with each attempt.

My heart raced and I felt an obligation to help immediately, but at the same time I felt a strong hesitation pulling me back to the ship. I reached down and pushed on the levers allowing the jaws of the trap to open. The deer scampered away.

The sunlight faded quickly, as if dialed back, casting the forest into an ominous late evening darkness. When I turned around, the treeline was peppered with a sea of eyes staring at me. Their stillness was petrifying, at first, causing my heart to race again. Then, as before with the rabbits, their thoughts flooded over me like a tidal wave.

"Is this him?"

"He looks awfully pudgy; does he eat deer?"

"Quite a puzzling thought, he is, for sure."

"Should we bring him to Aarth?"

My heartbeat slowed, as I realized they meant no harm. They began to depart slowly, all walking together back through the woods, and I felt myself drawn to them with a childlike curiosity. We spent a good half hour traversing up a steep incline before reaching a mountain peak with an amazing view of the forest below. It stretched on to the setting sun on the horizon.

Finally, we reached an adjacent mountain peak with bushes packed together like a giant couch, and a single moose stretched out, leisurely surveying the area while, somehow, smoking a joint.

"Ah, the helper. Good to see you man," the moose was so casual in its speech, as if it had been waiting for me. It tapped the joint against a rock and took another inhale. I am not sure how this was possible, the logistics of it were beyond me.

"Hi?" I thought, stupefied. With my mouth agape and my brow dipping, I'm sure I appeared like a deer in headlights.

"Yes, hello, and all those foolish human formalities. I can imagine you're confused about the whole thing, understandable. We've been watching you for a bit now. You're the second human we've found to be 'sensitive' to our language."

I continued to stare at the moose, perplexed.

"Look man, truth is, the track record for humans and, er, what do you call us? Moose? It hasn't been the greatest, and it's gotten even worse during the storm. We

need someone to step up and take the reins for us, to use a very human analogy.

"*We've been able to read humans for a while, and there's unfortunately not much to like. Humans have subjected Moose and other animals to some pretty dire conditions, sticking us in cages, running us over with vehicles, feeding some us some god-awful gruel stuff, which to be honest, is absolutely disgusting food that — highly unrecommended. I must say, you name it, humans have done it, and that all really has to stop.*

"*With the storm happening, human behavior has only gotten worse. Humans are killing us left, right, and center in a mad panic to survive the storm.*

"*We're not sure how you've been able to understand us, nor how you've managed to visit us in our ethereal home, but this violence has to stop. We're all working together to beat this storm, and it's time you joined our pacifist fight instead of being an enemy in it.*"

"*Uhm. How exactly can I do that?*" I asked.

"*Ah, yes, my dude. As you're beginning to figure out by now, but this whole construct you've spent the last hour in has been our best effort to communicate with you. It's not real. It's our best mutual exclamation of peace between our worlds.*"

I paused. It wasn't real. This made sense. It was all some sort of illusion. So, if that was the case, where the hell was I?"

"*You say you want me to help,*" I said, "*but I have no idea where the hell I am or what I possibly could do to help. Being a spokesman for an entire species isn't in the job description, especially not in the midst of an apocalypse. I'm just a medical responder, and not that good a one to boot. Given the events of the past few hours I'm quite ready to quit this whole first responding business.*

The moose pulled his joint out of his snout, and exhaled a puff of smoke in my face, sending me into a coughing fit. "*Woah there, man, settle down. I've never seen anyone so high-strung. You're our best hope right now. Buck up, have some faith in yourself. Anyway, look, there's a world far from here — Kostroma — where a group of our species — The Bies — has gone wild in retribution against humans. We don't know how exactly you can do it, but if you can get there, you can help stop them by trying to reach a truce between them and humans. Just reason with them. We've tried, but they've become exceedingly aggressive since the storm, mirroring the humans that once lived there.*"

The moose again inhaled smoke through its lungs, and exhaled, causing the puff to swirl around its head, reminding me of the storm. As I stood there considering the situation, I felt the whole landscape shaking. I reached out to the moose for help, but everything went black.

◢

"Fathom! Fathom!"

My body shook with a brutal force. I felt myself shake from a sleepiness to come face-to-face with Bailey.

"Hey, he's not dead!" she said. "How comforting."

"What…happened?"

"You were out for a good hour!"

"I…" My speech drifted off as I stared out at a massive colourful nebula in front of us which was interspersed with the white snowy powder of the storm.

"Goddamn ship took 'us right up into space!" Myles said from the back seat.

"Yes, and we'd really like to try to get back to earth *right now,*" Cabell said.

"Move aside, first responder, I'm going to bring us home." Bailey pulled me into her seat and took the wheel.

BAILEY PILOTS

As Bailey took the pilot's seat, wiry tentacles jumped out and wrapped around her skin. The ship jumped headfirst into the storm. The entire interior glowed a bright green as the ship rotated in circles. The view through the windshield was blocked by the intense white of the storm. And then all grasp on reality seemed to acquiesce to that of another…

The frosty white of the storm dispersed, revealing a bright azure sky with a beautiful orange-red sun settling along the dusky beige of the rocky Nevada mountain range. With a blurry haze, it was an incredibly realistic memory of my military deployment when the world first encountered the storm. The nostalgia was bittersweet. In these last days, the world was incredibly naïve to the severity of the storm.

"Ten bucks says you hit the cactus Bailey," Jim laughed. To my left, his bronzy calloused face beamed with a silly grin as he passed me the bow. Ah, archery. It was the one escape that we all loved.

Publicly, we were deployed to monitor for UFOs due to increased sightings as the storm grew more prevalent. But we were really tracking the Storm Ninjas: a cult of UFO conspiracy theorists that believed the universe was run by alien lizards disguised as politicians. At first they were harmless, carrying out ridiculous attempts at storming Area 51. But over time, they'd obtained some serious black-market weaponry, and had carried out some moderately successful attacks.

"Ten bucks is nothing," I snickered. "Fifty bucks. Bullseye."

Jim and the others laughed knowing full well no money would change hands. I took the bow and grabbed an arrow. I pulled it back against the string as I lined up my shot. Before I could shoot, an arrow whizzed past my head.

I blinked twice. Someone else had taken a shot. The arrow was lodged in the centre of the board. I turned my head to see a man placing his bow on our table, his back to us. It was our Major, Richardson. I instantly remembered his shape in the camo uniform. With decades of experience, his skill as a soldier was far superior to ours. He had a passion for the field and an unending ambition that had become non-existent nowadays.

As he faced us, it quickly became apparent that this was not Richardson, but a man with a graying beard and a toothless smile. I lowered my bow, trying to re-call where I'd seen his face before. But the colours began to fade as the dusty storm closed in once again. The white cold surrounded me.

Could that have been Hylotz?

PART TWO | ATAVIKA | WITH: BAILEY

I

The bitter cold pulsed through my body. The ship's steering wheel shook in my grip. The storm obstructing the windshield disappeared in brief moments, offering glimpses of a giant sun on the horizon. The others screamed as we continued to jolt violently back and forth in our seats.

Clearly this was my version of hell. I'd detested mandatory flight train-ing so strongly it had nearly turned me off the military completely. My first experience in a virtual flight machine drove me to vomit on my co-pilot, bestowing me with the nickname 'Palely Bailey.' That familiar nausea re-turned.

The storm receded as we entered a clearing with misty clouds scattered below like a rink in a stadium open to the vastness of space above. This mo-mentary serenity fleeted as the ship dropped into the clouds below, skim-ming along like a stone on the ocean. Try as I might, I could not regain con-trol. Through the motion blur of clouds, quick brushes of green appeared peaking through the white like blotches on a canvas. Trees. But hardly the 'happy little trees' of Bob Ross; these trees were monstrous, daunting.

With the volatility of the ship, we'd be on a crash course if I didn't act fast. I put all my force against the wheel to push it up. As if mocking my incompetence, the ship took a nosedive into the sea of clouds below. Before I could realize my error and correct it, we abruptly hit a tree, and the ship spun and convulsed as we hit another tree and all control was lost. The ship hopelessly tore through branches. I shivered, realizing I may just have sealed our fate.

My head was spinning. A static of rain persisted from outside. Glossy verdant leaves drooped over the windshield. I reached for the door and the ship teetered at my movement. The others stirred.

"Be careful," Fathom said. "We're barely stable."

The ship eased back as I pulled my arm away from the door handle. Again, I remembered my first training missions, where the door to the VR machine was like a lifeline. That sense of security was stripped from me now.

"What's out there?" Myles asked, trying to get a look through the windshield. The view was severely obstructed by the tangled leaves, but a maze of vines stretched beyond into the distance.

A jungle. Somehow, we'd landed right in the middle of a goddamn jungle.

"It's incredible," Cabell said, "how this ship has transported us so fast. This technology is mesmerizing."

"I'd be happy to have never found it," I said. Again, I felt a magnetic pull towards the ship's door, like the reflexive impulse to lock up Last Bastion. My conditioned instincts emboldened by years in security were useless here. "We can't just sit here. We've got to do something." Again, I reached for the handle.

"Bailey, no," Myles said, but it was too late. As I reached, the ship tipped with my weight. I was careful, but it had now gained a momentum of its own.

"Oh my God," Fathom said.

"Jump out," Cabell yelled, and we all grabbed for the door handles causing the ship to lose its balance, falling off whatever was holding it up.

I jumped out through door's opening and soared through the air. One of the vines I'd seen earlier came into view and I desperately reached for it, barely holding on. The screams of the others faded into echoes below as my freefall momentum came to an abrupt smack against some surface.

A sweltering heat much heavier than a sauna struck me with unrelenting ferocity. The only salvation was the constant showering of raindrops soaking through my clothes. Slowly, I pushed myself to a sitting position and removed my jacket out of a pure primal desire to reduce the heat.

Beyond the insulating sound of rain there was a dull chorus of cicadas occasionally interrupted by the chirping of birds and the occasional grunts of monkeys. I shivered from chaos of it all. What other animals could be out there?

The glowing light of the sun loomed high overhead, beaming through a bushy canopy revealing a daunting maze of jungle trees before me. The trees themselves had trunks thicker than skyscrapers and were laden with tangly vines. The surface below me felt rough and bumpy; a rugged dark bark of a tree branch that extended down far below. I crawled to my left to try to look over the edge, but no jungle bottom was visible. The view extended into darkness. The view upwards was equally indeterminable, and the storm was vaguely visible through the trees in the distance.

My memory was drawn to the war movies I'd seen as a child and revisited many times throughout my life: Arizona Blood and Hurting, but also classic remakes like Apocalypse Now, Rambo and Jurassic Park...there were so many that reflected the dark, ominous scene before me. A rumbling of thunder in the distance disrupted these memories.

"The first rule of operating a spaceship is don't open the door," said Cabell, his voice seemingly appearing from nowhere.

"Christ," I said, jumping back. I looked up to see him standing above me. "How about 'the first rule of crashing in a jungle is don't sneak up on the pilot,'" I said with a frown.

"I'm sorry, but you have really landed us in a situation here. Myles and Fathom are nowhere to be seen. It looks like they may have fallen to their death."

I shuddered. Was it so? Had my action led to their deaths? It must be so. The drop was deadly. I needed to process this.

"Our major rainforests were irreparably damaged during at the start of our current phase of the death storm, but this one is unscathed. It looks like you've taken us *very far* from—"

"Just hold on," I said, raising to my feet, "You know damn well that ship is a wildcard, there's no controlling it. Fathom drove us up into space. I could barely land the thing, and—"

"Of course, I know that," Cabell said, his glasses blurry and wet from the rain. He was awkwardly holding a giant leaf over his head which had very little shielding effect. The poor fool was raised with a silver spoon. He was the type who couldn't operate an umbrella and would just give up and throw it away when he couldn't close it. "Look, lets just focus on getting out of here and back home, OK? We need to find the ship so I can get back to my office."

"You you *you*, everything is about *you*." I frowned at him. He had never faced a real struggle in his life. No appreciation for the common man, endlessly protected by the naïve leisure of his ivory tower.

"What the hell is your problem with me?"

I shot him a resentful glance. "Must be your glasses. Have you tried corrective surgery?" He shook his head.

"Look, we've got to work together if we're going to get out of here. When I jumped out of the ship, I landed on this branch, and the ship continued falling through the branches below. It has got to be down there somewhere. So let's start working our way down."

Ahead of us, the branch met a steep decline which was unpassable. We chose to follow the branch behind us, which extended off into the distance. We began our apprehensive descent downward.

⬧

We passed over curious platforms formed of wood planks. Clearly, there was civilized life here. It was a relief.

"Lets just hope they're friendly," Cabell said.

As we headed downward, the surrounding sounds grew louder, and we were occasionally bothered by eyes watching us from dense bushes growing on the branches.

Our spirits raised again, when we reached a vine bridge that joined two branches. The bridge itself was small, with the same wood used for the platforms. Vines roped it together. It was dangerous but passable. We cautiously edged along it.

"It can barely support our weight," said Cabell. "How small can the folks who created it be?"

A branch snapped behind us. We spun around. Nothing.

"Who's there?" I demanded. Still nothing. I shivered. We continued.

"The consistency of the wooden plateaus and the bridges indicate some form of civilization," said Cabell, "however their level of intelligence—we can't be sure."

Another snap. We spun around on our bridge. Again, nothing. I reached down for my trusty taser. Still there, thank God.

The rain was a serious impediment to our progress, and we quickly tired of it. The stress of the past few hours was finally catching up and I realized that I needed rest.

"Where can we stop?" I said, as we hit another plateau. Cabell turned and looked at me, then scanned the area.

"Well, I don't know. We'll have to keep going until we find something. If there is something following us, I mean—let's just keep looking."

I nodded.

We continued for another good twenty minutes or so. I felt like I'd pass out at any moment.

"Here, look at this," Cabell said, "there's some crack in the trunk here but it's…it doesn't look natural. It looks forced open. The edges here are carved as if…cut by a blade."

We edged inside through a narrow opening. My claustrophobia started up, but as soon as I hit the floor on the inside, it was quickly suppressed by my desire to sleep. I began to address Cabell and I think he said something, but any recollection of a conversation quickly faded as I fell into a deep, highly anticipated, sleep.

"They're in the mountains!" Jim's voice crackled over the chilly mist of the enclosing storm as we followed in hot pursuit of the Storm Ninjas. Capturing them in their desert base was exacerbated by the storm, but we had finally cornered them.

Gunfire echoed across the mountains. I shuddered at the memory. Richardson ordered us to withdraw and regroup temporarily to come up with a better plan.

"We need to get out now," I'd insisted.

"We've never had a better chance to get them than now," Richardson said. We knew there was no going against his decision. He would never have ordered the attack if he didn't have to. I hated that he'd been forced to put us all in harm's way.

We took an offensive approach from left of the base, but somehow, they'd known. To this day I don't know how they could have known. They attacked us with assault rifles in an amateurism so irrational, it could have only worked in the hands of the insane.

We were forced to draw back, but not before Richardson took heat. His cry still tears through my nightmares. I'd tried to go back but the gunfire was too intense. We were forced to retreat and make it back home in the deadly storm which had rendered our navigational instruments useless. Richardson became one of the first deaths by cause of storm exposure.

A loud roar reverberated through my bones. It shook me awake. The air was hot and humid. I put my hand out to feel the dry, rough texture of the tree. I remembered the jungle. Christ. How was it possible to wake up to a worse reality than Nevada?

I reached for Cabell, but he was not nearby. I found his glasses on the floor, only to be shaken by another terrifying roar, much closer.

II

I waited. There were no sounds outside. I carefully edged my way out through the hole, cautiously peeking out.

There was no rain. A noxious smoke filled the air. It was rising from down below. This was worse than the Last Bastion base. I coughed. A small figure about a yard away disappeared into a bush.

"Hey," I yelled. No response. They were too short to be Cabell. I walked out and looked around. Nothing. I walked towards the bush. The figure jumped out and ran down along the tree branch. They were dressed head-to-toe in leaves.

"Hey," I shouted, "I just want to talk."

A tiger-like creature jumped from a bush nearby. It roared. In a split second I ran, and the creature chased me, lashing out at my leg. I tripped and fell but picked myself up. The creature was positioning to pounce on me. I screamed and desperately dove over the edge of the tree branch.

I fell three or four branches down before catching a vine of one of the bridges, but it immediately snapped. The bridge fell and I fell with it. I came up hard against a tree trunk with just enough power in my legs to keep me from suffering the brunt of the force.

I struggled to climb the vine. Decades ago, I would have had no trouble. Still, I managed to pull myself up onto the branch, where I lay back with my eyes closed, panting. When I opened my eyes, there were two more staring back at me. I sat up quickly. A short, scraggly brown-haired woman stared at me. Her face was sooty from smoke. She was wearing an outfit composed of leaves.

"Hello," I said.

We stared at each other uneventfully for a good two minutes. Could she speak English?

"Hello," she replied. The silence seemed to go on forever. I had many questions snowballing inside me.

"What is your name?" I asked.

"Maya," she replied.

"I am Bailey," I said, unsure how she would respond to a handshake and realizing that formality would probably be lost on her. "Are there others like you?"

"We are the Uriah," she said, nodding her head. I coughed at the smoke.

"This is quite a transportation system you have set up," I nodded towards a nearby vine bridge. "But where is all this smoke from?"

"The Uri. They praise the gods of the forest." I nodded, unsure of the reasoning behind this custom.

"Maya, did you see a man with me?"

"There was a man. Yes. But when I came back, he was gone."

I coughed again. "Where can we get away from this smoke?" I asked.

"Follow me."

I followed her down the tree branch. We crossed more bridges. I had to cover my mouth at times to avoid coughing from the smoke. We carefully scaled vines secured down along a trunk. We made it to another trunk with water flowing over it from high above. Maya walked into the water and disappeared. I carefully followed. The tree had been hollowed out into an area with jugs crafted from wood that contained water. Light shinned in from slits carved in bark.

Maya passed me a jug and I drank much of the water in it. She passed a coconut cut into pieces. It was the first food I'd had in hours. She explained that she was a watercarrier for the Uriah, who lived high above in the jungle worshipping the sun. The Uri lived far below and were hated by the Uriah, who forbid any communication with outsiders. She had met a few Uri and smoked with them and wished to visit the great ocean below.

After our discussions Maya said that she had to bring water to the Uriah village above. I decided to stay in this small home, partially because I needed rest, and partially because I was afraid the Uriah would not accept me. When she left, I lay down and drifted into another sleep.

"So all you have to do is stare at monitors all night?" The young man grinned at me with his arms back, his fingers interlocked behind his head and his feet on the desk.

"Put your feet down," I said. "But yes, that's it. Just stick to the routine patrols and you'll be fine. No napping."

"This is a cinch."

"It's a good job, but you could be a little more respectful." He just stared at me, expression blank and naïve. I sighed. The kid's mother owned a security business downtown. Nepotism was rampant these days. Most businesses had closed, and it was unsafe to be outside for more than a day. Security positions were dying out, but big corporations still needed protection from the growing hoards of homeless people breaking into commercial spaces seeking refuge from the storm.

"Any reason why that barrel is on fire?" The kid asked. I glanced at an amber glow on one of the monitors. The alley at the back of the factory was vacant, but the fire was growing bigger.

"Looks like we've got some excitement. Got your taser? Good. This'll be a good exercise for your first day." I flicked on my radio. "We're investigating a fire in the back alley, will advise of outcome."

I locked up the security cabinet and grabbed the fire extinguisher, passing it to the kid. "Know how to operate one of these?" He rolled his eyes at me.

We stepped out of the security room and locked the doors, beginning the ten-minute walk down the hall towards the back of the factory.

The alleys were a target for loitering as they offered a little better protection from the storm. Although shelters were set in place for the homeless, they were overburdened and lacking in rations. Often, people would brave the storm to dumpster-dive for more food. It was becoming riskier, though, as the storm grew more volatile.

When we reached the door, I unlocked and pushed the door open in a single swoop. "Hello? Anyone out here?"

The cold night air was crisp with the type of chill that would quickly freeze your face. The snow between buildings was gentle, less stirred than in the streets, where it gained more momentum with the wind. The alley was vacant except for a dumpster near the corner, which led to another alley leading to the street.

The fire was not too far from the door. I nodded at the kid, who walked over and sprayed the fire, and I had to admit, I was surprised he knew how to operate the damn thing. Smoke from the extinguished fire rose along the buildings, disappearing in the pale white of the storm.

Something soared through the air and landed next to the kid, and he had to shuffle to the side to avoid it. A person in a hoodie emerged from behind the dumpster and ran out of the alley.

"Hey," I shouted, my heart pumping from the attack. It was rare these days to catch someone in the alley, and interactions were usually more amicable. Weapons were unlikely, but the possibility was always in the back of my mind.

I walked over to the kid. He was picking up the tossed item. He passed it to me.

A snow globe.

Ornaments like this had been a cash grab in the early days of the storm, where there was excitement for the new lockdown style of living. Within the globe, snow swirled around a small candle-lit cottage, nestled in a forest, protected by thick glass.

I shook my head and tossed the globe in the dumpster. "Come on kid, we've got another patrol."

Voices interrupted my dream. They were speaking in a language I didn't understand. It was dark. Night? Blurry lights glowed through the waterfall. They were getting closer. I fought back the urge to go outside.

A torch was passed around the waterfall and placed inside, then a small figure about the size of Maya jumped through the water, their face masked by a skull. The teeth were crooked, and the eyes were cut out. I screamed.

Another two figures in skull masks joined and ran to me, I fought them, but they knocked me over the head.

I woke, still dizzy from the knock. I had no idea how much time had passed. Light bounced around the room casting eerie shadows against the wall. In the middle, a fire had been set, and the skull masked figures stood around it. Cabell, Myles, Fathom and Maya were all strapped up against the wall and Fathom and Myles were struggling to break free. Thank God they were still alive. I pulled my arms forward realizing I had been bound. The voices of the skull group chanted in some unintelligible language.

"What are they saying?" I shouted at Maya.

"They say, 'we hate foreigners,'" Maya replied. "'Foreigners fill the air with poison. They burn the forest. They must die by their fire. The god of light will save us from the poison fools.'"

The skull group moved towards us with torches in their hands.

"They can't be serious," I shouted. "What have we ever done to them?"

"We don't have anything to do with setting the forest on fire!" Cabell shouted, but they ignored him. The others shouted and screamed to no avail. My chest tightened and my heart jumped into overdrive as the skull figure approached. I twisted my head in a vain effort to reject the inevitable scorching.

The tallest skull mask of the group was standing in the middle near the fire. He raised his torch , shouting at the others. They raised their torches above their heads. I closed my eyes fearing the blow. The familiar Nevada fear had returned.

III

I was sure the blow was imminent, but it did not come. I pushed through the fear and opened my eyes. The skull maskers had pulled off their masks. My attacker had a bald head, charred tattoos on his neck and colourful face paint. He looked just like a skinhead from a biker gang, like the many who went on to join forces with the Storm Ninjas.

A rage welled up inside me. I gritted my teeth. This was not right. Like the attack on Richardson, it was unwarranted. I directed all my anger against my attacker, thrusting my head towards him with teeth bared, viciously trying to break free. But his eyes were wild, curious, smiling almost, like he harbored no ill-will towards me.

Instead of attacking me, he turned with some of the other attackers and brought fire to the skull masker in the middle of the room. A struggle escalated into a frenzied fight with a skull masker literally burning to death. Someone set Maya free. In turn, Maya set me free, and we set the others free. By this time, the room was engulfed in flames, and we raced out through the falls.

"Come this way!" Maya was ahead of us, her torchlit face vaguely visible. We followed close behind, careful not to overstep the tree branch in the darkness. The heat from the inferno eased off as we got further away, and the jungle's heat was now more tolerable.

After carefully navigating across bridges and stairs we entered another crack in a tree which led to a room. The torch was placed in the middle of the room, casting a glow on our faces as we recovered. The skull masker that nearly attacked me was standing next to Maya, his mask discarded somewhere along the way.

"What the hell was that?" I yelled, pointing at the man. "We were nearly burned to death back there!"

"You are safe," the man said. "We were there to protect you."

"Could have fooled us," Fathom said. "You nearly burned us all."

"We are Uriah. We are friends," he said. "I am Keon."

"If you are friends, you sure have a funny way of greeting folks," Cabell said. "What happened back there?"

"We are friends. Many Uriah are not friends. Some of my tribe want to kill foreigners, like you. But they are evil. My group is not evil. We saved you. We are not violent against the Uri. We like the Uri. We want peace between all."

"Are you a dissenting group from the Uriah?" Cabell asked.

Maya nodded. "Many Uriah do not understand the Uri. But we understand."

"So the Uriah are overall a non-violent crowd," Cabell said, "but a fraction of the lot are turning the whole batch sour. And the Uri are…friendly?"

"Uri will hurt no one," Maya said. "They are all good. They are peaceful."

"So can we speak to the Uri and straighten all this out?" Fathom asked. "We really need to find the ship and get out of here. This is insane. And… where is Myles?" We looked around. Myles was nowhere to be seen.

"Myles?" I cried, panicking. Then the man from before approached me.

"You can relax. We'll get him. We always get our men." My racing heart began to calm. My apprehension and anger toward this man was misleading. His power seemed to shine through his rugged appearance. His words carried conviction. I could see the warrior within him beaming at me.

"We will win all of Uriah, someday," he said. "The path for future is peace for all. We will make it happen. Progress is slow now. But we are winning smaller battles. Now, rest. We will leave to find your friend. At daybreak."

We rested for a few hours. The light from the cracks in the tree began to grow. When it was safe to leave, we moved through the crack, and began on the path back to find Myles.

After a good half hour, we were back at the tree, and it was burning wildly. If Myles had not escaped, there was no way he'd still be alive. And his chances of escape were not much better than our own. Defeated, we paused to consider another plan.

The spears took us completely off guard. They flew from the surrounding bushes. Had our ambushers been waiting for us to return? We tried to see a way out, but there was none. We were surrounded.

◄

We must have looked ridiculous being marched along with our arms tied behind our backs. The expressionless figures with painted faces and sharp spears directed us across jungle branches and bridges and up tree stairs.

We walked over a network of plateaus. There were huts stacked with water jugs, bowls of fruit, and spears. Figures with leafy clothes watched us from inside. Over time, these huts became a city built high up in the jungle.

We passed through a bustling waterfall flowing over a tree trunk,and entered a big circular room with wooden tables lined with fruit. There were more figures eating and speaking in a foreign language. They became silent. At the far wall, water was flowing over a much wider opening that appeared to be a window to the village of huts outside.

A woman sat in a wooden chair at the end of a long table. When approached on the right side of the table by one of our guards, she gestured towards our captors. We stopped. She addressed us in a foreign language. We said nothing. Maya responded in their language, then spoke to us.

"They want to know," said Maya, "why has Uri sent you to spy on them?"

"There was a pause, then Cabell spoke up.

"We are...humans...from far away. We are not the Uri."

Another pause, then the woman at the table spoke to Maya, who translated again. "She asks why. Why do you spy from Uri?"

"We are not Uri," Cabell said, "we are from far away." He paused. "We want peace for all. We want both Uriah and Uri to be at peace."

Again, the woman at the table spoke. Then, a scared look passed over Maya's face. "She says, Uri cause problems in jungle, cause death, why do you do this? You must pay."

The man who had saved us from the fire attack spoke up, and he sounded very mad.

"We don't mean harm" Cabell said. "We just want to go back...to where we're from."

Maya spoke again, then relayed the message again. "She says that you must be Uri. Or outsiders. You do not belong here. You must be jailed."

IV

"Just hold on," I said. "We haven't done anything to you. We just want to leave here!" One of the guards pushed his spear up close to my face.

The guards spun us around and marched us back through the waterfall. My face was hot. The injustice of it made me want to grab a spear and attack one of the guards.

We passed over a new bridge. There was a movement from the bushes on a branch adjacent to the bridge. One of the guards yelled, either in anger or giving an order, I couldn't tell.

The guards raised their spears, shouting, only to be cut off by a barrage of arrows from a higher branch. It was a trap.

Keon kicked one of the guards, who fell back against another. "Go," he yelled, and we all ran back across the bridge the way we'd come. I looked back in time to see Keon barely dodge a spear. He picked it up and cut the bridge vine. The vine disconnected and one side of the bridge dropped. Some guards tumbled off and some desperately held on for their lives. We had more time.

We edged along a branch and stumbled across another bridge. Maya led us to an open plateau. We stopped for a moment to catch our breath. Soon after, Keon stumbled out onto the plateau and dropped the spear he'd taken earlier.

"Cut me free," he said, and Maya cut the vine linking his hands together. He did the same for her, and they cut the rest of us free.

"We have little time," Keon said. "The Uriah have many soldiers."

"Can you take us to the Uri?" Cabell asked.

Keon nodded. "I can, but the path is long, and we have to go fast."

"We have no choice," I said. "Let's go."

◄

We spent days travelling through the jungle. It all looked the same to me, but Maya and Keon said they knew the path well. Many times, we were approached by the same tiger-like creature that had chased me, but Keon turned it away with broad sweeping gestures.

Further down into the jungle, it became darker. Moss was more prevalent. One old tree was completely covered in the stuff. Keon led us through an opening in the tree to a flat piece of wood. He pulled a stick out of his leafy suit and pushed it into the wood. It opened. We moved through the threshold.

It was dark and humid inside. We walked along a wall until Keon asked us to stop.

"It's a long way down," he said. "You take the leaf, place it around your hand, and slide down. Be slow at first, then fast. Don't let go. It's important, do not let go."

"This isn't very safe," Fathom said.

"How far down is it?" Cabell asked.

"It's far," Keon said, "but leaves will protect you. I will go first, to show you. Wait before going."

"What exactly is—" Cabell began, but he was interrupted by the sound of Keon sliding down what I could only assume was a vine.

One by one we followed. I went last. I reached the bottom with a splash. Surprised, I sank below the water, before I doggy-paddled to the surface. It was much cooler down here.

A torch flickered beside a wooden door like the one above. The reflection of the torch glowed in the ripples of the water all around the room. The others waited along the side of the room next to the door . I swam ashore. Keon unlocked the door, and we stepped outside onto a new wooden plateau.

It was dark and murky. Torches were attached to huge trees continuing into the distance. They were perfectly mirrored in the glassy water below.

A foul, ashy smell reminded me of the smoke from earlier. Keon walked around the back of the tree we'd dropped down from. He returned pulling a small boat by vine, and directed us to jump inside. Maya was fascinated with the water.

The ride through the trees was eerie. We passed boardwalks built around trees and docks for fishing. A few had doors and people—presumably, the Uri—sat watching us. Some were smoking. The smoke rose upwards, between the trees.

The path became more obstructed by fog as we continued, and much colder. We had entered the storm, although it was of mild intensity. I shivered.

"Where are we going?" Cabell asked.

"You will meet Graeme," Keon replied. "Our leader. He is really chill, you will see."

We reached three trees with boardwalks. Keon docked the boat, and we jumped ashore. We walked around the tree and continued. The entire area was a big boardwalk.

Above, there were huts made of straw and wood. We continued up a stairway to new level, eventually making it to a hut. We exited on a wooden overhang much like a balcony. It was overlooking a collection of houses lit by torches and surrounded the water. It looked like a small outport fishing community.

Next to us, there was a man sitting on a chair smoking. When he saw us, he stood. He was much taller than any of the other figures we'd seen here.

He had black, greasy hair, and the familiar leafy clothing.

"Finally, we meet," the man said.

"You were expecting us?" Cabell asked.

"Of course, my friends. There isn't much I don't know of. You're the folks that fell from 'heavens,' eh? What are you wearing? This is your clothing? Strange." We had long since removed our winter coats. Ironically, we would have loved to have them back now.

"Who are you?" asked Fathom.

"Graeme here, your local Uri leader."

"Well, thanks." Cabell said. "It's great to speak to someone sensible for a change."

"Of course, look, we're not against outsiders like the Uriah. I mean, we're careful who we let in but…we are pretty good at judging character. And we don't blindly worship some ridiculous 'sun god.' We're much more sensible than that." He bent over to pick up a joint and smoked it.

"What kind of joint is that?" I asked.

"This? Oh, this is truly a miracle. Want to try some?"

"I'm good," I said, shivering.

"Not a chance," Cabell said, turning away almost repulsed.

"You never know, you might like it," Graeme said.

"We call it the Atavika 'lief," he continued, picking it up and turning it around in his hand. "This is one of the greatest blessings bestowed upon our people. In fact, it's been around since the very beginning. If it weren't for this 'lief here, we'd probably still be lost up there in the clouds with the Uriah, worshiping some ridiculous false god." He took a long puff, then exhaled. "It's powerful stuff. It'll warm you up really quick."

"That's great, but is there a washroom around here?" Cabell asked.

"A washroom?" Graeme replied. "Oh, you mean…I see. Just use the ocean."

"This is an ocean?" I said, looking down below at the water.

"For the most part, yes. I mean, there are areas where there is ice, like in the Fallen Sky, but other than that, it's an ocean that goes on and on."

"The Fallen Sky…do you mean the storm?" said Cabell. "The white mist from the sky?"

"Yes, that's it."

"How has this storm not permeated the jungle? How is it only in certain areas?"

"The jungle protects us. It always has. We worship the jungle, not as a god but as a physical entity. We quite literally worship the Atavika 'lief, which we smoke in our ceremonies. It protects us from the harshness of the Fallen Sky, an area that was once jungle before the great fire."

Graeme took a long drag on his joint. "Are you sure you don't want a puff?" He held it out for us.

Cabell took it, not to smoke, but to study it. We stared blankly at him. He looked like he was connecting a giant puzzle in his mind.

"This is really curious. The chemicals in this plant must have an adverse effect on the storm."

"Well, the 'plant' as you call it, protects us when we have to cross the Fallen Sky, which we usually avoid, as the other side is Uriah territory. But that's exactly where you want to go, isn't it? That's where your 'ship' is."

Each one of us stared at him for a moment.

"The ship?" Cabell said. "You know where it is?"

"Of course," Graeme said. "Your ship fell right on the border between Uriah and Uri territory. We were able to hide it before the Uriah found out about it, but given their intelligence forces, the secret won't last forever.

"We have to get to the ship," said Fathom. "It's the only way for us to get home. Please, take us there."

"Of course," Graeme said. "We'd be happy to. But if you're going to pass the Fallen Sky, you're going to need to smoke some of this," he said, holding out the Atavika 'lief. "This is the only thing that will keep you from succumbing to the Fallen Sky."

We looked at each other. Cabell was quite obviously not at all interested in this, but we all felt that Graeme spoke the truth. It was the only way out.

"We'll do what we have to do," said Cabell.

"Excellent. We're preparing a smoking ceremony soon. Before that, feel free to look around.

V

We crossed the community's boardwalks. Keon explained that he was originally of the Uriah, but had defected as the Uriah had become increasingly religious and oppressive over the years. Although they were peaceful, there was a radicalized group that regularly attacked the Uri. This was the same group that had tried to burn us. In many ways, the radicalized Uriah were like the Storm Ninjas.

"The power of the Uri is much stronger," he said. "We have better, stronger weapons. Our only disadvantage is...we don't attack. Only defend. The Uriah always know when the attacks will happen. We only attack when one of our own is in trouble. We attacked to save you."

I remembered the attack on the bridge. Of course. They were the ones that distracted the guards.

"You saved us," I said. "With the arrows."

"Yes."

"These are your preferred weapons? I have not shot one in years."

"Would you like to?"

"Yes, I'd love to."

With that, Keon led us through another waterfall gateway to an area which was enclosed by trees, torches, and boarded walls covered in moss. Two big waterfalls fell down from high above. A giant bird easily four times taller than me swooped down next to me, giving me a start.

"Relax," Keon said. "These are the Tal, they are friends. They help us. Like sentries they keep us safe."

Keon lifted a wooden lid covered in moss and pulled out a bow with a case of arrows. He handed it to me and gestured towards a torch on the wall. I lined up and took a shot. The familiar stance brought back memories of the archery we'd set up in Nevada. I hit the target dead on. I looked back at Keon, who was smiling with admiration.

"You are very good," he said. "We could use your skill."

I blushed.

"Much of our life here is peaceful," Keon said. "Uriah does not know of this area. They attack us in other parts of the jungle. Your skill could help us defend other Uri strongholds. With aim like that, you could save many lives."

I laughed at the idea. But I was smitten at the compliment.

"You may keep this bow," he said. I refused but he insisted. "You have a warrior's spirit. You may someday need it." I thanked him for his sweetness and accepted the gift. "Now, we must head back to the ceremony."

A fire blazed on a dock in the middle of the community. All occupants had exited their huts and were smoking by their homes all around us.

Graeme was standing next to the fire. He greeted us with a smile. Sitting on a log next to him, was Myles.

"Thank God you're alive," I said. Myles grinned at me with stoned eyes.

"Bailey! Just think'n about you. Here, have some Atavika 'lief, this is fine." I took the joint and smoked it. The others were hesitant to, but Graeme insisted it would protect them from the storm. The drug grew a warmth inside me that buzzed me unlike anything I'd ever smoked before.

"The Uri saved me after the fire," Myles said. "And man, do they have some setup here. They're free to do what they want all day. It's sweet. I wouldn't mind stay'n here myself."

"That's great," said Cabell, "But I, for one, am getting more than a little homesick, and I've needed to use the washroom ever since we first encountered that homeless guy and his ship."

I remembered Hylotz and the photo I'd taken of him. It seemed like a longshot, but I pulled out the photo and passed it to Graeme. "Have you ever—"

"This guy," Graeme said, "is incredible!"

"You *know* him?" Cabell asked.

"Damn right I know him! Mind-blowing dude. He introduced us to the Atavika 'lief! Without him we'd probably still be Uriah, climbing up the jungle, stupidly worshipping the sun. We're so grateful to have met him. He taught us to speak outside of the Uriah, he taught us so much!"

"His name is Hylotz," Cabell said. "He came from the ship that took us here."

"Where is he?" Graeme asked.

I laughed. "Now there's a question."

"We don't know," Cabell said. "But we're trying to find out. We think he might be at our home."

"Ah yes, your home," said Graeme. "Well, if we can help you get there, we will. In fact, the boat will soon be here to take us across the Fallen Sky." He produced several more Atavika 'liefs for us. "Take these. We may need to smoke more later."

The boat arrived shortly, and we all jumped in. As Graeme and Keon rowed us through the darkness, the frequency of tree trunks grew sparser as the mist grew thicker. The familiar cold of the storm was setting in, yet the warmth from the Atavika 'lief was so strong, it seemed to protect us.

The journey was long. I'd not been out in the storm more than an hour since…Nevada. I shivered at the memory.

After several hours, the storm began to fade again. The massive trees returned. We reached an area with trunks that had stairs ascending, lit by torches. The boat approached an island of moss, which was just a gigantic dead tree stump.

We climbed onto the island. Graeme and Keon walked to the middle of the island and brushed loose moss off several big leaves. They tossed the leaves aside, revealing our ship nestled in a small pool of water.

"I've never been so happy to see such a piece of technology in all my life," Myles said.

"You and me both," I said. We pressed up against the doors and they opened. It didn't appear to be damaged.

"We can't thank you enough for all you've done for us," Cabell said, thanking Graeme, Keon and Maya.

"Can I go?" said Maya. "I want to leave the Uriah." We looked at each other.

"I don't see why not," Cabell said.

There was a wild scream from one of the trees, then a barrage of spears. One hit Keon, and another grazed my head. Keon fell back and rolled, hiding behind an elevated part of the stump. Graeme pulled out his bow and began shooting. The others jumped into the ship immediately. I saw a skull masker shooting from above, and instantly I was triggered. I felt an adrenaline buzz I hadn't felt in years. I pulled out my bow, and took a shot, hitting the skull masker off of the tree. It felt good. I shot another, then another. For the first time in decades, I felt alive again.

"Bailey, get in," Cabell shouted.

"Go!" I cried.

They hesitated only briefly, before the doors closed.

I realized in that moment, protecting Keon and the Uri was more important than the decades I'd spent grieving aimlessly in fearful inaction. The Uri would not lose another soldier. They would gain one.

Who pilots?

Cabell	Maya
Continue reading	Go to Page 376

CABELL PILOTS

"Cabell did it. He saved us from the storm."

"Genius. And we thought it couldn't be done."

"What dedication. What discipline!"

The voices cut through static as the room warmed and the snowy storm dissipated. Through the stony window, the clouds of the storm rolled off into the distance, receding as the chemical spray we had dispersed deflected it. Below, the clouds remained, but since most of the world had elevated to tower heights it did not matter.

"You've finally done it Cabell." The voice replaced the static. "We're promoting you to champion of Earth, although that title isn't quite apt enough. We're having a contest to come up with a better title."

I stepped back from the tower window and sat on my leather sofa. I was happy, wasn't I? Finally, I had achieved what I'd set out to do decades ago. My whole life project had come to an astounding close. I heard a slow, consistent clapping.

"Congratulations." The man's voice came from the left of my leather chair. I turned

to see a man with a beard watching me. Hylotz. He was lost in thought. "Of course, there is still a lot of work to be done. That is your specialty, right?"

I stared at him, unsure how to react. This was some sort of dream. But how?

"Lots of work to be done," he said, again. "That's the why. But the how. What about the how?"

He took a joint from his winter coat and lit it, bringing it to his lips. He inhaled. As he exhaled, a green plant grew from his mouth, covering his face and his body. I jumped up and stepped back. The viny green plant would not stop growing. It grew over the walls and out through the window, compacting the small room. I ran to the window looking out over the storm. Below, I could hear the cries of others. I had no choice but to jump.

As I fell back into the storm, its icy cold consumed me again, and I shivered and shook from the dream.

LEBERWURST-57 | WITH: CABELL

I

The ship dropped from a dingy gray sky. Below, a forest appeared through the mist. It was boxed in by big gray towers. I turned the wheel left and right to avoid crashing into them. Pulling back on the wheel reduced the speed slightly. We hit the ground hard, sending a puff of dead leaves into the air.

All was silent. Outside, mist surrounded the ship. We opened the doors. The cool, wet air rolled over me. Were we back on earth? It did not seem like it. The towers I had seen during landing were not at all familiar. A red glow of lights could be seen in the distance. They were surrounding the entire forest.   "There's the storm," Fathom said, pointing up. There was a trail of white powdery snow where we'd just fallen from.

"I'm happy to be rid of that damn jungle," said Myles.

"This seems like a much more tenable atmosphere," I said. "This is something we can work with."

We walked through the woods, shivering from the cold. I wished I had my jacket, but we had long since discarded our winter clothes in the jungle.

We approached one of the towers I had seen from the ship. Its red lights loomed overhead. It raised high up into the dreary sky. I ran my hand along its cold, smooth surface.

"Steel," I said. "The architecture is advanced. I've never seen any man-made structures this strong."

We continued in the woods. There was an unsettling feeling, like we were being watched.

"Wait," I said. "What's that over there?" There was a web of antlers swaying back and forth. "Looks like we've got company."

The moose stepped out from behind the bushes and stared at us. Fathom stared back at the moose. He was transfixed; lost in thought. Then he frowned with a look of dismay.

"What is it?" Myles asked.

"The moose…just told me where to go."

Myles shook his head. "Fathom man, you're losing it."

"That's impossible," I said.

"It says there is a farm nearby where other animals are being held hostage. It's asking us to save them."

"Give us a break, Fathom," Myles said. "I get that this whole situation is bonkers, but you can't talk to animals, man."

"It says there is a man there, who is dangerous. It says that we should—"

"Seriously, Fathom," I said. "Stop joking around."

"I'm not joking. I'm completely serious."

"Okay so you can talk to animals now," said Myles. "Great."

"Don't you remember the moose back on Earth? It led us to Hylotz's backpack."

With a snort, the moose walked away, and Fathom followed. "What else do we have to go off?"

Myles shrugged at me and hurried after Fathom.

After a long walk through the misty forest, we came to a steel wall fencing us off. It was twice our height, spanning far off into the distance.

"Interesting," I said. "Could this be the farm? Who wants to explore? Fathom? Your moose brought us here."

Fathom shook his head with apprehension. For an emergency responder, he sure was hesitant to act.

"I will," I said.

"Me too," said Myles.

Maya and Fathom helped Myles and I over the fence. On the other side, lines of crops grew in parallel. There was a nearly dilapidated brown barn in the distance, and further beyond there was a white farmhouse.

Myles and I walked towards the farmhouse. While passing the barn, we could see there were cows, chickens and other animals locked inside in cages.

"These conditions are horrid," Myles said.

"Let's try to remain optimistic," I said. "Maybe there is a good reason for it."

Contrary to my optimism, a loud alarm blared through the air, its red lights broke through the mist.

We ran back to the wall, but we could not get over. We were stuck. The others yelled at us, but there was nothing we could do. Drones buzzed through the air and shot at us. I took a hit and fell to the ground with a burning pain in my back. Not long after, Myles dropped beside me. We were paralyzed by the shots. The drones continued to buzz above us.

An old man approached and tied us up with twine. The tightness strangled my wrists. He dragged us into a barn and dropped us next to a pile of hay while he pulled open a trap door, propping it up with his shotgun. He dragged us to the opening and threw us down into a cellar. It was dim with only a single lightbulb hanging from a wire. As we lay there motionless, the voice of an announcer blared from a radio on a table. The announcer was loud and direct with an authoritative tone, his voice dominating the air waves:

"One dissenter caught in Leberwurst-354, Quarter 2 (-263, 57). You are required to report all dissenters to your supervisors immediately or face imprisonment. You have been watched.

"We appreciate all your work; it is smiled upon and sincerely and severely by the Blessed Guidance as they bring us to higher levels of elation endowing each human life with qualities never before seen only appreciable through years of toil that you happily have embarked upon of your own free will on the day of enlightenment.

"Your break is coming to an end. Please report to the work floor in the next ten minutes or suffer the consequences. We appreciate your cooperation and understanding that no other civilization could thrive at the level of productivity we've reached without your sacrifice."

The radio droned on for a good half hour. Then, the old man returned with the others, one by one, dropping them down next to us. With his balding head and scowl, there was something terrifying about him.

When we were all lying on the cellar floor, the old man climbed down the ladder and took a seat at the table, laying his shotgun next to the radio.

"Explain to me, fools, are you spies?" he said.

We were silent.

"Are you spies?" he demanded, with elevated agitation. I will have you killed if you are. Do you hear me?"

We stayed silent. Petrified.

"The Goddamn Blessed Guidance thinks I'm not running a legitimate operation here, I can damn well tell you I am! It's bad enough this storm has destroyed the year's crops, let alone having the Guidance breathing down my neck."

We were too afraid to speak, so we just listened.

"I'll give you ten minutes to prove you're not with a spy. If you can't prove it, you'll be shot!"

Our silence was horrible. I could feel us all thinking heavily for a good five minutes. I considered a solution. It was scary, but it was the only thing I knew.

"We can help you protect your crops from the storm," I said.

"What?" The man cried. I heard others gasp quietly.

"We have a special 'lief that protects from the storm. It can be smoked. It could be cultivated to—"

The man burst into a genuinely unhinged laughter, almost coughing as he lost control of himself. It was terrifying.

"Special 'lief? Where the hell are you *from* you fool?"

"We are from…a place far away. We came here in a spaceship. You can have the 'liefs, just please, let us go."

The man paused. I could see his interest growing despite his disbelief.

"Where are these 'liefs, you fool?"

"In my pocket," I said, gesturing to my left side, where I had tucked the Atavika 'liefs that Graeme had given us.

The man walked over and took the 'liefs from my pocket, bringing them back to the table. He pulled out a joint that was already rolled and held it up to my face, accusingly.

"Is this the best you have to offer, fool?" he berated, grabbing his shotgun.

"Smoke it," I replied.

The man paused for a moment. Then he took out a lighter from his pocket and lit the end of the joint.

"If this is a trick, you know you will die before it can kill me," he said.

"It's not a trick," I said, nodding in acknowledgement.

After a few moments ofsmoking, I could see he was feeling the effects of the drug. He became relaxed and placed the shotgun down. In his eyes, it was like he was wondering where we had come from, and whether he could trust us. He came over to me, grabbed me and pulled me to my feet. The others screamed.

"You must think I'm awfully naïve to believe your spaceship story," he barked. "I've heard some tall tales in my day, but this one takes the cake."

"I can prove it," I said. "I'll take you to the ship."

He held my face up to his and stared deep into my eyes. His prying red eyes showed a subtle lack of focus. It seemed like he was trying to tell if I was being honest. He cursed.

"Fool, you're coming with me."

II

The old man pulled me up through the cellar door and awkwardly dragged me across the farm. The patrolling drones shared the same ominous red-light glow as the surrounding towers from before. He opened the door to the farmhouse and pushed me inside. I fell on the floor onto my side. I squirmed to a sitting stance. There were cupboards lining the walls and a white fridge with scrapes and nicks. Flies buzzed around the sink where dishes were piled nearly overflowing, and there was an old wooden table with a radio in the middle. The same authoritative voice from before droned on, this time it made me feel sick.

"I don't know who the hell you are," he said, "but you're not from around here," He pointed his shotgun at my face. "The Blessed Guidance doesn't smile on foreigners and neither do I. Give me one reason why I shouldn't blow your brains out right here."

I stuttered, squirming to my knees. I could see in his eyes, he was deciding to kill me and the others, and then he would take the 'liefs. His finger slipped over the trigger. There was a ring from his pocket, which momentarily brought a confused look to his face. The effects of the 'lief had dulled his focus. I trembled as he reached down pull his phone out and answer it.

"What? Yeah, no, I haven't seen anything on that dissenter. No. But listen, you got to get down here. I've got something you're going to want to see."

I jumped to my feet and plowed into him with all my might. He yelled out and the shotgun fired. It missed. He struggled against me, but I weighed him down with my body. The drones reacted immediately. Red laser shots blazed through the air outside, closing in on the house. I jumped up and ran. I had little time to react.

There was a knife at the edge of the sink. I grabbed it and dashed away from the sink as another shot rang out. I jumped around the table and ran down a hall, finding a stairway. I ran upstairs. Over the banister I could see that the old man was gaining his footing and turning around.

Shouts came from the direction of the barn. Had the others escaped? At the top of the stairs, I ran for the nearest bedroom. The door was open, and I quickly closed it with my hands. I was barely able to lock it.

I fumbled with the knife I'd grabbed and was able to free myself from my restraints. Outside, someone screamed. I ran over to the window. It was Myles. He'd escaped but was shot down by a laser. The drones turned towards me and approached my window. I pushed a bookshelf across the window to block it.

I searched for another weapon. There was a shotgun in the closet. I didn't know how to use it, but I had to try. There was a loud bang on the door. It was the old man. I held the shotgun tight and ran to the door.

"You're dead!" The old man jiggled the door handle, before a shot rang out, and I jumped back. This was it, I had to act now. I cocked the gun and pointed it at the door, closing my eyes and pulling the trigger, hoping for the best.

The blast recoiled, throwing me back against the hardwood floor. There was a thump outside the door. I cautiously moved to the hole in the door to see the old man—dead. A dark pool of blood was oozing from his chest.

A drone smashed through a window in the hall and shot at me. I pushed the bed up against the hole in the door. Outside the drones buzzed, swarming around the house.

Not long after there were voices of men outside the house. The drones were not attacking them. The front door to the house opened and I hid in the closet.

"They're shut off," a scratchy voice yelled. There was a noticeable drop in noise from the drones outside. I heard footsteps walking around downstairs. "I'm checking upstairs."

I bit my lip and held my breath.

The footfalls caused the old staircase to creak as the man ascended. Then, another shout from outside. "Get out here!"

The creaks turned into fast footfalls towards the front door. The unknown man had left the house.

I crept up to the window and listened. I carefully pushed the bookshelf aside enough to see outside. They had found the others. They had rounded them up and were taking them away. There was nothing I could do. I crept downstairs and looked out the front door. They were leaving the farm with their new prisoners.

III

Smoke from Atavika 'lief curled around my head. I gazed through the crack of the boarded-up farmhouse window to the misty sky outside. It had been months since we had arrived here, and I'd shot the old man dead. Grief gnawed at me in equal measure to the warm glow of the buzz from the joint.

A greasy long-haired kid appeared at the farmhouse deck and knocked on the door. I swatted and cursed at flies buzzing around my head. I'd tried numerous times to get rid of them, to no avail. Placing my joint in a dish, I grabbed the shotgun and headed for the door.

"Atavika," the boy whispered through the door. I opened it quickly and dragged him into the porch.

"Were you followed here?" I uttered.

"No," the boy cried.

"Where is it?"

The boy craned his neck gesturing at his backpack. I pulled it off his shoulders and searched through it. There they were. Five stacks. I pulled out the bag of the Atavika 'lief and passed it to him. The boy stared at me.

"Well don't just stand there," I whispered. "What? What do you want?"

"I just wanted to thank you," the boy said. "Before you came, the Green Resistance was just a small group of people disgusted with the Blessed Guidance. Now, so many tired workers are turning to this Atavika 'lief to escape the oppressive regime, and they are joining our cause to rebel against the system."

"Just keep quiet about the 'liefs," I said, closing the door on him. I sat back down at the table. I recalled the first day we had arrived here. After the others were taken away, I had locked down the farmhouse. I had scoured all available literature to learn as much as I could about this world.

The old man was a failing farmer who provided for the Blessed Guidance, an oppressive ruling class that lived high up in the towers and had forced most of the population into labor. I had continued in the old man's shoes. Since the Blessed Guidance only communicated by phone, they were unable to tell the difference.

Initially the farm was failing due to the storm, but I had successfully duplicated the Atavika 'lief, which provided a defense from the storm, creating tenable conditions for growth. In the interim, I had formed an alliance with the Green Resistance, an underground retaliatory group against the Blessed Guidance. I had provided them the powerful 'lief, and they had provided me with money to survive.

The others had been forced into manual labor. I had thought about them often, but I could not justify going to find them, it was too dangerous.

The phone rang. I reached into my pocket and looked at the Caller ID. It was a representative for the Blessed Guidance. Cautiously, I answered.

"We've completed testing on the 'lief you provided. This product has the potential to protect Leberwurst from the storm indefinitely. We are astounded by your level of genius. Your work must continue, and we have gladly prepared a spot for you in a local tower, where you can live out your years of servitude in conditions far surpassing that of a farmer. Do you agree to this?"

"I do," I replied. "But regarding my request to have selected local assistants…"

"This is not a reasonable request. Local laborers remain detached from tower servants. You will have colleagues that will be chosen for you, but your request is highly unorthodox."

"I understand," I said.

"Nevertheless, you yourself are a bit of an anomaly. How you have grown this genius from the role of a lowly farmer is…baffling. Yet if you keep your head down and keep up your work, you will continue to be rewarded with the necessities required for your position. Again, this is more than many will ever know."

"I understand," I replied. "Thank you."

I hung up the phone. I stared at myself in the kitchen mirror. My hair had grown long, and I now had a beard. The Atavika 'lief had become a part of me. It was the only way I could relax. I had wanted to leave this place many times. I had returned to the ship but, I was unable to bring myself to operate it. I had hidden it, determined to return the next day and leave, but I could not do it. Something was holding me back.

Now, the prospect of life in the towers was much more pleasing than the stress of farm life. I would have recognition. Colleagues who would understand and respect me. It was more compelling than my isolation at Last Bastion even, where no one understood the value of my work. The radio buzzed to life, interrupting my thoughts.

The three foreigners found on Leberwurst-57 Quarter 1 (35, 18) have been sentenced to death. Their verdict has been a long time coming. The Blessed Guidance have given you much to be thankful for, yet still dissension has become such a problem, we have been forced to take action. We expect that the death of the foreigners will evoke a new age of higher productivity and we welcome it. We wish only to show you how *efficient* you can be when you put your minds to something, and this ambition is wasted upon the dissenters. Going forward, if you are harboring dissenters or foreigners, you will meet an in-kind fate. You have been watched. May the most blessed of all guidance direct you to beautiful toil through diligent longevity.

I paused, taking a moment to stare at myself in the mirror. I was ashamed. I punched the mirror. I had to snap out of it. I had to take some sort of action. They were my friends. I could not let them die. I gritted my teeth and grabbed the shotgun from the table.

IV

I flung the old man's backpack over my shoulder and set out on the path towards the processing plant. Through the Green Resistance, I had learned everything I needed to know about the layout of the factory, which was guarded by drones.

I approached the familiar large rock at the base of a landslide. Pushing it aside, I revealed the small cave I had come for. I pushed the rock back in place. At the back of the cave, there was a stone wall. I knocked on it with in a memorized beat. The wall slid aside, and I was greeted by two Green Resistance soldiers with guns, ready to shoot.

"Cabell, what brings you?" the soldier said relaxing, his dusty face becoming visible as my eyes adjusted to the dim lantern lights.

"I'm infiltrating the factory," I said.

"No way! The drone security is—"

"Look I've thought about it, and I have friends in there that will be put to death. It has to be done."

"It's a suicide mission!"

"It doesn't have to be. I'll need more weapons. Muster up some of the extras. Jex, is the west entrance to the factory still accessible?"

"It is, but—"

"Look I don't want to talk about it, okay? I'm going to do it. After we return, there is no way they will find the underground headquarters. I will under no circumstances lead them to it."

The soldiers looked scared, but they nodded their heads and rounded up several more shotguns and pistols with extra ammunition. They brought me to the west entrance to the factory.

The factory was an old warehouse that at one time was used to store dead animals but had been long since taken out of commission. Dilapidated machinery lay strewn about. The Green Resistance had tapped into an old drainage system in the warehouse that offered an escape for dissenters.

I lifted the grate off, and I quietly propped my head up. After surveying the area, I stepped out and placed the cover back on the drain. I crept to a door which led to a hall, and made my way down it, entering a ventilation system which connected both old and new buildings. Not fun, especially with a bag full of guns.

When I reached the sweatshop, I had to move carefully. The drones prowled with blood red eyes. They flew back and forth along the walls monitoring the workers below. The workers operated along a conveyer line poorly lit by florescent lights.

With the help of the Green Resistance, I had listened in on sensitive recordings of schedules determined by the Blessed Guidance, and I knew my friends would be working on this shift. It was a disgusting job, the slaughter and processing of animals for mass consumption.

I made my way down a ventilation shaft and unlocked a vent door, sneaking into the processing room. From behind a bigger piece of machinery, out of view of the drones, I looked over the faces of the workers in their white suits. Most were unfamiliar, but my eyes landed on a shorter worker. It had to be Maya.

An alarm blasted through the processing area and a red light flashed. A laser shot towards me, but I dashed away and returned fire. A nearby drone fell to the floor. The other drones swarmed in, and I shouted at my friends. They ran to me avoiding the laser fire.

"The bag, guns in the bag," I shouted, while unloading on the swarming drones.

The others grabbed the guns, and soon we were all shooting the drones down. It was not going to be enough, every drone in the factory would be on its way here.

"Quick, we have to get to the door," I screamed and led the others to one of the doors. The door was locked, but a shotgun to the lock quickly fixed that. I busted through the door with the others, and we made our way down a long hallway towards a staircase.

Three drones ambushed us on the stairs, and I nearly took a shot in the shoulder. Myles shot the drone down.

We ran down the staircase with more drones behind us. We shot open a front door and flew out into the night air. There were more drones ready for us. We had to run along the side of the factory shooting them, until finally we found shelter in the forest.

V

We survived the run to the farmhouse without incident. Once inside, the others collapsed on the kitchen table.

"There's no time," I said, "We've got to go. More drones will be coming!"

The radio blasted to life.

Leberwurst-13 Quarter 4 (22, 09) has been compromised. The dissenters will be killed. Report any unauthorized movement immediately. Searcher drones have been dispatched.

Did they know we were at this farm? No. They were still searching, meaning any drone strike would not be too formidable. But they would be fast. Ten minutes. I re-activated the farm drones and turrets. If they wanted war, they would get it.

"We've got ten minutes before the drones show up," I said. "We have to go. Now."

We made our way across the farm and through the gates, where we were met by an army of attacking drones.

They came slow at first, succumbing to the farm's drones that were buzzing around the periphery. Then they came in full force. We were forced to take refuge in the barn. These were only the first wave of drones, though. The next wave would be much, much worse. After the drone war that ensued, only four of my drones were left remaining. We would not survive the second wave. We had to go.

My phone received a radio signal.

Full attack! Leberwurst-57 Quarter 1 (35, 18)

I undid the locks for the animal cages. I instructed everyone where to run for the ship, and we escaped the farm property just before the second wave of drones arrived. During our run to the ship, we could hear them buzzing in the distance.

We arrived at the same clearing where we had first landed. We all brushed leaves off the ship and jumped inside. My phone blared.

Dissenters identified at Leberwurst-57 Quarter 1 (156, 8), Shoot immediately!

I tossed the phone out onto the ground just before the ship doors closed. Maya jumped in the driver's seat and took the wheel. The ship pulled up off the ground just as the drones arrived. They shot through the windshield, but their blasts were easily deflected off the ship.

As the ship began to spin in connection with the storm, I sighed. I was happy to leave this horrible nightmare behind.

MAYA PILOTS

They yelled at me from above, their spears high in the white air. They chased me down under the bright hot sun until I stood at the edge of a tree branch.

"You aren't like us," they said. "We don't want you here. Go."

My face was hot with anger. They hated me, and I hated them. I turned away from them, gazing into the darkness below, and I jumped.

I hit the water with a big splash. The water was very cool. Light fell from above.

Through the water, there were more faces. Many figures. Feminine. Beautiful. Glowing. Purple and blue. Their arms were locked together with…a man? A big man. He had much hair. His face was flushed red. He was happy.

He smiled at me and unlinked one of his arms. He gestured for me to join them. A dark shadow eclipsed the light overhead. I turned to the bearded man and the women. I followed them.

PART THREE | ONDAS | WITH: MAYA

I

We fell.

Like Tal falling from the sky.

Down down down.

There was a fiery blaze. Out there. Over an endless sea. Reigning like a god. Between sleep and wake.

We were so small.

I felt helpless. I missed the jungle cricket chorus. I missed the monkey dances. I wanted them back.

The sea closed in. Our screams did not stop it.

We smacked into water. Sides opened. Water rushed in. Screams muted. We struggled, but no. I could not make it. I could not swim.

Something tugged me. A soft blurry face. Bright like the sky. Calming the waves of fear. I tried to swim up, but I could not fight sleep.

Ａ

I coughed. Raspy. Like a dying monkey. Struggling for a last breath. Arms and legs lashing out.

A face stopped my struggle. I forced free. I ran to the light. I fell into water.

"It's okay Maya," said Fathom. "You nearly drowned. We're all here. You're going to be fine. You can calm down."

My heart pounded. Like the drums of the Uriah celebration of God. I stared at him. Light running off the side of his face. Running into the water. Running out to the fiery blaze in the sky. The winds were loud. Cold. The sky was dark. The ocean was black just like the Uri village. But it was not

Atavika.

"There's no exit other than the cave's opening," Cabell said. His voice bounced. "Curious, though, the positioning of the rocks suggests someone was hiding out here. And that gigantic red dwarf on the horizon is—unsettling. We're definitely not on Earth."

"No kidding," Myles said. "Can we all agree we've bit off more than we can chew with that goddamn ship?"

"The question is, just what determines where we end up? This navigational technology is way beyond anything we have on Earth. There doesn't seem to be any rhyme or reason to it, yet it appears to be propelling us across massive distances in space."

There was a splash. Myles spun around fast. "What in the sweet mother was that?"

We stared out of the cave. No sound. Only ocean waves. Only angered winds.

"I'm ready to peace out," Myles said.

Cabell sighed "We all are, but our ticket out of here lies at the bottom of that ocean. How are we going to get it? We might be trapped here forever."

Myles groaned. "How the hell did we survive the crash anyway?"

"Didn't you pull me out of the ship?" Fathom said.

"Hell no. Cabell pulled me out."

"I didn't," Cabell said. "I thought that...well, if none of us did, then—"

The water splashed. Creatures dove out at us. Like giant sharks. I screamed. Too late. A creature tackled me to the ground. I tried to move but it locked my hands. The others yelled. It was no good. They had us.

II

The ocean roared behind us. Like the Uriah. Angry for me to leave. We walked up a dark beach. Rocks cut like razor teeth. Wind stung like a hornet's nest. I fell. A sharp pain in my back. Wrists tied. It was our captors. They pushed me back up.

We entered bushes. The leaves jumped out of the way. Like grasshoppers escaping attack. They were black. Like wet soil. They moved with a secret life.

Our captors looked dangerous. Sharp spikes on their backs. Pointy noses. Shiny skin like a fish hiding in the ocean.

We walked long through dense bush. We were in a forest now. Strange swaying dark trees. The ocean roar was gone. We walked for so long. The harsh winds froze us. The trees shielded us some. But that made the freezing pain worse. I never knew this type of horror before. I wished for death by tiger.

After many steps we stopped at a fire. I stepped back. The fire scared me. Ever since the great fire in Atavika. It always felt scary to me. But the trees were tall here. They swayed above in the wind. They offered some protection. A shark man disappeared into a cave. He returned with a man in old, hooded clothing and clunky glasses. The man was smoking something. The two spoke by gestures.

"Humans," he yelled with anger. "Where the hell did you come from?"

We were silent. Could we trust him?

"Well it's really quite something," Cabell said, "there was a ship—"

"The ship? Where is it!" the man shouted. We went silent again. "H-Hylotz is behind this. I know he has the ship. Where is he, Goddamnit? Where is he?"

Cabell paused, surprised. "Well, the ship unfortunately met an untimely fate with the ocean…"

"Shut up!" The man yelled. He stomped his foot in anger, dropping his glasses on the ground. I jumped back in shock. He searched for the glasses. "Hylotz will pay for what he's done! N-no one steals from Duncan and lives through it! You'll r-rot until we find the bastard! Onda," he gestured to the shark-like men. "Take them to the i-ice caves! They'll die there f-for all I care!"

Our captors marched us through the forest. No more trees. It was colder. A deep cold like I never knew. The ground changed. Slippery. No more trees. Very strange. Was this ice?

We reached a rock on the ground. After much time. The Onda pulled the rock aside. Stairs led down into darkness. The Onda took torches and forced us into the opening. Each step into the ground was colder. In time the walls turned to ice. Sharp spikes threatened us from above. Were Onda hiding in the ceiling, ready to attack with spears? Our captors opened another rock door and pushed us into a small cave. They locked the door in place. We were prisoners in this horrible cold cave.

III

"Ain't this is about as far from sanity as you can get," said Myles. "I'd kill that idiot for his smoke."

"Just what did that man—Duncan—What did he say about Hylotz?" said Fathom. "How the hell could he know Hylotz if Hylotz is on earth? I mean, if we really aren't on Earth, because this sure doesn't seem like it."

"It's upsetting for sure," said Cabell. "One would have to assume this is some crazy simulation on Earth, if it's not actually another planet. And our technology is nowhere near the level of such a simulation so this *must* be another planet. But why would Duncan give a damn about Hylotz?"

"I want to go home." I said.

"I second that," Myles said.

"Look everyone, calm down," Cabell said. "There must be a way out of here. Everyone, try to break free from your restraints."

We struggled much. I tried for a long time, and I escaped the trap. My knot was not so tight.

"I am free," I said.

"Oh man, seriously?" Myles said.

"Yes. I am free."

"Free us," Fathom said.

I tried to free them. But I could not. The knots were too hard for my tiny hands.

"Never mind that Maya. Feel around the room. Can you open the door?" Cabell said.

I checked the walls. Cold and slippery. But there was no escape. It was hard to feel through shaking. I felt a door, but it was solid stone.

"The door is locked. Walls cold," I said.

"Maya, you're doing good, just try hitting the walls with your fist. How hard are they?" Cabell said.

I did as asked. The walls were very hard. Except one space. It felt empty like hollow of tree.

"One space feels empty," I said.

"Maya, try to hit the space with all your force!" Cabell said.

I tried this. It did nothing. "I can't break it."

"Show me where it is, Maya."

I took his hand. Brought him to the wall. He hit it hard. Nothing at first. The others joined in. There was a cracking sound. They hit harder. Then there was a break. The wall broke apart and everyone cheered.

"Push the ice away," said Cabell.

There was much noise. They cleared a space.

"Maya, can you fit in there?" Myles said.

I pulled myself into the hole. It was big enough.

"Excellent. Be very careful and go slowly. See if you can find an escape." Cabell said.

I crept through on my hands and knees. My body was in much pain from the cold. Soon I came to a bluish light. It was at the end of the opening. It was brighter here on the other side with many ice spikes high above. The light bounced around a cave. Far above I could see its source. It was the fiery ocean god leading me to freedom.

The cave was bright and beautiful. If I climbed high enough, I could escape. But without the others. Should I leave them?

One wall was a deep blue. The ice was smooth. White circles of light rose behind the wall. I returned to it many times, placed my hand against the ice. I imagined what could be out there. Was there a way home? Back to the jungle? I remembered my home. I wished for it badly.

I saw something through the ice. In the water. In the distance. It was watching me. A bluish figure. Blurry. The reflection reminded me of my Atavika friend. Many times, I saw her reflection in a bucket of water, when we gathered water for the Uriah. I liked her a lot. Then one day, the Uriah separated us. I never saw her again. I missed her.

At first, this figure was shy, and it stayed far away. But it came closer. I felt a longing to know it. Like my longing to return home. But, more than that, I felt a new warmth. A longing to know something like myself.

Then, one time, it came very close. It matched my hand. I could feel warmth through the cold ice, like waves of heat from the jungle's sun. Beautiful green eyes. Bright blue, smooth skin. Soft, gentle hands and swift strong legs.

And the voice started. Slow at first. But then stronger. *Who are you?* The voice was from the creature. But there was no sound. Somehow, it came through the ice, like waves washing over me. I asked myself it the same thing. Who am I?

The questions continued. We spent more time together.

"Are you from the ocean?" the voice said.

"I am from the jungle."

"Why are you here?"

"A ship brought me here."

"Are you a friend of the bearded man?" I paused at this. I remembered the man who taught us how to smoke in Atavika. I remembered his friendliness.

"Yes. He taught me many things. In the jungle. I miss the jungle. My friends are very cold. We need to escape this cave."

"There are many of us. We may be able to help. What is your name, small one?"

"I am Maya."

"You are a very beautiful creature, Maya. I am Onesia. I live with many other Onda like me, in the ocean."

Onesia's voice was soft and caring. We shared a similar curiosity for that which we did not know.

I told Cabell and the others about her. They thought I was crazy, but we continued our talks.

During one of our talks, Many Onda appeared. They looked up and down at me. I stared at them, imagining. Then the voices washed over me like a flood of rain in a storm.

"She's so tiny."

"Where could she be from?"

"Was the bearded man, right? Are there really other worlds?"

"I don't know if we should help her. What if she is a spy for Duncan?"

"But her thoughts appear innocent. And she knows of the ship. And she can speak through the cold."

"If she knows the bearded man, maybe she can return him? We must at least try to help her."

Over time they appeared with a larger object in their arms. They pushed it into the ice. I stepped far back. They swam back. Then swam in fast. They pushed the ship into the ice. Many times, they did this. Then one time, they burst through. Water went everywhere. It came up to my feet in the cave. It knocked me back. I stood up and saw our ship surrounded by the Onda.

▲

I led Onesia to the hole. "I am here with new friends," I said, through the hole.

"They are tied," I told Onesia. She nodded, lifted herself up and pushed through the hole. Her hands were bigger than mine, she could untie them one by one. They were free. Slowly, they crawled through the hole. They were barely able to fit.

"Maya, I can't believe you saved us," Myles said. Water was coming up to his knees.

"I am good at these things," I said. Cabell laughed. They all bowed to their savours, the Onda women.

"This is amazing; these women are the Onda as well? They are beautiful," Fathom said. "But they don't speak, how did you convince them to rescue us?"

"They speak, through here," I said, pointing at my head.

The others stared blankly at each other.

"You know what, I believe it. Given everything that's happened thus far, I one-hundred percent believe it," Cabell said.

"Me too," Myles said.

"Well please tell them thank you," Cabell said. The water was up to his waist. "The only problem we have is this water, and there aren't any exits."

"I guess that's our cue to leave," Myles said, walking up to the ship. He opened the ship door. Water spilled out. "I suggest we get the hell out of here fast. I can imagine better fates than drowning in a cave. Let's throw the dice on this beast."

We all walked into the ship. We jumped inside.

"Will you bring the bearded man back to us?" Onesia asked.

"I will try, if we can find him," I thought back.

The ship doors closed. The Onda women stood around us with curiosity.

"There's only one problem," Fathom said. "How do we know we're not going to crash into the wall when we start this thing?"

"I really never thought about that," Myles said.

"It could be pretty dangerous," Fathom said. "This thing is pretty damn unpredictable." The water was up to the glass.

"Well, we better figure something out soon," Cabell said. "The ship is airtight, but the cave is filling up fast. I'm not sure if it can withstand it."

I looked at Onesia. She looked back with big beautiful green eyes. She knew what I was thinking. Then the ship bobbed. We felt weightless. Through the windows of the ship, we could see the Onda pulling us through the water.

"Woah," Myles said.

"Incredible. It looks like our friends are saving us again," Cabell said.

The ship moved forward, faster as the water came up over the edge of the glass. The blue light from above faded. We crossed the hole in the ice wall and moved out into the big dark sea.

IV

Down, down, down.

We moved down into the dark ocean, away from the ice above. At first, it was scary—the ship shook like when we first fell into the ocean. It felt like we would fall apart. But the Onda were strong. We soon felt a sharp tug, the ship felt warmer, it moved with great force.

"Ocean currents," Cabell said. "They can reach velocities of up to 1.5 metres per second. Perhaps we will go faster, with help from our friends here."

Fish appeared through sky light—an incredible sight. Beautiful blues, reds, pinks, browns and yellows, there was nothing I have ever seen like it.

We moved upwards. An ocean reef appeared, a great rocky mass, a cave filled with coral appeared. We moved through it. Many beautiful creatures were hiding in the coral. They poked their heads out to say hi, like the sneaky animals hiding behind bushes in the jungle.

We exited the cave into the coral reef that was a giant maze of more caves. Onda women peeked out at us from the caves.

"*This is beautiful,*" I thought, to Onesia.

"*This is our home,*" she replied.

We moved further up, But and the water grew colder. A white snow, like over our jungle, was in the water. We entered, and it became freezing, dangerous, painful. It felt like when I flew the ship.

We could only see white, the cold continued to get worse. I felt a wave of change come over me, and I felt it in the others. Not like before, more closely. I felt how they felt the same. I felt connected to them. I reached out to Onesia. My mind branched off into many paths. I felt my thoughts grow stronger, clearer, coalescing with the thoughts of others.

"*What is this?*" I asked.

"*A great magic,*" said Onesia. "*From the heavens.*"

There was no pain. My mind felt light, like I could move anywhere. I thought of the jungle and felt as if I was back there. I thought of other places untravelled. It felt like I was moving there too. I felt my friends, men and women, many different types, happy together. And I felt my mind change, growing a new strength, growing together with many, growing, and moving great distances, balancing a great power. Onesia spoke to me now, her voice had become different. Like she'd changed as well. She was speaking with her many Onda sisters through the storm. Then she spoke to me.

"*Maya, you're a strong one, quite small, yes, but very strong. I can feel you. I can tell from your thoughts where you come from. It's an incredible jungle, and you miss it dearly. You want to return, but you also love to explore, and you're curious about my people.*

"*The Ondas were once a strong and proud race. Male and female Ondas lived together in the ocean in harmony. This all changed when this great white storm met our world. At first it was intriguing, as the images and feelings it brought were celestial; it seemed to connect us to a broader world with greater potential. However, many Ondas got lost in it, and we believe many of them died. It became detrimental to our home, causing us to move to other parts of the ocean to sustain life.*

"*However, one day a ship just like this one dropped from the storm. From it two men appeared. A bearded man and an older man with glasses. We saved them, like we saved you in your ship when you first arrived. We left them on a beach. At first, they were horribly inept, so we brought them food and helped them build a home.*

"*The bearded man took a liking to the Onda women. Somehow, he was able to speak to us, and he taught us how to survive in the storm. The older man took a liking to the Onda men. He taught them how to survive on land, and how to build land structures.*

"But as the storm grew worse, there came a time when the older man changed. He taught the Onda men that the way to beat the storm was to fight it through strength. To become stronger. To live on land and build stronger settlements against the storm.

"He taught them that women were weak to remain in water. He taught that true strength could only be obtained through pursuits on land. He also became obsessed with finding the ship that they had fallen in.

"The bearded man remained patient and tried to quell this change, but he was unsuccessful, and one day a physical fight broke out between the two. The fight led the bearded man to hide out in caves, and eventually the Onda men grew such a presence on land that the bearded man was forced to leave, with the help of us women.

"The bearded man swam with us to an island unvisited by the older man. The island was good enough for him to live peacefully for a long time. It is this island where we take you now."

Hearing Onesia's thoughts, I felt how beautiful she was. She accepted me as I was. Even though I was different. She did not wish me away. She swam through the water with such ease. I felt a reflection of my own curiosity within her grow, as my mind changed to join hers. I dreamed of joining her diving in the waves, flowing through the many pathways of the storm, reaching out to visit the depths of the Ondas ocean, to many other places, and maybe someday even to visit back home in my jungle. I felt her dream of one day uniting the Onda men and women, I wanted to help.

And then, I felt a new change. The storm fell behind us. I felt as I was before. We began to flow up, my thoughts returned to normal. The ocean god appeared above—a great light in the sky.

V

We stepped out onto the small island. It was burning hot, windy. The sky was blue with a bright light. There was a small hut in the middle of the island. The wind was very bad. We all had to run to the shelter of the hut. It burrowed into the ground, big enough for all of us.

"Looks like someone was living here for quite a while," said Fathom.

"The rocks here in the middle suggest a fire," Myles nodded. "And there's no shortage of fishbones. And look—A pipe. Well well, what do we have here. Matches and black leaves everywhere. What do ya say we smoke some of 'em?"

"Not sure about that," Fathom said. "I mean, could be completely unsafe, we don't know how the body's going to…"

"Oh, come on Fathom. It'll be a laugh. What do ya say, Cabell?"

Cabell sighed. "Fine, whatever. I don't really care at this point."

"Yeah," said Myles. They created a smoke, passed it around. Was it like the Atavika 'lief? I liked that. I smoked it too. It felt amazing. Fathom liked it so much that he kept some.

"Given the climate here it's fair to say we're on a tidally-locked planet," Cabell said. "This section of the planet would be facing the red dwarf we saw earlier, and thus in perpetual daylight."

We looked out through a window in the hut opposite to our entrance. It provided a full view of the ocean. There were black rocks far in the distance.

Cabell pointed. "You can see where day turns to twilight. That's where we landed."

"That's where we met that crazy Duncan dude and his Onda minions," Myles said.

Onesia appeared at the doorway. Behind her, the other Onda women. We all stared.

"What are they thinking, Maya?" Cabell said.

I looked at Onesia and thought, *"are we safe from Duncan's Onda men?"*

"You are very safe." Onesia said. *"They have never been here."*

"We are safe from them," I said.

"Well, that's great, but I don't plan on staying here much longer," said Myles. "Let's move."

"Where will you go? Will you find the bearded man?" Onesia thought.

"We will try."

"I want to be with you," she thought. In my mind, I remembered the storm, the way her mind felt, her dreams of exploring, her dreams of reuniting the Ondas. Much like mine, I wanted us both to explore. Here, there was no Uriah to separate us.

"Wait," I said. "I want to stay with Onesia."

The others stared.

"If you want," Cabell said.

I stared at Onesia. *"Do you want to come and explore with us?"* I thought to her.

"To go would be fine, although I could stay," she thought.

"Onesia wants to join," I said. "She wants to explore." I looked at Onesia. *"Do you want to drive this ship?"* I asked.

"Yes, very much," she said.

"She wants to drive," I said.

Cabell paused, thinking. "You know, I guess it doesn't really matter who pilots, because wherever we end up...it seems awfully random."

"I'd really like to know what it's like to pilot," said Myles.

"Well, honestly, either of you could pilot at this point. We'll figure it out when we get to the ship.

Fathom stepped out through the doorway to head for the ship. "Oh no," he shouted. "The ship is floating away with the tide!"

We ran to the entrance. The ship was far away. The Onda women were gone.

"We've got to swim to it," Cabell said. "Go, quickly."

We ran to the ship. Into the water. But I could not swim. I yelled at the others. My arms struggled against the waves. I felt myself go under. I was drowning. I felt myself drift to sleep. Like when we first arrived.   But I did not sleep. Instead, I sank. I breathed in the water. It filled me. I moved my arms. I could still swim. I swam again. I was above the water again. I swam to the ship with the others. We all held on.

"What happened?" said Cabell. "We thought we lost you."

"I fell underwater," I said. "But I did not drown."

"As did I," said Fathom. "The water filled my lunges, but I didn't drown. Could it have anything to do with what we smoked?"

"Curious," said Cabell. "But we must decide. Who will stay and who will go?"

"I will join Onesia either way," I said.

Onesia   Myles
Continue reading   Go to Page 391

ONESIA PILOTS

The cold of the storm kept me locked in a floating iceberg. As it melted, I fell deeper and deeper into the water. The water was occupied by many of my fellow Onda women and men. The waves stretched my mind out over a vast distance, resonating with the lives of many Onda.

Somewhere out there, I could see an old friend. That old, bearded man, what gentle eyes he had. His warmth lighted up my soul. I could feel his smile forming from my lips. Like the first day, when he arrived, when Onda men and women lived together in peace. His smile was like a new beginning. He whispered that all would be happy once again.

I reached out to hug him, but somewhere, in the vastness of space, something changed. A darkness overcame me. The same darkness that divided our people. Ev-

erything went black.

ONDAS | WITH: ONESIA

I

The wind jolted us back and forth as we fell to the ground. Our direction was all off; I couldn't make a level landing. It was terrifying. We hit the ground so hard the front of the ship became stuck, cracks in the ice spread out like ripples across the sea.

We pried the doors open and spilled out. It was freezing.

"This is strange," said Cabell, "What a familiar ambiance. Are we on the same planet?"

We walked around in near complete darkness, but I knew immediately where we were. It was the great ice sheets that I'd explored as a child. *"This is Ondas,"* I said to Maya. *"We are still on Ondas!"*

"Onesia says we're back on Ondas."

"This can't be right. This hasn't happened before," Cabell said.

In the distance, through the bluster of the storm, several figures approached, including one with a lantern. Upon their approach, I knew it was the Onda men. With them was Duncan, in his puffy black coat and hood. His presence sent me into the same revolt I'd experienced in the cold dream.

"We have to get away, it's Duncan!" I thought to Maya. But it was too late.

"Thought you could escape, eh?" Duncan said. We remained quiet, ready to run, but saw that we were trapped in. There were many Onda men approaching us from all sides, closing in on us in a circle.

"You w-won't be escaping this time, my friends," Duncan said and pulled back his hood. His cold blue eyes focused on the ship. "How delightful of you to bring the s-ship right to me!"

As he approached, the Onda men captured each of us, holding our hands back. Duncan paused for a moment, then removed a small, wrapped collection of black leaves from his jacket and touched it against the candle at the inside of the lantern. He inhaled, his pupils growing and glowing in satisfaction.

"Let us go," Maya screamed.

"What is your problem dude?" Myles asked.

"My problem," he said, again inhaling the joint, "is you've been keeping my sh-ship from me. Do you know how much power this ship has? It very well may have the power to take us away from this cursed storm!" Again, he inhaled. "And conversely, it can shipwreck you on a planet like *this*, stuck with a blundering fool."

"Hylotz," Cabell whispered, under his breath. Then he spoke up. "You and Hylotz were stuck on this planet?"

"That thief," Duncan said, spitting on the ground. "Hylotz was an idiot. He w-wasted his chances of using this ship to advance us beyond the storm. We could be on the way to reaching out to other civilizations and establishing s-solid alliances, but instead he's used the ship as his own personal limousine, using it to take him wherever he wants. Our Marzanna village was burgeoning before he arrived. Before the ravaging storm. He did nothing but steal from us! He can r-rot in hell for all I care, wherever the h-hell he is."

"So you're going to leave us here?"

Duncan flicked his smoked joint to the ground. "Just like Hylotz did when he found the ship and left me here, alone with the Onda. Now in the interest of avoiding losing this ship again, you *will* be stepping aside."

The Onda pulled us back from the ship as Duncan opened the door and stepped into the driver seat.

"Well don't just stand there," he yelled at his minions. "Free the sh-ship!"

Many Onda men pulled against the ship to try to free it from its crater, but it was stuck too deep. Duncan shouted at them until he became so angered, he screamed.

"Oh, give it a rest, back up!" He shut the door. We stepped back as the ship ignited with a green-metallic glow, sparking to life. There was a very soft hum as the metal pushed tight against the ice, at first to no avail, but then the cracks across the ice spread like wildfire.

By the time everyone realized what was happening, the fragmented cracks were splitting ice miles away, and in a massive blast, the ice fractured and sent us all into the water with the ship.

A

As we submerged in the icy cold water, several other Onda women who I'd called to appeared below. A mad fight ensued between Onda women and men, each of us struggling to break free. I could see our new friends being pulled deep down below. Strange creatures, they could not breathe underwater, they would surely die.

An Onda man grabbed me and pulled me back. I punched him in the head and swam downwards. The only escape now was down. Up surely would be dominated by angry Onda men. I sadly realized there was no way to help our friends.

I thrusted my arms through the water as fast as I could. Despite their strength, the swimming of an Onda man could not rival the swimming of an Onda woman. I evaded the Onda men and swam much deeper down into the ocean. I swam through cracks in coral that led me to a glowing bright orange, volcano caves, I'd remembered from my childhood. It was much hotter here, but Onda men hated the harsh warmth, preferring the cool dark, like that of Duncan's dusky caves.

When I was sure I was safe from detection, I sent out a nearby telepathic sonar to my Onda women, a few of whom I found nearby. We searched for Maya and the others, but we could not find them. In a last-ditch effort, we dove down into the volcanic cracks deep below, braving the scorching hot conditions. To our surprise we found the ship there, with the door open. Duncan was nowhere to be seen.

We pulled the ship up, up through an underwater cave which led to the open chamber of an inactive volcano. Pulling to the surface of the water, we were able to push it out of the water and onto the ground.

Through the opening of the volcano there was a long, white, cylindrical column of the storm. I knew that I could reach greater distances by thinking through the storm, so I lay down with my head in the storm.

I could hear Maya's thoughts and I could sense her distance from me. She was alive. I could see the others but could not reach them through the storm. I alerted as many Onda Women as possible to go for Maya, as Maya searched for the others, and direct them to the volcano.

Maya finally arrived with the others. She ran into my arms and kissed me. *You saved me again!"* She thought. *"I love you. I want to stay with you forever."*

"I love you too," I said. *"You can stay as long as you want."*

"Thank you for saving us Onesia," said Cabell, "we are truly indebted to you. But it was strange, how were we able to breathe underwater for so long?"

I thought back to the bearded man and his journeys with us, and I realized the answer.

"The 'lief of the bearded man, this 'lief helped him travel with us underwater, and it has let you breathe underwater," I said.

"The 'lief we smoked lets us breathe," said Maya. "Onesia says the bearded man used it. To swim with them."

"Incredible," Cabell said.

Cabell was interrupted by a splash from below. It was Duncan, running to the ship. He punched Maya in the face, and she fell, but she tripped him briefly. We all ran to him as he opened the door.

"Get the hell away!" Myles yelled. Duncan punched him and jumped in the ship. He tried to close the door, but I stopped him. I pulled him with help from the others and we pushed him out of the ship as the others blocked the door. They jumped inside and Myles took the pilot's seat.

Suddenly, Duncan grabbed me by the throat and strangled my neck, but Maya ran into him with her entire force, causing him to fly back against the floor. Lifting from the ground the ship exited the volcano caves, as the Onda swarmed in and restrained Duncan in his rage.

MYLES PILOTS

Bitter cold winds swirled around me. As the storm eased off, I could see I was holding on to the edge of a cliff. Above me was a figure. My father? He guided the way as we climbed up the perilous surface.

The storm below disappeared to reveal a pleasant mountain village, shopkeepers opening their businesses. Children playing in the streets. By all accounts it was a lovely scene.

The figure above turned down to face me. It was not my father, but Hylotz. I shouted at him over the howling winds, asking him what the hell this was all about. He just winked and pointed up. A shot rang through the air, and he fell over the cliff.

A familiar fear waved over me. I trembled as I had to catch myself from falling. As I looked up, the storm clouds returned. They surrounded me once again. The cold froze my body.

PART FOUR | MARZANNA | WITH: MYLES

I

Days.

It felt like goddamn days since I'd had a smoke. That crazy black weed we had smoked was intense, but it doubled my craving.

Yet here we are in this godforsaken ship, float'n around the universe look'n for some crazy old homeless man, for what? So we'll all just perish in an intergalactic storm? And yet here we are. Parked right in a flip'n snowbank. Freeze'n our asses off.

What led us here? Cabell's aspirations of saving Earth? Bailey's wish to escape the mundanity of urban life? Maya's chasing her own reflection? I pulled my foot out of the Ondas ocean water which had pooled at the bottom of the ship. No matter how we got here, it was a frig'n disaster. And I could really use a goddamn smoke right about now.

"Where the hell are we?" Fathom said, looking out the window of the ship.

"Your guess is as good as mine," Cabell answered.

"Ain't nothin but blowing snow out there," I said. "Looks rough. Y'know, we *could* be back on Earth. Looks about the same as when we left it."

"I hope so. Last Bastion's bathroom would be heaven right about now."

"There's only one way to find out," said Fathom, reaching to open the door. "It's not budging."

"We're in a goddamn snowbank, that's why." I nearly spat my words out. "This is a frig'n disaster." We tried our doors to no avail. What a waste of time. "Well what's the plan now?" I dared someone to step up and pierce through this shitstorm we'd got ourselves stuck in.

"Rock the ship! Maybe we can rock our way out of it," said Fathom.

Fair enough. Decent point. We started rock'n to and fro, working with staggered momentum. It was minimally effective. Mostly pointless.

"Right. Pretty much an exercise in futility. Never hurts to perform one of those though, eh Cabell?"

Cabell was about to respond before he was interrupted by a roar outside the ship.

"Jesus, Cabell, I know it's been a while since we had a good meal, but you really gotta get a handle on that stomach," I said.

"Shut up Myles. What the hell is out there?"

"Not sure I want to know," Fathom said.

"We may be proper screwed this time, for real," I said.

The ship shifted hard to the right, not through any action of our own. Must have been a goddamn beast outside.

"This ain't good. Not good at all," I said.

Light from the window was eclipsed by a figure with teeth gnawing into the glass.

"That's a lot of nope for me," I said.

"Look, let's just calm down and wait it out," Cabell said.

"Brilliant idea. Keep doin' what we're doin'. That's why they pay you the big bucks."

Cabell frowned, but didn't respond. He was more generally irritated than specifically angry at me. And to be fair, I wasn't really pissed at him as much as the situation.

We must'a spent hours in that goddamn ship, just wait'n. To be rescued? Naw, probably not. It reminded me of the road trips I took with the old man as a child. What a beast he was, constantly either on the booze, hook'n up with some woman or revel'n in the beauty of nature. But sit'n in this goddamn ship goin' nowhere brings back those memories now. In some ways he was a monster of a man, but hell, he got shit done. And, God bless him, he did show me how to deal with shit in life. Least postmodern urban life where drugs are available 24/7. Jesus, I need a smoke.

I woke up to a biting cold, howl'n wind, icicles form'n under my nose. Christ, I was out in the goddamn snow. How th'hell did this happen? I must'a fell asleep. The others were nowhere around.

I rose to my knees, my face freezing. Snow everywhere; I couldn't see a damn thing. I was shivering, and dizzy. I tried to get to my feet, but the wind wrestled me down to my knees again. This storm was going to be the death of me.

In the confusion of the storm I fell flat on the ground. Again, I tried to stand up, to no avail. I edged forward on my knees, and damn, it wasn't easy, let me tell you.

In my disorientation, I landed on my back once more. I forced myself up with all my might, and I was on my feet and out of the storm. It happened so fast it was surreal. Was I just imagining this, or was I fly'n all over the place?

It was quiet, like I was in the eye of the storm, the snowflakes were swirl'n all around me. Then I saw it. Sweet Jesus. Two antlers in front of me, protude'n into my field of vision. And a vicious face. Teeth barred around a horrible roar!

In my mind, I was running away as fast as possible, but I didn't feel my muscles move. Through the dizziness I realized that I was back in the storm. It was the most bizarre feeling. I'd just witnessed some sort of horrible beast, and somehow got myself out of it, even though I didn't—

The roar came from behind me, and the sound of footfalls. It was chase'n me! I had to get out of there quick, but my body was stiff as a rock. I moved through the storm as best as I could; the beast's howling faded. Somehow, I was moving without even exerting myself. Strange as hell.

This dance continued for quite a while. I moved farther and farther from that horrible beast, until its howls became indistinguishable from those of the wind. It felt like the winds of the storm were picking me up and whisking me along. The cold was horrible. I wondered how my body could withstand so much damn cold without completely shut'n down.

I kept moving, vision blurred. And soon enough I found myself in a dark space. I fell to my knees. Damp, cold, flat, rock. Definitely rock. I was in a cave. And I was happy enough with it. I curled into a ball and, despite the best documentation on survive'n hypothermia, I fell asleep.

II

Through the hazy blur of sleep, I'd entered a dream-like state. I explored a village that appeared from the darkness. It was the same bustling village I'd seen while navigating the ship. It was full of lively youth, rich farmland and a government unified with its people to create a future full of young happy lives.

At first, the winters were not long. But after a few years, they got longer and the snow soon permeated all year round.

The shops stayed open fewer hours in the evening. The kids returned home from playing earlier and earlier. And the people began to get mad at the government for doing nothing.

Even still there was a notion—not only with the government, but with the others—that it would all go away. Surely, obviously, it's only temporary. Seasons change; it doesn't last forever. The day would come when it would all just turn out to be a bad dream, and the kids would play later once again.

But one year, when summer came, the snow did not cease, and the white spiral storms began to grow worse. It didn't help that, during that year there was a great food shortage. The people were angry at the government, insisting something be done. And the government turned to the people and said "It's not our fault. We're doing everything we can." But were they?

In this same year, the town was afflicted with a herd of moose, apparently looking for food and shelter from the storm. Rumors said that the herd was accompanied by a bearded man perusing the shops with the moose, long after they were closed.

It was not until one day that a shop was broken into, that the government took a stand, its leader with his dark-rimmed glasses suggesting "the bearded man is to blame for this theft. We will find him, and we will imprison him. If any moose are found roaming the city, given the food shortage, it is acceptable to shoot them."

✦

I woke from the dream, the cave was dark as hell, and I felt like absolute shit. I was starved for food and a smoke. If that beast had been in here, I would've torn its throat out and made a meal of it. 'Course that was a bit ambitious, nonetheless I knew I needed to find the others.

Was this Earth? It was possible, but the storm seemed worse than we'd left it. Visibility outside was near zero and it felt even colder than I've ever known Earth to be.

I edged my way through the darkness, finally finding a doorway. I made my way out into a narrow space and continued onward. To my relief, I saw a light in the distance. When I reached it, I realized it was a candle. So there was some sort of civilization here. Thank God.

I continued down the hall, and found another candle, then another. I followed candles until I found some stairs leading up.

I walked up several floors before finally reaching a wooden door, a candle on either side. I pushed it open slowly. It was a big room with light beaming down from a ceil'n that opened into the sky which was void of the storm. In the middle there were long, broad wooden cases of a greyish-white plant. I brought it close to my face, but it did not exude any smell; the leaves were shaped like stars. It looked a little like the Atavika 'lief. Was this a greenhouse for them?

I walked down another hallway to a wooden door. The door flew out with a gust; The howling wind pushed the door back and forth on its hinges. I could feel the familiar bitter cold of the storm pushing up against me, breaking my skin out into bigger and bigger goosebumps.

Outside, the edge dropped off into a dangerous cliff. I paused for a moment to consider my options. There must be some sort of civilization nearby, and I was starved. I needed to move on—find those people. There was no other reasonable option at this point.

I carefully edged along the cliff not know'n how far down the drop might be but expecting the worst. There was a roar in the distance that made my blood run cold. Goddamn beasts again.

I shivered, considered turning back to regroup. It was too dangerous. Before I could make any progress, there was another howl close by. Out of the snow came the same horrid beast from before, on the path I'd come from, blocking my way.

I backed away from it, but the beast closed in on me fast. I realized now that I'd reached another edge. There was a wooden bridge, but it was derelict; impassable. I edged my way on to it until I reached the part that had fallen apart. The beast roared from the cliffside. I was screwed.

The only escape was to jump to the other side. With a deep breath, I made a valiant attempt jump across the gap, but I was short. My fingers scraped across the frail wood, but I couldn't get a grip in the snow. At the last second, my hands grabbed a hold of a piece of wood on the other side. I had almost exhaled a relieved sigh when the wood shattered into pieces. I fell, but managed to grip hard onto the dangling rope. The damage was too much and the bridge snapped behind me. I fell, the rope I still clung too swung me forward and I slapped against the other side of the cliff. My grip was loosening. There was no way I could climb up. I held on as long as I could, but it was only a matter of time.

I felt fear rise inside me. If this was really the end, what was the point of it all? My whole life I'd followed in the footsteps of my father, using drugs to ease the pain, to escape from mundanity of life but also, in a way, to avoid having to face the reality that someday, it would all be ultimately lost in an unavoidable fate. Emotions that had lay dormant for years welled up inside me.

I almost gave up when a voice called to me from somewhere out in the storm.

"Do not be afraid, Aaron Myles. Feel the pathway forward through the storm, only when you are at peace, will you feel yourself rise above."

III

The voice seemed to come from above, and I didn't hear it as much as I *felt* it. I made peace with my fate, and I let go. I had lived as well as I could, I had pursued my own happiness and that of others, and I had tried to do the best for everyone. I had a hell of a lot of good times.

"Allow yourself to let go and rise with us. You can rise above by succumbing to your fallible nature."

Through my acceptance of death, I realized a way forward was beyond the physical nature of this world. I allowed myself to let go, but I focused on following the voice.

Then I fell…into nothing. Instead, I rose to the edge of the cliff. A hand grabbed my arm and pulled me in a doorway. The door closed and people lifted me up a stairway. My vision was blurry. I was barely able to move.

We entered a greenhouse like the one I'd found. Through the light I could make out the people that had helped me up here. Long white hair draped from the hoods of their dark cloaks, they looked like some sort of cult.

A woman approached me. She was young and beautiful with close-set eyes, a pale complexion, and bright white irises. "Aaron Myles. So nice for you to join us. We were just musing on how dreadfully lonely it is, living in a derelict castle on a dying planet amid a universal apocalypse. Marcus, please prepare a 'lief for our guest, he's awfully cold."

I struggled to sit upright, my eyes squint'n to make sense of the situation. A bearded man had taken one of the plants from the garden and was wrapping it in a small piece of paper. He sparked a fire with a fire striker and brought it to the paper, a motion that immediately cleared my blurry vision and it brought a great warmth to my heart. I longingly reached out for the spliff.

I felt it warm my entire body as I inhaled it, the warmth seemed to cast the room in a new light. The group of men and women became kindred; I felt as though I could see beyond their hardened features to their youthful essence. What's more, I felt I could nearly *see* their essence as humans. I felt almost like a child again. And the cold didn't bother me one bit. I'd acclimated to it.

"There you go," the woman said. "You're feeling much better now, aren't you?"

"Yes. Yes I am. Thank you.".

"This drug will keep you adjusted through the storm. To be completely honest, we're surprised you made it this far. Unaided humans can't survive a Level 4 storm more than an hour. We had you on radar less than an hour ago, hence our trip to find you."

"Where...am I?"

"Oh, apologies. I should have introduced myself. My name is Nivea and this is the planet of Marzanna. We're delighted to have you, although we're quite confused as to how your ship got you here, given that intergalactic space travel has yet to have been discovered by humans, to our knowledge. Ourselves, we have not even had the opportunity to engage in interstellar travel, and sadly our days are becoming numbered."

I inhaled another puff of the spliff. It was amazing. I was so relaxed, and more attuned to the others and the ambience of the cave. I felt so warm.

"I'm glad I found you," I told them. "But what about my friends? There are some nasty beasts out there—"

"Ah, the Bies. Yes, they have become a serious nuisance since their mutation. They will attack immediately, and we can not communicate with them. If it wasn't for our fortress, we'd be dead.

"Don't worry about your friends. We already have a search party looking for them. They will be fine. Now, lets head back to the castle and get you some food. You look like you've been shaken by the storm for way too long."

"I won't argue with you," I said.

I stood and found that the drug had dulled the pain from before. We made our way up through the greenhouse and out yet another door. At the edge of the cliff, there was an incredible view. The storm stretched out like a sea of mist, leading a long path to mountains in the distance. At the top of the mountain, there was a castle, beautifully resting high in the air above the encroaching storm.

"Now, Aaron Myles, given your temperament and vulnerabilities getting here, I believe it's quite evident that you are at best novice to the teleportative potential of the storm."

"The what?"

"Well, remember when I *spoke* to you when you nearly fell off that bridge?"

"Yes."

"Well, then, how did you survive?"

"I fell and I just...well, I just landed at the other end?"

"Right. You landed *up* at the other end of the bridge. In short, you *rode* through the storm. A Level 4 storm has teleportative capabilities. You can *ride* the storm for short distances. Eventually it will peter out, but it will last for a good five minutes or so, if you're good at it, and if you have assistance from the 'lief.'"

"You're not saying that..."

"Yes. That's exactly what I'm saying. We have to *ride* across the cloud to the castle. It's the only way. The divide acts as the castle's moat, keeping the Bies, and — at one time — unwelcome villagers away."

"You can't be serious. There's no way I can do that. I barely made it here alive, somehow, but I can't cross a massive distance like that in five minutes."

Nivea took my face in her hands and gazed into my eyes. Quite intimidating, considering her beauty. Through her eyes, she spoke, but not through speech.

"You can, and you will. How did you get here? How did you escape the Bies? There's no way you would have made it this far without leveraging the power of the storm to guide you through. We've watched you from when you first left the ship. You've traversed a great distance to get here. And how did you do this? By giving up? No. Risk exists in all ventures. The only antidote for fear is action in the face of adversity. We must constantly be throwing ourselves into the storm and growing to meet the dreams of ourselves along the way."

"Alright. I will try, but can you help me?"

"Of course," she said. *"Hold my hand and stay present with me. As long as you feel me close beside you, you will not fall. And the others, you can feel them too can't you? They will be all around us. Stay with us, and we will cross the storm."*

I let my fear wash away, like I did when I let go from the bridge. Holding Nivea's hand, we both fell into the storm.

IV

Through some unseen magic, I was surfing through the storm, and I felt a presence with me. I was again impressed with the vision of the village, but this time the view followed the man with dark-rimmed glasses. He traversed across a winter forest with a team of hunters, rifles strung over their backs, intent on finding something, or — someone.

Their journey came to an end as they hid in a cave and spied on an older man with a beard who was walking along the cliffside. He turned to face them, and with a shot, he fell over the side of the cliff.

Riding the storm turned out easier than I thought, 'course the drug they gave me was work'n wonders. My body felt cool, yet I felt warm inside. It was like I'd acclimated to the storm.

We came to another cliff's edge and worked our way along a cliffside and into a cave. This led to the foot of a gray castle that was intermittently cloaked by the mist of the white death storm and covered in the 'liefs I'd seen earlier. It was truly breathtaking.

The castle looked like something right out of Earth's medieval period, suggesting their civilization was less advanced. Though with Nivea's apparent clairvoyance, it seemed like they were considerably more advanced for their time. I wanted the answers to this, but was content to just take it all in, revelling in the drug's effect.

The gatehouse opened for us, and we passed through a beautiful stone court. We traversed a vegetable garden and entered a threshold into to the castle keep. We ascended a long spiral staircase, and the walls were covered with a viny plant that looked a lot like the 'liefs from before. At the top of the stairs, we moved into an open room that overlooked a vast sea of the foggy, white mist of the storm. Another planet loomed on the horizon. In the middle of the room there was a stone column, with flat surface and plates of food laid out for us. The thought occurred to me…had Nivea telepathically alerted of our presence?

Nonetheless, I quickly stuffed my face with the delicious vegetables and fruits provided, revelling in the first decent meal I'd had since this whole thing started. When I was finished, my eyes met Nivea's who was eyeing me inquisitively. Maybe she couldn't read all my thoughts and was trying to pry further beyond her capabilities.

"Thank you for the meal," I said.

"You're quite welcome, Aaron Myles."

"Look, I have a ton of questions, right, but the one foremost in my mind is, why so nice? Why are you treating me so well when you have no idea where I've come from?"

She laughed.

"Oh my, Mr. Myles, we have more knowledge of your origins than you expect. However, there is still more we'd like to know about what brought you here. Never mind that. Right now, your comfort is of our utmost priority. We want you to know that you can stay here as long as you want, and you're entirely safe. You can have as much food as you want, and your friends are welcome also. We have made contact with them now and are bringing them back to the castle."

"How do you know so much?"

"We are an old people, despite our appearance. Our planet has undergone a lot of political struggles leading us to an extended—medieval period, as your planet would say—but it's nothing we can't overcome through patience and compassion. Yet no struggle has been so poignant, so *enlightening*, as this white death storm." She cleared her throat, her brilliant smile gleamed as the gentle mist of the storm brushed along her cheeks.

"Our people—my ancestors—veered away from the medieval dynasties in rebellion against an oppressive regime, physically removing themselves from castles like these and retreating to villages where a democratic form of government lived on for ages unaffected by the withering regal class.

"Yet in my day, unwittingly, our democracy would elect a potential tyrant, William Duncan, a man who—while initially a strong, powerful and compassionate leader—would eventually lead us into ruin in wake of the death storm.

"To be fair, a lot of it was out of his hands. Any government coming up against an environmental catastrophe of this magnitude would be in over its head, but Duncan internalized it, and—perhaps through anger or some form of vengeance—found a scapegoat in the trickling groups of Bies that had sought food and shelter in our villages."

"Despite blowback from the majority of our people, Duncan enacted legislation which permitted slaying of the beasts, and a volatile right-wing minority group took this as carte blanche to initiate some of the worst conditions we've seen for animals in our history.

"As an admitted 'radical' left faction, we accepted defeat and mobilized from villages at a time when the death storm was ramping up to full force and the chances of survival outside the villages was dire at best. Yet we found salvation against the storm in the form of a drug: the Marzanna 'lief.

"The drug had several beneficial side effects when paired with the storm, the least of which being what you'd refer to on your planet as 'hallucination.' As we investigated further, we found these visions were more real than we first assumed. It became evident that this drug was a gateway. Not only to our own minds, but to the many others stretching beyond our planet, reaching far, far into the various worlds of the universe."

While Nivea spoke, the cylindrical column next to us slowly opened, revealing the white dusty air of the storm, which spilled out into the room.

"Beyond this—and of more immediate benefit—the 'lief had a property that allowed our bodies to survive for much longer periods within the storm. And that was just what we needed to sustain a liveable life outside the villages in—ironically enough—our former medieval homes.

"That is how the Breaus formed. We are a small people that have outlived most of our planet that has died in the storm."

Nivea paused, allowing me to take it all in. It was beginning to make sense.

"What happened to the village?" I said.

"The village is no more. The people there did not survive the death storm; they looked on us as treasonous and rejected us outright. They foolishly died in their own ignorance, despite our attempts to help."

"But Earth…" I said, "…how do you know so much about Earth?"

"In short, the storm. You see this column which allows for the channel of storm air? Well, when paired with Marzanna 'lief, *this* is what we use to learn about the universe. There are many others out there that don't respond, but many that do. They have recognized their own potential for communication through the storm."

"Planets like yours—Earth—have not yet recognized us as valid. Those that have responded to us have provided great information, but when they've gone to their leaders, friends, and family they've been, at worst, looked upon as insane. We have seen people confined to psychiatric institutions.

"Yet, we haven't given up hope. As Breaus, we remain focused and dedicated to reaching out and discovering worlds through the storm. We relish the information we uncover in the universe as paramount to our ability to someday survive the storm."

I stared at the column of storm air. If everything Nivea said was true, then the universe really must be a big place.

"Indeed, it is," Nivea said, reading my thoughts. "Incredibly so. And you're about to see just how big it is."

The wooden door opened to reveal another Breau bringing the graying Marzanna 'liefs on a platter, along with a fire striker, cloth and flint. The Breau took our food plates and left the room. Nivea began the process of rolling the leaves into the flint. My eyes watered in anticipation. Voices— other Breaus—could be heard echoing in the castle hallways.

I became hypervigilant to the sights sounds of the sounds around the castle in anticipation of smoking the 'lief. For the first time in my life, I felt part of something big. Like I was witnessing true magic, something that could really change the world.

A blaze of light and heat exploded into the air as Nivea hit the fire striker and lit the joint. She held it out to me, and I took several puffs. The warmth began to fill my body.

"Now Aaron Myles, I know you're excited for this," she said, taking my hand in hers, "but please remain grounded. I'll be here to help you through this, but you're about to experience something relatively few have, and perhaps few will. You must remain grounded; it is important not to let go completely. Although sometimes that may be tempting, we can't let you go."

I nodded. My eyes must have been growing feverishly wide in anticipation of the sensation.

"*Now,*" she spoke to me through the storm, "*please lie back. Feel your head cool gently against the airstream of the storm. Close your eyes. Breath deeply with me. You can hear me. The sounds of the castle will start to...drift, let...body... recede...*"

...distance, time, temperature, constructs, all constructs, floating far above Marzanna, through space, so many avenues, so many directions. Each action could lead a different way. Each road bears fruits to another world...

...Earth...somewhere, it is visible, still ticking along ravished with the storm. My family, further back in time, my father, I can feel him with me, somehow, my presence exists with him, all those adventurous trips into the wilderness, magic just like this, some kind of otherworldly dial leading in every imaginable direction...

...There are many Earths...many different versions, each with slight variations, the universe is so large. Look, there, is a planet like a flower in a multifaceted garden with a wild jungle where we met Maya and there are millions of different versions of it like reflections in a mirror...

...And Ondas where Onesia saved us, and other planets varying in habitability, vibrance and life, what other worlds exist out there? It's beautiful...

...And minds too, like this small planet Aquila with creatures defending against the storm foolishly with metal barriers..."they are protecting from the storm, my king," says a wild-eyed, short elvish girl with fire and passion in her eyes for her ruler with a face of great concern for his people—I can feel their thoughts as if my own, as if I am them...but they will die at the hand of the storm, I can see that is a highly likely outcome...

...And Marzanna, I can see now, it is a planet much like Earth, but it has been destroyed by the storm. The storm is at nearly its highest intensity, many lives have been lost...

...And the Bies...I can hear them, I can hear their anger, their hatred of humanity, their disgust and their "kill them all! Kill the humans! They killed our loved ones! Destroy them completely! They must face the same fate they thrust on us for the storm! All except the bearded man! They must die!"

...But the 'bearded man'...what about this? Nivea? He was a friend to the Bies, yes. I can see in their minds. He helped them through the storm. He— ("the effect wears off from one area if you stay too long," Nivea tells me)—he is...Hylotz. Terral B. Hylotz...Yes, Nivea, he was welcomed here by the Breaus during their

crucial time…he was compassionate with the Bies and helped them live…he was celebrated as a Breau and— ("the poignant effect only lasts so long,") *—he was celebrated…before…he—* ("the effect is disappearing…")

V

I sat up, my mind racing.

"Take a deep breath," Nivea said. "You will get over it."

"I've got so many questions," I said, panting deeply. "Hylotz, the bearded man. He…we saw him too. That is how we received the ship…"

"Terral, Breau Hylotz," Nivea said. "Yes, he was with us. He was the one who encouraged smoking the Marzanna 'lief. He was crucial to our survival. We have the highest regard for him before he…disappeared. Are you saying he is associated with this…ship?"

"Yes," I said.

Nivea paused, thinking. I could hear her thoughts echoing in my mind: *"he spoke of a ship, his mind was vivid with images of other worlds, could he have been literally travelling to them all this time?"*

"Yes," I said. "It must be!"

"This ship…we need to find it."

"Yes."

"No, Aaron Myles. Do you realize, how incredible this discovery is? However it's possible that this ship exists, it's now an essential part of our continued survival, and would be indispensable to our growth in the universe!"

"Yes," I shouted, standing up and walking around. The door opened to reveal Fathom and Cabell.

"Fathom! Cabell!" I cried in excitement. I ran up and hugged them both. "Marzanna 'lief, it's fascinating. The universe is massive, there is hope for saving Earth, and it looks like Terral Hylotz has been whirling around the universe and smoking up in the ship!"

They stared at me blankly.

"Don't you see? It's this 'lief! It lets you see beyond the limits of your perspective. You can unite with the minds of others in planets far away. Just like the ship has taken us here, somehow this 'lief can do the same thing with our minds."

"Aaron Myles, you should calm down," Nivea said. "Maybe we gave you too much of the 'lief."

"No, you don't understand. I'm virtually indestructible with this." I took a spliff lying on the outstanding platter and inhaled a huge puff before Nivea took it from me.

"Myles," she said.

"No, It's Okay. It's powerful, so poignant, I can see through the storm. I can see beyond the confines of these walls. Even now, I can see many Earths, many worlds, like ours, which thrive, and maybe someday we can meet them. And this 'lief, it *protects* from the storm. Don't you see! It will allow you to *exist* through the storm."

"Yes Myles," Cabell said, "We know that, but..."

"No, You don't. You see, I can actually *ride* the storm." I ran over to the ledge of the castle despite the yelling of the others. I suddenly felt I understood my father. He'd always been so much freer than I, ready for adventure at any whim. I'd always been the one to hold back. The truth is that no number of drugs could bring back the exhilarating rush of taking the world on, facing life instead of trying to stay safe along the sidelines.

There was something more to this feeling than the others knew, something much bigger, and maybe, somehow, I could make them see. I stood on the ledge despite their screams. They ran to me but, too late. I let myself fall back, like a scuba diver into the sea of storm clouds below.

Foolishly, they would cry as the Breaus stated, "he is no longer with us."

They'd return to the ship, but not without the valuable knowledge they now had: the Marzanna 'lief would allow its smoker to transcend the storm and survive within it for longer periods of time.

In a short time, they came to realize the ship operated in a similar way to transcendence, taking the pilot to destinations of his or her deep desires.

They learned more of the war between the Bies and the village that slaughtered them. They learned how Hylotz and the Bies were to blame for stealing food, and how Duncan had waged a war on the Bies who had mutated into vicious killing machines.

Could the Bies be quelled? The question was raised, and Fathom declared he was beginning to be able to communicate with them, although they were not receptive.

Yet Fathom was insistent that he could reach them, if only he could travel to Kostroma, moon of Marzanna. He was insistent that the Bies must be quelled, that is, after all, what we're all here for; the prolonged continuation of the many; the chance for something better for everyone.

They'd find the ship, surviving the mutated Bies, and they'd continue the journey, hopefully saving the Bies and travelling across the storm, with Fathom piloting, to... Kostroma.

FATHOM PILOTS

As the coldness melted away, my body became wet. I shivered. There was a crack, and then ice that surrounded me broke into a flood of water that splashed onto the floor. I gasped for air.

Nearby, a similar splash could be heard, and a woman with a clipboard dressed in a white nurse outfit walked up next to me, her brown hair drenched in water, her brow furrowed, her dark brown eyes were displeased with me.

"You?" she spat.

"I? uh…"

She sighed. "Alright, lets head down to the morgue, if we must."

The room was full of file cabinets for keeping medical records. She opened a door and led the way down a long staircase. It must have gone on for a good fifteen minutes, before she opened another door to a dark room lit by a shoddy florescent flicker. The far wall had cases built into the wall. They were for keeping corpses.

"I'm surprised you're even still around," she said. "I guess we need all the help we can get, these days."

I shrugged.

"We need you to finish up as quickly as possible. I know this is your first time, but there will be many more bodies soon enough."

"More bodies?"

"Shhh," she said, placing her index finger over my mouth. "Just get to work. The subject was mutilated, torn limb to limb by some awful beast. Just clean up the mess, okay? Do you think you can handle that?" She pointed at the wall where one of the cases was pulled out, revealing a sheet over a corpse. I gasped.

"What is going on here?" I said, turning back towards the nurse, but she was gone. The door we'd come from was closed. I jiggled the knob. Locked.

I walked over to the corpse. The sheet completely covered the body. There was a mop resting in the corner of the wall. It hit me. Was this Myles? A shiver ran through me.

I knew what I had to do. I had to remove the sheet. I took a deep breath and pulled it down and…nothing. There was nothing there, but an eerie chill rose through the room.

The cold grew and grew, and the brick walls began to crack. Slowly at first, then much faster, big chunks of brick were falling apart, and the cold was unbearable. The ceiling began to fall apart, and the walls and—I had to jump onto the gurney which was the only solid item left. I pulled the sheet over me, shivering, covering my entire head.

When the cold finally eased off a little, I pulled the sheet down just enough to peak outside. There was no gurney now. I was hovering in darkness. Stars were above, below, and all around. I was in space. A vacuum was pulling me in many directions, yet I remained intact. The sheet had dissipated.

"Thank goodness you're still here," a man said from behind me. I turned around to see he was bald, in a white lab coat. He also had a clipboard and was staring at me. "We had doubts you'd make it this far, but your talents now can be exercised. You still have a long way to go."

"My talents?"

"Yes. Many lives are at stake. Many are counting on you to step up and help end the suffering." The man pointed behind me. Again, I turned around. Behind me, there were moose, rabbits and many other animals staring expectantly.

I turned back to the man, but he had changed. He had a beard. He was Hylotz. Still in a lab coat.

"What's this all about?" I demanded.

"It's too cold," Hylotz said, with a smile. He raised a joint to his lips and took a puff. "Too cold to tell how it'll turn out. Help them. They will help you."

He took another puff, then handed me his joint. In the spirit of the moment, I shrugged and took a puff. As the warmth glowed inside me. That familiar peace returned.

"You'll be pulled in many directions," Hylotz said. "Help them all. Someday…" his voice trailed off. The storm was approaching from far off in space. It was encircling from all sides, closing in, and Hylotz had faded away. I braced myself as the coldness grew once again.

KOSTROMA | WITH: FATHOM

We gently landed in the snow, a puff of which flew up over the windshield temporarily obstructing our view. Not that it would matter; the storm was raging on just as bad as on Marzanna.

My mind was in disarray with the events of the last hour. Seeing Myles jump was traumatic. On Earth, you'd spend hours of counselling and mental health treatment, and the post-traumatic stress would last for decades. This wasn't Earth.

"I don't know about this," I said.

"The tragedy we've faced from the Bies has been horrible," Nivea said.

"We've lost many Breaus to these beasts. If there is any chance you can stop them, Jacob Fathom, we need you to try."

Nivea opened a brown sack she had taken with her and pulled out the spliffs, one for each of us. She struck a fire and lit them. We each took one.

"And what if it doesn't work? What then?" Cabell looked concerned.

"It will work. If it doesn't, we've got the ship. We can try to find another solution.

"Very well," I lit the joint and inhaled. The warmth flowed through my body and I began to hear the echoes of voices in the distance—the Bies—revelling in anger and disdain for humanity.

"They hate us," I said.

"Yes but, can you talk to them?" said Nivea.

"I...can't. They are too far away. My voice would just be an afterthought to them.

"Then you'll have to go out," said Nivea.

"You can't be serious."

"What other options do we have? Stay at a distance from them but try to reach one. We'll come with you."

"This is incredibly dangerous," said Cabell.

"We have to try," I said with a shrug.

We opened the doors to the ship and slowly made our way out into the storm. Upon entering the strong, powdery snow, the Bies' thoughts became amplified tenfold.

"The humans are here. I can smell them."

"They're coming to kill us."

"Stop them!"

I turned to retreat to the ship.

"Wait," Nivea said. "Try to reach them."

I paused and called out through the storm to them. *"We come in peace. We just want to help."*

"Anything?" Nivea asked.

I was silent for a moment, then the responses came.

"How can you help, foolish human. You caused this disaster, you killed many of us. You caused our anger!"

"We did not cause it. We are against it," I thought. *"The people who caused it are no longer with us. We seek only peace. We want to help you survive the storm."*

"You are the cause of it! How could you help?"

Suddenly a movement came from my left, a beast jumped from the snow and attacked, biting my leg and causing me to scream out in pain. I fell to the ground. Nivea and Cabell kneeled to my side, but we were surrounded by Bies ready to attack."

"*No,*" I screamed, through thought. "*We mean to help. We are suffering from the storm like you. We can help!*"

"*You are the storm. You are the anger. And now you will die as a result like you have done to all our brothers and sisters!*"

The pain was immense. I knew I would pass out soon from lack of blood.

"*We are vulnerable to you now. You can kill us. Just know that we know of the bearded man, Hylotz, we know that he helped you. He was human like us. He helped you live through the storm. Do you remember him?*"

Silence.

"*He helped you, and we seek to help you too. We know how to help you survive the storm; we want to give you a solution.*"

Reading their minds, I could feel them remembering their history, the history of Kostroma before the storm came, when they were once a great race living in a warm climate. The planet had been full of life, before the storm came and a bridge connected both Kostroma and Marzanna, exposing them to the village that massacred them.

"*We know of the tragedy of the village; the people of the village are all dead now. We are against their violence and always have been. We have a way to deal with the storm. Maybe someday Kostroma can be the world it once was, and you can survive to see it.*"

I grabbed the brown sack from Nivea and opened it for the Bies. They roared a horrible roar and in a dying pain and fear, I lost consciousness.

"*Hey man, sorry about that whole plan to kill you thing. We greatly appreciate your offering.*"

I opened my eyes to find I was in the ship. Nivea and Cabell had tied a cloth around my leg, and I was stable.

"*It's just that, you can't really expect to massacre so many of us without consequences, right? Anyway man, you dudes are alright. Like really alright. And this plant, this, what do you call it? 'lief? This is the shit, for real man. Some real good stuff. We haven't tasted anything this good since the bearded man was around, the 'Hylotz' dude you speak of. Capital guy, best of kinds. Absolute legend, himself.*"

"We gave them the Marzanna 'lief and lit it for them," said Cabell. "They seem to like it."

"They certainly do," I said. "They are quite mellow."

"*Look man, you guys are cool. We will pass on word of you to our brothers and sisters. You want us to lay off the viciousness, just keep producing this shit and we shouldn't have any problem convincing the others.*"

"What are they saying?" Nivea asked.

"They want us to manufacture Marzanna 'lief for them."

"Well that's definitely doable," she replied. "I can reach out to the Breaus through the storm. We can make it happen."

"We can make that happen," I said to the Bies. *"Absolutely."*

"Right on. We'll go now and let you get on about your business. Please prepare more of this stuff as soon as possible. Best of luck on your travels."

"Thanks," I said to them.

"Well, I think that actually worked," I said.

"Yes," Nivea said. "This ship is already working wonders."

"This is great," Cabell said. "But is there any way we can actually return to Earth? This 'lief could be really helpful to humans."

"Well, we can try to do that," Nivea said. "But the ship, despite its amazing power, doesn't appear to be a perfect science. We're lucky it even brought us here, to Kostroma. How did you make this happen, Fathom?"

"Like you said, Nivea. How you focus through the storm when you reach through it: with intention. And, to be honest, the drugs seemed to help. I focused my mind on Kostroma, but beyond that, I just felt the utmost need to help. Like, strongly, just like Terral Hylotz, I wanted to help the Bies. I didn't want them to continue to suffer the fate that had befallen them, I didn't want them to die in the storm, and I didn't want them to kill others. And like Myles said, in a way, I wished for this with my all. All of my emotions, all of my thoughts, all were centered around this one goal."

"Well," said Nivea, "maybe we could try to reach out to my friends in Aras as well. They are quite far away in the universe, but they are the strongest most advanced civilization we know of. They have lots of ideas that haven been effective for helping to mitigate the damage of the death storm, and they sure could provide some suggestions for Earth. While they have left their planet, they have not been able to navigate beyond their galaxy. Meeting them would be a positive step for the Universal Storm Alliance, and we could really take great strides towards ending this storm for good. I'd really like to pilot. I'd like to try to reach Aras."

"Well, lets go," I said.

Nivea took the wheel and the ship lifted off the snowy surface of Kostroma, bringing us on a new journey.

NIVEA PILOTS

I swam through a surreal universe, through space, in search of Saranyu. The storm began to fade, as did space, and I was left sitting on a rocky mountainside. Above, ships fought shooting lasers and missiles with ferocious accuracy. Mechanical robots attacked each other on rocky terrain that continued into the distance and met another planet on the horizon. A small moon was visible in space.

In front of me there was a fallen robot. I could feel Saranyu's presence, but I could not see her. An orb of light gently fell from the storm above. When it reached the ground, it expanded into vision of my old friend. His beard had grayed more with the storm. Terral Breau Hylotz.

"Nivea, some day you may help stop suffering of our world," he says. "But the path will be long and fraught with conflict, with many minds to sway. Remember to never give up on your friends. There is one race that is very dangerous—"

I wish I could have continued to hear him, but his voice trailed off as the storm swept in returning the familiar cold.

ARAS | WITH: NIVEA

I

The ship spun like a whirlwind as I wrestled to regain control. After a few spins, I adjusted. We exited the storm, and I was struck immediately by the beauty of the sunrise. A blazing pink sun partnered by two smaller moons brightened the sky, painting a beautiful landscape that some cultures might suggest was akin to divine.

Steadying the wheel remained a challenge. It was shaking beyond control.

We traversed a deep blue mountainous terrain with bright red vegetation that I recalled from my storm talks with Saranyu. The bushes swayed back and forth in waves with the wind. We had made it Aras. So, it was true. The ship really could connect you where you desired.

This thought alone was warming, but I was concerned with our ability to make it to Aras's city, as we were essentially flying blind.

"Look over there," Fathom said, pointing. It was another cloud of the storm spiralling up into space. I realized our potential to reach Saranyu was, quite literally, through the storm clouds.

"I'm going to try to land," I said.

"Be careful not to drive into the storm, it may drive us back across space," Cabell said.

The ship shook as we brought it down on a cliffside, close to the storm.

"Well, that's a great landing," Fathom said. "You're the first of us to not crash the ship. Impressive."

"Thank you," I said. "I've had a lot of mental practice with Saranyu. She has taught me flying techniques through the storm. Let us head to it, maybe we can reach her."

We stepped out onto the blue, alien mountain. The clay-like soil squished against our feet. The red trees swayed in a light wind. A nearby pond glowed pink in reflection of the sky above. We finally reached a summit that touched upon the storm. Fathom opened the box with the Marzanna 'lief and lit it for me. I smoked it, then walked into the storm.

My mind drifted up into space, across the universe, then back to Aras, where I could feel Saranyu's presence.

"Are you there? Saranyu?"

I waited for some time, before her image appeared in front of me.

"I'm here. And you are too, I feel it. You are on Aras?"

"Yes, I'm here, with friends."

"How is it possible?"

"We have a ship. We don't know where it came from, but it lets us travel through the storm."

"We are searching for your location with our systems now. Yes, if you can proceed northwest, you will reach us."

"Great. We will head back to the ship and begin—"

My speech was disconnected by a jolting of my body, I was being pulled from the storm.

"What is happening?" I cried. Fathom looked horrified as he stared up above.

"We've got to get back to the ship." He shouted, as he ran back down the mountainside. "Another ship is shooting at us!"

II

I followed behind Cabell and Fathom, running as fast as I could. We retraced the steps that had brought us here.

"What happened?" I yelled.

"Some ship from above was shooting down at us. It looks like it's land-ing."

When we finally reached our ship, another ship appeared in front of us, heading directly towards us. It looked identical to our own.

"Get in!" Cabell cried, and as we closed the door laser fire hit us, caus-ing us to sway left and right.

"This is crazy!" I shouted.

"Well, at least we know this ship is durable," Cabell said.

"Nivea, you're the one with the best knowledge of how to fly this thing," said Fathom. "Get us out of here!"

I wrapped my hands around the driving wheel and our ship jumped to life. We lifted off the ground but were now face to face with the ship that had attacked us.

"Look out!" Cabell yelled. As we changed direction, the other ship did as well. Both ships collided, but our attacker was sent it into a downward spiral and crashed into the ground.

"Go, go, go!" Fathom cried.

I brought us back up into the air.

"Fathom do you have a compass?" I asked.

"Yes."

"Get it out. We need to be going northwest."

"Turn to the left," Fathom said. "Just a bit more. Yes, that's it!"

We continued our flight, unhindered by the ship that had attacked us earlier. It wasn't following. We did not come up on anymore instances of the storm.

We flew for a good half hour before purple lights sparkled in our eyes. It was the sun reflecting off glass—the city of Aras. Spaceships wove in and out of great metallic glass buildings, rays of light bouncing off their glass in bright blotches, a flurry of spaceships bustling with their daily business.

I recalled that this would be a busy workday for Aras. They were a highly advanced civilization, highly focused on space exploration. Like many advanced civilizations, they were set on exploring the universe and finding a solution to the death storm. They had already expanded beyond their planet and into their galaxy.

The sky was filled with the roars of spaceships as they blazed through the sky. The sound frightened me more than it would if it were an actual threat.

"Well this certainly is a pleasure, compared to what we've encountered up until now," Cabell said. "Perhaps we could even find a reasonable wash-room in this place."

"What the hell is it with you and washrooms, Cabell?" Fathom asked. "Why don't you just go anywhere? That's what we've all been doing."

Cabell shot a frown at Fathom. "Paruresis is no joke, Fathom. Not all of us can just go anywhere. I'm just seeking…optimal conditions. And this place looks like it would have something."

"The Aras are highly advanced," I said, "and they have technology that counters the storm. However, it is not an infallible technology, and it is growing wearier as the storm grows in intensity."

We walked along the landing pad and entered an open space which consisted of tall building with ports for ships extending high up and down. An elevator took us up to a new level. We explored the area.

We were on a sidewalk of sorts, with ships flying back and forth along the street, which was essentially just a space between buildings; there was a pinkish haze. People walked beside us, dressed in very plain navy-blue clothes, a type of uniformed wear. There were shops lining the block we were on. The buildings rose high up into the sky.

There was a café with drinks displayed on a sign. We stepped in and made our way to the bar, sitting next to two others speaking in an alien language.

The Aras were a soft-spoken species, their language had an absence of harsher consonants, but there was much more subtlety of expression in facial recognition and body language.

A bartender approached and spoke to us in their alien language. Realizing our inability to understand him, he provided us with three drinks and proceeded to step into the back, speaking on what apparently was an electronic device attached to his ear.

"What is this?" Fathom said, swirling his brownish-yellow drink around in his glass.

"A turbo-brew," I replied. "This is a drink many Aras use to get them through the day. It is a mixture of caffeine, alcohol, and a multivitamin. Some people swear by it to the near complete absence of meals."

"How do you know all this?" Fathom asked.

"I have been in contact with this society for quite a while through the storm. I never thought I'd get to meet them, though, so as you can imagine, this is an immensely moving experience."

"I'm sold," Fathom said, taking a sip of the drink. "Ugh, it's disgusting!"

"Wait a moment," I said, "It's adjusting to your taste buds."

I watched as Fathom's expression turned from disgust to awe. Then, Saranyu appeared. Her narrow eyes welcomed us. Her dusky skin was an expression of her many years as a fighter pilot for Aras Defense, and her dark blue uniform matched her pupils beautifully. She handed us each electronic translator which we attached to our ears.

"It is good to finally meet you, Nivea," she said. We pressed our palms up against each other's and stared diligently into each other's eyes for a moment, a greeting I understood was customary for them.

"And this is your crew of discoverers?" she asked, smiling upon Fathom and Cabell.

"Yes, this is the crew. They are loving the turbo-brew."

"Terrific," she said, laughing.

"One thing I should mention, Saranyu, is that we were attacked by a ship on our way here. We have no idea where it came from. It did not appear to be of Aras."

"That's strange. I've been at Aras Defense Command all day; we didn't see anything on the radar. Well, we'll look into it, but for now, lets head up to my office and discuss this amazing discovery!"

III

The sun flitted through the window and as we road up an elevator. I could see ocean rigs in the distance.

The view of the horizon from Saranyu's office was breathtaking, and the walls were posted with planets and star maps.

"After Nivea advised us of it when you were all still on Marzanna, we have been reaching out to the Universal Storm Alliance, and we're unsure as to where this ship has come from," said Saranyu. "Certainly, it is outside of our galaxy which we have near fully mapped. We don't have the technology to travel beyond our galaxy yet.

"Initially we thought it could be Delexeeaon technology, but we have reached out to them, and they have never heard of such a thing. They are only able to perform smaller galactic stints, like ourselves. So, crew, what do we know about this ship?"

"Not a lot," said Cabell. "It can travel great distances in space, and it has brought us to some pretty crazy places, thus far."

"Do you have any idea where it came from?" asked Saranyu, walking over to the window to observe the ship from her office. The ship was now protected by Aras security.

"They have no idea," said Nivea. "It appears to have been piloted by Terral Breau Hylotz who, as you know, introduced us to the Marzanna 'lief. If that's the case, there is a whole other layer to this old man that we were not aware of.

"Eventually, the ship ended up on Earth, an alpha classed planet quite far from us, and that's where this crew found it. Terral never mentioned a ship to us."

Saranyu walked over to the window and looked out at the ship. "It's really a beautiful construction," she said, "How does it work?"

"That's another curious thing," said Nivea. "It appears to operate according to the pilot's own inner motivations. It seems to connect to your pulse, and by some alien technology, it appears to be linking the pilot to a uniquely suited location somewhere in the universe. My intention, for example, was to pilot it here, and it seemed to resonate with that intention and brought us here."

Saranyu stood idle, staring at the ship. "If that's true, this ship is powerful beyond our knowledge. Could this mean there is an alien species beyond our level of competence out there?"

"Yes. There must be. With that, maybe there is hope for defeating the death storm."

"This is incredible," Saranyu said. "I must pilot it."

"Certainly," I said. "However, the crew is now trying to return to Earth. We are hoping to make first contact with earth and help them cope with the storm, with the Marzanna 'lief." I pulled a Marzanna 'lief out of my brown bag. I laid one on the table for Saranyu.

"Ah yes, the Marzanna 'lief," Saranyu said. "This will alleviate the struggle Aras has when reaching out across the storm. The drug we use for transcendence has its limitations. It will be most helpful to us. Thank you."

"It's no problem," I said. "Now, lets head down to the ship."

The ship was protected by a small army of Arasans with big laser-guns. Saranyu whispered to a few. There was a congregation of people gathered outside looking upon the ship with the utmost curiosity.

"There's quite a stir about the potential of the ship, but we're keeping its origins under wraps," said Saranyu. "Not for much longer, though. They're about to see what all the fuss is about."

We walked over to the ship and slipped in. A shrill alarm blared through the air. I covered both ears, startled. A green laser blasted right next to me, causing a nearby cargo box to explode.

"Get in the ship," Saranyu yelled.

I jumped in the ship and we looked out through the window to see a fleet of ships, just like our own, soaring through the air.

"Where did they come from?" Fathom cried.

"They're just like the ship that attacked us when we first arrived on Aras," Cabell said.

Another explosion near the ship.

"Aras Defense, come in," said Saranyu. "We've got a whole fleet attacking us!"

We could hear the response from Aras Defense coming through Saranyu's radio. "We see them. We're overwhelmed. No idea where they came from. They are destroying the city. Pilot the ship and get out of here if you can. We'll deal with them. We have our fleet mobilizing."

Saranyu initiated the ship immediately and we were air bound. A ship came up on our tail and we dodged a laser shot.

"I have no idea how to access the weapons, if there even are any," cried Saranyu. "We're going to have to stick to evasion tactics."

Saranyu rolled the ship to avoid another laser shot, but more ships were appearing through the window following us. They seemed fixated on us and our ship. They were not attacking the city and they were right on our tail.

The Aras were shooting at them from below, but they were undeterred. I saw one ship to our right side take a hit, but it glowed a bright green with some sort of force field technology.

"Hold tight," Saranyu yelled, and she dove down between the high skyscrapers of the city, leading us directly into citizen traffic.

We came up on several other citizen ships heading directly for us. She evaded each one, but some of the attacking ships were not as lucky. One smashed head-on into an oncoming citizen ship and they both fell into the ground below.

"Damnit, they're not letting up!" I screamed, as a laser shot flew across the side of my field of vision. This was way more intense than I had ever expected in the stories Saranyu had told me, and I instantly regretted my decision to come to Aras.

Saranyu turned us around a sharp corner, and we came up quick on the glass of a building. I thought we were about to crash into, but we narrowly avoided it and managed to pull away.

"Let's see how fast this thing can go," Saranyu said.

We held on to the side of the ship as we ascended at a nauseating pace. Glancing below, I could not immediately see the ships. I was looking for the storm, but it was not nearby. Then I saw her plan.

She pulled high up into the sky, the pinkish sky gave way to darker hues, and the cabin became colder as we entered space.

There were no ships visible below, but Saranyu kept up the jostling pace. We were going faster than I ever imagined possible. After mere minutes, we were completely free of the planet. The ships did not appear to have followed. They'd dropped completely off our radar.

IV

"Who the hell were they?" said Cabell.

"They're after the ship," Saranyu said. "No doubt in my mind. Looks like there's a price to pay for this asset that's landed in your lap."

"Believe me, we've already paid dearly for this ship. I'd gladly give it to them if it actually returned us to Earth."

"What now?" I asked.

"There's somewhere we can hide out for now. It's a research station behind Aris, Aras's first moon. It's a station where they study the storm. We should be good there for a while, and we can reach out to Aras as my local communicator won't reach them now."

We travelled through space for about a half hour before we came upon a circular object slowly rotating in space. It looked like a giant metal plate, but as we got closer, I could see windows along the edge.

We slowly glided over the top of the space station, and Saranyu's communicator flashed.

"State your Aras credentials," a voice boomed from the communicator.

"Saranyu Gem, Aras Defense Pilot, Officer Number 6137."

"We have no record of your planned visit. What is the situation?"

"Aras is being attacked by an unknown enemy. Defenseless, we have escaped the onslaught, but we fear Aras may be at serious risk. We request to enter the station and contact Aras."

A giant metal door opened to a blue forcefield. Once we reached the inside, the ship landed softly. We opened the doors and stepped out. It was a giant cargo bay with sturdy metallic walls. Ships and iron crates littered the area. It was silent for a few moments. Then a door opened along the back wall.

"Please enter the elevator and choose 'S' floor," beamed a voice through speakers.

We entered a circular glass elevator. We descended into a gigantic open room with big glass windows for walls. The windows provided an exceptional view of space, and the nebulous storm mass in the distance. There were trees growing throughout. They were scrutinized by men and women in white lab coats. When we stepped into the room, all attention fell entirely upon us. A man with short black hair and glasses approached us.

"Hello, I'm Mandell. We are contacting Aras now. Please, follow me to the command centre and we'll try to straighten this out."

We followed him.

"This is quite a station," I said. "What are you studying?"

"We are studying samples of the storm and its interaction with various flora. Aras has been lucky to avoid the storm, for the most part, at least compared to other planets in Archived Thought, however given Aras's orbit and the growing nature of the storm, it's only a matter of time before the planet is fully consumed."

"Are these trees resilient to the storm?"

"No. Even though we have altered their growth to strengthen them, they are still susceptible to consumption by the storm, and eventually will deteriorate."

"If you are studying the relationship between flora and the storm, why have you not placed the station in closer proximity to the storm?"

"The storm is near Aris; however, we can not place the station within the storm as it will break down the composition of the station within a relatively short time."

Cabell paused in contemplation.

"We have some samples that may be of interest to you. In our travels, we found a curious planet, 'Atavika,' which seemed especially resilient to the storm. We met a man, who provided us with samples of the Atavika 'lief, a special plant that grew there. It deflected the storm and shows great promise for future development. We have the samples in our ship."

"We'd be most interested in this," Mandell said.

"And the Marzanna 'lief, as well," I said. "The 'lief best known for adjusting one to the storm and allowing one to transcend it. We have samples of this you may study as well."

"This is excellent," Mandell said.

We reached an office area with many computers, and a communication link to Aras. A blue-uniformed Aras officer looked up and spoke directly to Mandell, with a look of panic.

"It's bad," he said. "The city has lost many turrets and defense ships. The only conciliation is that the attacking fleet has left, but unfortunately it looks like they have pursued the ship with our friends. We may be in danger."

"They want the ship," said Saranyu. "We are a peaceful race. We do not wish battle with them. However, we can not sacrifice the ship without stranding our friends here on Aras, when they wish to return to their homes. Perhaps we can lead them out of Aras, into the storm? It's dangerous, but we must protect Aras. Evasion has been our only ally thus far; their technology is advanced. They are definitely not of our world."

"Agreed," I said. "We've seen their ships; they are identical to ours. Perhaps we can lead them into the storm and escape them for good."

"The ship really appears to bring you somewhere unique to your own desires," said Cabell. "With that type of navigation system, it's probably a safe bet that we can completely throw them off by entering the storm."

"Agreed," said Saranyu. "Let's do it."

"Wait," said the officer at the command station.

"What is it?" Mandell said.

"Sir, we've got a situation here. An anomaly is coming up on the radar. I can't make out what it is, but there are numerous heat signals...right in front of the station?"

We turned and stared out the window. It was eerily quiet and still. I stared into the stars, then I saw something that made my blood run cold. The light from one of the stars in the distance seemed to move slightly.

We had no chance to react as a series of shots fired directly at the window, deflected by a blue forcefield around the station. A couple dozen ships appeared, striking us with an immense laser power.

"I'm guessing they're not willing to chat," Saranyu said.

"There's no telling how long the forcefield will last," said Mandell, as we all ran to the elevator. "This station isn't built for such an assault!"

"Let's get out of here and drive them away," Saranyu said.

The station shook as we rose in the elevator, away from the constant laser-fire of the ships. We made it to the cargo bay and beelined to the ship.

We passed 'lief samples to Mandell, when the metal door shook.

"They made it through the forcefield." Cried Mandell."

"We've got to go. Now." shouted Saranyu.

Mandell ran back to the elevator and Saranyu took the wheel as the cargo bay broke open with laser fire. It fell completely apart. Our ship burst through the rubble and shot out into space, hotly pursued by the fleet.

V

Saranyu's maneuvering of the ship was exceptional, but we couldn't outrun them forever. As she approached Aris, the storm appeared with Aras visible in the distance. We came up on it fast.

"They're gaining on us," Cabell yelled.

"We're almost at the storm," Saranyu said.

As we closed in on the storm, Saranyu began to spin the ship to avoid the fire, but one of the enemies was on our tail.

"Hold tight!"

As we held on to the sides of the ship, she took a sharp left, but hit something. Another ship was right next to us.

The storm closed in fast.

"Look out," Fathom yelled, as the new ship tried to knock us off course.

"I can't turn," Saranyu shouted.

We hit the storm.

SARANYU PILOTS

The cold storm faded leaving me with a warm memory of first days of training. We were so young when they first put us through the academy. The lockers of the old school scrolled through my mind, leading to the hangers, where we spent a good many days learning defensive flight training.

I'd excelled in the computer simulations, and many of the boys had grown quite jealous, some even attempting to thwart my progress. But I couldn't be stopped.

Was this my first day of actual flight training? In the hanger, my instructor sat in the pilot's seat of the first ship I'd ever piloted. As I walked up to him, he jumped out of the ship and removed his helmet. I expected his calm but stern face with that tangly black hair, but instead I was faced with an older man with a graying beard. The man smiled at me. How strange. Who was this man?

"No matter what, Saranyu, in the end, remember to follow your heart," the man said, and he threw his hand out for me. I reached out and he helped pull me up into the ship. Together, we flew off into the turbulence of the storm.

SULLAMECHA | WITH: SARANYA

I

We slowed rotation from the spin as we departed the intergalactic portal of the storm. The ship thrust through space at a rapid pace. Such a clever ship; the steering was highly responsive, allowing it pull off evasive maneuvers I'd never thought possible.

An orange and red hued planet grew before us, glowing an intense neon. It brought to mind the brilliant flash of the flares we had shot when surrendering during a training exercise. A sun in the distance was setting it aglow. I slowly brought the ship into orbit, and we approached the atmosphere carefully.

I'd been to many planets within our solar system, but this was unlike any I'd visited before. As we dropped closer to the surface, the bright orange glow dampened to reveal a dusty beige that permeated the entire surface with a familiar undulation of a desert.

"It worked," said Cabell. "Looks like we've lost them."

"Yes, but this planet doesn't look especially hospitable," Nivea said.

She was right. As we descended, it was clear that this was a hot, dry desert planet with many sand dunes. I recalled my years of training as a pilot on Aris. The military freight hauler that brought us there was slow, but Aris's gray deserts were a sandbox of fun.

We cruised over the dunes for a good twenty minutes without finding any signs of life, but we did find a curious anomaly: a bump in the sand, with an opening. We decided to land the ship and investigate. I pulled back on the wheel to reduce the thrust, landing it in the sand close to the anomaly.

Outside of the ship, it was incredibly hot and sweat ran down my forehead. A gentle breeze brushed my face and blew against my brown hair. I reached down to feel the sand. Its warmth seemed to swell in my hands. The grains were very fine, and the sand fell through my fingers.

"If there's any source of water, this would be a pretty habitable planet," said Nivea.

"It's likely that there are some water sources. Look at that," I said, pointing towards a smaller spiky cactus at the bottom edge of the dune. Fathom walked down the dune and went to touch it.

"Be careful," Cabell said. "Those spikes can do you some damage. Cacti may be lush with life, but from the outside they are potentially deadly."

We walked down the dune heading to the area we'd spotted from the ship. It was the opening of a cave. We carefully edged our way inside. It was so dark; we couldn't see anything. Nivea produced a fire which cast a light over the space, revealing a small mechanical device. It was only about as big as a suitcase.

Upon close inspection it looked like it had an engine attached to the back of it. In the front, there was a black screen which stared back at us. Whatever it was, it wasn't active, at least it didn't appear to be. I knelt down and stared into the glass. I could see my long brown hair and blue eyes in the reflection.

"It looks like there may be a presence here after all," I said. "Although, just what kind, it's hard to say."

A small red light appeared on the machine's screen. We stared at it. A bright white light flashed there, and the small device shot to life, wings shooting out of the sides of it. We ran out of the cave, but it followed us, flying at an aggressive rate. It shot red lasers at us as we ran up the dune, but we managed to close the ship's door before being shot.

It continued shooting at us, knocking the ship back and forth, so we quickly ignited the ship thrusting ourselves up into the air, in an attempt to evade it.

"It's some sort of defense drone," Nivea said, as we raced over the sand dunes, the drone still shooting at us at every turn. I swerved to avoid the fire, but when we were forced to absorb the shots, there didn't appear to be substantial damage done to the ship. It was sturdy, for sure. Most likely some sort of shield was protecting us.

The robot proved to be clever, though. Its movements were like no AI I'd faced before. We were at a loss as to how to escape it, and we really had nowhere to take cover.

We were about to ascend into space, when several dark objects appeared on the horizon. As we came closer, it was clearly a city, but with old ironclad buildings covered in sand. It looked inactive, as though it had been vacated a long time ago.

I took the opportunity to evade the drone by swerving around the dull gray-black buildings. Still, it was incredibly difficult to shake off my tail. I made a quick turn around one massive building, and then another, and again. We were now flying in a slightly different direction, and it appeared as though we had left it in the dust, for now. We had the speed advantage.

I darted my eyes left and right looking for a way to exit the village without arising the suspicion of the drone. Surely, it would see us if we rose. I made the decision to park the ship in an alley tucked between two bigger buildings, and we waited.

"Curious," said Cabell. "It definitely looks like this place has been abandoned."

"Yes," I said. "And they appear to be impervious to entry. I haven't seen any windows or doors, it's like they're just deadweight, or locked shut. Highly fortified."

"Would it kill us to explore a little?" Nivea asked.

"It very well could," said Fathom. "This place hasn't been too friendly thus far."

"Don't be silly," I said. "There's nothing wrong with exploring around the ship a little."

With that I opened the door and stepped out. The air was a lot danker here. The buildings were high, but not as high as they were on Aras. Though they were, without a doubt, incredibly durable. I walked up and touched one with my hand. It was dry and matte but did offer a dull shine.

The others joined me as I walked along the side of a building. I found a small opening which led downwards along a slight decline. I looked down into the space to see a glossy object reflecting light. The area appeared to be safe, so I began to head down.

"Be careful," Cabell said.

"It's fine," I said. "There's nothing down here."

Despite my confident display there was an unusual quietness to the area, and I wondered if we were being watched. When I reached the object at the end of the small decline, I could see it was a sort of glass circle embedded into the building, built into a larger circular space that possibly could be a door. As I stared into sphere, I once again recognized my reflection. Cautiously, I reached out to touch the object.

As with the drone, there was a flash and a red light that grew from within the shiny globe. I fell back on the ground. The light did not stop there, though, it ran along the edges of the building in diverting lines, like blood flowing in the veins of some hidden beast.

I promptly jumped to my feet and called to the others to go back to the ship. As we ran, the red lights blazed across the city walls as if we'd excited some dormant monster.

"Run," I cried, a sense of impending doom gripping my stomach. We jumped into the ship, and though there was no apparent threat, the walls were glowing bright red.

Suspecting there may be imminent danger, I thrust the ship up into the air and we began dashing through the city walls. And that's when we saw them. A swarm of drones appearing above the city. Then, they were appearing left and right, behind us, down every corridor. The damn drones were everywhere! They quickly closed in us with their blood-red eyes and startling accuracy.

We would give them a good run. Finding a long stretch, I thrust the ship ahead as fast as I could muster, and we were able to swerve around the appearing drones. They loomed above in the star filled sky, and I feared that we could not keep this up for too long.

"Look," cried Fathom. He was pointing along the alleyways to the right which, through intermittent glimpses, we could see the desert sand once again. There were no drones in the desert.

I slowed enough for the drones to catch up and although our ship took another shot, we made a quick turn and blasted into the desert.

The city disappeared behind us, and we once again surfed the dunes of the desert. But almost as quickly as we'd entered the desert, the sand gave way to rocky, mountainous terrain. Cliffs rose high into the air—we were in a massive chasm that grew deeper and more enclosed. We had no space to move.

"They're still chasing us," cried Nivea, who was looking through the side window.

"Look," cried Fathom. A quick glance to the side of the chasm revealed pathways and larger pieces of machinery strewn along cliffside. Almost immediately, one began shooting at us. Turrets.

Gigantic robots stood up. They fired at us with red lasers, with a stupefying accuracy. Our plight had quickly become desperate. We could not travel up as the top of the cavern was closed off with ledges. We had to keep moving forward.

Drones appeared from the cracks of the chasm. They fired with a steadfast determination. I realized I could not overcome the firepower. We had to land somewhere, now!

We dove down further into the chasm. The path forward became rockier and more enclosed. A laser shot set us into a spiral and I tried to steady us, but we veered off course and knocked into a ledge. The ship bounced to the side, then hit a rocky surface, skidding before crashing to a halt.

II

The ship wouldn't restart. The turrets were still firing at us, pushing our ship off the ledge. There was an open cave to our left. Given the volatility of the shots, we made the decision to ditch the ship and run for shelter.

We dashed through the laser fire into the cave's opening. Having escaped the onslaught of lasers, we took a moment to look around the cave. There was no other trace of human life. It was small, but the back appeared to go on for a while into darkness.

"What now?" Cabell asked.

"I'm betting those drones won't have too much trouble finding us," I said. "Quick, head into the dark and hide, if you can."

We hustled to the back of the cave. The lasers were still shooting at the ship outside, and we feared an attack from the flying drones.

"Wait," Cabell said. "Right here, there is a very narrow crack in the wall. And…is that a dim light back there?"

We moved over closer to Cabell, and indeed, there was a dim light visible through a very small crack in the wall.

"Kick it, punch it, whatever you have to do, break it open so we can fit through."

Outside, we could hear the drones swarming around the ship. We each took turns beating at the crack in the wall, and eventually it gave way enough for Cabell to fit through. We followed him, and soon we were in a narrow hallway leading to a dim light at the end.

The laser fire died down as we progressed further into the cave. Reaching the end of the hall, Fathom knocked his foot on some sort of cargo box. At first, we thought it was locked, but it opened to reveal a big electronic device.

"Strange," Cabell said. "It almost looks like a giant battery, but for what? The robots outside?"

We roamed for some time, before reaching a bigger room with terminals built into the walls. There was broken robotics machinery strewn about, similar to what we'd encountered outside. As well, there were two walls which were of a similar dull metallic substance to the buildings of the city, and they contained the globes we'd seen earlier. They were doorways, maybe, but they were closed.

"Curious technology," Cabell said.

The buzz of drones and laser-fire could became louder. The drones had entered the cave.

"What do we do?" Nivea cried.

We looked at each other. The lasers continued.

"Somehow they know we're in here," Fathom cried.

"This is bad," Nivea said.

We exchanged dashed glances. In a fit of anxiety, I jumped over to one of the globe doors. I placed my hand up against the globe, which instantly lit up with a red light, just like before. I pulled my hand back quick, and the screen flashed to life. The familiar red veins flushed out over the entire door.

"What have you done?" cried Cabell.

The door opened, and a giant mechanical creature immerged, shooting lasers at us. Nivea was hit, then Cabell. Fathom and I ran down the hallway only to be hit by a laser as well. I held my leg in pain and looked up to see the first drone approaching from the cave before I blacked out.

III

I awoke to blurry lights rising above. I was dropping. I could feel that we were falling, fast. I squirmed, but I was bound to some sort of gurney. The lights kept strobing over my face and, with my eyes closed, it felt as if they were probing into my mind.

I opened my eyes and turned my head to see the others who were also incapacitated. There, next to us, were two giant robots just like the one that had opened up the door and shot at us. I tried to speak, but my mouth was bound.

The strobing lights gave way to darkness. Then, slowly, rock stalactites came into view, and a cavern appeared through a window. Extremely high computer terminals were stacked inside. Robots and androids stared at me. The vision lasted briefly before disappearing into darkness again.

After about five minutes the door opened. The robots next to me pushed me into a dark room, then left me and the others there.

The light increased slowly, attenuating brighter until it filled the entire room. There was medical supplies and machinery, but no scientists. There were operating tables all around, but no doctors. What kind of creepy operation room was this?

Two figures moved towards us. Androids. Highly sophisticated humanoid creatures with white strips instead of eyes, silvery metallic heads and speakers for mouths. As I struggled to move, one of their white light strips flashed, scanning me.

"Relax, Saranyu," one of them said. The audio beamed through the oval speaker on their head where a human mouth would be.

"Yes, relax fighter," the other said.

"You are quite an evasive pilot," the first android continued. "Your friends here have not yet woken, yet here you are, already trying to escape. Don't bother. It isn't possible. You're in a highly secure vault facility quite far from any other organic life forms."

"How do you know my name?" The light flashed again.

"We know your name through a simple temporal lobe scan. A full brain scan will tell us more about your origins. You will be sedated for this scan."

I struggled to no avail.

"Just relax, Saranyu. You have no recourse. You will be sedated. Once we find what we need to know, your fate will be determined, as will the fate of your friends."

I struggled in vain as an android brought a needle to my neck and pierced my flesh.

A woozy, disoriented vision appeared. I was veering left and right, but after an extended period of nausea and dizziness, my shaking head steadied, and through a blurry fog my familiar cockpit came into view. The windshield sparkled with bright beams of sunlight.

"They're attacking! Throw them off." The command came from my headset, the voice was a commander I'd who trained me, his voice always carried stressed orders even in the tamest of situations.

I looked at the radar to see that we were being followed by several triangular ships like the ones that had attacked us on Aras. I dove into a tailspin to evade them, which was effective, but we were outnumbered. We could only keep this up for so long.

After a series of successful evasive moves, I took on fire, and my aircraft dove towards the water. I ejected with my parachute, and when I finally hit the water, I detached my parachute and began swimming.

My desperate swim ended when I found a beach. I stumbled out of the water and fell into eerily familiar soft sand. I twisted my head up to see that I was on an island just like that of the virtual reality training island on Aras. We had been given many training missions on this island, and I knew it inside out. I'd always had a fondness for it, but never actually existed on Aras, it was only a simulation.

In the sky above I could see several black and silver ships attacking, the same ones from my recent memory. One shot down at me. I ran into a nearby woods, finding refuge in a cave.

No sooner did I step in the cave then the entrance disappeared, and I was forced to walk further into the cave. I entered a room with a light that grew from above. The room was full of broken robot parts. I jumped back, falling onto my backside, as a man stepped into the light. He was tall and thin with long messy hair, a kempt beard and notable red eyes. There was something off about him.

"You are quite the pilot," he said, staring at me with a pensive gaze. He spoke absently, but his eyes seemed to penetrate mind. "We share the same enemy."

"Who are you?" I demanded.

He paused, as if carefully considering what to say.

"Call me Dem. You know, you are awfully lucky to have found yourself in the hands of a benevolent race."

I looked at him apprehensively. I did not yet trust him. I recalled our capture and the elevator ride. I needed to know more.

"Benevolent is a pretty funny word to use for what we've experienced so far. Are you behind these androids that sedated me?"

The man walked over to a broken android, knelt, then pulled it up to face him.

"Ah, the APEX model. Yes, it's one of the better models, for sure. There are many capable androids. The ones you met were in charge of sedation and brain scan technology. We have the power to insert this technology into any organic or inorganic matter."

"They were quite rude. And you're not much better. Could you kindly explain what the hell is going on?"

"Look, we're not sure how much *we* can trust *you* yet."

"Are you joking? You capture me and my friends, you sedate us with God-knows-what, you infiltrate our minds. What do you hope to accomplish?"

"Look, I know you're upset, but we have to take serious precautions against our adversaries. If you're not connected to them, you should take the same precautions."

"Who the hell are they?"

The man stood up again and walked over closer to me, his red eyes glowed as his gaze locked on me.

"They are an extremely violent race set on colonizing the universe for their own gain, at any cost. They destroyed most of our great city and they have attacked our planet multiple times in an attempt to steal our technology. They won't get it though, not as long as we're alive."

"And *who*, exactly, are *you*?"

"You may call us the Sulla. We were once a great civilization. Now we are the remnants of that. We are developing a new technology capable of leaving this planet, finding our adversary in their home world, and fighting them in retribution for the pain and loss they have caused. With the exponential rate our technology is growing, that will one day be possible. For now, we're hiding from them."

"How are you talking to me in this dream?"

"That's enough about us. How did *you* get here?"

I paused, glaring at him. There was no way he was going to tell me more, I knew that. Given that I was completely at his mercy, it was just as well I was forthright.

"My friends and I, we came from a planet called Aras. My civilization is technologically savvy as well, but our skill is in ship building. We build powerful spaceships, and we have explored far in our galaxy."

"Intriguing," Dem said, with an apparent genuine interest. "But we have seen the ship you came in; it is the ship of our alien adversaries. How is this so?"

I considered this. So, the spaceship we had, it was of the hostile alien race. The technology belonged to them. This made a lot of sense, given our experience with the fleet that attacked us.

"This ship was found by my friends, on a planet far away called *Earth*," I said. "They received this ship before they travelled to me. The ship has a technology that can travel through the storm…"

"Storm? What storm?"

"The…storm. You don't know of the storm?"

"We do not know of it."

"There is a storm that is ravishing the universe. It is near your planet, and one day it may consume it."

"The anomaly? Oh…yes. We know of this. However, we have never studied it with great intensity. It has never actually breached the atmosphere. You are saying that it acts as a sort of, portal, for space travel?"

"Yes. And communication across great distances."

"Incredible. We watched you from when you first landed on the planet. Your piloting abilities are very strong. Your race must be very proud. Well,

Saranyu, although my colleagues are very weary of your entry in the ship, your intentions seem innocent as far as I can see. I will be vouching for your freedom, but it's unlikely the masters will allow you free anytime soon. We'll do the best we can to get you out of here as soon as possible."

"You're telling me that you're going to keep us trapped here?"

"Your fate is beyond my control. I will try the best I can. Look, most likely you will be listed as a minor risk, and you will be given a temporary freedom on our android deck, where you will be fed and live fairly peacefully for the time being. However, this floor is restricted and under our control, so you won't be able to escape it. I have to go now. I hope to meet with you again, soon."

I felt the dream subside into darkness.

IV

I awoke, again, in the hands of androids. This time however, we were confined to bedrooms. The androids fed us, and we were cared for like sick children. I had a feeling that we were being watched and assessed.

A few days passed like this, before we were finally allowed to leave the confines of the sleeping quarters, and we were permitted onto a giant floor stacked with machines and electronics that was maintained by the androids. They allowed us to explore, but we wore bracelets which would stun us if we tried to leave. Not that we could leave anyway, the doors were highly secure.

We had gotten used to our new home and even grown friendly with the surprisingly lifelike androids. Then one day we were called to a room of computers, where we were instructed to lie down on soft cushy beds and close our eyes. The beds slid back into a wall, and we were instantly whisked away to a virtual reality, where we were trained on how to operate spacecraft. My trainer was Dem, and he was incredibly diligent instructing me on how to fly their virtual drones and mecha robots.

It was a walk in the park for me. I was mesmerized with how intelligent Dem was. He knew everything about drone operation, right down to the intricate circuits that allowed them to operate. We learned how to fly them, we learned how to shoot enemies, we learned how to stealthily collect information and we learned how to pulverize the enemy with a suicide move; one that sent a pulse of electricity out over a network rendering it inactive, while completely deleting the content of the drone.

The exercises grew old, but we had grown great friends with the androids. Although we were led to believe that the androids were autonomous, there was doubt amongst us, but we never fully articulated it, suspecting that we were being watched constantly.

The robots were definitely self-sufficient, but the androids appeared almost too life-like at times, and we suspected they were being controlled by some other entity, but there were no clues provided as to just whom that entity might be.

Then there was Dem and a few other 'virtual illusions' who professed to be programs, but would not go into any details on the great civilization that once existed on Sullamecha. There was something suspect about it.

Regardless, they were essentially friendly, although they said they couldn't let us go until they were sure we could be trusted. The ship that we'd come in had been taken and quarantined, and the technology was being studied. We didn't mind; again, we didn't really have much choice in the matter.

One day, we were interrupted from our virtual training by an ominous alert.

"We have spotted numerous unidentified objects incoming," Dem said, interrupting my drone navigation simulation. "We've got Tier 1 drones on it, but they're being overtaken. We're going to link you up to real-time Tier 2 robots, we need your help in taking them down, Saranyu. There are a lot of them."

"Why are we only hearing of this now?"

"We are only aware of it just now. I'm linking you up immediately. Saranyu, remember, no matter what, I'll be here the background to help. Okay?"

"Okay."

My vision blurred and then adjusted to a bright, white light which dialed back to darkness. I initiated a launch sequence and sent a sleeper drone up into the air, thrusting it left and right through a narrow cave and out into the bright sunlight of the dunes of Sullamecha.

The radar indicated there was a fleet of ships attacking from above. This was bad. I lifted the drone up into the air and fired on every ship I could. I successfully took down three or four before I sustained significant damage and took a nose-dive into the ground.

I switched to another drone and rose it from its sleeper cave. I managed to destroy another three enemy ships before my sleeper drone was taken down. This was not a drill; my success had been a lot better in virtual reality.

I repeated this for another good five or six drones, before I heard Dem speak to me from the background.

"Good Saranyu, but we've got another fleet following them and the drones are not cutting it. We're going to have to move to the Tier 3 robot-operated ships. Are you ready?"

"Never more ready," I said.

I felt the vision shift to a robot's eyes in a sophisticated ship. This was more like it. The Sulla had a whole army of android ships attacking, but there was no defence like a human-guided ship.

Navigating a hidden cave location, I burst out into the chasm with lasers already firing at the ships I'd been tracking by radar. They didn't last long. I took down five at the same time, then plowed on through another three before sustaining significant damage, but I evaded the attack and did a nosedive downward, going head over heels before flying back up and twisting around to fake the fleet out. I managed to take out another seven ships before my ship took fatal damage.

"Great job," Dem said.

I switched to another ship and began attacking again. With the others, we managed to take out most of the fleet. But Dem spoke to me again from the background.

"Saranyu, you've done good but we need you to disengage."

"What? No! I've taken out nearly the whole fleet!"

"Saranyu, you need to disengage now, or we will force you to."

"Why the hell would you?"

"There are multiple fleets approaching the planet. This is very bad. We don't have the capacity for—"

"No, I can take them. All of us working together, we can—"

"I'm not going ask you again."

I glanced at the radar. There were no more ships visible, but the radar did not span far beyond the planet. Dem had a broader view. There was no reason to doubt him. But then, weren't we good enough to take them? There were several of us were prepared for—"

My vision became blurry.

I awoke shaking on the bed in the computer room with the others standing around me.

"We have orders to move to a safer area," Cabell said. "The androids will take us. It's looking really bad. They're not sure if—"

"I almost had them," I yelled.

"Saranyu," Nivea screamed. "We have to get to safety. It sounds really bad."

I turned to two androids that were coming towards and gesturing for us to follow. Jarring back to reality, I ran with the others.

V

We ran to the elevator and began descending with our four android chaperones. The floors that flew past us appeared to show more electronic storage, wires, and mainframes. We descended many floors before the lights dimmed and we were left in darkness.

The androids operated the control panel to the elevator to no avail.

"This is not a good sign," Cabell said.

We waited for a good thirty minutes, before there was a loud banging coming from outside the elevator.

"What the hell is it?" Fathom said.

We stood silent, until the impact became visible on the side of the elevator. Then we screamed.

The androids again fiddled with the control panel, and prepared their lasers. Hesitantly, they gave us spare laser-guns they had hidden.

When the side of the elevator split open, we jumped back against the opposite wall and the androids shot madly at the hole that had opened. Whoever was trying to break in must have been stunned by that attack, but quickly laser shots followed from outside and the iron of the elevator was torn open.

We knelt down for protection as the laser-fire raced on like a game of quantum ping pong. Two androids dropped in the crossfire and the other two slid down to a sitting position, still firing.

"Run," the androids said, as it became clear our attackers were not ceasing. Surveying the outside area, we could see our attackers were approaching from the long end of a cavernous terrain, and the androids had successfully kept them at quite a distance.

We had enough room to run for a nearby maintenance hallway. In the moment we were exposed to high temperatures, I could see our attackers out of the corner of my eye. They were tall and wore gray suits. Their heads were protected by glass helmets and were much bigger than any humans would be. Their skin looked to be black.

We dove through the hot cavern and into the hallway which was absent of attackers. It appeared to be some sort of facility service hallway, as if it were meant for the upkeep of the base exterior and was not for regular use. It was lit by an electronic light and covered with metal panels. The aliens saw us and attacked, but not in time to be able to hit us. We ran down the hallway.

An alien shot a panel causing it to spray electrical ash. It was overwhelmingly hot. The laser-fire continued behind us, and Fathom and Nivea fired back when they could, but for the most part we just ran as fast as possible.

The race continued into a brighter area with a glass walkway. Outside there was strangely reddish substance, it was like lava but thinner. The temperature was so high that a human would not survive long, whereas an android could last much longer.

The aliens did not stop their pursuit. We fired several shots then crossed the glass walkway. Just after turning a corner at the end of the hallway, we heard a crash.

"They destroyed the walkway," Nivea shouted.

We continued running into another cavernous area until we reached a door that would not open, despite our screams.

I saw a globe and pressed it with my hand. A red light appeared within the globe, but it just remained there. The door did not open.

"The destroyed walkway should hold them," said Cabell, "but perhaps not for long. We need to get in."

Our screams grew more desperate as we continued knocking on the door. Finally, the door burst open, and we jumped inside. It closed and locked, as if operated by some higher power.

The room we now found ourselves in was curious. There were monitors showing many different areas of the underground facility. It seemed to be some sort of security station. The computer interfaces were unusual though. Most of the interfaces around the underground facility were direct links which robots operated by physically linking up to and were inoperable by humans. The interfaces in this room were much more human-friendly.

"Look," shouted Cabell, pointing at a monitor that showed another cavernous area that appeared to be a bay of fighter ships and drones. One in particular stood out. It was our ship.

"They must have held it for study," Nivea said.

"By the looks of these security cameras, there may be a crack in the ceiling leading up to the surface for the drones. So, if we can get to the ship, we should be able to get it out of here. How can we get to it?"

"Look," I said, pointing at the left wall. "There's a map of this area. If we take the next left service hall, it should take us right to it."

The aliens hit the door with lasers.

"We've got to go, now." Nivea said.

"I can buy us some time," I said, opening a virtual reality bed and jumping in. "Push me in the wall, they'll never know I'm here. I'll be able to operate the drones and give you cover to the ship."

"That's dangerous," said Cabell. Are you sure?

"Of course, I'm sure. You want to get back to earth, don't you? You need me to buy you extra time so you can get to that pilot's seat, Cabell. It's so close, all you have to do is get into the ship's bay, and I'll easily cover you. There's no way they'll be able to get you with me protecting. Don't worry about me, I'll be fine.

Will Saranyu go or will Cabell pilot?
Saranyu Goes   Cabell Pilots
Continue Reading   Go to Page 438

SARANYA GOES

A laser ripped through the door.

"We've got to go," screamed Nivea, grabbing my arm. We dashed through the second entrance, down the hall until we broke into the bay area with the other ships. The aliens burst in.

"There it is," I shouted, pointing at the ship. We ran to it and opened the doors and I jumped inside as the lasers came closer.

I took the wheel but was immediately torn from it by a figure outside the ship. The figure shot the others and threw me into the passenger seat.

I looked up to see the ship moving. It burst through glass into a cavernous area with the reddish lava-like substance, and then up, up through a crevice in the ceiling.

Another of the many worlds we've travelled, for that foolish creature and his stupid furry face, and here, our ship is in the hands of a known enemy.

But no more. We have the ship. We're in the storm. Heading home. No more will the ship be in the hands of a boundless fool.

The image of him is out there, somewhere, pale and pathetic, begging for the ship back, begging for our acquiescence, helplessly trying to reason, but despite our efforts, despite our numerous attempts to find him, we've come up empty handed.

Regardless, we have regained the ship. Our mission is complete.

UNKNOWN STARSHIP | WITH: UNKNOWN PILOT

I entered the landing bay at impulse power. Stabilization completed. Forcefield powered off. Shields were down. The landing was successful.

I stepped out into the familiar oxygenated bay of our ship. Our fleet joined me, each ship landing one at a time from space. A veteran pilot, my old friend, stepped up to me, his black tentacles capped by his helmet.

"Are they out?" he asked.

"They're stunned. Bound, captive, secure in the ship."

"Take one of them and report to command with news of the successful mission."

I opened the back door of the ship and pulled one of the unconscious aliens up into my arms, her long brown hair falling to the side.

We approached the storm teleporters. Channelling through the storm we arrived at the main bridge. My companions greeted our arrival with tentacle nods indicative of a successful mission.

"How long since the last communication with the League," I asked.

"Five days. You have been gone for nineteen days."

I walked around the deck observing our crew who were of excited in reception of our arrival.

"Have there been battles?"

"One battle, an inferior race miscalculated our dominance, their ship was quickly obliterated. We had to fly through a benign civilization in chase with the ship. The pilot was formidable."

The bridge screen provided a view of our current location, a destination quite far from our homeland. The exploration in our absence had yielded no suitable planets for settlement, otherwise we would have begun colonization.

"Any new notes on exploration?"

"None. We explored a planet which showed potential, but quickly became a false hope when scientific tests indicated the storm gains virulence when exposed to the atmosphere. It nearly cut through our suit technology. We aborted the mission immediately."

"Any word from homeland?"

"They are awaiting your arrival. They are in disarray. The storm has rendered the planet nearly uninhabitable; all remaining species are being transported to suspended animation in space where possible."

I turned to a nearby aid, passing the alien thief to him. "Revive her. We will bring her through the gate."

We entered a dark room with the storm-gate machines. We hooked our minds up to the system waiting for the familiar wash of information to flow over us as we connected to the storm, our bodies shook with an overwhelming amount of pain and pleasure.

And we were in. Homeland was in the forefront, ravished by the storm since our departure, it was painful to see. My mind's eye fell upon a group of faces superimposed upon the image of our homeland. On the periphery the other planets of the Defense League remained attentive as the League Master spoke.

"We have been advised your mission has been successful and the entirety of the Defense League is thankful. The Science League is of excited to learn that the storm-force ship technology has been successful in achieving universal travel. We will be holding a celebration in the next month to honor you with the highest notch for bravery. Please disclose now your details of the mission."

"Travel was not easy. We landed on many worlds irrelevant to our objective, and some worlds in which we only just missed the thief. Many worlds were habitable, providing promise for colonization."

The minds of the others buzzed with unique new fires, their ideas swirling in thought columns that I did not choose to explore at the time.

"We did not find the original thief, but through concentrated focus of his travels, we tracked him to a planet named **Marzanna**. *A connection here led us to a world named* **Aras**, *a unique planet ripe with alien creatures of considerable intelligence, but little threat. We explored the planet and found them in a city. They escaped to a nearby space station, but we did not catch up to them in time due the maneuvering of a formidable pilot.*

"We spent the remaining days trying to catch up with the thief to no avail. We found many unique worlds, but no imprint of their presence in the storm. It seemed as though they'd escaped off the radar of the storm.

"Then, we picked up a bizarre biological heat signal on **Sullamecha**, *the potential settlement we have been pursuing for quite a while, which is home to a highly intelligent species that has built up a technological barrier that we've been trying to destroy for ages."*

"We touched down on the alien, desert landscape to fight off the usual aerial attacks, but we followed the heat signals down deep into the planet's underground, where we infiltrated an android-built defense and found the prisoners and the ship there. We have brought the female alien pilot for your consideration."

"You may revive her," The League Master said.

I broke from the storm long enough to revive the alien woman and connect her to the storm. She woke, opening her consciousness to us for exploration. Immediately we perused her mind looking for more information about the original alien thief and the nature of this alien's native world. As she woke within the storm, her eyes darted madly around, a normal response for a novice in the storm.

"What is this," she cried.

"Alien woman, your name we find in your consciousness to be... 'Saranyu,' your kind has engaged in terrorism by taking possession of our highly sensitive technology, the damage caused is potentially unknowable from this vantage point."

Saranyu blinked, looking around, unable to penetrate the mind defenses we had now raised as a result of her cognizance. Then, seeming to come to grips with the apparent insanity of her situation, she spoke again.

"You are a species that has captured us? What are your demands? We mean

no harm."

"You are an inferior species," the League Master said. "But you are of close competence. Your air force capabilities are of interest to us. You will be compliant in advising us of your defense methods against the storm."

"We will not comply with tyranny. What are your intentions?"

"Our intentions are that which we carry on now," the Master said. "We will be visiting your world again, with your help. You will be giving us information, that we are now obtaining from your mind, that will lead to the successful colonization of our species in a new habitable world, at any cost."

"We will never bow to tyranny," Saranyu said.

"You can and you will. We have captured enough of you to explore new worlds in the storm, based on your unique biochemical anatomies. Within each of your individual minds, there is endless potential for exploration of worlds beyond our area of the universe. Your capture has opened the door to an entirely new dimension of space travel never before known."

"We will never comply. We will fight."

I ignored her foolish pleas and reached into her subconscious for any information that might give us insight into potential planetary settlements, especially with regards to Sullamecha, *the planet where we found her.*

This planet was one of the best options for settlement as it was within the same galaxy as our homeland, it contained many resources, and fell at a very low probability of storm consumption. At the same time it remained in close proximity to the storm.

I dove into her subconsciousness, where I became audience at a small island with ships flying overhead. It was an island that seemed to resonate with her youth. I followed her knowledge in the form of her self as she explored the island, and came face to face with a man of curious existence. His face looked of alien life, but there was much more standing up behind him. He was like a wall of information. I could sense something beyond him that was highly defended by a wall of technology.

As they began to talk, I tried to push against the man's façade to discover if his location was on Sullamecha. At first, I was unable to. But I began to make progress slowly. As I pried, he picked up a broken android, explaining something about its defenses, and suddenly he smiled a knowing smile, his red eyes glaring at me as the android flashed..."

I was shaken out of the storm by another.

"What is it?" I shouted.

"Our defenses have been compromised! There's been some sort of electronic surge! We are powerless!"

I jumped up and ran to the bridge. There was no power.

"Why aren't we on backup power?"

"There's nothing! We've already tried."

I paused.

"Get that alien woman out of the storm!" I shouted. "Subdue her!"

The crew did as asked, and after a good amount of work, the tech division managed to revive the ship.   "There is unauthorized movement of a ship in the landing bay."

"Turn on the force-fields!" I yelled.

We brought an image of the landing bay on screen just in time to see the recovered ship leave through the undefended landing bay door.

CABELL PILOTS

The familiar deathly cold raged through me, but I overcame it. Now, my veins flowed with a beauty unlike I'd known before.

In front of me, brilliant waterfalls rained down on placid lakes. Colossal skyscrapers dazzled in radiant sunlight. Verdant forests grew with an undying ferocity. The images flushed over me one after the other as if testing my capacity for awe. They were like earth before the storm, but there were many otherworldly variations.

The images continued to cycle, until one stayed. It was a snowclad forest, with a city in the distance. I watched from a mountain as a familiar traveler on a snowy mountain trail sauntered through the forest. Behind him, a city was vaguely visible through the throes of the storm. With his snowy beard and Santa hat, it was clearly Hylotz. I waved at him and he waved back, but he appeared resolute, like he had made a heavily weighed decision. It was the first time I'd seen him unhappy.

In a moment, he turned away from the city and back towards the forest and continued down the path. His footprints wove back and forth erratically like they had when we had first tried to find him.

Ahead of him on the trail, there was a flash of light, and he disappeared in the storm.

PART 5 | TERRA BETA | WITH: CABELL

I

We emerged from the tangled web of the storm, the ship weaving left and right through a desperate darkness like a rain-soaked leaf. Where were we now?

The steering wheel shook against my wrist as a new planet appeared through the darkness, its gray inhospitable alien atmosphere was hardly a welcome sight for its weary guests.

"Pull up," Fathom yelled, just before we slammed into the dusty surface, bouncing against the alien regolith multiple times before skidding to a stop.

Through the window, the terrain was clearly uninhabitable. It stretched out to the horizon. Bleak and desolate, it was more akin to the moon than Earth. This seemed to fly in the face of our theory about the ship's ability to travel to destinations of our innermost desires. When I took the wheel, I focused heavily on Earth, so how did we end up in this alien place?

"Not looking too friendly," Fathom said. "Should we get out and explore?"

"Absolutely not," I ordered. "Don't open that door. The absence of stars suggests a depleted atmosphere. You wouldn't last fifteen seconds without losing consciousness."

Fathom frowned. "Well, what now?"

I paused. The most obvious solution would be to take off again, if possible, to give it another shot. The harsh conditions of the planet suggested it simply wasn't worth the stay.

"Cabell, why don't you try piloting us out of here?" said Nivea. "Maybe our next stop will be brighter."

"It's really our only option," I replied. "Okay, lets give it another go."

I grabbed the steering wheel and waited for it to connect to my pulse. Nothing.

"Are you grabbing it tight?" said Fathom.

"I am. The damn thing isn't connecting."

"With that landing…I hate to ask this but, is it broken?"

I paused. With great disdain I was forced to digest that unfortunate truth. I made several other attempts to initialize the launch, to no avail.

"Well?" Fathom asked.

I felt like my whole life on Earth flashed before my eyes. Decades of research papers. Environmental tests. All the excitement of site visits, was it all for this? To be stuck on some lonely, uninhabitable planet at the desolate edge of the universe, left to die in a tiny vessel? Was this the fate of joining with the others to try to help some old homeless guy?

"I'm afraid we're trapped," I replied.

II

We were on our second day of being trapped without food and we had only limited water. Fathom stared hopelessly out the window. Nivea had resorted to obsessive introversion which was unhelpful. She was obviously accustomed to being connected to the storm on any whim.

"I could really use a smoke," Fathom said, pulling something out of his pocket. "Cabell," he asked, "remember when we were on the island, and we smoked the Ondas 'lief?"

"Yes," I replied.

"It helped us breathe, didn't it? Underwater?"

I paused to consider this. Indeed, the Ondas 'lief appeared to have oxidizing properties. It could help humans breathe underwater. Could it possibly help humans breathe in harsh oxygen-absent environments like this one?

"It's seems pretty risky," said Fathom, "but could it possibly let us breathe outside the ship?

"It's...plausible," I said.

"We don't have many options left at this point," said Nivea. "The Breaus have seen many planets through the eyes of civilizations, and we have seen many utilize the power of 'liefs to their advantage."

"It's crazy...but you're right, we don't really have any other choice," I said. "We'd starve to death if we choose to do nothing."

Nivea prepared the Ondas 'lief for smoking. "Now, what if we add this?" she said, pulling out some Marzanna 'liefs as well. "If we encounter the storm, we'll be able to connect and maybe gain some more insight into our situation." She prepared the 'liefs and provided us each with a joint. We smoked.

Fathom stared out the window. "Well, if this doesn't work, it was nice knowing you," he said.

"It's our only hope. If it works, this could open the door to some interesting scientific possibilities."

Fathom looked at me with a stronger resolve, with his anxiety calmed by the 'lief. With no hesitation, he reached toward the door to open it.

"It's been a blast," he said, and he opened the door.

Struggling to breathe, we passed out.

III

When I came to, the door was open. The others were not in the ship.

"Cabell," Fathom yelled. "Come out here."

I opened my door and jumped outside. The soil was a dark gray, much like the moon's regolith, and the blackness of space made me feel woozy.

"Well, we're still alive, so obviously the Ondas 'lief works," I said. Nivea stood behind me, pointing.

"Take a look, Cabell," she said.

I turned around to see a swirling mist of the storm in the distance, just over a small hill. Obviously, we had flown from that as if spit out of a tornado.

"That's our lifeline," Nivea said. "If we can get to that, we can reach out beyond the planet. It's a shot in the dark, but maybe we can reach someone through the storm that can help."

"Can we make it that far?" I asked.

"We have at least two hours, based on our previous smoking of the 'liefs." Fathom resolved. "Let's set out."

As we made our way up over the hill, I had to walk in a haphazard fashion to avoid some bigger objects in the soil. Rocks? I bent down to study them.

"What is it?" Nivea asked.

"These…rocks. They actually appear to be some sort of brick. Is it possible there was a civilization here?"

Nivea came to my side and investigated the artifacts. "It's quite possible, but let's press on, we don't have too long. Keep a couple of the artifacts."

We moved up on over the hill until the storm was in view. In front of the storm, there appeared to be the outline of a deserted structure. Could this have been a building? It's long vertical elevation looked familiar. As we got closer, we could see that on the roof there was a device that looked a lot like a telescope.

"Looks like an observatory. But could it be human?" I mused.

Nivea pondered the sight. "It looks as such."

"The storm is just over there." I pointed.

"Okay," Nivea said. "Now, there's no telling what the effects will be like considering we've smoked the Ondas 'lief as well as the Marzanna 'lief. So, proceed cautiously. When you enter the storm, direct your mind to any nearby life forces you can sense, and if that doesn't work, reach out as far as you can to try to gather as much knowledge about this planet as possible.

We walked into the storm.

The storm lifted my consciousness up, up into space, although I still felt like my feet were connected to the planet. I was able to reach out into the universe.

I sought to find Earth, but I could not find it through the storm, instead I kept falling back on our current planet. Amateurism with the storm, perhaps. Nevertheless, I was bound in close proximity to my friends, and I could sense their minds exploring beside me.

Nivea, for example, was reaching out to her Breaus in Marzanna, carrying on a conversation with a Breau that must have been present in the storm there. Fathom was also searching for Earth, but also his obsession was with some other energy which didn't hold a distinguished physical shape but remained fully present.

So, I focused on where we were. I tried to map the entire planet, but it was impossible. The storm did not reach over the whole thing. I transcended the storm to recreate an image of everything it touched. There was no life, yet there seemed to be a residue of something left over, as if there had been something significant here.

As I concentrated harder, an image became more prevalent. Closed shops. Unfriendly glances. Callous, inhospitable faces. Turned away. Cold winds. The memory of a home once ripe with life now torn, thrown into an unfamiliar terrain, a void of nonexistence.

Falling apart on street corners, hungry, cold, without food, without friends or family, at the precipice of a great unknown. A freezing. Cold. White. Wasteland.

Years turned to decades. Faces grew apart. Dark glances left only coldness behind, each striving to build its own barriers, mere fallible defenses against the unbeatable storm.

Alone. In the most unforgiving of conditions. What more is there to do than leave? Like footprints through the snow into the forest, what secrets could the forest hold? What other worlds could exist?

Still, there is life after leaving. Life in everything. Life in the forest. Life in the jungle. Life in the ocean. Life in the mountains. And yes, life in the storm. There is life in the storm, somehow.

The footprints flash through my mind like when we first saw him, when we first tracked him. Footprints leading into the woods, weaving through the stars, somehow the path led here, to this dead world. Somehow, it is the same. This existence, despite emptiness, it is the same.

Still, there is life.

I could feel the planet now, in my grasp. And I could sense a warmth present. A new beginning. Within us? Yes, but more. There were more voices here. Many voices, many minds, many memories, all of rejuvenation. Rebirth. Despite past failings, despite past conflicts, there would be a continuation. The forest never completely frees of the threat of fire, but after the fire, the trees grow back stronger. The

world can't escape the storm, but there can be relief from it.

I could feel the others tuning in to my experience, wide-eyed with curiosity. Perhaps for the first time, I was truly glad they were there. Without them, this planet, this universe, was a desolate place. We all felt something more, something new, with the traces of what we'd be left with: A great puzzle to solve at the behest of a great explorer whose journey never ended. There was still something here that needed to continue, something of value that could be saved, something to start anew.

I fell out of the storm.

"Cabell, I saw it too," Nivea said.

"And me," Fathom said.

"It was powerful," Nivea said. "My heart felt like there was still something here from a time long ago that was nearly completely destroyed."

"Yes," I said. I paused, marinating with the new ideas. *After death, there is still life. After fire, the trees grow back stronger. The leaves grow back stronger. The...'liefs, grow back stronger.*

"Nivea," I said. "The Atavika 'lief. What if we could keep growing it?"

Nivea paused, deep in thought. "When I was regularly connected to the storm, we maintained information in our thought archive on several planets with dire conditions. Many of these planets appeared to have no long-term sustainability for life, yet still they grew into vibrant worlds, due to the flora growing on them. Are you suggesting that the 'lief may be like the flora we found, capable of terraforming?"

"Yes," I said. "Atavika was lush with life and impenetrable from the harsh effects of the storm. What if we could replicate that on a planetary scale?"

"It's possible. We have the water from Ondas, the sun of this planet and the Atavika 'lief. And we have soil that may be tenable. But we'd have to find food to survive."

"The plant grows fast."

"At this point, anything works," said Fathom.

"It's decided then. Back to the ship," I said.

IV

We returned to the ship and spent the next few hours planting the Atavika 'lief. After a few days, the plants had grown quite large, shooting up towards space. We had tried to operate the ship multiple times, to no avail, surviving only on water collected in the ship from Ondas, and the new Atavika 'liefs that had grown.

It was looking like we would be able to sustain life here for a longer period of time than we'd initially thought, although the storm was leaving our area which meant we no longer were able to reach out to Marzanna and other planets for possible communication. We were in dire need of food.

Then, one day, we all jumped into the ship and closed the doors. I took the pilot's seat. With numerous attempts, there was a remarkable boost and, the thing jolted to life. I shivered as the ship shook and we flew through the Atavika plants now growing up towards space.

Quickly though, the launch became horrifying. My piloting skills were rough. Instead of twirling into a spiral that sent us up into space, the ship sputtered and shook left and right, nearly dropping to the ground.

We must have been fifty stories up when we took a dive downward, straight towards a peak of soil. Nivea screamed and Fathom gasped; we all braced for impact. At the last moment, before hitting the soil, I grabbed the wheel and pulled down. We cleared the peak of soil by mere inches. We pulled up over the hill safely stabilizing at a reasonable height.

As we cruised over the gray regolith, there was static sound emitting from Fathom's jacket. The two-way radio! Fathom pulled it out. A station came in clear.

"…Have we got a story for you! The *Revisit* craft has been actively exploring our Terra surface, with its intelligent robot Talus, and it's found quite a treasure this time! In the former Vancouver, now a wasteland of ash consumed by a Level 6 storm, Talus found an anti-storm respirator! Hard to imagine we once relied on these things. Astrologist Jill Fleming joins us to discuss the ramifications of this amazing discovery."

"Thank you, Olivia. Yes, it's been exhilarating to be on the team responsible for discovering the respirator. It reminds us that, in the early seventieth century, when the planet was grasping with a solution to the storm, anti-storm respirators were a temporary solution used to create a breathable atmosphere. That was foolish, of course, but it led to some interesting stories from crackpot stoners who ventured into the storm, raving of crazy planetary worlds existing beyond our planet.

"But this is the time that the concept of creating a breathable atmosphere really did gain momentum, which led to the forcefield technology we have today. Ironically, we celebrate the anniversary of this technology at a point where it has become perilously outdated, and we once again are seeking a sustainable solution to the storm."

"Thanks so very much for that brief on the respirator Jill. Now let's head to Jena for the forecast."

"Thank you, Oliva. In celebration of surviving the storm for a decade, Dome Environmental Control will be scheduling a special surprise for tomorrow: a snowstorm! Pull out your old snowsuits and prepare for a trip down nostalgia lane. This storm's gonna be a doozy!"

V

"Are we on earth?" Nivea asked, staring at me.

I stared blankly ahead as the ship continued cruising towards the horizon. "We…we can't be. This planet is desolate, uninhabitable. It can't be earth."

"But the mention of Vancouver," Fathom said. "The radio broadcast… it just sounded so real. Just like earth."

"Many worlds," Nivea said, staring at the two-way radio that was now emitting static. "The universe is vast. There are many worlds out there, many we have yet to discover. With the Marzanna 'lief, we have found and helped many simply through following mindful curiosity. It is the same mindfulness that brought us to Aras when I desired to reach Saranyu.

"It's what brought me to Kostroma, to free the Bies," said Fathom. "It's filled me with this…calm."

"It wouldn't be possible without this ship," said Nivea. "It truly is…a gift. From Hylotz. What did you want when you took the wheel, Cabell?"

"The same thing I've always wanted. A solution to the storm. To save earth. To find Hylotz. But beyond that, I guess I wanted to connect. To find others that recognize that common goal. To *feel* life, rather than just research about it. And, of course, I wanted us all to return home."

As I finished speaking, a structure appeared on the horizon. It took a few moments more before we realized what it was. It was a forcefield dome. The radio signal was correct, there was life here.

We cheered as I guided the ship towards the forcefield, when suddenly the two-way radio jolted to life with an intermittent flickering voice.

"This is Dome Defense, come in, over."

We glanced at each other in excitement. Fathom took up the two-way radio.

"Roger, this is Fathom."

"Please identify yourself and explain exactly where you have come from and how you got here."

Each of us looked at the other in disbelief.

"We…are from Earth. We found this ship, and…it's a long story."

"We have detected three humans in your unidentified spacecraft. Do you represent a stranded faction of survivors of the storm?"

"We are survivors of the storm, but when we left Earth, we left it in a much different condition than this planet."

"This planet is *Earth. Are you suggesting you are from a different planet?"*

Again, we looked at each other.

"We don't know," said Fathom. "We just know that this is not the Earth we remember. The Earth we left, not long ago, was dying in a storm."

"It has been decades since we found a tenable solution to the storm," said the voice. *"…albeit a fallible one. Your ship is entirely foreign. It is as if you have fallen out of another world. Regardless, we welcome you and we hope to learn more of your origins."*

I reached for the two-way communicator.

"I just have one important question for you," I said. "Where is your nearest washroom?"

Roxy Buckles
AND THE FLIGHT OF THE SPARROW
NICOLE LITTLE

CHAPTER ONE

Suki's eyes widened and shock spread across her face in discernable waves as she took in the gruesome sight before her; it ended at her mouth, which had taken on the shape of a perfect O.

"I know. I know." Roxy grimaced. "Shower-to-go isn't going to fix this, is it?"

"No chance in hell."

They stared at each other; neither blinked.

"It's starting to dry." A pause. "I think."

Roxy swiped a hand across her forehead and Suki watched in horrified fascination as a thick black glob rolled down Roxy's cheek and along her jawline. It quivered obscenely at the peak of her chin for a fraction of a second, and then hit the floor with an audible plop.

"Guess not."

"Get out! Go now!" Suki roared. "We're going to need a hazmat crew if you keeping dripping that… *stuff* all over the place."

Roxy shrugged helplessly, the movement dislodging even more gunk from somewhere beneath her jacket. She began to slink backwards out of the room, cringing at the ropy footprints she was leaving behind.

Suki's nostrils flared.

"Now I'm going to have to clean that up." The words, a low growl, reminded Roxy of exactly why she never wanted to be on Suki Kwan's bad side. "I don't like cleaning."

"I'm sorry Suki. Really!" she implored. "But what about the Witchlet meeting? I can't miss that."

"I'll have Mrs. Lester wait in your office for a few minutes once she arrives. She won't mind. Now go!"

"Go *where* exactly?"

"Down to transport. I'll just let them know you're on the way." She tapped a few keys on her wristlet communicator and with deadpan delivery: "They can hose you down with one of the Zip Ship power washers."

"One of the wha…" The auto-door swished shut on Roxy's startled expression and Suki snorted.

She wheeled her chair out from behind the desk and towards the hall closet, seeking out their meagre cleaning supplies: a threadbare mop and a spray bottle of funky green chemicals. Suki gave a long-suffering sigh. It would have to do.

"Revenge is a dish best served cold Roxy Buckles," Suki muttered, as she scrubbed ineffectually at the mess on the floor. "Cold and *wet*."

***

Roxy paused for effect outside the automatic doors, then, with as much dignity as she could muster, flounced inside - she was still dripping.

Much to Suki's relief, it was just water this time.

Roxy's short blonde curls were dark with moisture and she was fresh-faced, scrubbed of the dark mascara and bold red lipstick she favored. She was clad in a faded mechanic's suit: she'd left the overalls open at the neck and had rolled the bottoms up to mid-calf; she was barefoot. Suki watched with rapt attention as a droplet of water slid from a ringlet of Roxy's hair and trickled its way down into ...

"Like what you see?"

Roxy smirked and sashayed past Suki.

"Roxy..."

Roxy paused, and waited for the apology she felt sure was coming.

"You smell *so* much better now."

The reply came swiftly, in the shape of one perfectly manicured finger. Suki dissolved into a fit of laughter.

Roxy stopped, just short of the door, her voice indignant but lowered in deference to the client waiting in the next room, "I cannot *believe* you had them *hose* me down like I was some sort of... of... *soiled* vehicle."

Suki stifled her giggles, chagrined, and raised her hands in defeat. "I'm sorry Roxy, it was the quickest way I could think of to clean you up."

Roxy groaned dramatically and gestured to what she was wearing. "Not very professional now is it?"

"I am absolutely certain that Ethel-Beth Lester doesn't care what you are wearing as long as you do your job." She lowered her voice even further: "Do you think you'll be able to bring him back this time?"

Roxy's face was grim. "My theory? He's been served up for lunch long before now." She sighed. "But I suppose there's always a chance. So, I have to try. He might have hooked up with a Witchlet who's particularly sadistic. She might try to make it last a little longer, use him up for a couple of days to savour the kill. I guess I'll bring back whatever I can find."

She shrugged as she stepped away, plastered a smile on her face, opened the door to the inner office and closed it behind her with a faint click.

Ethel-Beth Lester sat waiting, patient as always, in one of the supple leather chairs placed in front of Roxy's desk. The woman gazed out the window, lost in thought, her mouth set in a thin line. Roxy cleared her throat softly so as not to startle her. She flinched anyways.

"Good day to you Mrs. Lester. I apologize for making you wait. I was slightly… indisposed. But now, I am prepped and ready for my trip to Salemmas. Once I know more about the situation, I will have someone contact you immediately. Most likely my associate Ms. Kwan."

She was but a wisp of a thing, Mrs. Lester, but Roxy knew there was a steely resolve beneath the soft exterior. "Thank you."

Roxy ran a finger along the inside of the coarse collar of her borrowed overalls. The tag at the back was irritating her neck. Who would wear these damned things by choice? The boorish mechanic hadn't been too keen on handing over the extra suit but his interest had definitely been piqued when he realized that Roxy intended to strip out of her saturated clothes right where she was standing. Her polite request that he avert his eyes while she did so had been met with some reluctance.

So, she'd thrown a wrench at him.

Okay, several wrenches.

She figured he was probably still running.

Roxy would get Suki to report the incident to Marcus MacLeod, head of building security and the man in charge of operating systems, before he left for the day. She could not do her job effectively if she was surrounded by a bunch of degenerates. Throwing tools at tools was not a part of her job description.

"Do you think Charles is still alive?" Mrs. Lester's soft voice snapped her back to the present.

"I wouldn't be able to say for sure, not until I see for myself. The length of the courting process varies, as you know, but we may still have a small window of opportunity." She paused, uncertain whether she would be crossing the line if she continued: "Look, I like you Mrs. Lester, so I am going to be straight with you because I don't want to give you false hope. This is the third time Mr. Lester has left with a Witchlet. If I can find him… are you sure you even want him back?"

To her surprise, Ethel-Beth laughed. "I wonder the same thing myself sometimes Ms. Buckles. I suppose I'm stubborn. I'm not ready to give up on him just yet."

"Then I will do my best."

"I know you will Ms. Buckles. You always do. Thank you once again for all your help."

"My pleasure," Roxy replied.

Roxy followed Mrs. Lester out of the room. She frowned as the doors slid shut behind what was her most frequent client. She hoped she would be able to do right by her. *Damn you Charles Lester.*

Roxy's job as an Exterminator, a bounty hunter-cum-mercenary, was not always pleasant. In fact, it very rarely was. Chasing down toxic pests, aliens, and invasive species was only one small part of her repertoire. Sometimes she had to go after the big guns, the worst criminals imaginable, and sometimes, things got a little dirty. People came to her during the worst moments of their lives and she tried to make things a little better when she could. She wanted to bring back good news and lost loved ones to their family members but, sometimes, the best she could do was a handful of scorched remains.

She closed the office door behind her and turned her attention to Suki Kwan, bouncing in her chair with excitement.

"Roxy." Suki gestured towards her desk. A flat rectangular package sat there. "I got a little something for you - a peace offering. The delivery drone dropped it off a short while ago. I gave very specific instructions to the boutique so; I hope you like it."

Roxy opened the embossed white box and eagerly removed a pair of form fitting black pants, a sleek red body suit and a cropped black leather jacket. She could not have chosen better herself.

Those overalls were history.

"You are the absolute best." She leaned over and pressed a loud affectionate kiss on Suki's cheek.

"Are you blushing Suki Kwan?"

"No. Absolutely not. Now enough of this mushy shit. The Zip Ship is fueled up and ready to go, so… go!"

CHAPTER TWO

Salemmas was distant, dark and desolate, a planet found nestled along the Daemon Belt. One of the least hospitable in the solar system, they welcomed visitors not with open arms but with open mouths and bared teeth.

At least it's not Mars, Roxy thought to herself, shuddering. She hated those damn dinosaurs.

The Zip Ship hovered, just above the Salemmas stratosphere, as Roxy doused the landing lights and prepared for descent. She would have to go in blind for this one. It was fortunate for Roxy, and for Ethel-Beth Lester, that Roxy was an acquaintance of the High Queen Witchlet Moll and as such, was permitted to come and go when necessary. There would be no fear of reprisal from the vicious creatures, but still, she was reluctant to announce her arrival. Roxy rarely set foot on the miserable planet and then, only when she had been hired to do an extraction. The hazard pay she planned to tack onto this particular invoice wouldn't hurt either.

This sort of job was usually grab and go; quick and dirty and usually not very successfully. At least for the women who hired her. Roxy's return trips to Aurora often saw her accompanied by nothing more than a small box of scraps; perhaps a fingernail or a tooth, a button from a shirt. If she was lucky enough to find anything at all.

She maneuvered through the cloud cover and eased the ship down onto the unfamiliar soil. It was black as death, despite the fact that it was mid-day. Tall, barren trees, their pale bark luminescent even in the dim light, towered overhead, their branches bowing outward in a tangled canopy over clusters of small dome shaped structures. These, Roxy knew, were the nurseries. From a distance, she could see the bright red lights of the main habitat - a large low unattractive building that did not inspire a welcome. She knew that deep below the rudimentary structure there were intricate tunnel systems, leading off into cavernous rooms where the Witchlets lived in groups of three. The nurseries, where the younglings were incubated, had to be kept near the outer limits of the planet to ensure the safety of the little ones. If a Witchlet were hungry enough or simply in the mood for fresh meat… well, it was better to remove temptation completely. Witchlets had enough population problems as it was.

Roxy exited the Zip Ship, landed solidly on her feet and remained in a crouch; she edged her way across the uneven terrain, trying to ignore the eerie snuffles and shrieks inside the nursery as she passed. Her fingers hovered at the weapon holstered on her hip. She knew from experience how painful a Witchlet nip could be and hoped she would never have to experience that again.

Her plan was to approach with caution initially, do re-con, and figure out what approach was necessary. Taking a quick glance inside the smudged windows, she saw workers in aprons busily placing bowls and plates along a banquet table; brightly colored fruits and lush green vegetables edged around the buffet. The focus though seemed to be on the middle of the table - the pièce de resistance - which had already been greased up, plump and prepped for roasting.

The pièce de resistance was, of course, Charles Lester.

His face bore an expression of dreamy disconnect; he lay there contentedly, simply awaiting his fate. The deed was nearly done. His purpose nearly fulfilled.

That decided it. Roxy breached the entrance with a stiff kick, a guttural roar escaping her lips. She was a tall woman, but in her high heeled black boots she cut a formidable figure. The Witchlets screamed and scattered as Roxy smashed her way through the entrance. They scurried through the first open doorway they could escape through.

Roxy snorted. Her reputation often preceded her but this was something else entirely.

She walked across the room to give Lester the once over. He seemed relatively unharmed and when she leaned in for a closer look he was still breathing. Witchlet poison was a powerful sedative and while its purpose was to make the victim docile, it very often slowed their heart rate. Sometimes it did a little more than just make the victim compliant.

Distracted, Roxy didn't feel the arm come from behind her until it was wrapped around her neck. The arm wrenched her backwards, knocking over several pieces of crockery. Broken glass and food carpeted the floor beneath their feet.

The fetid exhalations of the Witchlet who'd seen fit to grab her wafted into her face.

Minty fresh, it was not.

"Got youuuu." she intoned, her giggles high pitched and eager.

Roxy rolled her eyes. Yeah, you keep thinking that, fucker, Roxy thought and allowed her attacker to gain confidence - let her think that she was going to win. They waltzed around the room - a macabre dance - squashing mangalo fruit and tomates beneath their feet in the process. The Witchlet tightened her grip on Roxy's neck; her breath was hot and fast in Roxy's ear.

Roxy did not even try to suppress the shudder of revulsion that rocked her as the Witchlet rubbed against her obscenely.

Clearly, she was expecting both dinner *and* dessert tonight.

Okay, bitch, play time is over. Roxy let herself to go limp. As expected, the Witchlet loosened her grip. Before she had a chance to realize that things were about to go *very* wrong for her, Roxy had tossed her to the ground and pinned her there, the Witchlet's arms braced behind her, Roxy's knee in the middle of her shoulders. Subdued.

"Got youuuu." Roxy mimicked.

"Please," came the muffled plea. "I swear I wasn't going to hurt you. It was a joke."

Roxy hissed a breath from between gritted teeth. These bloody things were so exasperating to deal with. Conniving and clever. But not much got past Roxy.

"You seriously cannot expect me to believe that." Roxy retorted; her eyes ablaze. "You attacked me from behind. I think we all know where *that* was headed."

"Okay, fair enough." The Witchlet giggled again, nervously this time. "But in my defense, that was before I realized just who you were."

Roxy tightened her grip, wrenching the Witchlets arms high towards the middle of her back, grinding her knee cap into the Witchlets spine.

"Ow. Stop, please. Okay... Roxy Buckles, right? What if I told you, I have some information that could be very valuable to you?" she stammered, the words running together in her haste to get them out, muffled by the floor and the squashed food her face was pressing into.

"I'd say you were full of shit." Roxy remarked, growing bored with the exchange.

"I swear. It's *good* info. And you're definitely going to want to hear it. All you have to do is let me go and I'll tell you."

Roxy considered the options. She could definitely take on one Witchlet, especially this one, with an arm tied behind her back. But, if she screeched for her coven, then it became a three on one scenario; that would be a problem. Roxy did have to admit, as much as she was sure the Witchlet was having her on, she *was* intrigued.

"If you scream, I'll cut off your -."

"I won't," the Witchlet gulped, knowing exactly what Roxy would cut off.

With a sigh, Roxy released her. The Witchlet scrambled backwards on all fours until she came up against a wall. For all her bravado, she certainly seemed inclined to put some distance between herself and Roxy. The green opalescent scaled skin, long red hair, wickedly sharp nails and pointed teeth

Roxy placed her hand on her weapon; she was curious but she was not stupid.

"What's your name?"

"Verbena."

"And why should I believe anything you have to tell me?"

"I'm a Scout, you see. Queen Moll, she sends me out to different planets looking for ... uh ... companions. There've been a lot of rumours lately. Your name came up several times."

Roxy drew her weapon and spun the dial. It whirred menacingly, it's light flashing through a myriad of colors before it settled on an angry red. It beeped once and a small dot between the Witchlet's two eyes. Roxy took a step closer. Beads of sweat sprung up on Verbena's scaly forehead. She pressed back against the wall.

"Rumours don't pay the bills Verbena."

"It's about a man." She whimpered, really laying it on thick. "He's been on the run a long time. A fugitive. I think you might know him."

Roxy's breath caught in her throat. *Was it possible? Could it really be after all this time?* She wondered. *Dare I hope?*

Abruptly Roxy deactivated and re-holstered her weapon. She crouched down and scrutinized the Witchlet for signs that she was lying. Roxy tried not to appear too eager but the Witchet knew she had her now.

"Talk," Roxy barked, her mood quickly darkening.

Verbena sat forward and eyed Roxy with smug satisfaction.

"Sam Sparrow."

CHAPTER THREE

Charles Lester was still unconscious but his vitals were steady when Roxy returned him home safe and sound. Safe at least until his wife got her hands on him. A sleek Servo-Bot whisked him off down a long hallway while another bot went in search of Mrs. Lester in the stately hover-mansion. Roxy followed along, curiosity getting the better of her once again, and caught a glimpse of a stylish but simple bedroom on the main level.

The Servo-Bot had tucked Mr. Lester into a single bed. Roxy pretended not to notice the bars on the windows or the elaborate locks that had been installed on the outside of the door, though she was impressed by Mrs. Lester's ingenuity and refusal to give in. She quickly retreated, not wanting to get caught snooping by one of her nicest and most lucrative clients.

Mrs. Lester bustled into the foyer a few moments later and offered profuse thanks to Roxy. A small blip from the device around Roxy's wrist indicated that she had been paid in full for her services, plus, she noticed, a generous tip. She bid adieu to the Lester's and silently hoped, for Ethel-Beth's sake, that she would never have to see them again.

The short jaunt across New Cosmos saw Roxy arrive back to the office building quicker than she would have liked. She'd had a lot of time to think between Salemmas and Aurora but she'd also had a lot to process. She sat aboard the Zip as it powered down, wondering how long she'd be able to hide out here before she was discovered.

She'd had a lot of difficult conversations in her lifetime. She'd delivered terrible news to good people; she'd made bad people pay for terrible crimes. But the news she was about to share – it was not a discussion she was looking forward to.

She took a deep breath and unsnapped her seatbelt, slid out of her seat and pushed aside the door before dropping to the ground.

Times like this, she wished there was still something left to pray to. In lieu of that, there was always liquid courage.

***

The Oasis was blocked. Nothing unusual for this time of night. She tossed back a shot of *Soju* and rapped on the bar for another. Roxy was doing what Roxy did best – avoiding.

Patrons from all walks of life lined the bar, jostling each other amiably while they waited to be served, swaying to the music, shouting to be heard. Roxy didn't have to wait though. She was a good customer, though she usually spent her time there out back, in one of the private suites.

The reverberation of the music beat in tune to Roxy's heart. She closed her eyes, remembering - none to fondly - of a time two years prior when silence had fallen on The Oasis. For a spot where the party never stopped, it was almost a death sentence for the popular establishment.

It wasn't obvious at first, the infestation. The constant flow of intoxicating beverages led to carefree, inebriated revellers; no one took notice of the small winged creatures landing on their arm or their neck, nor the tiny, seemingly insignificant bites of the Succungei. Native to the darkest regions beyond the Daemon Belt, the minuscule vampire-like spider, fond of human blood, secreted poison in its saliva as it licked a wound clean. It caused a painful allergic reaction. The fever hit first, then a swelling of the face and watery blisters; bleeding from the eyes and ears was the final sign. These major symptoms lasted only forty-eight hours but those who suffered from the effects of the poison were often left to deal with vision and hearing issues for years to come.

The Oasis was inundated – both with Succungei and angry victims.

The owners, Lars and Bell, were desperate to save their business, and to ensure the safety and comfort of their loyal patrons. All they needed was someone willing to take on the enormous task of exterminating the building.

Enter Roxy Buckles. She enjoyed a challenge and a challenge this would be, she was absolutely certain. Slathered in a thick layer of her own patented No-Bite body spray, Roxy was able to enter The Oasis and easily eradicate the space of its smallest invaders… but the Queen, well, that was a whole different story. The vast bulbous arachnid, carpeted with wiry gray hairs and eight protuberant eyes, had not gone down without a fuss. Roxy shuddered at the recollection. Sure, there had been a little damage from the flame thrower but Lars and Bell had been so thankful to take back possession of their business, they were willing to over look a few scorch marks.

A pleasant scent of light citrus teased her nose, teased her out of her reverie. Cologne. She opened her eyes. The guy eased himself onto the barstool next to Roxy at the same time the bartender slid another drink in front of her. It was gone within seconds. She hoped he would be too. She wasn't feeling very social.

"Haven't seen you here before." His voice was gravelly, like he spent a lot of time smoking, or screaming orders. Maybe a bit of both.

"That's because I like to drink alone."

"Fair enough," he held out his hand. "Alexzander S. Zillinger."

Roxy ignored it. "That's a bit of a mouthful."

He winked. "My friends call me Zillo."

"Is your next line going to be something about me needing to know your name 'cause I'll be screaming it later?" Roxy deadpanned.

He threw back his head, his raucous laughter discernible even above the pulse of the music. "I like you. Let me buy you a drink. No strings attached; I promise."

Roxy turned to face him. He had dark eyes and dark hair and the grin on his face suggested knowledge of dark and dirty deeds.

Just the way she liked 'em.

"Okay, I'll have a drink with you. But I buy my own." Roxy waved to the bartender. "I'll take the bottle Suzie, just put it on my tab." She crooked a finger at Zillo. "Let's grab a booth in the back."

***

The bottle in the middle of the table held only an inch of clear liquid. Roxy had consumed most of it. The tension had finally seeped from her shoulders and she was starting to forget her troubles. She let go, began to enjoy herself, the company and the conversation. It had been a long time since she had talked this much.

She was having fun.

She might have been a little bit drunk.

"Wait, you're telling me the guy was keeping a *LanQuid*… in his *bathtub*?" Zillo stared at Roxy, a bemused quirk to his brow. "You know I've always wanted to visit Earth but now I'm not so sure."

"Ah they're not all bad. Maybe just a little naïve." Roxy smiled as she thought of Ed Farris and wondered how the poor guy was doing. And if he'd ever gotten the LanQuid ichor out of his carpet. "We all are, at times."

He watched her, shrewd, assessing. "This ex of yours. He's on the up and up then?"

Roxy nodded slowly, the liquor had loosened her tongue and she'd confessed the whole sordid mess. "Sure is," a heavy sigh escaped her lips. "I fucked up."

"Don't blame yourself. You did the best you could with the information you had at the time. I bet he doesn't blame you for it either."

She fiddled with her glass, "maybe."

"Think you'll get back together with him after all this is over?"

"I'm afraid that ship has sailed Zillo."

"That's a real shame, doll. Sounds like you really cared for each other."

"Maybe," a shrug of her shoulder. "It is what it is."

They sat in companionable silence for while, the beat of the music throbbing in their ears, the *Sujo* coursing through Roxy's veins.

"Well, Roxy, it's getting late." Zillo cocked his head to one side, pursed his lips. "What do you say we head back to your place now?"

"I think that's the best idea I've heard all day," Roxy replied.

They stood. Zillo threw an arm around Roxy's shoulders and she leaned into his side with a sigh, her head on his shoulder. They left the bar together and headed off into the falling dusk.

***

"You going to be okay to get upstairs by yourself? I can walk you up if you're feeling too wobbly."

"I'll be fine Zillo, thanks." She hiccupped, then giggled. "Oops. Sorry. I really appreciate the ride home and the chat. It was good to get it off my chest. I've never met an Engineer that didn't drink before."

"One's my limit. Get some sleep doll. Keep in touch, and like I said, call me if you ever need anything. Or even if you don't need anything at all." Zillo winked and pulled away. "Stay safe," he shouted out the window.

Roxy waved. *Who knew?* she thought to herself, *guess you really could find friends in low places.*

***

She flopped back on her bed, fully clothed; let her eyes drift shut. It was certainly not the way Roxy had expected the night to end. *Or the morning to begin*, she thought ruefully to herself as the first pale streaks of dawn penetrated the room, caressing her face with weak sunlight. She turned on her side and curled into a ball. A few hours of sleep were all she needed.

The jarring bleep from her wristlet pulled her back from the edge of slumber. She sat up abruptly, noting the name of the caller on the display. She groaned.

"What's up?"

The voice on the other end of the call was brisk, but Roxy listened attentively, eventually nodding and rising to her feet.

"I'm on my way."

CHAPTER FOUR

Sam Sparrow was dead.

Deceased, departed, lifeless, gone.

Or at least he *would* be… once Roxy caught up with him. He'd finally been spotted. A credible tip from a reliable source this time. It checked out and there would be no mistakes this time.

Yeah, you've already made enough of those, she thought to herself.

This might be her last chance to set things right and she planned to grab that opportunity by the balls. And twist.

Roxy had always thought Sparrow had had help with his escape. She'd never been able to pinpoint just who had been his accomplice but that person was second in line on her most wanted list.

She perched on the corner of her desk, tossed back a third caf-tab and prayed it would keep her upright and moving for the rest of the day. She drummed the fingers of her right-hand rhythmically atop the gleaming surface and stared through the glass windows of her high-rise office. The hazy azure sky proved an inadequate distraction as she ruminated over the logistics of her plan. Her brain was shifting into full prep mode as she neared go time.

There was just that one last little thing that she needed to do.

She couldn't put it off any longer.

"Suki," she shouted through the closed door, the slight waver in her voice only a small indication of the trepidation she felt. This would be a difficult discussion. She waited a few minutes, then louder, "SUKI."

In short order the door banged open and a harried Suki Kwan appeared at the threshold, hands clenched on the wheels of her chair as she pushed herself forward. "You know; you *could* call me on the intercom occasionally. I distinctly remember showing you how to use it, so you have no excuse."

Roxy chuckled, "but how else would I get to see that gorgeous face of yours?"

The quirk of an eyebrow but no response.

Roxy tried again. "I thought you deserved a break?"

The corners of Suki's mouth fought to curl into a smile. A break. Sure. "You're trying to butter me up. What do you want me to do now?"

Roxy paused, her demeanor growing serious. "I need you to clear my schedule for the rest of this week. Maybe even the week after as well."

Suki examined her boss through narrowed eyes, "you're joking."

"Sorry," Roxy said visibly deflated, hoping the sincerity of her apology came through. "I am not."

Suki was not convinced. She launched into a tirade about responsibilities, their reputation as a company and the potential loss of valuable clients. Roxy winced and collapsed into a chair. She placed her forehead against her cool maple desk and allowed Suki's rage to wash over her. She was right of course but alas… Roxy had to raise her voice several decibels to be heard above the indignation: "I've got a lead on Sparrow."

Silence. Suki Kwan being speechless, that didn't happen very often. Sparrow was a topic they avoided at all costs and here was Roxy just dumping him into the middle of the conversation like a rotting corpse.

Suki's expression ran a gamut of emotions before she quickly composed herself - the defeated slump of her shoulders though; it made Roxy's heart ache. She waited it out, knew Suki would be mad if she intervened with platitudes or pity. When she sensed that Suki was ready, she began to speak again, sharing the information she'd gotten from the Witchlet and the plan she had formulated. It was a damned good plan too.

"Are you sure Roxy?"

"I am."

"It's been such a long time, is it even worth it now?"

"Yes, Suki, it is."

Suki nodded her acceptance. Once Roxy set her mind to something, well, there was no going back.

Roxy stood, with a determined stride she rounded the desk to crouch and take Suki's hand in hers. She brushed her thumb gently across the pale scars that crisscrossed Suki's knuckles: "It will *always* be worth it my friend. You deserve justice. And I sure as hell plan on making sure you get it."

***

Home.

Alone.

With nothing but her thoughts for company.

Nibbling absently on a PWR Protein Delite™, she briefly considered giving in and finally buying herself a robo-pet. Something other than silence to greet her when she walked in the door.

Yes, there were a million other places she would rather be right now than this godforsaken condominium but she had sworn to Suki that she would not leave Aurora until the morning. Transport wouldn't prepare a Zip Ship for her until then anyways. Suki made sure of that.

She frowned at the tasteless snack in her hand, as if only just realizing it was a mediocre excuse for dinner. With a sigh, she tossed it, half eaten, in the trash.

Roxy selected the pre-programmed shutdown mode on her Condo-Comm Interface (or CoCo for short) and the windows overlooking downtown New Cosmos turned opaque and dark. The perfect accompaniment to her mood. A hush fell over the apartment as the state-of-the-art system blocked out the constant rush, rush, rush of the busy metropolis below. All Roxy wanted to hear was the sound of wine being sloshed into a glass. A lot of wine. Into a very large glass. But first, a more adequate shower than the one she had so abruptly received earlier.

She wandered into her bedroom, peeled off the clothes she'd worn that day and with them, her composure.

She stepped into the stall; the one place where she allowed herself to let go, the scalding water washing away the stench of the city, and the scorch of her tears. She scrubbed until her skin was pink.

Afterwards, wrapped in a thigh skimming oversized sweater and little else, Roxy folded herself onto the sofa, careful not to spill the generous glass of wine she had poured for herself. Using her wristlet, she ordered what would prove to be too much sushi for one person and finally admitted to herself that there was only one thing she would be doing for the rest of the night... and it would not be sleeping.

CHAPTER FIVE

"CoCo, open file A241-M93, cast for display."

"Happy to help, Roxy," came the smooth computerized response. Instantly, the wall in front of Roxy was transformed into a screen and became awash with high resolution photographs. Smiling faces beamed out at her: a blast from the past. She selected one in particular, sweeping aside the others with a flick of her wrist. She grasped the image in mid-air and zoomed in on the happy group.

The good old days. Before everything went to shit.

Roxy waved her hand and the pile of photographs fanned out in front of her again.

"Slideshow."

"Would you like music to accompany your presentation?" CoCo prompted.

"Fuck no."

"As you wish."

The lights dimmed automatically, and in succession, Roxy's early life played out before her eyes. Those blissful years at The Academy, when they were young and unaware just how bad things would get; before they'd experienced horror, loss and sadly, for Roxy, unimaginable betrayal.

She took a hasty sip of wine as a picture of an 18-year-old Suki Kwan came into sharp focus. Roxy's heart swelled. Long, straight, dark hair framed a cherubic face as the vibrant girl posed cheekily against a backdrop of sand and sun. No scars yet marred her perfect complexion. She was happy and healthy. While Suki continued to recover from her injuries, a wheelchair provided freedom and a sense of independence, and as she grew more confident, sometimes just a single cane. Roxy's closest friend. She owed her so much.

Roxy punished herself like this often. Penance. There were some things she just couldn't forgive herself for. Tonight, though, this was different, she was using this to fuel herself for the fight ahead; to get fired up before she would head out in the morning to finally exterminate the one crim that got away.

No one ever escaped from Roxy Buckles. They didn't call her the best in the business for nothing.

And then, there he was, as if her very thoughts had conjured him up out of thin air: winking at her from the slideshow; nearly life-sized, the photo sent shivers coursing down Roxy's spine and the alcohol in her stomach turned sour, the bile rising in her throat.

Sam Sparrow.

"Pause."

She unfurled from her seat, her long legs quickly bringing her eye to eye with the piece of human garbage who'd nearly stolen everything from her. His image was already burned into her mind but she still examined him in great detail, his square jawline, his aquiline nose and the full lips that stretched across those perfect white teeth. He was posing with cocky confidence next to a Zip Ship, the day of their first practice jaunt; young and brash, and full of promise.

But promises get broken.

A bell jangled loudly. Roxy jumped, her arm jerking; the wine in her half full glass sloshed over the rim and spilled. She cursed fluently as red blossomed across the wall next to her, splattering close to the ceiling and running in bloody torrents to the floor.

Roxy activated call mode on her wristlet, mentally chastising herself for not having turned off the damn notification sounds when she had arrived at home like a sensible person would have done. "Aeyo, Roxy Buckles speaking."

Eyebrows disappearing somewhere in the vicinity of her hairline, Roxy sat abruptly on the sofa as the voice on the other end of the wristlet identified themselves – not that they needed to. Roxy would have known that voice anywhere. No, it wasn't every day that she received a personal call from the Commander of the Planetary Regulation Committee.

"Commander Carmine." Roxy tried to keep her voice even.

"Ms. Buckles. We may have a job for you, if you are interested."

If she was interested? Roxy thought, astonished that it was even a question that required any sort of consideration.

"Of course, anything at all I can do to help the Committee sir," Roxy replied, trying to keep her voice level.

"Glad to hear. Please be at The PRC Plaza at nine tomorrow morning. My assistant Flavia will meet you in the lobby."

"I will definitely..." Roxy trailed off at the sound of a loud click. The Commander had already ended the call. "... be there." She ended breathlessly.

Bubbles of anticipation tickled their way through Roxy's stomach, effervescing through her mouth in an exultant shout: "YES."

It had happened. Finally. All her hard work was paying off. Roxy flailed about the room to a song heard only in her head; her arms in the air, her hips gyrating un-rhythmically in what for her was a close approximation of a dance.

Bzzzz.

The takeout food had arrived, interrupting her jubilant celebration. She giggled and straightened her clothes and hair. As she went to answer the buzzer her eyes flicked to the projection still up on the wall and her elation drained away. She slammed back to reality with a jolt and realized with a sinking dread that this meeting with Commander Carmine might mean putting any other plans on hold. *Damn.*

She opened the door and graciously accepted the package of food from the delivery drone. It beeped its thanks and zipped away. Roxy tore into the packaging and, standing at the kitchen counter began devouring her dragon rolls, salmon maki and crab nigari with relish. She washed it down with long pulls of wine from the bottle, swiping her mouth with the back of her hand. All the while she stared daggers at the picture of Sam Sparrow still larger than life on her condo wall, as a crimson stain darkened on the wall behind him.

She nodded decisively.

Soon.

CHAPTER SIX

The next morning, on the mosaic patterned portico that led into The PRC Plaza, Roxy found herself gazing upward in wonder at the unapologetic opulence of the building. The aptly-named *megatall* skyscraper soared beyond the clouds, disappearing into the miasma of morning, its dark tinted windows mirroring distorted ghostly images of passing ships, cargo-carriers and biomorphic robotic birds.

"Excuse me." A tall muscular dual-headed man that Roxy recognized as a local meteorologist grinned at her from both faces as he walked past her on the sidewalk. "Nice day we're having." One head winked and Roxy returned the smile.

It was then she realized that she'd been standing there, slack-jawed in front of the building, for an embarrassing length of time. She clamped her mouth shut and pretended to fiddle with her wristlet until the heat in her cheeks subsided.

She could not - would not - blow this. Ever since she had graduated from the Academy and been given the official designation of Exterminator, she had dreamed of being called upon to serve the Planetary Regulation Committee. And now here she was.

Better late than never, Roxy thought to herself. Stiffening her shoulders, and her resolve, she approached the entryway where the automatic doors whooshed open to permit her access. The chill of the controlled climate inside was a welcome embrace.

The scene that greeted Roxy was absolute chaos. People scurried in all directions and though no one quite seemed to pay attention to where they were going, they avoided each other, and potential collisions, with an ease born of practice.

The place had seen a lot of upgrades since Roxy had last been there a decade ago. That included a large floating electronic notice board that she had to crane her neck to see. Advertisements and announcements flashed across the display.

A tremor passed through Roxy as a large picture of a Witchlet projected onto the screen. She had seen enough of those damned things to last a lifetime. The picture was accompanied by scrolling text encouraging any civilians who had been affected by the recent increase in kidnappings to please contact Sergio in the Complaints Department.

A petite young woman, her short hair the color of ripe blueberries advanced on Roxy, waving impatiently, "I am Flavia, Commander Carmine's executive assistant. Follow me." She turned, not waiting for a response from Roxy, and dashed off in the direction of a bank of elevators nestled in an alcove beneath a busy mezzanine. Roxy followed behind hurriedly, trying to keep Flavia in her sights while she dodged a person swinging a briefcase and shouting loudly into their wrist.

"Level 220," Flavia ordered, barely allowing time for Roxy to slip inside the swiftly closing doors. Roxy shot a surreptitious glance in the assistant's direction; Flavia was staring straight ahead at the floor designators.

The elevator rocketed upwards, numbers blurring on the monitor as the speed increased. Roxy suppressed the urge to fill the awkward silence with small talk and instead, stood quietly, willing her nervous body not to sweat through the armpits of her recently purchased silk charmeuse blouse.

The elevator pinged, announced their arrival, and the doors slid opened. Roxy gaped. The office of Commander Seth Carmine encompassed the entire 220th floor.

"I will leave you here. Please wait in the atrium until you are called." Flavia gestured for Roxy to exit the elevator.

"Thank you."

Flavia gave a curt nod and then she was gone.

Wow. Suki deserves a big *raise*, Roxy thought.

"Ms. Buckles."

The mellifluous voice came to her from her left and she shifted to acknowledge the tall, well-dressed man who stepped out of the shadows, his hand extended. His thick head of salt and pepper hair was perfectly coiffed. Beneath the curve of his enigmatic smile was a neatly trimmed goatee.

He clasped Roxy's hand in his. His handshake was dry and firm.

"Commander Carmine, it is a pleasure to meet you."

"Ms. Buckles, the pleasure is all mine. Please, join me in the lounge. I've had Flavia come in early and prepare us a breakfast tray. She makes a wonderful cup of coffee."

"I would be delighted and please, call me Roxy."

He grinned. "Excellent. We will be Roxy and Seth then."

Roxy could have fit her entire condo just inside Commander Carmine's lounge. The lavish furnishings were monochrome black and grey; one entire wall was made of glass and looked out onto a tiffany blue sky. The opposite wall was bare, save for a large abstract painting of serpentine swirls.

Feeling strangely out of her element Roxy waited until the Commander indicated she should take a seat before she settled herself on the edge of a stiff leather sofa. A Servo-Bot materialized at Roxy's elbow, poured her a cup of coffee and then dashed away as quickly as it had come. Commander Carmine served himself from a crystal decanter of light amber liquid. Roxy took a small polite sip from her cup; it was good coffee.

"You'll forgive me Roxy if I skip the pleasantries and get straight to business?" He did not wait for a reply. "The PRC have had eyes on a sect of rebels for a while now. Years even. Recently, there have been some rumors of an uprising. They call themselves The Bastent and we have reason to believe that the recent increase in intergalactic crimes have a direct correlation with their... activism."

Roxy leaned forward; her curiosity piqued. An idea was beginning to take shape in the back of her mind. *Sparrow? Lynx? Was it possible?*

Carmine continued: "Your recent LanQuid problem, for example. Who do you think sent that particular pest Earthside? And I believe there was a rather unpleasant Succungei infestation not that long ago as well? Dare I mention that our Complaints Department is working overtime dealing with all the hysterical women bemoaning the loss of their poor stupid husbands. Damned oversexed aliens." He slammed his glass onto a side table.

"This group has zero interest in negotiating for peace." He grimaced. "We have tried of course, but they are spoiling for war."

"What can I do to..."

"You must infiltrate the contingent." He pushed on, as though he hadn't even heard her speak. "And apprehend their miscreant leader. According to our sources The Bastent have been very, very busy." His upper lip curled in disgust. "Recruiting criminals and other outcasts that they have convinced to commit to their cause. They are running amok all over this solar system and far, far beyond."

Roxy, her coffee long forgotten, placed her cup back on the table. It clinked against the marble top and Commander Carmine jolted. He was so caught up in his impassioned speech, he seemed to have forgotten that there was someone else in the room. He stood and shed his jacket, rolling the sleeves to the elbow. He approached the bank of windows and gazed thoughtfully into the distance. Clouds billowed past, obscuring the view. The silence stretched.

Roxy finally spoke, unable to stand the suspense any longer. "This leader, Commander... Seth... what is..."

"River Lynx." He interrupted, spitting out the name as though it left a bad taste in his mouth. "From Mauw. They have been a thorn in my side for far too long. It's personal now."

Roxy struggled to keep her face blank.

Carmine scrutinized her from across the room. "I am sure you can understand that yourself Roxy. From what I have heard, you know a little something about personal grudges." He stopped just short of a satisfied smirk.

Seth Carmine was a shrewd bastard. But he wouldn't throw Roxy off her game. She knew that her need for vengeance against Sparrow was common knowledge and she could accept that. It also wasn't beyond reason that The PRC would be keeping tabs on her, putting her directly on Carmine's radar.

"I can leave today," she said decisively.

"Excellent." Commander Carmine tented his fingers. "I will have Flavia forward you the coordinates to Mauw and the file we have on The Bastent. I have heard very good things about you Roxy, I can see a bright future for you with The PRC."

"Thank you, Seth. I appreciate the confidence you have in me."

Roxy rose and smoothed the palms of her sweaty hands down along the thighs of her pencil skirt. She glanced up to find the Commander had moved closer. *Was he checking her out?*

Roxy cleared her throat to break the tension. "Any special instructions that you have for me?"

He reached down to pick up the drink he had poured earlier, threw it back, his throat working as he swallowed the amber liquid. Sweat glistened on his forehead.

"Just get the job done."

"And for clarification, this leader of The Bastent... how do you...?"

"Dead or alive Roxy." His face spread into a sinuous smile. "But preferably dead."

CHAPTER SEVEN

Roxy decided to walk the ten blocks from the business district to the Chaffey Building and the offices of Buckles & Associates. She grabbed an order of onion bhajis from a street vendor and ate as she strolled. Having missed out on breakfast, she was starving.

By the time she arrived back on her own turf, her feet were sore but her mind was clear.

It was unusually quiet when she let herself into the office. She glanced at the time and was surprised to see that the afternoon had crept up on her. Suki was likely out for lunch. Wearily she removed her heels and limped towards her inner sanctum. She sank into her chair with an audible groan of relief.

An eerie sense of calm had come over Roxy the moment she had learned that Commander Carmine was sending her to Mauw. Suddenly everything she had learned as of late made sense. She thought back to the information she had gleaned from the Witchlet Verbena before she'd exterminated her, and felt a tiny twinge of guilt for having gone back on her word.

River Lynx and Sam Sparrow were working together; Roxy was absolutely certain now. It was all coming together. And they had to be stopped.

Roxy would leave for Mauw within the hour.

She was about to kill two birds with one stone.

***

Her mood matched the gloom of the sky outside her window. Thunder grumbled in the distance.

Roxy wasn't very good at goodbyes, even the thought of them, so she busied herself: a mediocre distraction. Within a few minutes she had arranged passage on a cargo-carrier out of Aurora that evening, calling in a favor to keep her name off the official manifest.

She would leave the Zip Ship behind this time. Flight plans meant she could be tracked and she saw no reason to give warning that she was on the way.

Her wristlet beeped: a message from Commander Carmine's assistant Flavia as promised. Detailed dossiers on River Lynx and The Bastent were attached. She would read those on the trip. And then there was her contract. *That* she would read now. Roxy gave a low whistle at the payout she was due upon completion of her mission. That would buy a *lot* of sushi. A non-disclosure clause near the end spelled out in no uncertain terms that no one was to be made aware of the nature of her travels. Roxy hated keeping things from Suki but this time it would be a necessary evil.

From the closet she retrieved a change of clothes – she wouldn't be caught without one again – and quickly shrugged out of the blouse and skirt she had worn to The PRC meeting. Slim fitting dark pants, black shirt and jacket replaced them. She hauled on worn combat boots. In front of a mirror, she slicked back her short bouncy curls with gel until they were smooth against her head, and with a precision born of practice, lined her eyes with thick kohl and traded her signature bright red lipstick for a slash of deep maroon.

Roxy stared at herself for a moment, stiffened her shoulders like a good soldier. She grabbed her Go Bag and stepped out of the room, closing the door softly as she turned.

"Roxy!"

Roxy jumped. Suki had returned from lunch. "Shit, you scared me."

"You look..." Suki trailed off as she took in Roxy's changed appearance.

"I believe the word you are searching for is *delicious*." Roxy smirked.

"Wait." Suki knitted her brow, her eyes roving to the travel bag that Roxy held in her hand. "Were you leaving without saying goodbye?"

"You know I'm not good with this stuff Suki," Roxy replied, bravado gone.

"You were going to send me a Holo-Gram once you were in the air, weren't you?"

"Maybe." Roxy grimaced. Sometimes she wished Suki didn't know her quite so well.

"You don't have to do this Roxy. It's been ten years since Sparrow went AWOL. He's kept his head down. Maybe we should just leave the past where it belongs – in the past."

Ignoring Suki's plea, Roxy leaned over to place a lingering kiss on her forehead. "Remember what we used to say to each other, back at the academy, before we left on our practice missions?"

Suki snorted. "You were the one who came up with that particular gem. And *you* were the only one who ever used it. But I remember." She paused. "How long do you think you'll be gone?"

Roxy reached down and grabbed her bag. She walked to the automatic doors and stood in front them, frozen.

"Roxy?"

Roxy shook her head once, plastered on a cocky grin and glanced back over her shoulder: "Goodbye, don't cry, you'll see me soon!"

Suki groaned. "Is that a promise?"

Roxy hurried through the door before Suki had a chance to ask any more questions.

For once in her life, Roxy didn't have the answers.

***

She slipped aboard The Orbiter 3000 under cover of darkness, a wink and a nod from the porter as he unlocked the cargo hold and walked away whistling. Roxy grabbed a pile of old netting and made herself comfortable between a crate of mangolo fruit and a stack of pallets containing automatic solar trackers.

She lay back against the makeshift bed, duffle beneath her head, and scrolled through the files Flavia had sent. The report consisted mostly of third-party information and tips from shady informants. There was no solid evidence that Roxy could see. She frowned. She'd expected more. The

Mauwian's were, in general, a peaceful species. There had never been a reason to visit their planet until now and they rarely, if ever, travelled outside their own. Roxy couldn't help but wonder why the Mauwian's would all of a sudden turn hostile and instigate war.

Sparrow's influence no doubt, Roxy sneered.

She yawned, her eyes heavy from reading the files in the dim light. It had been a long day. She felt the vibrations of the motors as they revved up to lift the ship from its moorings and before long, the gentle rhythmic sway of open space became a soothing lullaby and Roxy succumbed to sleep.

CHAPTER EIGHT

A heavy thump roused Roxy from her slumber. The ship had docked on Mauw. She blinked several times, driving the sleep from her eyes. She grabbed a PWR Protein Delite™ from her bag – matcha flavor this time – and ate it quickly, needing the burst of energy. She slipped the straps of her bag over her shoulders and then lingered in the shadows near the door of the cargo hold, waiting for the signal.

Three sharp raps on the door. Roxy would have mere seconds to leave the ship and find cover. Being caught as a stowaway was not an option. She detected the low whine of the gears as the door eased open and then she was out.

She ran in a low crouch and did not looking back. The sound of blood rushing and the frantic pounding of her heart was all she heard. She plunged into the gloom of a thicket of trees, dodging branches that whipped at her face as she ran. She stopped only when she could no longer see the lights of the spaceport behind her. She threw herself at the base of a large sequoia hybrid, her breath rasping loudly.

She glanced at her wristlet. No time to rest. Suntwin was rising and she still needed to do recon.

Roxy scrambled to her feet and looked for a place to secret her bag. Her eyes alighted on a natural indentation near the roots of the sequoia. She brushed away dirt and detritus and grunted in satisfaction. The opening was large enough to stuff the bag inside. She kicked leaves and twigs in front of it and stood back. It would have to do. She wiped her dirty hands on her pants and set off at a steady pace. If she remembered correctly, from the brief glance she had gotten as she left the cargo ship, there were lights to the North. Lights meant civilization.

She had gone no more than a few yards when she heard the unmistakable sound of a twig snapping beneath a foot. She slid behind a tree and became still.

"'Ello there," came a friendly voice. "Would you please come out from behind that tree? There are many of us I am afraid. I believe on your planet they say, 'you are surrounded?'"

"Dammit," Roxy muttered.

"Please do not be alarmed. We will not hurt you."

Roxy took a deep breath and stepped out from her hiding place. Any words she might have said died in her throat. Before her, in the low light of dawn, was the most stunning creature she had ever seen. Tall and covered in sleek ginger fur, festooned in khaki shorts and shirt, the Mauwian grinned at her, displaying tiny sharp teeth. Cerulean feline eyes winked at her from beneath the brim of a matching khaki beret.

"Ello." Their voice was gravelly but amiable. "My friends and I would appreciate it if you would come with us. I will walk towards you slowly and then I will take your arm."

The Mauwian seemed to be waiting for her consent.

Roxy gave a curt nod. They approached her calmly. "I am Bareen. It would be my pleasure to escort you to meet our sovereign."

Roxy's lips thinned with fury.

She'd been set up.

From behind, and to either side of Roxy, smaller but similarly dressed felines appeared. One, striped with long fur, waved cheerfully.

Bareen gently took Roxy's hand and placed it in the crook of their elbow. Arm in arm, they strolled out of the forest and along a well trodden dirt path, the other Mauwian's chattering and laughing behind them. Bareen's arm was soft and warm.

"River will be very pleased to meet you," Bareen murmured, patting Roxy's hand. "They have heard many good things about you."

It was the oddest capture Roxy had ever experienced.

The dirt path wound a circuitous route that stretched on for miles. Suntwin had reached its zenith in the sky by the time they emerged into a lush green meadow. The smaller Mauwian's dropped to all fours and loped through the grass, chasing each other, their tails high above their backs.

Bareen chuckled indulgently at their antics. "Kittens."

Roxy kept her mouth shut.

Just beyond the meadow lay a large cluster of modern wooden buildings. High above those, in the sturdy branches of the sequoia hybrids, were hundreds of tree houses. Homes, Roxy realized, taking note of a multitude of tiny faces that peered at her through the windows. Some of the treehouses were connected by large patios, others by enormous branches – both scored deeply with scratch marks and gouges. Vibrant green foliage grew unchecked on and around the houses, providing natural shade but also allowing brilliant light to filter through.

Roxy could see several fully grown Mauwian's luxuriating in the Suntwin's rays, one lay curled up on a branch nose to tail. Roxy could hear them snoring, despite the distance.

Bareen corralled her towards the largest of the low structures and Roxy reluctantly dragged her gaze away. It was a utilitarian building; two windows and a door, a small deck ran the length of the front and was home to a multitude of lush potted plants that Roxy quickly identified as Nepeta Cataria or, in layman's terms, catnip. Roxy followed Bareen up the two steps that led to the deck, eyes roving, taking notes.

It was cool inside, a welcome relief after the long walk.

"Please wait here, River will be with you shortly. I will bring you a drink."

This was the main room of a meeting hall. Chairs were fanned out in front of a podium, and next to that, a whiteboard was cluttered with tiny cramped handwriting. In the corner, filing cabinets were stacked in a neat line. This must be where The Bastent gathered. Their headquarters.

"Bareen will return shortly with your drink."

Roxy jumped. She spun around, chagrined at having been snuck up on again. She was losing her touch.

"I am sorry to have startled you Ms. Buckles. Sometimes we forget that humans do not sense our approach."

So, this was River Lynx. Of average human height, with golden eyes and wearing the same khaki uniform as the others, their Bengal coat gleamed as they approached Roxy, a paw extended in greeting. Roxy ignored it.

"I am sure you have many questions and there will come a time when I will answer those for you. You have my word. In the meantime, to alleviate your curiosity, the young porter who snuck you aboard The Orbiter… he is a friend of The Bastent."

Roxy's nostrils flared. Heads would roll if she ever made it back to Aurora.

"Please do not be angry with him Ms. Buckles. He meant well."

"What do you want from me?" Roxy burst out.

"It is not *I* that wants anything from you. Although I am very pleased to have you here. Please, take a seat."

"Why don't *you* take that seat and shove…"

"Roxy."

Roxy gasped and spun around. Shock rippled across her face and she felt herself go cold.

He was older and a jagged scar crossed his forehead but it was him. "It's been a long time."

And then he had the gall to smile.

White hot anger exploded in Roxy's chest and her vision blurred. She launched herself across the room, tossing chairs as she went, her hands reaching blindly for Sam Sparrow's throat.

From the corner of her eye, she saw something furry launch itself in the air. She felt the jarring impact, the nothingness of freefall and then the sharp pain as her head cracked against the timber of the podium.

There was a rush of sound, voices shouting and then… nothing.

CHAPTER NINE

The terse whispers were barely audible above the steady drum of pain that threatened to rip her skull apart but they teased her to consciousness nonetheless. She blinked the room into focus.

It was a small bedroom, sparsely furnished with roughly hewn timber walls. The bed upon which she rested took up most of the space. There was a small table next to the bed that held a glass of water and, in the corner, a tall structure that Roxy thought might be a scratching post. It contained nothing else and Roxy wondered, vaguely, if this was meant to be a holding cell. An unidentifiable though not unpleasant floral scent was heavy upon the air, drifting in through the window on a gentle breeze. Gauzy drapes had been drawn against the light; they undulated lazily in the draft. The window was really all she needed to facilitate her escape.

Roxy was lying atop a firm but comfortable mattress; a downy pillow cradled her head and a delicate pastel colored muslin blanket covered her legs; a patchwork quilt was draped across the footboard. She struggled to rise from her prone position, her hand flying to her head, and the bandage that covered it, as starbursts flared, eclipsing her vision.

She had one hell of a headache.

The door, slightly ajar, funneled the words of whomever was speaking outside it. Their voices were soft but Roxy had heard enough to know that she was the topic of conversation. She swung her feet over the side of the bed, wincing at the fresh wave of agony that the small movement caused. She pushed through it.

Get it together, Roxy, she chided. *You've dealt with far worse than a knock to the head.*

Roxy slipped from the bed and, keeping an eye and an ear to the door, tiptoed across the room, grateful that she was still wearing her shoes. Putting those on would have taken up precious time. She cringed as a floorboard creaked. She brushed aside the curtains with a trembling hand and squinted into the mid-afternoon light. If her estimates were correct, she had been unconscious and at their mercy for several hours at least, perhaps even half the day.

Sitting gingerly on the window ledge, Roxy eased her legs through the window. Giving herself a little push, she landed softly onto the green grass below, thankful that she was being held on the ground floor. She rounded the side of the building and leaned against the back wall, breathing heavily. She swiped at the greasy sheen of sweat that coated her brow and glanced back to confirm that, this time, she had not been followed. She was in the clear.

She slipped into the heavy copse of trees beyond and was swallowed whole.

For hours Roxy followed the signal, the tracker on her supplies sending coordinates to her wristlet, leading the way back to where she had left her bag beneath the tree. She concentrated on putting one foot in front of the other, though her limbs felt impossibly heavy and her boots like weights upon her feet. She stopped only once, leaning her forehead against the rough bark of a tree, struggling for the strength to carry on. Her bandage caught on the husk as she pushed herself upright. She ripped it off, cringing as it stuck and then tossed it aside, taking vague note that the bleeding seemed to have stopped. Small blessings.

She was desperate for rest, even more desperate for water but the thought of the bag of supplies that she had hidden beneath that sequoia kept her plodding on, even when she wanted to give up. She would never be able to forgive herself for getting busted when she had first arrived and, even more so, for having been cocky enough to leave her weapon behind before she had set out in the first place.

It had been a rookie mistake.

She would not let it happen again.

As Suntwin began its descent in the sky, Roxy broke through what seemed to be a familiar thicket of woods. Assured by the coordinates on her wristlet she made her way through the dense foliage, dodged branches, tripped over roots and snapped twigs until she reached the point from which she had started.

In the rapidly fading light, she dug frantically with bare fingers, her short nails gouging viciously into the lush earth beneath the tree. She pulled the mud-speckled bag free of its confines and with shaky, dirty hands, dug around inside.

A small cry of victory: she hauled open a sealed package and threw several blobs of *Quencher* - portable drinking water that was encased in an edible membrane - into her mouth. The relief was immediate; the liquid exploded on her tongue, drenched her parched mouth and soothed her burning throat as it went down.

Her thirst momentarily satiated, she gnawed on a strip of eggplant jerky while she gathered her things together. Using a fallen frond, she brushed the dirt back into place, hoping what she had done would look natural should anyone come searching in the area.

Sleep was not an option but she badly needed it. Sitting beneath the tree she rifled through the bag once more and exhaled joyously through her teeth as her hand brushed against the small injector pen at the bottom of her bag. She'd forgotten it was there but she was damned happy to find it. Removing the cap, Roxy slammed the auto-injector into her thigh, delivering a high dose of pain relief medication directly into the muscle. It quickly spread throughout her body bringing reprieve when it was desperately needed. The cessation of the throbbing pain in her head was nearly instantaneous and the aches and discomfort of her breakneck escape and endless run into the woods seeped away.

Feeling relatively back to normal now, or as close as she was ever going to get at present time anyways, Roxy pushed herself to her feet and brushed the bits of dirt and broken leaves off of her clothes. Her hands were filthy. She touched her head and winced; she felt dried blood and was certain that she must be covered in blood and gore. She would never dare to use a *Quencher* to clean herself. Roxy had no idea how long she'd be on her own here and water was precious. She would have to ration.

As nice and quiet as it was here, despite the peaceful solitude of the night, she definitely could not stay where she was. It would be the first place they would check once they realized she was missing, if they hadn't already. She would not underestimate them this time.

Brain churning, tossing out different scenarios and how they might play out, she tried to formulate a plan. As far as Roxy was concerned, she was going to have to go bold or... well, there would be no going home for her.

She slipped the bag over her shoulders, tightening the straps around her chest and waist so it wouldn't bounce if she had to run and secured her weapon to her thigh in a holster for easy access if she needed it. As content as she would ever be with the plan she had made on the fly, she soldiered on, heading back in the same direction from which she had come only a short while ago.

Under the cover of darkness, she would slip back into their lair.

Only this time, she was ready for them.

Roxy had claws too.

And she damn well wasn't afraid to use them.

CHAPTER TEN

"She could not have gone far. That was quite a knock to the head."

"You don't know Roxy." Sparrow gave a long-suffering sigh.

"No, I do not." There was a pause. "Forgive me my friend, but perhaps, after all this time, neither do you."

Though she was tempted to sneak a look, Roxy stayed hidden, cloaked in shadows; eavesdropping. The pain in her skull had lessened to a dull throb but she seethed with anger. It was something she knew she had to get under control. She would need a clear head for what was to come.

There was a rustle above her - someone was standing at the window. They pushed aside the drapery; a glimpse of dark calloused hands on the sill told Roxy it was Sparrow. She shrunk back, flattening herself against the exterior.

"We *have* to find her River."

"We will. Tonight, we must rest. In the morning Bereen will lead the search party. They are one of our best trackers."

"I'm going with them."

Their tone, firm: "No, you will not Sam."

There was a muttered curse and the window abruptly slammed shut. Roxy released the breath she'd been holding.

Guess Sparrow isn't the one calling the shots after all, Roxy thought, puzzled. *So, what the hell do they want with me?*

She waited until the lights in the room were extinguished and then crept back to the shelter of the trees behind the meeting hall. Things were quiet in the small Mauwian settlement; tree houses were dark and nothing but the quiet subtle sounds of night drifted through the windows high above.

Still, Roxy would maintain her vigil.

The faint sound of footsteps drifted to her ears and a dark shape paused at the periphery of the forest. *Sparrow.* He began walking in the opposite direction of the village. Roxy waited a few beats, then followed, keeping close to the treeline, her dark clothes blending in with the night.

After hiking a short distance, a separate dwelling loomed out of nowhere, all on its own. Sparrow climbed a short ladder and entered a hut that rested on the lower branches of another massive sequoia. It was octagonal like the other tree houses she had observed but smaller: big enough for just one man. She heard muffled sounds issuing from inside and then, a few minutes later he re-emerged, drink in hand and leaned a hip against the railing that surrounded the platform of the house. He rubbed absently at the scar on his forehead.

He looked a little worse for the wear she had to admit, his hair was longer now; there were several days of bristly growth on his face and his clothes were rumpled and sweat-stained. Roxy felt a twinge of something that might have been pity. This was a different Sam Sparrow than the one she had known. How the mighty had fallen. He looked... defeated.

No. Roxy shook herself mentally. Now was not the time for sentimentalities. She needed to focus on what she had come here to do. Once that was sorted, she would do the job The Planetary Regulation Committee had hired her for. She'd found herself rather underwhelmed by River Lynx, despite their reputation as a tyrant and leader of a fascist regime. Roxy expected they could be disposed of with very little effort on her part, a quick slice of a blade; up close and personal.

She watched from the shadows as Sam tossed back his drink and with a deep sigh that was audible even from the distance that separated them, he went back inside. She would bide her time. He'd have to sleep eventually.

Afraid that the light from her wristlet might alert someone to her position, Roxy sat in the shadows with nothing but her dark thoughts to keep her company:

And she was right back there. It was immediately after the explosion. Smoke, dust and the incessant keening of an alarm filled the burning air. She staggered through the rubble, trying to blink dirt and blood out of her eyes. She heard shouting, crying and then suddenly realized that it was her: she was screaming their names, struggling to be heard above the cacophony of disaster.

"Ma'am? Ma'am are you alright? Do you need help?"

The voice came from behind her, muffled. Her ears still rang from the blast. She'd been one of the lucky ones, if you could call it luck: she'd been on the lower levels, about to exit the building, when the blast hit and she had been able to drag herself free.

"My friends! You have to help them!"

"Were they down here with you?" The man in the high-tech rescue gear had to yell to be heard above the whir of rescue helicopters over head and the sirens of emergency vehicles on the ground.

"No... no they were on the 180th floor."

The look on his face told her all that she needed to know.

Well over an hour passed while Roxy remained lost in her memories. She was stiff from sitting in the same spot for so long; she stretched and flexed and emerged from hiding with renewed focus and determination. The time had come. She crept up the ladder, kept her body low to the floor and effected an army crawl along the platform. She would avoid the front door in case it was secured. The windows had been left open though, allowing a balmy breeze to circulate the hut. Roxy risked a glimpse inside. She couldn't help as a small gasp of surprise escaped her lips. Roxy had expected a sparse hideout at best, a place to hunker down and lay low for a while before moving on again, but… Sam had made a *home* here. There was even a vase of flowers on the kitchen table.

Roxy inched around to the next window. A low lamp had been left on in the far corner, a faint blush of light illuminated the man on the bed; a simple white sheet covered his lower half and one arm was flung above his head, across a pillow. He was breathing deeply, sleeping soundly. *Of course.* Roxy averted her gaze but not before getting an eyeful of firm golden male skin.

Nothing you haven't seen before Roxy, she scolded. *Stop stalling.*

She threw one leg through the opening, easing herself across the sill. The floor beneath her boot creaked and she froze, her heart in her throat. Sparrow stirred and the sheet slipped, perching precariously low across his hips. But he did not wake. Roxy sent up a silent prayer of thanks and swung the rest of her body inside. She knelt and pulled a short knife from her boot and stealthily crossed the room.

When Sparrow's eyes popped open, he didn't seem all that surprised to find Roxy straddling him, the sharp edge of her karambit pressing against his throat. He searched her eyes and an expression of something akin to sadness flickered across his face; it happened so quickly that Roxy wondered if perhaps she had imagined it. It was promptly replaced by calm indifference.

Roxy defiantly held his gaze. She'd waited a long time for this moment and the thrill of it thrummed through her veins.

"Any last words Sparrow?" Roxy whispered.

"Not really," Sam drawled. "Only I seem to recall that the last time you were in this position, it was a lot more enjoyable for the both of us."

A lazy grin spread across his face and Roxy's eyes narrowed. With one judiciously aimed blow to the temple, Sparrow was out cold. Roxy sat back and let loose with a string of profanity she was sure would have made a sailor-bot blush.

Dammit. Now she would have to wait until he came to. Despite her reputation, she wasn't the type who would slit the throat of an unconscious man. Even scum like Sam Sparrow.

Roxy began a thorough search the house. She pulled contents from drawers, rummaged through cupboards and poked through the cedar chest at the foot of the bed. Blankets, books and papers; she brought up short when she hauled out a framed photograph. It was Sam... and Roxy. She was looking into the camera, her arm thrown around his shoulders, a wide grin on her face. And Sam. Well, Sam was looking at her. They looked happy. In love.

She quickly jammed the frame back beneath the blankets and closed the lid of the chest. More rattled at the discovery than she cared to admit, and not having found anything of worth, she grabbed the sheet from the bed and, using her knife, sliced it into serviceable strips. With practiced movements - ignoring the now naked fugitive on the bed - Roxy tied Sam's wrists and ankles tightly to the bedframe. She dragged a chair in from the other room and sat next to the bed; her anger a slow simmer just below the surface.

Okay. She would wait, get some answers from him first.

Because she sure had a lot of fucking questions.

And *then* she'd kill him.

CHAPTER ELEVEN

Boots resting on a bedside table, feet crossed at the ankles, Roxy was flipping nonchalantly through the pages of a book on deep space flora, when Sparrow began to slowly regain consciousness. A smirk played across her lips. She watched from the corner of her eye as he examined the makeshift restraints. He glared at her as she continued to flick through the pages.

"That was my best sheet, Roxy."

Roxy rolled her eyes and tossed the book to one side. "You're lucky it was just the sheet."

He grimaced. "Untie me."

"No."

He struggled, yanked on the bindings, but Roxy knew she had tied a damned good knot – he wasn't going anywhere, and his struggles were only making them tighter. She could see his frustration was mounting and a pleasant shiver of satisfaction coursed through her. She was in charge now.

"Could you at least throw a blanket on me then?"

Hand on her hip, Roxy raised an eyebrow in mock disappointment. "Why Sam Sparrow, have you gone and turned shy?"

"You don't have to be so goddamned smug you know."

"Why shouldn't I?" Roxy growled, giving him a glimpse of her anger. "I have you exactly where I want you."

"Naked and tied up in bed?" Sam chucked, his eyes raking over Roxy. "Darlin' all you had to do was ask."

Roxy swore in frustration and stomped from the room, Sam's throaty laughter following close behind her. She grabbed a checkered throw blanket from the back of a chair and returned to toss it hastily across the lower half of his body.

"What exactly do you have to laugh about? I could kill you right here and right now without absolutely any remorse."

"Why haven't you then?"

Roxy blinked. "I… I have questions."

"Don't we all." He muttered under his breath then, "Listen, Roxy, I'm not the person you seem to think I am."

Roxy laughed mirthlessly. "I thought I knew who you were but that's not the real Sam Sparrow at all."

"I'm telling you the truth," Sam interjected. "I have been all along. I had *nothing* to do with that explosion. I would never…" He trailed off and shook his head. "I would never hurt anyone like that."

Roxy glared at him in disgust. "You were arrested. Convicted in absentia. Guilty as charged."

"I am innocent."

"Yeah, they all say that." Roxy rolled her eyes.

"Come on Roxy," Sam bellowed. "You *know* me. How could you ever think…? I would never put the people I love in danger like that. Not Suki… and definitely not you."

"Don't you dare talk about love." Roxy shouted back. "Suki almost died, spent *months* in hospital. Months of pain and surgeries and physical therapy. That is on *your* head. I *never* knew you."

Roxy glared at him, struggled to control her breathing. The pounding in her temples amplified. She turned away; head bowed.

"Look at me, please. It was a set up Roxy." Sam tried to catch her gaze, his eyes pleading. "They needed a scape goat and I was the perfect choice. Who would believe me, some cocky fly-guy fresh out of the Academy who was already butting heads, over the word of the Commander of The PRC?"

Roxy gaped. "Are you trying to say Commander Carmine lied? That he *framed* you? Wow. You are even crazier than I thought."

"I am not crazy," Sam erupted. "Why won't you believe me. I did not lie."

"Fine then," Roxy shrugged her shoulders, calling his bluff. "Prove it."

Sam looked defeated. "What about my word? That used to be enough for you."

"Innocent men don't run."

He looked at her, his eyes pleading for understanding. "I had no choice. They would have executed me if I'd stayed."

Roxy stood, nodding in agreement. "And rightfully so."

"Roxy, please…"

She crossed her arms, remained silent.

Sam swore under his breath. "We, Rover and I and The Bastent, plan on exposing The Commander and his flunkies at The PRC for what they truly are. Something is coming Roxy. Something big. And he's behind the whole damned thing."

"Or so you say."

"A long extinct species suddenly reappearing… Earthside of all places and a LanQuid of all things. Look at all those Witchlet kidnappings; you don't think The PRC keeps eyes on those things? Why haven't they put a stop to it? I think you know why. Because it benefits them. You don't even know the half of it. The things they've done and continue to do."

"Why would Seth have sent me *here* then?"

"Oh, it's *Seth* now, is it?" Sam gave a short bark of laughter. "Because he's getting scared. He's finally realizing just how close we are to taking him down. And he knows all about your vendetta. He's using you to get rid of me and River. Once we're gone, The Bastent will collapse and he can go right back to doing whatever the hell he wants."

"That's ludicrous." Roxy scoffed, "Commander Carmine wouldn't have even known you were here."

"No? For fuck's sake Roxy, when did you become such a goddamned sheep? Seth Carmine is the one who helped me escape."

Roxy gasped. "Will you stop at no lengths to…"

"He threw me the keys to a PRC Zip," Sam continued, raising his voice to be heard. "Told me to run. It was all a part of his plan. He's known where I've been this whole time. You can ask River. They granted me asylum on Mauw and I've been here ever since. You're smart. Think about it."

Roxy gnawed on her bottom lip and then appeared to reach a decision. She bent to retrieve the karambit from her boot. Sam collapsed back against the pillows, frustrated, and sighed in defeat. Roxy stood over him, the light from the lamp in the corner glinted wickedly along the blade as she ran her thumb across its edge.

"You know what Sam; I don't like liars." She paused and studied his face, "But I also don't like being someone's bitch."

She leaned over and began to slice through his restraints.

"Take me to River."

CHAPTER TWELVE

A match flared in the darkness and the sweet scent of herbs permeated the air.

"Did you know Roxy Buckles, that a Mauwian's olfactory sense is thirty times better than that of a human? And that despite this delightful nip that I am partaking of, I can still smell you there?"

"Oh yeah?" Roxy snarked. "And what do I smell like?"

River inhaled deeply, then on an exhalation of smoke: "Melons."

Sam coughed to cover a laugh and Roxy glared at him in the gloom.

River Lynx chuckled. "It is safe to approach. I will not harm you Ms. Buckles. You have my word. As long as I have yours that you will not use that knife on Sam."

"Maybe you should have mentioned that to your friend from earlier," Roxy returned, wincing. The tender spot at her hairline and the still present headache were a not so pleasant reminder of the encounter.

"I am deeply sorry that you were injured Ms. Buckles. I have had a word with Kashmir and they will be scooping litter for months to make amends. They are young and were trying to protect Sam."

Roxy rolled her eyes. *Sam, Sam, Sam.* "Not only harbouring but protecting a known fugitive?"

River Lynx stepped into the pool of light that bled from the windows of the large hut behind them. A tendril of smoke curled around their head and Roxy could see the flash of shrewd feline eyes as they assessed her.

"You have much to learn Ms. Buckles."

"Is that right?" Roxy nudged Sam forward with an elbow. "Perhaps you'd care to enlighten me then," she added dryly, her words dripping with skepticism.

"I would be delighted." River gestured with the sweep of a paw for Roxy and Sam to follow, dropping the end of their still smoldering cigarette into a small jar of liquid on the balcony of the hut. "But first, I will need you to sheath your weapon."

Roxy hesitated. Trust was not something that came easily to her. *Well, they've already had multiple opportunities to kill you if they really wanted to,* she reassured herself. She gave a curt nod and slipped the knife back into her boot, comforted by the fact that it was easily accessible if she needed it. Sam followed River into the dwelling, with Roxy close behind.

River's home was larger than Sam's by half. Built in book cases lined the walls, overloaded with a haphazard assortment of scientific journals and large volumes of fiction, it looked ready to collapse; a large basket of yarn was filled to overflow in one corner. The rooms were neat and tidy with large overstuffed furniture. Throw blankets and large pillows were in abundance and lush green plants covered every available surface.

"Please take a seat. May I get you a drink?" River offered, the epitome of the perfect host as they poured themselves a saucer of cream. "I have herbal tea, or ice water if you'd prefer."

Sam lowered himself onto a bench. "Water would be great, thanks River."

Roxy crossed her arms and glared at the both of them.

"As you wish Ms. Buckles."

The conversation that followed left Roxy reeling. She crossed the room and collapsed into a chair.

Ten years of her life – she'd been living a lie.

Sam sat quietly, watching Roxy intently as she absorbed the news. River presented their case - cold hard facts and evidence that Roxy could not ignore. The most damning of all, grainy footage obtained from the damaged front-end camera of the PRC Zip Ship as Sparrow flew away from Aurora for the final time – there was Commander Seth Carmine standing on the tarmac, watching… completely and utterly fine. No bruises, no cuts or contusions, nothing to indicate a severe concussion; no blood from the brutal beating he had claimed Sparrow had inflicted on him.

River spoke passionately but not fanatically; they were articulate and well informed and remarkably calm for someone who had just dropped the emotional equivalent of an atomic bomb.

"The Commander is hungry, his appetite for power continues to grow. Do you understand Roxy Buckles?" River implored. "If we do not take him down, if we do not put a stop to this, many more innocents will suffer and die."

Roxy nodded, then stood and stepped through the door of the hut, her breathing ragged as she leaned over the railing of the balcony, trying to blink away the shadows that encroached at the edge of her vision. The familiar burden of guilt and regret weighed heavy on her shoulders.

She had been presented with irrefutable proof that Commander Carmine was corrupt.

And that Sam Sparrow was innocent.

She desperately needed to speak with Suki and cursed at the uselessness of her wristlet and its inability to communicate at this distance. Suki was her connection to the real world, to home, and without that tether, she felt adrift and alone.

Roxy heard the soft pad of paws approach her from behind. River Lynx joined her at the balcony and stood in quiet contemplation.

"What?" Roxy barked, finally, when the silence became too loud.

"I understand you are in turmoil, Ms. Buckles and I am sympathetic to your pain. But now I want you to imagine how Sam has felt for the past ten years." They paused, watching Roxy with judicious eyes. "I have had Kashmir prepare a space for you for the night. I will take you there. You should rest."

"I'll show her the way River," Sam eased himself through the doorway of the hut.

Roxy put her head down and threw her walls up. A terse, whispered conversation between River and Sam lasted less than a minute and then Roxy and Sam were alone.

"Well, you *were* looking for a bad guy to kill." Sam shrugged, his attempt at a joke to ease the tension falling flat. "It's just a different guy now."

Roxy took a calming breath. "When's the next cargo ship out of here? I need to get back to Aurora and fix this mess."

Sam cleared his throat. "We're all going. We still have the PRC Zip Ship in dry dock. It's not as modern as the new ones but I repaired it as best I could, it'll get us there."

Roxy finally looked at Sam. "You'll be arrested on sight."

"I'll have to take the risk. I won't let you and River fight this alone."

"I can handle it."

"I'm not saying you can't but goddamn it, Roxy, that man took everything from me. I *need* to do this."

Roxy pushed past Sam and down the steps of the treehouse. She set off at a brisk pace with no particular destination in mind, just a desire to put distance between herself and the past.

"Roxy! Wait up." Sam called to her from across the clearing.

Her footsteps slowed - she owed him that much she decided - and Sam jogged up beside her.

"There is just one more thing we need to discuss."

"What could we possibly have left to talk about?" Roxy demanded, frowning.

Sam regarded her with a mixture of sadness and longing, "us."

"There is no *us* Sam."

"Roxy..."

"No."

He sighed. "You've heard River out. At the very least, let me tell you my side of the story, in my own words. Please."

"Okay, Sam," she took a deep breath. This was harder than she would have imagined it being. "I guess it's time. I'm listening."

CHAPTER THIRTEEN

Sam flattened himself against the wall, the chill of the brick exterior penetrating easily through the thin white fabric of the threadbare shirt that served as part of his prison garb. He gasped for air, his chest heaving; those daily runs on the treadmill having done very little to prepare him for the eventuality of long distance running and dodging the law. Sweat dripped into his eyes; he swiped a trembling hand across his forehead surprised to see it come away stained with blood. The prison guard hadn't gone down without a fight that was for sure.

He quickly considered his options.

Well, he could turn himself in.

He stifled a short bark of laughter.

Fuck no, that wasn't happening. Not when he had worked so hard to get away.

So, there was only one choice left: he would have to keep running until he was able to prove his innocence. All he had to do now was make it off Aurora alive, dodging both the Gendarme and the wrath of the very people he had thought were his friends... who he thought would always stick by his side. The betrayal left a bitter taste on his tongue. No, he had to get out of here and get out quick. Along the way he would have to avoid all the check points he was sure had been set up by now, the roadblocks and the air patrols who'd all be on the lookout for him.

He'd bet money they'd been given the order to apprehend at all costs.

Dead or alive.

But somehow, before undertaking all of that, he had to remove the tracking device they'd implanted in his forearm. He'd never make it otherwise.

Piece of cake, he thought ruefully.

He inched along the wall, desperately seeking cover, knowing he had to act quickly before they caught up to him. Quietly gaining access to a building would be ideal. The warehouse district in which he currently stood was rife with abandoned business fronts and condemned buildings. This was one of them, Sam was sure, the one he currently leaned against – the burned-out vehicle in the parking lot was as good an indication as any. As he rounded the corner at the back of the building, he lowered to a crouch preparing for what might be an ambush on the other side. Relief weakened his knees – there was nothing, no one in sight. He'd given them the slip.

For now.

Ah but there *was* a door. Sam worried about the noise he was about to make but considered it a small price to pay. He threw his full weight against the door, grunting with the effort, the tendons in his neck straining. He gave a soft cry of triumph when the flimsy lock gave way and the door swung inwards. Success.

It was dark and dank inside the building but it was quiet and it was empty. Refuge. Sam kicked his way through detritus and debris that had been left behind when the owners had hauled up stakes, and the trash left behind by squatters and hoodlums who'd been looking for a place to party or do drugs. Everything was coated in a thick layer of dust and grime and things Sam didn't even want to think about.

Across the wide expanse of the warehouse, Sam spotted what was probably once an office space; a hidey hole for the boss where he could keep an eye on his employees. The door was angled at a heavy lean; Sam pushed it back against the wall, one rusted hinge squawking in protest. He took stock of the meager furnishings inside: a wooden desk, a swivel chair, a filing cabinet and a shelf. All sagging or rusted. The heavy smell of mildew assaulted his nose.

Sam pushed the chair to one side dislodging a torrent of mouse droppings from a hole in the stuff. He shuddered but a search of this room was essential. The desk drawers were warped with age and water damage and gave protest when he tried to open them. But Sam was persistent. With a hideous screech the drawer released and spilled forth its contents. Nothing more than some faded receipts and a letter opener. He continued his exploration. Inside the larger bottom drawer: a half bottle of amber liquid and a small tumbler. Sam gave the bottle a sniff – definitely alcohol. The letter opener he'd found in the first drawer would have to do; he didn't have many other options.

He splashed the booze onto the letter opener, took a couple of deep breaths and with prodding fingers located the small lump on his forearm that indicated the injection site of his remote tracking device. He closed his eyes, and steeled himself. Ready as he would ever be, he placed the pointed edge of the letter opener against his bronzed skin and then he pushed as hard as he could, drawing it down and across his flesh. His vision narrowed to a point. He closed his eyes. Starbursts exploded behind his eyelids and he fought for control.

He was panting heavily, sweat beading on his upper lip and forehead, staining the underarms of his shirt, by the time he'd dug the small device out of his flesh. Waves of darkness threatened to pull him under but he gritted his teeth against the seduction of oblivion. He threw the capsule sized device to the floor and stomped on it with his combat boot, smashing it to bits.

Foregoing the dusty drinking glass Sam pounded back the liquid in the bottle, swallowing convulsively until it ran dry. His eyes watered and he coughed. He wondered how old the drink had been but figured that it was probably the least of his worries today. He ripped a sleeve off his shirt and bound it clumsily around the gaping wound in his arm. Red slowly seeped into the makeshift bandage. He probably needed stitches but at least at least now he was flying under the radar.

He took a shuddering breath.

Now he had to get the hell out of dodge.

CHAPTER FOURTEEN

A quick search of the warehouse turned up a motheaten peacoat, a baseball cap that had seen better days and an old Swiss Army knife that was better than no weapon at all. Sam eased the coat over his injured arm, pulled the hat low on his head and slipped the new found weapon into a pocket for easy access. He scanned the area outside the building as he slipped through the door and back into the light of day. He blinked; his eyes slow to adjust to the change from dim and dank to Suntwin.

He had no idea where to go. With a pang, he thought of Roxy but quickly dismissed the idea. Their meeting at the prison hadn't gone as he had envisioned. In his head he'd imagined tears, Roxy insisting he'd be freed and then her promise to prove him innocent, maybe even just a hug. Instead, the guards had had to hold her back from strangling him with her bare hands. He was still in shock that she could believe he would do such a thing. He thought of Peter, Erik, Johanna, Mel, Dr. Kristina, Lizzie and so many others... gone in the blink of an eye. And Suki. He hadn't been permitted to visit her at the hospital. From what he had been told, she wouldn't have known he was there anyways.

The shock waves of the bomb had spread out and up. Suki had been a mere three floors above the center of the blast. It was a miracle she had survived at all. Her saving grace – she'd been in a class demonstrating the use of tactical gear and had been suited up in full regalia. If not for the helmet…

Everyone else in that room had died that day.

They'd shown Sam the photos of the aftermath during his interrogation; the mangled bodies, the severed limbs, the blood and brick, the dust and debris. Suki covered in bandages, tubes and wires everywhere, surrounded by machines keeping her alive. If they hadn't told him that it was Suki there in that hospital bed, he would have never believed it.

Those images would haunt Sam until his dying day.

He eased himself around the corner of the building. All clear. He'd have to sprint across the wide-open expanse of the parking lot to make it to one of the other warehouses. Behind that was a highway – he might be able to hitch a ride or sneak onto a Transport Barge.

The blow above his left ear sent Sam reeling. He dropped to the ground like an anvil, the rush of blood roared in his ears.

He had little time to get his bearings, the shiny tips of expensive crocator shoes entered the periphery of his vision and then everything went hazy as his tenuous grip on consciousness slowly began to ebb away.

***

It was cold when he awoke, face down on the freezing asphalt. He raised his hand, touched his fingers tentatively to the space behind that throbbed in time with his heartbeat. It came away slick with blood. He groaned.

"Oh good, you're awake. I thought I was going to have to throw a bucket of ice water on you."

The familiar voice crashed into Sam as he opened his eyes. His vision swam but suddenly he was all too aware of where he was…. and just who was talking to him.

"Well come on then. We don't have much time. Very clever removing that tracking device Sparrow, but that's going to leave a nasty scar you know."

Commander Seth Carmine's mellifluous tones were laced with humor, but underneath Sam could sense something cold and reptilian in the man. Seth Carmine was the type that would eat his own young. Or toss them at monsters without looking back, just so he could get away.

Sam stumbled to his feet. He swayed, took deep breaths as he struggled to regain his balance.

"I suppose you're wondering why you're here?" Carmine remarked, quirking an eyebrow as he casually examined his fingernails.

Standing beneath the portico of the Zip-Ship launch at The PRC high-rise Sam did indeed wonder why he was there and why he was not immediately sent back to lockup or why he hadn't found himself on a one-way, all expenses paid trip to Brig-5.

"You could say that," Sam drawled slowly.

Carmine tossed something in Sam's direction. He grabbed it in mid-air before it could smack him in the face.

"Zip keys?" Sam questioned, incredulous as he stared down at the item in his hand. "What the fuck is going on here?"

"Go," Carmine said.

Sam shook his head, bewildered. He stayed stock still, waiting for the catch.

"Did I stutter?" Carmine burst out. "God damn it Sparrow. Go. Get out of here right now. The Zip is fuelled and ready to go."

Sam's jaw dropped.

Carmine jerked his chin in the direction of the Zip. "Now."

Sam studied him for a moment, calculated his chances if he didn't jump at this opportunity. This could give him time to prove his innocence. And doing so should be a piece of cake with the Commander of The PRC on his side. With a sudden burst of clarity, he realized exactly where he needed to go. It would be safe, quiet, and impartial. They would help him there.

Sam ran for the Zip. He quickly did pre-flight checks. The ship had just enough fuel to get him where he needed to go. With the flick of a few buttons, Sam was airborne. As the vessel began to gain altitude Sam hovered just above the tarmac. He locked eyes with Carmine and held his gaze. Before the Zip banked, he saw the Commander casually wave, his blazer flapping in the downward breeze created by the ship.

For some reason, Sam could not bring himself to wave back.

***

There was an uneasy silence when Sam finished speaking. His voice had grown hoarse near the end; it had been a long time since he had talked this much. Roxy had listened respectfully, for once not interjecting or interrupting to ask questions.

Sam searched her face for a hint of what she might be thinking.

"You don't believe me," he finally murmured, his expression bleak.

"I'm sorry Sam."

The breath he'd been holding spilled out of him in a rush. "It's okay Roxy. I understand. I can't expect you to… "

"No Sam, I mean I'm sorry for everything. I do believe you. And now, I have to go and make things right."

CHAPTER FIFTEEN

There had been a tense sort of calm inside the Zip for the first half of the jaunt back to Aurora. With each of the three occupants lost in their own thoughts, small talk and any sort of conversation had been off the table. At one point, Sam had fallen asleep, lulled by the rocking of the ship and what had probably been ten years of restless sleep.

Slumped down in the co-pilot seat, twitching occasionally, head back and mouth open he'd begun to snore loudly - much to the chagrin of his travel companions. The raucous noise had served one purpose though, to break some of the tension between Roxy and River who had now joined together in a solidarity born of annoyance.

"I suppose it would be in poor taste to throw him off the ship?" River remarked dryly.

Roxy stifled a laugh. Though the atmosphere inside the Zip had become cordial, it still hadn't stopped River from questioning everything that Roxy did: nitpicking about her speed, alternatively suggesting she slow down and then go faster; shouting if they thought Roxy was going to hit something and using a death grip on the arms of their seat, so much so that they left claw marks. They had been a typical backseat driver the whole way from Mauw and it had chewed away at Roxy's last nerve. Their squabbling had eventually woken Sam who refused to believe he'd been snoring.

"Okay!" Roxy shouted. "Everyone just shut up and let me fly."

A blessed silence had ensued for the duration of their jaunt. Roxy let out the breath she had been holding since liftoff. Nearly there.

***

"Here. Take these." As their ascent approached, Roxy reached inside her coat and, with the quick flick of a wrist, tossed a small sealed plastic packet across the bridge to Sam. The ancient Zip Ship she was piloting did not have autopilot capabilities, she needed at least one hand on the steering gyre at all times. She'd forgotten how advanced these things had become in the past ten years, thinking of her own fleet back at Buckles & Associates.

Sam ripped into the package; two small white capsules fell into his hand. He passed one of those behind him to River, sitting in the jump seat.

"And what are these exactly?" River inquired from the back, a note of scepticism in their voice. Roxy groaned internally, steeling herself for an argument she felt certain was on the way.

"*NoTraks*. They block scanning systems and interfere with surveillance cameras and facial recognition software. It gives us a brief window of opportunity to get you into Aurora undetected. Should last long enough to get you inside my condo. I have my own set of security features there so you'll be safe. Take them now so they have time to kick in."

Sam raised an eyebrow. "I didn't know this existed. I guess there are a lot of things I don't know about now." He was right. Ten years was a long time and Aurora had advanced by leaps and bounds in that time.

"Well, they aren't easy to come by," Roxy admitted cagily, "but I know some people."

"I bet you do," River murmured.

Roxy glanced back over her shoulder. Surprised, she watched as River tossed the capsule into their mouth, swallowing without further complaint. It was the first real indication of trust Roxy had gotten from the Mauwian. She felt some of the tension seep from her shoulders.

"We're about fifteen minutes out." Roxy assessed the instruments that were lit up in front of her and flipped a switch; a gridded map illuminated on a screen, coordinates flashing in red. "I'm heading straight for my office building. We can park the Zip in the garage. I need to speak with Suki first. She'll be worried."

"Look, I've been thinking Roxy," Sam hesitated, then seemed to make a decision. He plunged ahead: "Perhaps it would be safer for Suki if she didn't know about this until… until its all over and done with."

"Sam is right," River agreed, leaning forward to touch his shoulder in support. "In the long run it may be better for your friend to remain ignorant to our plans. She will have plausible deniability. From what Sam has told me, Ms. Kwan has suffered enough at Carmine's hands."

Roxy bit her lip, torn. Was she being selfish, rushing to see Suki, did she simply want to assuage her guilt? As much as she hated to admit it, Roxy knew Sam and River were right. Suki had to be protected at all costs. She had suffered enough. Roxy swore loudly and leaned forward to reprogram the coordinates into the grid map, so that the flight plan ended at the condos parking garage.

"You're right. The less people we have involved the better. What Suki doesn't know can't hurt her."

She saw Sam and River exchange relieved glances. They'd been expecting a fight.

Roxy took a deep breath. "Five minutes out."

"Wow. It's certainly changed," Sam observed with a low whistle, his eyes wide with wonder as the vista of Aurora unfolded below them. The lights of the city, auspicious and grandiose reached out towards the Zip Ship welcoming them into its burnished embrace. Though Roxy did this frequently, this re-entry into Aurora was a new experience every single time. New buildings sometimes seemed to appear over night in the ever-growing capitol and she was always a little bit dazzled as her home planet came into view.

"Time has a way of doing that," Roxy remarked after a pause. She glanced at Sam. He looked like he hadn't heard her at all, his face pressed against the window of the ship like an Earthside child, peering wide-eyed into a candy shop. She felt a twinge of guilt along with a mix of emotions she refused to acknowledge.

"Are you sure this is going to work?" Sam inquired as the Zip made its final descent. "I hate to stand by, idle, while you do all the setup work. There has to be something I can do."

"You can hang tight and try to relax. It's nothing I can't handle," Roxy insisted, as she wrestled with the gyre, vibrating in her hands as it fought the descent. "Just let me set things up with Carmine. We can't risk either of you being seen by him or any of his goons. Not right away at least. We need the element of surprise."

Sam huffed an audible sigh of frustration. "Okay, and then what will you do?"

Roxy turned to meet Sam's eyes; her face set with grim determination. "What I always do Sam. I'm going to kill the monster."

CHAPTER SIXTEEN

"Roxy Buckles! To what do I owe the pleasure?"

The warm greeting at the other end of the call poured over Roxy like molten honey and for a moment she simply enjoyed the feeling it evoked in her, the rush of calm.

"Roxy?" The voice immediately grew heavy with concern. "Everything okay?"

"Remember when you said if I ever needed your help, all I had to do was call?" She paused, uncertain whether she was doing the right thing or not. She didn't want to drag someone else into the fracas. "Well, I'm call-ing."

Zillo had access to a range of technology and equipment Roxy could only dream of. Buckles & Associates just didn't have the budget. Maybe, after this job, it might.

The low husky chuckle reverberated down the line. "I meant every word of it Roxy. Anything at all. What can I do for you?"

Roxy explained, briefly, the plan she had already set in motion and how he might be able to help.

"Come by my office. I've got just the thing."

Relief flooded Roxy. "I can't think you enough Zillo. I'm on my way."

***

CommsLink was located in the Warehouse District of New Cosmos. Major upgrades had been done to the area over the years and now it was booming. Zillo's company was housed in a squat non-descript brick building that backed onto the highway. A simple black and white sign hung above the main entrance. Roxy doubled checked that she had the right place and tried not to be underwhelmed. Greeted by an old manual door that had obviously not been replaced since the original construction, Roxy leaned into it, trying to push her way inside only to discover she actually needed to pull. She cringed in embarrassment as she stepped over the threshold.

Her jaw dropped.

The inside of CommsLink was in stark contrast to its outside. *They weren't wrong when they said not to judge a book by it's cover*, Roxy thought to herself as she tried to take it all in. State of the art yet stylish, the foyer dazzled. A transparent glass desk to the left of the doorway was staffed by a young woman, from Earthside if Roxy was not mistaken. She smiled at Roxy.

"We've been expecting you Ms. Buckles."

"Thank you, Bridget, I'll take it from here."

Zillo raised his hand in an eager greeting to Roxy, his voice booming across the marble floored lobby. He embraced her enthusiastically and Roxy sank into his arms with a mixture of relief and something she couldn't quite describe.

Maybe it was hope.

Maybe it was lust.

She was all over the place these days.

Zillo made Roxy think of long nights at home and easy mornings lingering over coffee, walks along The Esplanade, holding hands, and wine by the fire; holidays and celebrations and…

Oh god. Zillo made Roxy think long term. And Roxy Buckles did not do long term. Not anymore.

And Sam. Sam made Roxy think of things she'd buried long ago, things that she had worked hard to forget. Once upon a time *he* had been her long term.

She groaned internally. Things were getting far too complicated. What had happened to the simple life she had come to enjoy? She would definitely need time to eat her feelings once this whole thing was over. An entire sheet cake and a case of beer sounded good right about now.

Zillo was dressed for his office persona. A crisp white shirt fairly shone beneath a sharp black pinstripe suit. It hung on his shoulders as only something *that* expensive could, it hugged his biceps and stretched across his broad chest as he moved towards her. The cufflinks at his wrists were gold inlaid with black opal. But his shirt had been opened at the collar; his tie loosened; he clearly hadn't shaved that morning – possibly not even the morning before that. A smear of grease streaked across his forehead his forehead. Roxy tried unsuccessfully to smother a grin.

"What so funny?" He asked, his brow furrowing, his smile uncertain.

Roxy stepped up to him, yanked a white handkerchief from his breast pocket and leaned in close, her breath mingling with his as she gently wiped the dirt from his face.

Roxy returned the once pristine handkerchief to his pocket.

"I guess I missed a spot." Zillo blushed charmingly. "Come with me."

He grabbed her hand as though it were the most natural thing in the world and pulled her along to the glass elevator located at the center of the main foyer. Zillo waved his free hand in front of an illuminated panel and the door whooshed open.

"Daedalus Lab," Zillo spoke aloud and winked at Roxy.

"No offence Zillo because I know the crazy amount of tech you produce out of this place, but... how in the world can you do that in such a small space?"

Suddenly, the elevator dropped and Roxy gasped.

Zillo chucked. "Sorry for not telling you. I wanted to see the look on your face."

Roxy would have smacked him had she not been so busy looking at the incredible views that surrounded her. To stave off the claustrophobia of travelling underground, through what was, at times, solid rock, the elevator walls projected moving images of stunning vistas, rolling hills and ocean views. She felt Zillo squeeze her hand. His boyish enthusiasm was contagious.

Mere moments later the elevator coasted to an easy stop and the doors opened to reveal a long white, seemingly endless hallway with numbered doors on either side.

"How far down are we?" Roxy asked in a hushed tone.

"Two point five kilometers." He stated proudly. "Upstairs we have a few boardrooms and offices; I use one floor as an apartment and I stay there sometimes when I'm working and don't want to waste time going home; there's a bit of storage but, to be honest, it's mostly for show. The real magic happens down here."

Zillo pulled her along the corridor until they came to a door near the end of the hall – number 144. Zillo's handprint opened the door and the lights came on automatically as they entered. The room was larger than Roxy had expected, air conditioned to keep the temperature suitable for all the computers and hard drives. Work benches lined the walls, their contents organized chaos. Screens and touch tables filled every other available space around the room. A large antique mahogany desk had been pushed to one side near the door and was stacked high with books, papers, and electronic components. There were no chairs. *Does he ever sit down?* Roxy pondered.

Zillo gave her hand another squeeze and then released it, tugging off his tie, shrugging out of his jacket and rolling up the sleeves of his shirt.

"There. That's much better. I had a meeting this morning," he said in way of explanation and grimaced to show how little he had enjoyed the experience.

Roxy lingered near the doorway. Her hand still tingled from the contact with Zillo. She pushed the confusion that swirled within her to the back of her mind to ruminate on later and forced herself to ignore the feeling. She followed along behind Zillo as he walked to the longest table at the back of the room.

"I've been working on a little something. It's relatively new but has passed the first, second and third rounds of experimental trials in the lab. We will be ready to launch to the public soon. But you, my dear, are getting first dibs!"

With a flourish he presented a small clear patch in the palm of his hand, about the size of an old-fashioned book of matches. "Tada!"

Roxy blinked and tried to think of something nice to say. "Um…"

"I thought you would be impressed," Zillo sounded genuinely hurt and Roxy stammered for a moment before she caught the gleam in his eye.

"Damn you Zillo!"

He laughed. "Sorry Roxy, I couldn't resist."

She did smack him then, though gently and in jest, on the arm, "well, what is it? Can you tell me how it works?"

"Gladly."

***

They returned to the main lobby, Roxy's head was filled with information and detailed instructions and many other things she didn't have the energy to deal with in the midst of everything else. She took note of the time on her wristlet and discovered she had spent much longer with Zillo than she had originally planned on.

Time flies when you're having fun, a voice whispered in her head. She told it to shut up.

"You should come back again… when this is all over, I mean. I'll give you the grand tour."

"I'd really like that," Roxy replied.

"No pressure eh, Roxy. Just a tour. That's it."

"I know Zillo." She knew he wanted more but he would never push.

"Best of luck, sweetheart. I hope it all works out for you. *All* of it." He raised a brow meaningfully.

Roxy knew that Zillo believed that there was unfinished business between her and Sam and perhaps he was right to a certain extent. "I've told you Zillo, that ship sailed long ago. It's gone so far that it's not even a speck out on the horizon." Roxy smiled sadly, but her voice held an air of finality and there was a flash of steely resolve in her eyes. She was slowly learning that she had to leave the past in the past. Once and for all. Where it belonged.

"Call me. Let me know how things go. And that you're okay."

"I will. I promise," Roxy replied, breathlessly. She turned to leave. Clinging to the package she'd acquired in the Daedalus Lab as if her very life depended on it. It probably did. Hers and Sam's and River's.

She didn't need to look back to know that Zillo was watching her leave. She knew he would watch through the window until she was long gone. She also knew that he wished she would stay.

The best she could offer was that she would come back … in time.

The stomp of her boots against the concrete echoed down the street behind her and for a moment she faltered, squinting in the bright mid-day light of Suntwin. *Was this the right decision?* She asked herself for the millionth time. She swallowed hard against the lump in her throat. She was leaving behind what could very well be her future… to dive headlong into the churning, murky waters of her past.

This would be the last time.

Squaring her shoulders, she picked up the pace, and kept on walking.

CHAPTER SEVENTEEN

A siren blared. Someone nearby was playing music – very loudly. A succession of *SkyShaw's* zoomed by, their passengers whopping and laughing.

She didn't hear the approach from behind.

"You seem troubled, Ms. Buckles."

"That's a bit of an understatement." Roxy forcefully blew a breath out through her lips and ran a hand through her hair. She winced as a finger brushed against her still fresh head wound.

Roxy was reclining on the balcony of her condo; her feet propped up on the railing. River Lynx stepped through the sliding door and closed it behind them softly before padding to the railing and leaning against it. The night was balmy; the temperamental breeze was just enough to keep them from overheating. A glass of water next to Roxy was sitting in a pool of condensation, too tepid to drink now; she hadn't really wanted it anyways. She had poured it for something to do with her hands.

"Would you like to talk about it? I have been told that I am a good listener. It is okay to be vulnerable you know. It is not a sign of weakness."

Roxy shot River a covert look from beneath her lashes.

"Or I could contact a friend for you. If you would rather that. I think perhaps the time has come for you to unburden yourself of what is evidently weighing you down."

Roxy sighed in resignation. "No, no it's fine. I tried earlier but I can't get in touch with Suki at all. I've called the office, her house, and blipped her wristlet. Nothing. She's probably too busy working on the mess I left behind for her or maybe just too pissed off at me to talk. I'll give her some time to cool off." Roxy stood up and leaned against the railing, her shoulders tense. She was embarrassed to have admitted to River that she really only had one close friend.

Unless you counted Zillo.

Though Roxy wasn't sure exactly what he was to her at the moment. She knew what he *could* be – all she had to do was say the word. *But what about Sam?* Her traitorous heart whispered.

"Shut the fuck up," she muttered.

"What was that?" River inquired, as she glanced away from the view of New Cosmos. She had been intently studying a flock of biomorphic robotic birds that had just soared past.

"Sorry," Roxy blushed. "I was just talking to myself."

"It is very bright here on your planet," River observed. "And loud. On Mauw we cherish the silence. It is in the silence that we are able to hear what our heart and our mind have to say. We also very much enjoy naps. Sleep is restorative."

Roxy didn't know how to respond to that but she considered how New Cosmos might appear to outsiders. Roxy loved how *alive* Aurora was. How it never stopped moving, how it was never quiet, how it never slept.

She probably liked it for the very reasons that River did not.

Roxy looked at the earnest faced Mauwian standing across from her and did the exact opposite of what she would normally do: she spilled her guts. By the time she stopped her throat was raw and she felt a bone deep weariness that could only come from such a cathartic experience. She grabbed the glass of water and gulped it down.

"Ms. Buckles."

"River, after everything I just told you, I think it's fair to say you can call me Roxy now."

River nodded. "Roxy then. Your friend Suki is right to tell you to ask for help when you need it. You should listen to her. She sounds very smart. I also think that you yourself know that you cannot keep this up long term. It is not fair to Sam and it is not fair to your new friend Zebra."

"Zillo," Roxy interrupted.

"Yes, that's what I said," River nodded assuredly. "Neither is it fair to yourself, this situation you have come to find yourself in. Look, I know you are confused right now. A lot of information has come your way in a short period of time and you have every right to be distracted. But you cannot continue to string them along in this way."

Roxy dropped her head into her hands and groaned.

"And despite what you think, Roxy, *you* also deserve happiness." River remained silent for a moment, then gently asked, "Do you still love him? Sam, I mean."

Roxy pondered the question in tense silence and then, in clipped tones that belied the emotion beneath them, she finally replied, "I *made* myself hate him, you know. When I saw Suki, the way she was in her hospital bed. She looked so broken. We didn't even know if she was going to make it. And the way she struggled to learn how to do everything again - it really wasn't all that difficult to push him out of my heart." She cleared her throat against a sudden rush of tears. She would not cry. "A part of me will probably always love Sam, but its the part of me that I've had to lock away all these years. I'm afraid to open that door again."

"Sometimes the past needs to stay where it is," River nodded, gazing once again out over the vista of New Cosmos. "Now, Roxy, we really must do something about the state of your kitchen. You don't even have any..."

A call came through to Roxy's wristlet, startling them both. River went quiet as Roxy answered and replied to the caller in clipped tones.

"Trouble," they purred, more of a statement than a question, their whiskers twitching.

"Always is, River," Roxy replied, grimly. "Always is."

"What can I do to help?"

"Well, River, I'm going to need you to punch me in the face. Several times. Use the claws. And make it believable."

River's eyes grew wide with astonishment but then as realization set in, a toothy grin spread across their face. "It would be my pleasure."

CHAPTER EIGHTEEN

There was no hesitation in Roxy's stride as she stalked her way across the lobby of The Planetary Regulation Committee building. She did not pause beneath the large bulletin board screen this time, did not stop and gaze in awe at the opulence of the foyer or the rushing crowds inside the plaza. She did not acknowledge the shocked, open-mouthed expressions and audible gasps that resounded from the people as she passed.

She smashed a finger against the call button for the elevator and waited, the flare of her nostrils only a minor indication of the volcanic fury that bubbled just below the surface.

"Level 220," she barked when she had been permitted entry. The doors whooshed shut and Roxy stiffened her shoulders. *Deep breaths*, she muttered to herself. It was almost show time.

The elevator dinged, announcing her arrival, and she stepped into the lavish office for only the second time in her life. She feverishly hoped it would be the last.

"Roxy, you're returned already. Well done." Carmine emerged from his inner sanctum; Flavia was close on his heels. Flavia gave a muffled squeak as Carmine continued to speak, "I... uh... trust that you were successful in your endeavours?"

Roxy expected it was a rare occasion that found Commander Seth Carmine at a loss for words. She felt a rush of satisfaction. Roxy watched coolly as the Commander assessed her from head to toe. Roxy was covered in splatters of blood. As she moved, glimpses of raw looking scratches along her legs and arms could be seen inside the tatters of her clothing.

"It's done," Roxy confirmed.

A Cheshire grin spread slowly across Carmine's face and he rubbed his hands together in glee. Turning, he spoke in a low tone to Flavia who nodded and scurried out of the room. "Let's have a seat." He gestured towards the lounge area. "Uh… try not to get too much blood on the upholstery if you can help it."

Roxy plunked herself down on a white leather armchair, and leaned back pretending not to notice as Carmine's face blanched.

"Now, tell me, how did you do it – give me all the gory details. Did it beg for its life?" Carmine leaned forward, virtually salivating in anticipation.

Roxy had to suppress a shudder. "As you can probably tell from my appearance," Roxy gestured to her wounded arms and a trio of red scrapes that marred one cheek, "Lynx went down fighting." She forced a chuckle. Roxy began to describe, in painstaking detail, the fabricated torture and eventual extermination of River Lynx, a story they had constructed together before they'd left Mauw. "So, then I grabbed a fistful of fur and slit their throat."

Carmine leaned back against the sofa where he sat, nodding appreciatively.

Roxy was appalled, both at the Commanders unbridled delight at the description of such a cold-blooded murder and also over her own ability to easily tell such bald-faced lies.

"I can see a very bright future for you with The PRC Roxy. Very bright indeed." He rose from the sofa and crossed to stand in front of the glass wall that overlooked a stunning azure sky.

"Thank you, Commander." Roxy inclined her head in acknowledgement. "There's just one more thing though. Sam Sparrow. River Lynx has been harboring him on Mauw He has been conspiring with, and aiding, The Bastent *this whole time*."

Roxy had to give it to Carmine, he had the grace to at least try and look surprised by the revelation. "That is incredible. And were you able to take care of your little *problem* with him?"

"No. The bastard had already absconded from Mauw by the time I'd beaten the info out of Lynx," Roxy growled, fists balled tightly in her lap. A dark shadow passed over Carmine's face as Roxy dropped the news; he quickly shuttered it, a stony mask taking its place. "I *was* able to ascertain exactly where he has fled to Commander: Sam Sparrow is on *Aurora*. And he's out for blood."

Carmine cleared his throat, a sheen of sweat glistened on his brow. "Is that so?"

"Yes," Roxy replied. "And from what I've heard, the blood that he's after... it's yours."

Time seemed to slow down. Roxy's heart beat a wild tattoo beneath her breast as she waited to see if Carmine would take the bait.

He laughed, but underneath the cool façade Roxy could detect a whiff of nervousness.

"Me?" Carmine questioned. "Why... why would Sparrow come after me?"

"He seems to be harboring some delusion that *you* are responsible for the explosion at The Academy." Roxy injected as much disbelief as she could manage into her speech. "He's claiming that *you* set *him* up."

"That's preposterous," Carmine spluttered, turning to gaze out the window. Roxy watched in amusement as he reached up to loosen his tie.

Hook, line and sinker, Roxy thought. "Of course. Imagine the audacity," she exclaimed. "As if anyone would believe some filthy criminal like him over you, a respectable businessman and leader."

"Thank you, Roxy for your – "

"One other thing though," Roxy interrupted, lips pursed in thought. "He's claiming to have proof of his innocence. Surveillance videos that had previously been doctored; witnesses who have since come forward to say that their testimony was a lie and that they'd been paid well to do so. It's quite damning."

Carmine swung around; eyes narrowed as he assessed Roxy. "Well obviously he's full of shit."

"Yes," Roxy remarked. "Something definitely stinks here."

Carmine tightened his tie, fiddled with the cufflinks at his wrist and rebuttoned his jacket. "He *must* be stopped."

"Well, lucky for you Commander, you already know someone who's perfect for the job." Roxy grinned, gathering her focus.

She saw Carmine visibly relax. "Indeed, I do."

Roxy stood. "I have some leads I plan to follow up on this evening. I'll be in touch."

"Please do Roxy. And thank you for cleaning up this mess. From the moment we met, I knew you wouldn't mind getting a little dirty," he winked. "You never let them get away, do you?"

"No, and you can count on that." Roxy threw over her shoulder as she strutted out of the room and through the doors of the waiting elevator, shoulders back and her head held high. "I *always* get my man."

CHAPTER NINETEEN

The pain behind her temples throbbed in time with the wailing of the alarm. Suki massaged her forehead and the bridge of her nose with little success at alleviating either the pain or the annoyance.

Reorganizing a schedule that had already been reorganized to within an inch of its life was pushing Suki's patience to its limits. She loved Roxy. She loved her job but... Suki leaned back in her chair with a sigh and for a moment allowed herself to fantasize about what life might have been like. What would have happened if she'd been able to graduate from The Academy. Where would she be right now if things had gone according to plan?

She'd applied to The Academy on a whim. Their training programs were second to none and her friends had already been accepted. Her marks were good enough for a scholarship and so she'd written the entrance exam. How far would she have gone – would she have risen to the top? Would she now be teaching at The Academy if Sam Sparrow hadn't blown it to smithereens? Truth of the matter was, after so long – it didn't really matter anymore. She may not have gone where she intended but right now, she was exactly where she needed to be.

Suki tapped on the buttons on her intercom with more force than necessary and waited not so patiently for a response at the other end.

"We are sorry Ms. Kwan. We're still working on it."

"It's been an hour."

"Again, I am sorry. I have everyone in security working on it. We can't figure out why the alarm is going off. We may need for push a full restart of the system."

"How long?" Suki demanded.

He sighed. "I can't say for sure. Look, most places have closed up shop for the day. Maybe you might consider doing the same?"

"Not a chance," Suki muttered before she ended the call, her gaze taking in the myriad of papers strewn across her desk, the two glowing screens showing the color-coded schedule she still had to completely reorganize. She'd be lucky to get home for bedtime.

The wail for the alarm continued through the afternoon. Suki typed and filed at a breakneck speed, not even pausing for lunch. As Suntwin finally set over the bustling downtown metropolis, Suki leaned back in her chair and sighed in relief. Her work for the day was done.

She quickly turned off her screens and carefully arranged her paperwork into three neat piles: *Urgent, slightly less urgent,* and *can wait.* She was contemplating dinner when it happened.

If not for the growling of her stomach, Suki might have thought she'd gone deaf in the ensuing silence. The cessation of the alarm was a welcome relief. It would have been even more welcome – Suki glanced at her wristlet – seven hours ago.

The pounding pressure that had wrapped itself around Suki's forehead like a band had only increased as the day wore on. She thought longingly of stuffing her face with something sinful and collapsing atop her bed with the relief of a *No-Graine* strip stuck to her forehead. It would knock her out until morning; a welcome reprieve.

Suki had already tapped in the first three digits of the alarm code before she noticed it was not illuminated as usual. The eerie green light was absent in the dimness of the office as Suki lowered the overheads with the wave of her hand.

Security had obviously opted for a restart of the system. Suki carefully treaded her way back to the desk and pulled a set of tarnished keys from within a deep drawer. They were fossils in Suki's opinion, archaic and unnecessary, left over from a bygone era but Roxy insisted on keeping them in case of an emergency. Suki would never be able to tell her about this – she'd never live it down.

It took her a few minutes to figure out the mechanics. She found the correct key for the office door and smiled, pleased, as the rarely used lock slid into place with a satisfying clunk.

"How quaint." Suki tossed the ring of keys into her satchel and exited the building, thinking that the alarm system would be back up and running in the morning, the keys could be returned to the place at the back of the drawer and Roxy would never have to know she'd been right about them.

And if Marcus told her, well… Suki smirked. Yeah, that wouldn't happen on her watch.

***

The murky grey dawn that greeted Suki the following morning did nothing to stifle her cheery mood. It had just turned 5 am, her headache was gone and thinking ahead to her day, Suki knew she had only three items on her desk marked as urgent. Maybe she'd grab lunch on the Esplanade this afternoon. An extra-long lunch to make up for yesterday. She'd charge it to Roxy's business account. Satisfied with her plan, Suki quickly dressed, slicked a sheen of lipstick across her lips, pulled her dark hair into a sleek chignon and decided she felt well enough today to leave for work with just her cane.

She arrived at the office, looking forward to the day ahead, for once. When her ID card failed to allow her entry, she shielded her eyes, trying to peer into the exterior beyond the glare of the reflective glass. No one in sight. She banged on the main door and when this yielded no results, she used her wristlet to call the main operator. The disembodied voice of the automated answering system informed her in a monotone voice that there was currently no one available to take her call.

The electronic buzz that accompanied the opening of the main door finally reached her ears.

"About bloody time," she muttered, trying to see into the interior to thank the good Samaritan who'd let her in.

"Marcus!"

"Sorry Ms. Kwan. Still having some issues. The whole building is operating on backup. At least the alarm stopped sounding?" His attempt at a joke failing, the grin on his face dissolved in the shadow of Suki's displeasure.

"Please excuse me Marcus, I have work to do."

Fishing the ancient set of keys from her satchel, Suki let herself into the office, flicking on the overhead lights. She strolled to the desk, powering up her screens. She noted a surprising lack of messages requiring her attention and nodded her head in approval.

Suki sniffed. Something smelled repulsive. Had she inadvertently missed a glob of LanQuid goo when she'd cleaned up? No. That wasn't it. It was more like spoiled food masked by some off brand air freshener or body odor mixed with cheap cologne. Suki froze. A frisson of fear tingled along her spine.

A shadow moved behind the shades in Roxy's office.

Suki was not alone.

She reached for the alarm button beneath her desk only to realize, her stomach sinking, that it would be of no use with the entire security system down. Suki muttered a curse beneath her breath and began backing up towards the door.

"I don't think that's a very good idea, Ms. Kwan."

Suki whipped around, "Marcus!"

He had the grace to look embarrassed. "I needed the money. My daughter. She wants to go to school on Earth." He shrugged. "That shit ain't cheap."

Suki heard the door to Roxy's office swing open and a large greasy Cro-Magnon type grinned at her, cracking his knuckles. With alarm, Suki realized the man was wearing the uniform of the PRC Gendarme. Her heartrate spiked. He wasn't even attempting to hide his identity. Which meant her didn't care that Suki knew who he was.

That wasn't a good sign.

She tried to stall, distract them, hoping they wouldn't notice her activate the emergency alert on her wristlet.

"That door was locked!"

Marcus and the Gendarme chuckled together companionably. "Those old locks are easy to breech."

The Gendarme rushed forward and wrenched her arm behind her back. He had moved so fast for a beast of his size that Suki barely had time to register the sharp pain in her shoulder before he had relieved her of her wristlet and tossed it to Marcus.

Suki's cane clattered to the floor.

"You said she keeps a chair here?" the Gendarme growled.

"Yes." Marcus fumbled with the closet door, producing a compact wheelchair Suki used on particularly bad days. "See JB! Told you!"

The Gendarme grunted in satisfaction. "Put her in it. We've got places to be." He sneered at Suki and licked his lips.

There'd be no long relaxing lunch for Suki on the Esplanade today.

If ever.

CHAPTER TWENTY

What the hell? Roxy thought as she stood outside the entrance to her condo. She was sure she'd heard yelling inside and then, *was that a hiss?*

The atmosphere inside Roxy's condo was thick with tension when she walked in. She could have cut it with a *karambit*. She found Sam pacing the room like a caged animal while River was doing their best to get him to sit down, to eat something, drink some water; anything other than this frenetic marching from one end of the room to the other.

River had not been impressed to find a half-empty fridge with nothing more than a few languishing bunches of kale, expired condiments, beer and crusty take-out food, still in its containers. They'd been forced to settle for an old can of tuna, found languishing at the back of a cupboard, probably expired. It still sat, uneaten, on the table in front of them.

Sam rushed to Roxy's side as she walked in the door, his expression hesitant but hopeful. "Well?"

"He bought it." Just saying the words out loud to someone instead of merely thinking them gave her a rush of energy and excitement. It was the best part of the job.

She glanced at her wristlet. "My contacts are now on site. We'll give it a little bit of time to do their normal thing and then one of them will rush to report that you've been sighted at the old grounds of The Academy. Carmine won't want to do the dirty work himself, I'm sure; he's too much of a coward. He'll leave that up to me, that's why he wanted me in on this to begin with - but I don't think he'll be able to resist turning up to confront you and lord it over you that he's 'won'."

"And then it will all be over," Sam whispered, wonder in his voice. "Finally."

Roxy met River's eyes across the room and an unspoken promise passed between them. Tonight, they would make things right… one way or another.

***

The cool air was stark relief against her flushed cheeks. It had been a long but fruitful day. Roxy stood on the balcony gazing out over the blinding lights of New Cosmos, the faint sounds of late-night revellers rising up to greet her. She smiled. The city never stopped. She couldn't think of anywhere else that she would rather live.

"Roxy…"

She froze, her name so raw upon Sam's lips that it sent her stomach into a somersault.

"We should talk."

This again; he was relentless. Roxy braced herself because he wasn't going to be happy with what she had to say. "I didn't realize you enjoyed my conversation quite so much, Sparrow."

"Cut it out Roxy. I know what you're doing. You only call me *Sparrow* when you're trying to shut me out. I know you've had a lot thrown at you over the past few days. You haven't had as much time as I've had to process this whole mess."

"I am fine."

"Are you really though Roxy? Because I see your hands shake when you brush back your hair or when you lift a glass or pick up a file. I see that faraway look you get in your eye when you think no one is looking because you've gone some place inside your own head." Sam sighed, his frustration mounting. "Come on. Talk to me."

"I am so tired, Sam. Tired of talking, tired of being in the dark and being the last to know everything. I *need* to finish this. Once it's all over, then there will be time to talk."

"Why do you have to be so goddamned stubborn, Roxy?" Sam slammed a hand against the railing, his shoulders tense and his face grim. "What about us then?"

"Us?" Roxy laughed, though she found little humor in the situation. She turned her back to gaze out at the cityscape, the lights and the buildings filled with people. She wondered what they were all doing tonight. If they were happy. Truly happy. Or just living a lie like she had been for so long. "There is no *us* Sam. Not anymore."

"Are you sure about that?" he whispered, his voice low and husky.

"Yes," she replied, firmly, wanting to shut this down before it even got started. But the quaver in her voice betrayed her.

"Is there someone else? Is that why?" Sam asked. He held his breath waiting for a sign from Roxy that his worst nightmare hadn't come true. That he had lost her once and for all, that the one last thread of hope that he had been holding on to had been permanently severed.

The silence grew. And with it, Sam's confidence that Roxy still felt *something* for him.

Roxy felt Sam draw nearer, step up closer behind her; it was a subtle movement but, then again, she had always been in tune with the movements of his body.

"You should get some rest Sam. You'll need it. I have things to do."

"Do you really? What things to do you need to do?"

"There's a lot that needs to be done tonight," she insisted.

"Do you *want* to go Roxy?" Sam asked.

Roxy turned around, her eyes pleading: "Don't do this Sam, please. It's not the time."

"Do what?" He stepped closer, and then closer still, until they were barely a hair's breadth apart. "This?"

Sam ran one calloused finger down Roxy's jawline, stroked it gently across her bottom lip. Her breath caught in her throat.

"Or this?"

He leaned towards her until his forehead touched hers. She closed her eyes, memories rushing back. Happier times. Her and Sam.

"Or this?"

His lips brushed against hers tentatively, seeking her permission. She sighed and leaned into the kiss, deepening it. She felt a shudder pass through him and thrilled at the knowledge that she could still make him feel this way. She felt powerful and alive. She slid her hands up his broad chest and across his shoulders before reaching up to tangle her fingers in his hair; she tugged gently on the too long locks, scraping her nails across his scalp; he groaned and nipped at her bottom lip. He spread his hands across her back, and then lower still, crushing her against him.

Sam trailed a line of scorching kisses from the corner of her mouth, and along her neck pausing to taste the pulse raging above her collarbone. He broke the connection, his breathing ragged, "stay with me tonight?" he pleaded. "I've missed you."

Roxy met his eyes, heavy-lidded with desire. This loaded question; she knew it was about far more than just tonight. And she didn't have an answer. Especially not the answer she knew he wanted. She dragged her tangled hair out of her face, took a deep breath and moved from Sam's embrace, stepping towards to the door that led back inside.

"I can't do this Sam. I'm sorry."

She closed her eyes before she could see the expression on his face. She hated seeing him in so much pain. She stepped back through the door and left him there, alone, on the balcony.

And though she wanted to, she did not look back.

CHAPTER TWENTY-ONE

Suki swam to consciousness slowly, like a deep-sea diver ascending from the briny depths. Her head felt impossibly heavy; her ears stuffed full of cotton, her mouth dry and her tongue like sandpaper. She'd kill for a blob of *Quencher* right about now. Or two. The feeling was quite similar to the worst hangover she had ever experienced... only Suki didn't drink anymore, and she hadn't taken a sip of alcohol in well over ten years. Her eyes popped open as reality slammed into her.

She vaguely recalled the pinprick of a needle and reached up to rub her neck. There was a tender spot - an injection site - a few inches below her left ear.

She'd been drugged.

Recalling the scene back at the office, ambushed by the head of security and that disgusting piece of garbage, JB, Suki used her anger to bolster some courage. She put her hands to the floor and pushed herself into a sitting position. A gasp escaped her lips; the flare of pain in her hip was fresh and sharp – she gritted her teeth and kept pushing. Leaning back against the wall, sweat beading on her forehead, she breathed a sigh of relief, thankful for small blessings.

If she somehow managed to get out of this alive, she was going to make sure that Marcus got his ass fired. And then sent off to Brig-5 as fast as humanly possible. Scum like that deserved to rot in prison.

"Suki shivered. The room was pitch black and the tantalizing sound of dripping water resounded somewhere close-by. She licked her chapped lips. She was desperate enough to consider it. A foul stench of oil and rubber permeated the air and Suki tried to breath though her mouth. She was beginning to realize the enormity of the situation that she was in, but Suki simply did not have it in her to give up easily.

She raised her hands, waved them around slowly, reaching blindly out in front of her. She scooted herself forward a few inches, ignoring the pain, and repeated the action. If there was chair, a table, or some other piece of furniture she might be able to use it to haul herself up. After lying prone on a cold stone floor for an extended period of time, her muscles had seized up, her legs less than cooperative, failing to follow her commands to *move*. What she would do once she had managed to accomplish that feat? *Well,* Suki thought, *we shall cross that bridge when we come to it.*

The echo of approaching footsteps snagged her attention and, knowing she had mere moments, she slid herself backwards and eased her body back onto the floor, to make herself look as pathetic and defenseless as possible. She heard an old manual lock disengaging, the click of a switch, and then light flooded the room, blinding her. She raised a hand to shield her eyes against the sudden glare.

"Rise and shine, sleeping beauty."

Suki recognized the guttural tones of the apostate Gendarme who, in cahoots with Marcus, had kidnapped her and taken her… wherever she was right now. She blinked up at him and then surreptitiously looked around the room. It was completely bare, the floor filthy and covered in debris, a leak in the far corner moldered its way down the wall. Suki was glad she hadn't gotten that far.

And she was certainly thankful that she happened to be up to date on all her vaccinations.

"Get up."

"I can't get up, you stupid prick," Suki spat, bristling at being ordered to do anything for this barbarian. "In case you haven't noticed…?" She gestured wildly to her legs, crumpled beneath her.

"You're spunky. I like you."

Roxy rolled her eyes. "The feeling is *not* mutual."

He had no weapon that she could see but she was harboring no allusion that she would be able to take down this behemoth of a man all on her own. She would just have to bide her time until the moment came, when the feeling came back to her feet and her hands weren't so still. She would know when. *They hadn't killed you yet,* she surmised, *so obviously I am meant to serve some other purpose.* She would try and use that to her advantage.

He lurched toward her and Suki willed herself not to cower beneath his towering frame. She would not give him the satisfaction of knowing just how scared she was. He grabbed her by the arm.

A small cry of pain escaped her. "Watch it asshole."

He hauled her up from the floor as though she weighed nothing.

"I suppose Marcus is back at The Chaffey Building now, working as if nothing ever happened?" she asked, trying to stall for time. "There never was a problem with the security system, was there?"

"Can't get nothing past you, hey?" JB smirked and jerked her forward, wrenching her shoulder. "But I'm afraid our friend Marcus has outlived his usefulness. He's had a bit of an *unfortunate accident* earlier this afternoon. Now shut the hell up and start walking."

Suki limped from the room, pain shooting from hips to ankles, pins and needles in her calves; her left foot still partially numb. JB half supported, half dragged her from the room before unceremoniously dumping her into the wheelchair he'd stolen from the office.

He pulled a rag from his back pocket. "As much as I have enjoyed our chat little lady, I'm going to need you to be extra quiet now, got it?" He stuffed the rag in her mouth, walked around to the back of the chair and pushed her toward what looked like a large service elevator.

Suki tried not to gag as the cloth pressed against the back of her throat. She blinked the water out of her eyes and as they adjusted to the dim light of this new location, she tried not to let on that she knew exactly where they were.

The storage units on the lower levels of The PRC Plaza.

Realization slammed into Suki with the force of a battering ram.

This was an inside job.

Roxy was gonna be pissed.

CHAPTER TWENTY-TWO

"Would you like a caf-tab or a regular coffee?" Roxy offered, shifting from one foot to another in the middle of the kitchen.

She was in no mood to play hostess but anything to break the damnable silence that had hung like a heavy cloud over her condo since she'd returned from her first visit to CommsLink.

Sam leaned his elbows on the table, ran a hand over his face. He looked exhausted. "No Roxy, I don't want coffee. I want to…"

A sharp beep emitted from Roxy's wristlet and she quickly pressed a button to silence it.

Saved by the bell.

Her face hardened as she read the message that had arrived with the notification. She glanced up and her eyes locked on Sparrow's. He had a way of looking at her that was equal parts want and what the hell. It was not something Roxy was ready to deal with quite yet, especially after what had happened earlier in the night. And especially after her stolen moments with Zillo. There was enough on her plate already.

She quickly looked away, calling out to River Lynx who was napping in the other room: "Lynx! It's time."

The trap had been set. It was now or never. Sam and River grabbed their bags and with a nod at Roxy to indicate that they were ready, followed her out of the condo. They would bypass the front doors of the building – too risky – and instead a *Roamer* (an off duty rapid transit *SkyShaw* driver looking to make a little extra cash) would collect them from the roof and deliver them across the city, no questions asked.

Thunder rumbled in the distance and a streak of lightening kissed the sky in brilliant hues of violet and blue. River eyed the swirling mass of murky pregnant clouds above their heads with concern. Under different circumstances Roxy might have been amused. Clearly, the idea of a rain storm did not appeal to Lynx. Roxy was really starting to like that feline.

"We'll test the device when we arrive." Roxy, sitting between River and Sam, spoke low so the *Roamer* wouldn't overhear.

Sam gave a curt nod. Roxy wondered for a moment if he might be nervous but then dismissed it just as quickly. He'd never been the type.

The plan was simple: Roxy and River would secret themselves amongst the ruins of The Academy, staying within earshot should Sam need assistance. Sam's job was to allow Carmine to "catch" him hiding there. Carmine would use it as an opportunity to gloat of course, to lord it over Sam that he, Carmine, had finally won. They just needed him to say the words and the entire confession would be broadcast live across every single electronic device on Aurora via the CommsLink System wired to Sam. Roxy had called in a *big* favor.

Carmine was going down.

"We got this." She said aloud, to assure herself as much as the two sitting beside her. She felt Sam grab her hand and squeeze.

This time, she couldn't bring herself to pull away.

***

The *Roamer* set them down half a mile from the former grounds of The

Academy. The driver grinned at the generous tip and zipped away whistling a jaunty tune, the extra money ensuring his discretion.

Sam was a bag of nerves. He paced and ran his hands over his head as Roxy and River discussed the whens and wheres of their mission using the projected map on Roxy's wristlet.

In the moments before they walked down to the road, their final steps before the denouement of this wretched night, River pulled Sam gently to one side, paw on his shoulder as they spoke in hushed tones. Roxy saw Sam nod and the two embraced. She tamped down on the wave of jealously that threatened to swamp her. *You forfeited that particular right, Buckles*, she admonished herself. She quickly turned away.

"Let's test that CommsLink System shall we?" Roxy called over her shoulder.

Sam approached, hauling his shirt over his head.

Roxy cleared her throat. "So, uh, this small patch gets applied to the chest right... uh... here and is absorbed by the skin. It remains an active mic for three hours." She pressed the thin membrane against Sam's chest. His skin was warm and alive beneath her fingers. She snatched her hand back as though she'd been burned.

She heard Sam chuckle as he put his shirt back on.

"Don't you start." Roxy snapped.

"How'd you swing this anyways?" Sam asked. "This kind of equipment is above even your pay grade."

"I know a guy," Roxy said with finality. And boy did she owe Zillo big time.

"A guy hey? What kind of guy?"

Roxy's eyes flashed. "A friend. Not that it's any of your business."

"It *is* my business if you've dragged some stranger into this whole thing without... "

"I would never," Roxy snapped. "He owns CommsLink and he wanted to help. He's a good guy. Not that you'd know anything about that."

"Hey, now that's not fair Roxy." Sam sounded genuinely affronted.

"Okay lovebirds." River interjected, rolling their eyes. "Are we ready to go now?"

Roxy glared at them but bit back her retort. "As much as we will ever be," she finally replied, her mouth set in a grim line.

Sam hefted a backpack onto his shoulder. "This is going to work... right?"

Neither of them replied. The time for reassurances had long passed.

They set off at a steady pace, one in front of the other with Roxy taking the lead. They kept to the shelter of the treeline, at the side of the road.

There were fissures in the asphalt, weeds snaking through the cracks; the trees at the sides, once trimmed and neat, now lorded in a canopy over the road. As they passed through the broken and twisted gates, the hulk of the former Academy slowly emerged from the darkness.

The smell of ash and smoke and death still hung heady on the air. Or perhaps it was just an olfactory memory for Roxy, throwing her back in time as the sights and sounds of that terrible day all came back to her in a flash:

"My friends! You have to help them!"

"Were they down here with you?" The man in the high-tech rescue gear had to yell to be heard above the whir of rescue helicopters over head and the sirens of emergency vehicles on the ground.

"No… no they were on the 180th floor."

The look on his face told her all that she needed to know.

"No. You need to do something. Now." Roxy coughed, the deep hacking by-product of smoke inhalation. Blood poured from a gash at her hairline, dripped into her eyes; bloody tears ran down her cheeks, cutting tracks through the mask of dust and soot that covered her face.

"Ma'am, you should really be seen by the medi-droid."

"Well, sir, you should really suck my – "

The blast shook the ground beneath their feet, nearly knocked them to the ground.

"Secondary device. I repeat, a second bomb. Fall back, fall back!" The guy screamed into his comms, turned and waved his arms for the rest of his men to follow as they headed for cover.

And Roxy, well, Roxy turned and ran back into the building.

Or what was left of it anyways.

"Wow." Sam's soft shocked exhalation right next to her ear snapped Roxy back to reality with a jolt.

She had almost forgotten the enormity of the destruction the explosion had caused. She was glad she wasn't seeing it in the harsh reality of daylight. A shudder passed through her as she took a deep breath, seeking equilibrium.

The past and the present were colliding and Roxy was holding on for dear life, trying to ground herself in the here and now.

"Places everyone," Roxy muttered, low and deliberate. "Let's do this."

The scrape of a boot behind them, then, "Fancy meeting you here, Roxy Buckles."

Well fuck.

CHAPTER TWENTY-THREE

Commander Seth Carmine materialized from behind a towering pile of scorched rubble like a magician emerging from a cloud of smoke; smarmy and with a cocksure swagger – the only thing missing was the cape and top hat. He snapped his fingers and his tall, lumbering assistant emerged from the overgrown foliage across the blackened courtyard. The flunky had greasy dark hair, It was slicked back from a sloping forehead; his burly muscles rippled beneath the garish green uniform of The PRC Gendarme that he was wearing and a twisted smile spread across his face.

In front of him, weeping softly behind a gag stuffed in her mouth was Suki Kwan.

"Suki!" Roxy took a step forward, her intentions quite clear, but stopped short at the sight of the large, wickedly sharp knife that the Gendarme had pulled from behind his back. She realized, to her chagrin, that Seth Carmine had also devised a plan. And it looked like his was the only one going accordingly. Roxy would never forgive herself if her own hubris got Suki killed.

"Now, now Roxy." Carmine tsk-tsked. "Behave yourself. If you keep that up, JB there might have to use that knife. And trust me, you do not want JB to use his knife. Are we clear?"

"Very." The word was spat through clenched teeth as Roxy tried to stave off the combination of intense anger and fear pooling in her stomach.

"Please remove the weapon you have holstered on your thigh and slide it towards me."

Roxy stared at him; her chin tipped in defiance.

JB brandished the knife towards Suki with gleeful exuberance. Roxy felt River Lynx slide closer to her and whisper, "You may not want to *chaton*, but you must do as he says."

With a deep sigh Roxy acquiesced. She unclipped her weapon and flung it as far as she could behind her. There was no way in hell she was giving Carmine and his goon any extra ammunition.

"Not very good at following orders, are you?" Carmine asked, incensed.

Roxy quirked an eyebrow and shrugged.

"You want your friend over there to die right now?" He nodded towards Suki. "All I have to do is say the word."

Sam let loose with a string of curses but was instantly drowned out by a sharp crack of thunder. The ground trembled beneath their feet and Roxy's nose detected a faint whiff of ozone.

An opportune distraction that River Lynx seemed more than happy to take advantage of: while the sky still grumbled and while gazes were drawn towards the dusky blue, River touched Roxy on the shoulder reassuringly and then bounded off into the shadows, disappearing out of sight; the tip of their tail blending in quickly amongst the tall willowy grass.

Perfect, Roxy thought to herself, *at least something is going according to plan… even if everything else has gone to shit.*

"You really seem to draw these cowardly types to you, don't you Roxy?" Carmine sniggered, his expression one of distaste. "Perhaps it would be wise of you to find yourself some better friends." The Gendarme joined in on the joke, cackling, though Roxy was certain, being more brawn than brains, that he knew absolutely nothing about that was actually going on.

"You applying for the job, Commander?" Roxy snarked. "Sorry, but your resume leaves a little something to be desired."

Shooting daggers in Roxy's direction, his face flushed an ungodly shade of purple, Carmine pulled himself to his full height: "You should be so lucky to be a part of my inner circle."

Roxy laughed. "Stuck a nerve, did I? You see, it doesn't count when you *pay* people for their loyalty, Commander. You really think JB over there would have your back if you didn't have him on the payroll?"

Carmine stammered. Roxy saw his eyes shift to JB and narrow.

JB, slack-jawed with incomprehension, did not exactly inspire confidence.

A shout: Suki had somehow managed to free a hand from her bindings, yanking the gag from her mouth. "Look out!"

Roxy barely had time to register the movement before Sam exploded past her, knocking her to one side. She stumbled, blinked, and before she had a chance to process what was happened, Sam had launched himself at Carmine, slamming into him at full speed – the small handgun that Carmine had pulled from inside his coat tumbled away into the rubble.

Both men tumbled to the ground in a tornado of fists and fury.

Roxy heard Suki's frantic exclamations as she worked to free herself from her second binding. Sam had pinned Carmine beneath him. Grasping one of the Commanders lapels in a tight grip, he used his other fist to smash repeatedly into Carmine's face. A jagged flash of lightening zigzagged across the sky, illuminating the scene in sporadic bursts, momentarily blinding Roxy.

She watched the chaos with mounting terror.

The gargantuan Gendarme backhanded Suki, her chair rocking back on its wheels from the force of the blow. She cupped her face, her right eye already beginning to swell. JB didn't spare her a backwards glance as he ran to his boss' aid.

Wincing in pain, Suki determinedly returned to working on the tape that still held her left wrist. Roxy surged forward, sprinting across the distance that separated them. She bent down and began wrenching at the tape.

"Roxy. Roxy, you have to help Sam. I can finish this. Please!"

"I've almost got it," Roxy insisted, as she felt the tape start to rip.

"Go, dammit. I've got this."

Roxy cursed, turning towards the scene that was playing out across the courtyard. She could do nothing but stand there as JB flung Carmine to safety behind him and suddenly surged forward, slamming his knife into Sam's back in one smooth brutal motion.

Roxy heard someone scream.

In an instant, she realized that the bloodcurdling cry had come from her.

Sam bucked as the knife sliced through his skin, the soft area just between his shoulder blades. He twisted away from Carmine, who lay heaving on the ground, spitting out blood and what might have been teeth. JB leaned over and yanked the knife out of Sam's back. Sam rolled over and away from Carmine; fists already clenched – ready for another fight.

Only he didn't get the chance.

JB dropped to the ground and straddled Sam, smashing the hilt of the weapon into his face. The Gendarme's greasy hair hung in his face; his eyes gleamed as he held the knife aloft.

Carmine pulled himself to his feet, swiped his sleeve across his lips and grinned through a mouth of bloodied teeth. He threw back his head and laughed maniacally.

A madman.

"Finish it." Carmine gave the order with relish.

"With pleasure boss."

"No!" The ragged howl burst from Roxy's throat as the Gendarme plunged the knife into Sam for the second time. Sam coughed, choking, as a mist of blood plumed from his mouth, splattering over his chin.

The ruthless assault had taken only seconds.

Roxy heard Sam call out her name.

But she had already started to move.

CHAPTER TWENTY-FOUR

Thunder detonated above them; lightning clawed its way across the dusk in jagged bursts as night claimed its dominance over the sky.

Roxy let loose with a primal battle cry as she ran and leaped onto JB's back, her arms encircling his trunk-like neck as he struggled to his feet, her weight throwing him off balance. Out of the corner of her eye she saw Carmine scrambling, searching frantically amongst the rubble for the small pistol he'd lost earlier.

JB jerked around, trying to shake her loose. He tossed his head, attempted to grab at her with his beefy hands; his broad shoulders and chest leaving him at a disadvantage. He was also dumb as fuck and evidently not used to people fighting back. Roxy dug her knees into his sides and held on for dear life. She clawed at his face with her nails and bit into his ear, gnawing viciously; gone half feral with grief and anger and fear.

The Gendarme roared. Roxy spat blood and gristle to the ground and screamed for River. "Lynx! Now would be a good time to show yourself, god damn it."

Carmine sauntered over to Sam, who had rolled and was now trying to drag himself towards the madness. Roxy had no idea how he was still moving.

"I win, Sparrow." Carmine drew back his boot and smashed it into Sam's ribs with a sickening crack. He straightened his tie, smoothed down the front of his jacket, seemingly oblivious to the bloodstains that marred it.

JB abruptly stopped trying to toss Roxy from his back. He went still, as though making a decision, then threw himself backwards. Roxy had no time to react. She hit the ground with a sickening thud, the air rushing from her lungs as the hulking mass of the Gendarme landed on top of her. Instinctively she let go, gasping for breath. JB rolled to his knees and bent over Roxy, sneering at her as blood dripped from his ear. "Fucking cunt."

Roxy saw the fist coming towards her in slow motion. Pain ricocheted through her jaw as the punch landed with devastating accuracy. Her teeth snapped against her tongue and blood flooded her mouth. She closed her eyes against the wave of pain.

"Nice work JB! Carmine nodded at his cohort in approval. "Now take care of that other bitch."

Suki, who was tugging frantically at the last vestiges of tape that held her to the chair, flinched as the Gendarme sent a wolfish grin in her direction. "Happy to. Been waitin' all day."

And that was when the heavens opened up.

A stormy gust of wind surged over them, rain hammered against Roxy as she lay on the ground, plastering her hair to her scalp. She gasped as the icy water drenched her, thankful though she was for the clarity it brought. She clambered to her knees.

Sam was on the ground a short distance away, silent and still as a pool of blood expanded beneath him. He'd gone down fighting, the way he would have wanted. The knowledge did not make Roxy feel any better. She wanted to run to him, curl up by his side and tell him that everything would be okay. Old habits died hard. She forced herself to push him from her mind.

She locked eyes with Suki across the battered ruins of the once magnificent Academy for Intergalactic Law Enforcement. JB stood behind her, his knuckles fisted in her dark tresses; he had nearly lifted her out of her chair as he pressed the tip of his knife into the delicate skin at the base of her throat, just waiting for the word to cut.

"Look what happens when you double cross *me*." Carmine sneered as he towered over Roxy. "All you had to do was follow my instructions. You could have gone places. Now the only place you're going is the morgue."

"Tell him to let her go." Roxy's voice oozed malice. "She's done nothing to you."

"I'm afraid I can't do that Roxy," Carmine replied, amused. "She's my insurance policy, you see. And now, she knows just a little bit too much."

Where the hell was River? Roxy squinted into the driving rain, straining to see beyond the shadows of the charred brick walls, rising jagged from the broken foundation. A dark sleek shape appeared suddenly before merging fluidly back under the cover of darkness. Roxy wondered if she had hallucinated it. Or maybe, just maybe, help *was* coming after all.

She needed to stall.

"Why?" Roxy staggered to her feet. "You owe us that much don't you think?" She didn't dare look back at Suki. Perhaps, if Roxy could hold Carmine's attention for long enough, she could buy some time for her.

This was all her fault.

She'd been arrogant.

And now her friends would pay the price. Guilt enveloped her.

Focus, Roxy, Focus, she admonished herself.

"I don't owe you a damned thing, Buckles but the answer to the question should be obvious, especially to you. You're all about *justice*," he mocked, rolling his eyes. "The *Academy*. What a joke. Churning out brainless twats who memorized and then regurgitated the very laws they had no intention of upholding; a mockery of the uniform they had the privilege of wearing. It had to stop."

Roxy blinked the rain from her eyes and stared at him, baffled. She was drenched to the skin. Under the umbrella of his own audacity, Carmine seemed unaffected by the downpour.

"Wait. You're telling me, you *broke* the law because you wanted to *uphold* the law?" She asked, incredulous. "But that's preposterous. People died! *Good* people. And not only that – you destroyed a man's life. A *good* man." Roxy didn't dare glance at the motionless form of Sam Sparrow sprawled out on the ground. She swallowed, hard. "There had to have been an easier way than that."

"Collateral damage." He shrugged, indifferent. "It was for the greater good. There was no need for a training academy. A waste of time and money. I could have easily handpicked our law enforcement to ensure we had the cream of the crop. Like I do now. It works well."

"Works well for *you*, I'm sure, but what about everyone else?" Roxy retorted, swiping rain from her eyes. "How many others have you double crossed or set up... or murdered to get your own way?"

"I'm right and you know it." He argued, ignoring her accusations. "Do you really think scum like Sam Sparrow, the so called *best* that The Academy had to offer, would have brought anything other than shame and embarrassment to The PRC? Strutting around like a cock of the walk. Useless piece of shit. What's a few casualties when you end up winning the war. Give up this ridiculous fight. I might even reconsider bringing you into the fold... if you're willing to follow my rules." Carmine raised an eyebrow, a self-satisfied smirk playing across his bloodied lips.

"No fucking way," Roxy spat, enunciating each word.

"Then I guess *you'll* get what's coming to *you*."

"No, Commander, you'll get what's coming to you." Roxy gloated, as River Lynx glided from the shadows behind Carmine, stealthy and silent. They pounced; claws extended. Seizing him around the neck in a lethal grip, Lynx dragged him backwards and off balance. They hissed into Carmine's ear, whispering sweet nothings – but there would be nothing sweet about the plans they had for him.

Roxy saw his eyes go wide.

Gotcha.

CHAPTER TWENTY-FIVE

The deluge ended just as suddenly as it had begun: a tempest in a teapot. In the ensuing silence, the echo of a gunshot was particularly loud.

Roxy flinched, the noise unexpected and assuredly, unwelcome. She raised her hands instinctively and froze in a half crouch. The retort had come from somewhere behind her. As the seconds ticked away at a snail's pace, a thousand different scenarios played out through her mind – and none of them were good. She saw River's pupils dilate as they watched the scene unfold across the charred remains of The Academy. River tightened their grip on Carmine as his eyes bugged and he fought against them with renewed fervor, trying to break free.

Roxy turned around slowly, remaining in a defensive stance, her heart in her throat but ready to fight. *Please, not Suki*, she begged the universe.

Carmine's henchman, JB the Gendarme who had brought shame to the title, lay in a tangled heap on the ground, blood trickling from a wound at his temple. He was clearly unconscious and, quite possibly, dead. And, Suki… well, Suki was holding a gun. It wasn't a very large gun, no, but one that had certainly served its purpose.

It was still smoking.

And it was now pointed directly at Commander Seth Carmine.

"Where the hell did that thing come from?" Carmine squawked, fear causing his voice rise several octaves as he continued to fight against River's hold on him. They hissed in his ear, Carmine flinched and Roxy watched dispassionately as River raked their claws down Carmine's cheek. He began to weep, softly, finally accepting defeat. He wasn't going anywhere.

"I always carry a gun; you piece of shit." Suki shouted, her voice, and her hands, both strong and steady. "Guess it never occurred to you to frisk the 'cripple,' did it?" Her face twisted in anger and the fire in her eyes made her suddenly look very imposing.

Carmine blanched as Suki expertly chambered another round. "But… But JB…"

"But… But JB." Suki mocked. "JB is - my bad, *was* - as dumb as a bag of onions. Was he really the best that you could find for your Gendarme elite?" She laughed. "Not once did he check me for a weapon. He had ample opportunity to frisk me if he wanted to. Old JB here would have flunked out of The Academy within his first semester."

Carmine remained reticent, silenced by fury or fear, perhaps further cowed by Suki's verbal barrage. It might have been all three. His satisfaction over Sam Sparrow's destruction seemed to have ebbed away.

No, Roxy told herself firmly. *Put Sam out of your mind now, you must focus on Suki.*

"Suki," Roxy cajoled softly, in what she hoped was a reassuring and calming tone. She began a slow approach towards her friend, keeping one eye on the loaded weapon while her mind frantically went over her options might be here. She gave a short shake of her head to River, hoping that the message to stay put got through to them. They needed to keep Carmine subdued. She knew River longed to go to Sam - as much as Roxy did.

"Don't you *Suki* me, Roxy Buckles." Suki's eyes flashed with anger but her gaze did not waver from her target. "Revenge, remember? Finally bringing these lowlifes to justice? Here's our chance. He took so much from us both, Roxy. And Sam." She choked on a sob. "We have to make them pay!"

"You don't want to do this," Roxy prompted.

"Like hell I don't." Suki gave a derisive snort. "Don't you know what he did?"

"I do," Roxy replied softly. "I know everything now."

Suki carried on, not really needing a reply, "Because I know *exactly* what he did. He planted that bomb, he killed all those people, and then he framed Sam for his dirty work. He had one of his goons beat him up – probably this scumbag here - so it looked like he'd been assaulted by Sam before his escaped. It was him all along. Sam was just the scapegoat." She swallowed with difficulty, trying to control her emotions, and then, her voice dripping with scorn, "The *Commander* didn't mind telling me all the sordid details before you arrived. He was going to kill me anyways, you see."

"I know you want him to pay and he will, I promise you." Roxy insisted as she inched closer. "Just not this way."

"His kind don't understand any other way, Roxy."

"No, Suki, they do not. *But* you are not *his* kind."

Suki wavered for a moment, the gun shook in her hand and the barrel drooped towards the ground. Roxy felt the tight knot of tension in her gut begin to unfurl. She was nearly there; just a few more steps and she'd be close enough to safely disarm Suki. Then it would end.

"You're River Lynx, right?" Suki shouted across the ruins towards the Mauwian sovereign who still held Seth Carmine in a death grip, despite his defeated demeanor. "You have excellent reflexes I would imagine."

River glanced at Roxy, their confusion was evident, but finally they nodded in response to Suki's question. "What you have said is correct, Ms. Kwan."

"Good. You should move. Now."

River did as they were told. Something in Suki's voice telling them that this was not the time to hesitated.

It was not a moment too soon.

Roxy recoiled as the gun blast went off right next to her, an arms length from Suki, loud enough to make her ears ring. She watched in horrified fascination as the bullet slammed into Carmine. He was lifted by the hit, a marionette on a string, before he crumpled to the ground, shrieking as he clutched at the bloody mess that used to be his knee.

Roxy gaped at her friend. "Suki?"

Suki let the gun fall to the ground and then scrubbed her hands along her thighs. She turned towards Roxy as the high-pitched wail of sirens whooped in the distance and the low, steady *chuff, chuff, chuff* of air-ambos hammered the sky as reinforcements drew closer to The Academy, just a little too late to do much good.

With a smirk on her face, Suki tossed her sopping wet hair over her shoulder: "I guess the other bitch got taken care of after all." Her face crumpled. "Roxy. *Sam!*"

Roxy was already halfway across the courtyard, River not far behind her. She knelt on the ground next to Sam and tentatively reached out to touch his face. She snatched her hand back and held it to her mouth, too afraid to speak.

"Roxy?" River stood next to her, their tail flicking with concern. "Is he…?"

"He's so cold, River. So cold."

CHAPTER TWENTY-SIX

Roxy sat, quiet and still, staring into the mirror, not quite recognizing the face staring back at her, though she supposed it must be her. Atop the vanity, sat a small first aid kit. Open, its bandages and plasters spilled out amongst the assorted quick-fix ointments and easy to apply stitch-stickers. She'd refused treatment at the scene, likewise at the hospital, choosing instead to pace the halls with her arms wrapped around herself. Mascara had run in milky gray rivets down her cheeks, a startling contrast against the pale and peaked mask of skin she currently wore.

She couldn't look away.

She raised her eyes to the hair matted with blood, raised a shaky hand to the gash on her forehead. Those hands: crimson stained, dark and crusty around the nail beds where the gore had dried and cracked.

With a small cry, she swept the first aid kit from the desk, its contents flying asunder across the floor. She stood so suddenly that the small chair upon which she had sat fell backwards with a clatter. Wincing, Roxy wrenched the cropped leather jacket from her shoulders and tossed it into a corner. She'd never wear it again. She was no longer wearing her boots. Surely, she must have removed them when she'd arrived at home but she had no recollection of any such event.

She stumbled into the bathroom.

"CoCo, shower mode 5, no auto-shut off this time."

"As you wish Ms. Buckles," came the smooth computerized tones. "Full jets activated. Enjoy."

Stepping into the stall fully clothed, she closed her eyes as the scalding hot water cascaded over her. It pooled for a moment at her feet, pink and foamy, before it circled the drain and disappeared.

The blood and dirt, the sweat and tears – that wasn't all Roxy hoped the water would wash away.

***

"God dammit, Roxy!"

Shivering, Roxy, who lay crumpled on the floor of the marbled shower, still in her clothes, gazed up at Suki, confused. Suki threw a plush white towel around her friends' shoulders and helped her to stand.

"Let's get you out of these wet clothes, hey?" Suki continued in a much gentler tone. "You'll feel much better then. River has ordered us some food."

She led Roxy out of the bathroom and sat her on the bed. "Do you mind if I help you with this?" Asking permission before she tried to peel the sodden clothing from Roxy's quaking body.

"Nothing you haven't seen before, right?" Roxy shot back quickly.

Suki smiled. It was a small spark, but a spark nonetheless. Roxy's reticence had been starting to scare her.

Roxy allowed herself to be undressed though it was difficult for her to feel this vulnerable. Suki dried her briskly with the towel, taking time to squeeze the water gently from her dripping blonde tresses. She helped Roxy slip into a pair of soft pants and a warm, oversized sweater, sliding thick socks onto her feet. Stumbling slightly as she rose from the floor, Suki caught herself on a bedside table. Roxy's hand shot out to steady her.

"Are you sure that you're alright?" Roxy asked, concern evident in her voice, superseding, for the moment, her own discomfort. "It should be *me* looking after *you*, Suki, not the other way around."

Suki stroked Roxy's hand where it lay upon her arm. "Let's look after each other then, shall we?" A smile teased at the corners of her mouth. "Now how about we see what River ordered for us to eat. I'm starving." She frowned. "Fuck. I hope it wasn't fish."

Despite herself, Roxy laughed.

They left the clothes and towels where they lay. A problem for another time, when menial tasks wouldn't feel quite so insurmountable. They closed the door behind them as they headed for the kitchen.

The mouth-watering aromas of *Pad See Eiw*, spicy *Tom yum goong*, *Khao Pad* (a savory fried rice) and Roxy's favorite red curry, *Gaeng Daeng* permeated the condo. Roxy took a deep breath and pressed a hand against her stomach as it grumbled in anticipation of the feast.

"Good. We are ready to eat now." River gestured towards the spread of takeout boxes that covered the entire surface of the countertop island. They held up two paws, both were holding bottles of wine. "And we are also ready to drink."

As River dug into their *Yam Pla Dook Foo* with relish - a dish of Fried Catfish with Green Mango Salad - Suki met Roxy's eyes above the feline's head and quirked an eyebrow. Roxy jammed a spoonful of shrimp soup into her mouth to stifle her laughter.

No, things weren't perfect right now. But they were pretty damned close.

***

River and Suki were discussing the unionization of *SkyShaw* drivers and what it would mean for the future of transportation in the city. They were speaking and gesturing vigorously while shooting Roxy surreptitious glances to ensure that she remained involved in their conversation, keeping her distracted. Roxy was sure Suki and River also had a lot on their mind but she was glad for their company and their concern. She was glad that she wasn't alone. No robo-pet could ever compare.

Suki had been fielding calls and messages all day: reporters, representatives from The PRC; even Ethel-Beth Lester had called to check on Roxy. The take down of the Commander of The PRC was big news; the corruption that had been exposed was a scandal that reverberated throughout New Cosmos like a shock wave and would continue to do so for ages to come. Those who hadn't heard of Roxy Buckles already, sure knew who she was now.

Finally, Suki had shut down all communication devices and left word at the front desk that no visitors, flowers or packages would be accepted at the condo.

Zillo had called five times, Suki had hesitantly told Roxy as she sloshed more wine into the half empty glass. Roxy nodded in acknowledgment, but turned to look out the window, saying nothing. She made no move to retrieve her wristlet which lay on a side table on the other side of the room, off. In the reflection of the glass, she saw Suki and River exchange a look so she rejoined them in the kitchen. She smiled and smiled and sipped more wine until the whine of a siren, down below, on the streets assaulted her senses. Someone, somewhere else in New Cosmos was also having a bad day too.

Her mind drifted and the sound of River and Suki chatting died away. She could smell the damp earth, saturated from the sudden storm; she could taste the metallic sharpness of iron on her tongue; the pounding of her heart, the rush of blood in her ears.

She could also remember the immense flood of relief she had felt as River had bent over the man who lay prone on the ground only to wave frantically to the first responders, shouting, "He's got a pulse!"

CHAPTER TWENTY-SEVEN

Roxy blinked back to reality.

Suki and River were holding a whispered conference at the other end of the table, heads bent together, their backs to Roxy. Just how long had she been lost in the reverie? She flushed, embarrassed.

"What are you two scheming about now?" Roxy tried to keep her voice light and airy.

"We were thinking that perhaps it would be a good idea for you to get away for a bit. Until some of this fervor dies down." Suki suggested hesitantly.

"What do you mean?" Roxy asked, immediately suspicious.

"You are everywhere, Roxy. Buckles & Associates has received 4698 calls in the past twelve hours. When that CommsLink System went hot, it pinged every computerized interface on this planet. The driver of a Transport Barge was close enough that he was able to broadcast the whole thing as it happened via *FaceGram Live*." Suki sighed. "It's gone beyond viral."

"I guess it's good for business?" Roxy joked.

"Roxy, for every one hundred people who love you, another one hundred hate you. With a passion." Suki cringed. "We've tried to keep you from the news reports. The PRC is scrambling right now; the entire Gendarme has been abolished until they can weed out the ones who were loyal to Carmine from the ones who are loyal to the badge. There was a bomb threat at the Chaffey building just this morning."

"There are some that would have your head on a silver platter, Roxy." River interjected, blunt as ever. "It will take time to separate the wheat from the chaff as Suki has said. You will go underground. Until it is safe. No contact with anyone. Not even your friend Zero."

"Zillo." Roxy replied, dryly

River blinked at her. "Yes, that is what I said."

Roxy shook her head. "Okay, okay." She went silent, processing the information, then squared her shoulders. "So, what do we do?"

"That is where I come in." River replied. "I believe that I can provide a solution to your problem."

Roxy gave a slight nod to show she was listening.

River continued: "You will return with me to Mauw. No one will know where you have gone except the three of us here. We will provide you safe haven, much as we did with Sam. You will stay as long as you need to until things calm down here on Aurora."

Roxy lowered her eyes at the mention of Sam. "I… I appreciate this very much River but I don't see how I could possible leave right now. There's too much to do. Suki can't…"

"With all due respect, Roxy," River interrupted, pupils dilating. "Suki is *more* than capable of handing things here. I believe in her and you should too. She has proven herself time and again."

Suki blushed. Roxy took in the purple and black bruise that had spread across Suki's forehead, the split and swollen lip, the battered knuckles and bandaged wrists, raw from the tape that had bound her to her chair. And yet here she was, still fighting at Roxy's side as always.

"I'm sorry Suki. I don't give you enough credit," Roxy acknowledged, clearing her throat that was suddenly tight with suppressed emotion. "River is right. You *are* more than capable."

"Thank you for saying that, Roxy. Will you go with River? They've arranged transportation for you both. I think this is for the best, at least for now.

"What about you? Will you be safe Suki?"

"Don't worry about me, Roxy. I have everything under control."

"Alright then," Roxy finally agreed, relenting in the face of common sense.

Suki sighed audibly; her relief evident. "Good."

Roxy smirked. "Now, which one of you is going to help me pack?"

***

As Suntwin set, and the last fingers of hazy tangerine caressed the horizon, Roxy and River departed for Mauw. Roxy fell asleep almost instantly; the heavy vibrations of the motor, too much wine and too little sleep, a heady combination.

She stirred just as the ship set down on terra firma; her arrival this time a little less clandestine than the last. River rose sinuously from where they had sat, stretching and yawning broadly. Roxy hadn't been the only one to grab a cat nap on the way to Mauw.

A small group of Mauwian's greeted her and River as they stepped down from the gangplank of the ship. Roxy recognized Bareen, who bowed deeply.

"Welcome back, Ms. Buckles."

"Thank you, Bareen." Roxy wasn't sure if she was supposed to bow back in greeting. Ruffled she did a sort of curtsey which seemed to please both River and Bareen.

River turned to Roxy, "I believe you might also remember Kashmir?"

A younger Mauwian stepped from behind their brethren and hesitantly waved at Roxy. "It is nice to see you Ms. Buckles."

Roxy was quite sure that she would never forget Kashmir.

Smiling, River addressed Roxy once more, "Kashmir was quite eager to prepare lodging for you. They wanted to place you in one of our immediate clusters but I thought perhaps you would prefer some privacy. If you are up to the walk, I can show you to your accommodations."

Tossing her duffel over one shoulder, Roxy summoned a smile. "Lead the way."

***

Roxy climbed a tall ladder and emerged onto an octagonal deck that wrapped around a medium sized treehouse, nestled in the thick branches of the hybrid sequoias that were a signature of Mauw. River had bid her adieu on the ground, having urgent business to attend to; much had accumulated in their absence from heir home planet. The Bastent still required its leader. Perhaps now more than ever.

She poked her head in through the doorway. Kashmir had really outdone themselves. Bowls of fruit and jars of flowers lent a pleasant fragrance to the previously unoccupied abode, giving it an air of hominess. Roxy dropped her bag near the entryway and turned in a full circle. The kitchen was well stocked: bottles of milk and a carafe of thick cream; rice and fish, there was spinach and kale, bunches of fresh herbs and crisp root vegetables; Roxy even thought she spied a bottle of white wine behind several loafs of grainy bread. A small pantry was full of lentils, coffee, flour, sugar and other staples. Roxy would not go hungry.

The small kitchen led way to an equal sized lounge area. A soft throw lay atop an invitingly plush couch; several large cushions and a beanbag chair looked just as comfy. A pile of books sat on a side table next to a potted plant – some type of fern if Roxy was not mistaken – and a small jar of sweets. Through another doorway was the bedroom. A lamp in the corner lit the room softly in rosy hues. Roxy was exhausted; it could have been a dump and it still would have looked like heaven. Roxy had been given directions to a small waterfall nearby where she could clean up. Mauwian's had no need for such amenities but Roxy was certainly thankful to have the option.

Clean now but with little energy for much else, Roxy collapsed into bed, pulling a single sheet over her nakedness. She was asleep within seconds.

***

A loud thudding sound penetrated the fog of sleep as Roxy struggled to shake off the last vestiges of what had been a very pleasant dream. She stumbled from the bed and headed towards the sound.

"I'm coming, I'm coming!" She muttered as the noise continued.

"Please excuse the very early wakeup call, Roxy but we seem to have a bit of a problem."

"What now?" Roxy groaned and yawned widely, standing in the doorway of the treehouse, the sheet clasped modestly to her chest as the early dawn light bloomed violet and pink behind River Lynx. The look on their face was somber and Roxy quickly came to her senses.

"River," Roxy's voice was now thick with concern as she watched the normally unflappable Mauwian wring her paws. "Tell me what's is going on. Is he…?"

"No, Roxy, not that," they paused. "But, well, it would seem as though Suki Kwan has been arrested."

CHAPTER TWENTY-EIGHT

"A minor inconvenience."

"Suki, they dragged you off in handcuffs." Roxy was incensed. "I'm coming back right now."

Suki, unruffled, laughed at Roxy's indignation. "Stay where you are.

It's nothing I can't handle."

"How did this even happen? It's preposterous. It was clearly self-defense."

"Someone got a little too enthusiastic. And now that someone will be riding a desk for the foreseeable future, if they want to keep their job." Suki replied, wryly.

The encrypted software tech that Suki was using to speak with Roxy, that had patched into her usually ineffective at long distances wristlet, emitted a sharp beep indicating that the time for safe and secure conversation would soon pass.

"How did you even get this contraption, Suki? I didn't know such a thing existed. It must be new?" Roxy asked, holding her breath, afraid of the answer but needing to know all the same.

Suki hesitated. "Zillo," she whispered. "I'm sorry Roxy. I felt really terrible so I returned one of his calls. All I told him was that you were okay and that you were safe. I didn't say a word about where you were or even that you'd gone off planet, but he's smart and I think he read between the lines. He wanted to help. He's a good guy."

"I know." Roxy demurred.

Beep.

"I think our time is coming to an end," Suki interjected. "Look everything is under control, I'm fine and I can promise you no one else will try and lock me up again. I can get back to fixing things up around here. And then we can get you back. I don't want you to worry about it anymore, got it?"

"Got it. But... you're sure that you're okay, Suki?"

There was a long pause, then Suki giggled. "If I'm being honest Roxy, and please, I hope you don't think badly of me when I say this but... I am fairly certain this has been the most exciting week of my entire life."

Roxy gave a throaty chuckle. She could definitely understand that.

Beep.

Sobering quickly, and before she could lose her nerve, she asked, "Have you been able to see him?"

"No, but not for a lack of trying. They wouldn't allow it. Something about following protocols... they wouldn't give me a lot of details."

"He's... he's going to make it though, right?"

The device gave one final ear-splitting beep and then the line went dead.

***

Roxy spent her time on Mauw trying to do the one thing that she was not very good at: relaxing. The time went by slowly; the first week that she was there felt indeterminable, she felt sluggish like she was trying to push her way through syrup. But it was not entirely unpleasant once she got into a routine and stopped feeling so sorry for herself. She went for long walks, exploring, and collected wild flowers that she delivered to the Mauwian elders. She cooked elaborate meals for herself, read books for pleasure and somehow managed to keep that one fern alive. She went swimming at the falls nearly every day, floating on her back in the heady rays of Suntwin, her eyes closed, striving to keep her mind blank. To just enjoy.

The bottle of wine remained at the back of the fridge.

She regularly attended meetings of The Bastent, though she mostly sat at the back of the room, listening quietly and taking it all in. Roxy would never be the type of person who would completely turn the other cheek in a dangerous situation but she was beginning to realize that, perhaps, there were a few other things she could try first rather than storming in, half cocked, guns ablaze. It was quite the epiphany for her.

She had long chats with River; there was an easy trust between the two now and Roxy was learning that friendship meant an equal give and take and that she didn't always have to be in control. And that sometimes people were more than capable of taking care of themselves.

The seasons changed but it was subtle shift on the planet Mauw. The days got a little bit shorter and a little bit darker, a cooler wind blew every now and again but everything else remained much the same. On Mondays, Kashmir came by Roxy's treehouse. They were attempting to teach Roxy an elaborate board game that was comparable to chess and, while the skills were slow in coming to Roxy, she kept trying; Kashmir was a patient teacher.

It was during one of these sessions that Kashmir, finally having worked up the courage, asked, "Ms. Roxy, will you teach me how to fight. I want to be able to defend my brethren. No matter what it takes."

Roxy contemplated her answer, knowing that the eager young Mauwian was at an impressionable age. "Well, Kashmir, fighting isn't always the answer." Roxy surprised even herself with that response. "There are many other ways to defend yourself, and your friends, without killing. Justice... it isn't always so black and white."

And, so, that was how Roxy ended up teaching mixed martial arts to the oldest of the kittens, twice a week, in the community hall. They were rowdy but Roxy appreciated their enthusiasm and it gave her something physical to do. She felt alive.

It was, all at once, the strangest, but also the most normal time, of Roxy's entire life.

Roxy had dragged the beanbag chair and a soft blanket to the balcony. She sat watching the day reluctantly give way to night, the blanket across her lap as she nursed a cup of lukewarm herbal tea. She heard the soft sound of company padding its way up the ladder. River emerged through entryway; a shawl wrapped around their shoulders.

"River, to what do I owe the pleasure? Not that I'm complaining now, mind you." She felt her smile falter as River stood there, stoic faced.

"It's over Roxy."

Roxy rose from her beanbag, the blanket falling to the deck to pool around her feet. She had longed to hear those words. She was afraid to speak, lest she break the spell and wake up. She had now been living on Mauw for six months… while things had gone straight to hell and back on Aurora.

"Really?" she whispered, breathless, hand at her throat.

River nodded. "Suki has sent word. It's safe now, Roxy. You can finally go home."

EPILOGUE

"Load 'em up!"

The call echoed down the long bare hallway and out into the obscurity of night as a line of chained and shackled prisoners were led one by one from a squat brick building and across a darkened and rutted tarmac. Awaiting them with open doors, lights ablaze and motors humming, was *The Quentin*, a passenger carrier specifically equipped to safely and effectively transport convicts.

A man at the end of the line limped along slowly in his ankle restraints; his drab, faded grey prison uniform and black canvas sneakers were not at all like the clothes he had grown accustomed to as a part of his lavish lifestyle. There were no extravagantly tailored suits or costly *crocator* shoes where he was going. No meals paid for on the taxpayer's dime, no hush money deposited into various off-planet accounts. It would be a whole new ballgame.

"Move it along there, *Commander*," Fredriks sneered with as much malice as he could muster. Being one of the newly appointed Gendarme under the direction of Hadrian Durand, Freddie Fredriks had little time for scum like the former leader of The PRC. He prodded Seth Carmine sharply from behind with a long black baton, a quick jab to the ribs. "We ain't got all day."

"My knee." Carmine whined, his face screwed up piteously, lower lip trembling as he sought sympathy from the guard.

"Barking up the wrong tree, mate." The guard remarked scornfully, looking down his nose at Carmine, of disgust written all over his face. "You're lucky that little lady didn't shoot you a wee bit higher. Then you'd really have something to complain about." He smirked. "Now get a move on before I *make* you move."

Each prisoner was led aboard the ship and taken to their individually assigned cryo-pods. Once inside, they would remain in stasis for the entirety of their journey. And quite a long journey it would be.

Brig-5, the prison planet, was located in the X-Sector – an otherwise undeveloped region at the furthest reaches of the solar system. It would take the better part of a year before they would reach their destination, and equally as long to return to Aurora.

A short while later, all twelve prisoners had been prepped for the trip, locked within their cryo-pods and sent off to dreamland, despite their loud and lengthy protestations of innocence. Fuel reserves had been filled and final checks had been done on *The Quentin* as per the pilots' instructions. It would ensure a smooth and problem free foray into the beyond.

Take off was now imminent.

"Captain? We're ready when you are." Fredriks called out, speaking for the rest of the small crew that would accompany the ship on its excursion. There were not many that would volunteer to take this particular job but for those willing to give up two entire years of their lives, the pay would be quite handsome indeed.

"Thank you, Fredriks." Sam Sparrow stepped out from the cockpit, handsome in his trim pilots' uniform, a line of gleaming gold and silver medals pinned across his breast pocket. "Certainly glad to have you along for the trip. I know it must be very difficult to leave your family behind."

"Aye, they'll keep. I'm glad to be here, Captain. And yourself, do you got anyone waitin' for you when you return?"

Sam gazed thoughtfully at Fredricks for a moment and then gave a small, clipped smile as he turned to re-enter the cockpit: "I sure hope so Fredriks. I sure hope so."

www.ingramcontent.com/pod-product-compliance
Lightning Source LLC
Chambersburg PA
CBHW031950060726
47497CB00016B/978